The Huachuca Conspiracy

Rescuing Our Children at Risk

A Novel

Will Rogers

iUniverse, Inc.

New York Lincoln Shanghai

The Huachuca Conspiracy
Rescuing Our Children at Risk

Copyright © 2007 by Will Rogers

iUniverse books may be ordered through booksellers or by contacting:

iUniverse
2021 Pine Lake Road, Suite 100
Lincoln, NE 68512
www.iuniverse.com
1-800-Authors (1-800-288-4677)

This is a work of fiction. All of the characters, names, incidents, organizations, and dialogue in this novel are either the products of the author's imagination or are used fictitiously.

First Edition: December 2006

Summary: The connection of child abductions to slave labor, prostitution and pornography. Action-packed elements help one digest serious subject matter in an unforgettable manner. Valuable involvement information in end notes.

ISBN: 978-0-595-39835-5 (pbk)
ISBN: 978-0-595-84239-1 (ebk)

Printed in the United States of America

In loving memory of my precious son, Nathan Andrew Rodgers ...
Nathan, you passed away in my arms, which ache to hold you again.
I shall never forget you, my precious son.

To all our precious children who bring us joy everyday ...
You fill our hearts with happiness and hope.
Let us never forget you are our future,
the answers to our prayers for a better tomorrow.

To all those united by a consecrated heart that beats with compassion ...
Your courageous determination to protect our future, our children,
is that which may hopefully enrich their lives, giving them a head start
towards becoming like-minded compassionate individuals.

To my dear, faithful wife, Audrey ...
You gave me much hope and inspiration to complete this book.
To all these, this volume is gratefully inscribed.

◆   ✧   ◆   ✧   ◆

Introduction

Mike is about to embark on the most terrifying ride of his life ... an excursion composed of harrowing thrills, twists, and turns that will whirl his mind into a tailspin. Mike is feeling rather vulnerable and alone, having already lost his parents to a plane crash and, later, his grandparents to a hotel fire. Now he's left wondering if he will ever see his little brother—his only sibling—again. About this time, he meets and teams up with a mysterious, beautiful young woman with whom, he soon learns, he has something in common. They promptly find themselves embarking on one of the deadliest adventures of their lives.

Together, Mike Taylor and Audra Heyburn uncover one of the most horrifying secrets in the history of the United States. What started out as being considered an isolated abduction—until Mike meets Audra, whose brother was also abducted a few years earlier—leads to their discovery of a conspiracy beyond imagination: A vile underground empire exists. These malicious malefactors have been abducting children for many years, for the most diabolical reasons imaginable: slavery, sexual exploitation, or to be trained—by force—as part of a subversive faction ... one that may one day return to the States to take over. For the sake of not only the citizenry of the United States, but especially for the welfare and safety of their own children, this network must be overthrown.

Can Mike, a conservative nursing student, and the young, unconventional, Miss Heyburn help put a stop to this evil before it is too late? So far, they have been turning up dead-ends ... until, that is, they enlist the aid of their heroic associates—including Audra's *Green Beret* father, and a former Scotland Yard investigator—hence, becoming involved in one of the greatest rescue attempts of the century!

♦ ✧ ♦　　based on true world events

Preface

The qualifications for writing realistically about a tragedy as painful as losing a dear, sweet child—a beautiful gift from God—only come from having experienced the same. I have waited through the long, sleepless nights … realized the horrors of a beloved son slipping away … and the feeling of such utter helplessness that comes to those who realizes they cannot help their own child at a time like this. Finally, I have lived through the agony of the heart, mind, and soul that overtakes those having to accept the reality of what has just happened, as I held the lifeless body of my son … my only son … in my aching arms. Through these, I somehow feel unfortunately qualified.

Since my own son's death, I have poured my heart into children … thereby witnessing many broken hearts. I have sat in support groups where fellow members have suffered the death of a child, often abduction-related. Seeing the heartrending despair experienced by the participants, I have come to believe that the most tragic event a parent or guardian could ever endure is the loss of one of God's angels … a precious daughter, or son. This not altogether altruistic act is that which has contributed much towards my own healing. Now, to be sufficiently knowledgeable to help others avoid the heartbreak witnessed there, I find myself spending countless hours thoroughly researching child exploitation and abductions … both the theoretical reasons behind it and the horrors thereof.

Research has indicated that our society may sometimes be too apathetic regarding things not touching our own back yard. Yes, subjects of a sensitive nature are more conveniently ignored than dealt with. However, we would do well to consider the victims and—in spite of the uneasiness such subjects might cause—press on, working towards a cessation and eradication of this terrifically heinous crime which this volume attempts to vividly portray.

I especially take pleasure in acknowledging my wife, Audrey Rodgers, for all her input and advice. Her efforts and sacrifice will always be remembered.

Thanks goes also to all those who have inspired me to return to my long-held goal of becoming a *bona fide* writer. These people include my father, Wayne Rodgers; my mother, Cherié; my wife, and a special author and friend who also prodded me, saying, *"No matter what others say, you can do it!"* Thank you, Wanda, for your most encouraging words.

I also want to acknowledge the Cochise County Sheriff's Department and the Sierra Vista Police Department for their kind assistance. I extend my special thanks and acknowledgment to all the wonderful people of Cochise County who were very helpful in making this book more realistic. We also want to especially thank the people who made it possible to enrich this volume by giving me their consent to use their titles or the names of their businesses. Thank you, Mark and Maggie, Jessica, Mark D., Pat K. and Bill, David U., Mark C. and the wonderful people at the Windemere Hotel—along with many others in Hereford and Sierra Vista whose brilliant input allowed me to add much local color to the novel.

Special thanks and appreciation to the outgoing folks in Bisbee who shared much input about their majestic mining town, and pointed out all their very quaint special attractions in their colorful community. I am very grateful to Phelps Dodge for all their kind input, as well, and for consenting to allow me to mention the historic and beautiful mine tour in Bisbee. Thank you, Tom, Donna, and company from the mine tour. Thank you, Brad and Kelly.

I also wish to recognize our Officers at Fort Huachuca, who kindly allowed me access to their intelligence museum, and information that allowed me insight into how our courageous *Special Forces* operate to safeguard our nation. I am very grateful for all the advice and knowledge shared by Colonel Noel Habib, as his expertise in military protocol was extremely helpful. I salute the *Rangers, FBI,* and all our service men, at home and abroad.

I also wish to praise the creator behind the Sonoran Desert, from the spectacularly ominous, colorful mountains to the gentle plains of the San Pedro Valley. The desert captivates our souls with all its diverse semi-arid and sub-tropical vegetation, from the various range grasses—such as beautiful purple three-awn, gramas and Kentucky blue grass—to large Arizona white oaks, cottonwoods, and the ever aromatic pines and spruces. The desert is now in bloom and, as I look out over the lush, flowery landscape, I pray I have administered justice in describing the beauty of Southwest Cochise County.

◆　　　◇　　　◆　　　◇　　　◆

The Huachuca Conspiracy

"Hey, Bobby, grab the water jugs! We've got to get moving. If we don't get out the door soon, we may as well stay home!" shouted Mike.

"I'm moving as fast as I can, and you promised we'd hike the peak today. You can't back out now just because it's getting a little late."

"Yeah, I know, but it still gets dark early now, so we do need to hurry," explained Mike.

Mike, a husky twenty-one-year-old college student, looked at his younger brother and smiled. They loved hiking *Tucker's Peak*. They enjoyed the calm serenity and the beauty of the mountain's majestic cliffs and deep gorges. The mountain displayed a dry desert look on the east side, yet on the west side, green shrubs and vegetation grew in great abundance, due to the rain clouds that dampened the mountains' western slopes. However, before the clouds cried down any precipitation worth mentioning on the eastern slopes, they usually broke apart owing to the height and rugged structure of the mountain range.

Bobby grabbed the water jug and bustled out the front door, "Race y' to the Jeep Bro!" shouted Bobby.

Mike looked at the back of his thirteen-year-old brother's head as Bobby disappeared out the door. "Does everything have to be a challenge with you!" hollered Mike as he dashed out the door and barely beat Bobby to the Jeep.

"Hey! You almost lost!" laughed Bobby.

"One day I probably will, Little Brother. Oh no! I forgot to shut the front door. See what you made me do?" laughed Mike.

"Ha! Well, don't blame me if we're late now!" exclaimed Bobby. Mike turned and swiftly raced back to the door, grabbed the doorknob, closed the door and locked the deadbolt. As Mike turned to walk back to the Jeep, he could not help but think how Bobby reminded him of the actor that played the part of

Bobby on the hit series, 'The Brady Bunch.' His dark hair and facial features were striking in comparison. Mike cherished his little brother. They were very close and for good reasons. Mike and Bobby's parents passed away in a plane crash only a year after Bobby was born. Mike was nine years of age at the time. He remembered the call on the phone, as well as the social worker that showed up with the police. They walked into their home and gently spoke to Mike. Sandy and Jim Taylor loved airplanes, so when Jim, a jet mechanic for American Airlines, received his private pilot's license, they purchased a *Cessna* and began to fly their own plane to visit relatives, instead of booking flights on American Airlines.

Mike's mind played back the tragic scene. He recalled the pleasant social worker lowering her head as she spoke very tenderly to Mike. She told him what had happened. Mike sat in his favorite leather chair in the family den listening eagerly for the lady to say that his mother and father received a few bruises and scratches but that they would be okay. He did not believe the social worker when she gave him the sad news that his parents had died. Mike quickly went into denial, and ran off to his room.

"She *has* to be mistaken!" he sobbed. "The police and this lady have to be wrong. They have the wrong house, the wrong people, and the wrong plane. My father wouldn't crash! They're all wrong!" They had just taken the plane for a short flight. Mike shook as he finally managed to cry himself to sleep that night.

Mike looked grimly down at the sidewalk for a moment, "Man, they died so quickly. While Bobby and I were at home with a babysitter, our parents perished in a plane crash ... just like *'that.'* There sure is a very fine line between life and death," whispered Mike to himself as he walked over to Bobby.

"What'd you say, Mike?" Bobby inquired. Mike did not want to let on that he had been thinking about their parents' death, so he looked at his brother and spoke, "I said I'm almost out of *breath*."

"Gosh, y' big wimp! You'd better catch it quickly 'cause we've got a lot of climbin' to do, Mikey!"

"Yeah, no kidding, Squirt!"

"Hey, who you calling 'Squirt!'" Bobby protested.

Mike feigned scanning the area for any other possibilities. "Well, I don't see anyone here but you!" Bobby doubled up his fist and slugged Mike in the arm. "Oh my, that hurt!" laughed Mike.

"Oh, you want some more, do you? I'll hit you so hard that when you wake up your clothes will be out of style!" shouted Bobby.

"Oh, no! Please have mercy on me, Bobby. Please don't hurt me!" pleaded Mike playfully, as he chuckled. Bobby slammed his fist into Mike's shoulder again. Mike's muscular frame absorbed the blows with little consequence.

"Okay, champ, you win. Now, let's get going. Last one in the Jeep's washing the clothes when we get back!" Bobby shot into the Jeep like a rocket.

"Ha! Looks like you get macerated hands when we get back this time," roared Bobby.

"'*Macerated*' hands? Where did you learn that one?" asked Mike as he stepped into the Jeep Wrangler.

"It means, like, '*pulverized*' or '*mushy,*' like when they get *verrry* wet."

"I know what it means. I meant where did you learn that silver-dollar word?" Mike started the engine.

"In school," explained Bobby.

"You always amaze me, Little Bro," laughed Mike as he slipped the transmission into gear and cautiously backed out of the carport. Once on the road, he looked over at his brother with a sense of pride. He loved his brother dearly. Bobby loved school and academics; his high GPA proved this. He was a gifted child with a brilliant personality and a great outlook on life. He gave Mike a lot to live for. If not for Bobby, Mike's world may have fallen apart after his mother and father died.

As Mike drove on down the road, he hunted for his CD case. He fumbled around in vain and almost went off the road.

"Hey, speed racer, what are you trying to do, get us killed?" squawked Bobby, as he gripped the edge of the leather bucket seat he sat in.

"Sorry, Bobby boy. I thought I left our CD case in the Wrangler, but I guess I didn't."

"Oh, oh!" exclaimed Bobby.

"Oh, oh, what?"

"I'm sorry, big Bro. I took them out last night before I cleaned the Jeep. I must have left them in the house. Rats! I'm at a loss for words!" Bobby profusely apologized.

"You sure use that saying a lot," said Mike. a bit irritably.

"Hey my Sunday school teacher, Dennis. says it all the time. 'Guess it rubbed off on me. I am sorry about the CDs, big Bro," sighed Bobby.

"Eh, no biggie. I'll find some tunes on the good old-fashioned radio," Mike assured his penitent little brother.

"Yeah, let's hear some Snoop Doggy, man!" laughed Bobby.

"Yeah, right! The day I listen to that headache music will be the day I am inches from full-blown dementia," chuckled Mike.

"Some of it's not so bad, Mikey-y-y."

"Oh, oh, what? not so bad, Mikey-y-y."

"I'm sorry, big Bro. I took them out last night before I cleaned the Jeep. I must have left them in the house. Rats! I'm at a loss for words!" Bobby profusely apologized.

"You sure use that saying a lot," said Mike. a bit irritably.

"Eh, no biggie. I'll find some tunes on the good old-fashioned radio," Mike assured his penitent little brother.

"Yeah, let's hear some Snoop Doggy, man!" laughed Bobby.

"Yeah, right! The day I listen to that headache music will be the day I am inches from full-blown dementia," chuckled Mike.

"Some of it's not so bad, Mikey-y-y."

"Well, maybe some of it, but the majority of it just rocks my brain into fits!"

"What brain?" jeered Bobby.

"You little whelp! I'll get you for that one, Mister."

"Oh, now y' got me shaking in my little booties!" Bobby sarcastically quipped. Mike admired his little brother's humor, "Bobby, you've got a quick wit, I'll give you that much."

"And you're all right, too, Big Brother … especially when you're sleeping," yowled Bobby.

Mike scanned through various stations on the radio. He tuned into a public radio program airing a provocative conversation between two expert doctors concerning stem cell research.

"Doctor Banes, what I'm hearing from you is that you are suggesting we should only use cord blood stem cells in recipients until embryonic stem cells are perfected—then cord blood cells should only be used on the donor. Why do you say this?" inquired a masculine voice, belonging to a Dr. Shaw.

"Well, we believe that umbilical cord stem cells give rise to a greater chance of graft versus host disease and, unlike embryonic stem cells, they cannot be proliferated in-vitro, and widely distributed to those in great need of cure," Dr. Banes stated clearly, with a deep, calm voice.

There was a slight pause. "I understand this; however, there are plenty of claims made today that some countries whose scientists are more active in cord blood cells are achieving cord cell proliferation. They suggest that the United States is obsessed with embryonic stem research, to the extent of possibly not looking closely enough at cord blood cells, which are much easier to access and are definitely controllable. In addition, I do not agree with your position on cord blood cells hosting a greater chance of disease. These young, virtually undeveloped, cells have yet to acquire antigen-like qualities that might cause disease, or rejection. Furthermore, any abnormalities are carefully screened out before they are introduced into the host or recipient," explained Dr. Shaw.

"Doctor, Shaw, there is no proof to substantiate your claim. Name one country that is achieving proliferation with cord blood cells," growled Dr. Banes.

Dr. Shaw spoke up immediately. "A Korean news channel announced that Chosun University professor Song Chang-Hun, gained global prominence last week with the case of a miracle stem cell cure. Song surprised the world by announcing that a person with a spinal-cord injury had successfully been treated with stem cells from umbilical cord blood. Hwang Mi-Soon, who had been paralyzed for the last 19 years due to a back injury, took a few steps with the help of a walker following stem cell therapy, and she is gaining more use of her legs and limbs each passing day. I am surprised you do not keep up with the latest issues!" he added with passion.

Silence followed. Then Dr. Banes began again, "This is only one isolated case...."

Dr. Shaw interrupted, "Not so! There are also other cases in Korea, and even here in the United States. Listen, Dr. Banes, I realize you and your colleagues want to help, but we face a responsibility as human beings. I believe our scientist need to examine blood cord stem cells more closely. They should join other countries in cord stem cell research, instead of focusing so much attention on embryonic stem cells, which are uncontrollable and lethal. You and I both know that embryonic stem cells have a dangerous tendency to form teratoma (cancer or tumor of cells) when injected into animals or human beings ... something that doesn't happen with adult stem cells.

"All in all, embryonic stem cell studies have yielded little in the way of concrete results while we are now conducting clinical trials with cord blood stem cells. This is not just me talking, but many other scientists also know this to be fact," Dr. Shaw emphatically continued the argument, convincingly.

"Listen, we cannot abandon the cause! We cannot afford to postpone or alter our embryonic stem cell research! We *will* discover how to fully control embryonic stem cells, and we *will* be the first in the world to do so. Then, these other nations we hear of will understand how viable our research is and join our endeavors," a frustrated Dr. Banes countered, loudly.

"You do realize you will be facing moral issues, and chop shops set up to exploit our women and our unborn might become an heated issue?" questioned Dr. Shaw.

Dr. Banes had barely started to respond when Bobby hollered out, "Okay, okay! Enough already! I've heard enough, Mike! It all sounds like a horror story. Nobody's getting *my* stem cells!" Bobby opined vehemently.

"No kidding, although I've got t' admit I do enjoy debates like this one," Mike answered. Discussions on the radio and television containing thought-provoking information fascinated Bobby also, but his mind was on having fun and letting go. The last thing he wanted to hear was a heated debate about stem cell research.

Mike depressed the scan button and found a station that played a variety of songs. He glanced over at Bobby. "Hey, Little Bro, you don't have t' worry about your stem cells. anyway. Nobody would want your crazy cells. Heck, if they injected your cells into someone, they'd probably turn into a werewolf or Frankenstein's monster," Mike teasingly laughed.

"Laugh it up, fuzz brain. If they injected your cells into someone, they'd probably turn into a little, fat worm or a maggot!" jeered Bobby.

"Hey, how would you like to walk the rest of the way, wise guy!" roared Mike.

"Be just like you to drop me off so some mean person can hurt me," sighed Bobby.

Mike felt badly, but he also knew Bobby's harmless, manipulative ways. A very serious look replaced Mike's smile "Bobby, if anybody ever dares lay a hand on you, I'll break them into pieces." Mike's voice became very sober, while Bobby felt much more secure, hearing his brother's protective assurances.

"Thanks, Mike. I feel the same way about you, too," chuckled Bobby.

The *Ballad of the Green Berets*, sung by the artist Barry Sadler, came across the airwaves, and Bobby began to sing along with him.

Fighting soldiers....

Mike broke in, "You really love that song, don't you?"

"Yeah, so did Grandpa … and you sang it a lot with him, too."

Mike began thinking about his loving grandfather, a Vietnam vet. Then he joined Bobby, as both sang along with the chorus. They continued singing, as they drove on to their destination.

Bobby looked affectionately at his older brother. "Hey, Mikey, can we get a *Big Gulper* at Brown's store? It's just up a little ways from here."

Mike smiled and rubbed the top of Bobby's head affectionately. "I was hoping you'd ask for a soda. Let's do it." Mike pulled into Cal Brown's store. Bobby and Mike jumped out and bolted into the store. Cal and his wife, Linda, stood behind the register talking to a customer about the rising cost of gas.

"Hey! Bobby, Mike—'good to see you today. Where are y' headed?" Cal was a fun-loving fellow with a bright smile, a few wrinkles and graying, dark brown hair. His wife Linda, a strawberry blonde, wore a smile, also. Mike noticed how nice she looked with a turquoise headband and a bright-red bow holding her ponytail together.

"Ah, we're headed up to our favorite place to go hiking," explained Mike.

"Oh, the hill you call the '*Taco Stand.'* Well, that sure does sounds exciting," laughed Cal.

Mike turned to see two rough-looking men wearing faded blue jeans and dirty T-shirts, standing opposite Bobby. One of the men, a blond-haired fellow, turned and poked his friend in the ribs. "Hey! That's Mike Taylor and his brother."

"So?" replied the dark-haired ruffian. "Well, they came into a lot of money after their parents and grandparents died. He sure loves that little brother of his."

The other man looked puzzled. "What does that have to do with the price of beans in Alaska?"

"He'd do anything, and give anything, for his brother. His brother is all he has now."

Mike saw the sinister look on the blond-haired man's face as he watched young Bobby. He excused himself from Cal and Linda and boldly forced his way in-between the two men. The man immediately took offense. "Hey, rude dude! What gives?" he scowled.

Mike looked at the man with cold, piercing eyes. "I need a soda, and you seem like two kind gentlemen that wouldn't mind sharing the fountain."

"*You* got nerve, stranger!" the crude specimen of a gentleman growled angrily, his scowl deepening. "I think you're mighty rude."

"You know, you little blond twerp, I don't like the way you looked at my brother. I think you're hairy."

"Why you two-bit yellow-bellied snake!" The man threw a wide right at Mike. His fist was caught mid-air, and agonizingly squeezed, sending him to his knees as his knuckles cracked. As the man sank to the floor, he begged Mike, "Okay, okay! Please stop! I didn't mean anything. We were just talking. We aren't here for trouble!"

Mike lifted the man clean off the tile floor and said, "If I ever catch you around my little brother again, I'll break your fists and your arms. Now, get out of here, and make sure you pay for your merchandise before you leave!"

The men ran to the register threw down a fin, telling Cal and Linda to keep the change; they couldn't get out the door fast enough. Bobby and Mike walked over to Cal and Linda.

"'Got to admit you have a way with people sometimes, Mike," Cal joked.

Mike smiled, "You know I'm just a pussycat, but when someone looks funny at my brother, the protective beast inside me roars."

"Well, I hope the beast within doesn't scare all my customers away."

"Cal, those two hooligans are better off staying *out* of your store. They smell bad, and look terrible. I think they could scare Godzilla away!"

They all laughed. Linda looked at Bobby with loving eyes. "Bobby, you don't have to pay for your *Big Gulper*, it's on the house. You know, as you grow older, you remind me so much of Cliff." Tears came to Linda's eyes. Cal hugged his wife.

Mike looked down, sadly, studying the floor. "I am so sorry."

"No, don't worry, Mike; it's not you. It's been eight years since we lost Cliff, but it still sometimes seems like yesterday." Linda wiped her tears from her eyes and bid the two Taylor boys farewell as she disappeared into the back of the store.

Mike and Bobby waved *'good-bye,'* as they exited the store. Cal called out, "Come back and see us soon, guys!"

Turning around to wave, Mike answered, "Will do, Mr. Brown … will do."

Chapter Two

A young woman stepped out of her Nissan pick-up and walked over to her brick, site-built home, carrying a backpack containing textbooks on biology and chemistry. Her day had ended as any other—classes at the college, followed by time spent at the institutional library—helping students operate computers and other library equipment, as well as finding periodicals and books for them.

Her dark auburn hair blew across her face as she opened the door and stepped inside. Her father, a colonel in the Army, sat quietly, snoozing in his recliner in the family den. The young lady softly sauntered over to her father and gave him a small hug. The colonel moved a little and let out a slight groan. "Hi, Aud. I hope you had a great day."

"Actually, Daddy, it was no different than any other. How was yours?"

Pat looked down at the carpeting, his depression very evident. "No change; everyday I go through the same old routine. I don't know how much more of all this I can take. I wish your mother were here … and well. I don't even have a wife anymore," he said, still staring at the floor. "She's a statue, not a human. I just do not understand how all this happened; it happened so quickly!

"It's just not fair! I don't think anything will ever be the same again, now that Todd is gone. We lost so much, so soon! We deserve a life, but what we have is hell on earth. Sometimes I think we will never have a life again. At those times, I just want to go to sleep, and wake up in heaven," Pat continued, so distraught he forgot that this would only mean one more loss for his daughter.

"Please, honey, I just want to be alone." Pat rolled over, as he closed his eyes, and was soon off to sleep again … something he'd learned long ago was a good escape from the interminably devastating reality with which they'd lived for the last several years now.

The young woman walked out into the living room and plopped down on the comfortable overstuffed sofa. She looked up at the ceiling in dismay. "Oh God, please send us a miracle … someone, or something, that will brighten our days—especially Dad's—and lift our spirits before it's too late." She collapsed to a prone position on the sofa, as tears began flowing profusely.

Dennis Perris walked nervously across his hotel floor in Tucson. Dennis had always thought of himself as a very kind and jolly type of guy that never worried about anything. He was a youth pastor for *Shiloh* in Sierra Vista, and he loved the children. If anyone could make the saddest, most unhappy, child laugh, it was Dennis. Why was his mind so troubled, and why did his spirit ache?

"What is wrong with me? Why am I so nervous and upset? I can't remember ever feeling this way." Dennis usually—in spite of his chosen profession— was not one to pray on impulse, but he found himself doing so today. He reached for his Bible, opened it and read a few verses. Then he knelt down and prayed for all the children to whom he normally ministered. In fact, he prayed for all those he knew at *Shiloh,* young and old alike, unsure as to why he felt so compelled.

Once he'd prayed, Dennis decided he must call his pastor at *Shiloh Valley Church.* "Hello, Pastor Richey speaking."

"Hi, Pastor Richey. This is Dennis. I'm just calling to make sure everything is all right. How is everybody?"

Pastor Richey paused for a moment. He did not expect this from Dennis, who was normally a rather complacent, happy-go-lucky sort of guy. "Everyone is fine. Why?"

"I don't know. I just have this strange feeling that something is about to happen, and I hope it's just a silly feeling and nothing more."

The pastor spoke calmly. "Dennis, I do not think you need to worry. I guarantee that all is fine. Now, just try to chill out, man! You do have a very big day tomorrow; you're probably just nervous about what's about to take place. So, just take a few deep breaths and relax, buddy, and we'll see you when you return from Tucson."

Dennis ran this through his mind. "Yeah, you're probably right. I think I'll get some rest, after I try to wind down with a bit of television. Thank you, pastor Richey."

"You're very welcome, Son. See you soon. Ciáo!"

The pastor hung up. Dennis turned on the TV, feeling much better after having spoken with his pastor-mentor. Everything was in order now.

Chapter Three

Bobby looked over at Mike as they drove towards their destination. "Hey, big, burly Brother, what was that all about in Mr. Brown's store back there?"

Mike looked out his window to his left as he spoke. "Let's just say I didn't like the way that blond-haired freak gave you the eye."

"Ha! If that dude wanted a battle, I'd kick him into next year, but I wouldn't have stopped squeezing his puny fist till it popped. And if that other geek wanted to rumble, too, I'd smash his smug face into the ground. But I wouldn't leave a trace of either one of them … and if…."

Mike interrupted Bobby. "Hey tough stuff, you sure are full of *'ifs'* and *'buts.'* You know what?"

"What?" asked Bobby.

Mike laughed,

> *"If, 'ifs' and 'buts' were candy and nuts,*
> *We'd all have a Mer-r-ry Christmas!"*

Bobby laughed aloud. "You know something, Bro? You are pretty darn witty yourself … a poet extraordinaire!"

"It's no wonder, hey! I hang around with *you,* tough guy; it sort of rubs off," Mike teasingly complimented Bobby, as he hugged him with his thick arm.

Finally, the peak loomed just ahead of them. Bobby looked up the slope of the mountain. He spied a large rock outcropping. "There's the *Taco Stand.* I can't wait to stand on top of it!" he excitedly exclaimed.

Mike peered at the jagged rock formation that he and his brother had earlier dubbed '*Taco Stand.*' The structure of the rocks that created this formation gave it such an impression, that it was a very befitting name. Mike stopped the Jeep. "Well, Little Partner, let's get our gear and beat a path."

"You bet!" Bobby enthused, as he bolted out of the Jeep and fumbled through the back bed of the vehicle. It only took the boys ten minutes to gear up and began their long hike up the mountain.

"Well, there's Morgan Wash that leads to Morgan Mine. Let's head north down the Wash, and then cut our way to the bottom of *Taco Stand*. I'd like to try a straight climb to the *Stand* today. 'You game, Bobby?"

"I'm always up for blazing new trails, Bro!" exclaimed Bobby. They began the rugged ascent up the steep slope through sharp rocks and rough foliage. They fought their way through a large pile of loose rocks, composed mostly of schist, granite, sandstone, limestone and displaced volcanic cinders. Mike gazed over the eastern slope at the scanty conifer-oak scrubs and sparse cactii. He liked the western slope because of the greater abundance of open oak woodland and the thicker grass.

They reached the top of the jagged rock formation and sat down to gaze at the beauty of the area below them.

"I love it up here. I wish our house was up here," said Bobby.

"Well, it'd be okay with me, but I'd rather live on the western side."

"Too much rain on that side. 'Might get washed away!" Bobby worried.

"I don't think so. The grass grows too thick on that side, and the trees are denser. There are more oaks and poplars, and they are much bigger."

"And there are bears on the other side that could eat us!" laughed Bobby.

"Nah, they wouldn't like us. We'd taste too bitter!" chuckled Mike.

Suddenly Bobby saw something move far below them. "Hey! I saw something moving down there!"

Mike squinted his eyes sharply. Since he was very young, Mike remembered squinting his eyes whenever he wanted to focus keenly on something. "I don't see anything," he replied.

"I could have sworn I saw something ... I know I wasn't seeing things," insisted Bobby.

"Bobby, I am sure you did. 'Lots of animals live up here, you know."

"Yeah, probably just a deer."

"Well, I'm pretty sure it wasn't a bear—*Gr-r-r-r!*" Mike roared, as he hugged his little brother.

"Stop it, Mikey-y-y! You're kind of giving me the jitters!" Bobby whined.

"Hey, 'sorry, Little Bro. I'll *try* not to *Gr-r-r-r* again!" Mike playfully teased one more time, as he rubbed his brother's head affectionately. They wrestled a little, and then moved on.

Mike looked at his watch as they stood upon the pinnacle of Tucker's Peak. During the summer when the days were much longer, they would usually climb a fourth of the way down the other side of the slope; however, today he knew they did not have the luxury of doing so. "Well, Champ, a few more fun hours and night will befall us, so I guess we'd better take in all we can before we start back down the mountain." They both looked in awe at the western slope.

"'Seems like every time we come up here, it changes," observed Bobby.

"Yeah, I can never get enough of this peak. Man! You look on one side and you see mostly desert. You look on the other side and you think you're in the wooded lands of Oregon—or something. Funny how this mountain is, ain't it?" inquired Mike.

"You mean, *isn't* it." Bobby corrected Mike.

"That, too, Mr. English major," retorted Mike. After one last look, the two brothers turned and started the journey back down. Traveling down the rocky slope was not as difficult as climbing up had been … 'only a little over an hour, and they were almost near the bottom.

"Well, we're almost at Sandstone Creek, Bobby," said Mike. He stopped when he received no response from Bobby. Mike had been walking ahead of his brother. He thought he was right behind him the entire time. "Bobby!" hollered Mike.

"I'm over here!" shouted Bobby. Mike followed his brother's voice. He climbed over a little stony knoll and started down a gentle slope that cut into a ravine below him. Bobby stood there hidden by a large sage bush.

"Hey, y' peeping Tom. I had to let go with the yellow flow, Bro!" laughed Bobby.

"Okay, but next time let me know when you've got to stop to go. I almost walked off without you," explained Mike. The strange, uneasy feeling that Mike had felt earlier was inexplicably returning. He had no idea why he felt so apprehensive and agitated—as if something was about to happen—something terrible. The sensation was familiar for some reason.

As he began to search his mind for when the last time was that he'd felt this way, Bobby shouted at Mike, "Hey man! I don't need an audience!"

"Well, I should hope not. I'll be up top waiting for you, but don't take too long … I want to get you home soon."

"Yeah, yeah … whatever," replied Bobby. Mike walked back up to the crest of the mountainside and waited for his brother. He reached down and picked up a stone.

"Hm-m-m, a little rhyalite … mixed with gneiss and granite. Well, the collection of precious metals and minerals is not too abundant—or worth talking about—in these particular mountains. It's not too far east, though, in the Mule Mountains, where the mineral content becomes rather precious," Mike mused. Then his mind went another direction. "God, you sure know how to fill our minds with wonder. How can one mountain range lack precious metals yet—

only a few miles away—another mountain range is packed full of precious metals and stones. Amazing!" exclaimed Mike, almost to himself.

Mike had just risen from a squatting position when he heard Bobby let out a loud, short cry. Without one second of hesitation, Mike bolted in the direction of his brother's cry. In no time, he was at the site where he had left Bobby for only a moment, giving him a bit of privacy. Mike stood shocked and perplexed—feeling a bit imprudent. "I'm letting my mind get the best of me," Mike told himself.

"Okay, Bobby, come on out from your hiding place, Partner!" shouted Mike with a sideways smile. He felt foolish. How many times had Bobby played games on him before? No doubt, this was just another game. Mike looked all around, waiting for Bobby to pop his head up over a boulder and laugh at him. But as the minutes went by, Mike became agitated—and a little worried, as well.

"Bobby! If this is one of your silly games, it is not funny anymore, Bobby! Bobby! Bobby! Bobby, come on out! We've got t' get moving … it's getting late. Bobby, I mean it! Let's go!" screamed Mike. Mike stood motionless, having gotten no response from Bobby. For a moment the world seemed to stand still. The only nearby sound Mike heard was the wind rustling through the oak and poplar trees. In the distance, a coyote yapped and a mockingbird cackled from a branch in an oak tree to his left. All else was quiet. Mike shot over to the area where Bobby once stood only minutes ago … nothing. Mike felt suddenly weak … numb with fear, as his mind raced frantically for answers. "What just happened? *How* did it happen? Where *is* Bobby?' he questioned no one in particular. His heart pounded, and his knees felt oddly weak, as he methodically scanned his surroundings with care.

Then he saw it. He focused his eyes on a prickly greasewood. He swallowed hard as he lifted a small torn and tattered piece of cloth from the jagged branch, a piece of Bobby's green flannel shirt that almost blended in too well with the shrubbery. Mike felt fortunate to have recognized it. He gazed down at the ground below the shirt. His heart sank even more. The broken sod and strewn sand told the story of a struggle that had just taken place. Mike fumbled feverishly for his cell phone. He was so confused and nervous, that he dropped the phone on the ground. Quickly retrieving the phone, his hands shook nervously in fear as he barely managed to press the numbers 911.

What happened next seemed like a blur to Mike. He later slightly remembered yelling at the dispatcher. However, he was so distressed that—after telling the authorities exactly where he was—he screamed at the dispatcher, wildly exclaiming the details of his brother's having vanished. He then demanded choppers, or whatever it took, to get the authorities at the scene to help him find his brother immediately. An officer told him to calm down and grab hold of himself.

"There is no proof that he just disappeared. Your brother may have just stumbled down the mountainside, and hit his head on a rock. He may only be hurt and unconscious."

"Sir, you might be right, and I hope you are, but I see boot prints where Bobby was standing that are not his … or mine. They look fresh, very fresh. I'm not sure, but it looks like someone might have taken him. I see signs of a struggle, along with those prints. I hope I am wrong, sir! I hope and pray he is all right, but it doesn't look good at all. Please, get up here immediately and help me! Don't waste anymore time!

"Oh God! Oh God! No! No! *No-o-o-o!*" Mike screamed frantically, as the feeling, the strange foreboding of earlier in the day, returned. He remembered now … this uncanny apprehension Mike was now feeling was akin to the anguish he'd felt the night his mother and father's plane crashed … twelve long years ago.

Mike frantically snatched many dry limbs from the desert ground. He tugged and pulled dead limbs from any shrub he could find, figuring the authorities would quickly spot his smoke. Just as he began to light the fire, his ears heard the familiar *thwack, thwack, thwack* of a helicopter off in the distance. For an instant, Mike thought how the slang word, *chopper,* aptly described a helicopter, as its blades surely sounded like it was actually chopping the air as it flew.

Mike threw some green leaves over the fire he'd made, and then began racing down the side of the ravine where he thought Bobby might have taken a tumble. Mike fell. He clawed at the ground in desperation. His mind could not think straight. His forehead broke out in heavy perspiration. His head was buzzing, and he felt dizzy. He ran around in a frenzy, screaming Bobby's name. He pulled back the thorny limbs of manzanita, briar and greasewood bushes, hoping to see Bobby hiding in the thick shrubbery. His efforts only left the flesh of his hands and arms torn and bleeding. Ahhh! Bobby! Bobby! Mike fell to his knees screaming louder and louder as tears ran down his dust-covered face. His heart felt as though it might burst through his chest at any moment.

The next thing Mike saw, when he looked up, was the police and the county helicopters descending from the sky. Some news choppers also hovered over the scene. The air filled with the loud noise of the helicopters' blades. Then he spied a few prints next to a boulder. He recognized the prints of Bobby's Nike hiking boots. Much larger boot prints lay next to Bobby's—then they strangely disappeared. Something told him to tug at the stones that hid a small crevice between two large rocks. He pulled and tugged with all his might.

"Ah-h-h-h! I'll get it open. I'm coming for you Bobby! Ah-h-h-h, You dirty pig! You filthy, evil child-molesting poor excuse of a man! I'll kill you. I'll find you and kill you all … you dirty bastards!" screamed Mike at the top of his lungs. Now he had seen enough to believe that someone had stolen Bobby from him. He felt weary and faint, but he continued to search. The scenes played out quickly. Out of nowhere, the Sheriff arrived with some of his deputies. They brought the K-9 division with them. Mike wondered if the men rappelled out of the choppers holding their dogs; otherwise, how could they have reached him so quickly?

Special trained police officers were combing the site, also. Mike heard the Sheriff shout at his deputies, "Get those dogs away from that rocky cliff! Set them at 20 meters apart and comb down the side of this mountain!" The Sheriff turned his back on his men and walked over to Mike who was, by this time, pacing alongside the ravine, confused and forlorn.

"Mike! Get a grip!" hollered the Sheriff. Mike looked at Sheriff Joe Tress. He shuddered as though in shock.

"Sh … Sh … Sheriff." Mike stammered, still feeling as though he were in the middle of a nightmare—from which he desperately longed to awaken.

"Mike, do you have anything that belongs to Bobby … anything with his scent on it?" demanded Joe.

"I …" Mike, drained from trauma, fought for words, "I … I've got a piece of his shirt. Yeah … a piece of his shirt," he mumbled, as he handed the small scrap he'd found caught on the greasewood bush to the Sheriff. Then with more clarity, born out of desperation, Mike spoke again. "You've got t' find him! You've *got* to save him from that pervert. You've *got* to!" Mike was literally screaming at Sheriff Joe, by the time he was done pleading.

Sheriff Joe looked into Mike's desperate eyes. "Mike, you must try to stay calm. We don't even know if there is a perpetrator. Bobby may have just fallen below, or maybe he saw something fascinating and ran off to investigate. You know how curious young boys are. Please, you must take care of yourself. My God, Son … you're bleeding and all tattered!"

"Oh! I'll get him if you can't. What good is the law, anyway?" Suddenly the Sheriff's attempts at calming him seemed to Mike as though he were merely brushing off of the seriousness of the situation. With a cynical tone, he continued. "They couldn't catch a cold, let alone a bastard child thief! Ah-h-h-h, Bobby! Bobby! Bobby! You're all I have. I'm coming, my dear Brother. I'll never leave you!" Suddenly something pierced Mike's arm. He winced a little, then he felt very weak. His eyes blurred. Mike fell to the ground, subdued.

"Wow! Now that was one fightin' fool! That was the third sedative we gave him since we've been here!" exclaimed one of the paramedics. The Police

Sergeant gave Mike a sympathetic look. "Lord, I am so sorry, Mr. Taylor, but you were on the verge of jeopardizing our entire mission."

The last thing Mike saw before losing consciousness was the Sheriff tucking something into his right shirt pocket, and pulling something out of his left shirt pocket at the same time.

Mike awoke early and walked into Bobby's room. There lay Bobby, still snuggled in his warm covers. Seeing his *Superman* blanket brought joy to Mike's heart. He reached down and stroked his little brother's forehead. "You sure gave me a scare, Bobby. I thought we'd lost you for sure up in those mountains." Mike lifted his brother in his arms and hugged him tightly, as he laughed and sang out for joy.

The big blanket wrapped around Bobby suddenly collapsed into dead air, as blood seeped down Mike's arms and over the edge of the bed. Mike let out a very loud cry, as he woke with a start from this surrealism. Mike felt his throbbing forehead, as sweat poured from his brow. His eyes focused in on the room. "Oh, God, I'm in a hospital somewhere. What a nightmare!" he cried, as he realized the pleasant dream he'd had was just that … a dream. Unfortunately, the nightmare of which Mike had just spoken was now his reality.

He looked at the nightstand beside his bed; on it lay an open Bible. Mike lifted the Bible and looked at the pages. He noticed some highlighting in the Bible. Someone had highlighted Exodus chapter 13, verses 2 and 13. Mike read verse two:

> *"Sanctify unto me the firstborn, whatsoever openeth the womb of the children of Israel. Both of man and of beast: it is mine."*

Then his eyes fell upon verse 13:

> *"And every firstling of a donkey you will redeem with a lamb; and if you will not redeem it, then thou shalt break his neck: and all the first born among men, you shall redeem."*

"What the heck is a Bible doing open on my nightstand? Who put it there … and why? What does it mean? And, *where* is Bobby?" Mike's mind began torturing him with questions, as he raised the Bible, opened the drawer beside his bed and began to place it in the drawer. However, something compelled him, instead, to place the Bible beside him in his bed until he could make sense of the verses. Then the reality of the verses' meaning hit him.

"Oh, God! Bobby!" he screamed aloud. Several nurses rushed into the room to witness Mike sobbing. Instantly they knew, his mind had cleared and his thoughts had returned. He knew Bobby was gone. "Where is Bobby!" demanded Mike. "Please tell me they found him."

One of the nurses looked glumly at the tiled floor. "We're so sorry, Mr. Taylor...."

Mike interrupted the nurse, "No! He can't be gone! They've found him—you're wrong—I *know* he's alive! Now bring him in here ... right *now!* Bring him to me!" Mike loudly demanded, as his voice boomed down the hospital corridor.

A doctor rushed into the room and whispered something in the ear of one of the nurses. The nurse left and brought in a syringe.

"No you don't! No! You leave me be!" Before Mike could get out another word, he felt the warm fluid flow through his veins. He sank back into a state of calm sleep.

When Mike awoke again, he looked around the dimly lit room. Something was different. Had his state of awareness been reduced to complete loss of memory? His eyes adjusted to the light and he realized it was nighttime, for the sun's rays no longer pierced through the heavy curtains of the windows. Mike felt much more at ease, yet he knew Bobby was out there—somewhere. He tried to not let his mind imagine the worst; instead, Mike began trying to put the puzzle together. His mind took him back to the scene where he'd last seen Bobby. He began to envision everything he had seen and heard. Once again, he started asking himself numerous questions, starting from the point at which they had left the house.

"Let's see ... Bobby grabbed the water jug ... I returned to the house—but, why?" Mike's brain was a little fuzzy from the sedative. As he lay in bed, he tried hard to remember. "Oh, yeah, I went back to close the front door—then we raced to the Jeep and drove to the mountain. Was anyone following us? How did this person—whoever he was—know that we would be at that spot today ... or was it just blind luck?" Mike stirred uneasily. He was a nursing student at Cochise College, and one thing that his schooling had trained him well in doing was problem solving—and analyzing situations concerning patients' cases. Now he was up against the greatest challenge of his entire life. His assumptions must hit the mark with great accuracy if there would be any chance to recover Bobby alive. His mind almost went into another dither.

"Got to keep a cool head. I lost it out there and they sent me to the hospital. I must maintain. I cannot help Bobby if I lose my mind." Mike told himself aloud. He forced himself to again play back the episodes that had taken place that day, meanwhile resuming his talking aloud. "Let's see ... who knew we were going to that mountain? Dennis knew ... Mr. Eldon, our next-door neighbor knew ... I always tell him in case we do not show up." Mike considered these two men for a bit. Dennis was an assistant youth minister at *Shiloh,* the church he attended. Dennis, he and Bobby were very close friends. Mike and Bobby practically grew up with Mr. Eldon. Mike remembered telling some of his peers at college about his and Bobby's trips to Tucker's Peak. Could one of them possibly be involved?

"Nothing seems to add up to one sound suspect. I don't remember anyone following me, so whoever it was knew we'd be there, and had a very good idea which path we'd take. I just can't pinpoint anyone! The only ones that would have any clue as to the path that we would take are Bobby's friends. They come along with us at times, but I know none of them kidnapped Bobby." Suddenly a thought captured Mike's mind. "Wait a minute, Mike. Of course—the children have nothing to do with it, but—children talk. That's it! One of the children probably talked about their adventure with us—and what path we took up the mountain—with the suspect."

Mike quickly drew up a list of the names of all the children that had ever gone with Bobby and him to Tucker's Peak. Then he made a mental picture of all their faces. Yet another thought entered Mike's mind. "Maybe those thugs at Mr. Brown's store knew more about me and Bobby than what met the eye. Maybe they followed us out to the mountains, hid well, and waited for the right moment—then they swooped down on Bobby and kidnapped him for ransom. I'll probably get a ransom note from those puke-heads as soon as I get home! Ah, Mike, get a grip. You're already wiggin' out. Come on, put on a cool head." He then allowed his mind and body to relax some, in an attempt to remain composed.

Mike knew that his life would soon be flooded with official agents from the *FBI,* and officers from state and local departments. "Lord, the inquiries that may follow will be exhausting, and they'll probably take up too much time—time I will need to begin my search. I know nobody will pour his or her guts into this case like I will. I can't count on the authorities … I have to find him before something happens!" Mike cringed at the thought of how wicked people can be. The child molestations and murders he'd often heard and read about almost sent him into a panic mode … yet again.

His eyelids felt heavy. The drugs were once more taking their toll on Mike's body. Just as he closed his eyes, he remembered watching Sheriff Tress tuck the flannel piece of Bobby's shirt in his pocket as he pulled something from his other shirt pocket. "Don't know what that was all about. Guess he had to blow his big old nose with his hanky," laughed Mike to himself. Mike felt a jolt rock his brain … the green cloth! The only reason the Sheriff would have wanted the cloth was that it had Bobby's scent on it. Why, then, did he put it into his shirt pocket, when he should have immediately introduced it to the dogs?

Finally, Mike began to believe he'd found a suspect. "Maybe I can dupe some of the Sheriff's deputies into answering a few questions that could lead me to a breakthrough in this horrible nightmare."

N

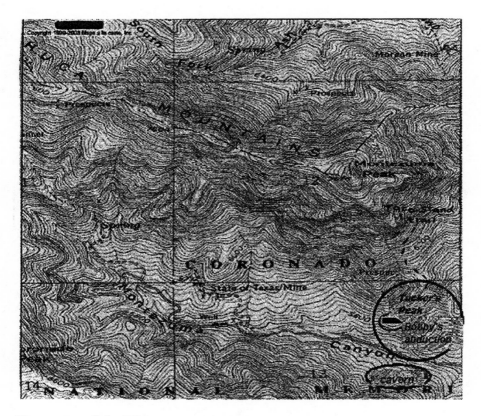

Topographic Map showing site of Bobby Taylor's abduction. Bobby was abducted just north of Montezuma Pass (Montezuma Canyon Rd). This is a partially paved road that winds through the breathtaking scenery of Coronado National Memorial Park. Vasquez de Coronado, Captain-General, led the *Conquistadors* through this very path, looking for legendary cities of great wealth from 1540–1542.

Also, note cavern opening. This is the cavern which Mike and Audra explored while looking for answers to Bobby's abduction. See story.

Chapter Four

Mike was all too correct about the inquiries, for he soon found himself surrounded by FBI agents, deputies, detectives, as well as the media. Mike felt much more clear-headed. The medication had worn off, leaving him in a very coherent state. He did his best answering all the routine questions each department asked; most of the questions hinged upon *when* and *where*. Because Mike was very time-conscious he was, therefore, was able to give very accurate time frames. He also painted very clear pictures of the places they had hiked. Not caring much for the media—they could be very intimidating—he gave Lucy Trent, one of the reporters, a very hard look when she began badgering him with groundless accusations, in the form of questions: "Mike, do you believe you may have been a little careless in your actions? I mean, if you would not have left Bobby alone, he might still be here with us."

"Ma'am," Mike asked in a controlled manner, "are you a mother?"

"Well, I don't see what that has to do with my question," said Lucy, a bit irritated. She obviously did not expect this kind of a reply. She thought Mike would break down and sob, "Oh, yes! It's all my fault. I should have done this … and I should have done that."

Again, Mike repeated the question, "Are you a mother, Ms. Lucy?"

"Yes, I have two children … a girl and a boy. Cindy is three, and Tommy is four—why?"

"Ms. Lucy, can you look me in the eyes and tell me that you never, ever once have left your son or daughter alone, either in the bathroom or in their own rooms and, can you tell me where your children are right now … at this very moment? I know they aren't with you," said Mike sharply.

Lucy felt frustrated over her interview script not being followed one whit. She wanted to strike out, but then she thought a moment about what Mike had said. "I'm sorry, Mr. Taylor, I see your point. However, I …"

A psychiatrist assigned to Mike's case cut Lucy off, explaining: "I believe that Mike has answered enough of your questions for one day, Ms. Trent. I think we should leave him alone now."

Mike looked up at his inquiring friends. "What has happened? What are we going to do?"

A tall dark-haired FBI agent leaned over. He looked down at Mike lying in bed and said, "Mr. Taylor, we thoroughly investigated the scene. We are convinced that you were right—unfortunately, it appears that someone did abduct your little brother. All the evidence we were able to collect points to this. However, we do not believe this to be a typical non-family abduction. We have reason to believe the perpetrator or perpetrators planned this. Why, we do not know; maybe there will be a ransom request involved soon. We hope so, because the agency maintains greater success at recovering children held for ransom than those that people randomly abduct without a cause.

"Most kidnappers that hold children for ransom slip up and when they do, we are there. I also want you to know we placed Bobby on *Amber Alert*. We are doing all we can—even Fort Huachuca is involved. Their intelligence HQ detached a unit to the site where Bobby disappeared, and they also sent probes all over the region."

The agent hesitated. "And ...?" inquired Mike cautiously at the delay.

The agent fidgeted some more, and glanced out the window, delaying further. "Nothing ... we cannot find a trace of your brother. It's like *Mother Earth* just opened her yawning mouth, and swallowed him whole."

Mike squirmed. "I don't believe it. How can he just *disappear?* He's probably right under your noses. I'll bet he's walking around Sierra Vista right now. Or, I'll bet he's at home. I bet you really didn't look well enough for him!" shouted Mike. Lucy smirked and rolled her eyes as though to say, "That's what you get for your irresponsibility, young man."

The FBI agent lowered his head. He reached down and placed his hand on Mike's shoulder. "I am sorry Mr. Taylor. I wish I could paint you a brighter picture. I wish I could tell you everything will be fine. I can say again that we will do everything within our power to bring Bobby home."

Mike took in a deep breath. He shook the agent's hand. Some of Mike's guests started to file out of his room. Mike tugged on a deputy's shirtsleeve.

"Yes, sir, what can I do for you?" asked the deputy.

"Please, please come back in before you leave. I want to talk to you alone," pleaded Mike.

"Sure, Mr. Taylor, I can do that much," said the deputy.

Lucy Trent turned and began to speak again but, before she could get one word out of her mouth, the psychiatrist, Dr. Rumsfield, spoke up quickly. "Ms.

Trent, I want my patient to get some *rest* now. You got what you came for … you have your story. There is no further need for harassment."

"Well, I … ah, *ohhh!*" Lucy left in a huff.

"Just got t' love the press!" Mike laughed sarcastically. Dr. Rumsfield laughed, also.

Then the doctor looked seriously at Mike and asked, "Mike do you know what day it is?"

"Checking my state of awareness, huh? Well, I … Wednesday, I was with Bobby and then I found myself here. I know it's daytime the sun's shining, and I know I'm in a hospital. I know my name, but I've been in and out of sedation. I guess that answers your question."

"Splendid, your responses have all been quite normal for surviving such a traumatic experience. Mike, I am terribly sorry about your younger brother. Please, if you ever need to talk, call me. Here's my number." Dr. Rumsfield handed Mike his calling card. "Oh … and, by the way, today is Thursday. I'm going to document in your chart that you are responsive and physically and psychological fit to go home today. No need for you to be penned up in here. Besides, it would be healthy for you to be around family and friends at this time," concluded Dr. Rumsfield. He had no idea that Mike's only family—except for his Uncle Bruce, who was too busy living a reckless lifestyle to bother with his nephews—centered on a young boy named Bobby Taylor.

Mike lay quietly for ten minutes looking out the window of his room. Finally, a faint knock came from his door.

"Come in, please," said Mike, hoping to see the deputy. The deputy carefully opened the door and slipped cautiously inside.

"Sorry, it took so long Mr. Taylor, but the good doctor stood at the nurses' desk longer than I expected."

"Why didn't you just tell them that I wanted to see you?"

"Wish it were that easy, but it doesn't work like that. You see, your psychiatrist works for the Feds … his orders are strictly followed—believe me! By being in here, I am putting myself out on a limb, partner," the deputy explained.

"Well, I'll take all the blame if anything happens," Mike replied.

"Yeah, I'm sure that will help," Deputy Seagle scoffed.

Mike looked at the deputy's nametag. "Deputy Seagle, you are my friend, and my *friends* are allowed to be with me, so relax," Mike assured the deputy.

"I'm also on duty and, even if I am your friend, I have to follow orders when I'm on duty. But sometimes—in cases like this—I hate following orders, 'cause it's more exciting not to!" laughed the deputy. Mike laughed, too. "Hey, call me Jeff; that's my first name," the deputy continued.

"Thanks Jeff. I really appreciate your coming back to see me."

"Hey, what are friends for!" exclaimed Jeff.

Mike laughed again. I like you, Deputy. I really think we can be friends," smiled Mike.

"I don't see why not," replied Jeff.

Mike leaned forward and started to ask the deputy questions. "Jeff, were you at the scene of the crime? I mean, were you at the mountain just after my brother, Bobby, was kidnapped? And, please, call me Mike. I don't want this conversation to be so danged formal … I'm up to here with formal," moaned Mike, as he extended his hand in a prone position above his nose.

Jeff smiled as he spoke, "Yes, Mike, I was. As a matter of fact, I was sent here today because I was one of the deputies at the scene. Actually, I volunteered. I wanted to come here. The Sheriff was called to an emergency or he'd be here, but I told him I'd fill in for him."

"Hey, that's mighty *'righty'* of you, Jeff," chuckled Mike.

"Thanks, Mike."

Mike's face grew more serious as he looked at Jeff. "Jeff, what do you remember about that day?"

The deputy looked up at the ceiling as though he was playing back the entire scene in his mind. He held this position for almost a minute as he hummed a little to himself. "Well, things did go by rather rapidly, and even though we are trained to retain as much detail as possible, I can only tell you what I heard and saw. You'd have to read the report yourself to get more detail," explained Jeff.

"I will, Jeff, but I've just gotta hear something now … please?"

"Ah, why not? Okay, I was ordered to recon the area below the path you and Bobby were traveling. Actually, I saw the evidence of a brawl that took place beside a sage bush or some kind of bush. I noticed scuffled footprints in the dirt and broken limbs. Sheriff Tress ordered me to take up with the K-9 unit and scout below. He really gave us all heck when he saw the dogs held up at a big boulder. "You'd think they were after a fox in a hole," Jeff chuckled a little at the thought, "Well, anyway we carefully and rapidly combed the area as we fanned outward. Usually I don't get too mixed up with the K9 division, but we were short-handed, and they needed cover, just in case of gunfire.

For just a brief ten or fifteen minutes the dogs began to snort and bark a little. We thought we had something, but they calmed down just as quickly as they started. "Kind of odd how they pawed at the ground and snorted. One of the dogs even started digging. His trainer shouted 'Hey, Red, we ain't got time for chipmunks or gophers! Come on!' We started back down the side of the mountain, but I've got to tell you Mike … we did not see or hear anything, and we were moving fast … double time. I'll tell you this much: if there were anybody in the area, we would have got him or her. Somehow, the perpetrator found a way out." Jeff stopped for a moment.

"Can't see how he could have gotten away. The dogs would have located his hiding place, and the skies were filled with choppers."

"Did you see any other people or vehicles in the vicinity?" asked Mike

"Yeah, we came across three children, a mother and father. They were all hikers. They looked very much worn down, and clueless. We detained them for awhile and took their names, addresses and license numbers for possible later inquiries; we were hoping they might have seen or heard something, but they just shrugged their shoulders. Other than this family, we didn't encounter anyone else."

"But what about fresh tire tracks? Weren't there any fresh tracks—anywhere—to be seen?"

"Oh, yeah, there were other tire tracks, some fresh, but my goodness, they were very common. Most were Michelin tires——like the tires you have on your Jeep. Those are very general. Mike, I just don't know what to tell you; we are all very stumped. This is a terrible tragedy, and it makes me sick. I have children of my own. I know Bobby was your brother, but in reality, you are more like a father to Bobby ... you've practically raised him. I know, as I saw the news and read the papers. I feel for you, Mike. Hell, if that happened to one of my kids I...." Jeff hesitated, then stopped. Mike looked curiously at the slim, brown-haired deputy. Mike thought about how wiry the man appeared. His tan arms blended in with the khaki beige uniform he wore.

"You don't have to tell me; I think I get the picture," said Mike. The deputy looked down at the tiled floor in Mike's room. He felt like he'd accomplished very little. He hoped he had helped Mike some; the last thing he wanted to do was cause more grief. The deputy bid Mike farewell. He told Mike he must get on back to work, and then he turned to leave.

"Hey, Jeff, I am very grateful that you took the time to come back and see me," said Mike loudly.

"Well, I'm sorry that's all I could tell you, Mike. I'm damned sorry about the whole thing. God knows we all wish this never happened. Well, I guess I'd best get on my way."

Mike watched on as the deputy started to open the door, "Hey, Jeff!"

"Yeah, Mike."

"Just a few more question, please," insisted Mike.

"Anything, Mike," said the deputy softly.

"How did the dogs even know how to pick up Bobby's scent?"

"Ah, well, the Sheriff brought over a piece of cloth that supposedly had his scent on it," stated Jeff.

"What do you mean?"

"Sheriff Tress handed one of the K-9 trainers what looked to be a torn piece of clothing that Bobby was wearing at the time he was abducted," replied Jeff.

"Hmmm … very interesting. So, the trainers shoved the cloth in front of the dogs' noses and away they went?"

"Yeah, kind of like that."

"Just curious, what did that cloth look like? I mean, what color was it?"

"Oh, let's see …" the deputy rubbed his forehead, "it looked like a piece of cotton or flannel cloth, beige in color," the deputy answered.

"Sure it wasn't green?"

"Pretty sure. I really do strongly believe it was beige," insisted Jeff.

"How did the Sheriff know mine and Bobby's name when he arrived at the scene? I know I didn't tell him."

"No, you didn't tell him, but you sure made Bobby's name and your name very clear to our dispatcher. He gave the Sheriff your names before he even arrived at the scene."

"Oh, hmmm…. Well, like I said, Jeff … thanks for your time. Hey, keep in touch, and if anything comes up, let me know," Mike requested.

"Here. I don't usually do this, but I feel led to, for some reason." Jeff wrote on a small piece of paper and handed it to Mike. "That's my personal cell number—not a station or official phone number. I want you to have it. You might want to talk some more, later. Anyway, I'd like to help if I can," spoke the deputy softly.

"Hey, you're all right for a cop!" laughed Mike.

"Yeah, you just get well and leave the search to us. I'll do *whatever* it takes to find your little brother, Mike," swore the deputy, sympathetically.

"You promise me that, Jeff?" Mike's eyes watered a little.

"Yeah, Mike, I promise … I really do promise." With that, the deputy stepped out the door and made his way down the long corridor.

Mike cupped his hands around the back of his head and laid back on his bed, "Darned bed is so narrow and uncomfortable, I can hardly think. Man, I've got to get out of here soon!" He looked at the walls and the ceiling. His mind replayed the entire conversation he had just had with the deputy. Nothing was making any sense at all. However, he felt as though he had covered a few important areas during his stay at the hospital. He made a very important friend that might help keep him posted on inside information, and he definitely felt like he already discovered a key suspect … Sheriff Tress.

Why would Sheriff Tress hide the torn green flannel cloth Mike had found, and give the dog trainers another piece of cloth? Another point of interest—which Mike found very peculiar—was the dogs themselves. Why did the dogs stop at a boulder and bark soundly, at it as though it concealed an animal? Mike tossed a bit in bed. "Hmmm, the dogs pawed and snorted at the ground, too. Maybe it was just a gopher, or could there be something more to the tale? The dogs picked up on some trail after the Sheriff handed that torn cloth to the trainers, but why?"

Mike tossed more in his bed. The ghastly crime was beginning to play out like some sort of crazy Sherlock Holmes murder mystery, and Mike didn't like it. "Why was the Sheriff so anxious to pull the dogs away from the boulder?" Mike tossed for a third time. He felt quite well, and he didn't want to spend any more time in the hospital. He glanced at his cut up arms and blistered hands. "Nothing but superficial wounds. It's time to check out of prison here and do what too much paper work and politics keeps the authorities from doing ... their *job*. I'll find Bobby. I'll bet I've mustered up more leads in the time I've been in this hospital than the FBI, police, Sheriff and all the other departments combined," roared Mike aloud.

Mike dressed himself and walked over to the nurses' station. "I want to leave now nurse, and I realize that my doctor must give his authorization, so I really would be grateful if you would please contact him and tell him that I'm gonna go crazy if I stay here any longer."

The nurse looked thoughtfully at Mike. "Well, Mr. Taylor, I must say I like your spunk and you do look very perky. Okay, I'll call Dr. Craig and tell him you want to go home."

Mike took hold of the nurse's soft hand and looked into her pretty, dark eyes. "Nurse Chelsea, I really did appreciate all your kind, loving care. Thank you." Chelsea blushed as she gazed into Mike's deep blue eyes. His charm captivated her.

"You keep it up, Mr. Taylor, and I might just find a way to keep you here," she laughed. Mike laughed also as he tenderly held Chelsea's hand in his and gently massaged the upper area of her hand with the ball of his thumb.

"I'm going to miss you, Handsome. We don't get many patients like you." They both laughed aloud as Mike made his way back to his room, while Chelsea thought to herself, "And they say chivalry no longer exists. Well, the girls haven't met Mike yet, I guess."

Two hours passed before Dr. Craig finally gave his approval to let Mike leave the hospital. After he made his rounds and checked Mike thoroughly, he left a few prescriptions with Mike and told him that he wanted to see him in his office in three days for a follow-up. Mike insisted he was fine, but he gave in when the doctor asked him if he would like to spend another day in the hospital.

Mike gathered his keys and his wallet, and then Chelsea escorted him down the corridor in a wheel chair. Mike protested, but Chelsea smiled and told him it was hospital policy. Mike explained that he knew this but he still thought it foolish.

"It's all a liability issue, Mike … and I know that you know this, 'cause you are a nursing student," scolded Chelsea.

"Yeah, yeah, yeah, I know. But we do seem to get carried away a bit sometimes, don't you agree?" asked Mike.

"To an extent." Chelsea stood outside the door to the hospital as Mike jumped out of the wheelchair. He turned and thanked Chelsea one more time. He told her he'd miss her—then he quickly walked over to his Jeep that one of the officers had very kindly driven to the hospital.

As Mike drove away, he felt very grateful to the officer who had performed such an act of kindness for him. He began to think about what he should do when he got home. The first thing he thought about was the Internet. Maybe he could find out more about abducted children and how the system worked.

As Mike drove into the driveway, his heart sank. He felt so alone. "Maybe I'll open the door and Bobby will jump out and shout, 'Surprise! We fooled y' good this time!' Yeah, sure he will."

Mike opened the door and slowly stepped into the dark house. He heard nothing except the hum of the refrigerator in the kitchen, and it even seemed to emit a sound of woe and melancholy. Mike felt very empty. He'd never dreamed how lonely the house could become without his little brother stirring about, shouting and laughing. He remembered the many times he had scolded Bobby for being too rambunctious; now he wished Bobby was around to scold. Already he realized that life without Bobby meant no life at all.

Mike found his way to his room and turned on his PC that sported *Windows Office 2000 Professional* as its main software program. He sat back in his chair and thought about how lucky he was to have so many friends in Sierra Vista that cared. Only a week ago, Mike's PC had broken down. He'd called *Monsoon PC* and spoken to Mark, a very efficient PC expert. Mark told him to bring his tower into his shop. Mark told Mike he would have his computer up and running in no time. True to his word, Mike had just driven into his driveway, and just walked into his house, when Mark had called and said he'd already repaired the computer.

Mike hung up the phone, grateful for Mark. "And to think, the big electronic store in Tucson wanted twice as much to repair my computer … and they said it would take them over a week to get to it," grumbled Mike as he searched the 'Net for articles on missing and abducted children. He came across some terms that sounded very familiar to him—*NCMEC, NISMART,* and *Child Find.* Why did these sound familiar? Mike sat in his chair thinking for a while.

"Of course! *The National Center for Missing and Exploited Children, National Incidence Studies of Missing, Abducted, Runaway, and Thrownaway Children*, and *Child Find* have been mentioned on *America's Most Wanted*," Mike suddenly remembered, "and I've seen displays before over at the college, too."

Mike lowered his head, as a wave of regret washed over him. "I wish I had turned the Jeep around and gone back home. We were starting out late, anyway, and that may have been a sure sign that something horrible was about to happen! 'Wish the Jeep had broken down. Why didn't God give me any warning? 'Wish the Jeep would have gotten a flat, even, to hold us up!" Mike sighed deeply. He knew beating himself up and blaming himself now would only lead to anger and depression, which would fog his mind.

"If only I could find somebody to help me. If only I knew someone that worked on cases like this. Better yet, I wish I knew the person who was working on this case." Mike pondered over this for a while as he wrote down numbers to different support groups for victims of abductions he had just found on the Web. "Let's see, there's the *Homicide Survivors Inc.*, *Knights of Kindness*, *Domestic Crisis Center* and chapters dealing with the plight I'm in, sponsored by the *NCMEC*. 'Looks like I may have to go to Tucson to receive any support. I'll call the division in Tucson tomorrow and see if they have any chapters closer to me. Man! I also have to go to college tomorrow and explain why I am going to pull out for a semester. I hope the director will understand." Mike spoke quietly to himself.

After three hours of surfing the 'Net, Mike's body finally grew a bit tired. He walked out of his room, and made his way into his brother's bedroom. At first, he felt very apprehensive about entering; however, he fought off the trepidation and bravely crept into Bobby's room. He switched the light on to see a picture of him and Bobby hugging each other, as Bobby held up a large stringer of fish. Mike laughed; he remembered the fishing trips as if they were yesterday. His mind envisioned Bobby at Parker Canyon Lake, alongside him, as they cast their lines into the fresh water hoping for trout or bass.

How Bobby always seemed to catch all the fish remained a puzzle to Mike. "Wow, Little Brother, you always made a fool of me when it came to fishing. Ha! But there is more at Coronado Forest than fish. You sure showed me up in fishing, but I showed you up in canoeing. 'What about the time at that old cave south of Montezuma Peak and Hartford. Why I ... I...." Mike stopped talking to himself. He paused for a long while. His brain was going full tilt. He thought about how close they were to that area the day Bobby disappeared.

"Tucker's Peak is not on the map, but it is close to Montezuma Peak. In fact, it's south of Montezuma Peak and closer to the cave. Hmmm ... I wonder if a topographic map of that area might be of help. When I go to see my counselor and the Director of the Nursing Department at the college tomorrow, I'll make a quick pit stop at the library, and dig out the maps. 'Should have thought of this sooner," Mike said aloud, though no one was there to hear.

Mike turned and studied Bobby's bed. His *Superman* blanket lay atop his unmade bed. Then Mike looked at the bed frame, made out of mahogany and cherry wood. He knew this because he had made the bed for Bobby. He, in fact, had spent an entire semester in Shop Class when he was a senior in high school carving away at the frame and the drawers. He routed it into the shape of a *1950 Ford Pick-Up* truck. Bobby loved the style of old Ford Pick-Ups back then. The bed of the truck supported the box springs and mattress. The sides built up for bottom drawers so Bobby could tuck his clothes or books in them. The cab actually had hinged doors allowing Bobby more space for clothes or other knickknacks. Bobby's eyes had almost popped out of his head when Mike presented him with the bed. It had been a cold, frosty Christmas day when Bobby walked into his room and saw the bed for the first time.

Smiling from ear to ear, Bobby laughed out loud and began jumping on the mattress. Then he pretended that he was hauling a load of ore from Bisbee to Sierra Vista. "Now I know why you wanted me to stay over at Brian's house last night. You needed to get this bed up while I was gone," laughed Bobby, as he bounded out of his wonderful bed and jumped on his brother. He gave him a big bear hug and said, "You're the *bestest* brother in the whole wide world. Promise you'll never, ever leave me, or let anything happen to me or you!" The words now echoed repeatedly in Mike's head, as this memory played through his mind…. "Promise you'll never, ever let anything happen to me or you!" Mike collapsed on Bobby's bed. He could still smell the scent of his little brother on the sheets and blankets.

Tears filled Mike's eyes until he scarcely could see. His mind felt numb as a huge lump formed in his throat. He could no longer hold back the intense grief as he screamed out, loudly, "I'm so sorry, Little Brother. Oh! Bobby! Oh! Ahhh …! Bobby! Bobby! Oh God! He's just a little boy … oh, God! Please don't let him get hurt! Bobby! I let you down. I let something terrible happen, the worse nightmare that could happen to a child. I let it happen to *you!*" Mike fell into Bobby's pillows and passed out, exhausted beyond belief from it all.

Chapter Five

Mike stepped into the Director's office and closed the door behind him. "Hello Mike," began Mrs. Marcy Stanford, a very kind and pleasant-looking woman, "I'm sort of surprised you are here today."

"Actually, I feel a hundred miles away … at least my mind does."

"Well, I can certainly understand that. Mike, I read the papers and watched the news. I know this is going to sound like a very silly question, but how are you holding up at present?"

"Faith and hope are holding me together. Dr. Stanford, the reason I am here is due to this recent tragedy that has occurred in my family. I truly do not want to miss any clinicals, or class work, but I have become overwhelmed since my brother's disappearance. I just…." Mike paused.

"Mike, I expected this, and I want you to know that because of your extreme circumstances, I am fully willing to honor your leave of absence. You are a *straight-A* student, with a glowing attendance record. I want you to know that I have already made arrangements to extend to you an *incomplete* status, which I will allow you as much time as possible to make up. Please do not worry. The college will still be here when you return," Dr. Stanford smiled at Mike and shook his hand. Mike felt very relieved and grateful.

"Mike, I just hope you do not do anything desperate," said Dr. Stanford with much concern in her voice.

"What do you mean, Dr. Stanford?"

"Well, if it were my child, I'd probably feel like killing myself—or *some*one!" exclaimed the good doctor. Mike turned away as he spoke, "Dr. Stanford, I really don't know what to do right now."

"Mike, try to leave this matter to the authorities. I have read that their techniques have improved considerably." Dr. Stanford was trying to be helpful and considerate, and Mike knew this, but he also knew that he had already made up his mind days ago. Bobby was all the family he had and most of the reason he kept going on. How could people really understand this unless they shared the same life?

Mike looked at Dr. Stanford and just said, "Thank you, Doctor; you are very kind and thoughtful. I will try to keep in touch. Mike turned and walked out of Dr. Stanford's office. Outside he spied a few of his friends and classmates. They were very busy discussing some topic. Mike thought they were probably analyzing some case studies or dealing with a tough pharmaceutical problem. Maybe they were in the middle of a serious pathophysiology debate. Actually, he could not care less what the topic might be. His next stop was to be the library.

Mike wasted little time walking over to the information booth for help. "Hi, Miss Ah-h-h...." Mike paused. He looked for the young lady's nametag, but in vain.

"Oh, I'm sorry. I left my nametag at home," explained the very pretty girl.

"Late for classes, huh?"

"And how! I barely made it to my chemistry lecture. Man! I can't afford to miss my instructors' classes. I can't afford to be late. Oh, my name is Audra, by the way. I just started this new job as the information clerk, but I really know the library well. Give me a topic and I'll point you straight," laughed Audra. Mike instantly fell in love with her cute dimples. Her wavy, dark auburn hair accentuated her tanned, oval face. Her big brown eyes sparkled as they spoke.

"Well, Audra, my name is Mike, and I am very interested in learning where you folks hide your topographic maps," said Mike.

"Maps, topographic, ah yes, they are right over here in the Map Room, under *Geological Survey*. Follow me, Mike … I'll show you. Actually, I wanted to get away from that boring booth, so I would be happy to help you find any map you need," laughed Audra. Her personality bubbled as she walked with Mike. She also thought that Mike was a very cute guy. As she walked beside the tall, husky gentleman, she envisioned Mike holding her in his strong arms. She wondered if Mike was thinking the same way about her, but she, of course, did not let on.

"Here we are. Now what is it you're looking for?" Audra inquired.

"I would like the map that covers the area close to Hartford, near the cave … the southeast section of the Huachuca Mountain range," replied Mike.

"Hmmm … let's see … okay, here we go. Hey, you're lucky; we just got the new prints a few days ago!" exclaimed Audra, as she pulled a map off the rack and unrolled it.

Mike looked carefully over the map. He even produced a magnifying glass from his pocket and began to search every inch of the map where Bobby vanished. "Okay, there's Montezuma Peak, and Tucker's Peak is close by—right there, and there's the Morgan Wash and Sandstone Creek. Let's see … aha! The ravine along the contour lines, next to the peak we were climbing!" shouted Mike.

"Hey! I know you. You're Mike Taylor!" blurted Audra aloud.

"That obvious, huh?" asked Mike.

"Well, I keep up on abductions ever since my little brother was kidnapped four years ago," Audra's voice sounded sad and distant.

"Oh Lord! I'm so sorry, Audra. It's horrible, I know. I am really sorry." Mike saw her eyes water.

"Yeah, so am I. Nothing has been the same since that day. We all die a little inside when we lose a loved one, but when they are abducted, it's like we die all over again each day, because we have no idea if they are alive or dead. It's terrible and, if I ever could find out who it was, I'd scratch out their wicked eyes!" growled Audra.

"I know what you mean, Audra. I really do," Mike affirmed.

Audra shrugged her shoulders. Now she felt more interested than ever in Mike. "Mike, if you will allow me, I would like to help you as much as possible."

"Audra, I am on a mission. I really don't believe that the authorities can single out cases. This is why I think their success rate sucks so badly. If they could focus on one child, they would probably find him or her, but if you have kept tabs on all of the missing children that flood just one FBI agent's desk, you'd understand why the abductions are so danged elusive! Mike gritted his teeth when he said the word *"elusive."*

"What is your mission then?" Audra wondered.

"I am going to increase my brother's odds, because I myself believe that if I focus all my efforts on his case, I'll find him," explained Mike, as he probed the map more thoroughly.

"Well, then, I'll increase the odds even more, by helping you," said Audra with a serious ring to her voice.

Mike looked at her beautiful face. "Thanks, Audra. I could use all the help I can get." He turned back to the map. "Hmmm … that's strange, I never noticed that symbol before. I am familiar with mining symbols, windmills, footmarks, railroads, creeks, rivers, washes and other road and trail symbols. I've even seen graveyard symbols, but what is that symbol?" asked Mike, pointing at a mark on the map. Audra looked closely at the map. As Mike held the magnifying glass over it, the mark jumped out at Audra.

"Maybe it's just a glitch, a printing error," surmised Audra.

"It looks too refined, like it was meant to be there. Audra, where was your brother last seen?"

Audra felt a little weak as she thought of that horribly sad day, but she felt a type of dedication to this cause. So she mustered up her courage and proceeded to speak. "He was at a camp meeting outside Globe and north of San Carlos, near Talkali Lake," Audra sighed.

"Pull that map, please, Audra!" exclaimed Mike a bit loudly. Audra stumbled through the maps. She took down the map hanger, and turned to the topographic map that revealed Lake Talkali and the surrounding area. Mike looked over the map very carefully. He scanned and scanned the map, but he saw nothing.

"Well, 'see anything in particular?"

"No, I guess you were probably right, Audra. The mark is just a silly glitch," Mike felt a little embarrassed. He also felt like he was getting nowhere, yet his pride forced him to believe he had suspects and clues. In his mind, he saw himself holding his brother and saying, "I love you, Bobby. You knew I'd never, ever let anything happen to you!"

"Hey! You still in there?" laughed Audra as she knocked lightly on Mike's crown, his daydreaming rather obvious.

"I think I'm home someplace in that thick skull!" laughed Mike. Audra laughed, too.

"Hey, Audra, would you like to share your story with me? I mean would you mind helping me? I mean, I...."

"Mike, I know what you are trying to say. You want to know how I've kept my sanity through such a tragedy. Yes, Mike, I would love to help you. I think a little dinner and a glass of strong lemonade would loosen me up enough to talk," giggled Audra.

"When do you get out of this big bookcase?"

"Five more hours, maybe six. I'll meet you at the Country House Restaurant, say seven-thirtyish. They make the best deep-fried zucchini. The food's great, and the prices are very reasonable—especially if you're a starving college student." chuckled Audra.

"Miss Audra, consider it a date."

"You mean, consider it your first support session," retorted Audra.

"Must women always be so business-minded?"

"Until we decide there's possibly something besides business involved, yeah, I guess so," laughed Audra. Mike helped Audra hang the maps back on the rack—then he bid her farewell, until later. He quickly left the library. He had another stop to make. Actually, he had many a stop to make, and he knew time was running out ... every second counted. Mike knew that time would soon become his archenemy, for time would slowly turn into a deadly, sharp blade, whittling away at his brother's life.

Mike hopped into his Jeep and drove west on Fry Boulevard. He pulled Bobby's picture out of the glove compartment. Mike looked into Bobby's sparkling blue eyes. Bobby smiled back with cute, deep dimples. Mike grinned from ear to ear. "I love you Little Brother, and I'm going to find you … I promise you, even if it kills me. I'm *going* to find you!" Mike pulled into a shopping plaza and bolted out of his jeep. He ran into the first store he saw and held Bobby's picture up to the clerk's face, as well as his patron's faces.

"Have you seen this young boy? He's my brother. Have any of you seen him?" Mike pleaded. The clerk and the customers sensed Mike's desperate soul and grief. They wanted to say, '*yes*.' Some even took the picture and held it closer to their eyes. Mike knew they all wanted to say '*yes*,' but they just shook their heads, helplessly.

One man sadly said, "I have three little children of my own. I can't imagine how you feel. I'd go crazy if I lost one of them." His head drooped as he walked away from the sad scene. Mike ran out of the store. He entered other stores along that stretch of road, repeating the same process in each of them, until it became a routine. With each store he walked into, he experienced this same result every time. Nobody knew anything. Some recognized Bobby from bulletins they had seen, and the television exposure Bobby was receiving. They offered their prayers and best wishes, but that was all they could do.

Mike climbed back into his vehicle, and roared west on Fry Boulevard. He turned down Coronado Drive, and worked his way south through all the housing developments. Mike felt compelled to start rapping on doors and showing all the neighbors his brother's picture. When he saw people walking down streets or sidewalks, he would quickly pull up next to them and plead his case, but still no positive replies.

He drove further south to Buffalo Soldier Trail and covered the entire area. Then he drove north on Buffalo Soldier Trail to Highway 90, where he next found himself in Huachuca City. He ran into the small town's convenience stores and showed Bobby's picture to the people inside—no response. As he traveled, he was hanging up posters of his brother in all of the stores he visited. Maybe somehow, someway, Bobby's kidnapper might slip up, become publicly visible, and someone would spot Bobby.

Mike drove back to Sierra Vista and turned left onto Fry Boulevard to continue his search. His heart was racing, and he was beginning to discover the futility of his search. He turned north onto North Avenue and resumed his search. He turned down many streets, combing the northern sector of Sierra Vista. There he met plenty of people, and showed Bobby's picture to all of them. But all he received was more negative replies, and best wishes … just as before.

Finally, after talking with officials at City Hall, the library, the Sheriff's substation, the Community Center and the Courthouse, Mike found himself coasting slowly into Veterans' Memorial Park, just north of East Fry Boulevard.

Mike sluggishly walked towards the park. He saw many children coming out of Sierra Vista Middle School, as he half staggered from exhaustion into the park. His eyes caught a familiar figure … it had to be Bobby! "Bobby!" Mike screamed. He ran for the lad as fast as he could. Bobby's back faced Mike, but Mike just knew it was Bobby. Mike reached for his brother and spun him around.

"Ah-h-h … who *are* you? Help!" hollered a young lad that looked very much like Bobby.

The young boy's mother ran swiftly to her son's rescue. "Let go of my son!" screamed the woman. She reached into her purse and pulled out a cell phone. "You crazy man! I'm calling the police!"

Mike quickly let go of the young lad and jumped back. "Please, Ma'am, you don't have to do that. I just thought your son was my brother."

The lady hesitated for a moment, noticing Mike's face looked just as startled as her son's face. "Wh … who are you?" inquired the woman.

"My name is Mike. I can't…. He's gone … he's really gone! Bobby is gone." Mike turned and walked away, his face void of expression. He dropped Bobby's handsome photo and slowly walked over to the grove of trees directly in front of him. He looked more like a zombie than a human. Mike dropped to his knees below the trees, staring helplessly at the green grass below him. He began sobbing as he dug up clumps of sod. "Oh, no … Bobby, no, no, no, no … *No!* You can't be gone. Oh God, please help me. Please, God, bring him back. Don't let my baby get hurt. He's all I have. Ah-h-h! Bobby! You were right with me. You can't be gone. Ahhh … Bobby!" Mike burrowed his head in the ground, and rocked back and forth, crying uncontrollably. Birds in the trees, overhead, cried out through the limbs, and a squirrel chattered loudly. Mike knew they joined him in his sorrow. He knew they were crying out to their creator to save Bobby. Yes, even the animals shared his grief.

Mike felt a warm, gentle hand caress his right shoulder. "I know who you are now, Mr. Taylor. I read the back of Bobby's picture." Mike slowly took the picture from the lady's extended hand. The lines on her face revealed the deep concern she had for Mike. Her dark hair softly swayed in the breeze.

"You look much like my mother did when she was alive. You are very pretty … like her, and your hair is the same color. No wonder your son looks so much like my cute little brother," sobbed Mike.

The lady began to cry, too. She felt the horrendous grief inside Mike. She hugged her son tightly. "Mike, I wish we could do more than just pray for you. I wish.... I am so sorry." She reached out and hugged Mike. Mike broke down in her arms, and wept bitterly upon her shoulder. Her son Ricky even cried a little.

Mike rose from the ground and gave the lady a long hug—then he told her he was sorry about the confusion. The lady apologized for her behavior, and told Mike her name. "My name is Amy, and this is my son Ricky. We want to help you, Mike. If you give us some posters of Bobby, we will pin them up for you."

"I don't have anymore," Mike lamented.

"Well, here is my card. It has my email and number on it. When you make more posters, email me some—or send them to me—and I'll pin them up," said Amy, as she wiped tears from her eyes.

Mike looked calmly into Amy's eyes. "Thank you, Amy; thank you for being here today. You may not know it but you have just inspired me. Thank you."

Amy gave Mike one last hug—then they parted. Mike shrugged his heavy shoulders. He felt weak all over, after this most unsettling encounter. He now knew the score ... he could not do it all on his own. He gave in to the fact that he would need help. Then he remembered that he was to meet Audra later.

Mike climbed back into his Jeep, and turned left onto Fry Boulevard, heading east. He began talking to himself again. "I'm going to find you, Little Brother, and I'm going back to the site you were abducted from, but not blindly. I need to know what happened that day after I passed out. I want answers. I need answers. And ... I know where to get them."

Mike drove straight through the intersection of Highway 90 and 92 towards Bisbee. His mind was on the dog trainers at the Sheriff's Department. He reached into his pocket and retrieved a card and his cell phone. "Well, Officer Seagle, you said if I needed help to call you. Here I come. The dog trainers will know more than I do about our canine buddies and, with a little luck, I may just discover what I already believe could be another possible clue," said Mike to himself as he nudged the gas pedal a little more to increase his speed. He felt very anxious, and he wanted facts.

Mike turned to a public radio station. He though a good debate might keep his mind off his problems for a while.

"As we examine the stats of the annual number of missing children, we discover an appalling number of cases each year. The *NCMEC* reports that nearly 2000 children are abducted in a 24 hour period."

"Hold that statistic for a moment," interrupted another individual partaking in the discussion. "When one does the math, we are telling our listeners that seven hundred and thirty-thousand children turn up missing each year. Now that is a very large figure, and very hard to believe. Mr. Thompson, that is like saying in twenty years the number of children abducted will be close to the entire population of New York City. That is a little difficult to digest."

"Mrs. Johnson, not long ago Senate Majority leader, Bob Dole; Senate Minority leader, Tom Daschle; House Majority leader, Dick Armey; and House Minority leader, Dick Gephardt, all appeared with former Attorney General, Janet Reno. This was in conjunction with the *National Center for Missing and Exploited Children (NCMEC)*—at a ceremony to raise public awareness of this problem. The cases have been well documented and, hence, your figures."

"But, doesn't the media actually over-inflate these figures?"

"Yes, it is safe to say that they may do so, and I also must add that I am glad that they do—if they do—because their figures have really grabbed America's attention about this horrible crisis we face today. And, this crisis seems to be growing much worse," added Mr. Thompson.

"It is my understanding that the media claims that two million are abducted annually. This is far short of the number given by the *NCMEC*; however, Louis McCagg, Director of *Child Find*—the nation's oldest and best-known missing children's organization—has stated: *'There's a tremendous scare on.'* He was once a strong supporter of the 50,000 estimate, yet *Child Find* now says that the actual number is even less than 50,000."

"Mrs. Johnson, Bill Carter, of the FBI's Public Information Bureau, has said,
> *'Their figures are impossible. More than 50,000 soldiers died in the Vietnam War. Almost everyone knows someone who was killed there. The numbers I've seen from missing child groups on abducted children range from 5,000 to 50,000. Do you know a child who has been abducted? That should tell you something right there.'*

There was a short pause then Mrs. Johnson began again. "Mr. Thompson, John Gill, the Director of *Children's Rights of New York,* has also stated, similarly:
> *'It's sad to say, but some organizations are exaggerating the figures to make their cause seem more urgent. Why, our schools should be empty if there were that many missing children.'*

Mrs. Johnson continued, "Furthermore, what do we consider to be the basis for these inflated numbers? The U.S. Department of Justice issued a report in 1990 that is highly informative but—due to a number of factors—is susceptible to easy misuse. The *National Incidence Studies of Missing, Abducted, Runaway, and Thrownaway Children (NISMART)*, breaks down *'missing'* children into five categories. These categories are: (1) family abductions, (2) non-family abductions, (3) runaways, (4) 'thrownaways' (children who were either told to leave their homes, were abandoned or deserted, or ran away, and the parent or guardian made no effort to get the child back), and (5) lost, injured, or otherwise missing.

"Here's where the potential for yet more confusion to begin ... each of these five categories is further broken down into '*broad scope*' numbers, and '*policy focal*' numbers. '*Broad scope*' defines the problem the way the affected families might define it. This definition includes both serious and minor episodes, 'that may, nonetheless, be alarming to the participants.' The '*policy focal*' approach, by contrast, defines the problem from the point...." Suddenly Mr. Thompson interrupted Mrs. Johnson.

"Mrs. Johnson, John Walsh, host of the television show, *America's Most Wanted,* has testified before Congress about this issue. He has placed the annual total number of abducted children at more than 1.5 million, adding that '*we don't have a clue what happens to over 50,000 of them,*' and that, '*this country is littered with mutilated, decapitated, raped and strangled children.*'

Mr. Walsh, who survived the tragedy of his own son, Adam, being abducted and killed—a case that received national attention—joined Janet Reno in officiating a recent ceremony. Now, these are their unadulterated official statistics. Whether you want to believe these figures, or not, is up to you. What we are trying to make the public aware of is that there is reason to be extremely cautious. We have to be on guard. We must take precautions, even to extremes if need be, to save the lives of our children."

"Mr. Thompson, the point my organization is trying to make is quite clear. We are instilling *fear* in our children. People are trying to coax parents into programs that validate the use of marking our children's teeth or imposing hidden implants in their bodies, so if they are abducted and later found dead—or, hopefully, alive—they can be identified. Now, the probability of being abducted and murdered is less than a million to one, literally. Yet, we continue to encourage fear in many of our children today. Some of the things people do out of fear are very harmful. To me it's even questionable whether parents ought to ingrain in their children a fear of strangers. What happens is that we end up with a society in which nobody trusts each other."

Mike snapped. He slammed his fist on the dashboard. "You're a little late with this information! I can't believe it! What a dirty trick of the devil himself!" Mike shut the radio off, and slumped back in his seat. "C'mon, Mike; keep cool. You must maintain. 'Got to keep a level head."

After almost twenty minutes of driving, Mike came to The Bisbee Traffic Circle. Several exits veered off the circle. One led to Douglas, off highway 80, another exit took off to the old Bisbee district and Bisbee junction, and yet another led to Highway 92—to Palominas and Sierra Vista. Mike turned left, and followed the road into the town of Bisbee. He passed the *Information* sign directing drivers to certain County facilities, one being the Sheriff's office. Mike drove carefully as he looked for Judd Drive, the road that led to the office. He turned left on Judd Drive and stopped at 205 N. Judd Drive. Slowly, Mike pulled into the sheriff's office, parked his vehicle, stepped out and walked into the station. An attractive female dispatcher, or receptionist, greeted him.

"Hi, ma'am, my name is Mike. I was wondering if Officer Jeff Seagle is available?" Mike expected the woman to answer with an affirmative, but she told Mike that he had to leave due to a traffic emergency.

"How long ago was that?" asked Mike a bit anxiously.

"Oh, the call came in about 20 minutes ago, but those accidents can be very tiring and untimely," added Veronica, the receptionist. Mike noticed her nametag.

"Well, Veronica, would it be all right if I sit here in the lobby and wait? Maybe he'll be back soon."

"Sure, I don't see why not. Was he expecting you, Mr.… uh …?"

"Just call me Mike, but my last name is Taylor and, yes, Jeff—I mean Officer Seagle—is expecting me at this time." Veronica's mind fidgeted with Mike's name. For some reason she thought it sounded familiar, but she dismissed it as a fluke, for she was exposed to so many names, she could barely keep track of them all. Still, the name seemed recent and of importance. Mike and Veronica talked between the calls she received from citizens of the County. Most of the calls were inquiries for information on specific legal matters.

Veronica patched the calls to the proper individuals that she hoped could help them. As she set the phone back down on the cradle so she could return to the conversation with Mike, the door opened and Jeff stepped inside. Instantly his face lit up. "Hi, Mike, I am so glad I finally got free of that little gig that took place on the highway, Nothing to panic about. Apparently, the driver was so engrossed in the scenery off Highway 90 that he did not notice he veered left of center until he sideswiped a vehicle. Thank God, he did very little damage, and no one was hurt at all. However, I had a little problem with the victim. Lord! He wanted to kill the poor guy that sideswiped him, but he finally calmed down when I mentioned the *'gray-barred hotel'* to him!" laughed Jeff. Jeff loved his occupation, and it showed in his voice.

Mike laughed also, "I think I'd back down, too, if an officer told me they had a vacancy at the gray-barred hotel for me if I didn't act civil!"

"Well, Mike, the paper work is complete. All I have to do is hand it in, and then I'll take you back to see Rick and Kevin. They've been excited to see you. You know, the only visitors they get come in the form of three-and-four-foot high, rambunctious little critters that love dogs!" laughed Jeff. Mike knew exactly whom Jeff was referring to as *critters*—children.

"Do they come often?" asked Mike.

"Nah, they usually only visit us during church or school outings," said Jeff as Veronica buzzed them through the metal door that led into the offices. Veronica finally put the puzzle together.

"Why, I'll be jig sawed—that's Mike Taylor, the young man who lost his little brother! I knew there was something about him ... about his name!" She felt a bit of remorse run through her body. "Poor guy, I wish I could tell him that his brother will be okay, but I'm too familiar with these cases; not good." Veronica lowered her head. She felt helpless and very uncertain for Mike.

Jeff led Mike outside to an annex building. The building was boldly marked *K-9 Div.* Mike and Jeff heard the dogs barking.

"Huh ... wonder what the ruckus is all about," commented Jeff.

"Maybe they have one of the trainers treed!" Mike humorously suggested.

Jeff laughed also, "Knowing those bozos, I wouldn't put it past 'em." Jeff stopped at the entrance to the large kennel, and told Mike to wait for him to return. "I just want to make sure the coast is clear before we step inside."

"Sure, Jeff, last thing I want is my butt bone bit in two by one of your police dogs!" Mike grimaced at the thought.

Jeff looked at Mike and said, "Well, that would be a first. They're actually more docile than you may think. You'll see! Once y' get t' know them, they'll love you," explained Jeff.

Mike smiled, "Oh I'm sure they are wonderful, and we ... well, Bobby and I ... love dogs." Mike's smile left him as Jeff lowered his noble head and walked inside.

As Jeff approached the *K-9* unit, he couldn't help feel sorry for Mike. Jeff had taken it upon himself to check out Mike's background, after meeting with him in the hospital a few days earlier. Here was a young man who had lost his mother and father to a plane crash and, several years later, his grandmother and grandfather also passed away. The state had awarded Louis and Mildred Taylor custody over the two boys, Mike and Bobby. However, about the time Mike reached his twenty-first birthday, his grandparents had perished in a hotel fire in Florida. That was only ten months ago. Because Mike was of age, the state saw no reason to separate Bobby from his brother. Plus, Mike and Bobby's parents—and grandparents—had left the kids a very handsome estate, and the hotel that burned down had awarded them a very handsome settlement. At least they were financially set, possibly for life.

Jeff also liked the young man's benevolent background. He gave of himself freely to coach young students in wrestling, and he taught Sunday school.

Except for a speeding ticket he received three years ago, Mike had a snow-white record. Jeff also had learned that Mike had a friend on the police force—Raymond Duke, a Sierra Vista police officer—one of Mike's best friends. Jeff knew Raymond a little, so had mentioned Mike and Bobby's disappearance to Raymond. Raymond had indicated to Jeff that Mike had a deep respect for the law, explaining that Mike had even thought about law enforcement at one time. However, feeling he could more directly help others by being a nurse, he had chosen that field, rather than law enforcement.

"I'd rather have a loving family than all the gold in the world," said Jeff to himself, as he poked his head around the corner of one of the dog cages.

"Well, looky who's spying on us, Old Red!" exclaimed Kevin Kline, one of the trainers. Kevin featured a round face with a big smile. His light complexion and thin blond hair added to his baby-face features. Old Red was busy chewing on Kevin's well-wrapped arm. Old Red looked at Jeff, and wagged his tail.

"Hey, Old Red, buddy, it's me ... Jeff!" roared the deputy. Red let go of Kevin and jumped on Jeff. "You big ole rascal, you! Hey, where's your buddy, Rick!" laughed Jeff as he caressed and patted Old Red. Actually, Old Red was not old at all. He was only four years of age but, due to his drooping hound dog eyes, he looked old, so the title stuck.

"Rick is outside in the yard with Lobo and Sherlock," grunted Kevin as he lifted himself off the ground. Rick walked proudly into the kennel with Lobo and Sherlock, two beautiful German Shepherds. Lobo was silver and black, with exceptional markings, and Sherlock was a standard brown and black. Lobo sported a prettier coat, but his tail was slightly hooked due to scar tissue from a healed bullet wound.

Rick dearly loved Lobo, because there was a time when he had almost given his life for him. Rick had been on a routine call to check out a camper under suspicion of drug trafficking, when Lobo began to bark and paw at the side panel of the camper.

"What's the fuss about!" exclaimed the owner.

"You tell me. My dog apparently has detected something behind that steel panel," stated Rick soberly.

"Well, I ain't about to tear the panel apart just cause your dog is making a fuss. Shucks, for all we know he smells some animal we probably ran over," bellowed the owner.

"Well, if that's all it is, then you have nothing to worry about, but that panel is going to come off ... now," ordered Rick. One of his colleagues stepped forward with drills and tools to begin the removal of the suspect panel. Suddenly, Lobo jumped at a man who was rounding the corner of the camper. Lobo hit him squarely in the chest as they both went down. *"Blam!"* the gun the criminal brandished exploded loudly in his hand. He missed his primary target, Rick, but the bullet partially severed Lobo's tail. Even in pain, Lobo disregarded his welfare, as he kept the criminal at bay. He held on tightly to the man's hand and bit down severely until the man dropped his 9mm automatic pistol. Rick ran over and swung a strong right fist into the belly of the assailant—then he kicked him sharply in the rib cage. The other officers pulled Rick off him, and led him away.

"The damned murdering fool! Lucky for him he didn't kill Lobo, or I think I might have killed the man myself!" shouted Rick. Lobo—bleeding and limping—crawled over to Rick. The poor dog whimpered in pain. Rick quickly placed Lobo in an ambulance, despite the medic's protest concerning the dog. Rick made sure the paramedics safely transported Lobo to the nearest animal hospital. Later, the police uncovered a large supply of illegal substances such as crack and marijuana from the RV. Lobo became a hero overnight that day, but his tail never was the same.

After Lobo healed and Rick felt better, the other officers made a loving sport of the traumatic affair. They would look at Lobo and say things like, "What a tail that was boy!

"Yep, the bad guy got him by the tail. The problem with Lobo is he's always telling tales. Tell us another tail-tale, Lobo!" The jokes never really ceased. Even today, the tales go on.

As Rick walked over to Kevin and Jeff, Lobo grabbed the cuff at the bottom of his trousers and sent him tumbling. Rick landed heavily on the ground. Rick laughed until he almost cried, as the two wrestled like children. It was easy to see the love between dog and deputy. Mike laughed loudly, too. His laughter startled the men, but not the dogs—they knew he was there. However, they sensed he posed no danger, so they did not bark. Kevin looked at Old Red, "Well, well ... some watch dog you are! Now, if that there young man was a crook, he'd have had us all!" grunted Kevin.

"Oh, man! I'm sorry, fellas. This is Mike. Mike, I got so caught up in all the hoopla in here that I forgot all about you. I meant to get you ... oh, well," sighed Jeff looking at Mike.

"Hey, I probably shouldn't have walked in by myself. I could have been misjudged by one of your dogs and ... who knows what could have happened," stated Mike, not feeling too slighted.

"Ah, the dogs know good character when they smell it, but don't do that again Mike, please. We had an incident before when a stranger walked in and ... phew! Well ... it wasn't such a great outcome." Old Red walked over to Mike, and licked his hand. Suddenly he jumped up on Mike and began sniffing his shirt pocket avidly. He even began pawing at it. Then he let out a little gruff bark, and stood wagging his tail, and looking up at Mike.

"Hey, young man, what you got in that shirt pocket—better not be illegal!" exclaimed Rick.

Mike laughed as he pulled out a hanky. "Well, if white handkerchiefs are illegal, then I guess y' better lock me up!"

"Hey, can I see it, Mike?" asked Kevin.

"Sure can," said Mike enthusiastically as he handed the cloth over to Kevin. Kevin held it to Old Red's nose. Old Red wagged his tail and barked a bit.

"Strange, Old Red acts like he knows that scent. Hey, I know, you are Bobby's brother, but them dogs weren't looking for you. They were hot on your little brother's trail. Why is this hanky so important to them?" Kevin looked puzzled.

"Well, Lobo, sure didn't make a fuss!" Rick interjected.

"That's because he's all tale and no walk!" laughed Kevin. Everyone laughed at this; even Rick saw the humor in the pun.

"Well, actually gentleman, Old Red may know the scent on that hanky. You see, that hanky is not mine ... it belonged to my brother. He left it in the Jeep before we began our climb the day he was...." Mike's voice trailed off.

"We all know. We hated that day. For some reason nothing jelled ... in fact, I was very perturbed. I never saw our dogs lose a man in a search like that one!" exclaimed Kevin.

"Yeah, it was too odd. We have arrived on scenes later than that one and found our suspects rather quickly. Old Red, our prized bloodhound, has the nose of a champ, and Sherlock and Lobo are fast as lightning on their paws—they make a great team! Old Red usually picks up the scent, and then the shepherds run down the culprit or culprits, but that day something went awry. What, I just do not know," stated Rick.

"Well, what fascinates me is how long they remember a scent!" exclaimed Mike.

"Heck, they got the memory of an elephant when it come to scents. Why, have you ever gone away from a dog that knew you? I mean have you ever been gone months, even years, from a dog—and then met up with that dog again?" Rick asked Mike.

"Well, yeah ... sure."

"And what happened?"

"Well, the dog barked and looked suspiciously at me, but then it seemed to remember me, especially ..."

"Especially when the good old boy smelled you or your hand—right?" Kevin blurted out, as he interrupted Mike.

"Why, you baby-faced booger! You stole my thunder. You're always stealing my punch lines!" moaned Rick.

"Oh, if anyone is being the baby right now, it's you darlin'!" laughed Kevin.

"And don't call me darling ... I ain't your darling!" Rick complained yet more.

"No, you're not, but when you whine and complain, you remind me of my wife, Darlene, so naturally I'll call you *darlin'* when you whine!" jeered Kevin.

"Oh, shut up!" scolded Rick, laughingly. Mike laughed with the deputies also, and then he began to speak with a thoughtful restraint.

"Hey, guys, I've been wondering. Do dogs really have an extraordinarily keen sense of smell? I mean could they pick up the personal scent of some-one if it was transferred from another individual who was, let's say, holding a cloth that had the scent of the individual on it, but then grabbed a different cloth and placed it in front of the dog?"

"I think I know what you're referring to, secondary transfer scents. Hmmm ... yes, I know Old Red can. Mike, you see, dogs like these are trained to pick up scents no matter what, but if you place the scent of an individual in front of the dog it helps. I mean it eliminates other scents and aids in choosing the main scent. The dog now knows to key in on that scent. Does that help any?" inquired Kevin.

"What if Old Red was to be given the scent of someone other than the main subject?"

"Well, he'd probably nose around for a few minutes wondering why he could not pick it up, but then he'd decide to sniff out the strongest scent of a human available," explained Kevin.

"But if Old Red caught a little of the main subject's scent from secondary transfer, would he know who the subject was then?"

"I would think so because the subject's scent would be very strong in the area being searched. He might be a little buffaloed for a spell, but as soon as his keen nose picked up the strong scent of the subject, *'zip!'* ... it's off to the races, howling and barking he'd go—like he did for awhile at the scene where your brother was abducted." Kevin stopped right there. "I'm sorry, Mike," he said sadly.

"Please, guys, let me talk ... and don't be afraid to bring Bobby into this. It actually helps me. I want to talk about it, please," coaxed Mike.

"Well, in that case, do you have any other questions about our dogs?" asked Rick.

Mike chose his words carefully. He did not want them to detect his suspicion in the Sheriff. "Actually, I do. Can dogs hear so well that they might be able to detect noise below the ground?"

Rick fidgeted for a moment. He looked up at the ceiling then down at the ground. "Well now, that's a good one. I'm sure you know that the earth is a great noise insulator. However, experts say that the rockier the earth is, the better chance noise has to travel. So, if the ground is stony, I suppose it's possible. Except I don't think those floppy hound ears of Old Red could hear very well, since they're covered by big flaps!" laughed Rick.

"Bull corn, and more bull corn! Those big pretty ears act like megaphones. They cup around the eardrums and capture all the noise. Why ... you remember when he put his ear to the ground during our search for Bobby, don't you?" asked Kevin excitedly.

"Yeah, and you told Old Red we had no time for gophers!" heckled Rick.

"Yeah, I know I did, but afterwards, I wondered if he had maybe heard something underground, after all."

"He heard a chipmunk chattering at her lazy ol' husband!" roared Rick.

"Then he can hear things underground," said Kevin triumphantly.

"You know what? I thought it was mighty strange the way those dogs attacked those boulders. You'd think they found something for sure," remarked Rick.

"Yeah, no kidding. I wanted to stay there and snoop around those big rocks, but the Sheriff insisted on heading further down hill," moaned Kevin.

"Well, no wonder; I didn't see anything there but rocks, and maybe a little crack in the boulders where a critter crawled into. That's probably what the dogs were barking at, anyway ... a silly critter," taunted Rick.

Mike interrupted the conversation. The boulder, or rocks, they were talking about seemed rather familiar.

"Hey, guys, that boulder you're talking about: did it kind of resemble a nose? I mean did it look odd and large, and was it outcropping from the south side of the ravine?"

They all looked at each other as their minds drifted back to that miserable day. Finally, Jeff spoke up, "Yes, Mike, now that you mention it, it did look like a nose—and it was on the south side of the ravine. Why?"

"Well, I saw that same boulder, and I noticed footprints below it. Didn't you see the footprints?" Mike wondered.

"Well, er ... not exactly. We were pulled off that area rather quickly by the Sheriff," explained Kevin.

"So, the dogs really might have discovered something there!" exclaimed Mike.

"'Guess anything is possible. I wish we would have checked that area out more thoroughly," said Jeff.

"You know. It was a little odd that Sheriff Joe pulled us off that scent *so* quickly … not that it means anything but, gee, it may have been a clue at least," griped Rick.

"Oh well, the Sheriff knows what he's doing. He did the right thing, I guess. Nobody but Houdini could have disappeared into that outcropping and, even then, it would have taken him a few years t' figure out how!" laughed Kevin.

"Yeah, guess you have a good point there, still…." Rick stopped talking when he saw Kevin giving him the eye.

"Well, men, I think I had best be hitting the trail. I still have chores to do, and it's starting to get a bit late," said Mike.

"Hey, anytime you feel like sharing a few laughs, or you want to know more about our prized pooches, you just drop in or give us a call," shouted Rick.

"Yeah, don't be a stranger; we love company, even if it is human!" chuckled Kevin.

"You guys are great. I'm very glad I stopped by. You were very entertaining and educational," said Mike.

Jeff escorted Mike out of the annex and into the main office. He told Mike he was welcome anytime. "Mike, please, if you ever need a friend to talk to, you know I'll be there," assured Jeff.

"You've said that before, and I'm gonna hold you to your word, Deputy," Mike slyly smiled. He shook Jeff's hand, then walked out of the office and into the lobby. Ironically, he met Sheriff Tress at the main door.

"Well, hello there, Mr. Taylor. I was told you might drop by sometime soon. How do you like the station?" Mike felt a bit nervous and uncomfortable. He already listed the Sheriff as a suspect, and now here he stood right in front of him, bigger than life. His tall frame sort of intimidated Mike, even though Mike stood six-two. This man stood every bit of six-four, and his shiny boots helped raise that height to six-six, easily.

Mike mustered up his courage, and looked into the dark eyes of Sheriff Tress. "Actually, I think you have a fine headquarters. I was here when I was a boy during a field trip. I don't remember it being so big, or so modern in some places," said Mike, trying not to seem suspicious.

The tall, pleasant-looking Sheriff smiled as he spoke softly. "Well, we have remodeled some, and expanded some, as well, due to a little more growth in the county. Say … did you talk to any of my deputies?"

"Sure did. You have a great bunch of guys, Sheriff. They are definitely dedicated to you and to law enforcement.

"How would you know?" blurted the Sheriff, a bit sarcastically. Mike wasn't ready for such a strong reply. Mike thought the Sheriff might more aptly just say, *'Thank you,'* as he beamed with pride. Caught off guard, Mike thought quickly.

"Well, since you put it that way ... because they speak so highly of you; that's all I meant." The glow had left Mike's face, and he became a bit irritated. Maybe the Sheriff was testing him. Maybe the Sheriff wanted to figure out if Mike suspected him. These were the thoughts that quickly entered Mike's mind, but he felt bold and rebellious now.

"I'm sorry, Mike, I didn't mean to sound so cantankerous. Still, I think that you must be around a person longer than an hour before you can judge their character ... or their loyalty."

"Sheriff, I beg to differ. I think I can judge some peoples' characters in five minutes or less. Haven't you ever been around someone whose manner of speech immediately betrayed their morality, their honesty—or lack thereof ... their concern for their fellow man—or lack thereof?"

The Sheriff looked sharply and coldly into Mike's deep blue eyes. He wanted to push Mike a bit further. For some reason, he didn't like Mike. He didn't like him from the get-go. When he saw him at the scene, he knew he wouldn't like this impertinent young man, no matter how intelligent or moral he may be. He certainly did not care for Mike's rude comment about the law, even though Mike was traumatized at the time.

"Mike, I must be getting along. I hope you keep your nose clean, and—whatever you do—leave the search for your brother to the authorities. I get the feeling you may be trying to take matters into your own hands."

"I beg to differ with you again, Sir. If I had taken matters into my own hands, the culprits would already be behind bars!" exclaimed Mike. Mike's audacity did little to win over the Sheriff's trust.

"Culprits! You say that as though you know something I don't!" an agitated Sheriff Joe sounded off.

"Just speculation, Sheriff ... nothing to get your feathers all ruffled about," said Mike a little sarcastically. The Sheriff pulled Mike to the side.

"Now, you listen, and you listen *good!* We're all you have now. You can't do a thing without us. Son, you need to learn that ... and fast. I'm only telling you this 'cause I care, and I don't want to see you get hurt anymore than you have already. I've come across strong, I know, but Mike ... I know you've been asking questions. If you know anything, you should let me know about it ... pronto. I'm your friend, not your enemy, doggone it! Think about that for a spell."

Sheriff Tress turned and walked over to Veronica, who could not help but overhear some of the words the two exchanged. She had rarely heard Joe talk like that, and It scared her. There was no good reason for it. Joe motioned to Veronica to follow him, as he walked back inside the office.

Mike quickly left the station and raced to his Jeep. He felt very flustered and angry. How dare the Sheriff play around with and manipulate his emotions like he did. Mike started his Jeep and roared out of the parking lot.

Once inside his office, Sheriff Joe looked coldly at Veronica. "Maybe you think I was a bit hard on Mike, but if he's going to make it through this, he's got to be tough enough to know that he has to let us do our job!" he bellowed.

"You know, Sheriff, sometimes you scare me!" exclaimed Veronica.

"What does that mean?" he barked.

"You figure it out, Sheriff." Veronica answered, as she walked back to her desk. She wondered why he had even pulled her to the side to talk to her. Was he feeling guilty about the abduction rescue being botched … helpless and culpable? "His team fumbled the ball and the crook got away! Guess I'd feel a little to blame, too," Veronica muttered to herself as she reached for the phone.

Mike made his way around the traffic circle one more time and drove towards the old section of Bisbee. He passed a huge man-made crater known as the *Lavender Pit*—a huge deep cavity, named after a long-gone mining engineer, from which hardrock miners extracted countless tons of copper ore. The copper and iron, along with a mixture of other elements, gave it an interesting shade of lavender. As he rode by the *Queen Mine Tour,* Mike's mind played back times when he and Bobby had toured the huge copper mine. He recalled seeing Bobby's face light up when they rode the train into the man-made, majestic cavern. He and Bobby both loved geology. To them, the mine was one of the most fascinating, beautiful, crystalline wonders they had ever seen in their lives.

Thoughts of the colorful, precious, crystalline minerals left Mike's mind as he entered Bisbee's historic district. He drove up Naco Road, stopping his Jeep for a moment alongside the street curve, and staring at all the porches—supported by elegantly carved wooden columns—up and down the sidewalks. A sign in one of the antique shops read, *'VaVoom.'* Mike knew the attractive young couple that owned the quaint little specialty and gift shop. Mike chuckled, as Bobby and their visits here began filling his mind. "Bobby, you sure did love running in there and looking at all the *Star Wars* memorabilia … and other old trinkets.…"

Mike wiped a tear from his right eye. No matter what he looked at … what he did … where he went, he saw Bobby's face. "Is this what it's like to go crazy? Maybe I'll find myself in a mental ward yet," said Mike aloud. The wind blew through his open window, making a lonely whooshing sound, as it caressed his cheeks. Mike's heart grew very heavy. The world appeared empty and bare, like one massive ghost town. Even the whining tires rotating over the asphalt road from passing vehicles sounded forlorn … mournful. Mike's heart wanted him to walk into the gift shop and say hello to Kelly and Brad, but his mind told him not to burden them with his problems.

He sighed and shrugged his shoulders, as he pulled back onto the road and drove on. As he did, he couldn't help but notice how glamorous all the little shops looked. Each time Mike was in Bisbee, he felt as though he had stepped back in time—when the west was young and unforgiving. He took delight in driving slowly by the many art galleries, gourmet restaurants, coffeehouses, bookstores and specialty shops. Mike also loved walking among the charmingly restored neighborhoods of Victorian-and European-styled homes, perched miraculously—if not precariously—on the hillside. At the moment, he was yearning to walk a spell, relax, and take in the scenery around him. Maybe a peaceful stroll would ease his troubled mind. However, this alluring leisure time would have to wait, as he had an appointment with a private investigator, and he did not want to keep the man waiting.

Mike studied the addresses carefully. Finally, he saw the right address. He parked his Jeep and walked into the rundown shack. Inside, the shack was actually cute. It had a clean potbelly stove and pretty striped wallpaper trimmed with roses. Some pictures of the town hung on the walls, and one picture of a young boy stood out from the others. Mike took a couple steps back for a better view of the boy. Mike spoke aloud to himself, "I wonder…."

"Yes! That's Danny. That's my son. Mr. Taylor, I presume!" exclaimed Matt Piper, the private eye that Mike had carefully chosen to hire on as an aide to find Bobby. Mike's heart almost skipped a beat.

"Well, you presumed correctly, but what do you mean by sneaking up on your clients like that!" griped Mike.

"Well, I guess I did startle you. Sorry, chap, but I couldn't help myself."

"So, you're a bit odd … but I guess that doesn't matter. I know who you are, Mr. Piper, and I need your help on my case," said Mike.

"Oh. We spoke so quickly over the phone—and I have so many other cases—which one would that be?"

Mike looked around the detective's office. No signs of pending cases lay anywhere in sight. However, Mike decided he could play along. "The Bobby Taylor abduction case is what we talked about over the phone."

"You mean the wireless, Chap. I do not own a phone line, just a fax line."

"Well, couldn't you use the fax line for both?"

"Nah, 'twould cost me more money, and I pinch every dime I can these days. 'Not that I can't afford the phones, but I like being frugal."

Mike began to think he'd chosen the wrong man for the job, yet the detective seemed rather humorous, so Mike decided to stay for a little while longer.

"My dear young man, why don't we discuss your dilemma over a spot of tea or coffee?"

"Sounds like a good idea, Mr. Piper."

"Please, lad, call me Matt ... or Inspector."

"Okay, Matt ... you've got a deal. Now let's find out if you're up to a challenge." Mike's voice sounded a little cynical.

"Well, now, that's a good question. First of all, do you know what the success rate is when it comes to recovery, especially live recoveries?"

"No, I don't but, from what I have read, not very good."

"Excellent observation. So, should you waste your bread and butter on me? Hmmm ... well now, I have three success stories. I have found two dogs and a little girl. The little girl's father abducted her, and I traced him down, once I discovered he lived in a small town in Alabama. He didn't even bother with unlisted numbers. "I merely called him on the phone and pretended to be a building inspector that needed to check his house for a possible violation for which the city would reimburse him. They have funny rules in some small towns, you see. In that town, if a contractor or developer messes up and creates a code violation, the city corrects the problem and recovers the funds from the builder—then they give the owner a share. But that's only if you live in one of the city's special project sites like the girl's father did. What a deal!"

After hearing yet more from Matt, the Inspector, Mike was convinced he'd found a clown instead of a legitimate investigator. The Inspector continued, "Ah, but in my youth—my younger days—I solved many other cases. I specialized in theft. I loved to catch a thief!" Matt took out a huge book full of clippings. He handed the clippings to Mike. The newspaper clippings revolved around all the theft cases that Matt had solved. He was popular over in Great Britain ... especially Scotland Yard. He solved many cases from trivial home thefts to grand thefts, including million dollar paintings and very expensive jewelry. Mike leaned back in his chair. Now he knew from whence Matt's English accent came. And maybe ... just maybe ... Mike had not hired a clown, after all.

"Matt, you were obviously brilliant in Europe, but what brought you over here?"

"Mr. Taylor...."

Mike cut Matt off. "Please, Matt, call me Mike, okay?"

"Mike, when news of my favorite nephew's abduction reached my household in Northern England, I rushed over as soon as possible. I thought, for sure, that I could find the bastard rascals. By Jove, I felt very confident about the case. If I could track down the most intelligent thieves known to mankind, I thought that I surely could wrestle down a child abductor."

"What about your family in England?"

"What family? If you think a man that is constantly on the prowl can hold down a family—no, not I. Oh I've had my jollies with the ladies, but never a real joy … know what I mean?"

"I can only imagine. But, let's get back to the real world now 'cause, frankly, I do not have much more time."

"Mike, all kidding aside, I *can* help you. I know all the bureaus to contact … I have access to all the files in this case, due to my license. I can help, but I can't even begin to offer you a guarantee of any sort."

"Matt, can you guarantee that I'll make it back home today without being killed in an auto accident?"

"Point well taken. You know, Mike, I poured my life into finding young Danny Thatcher. He was the only child my sister ever conceived, and he was like a son to me. Today I refer to him as my son. Anyway, my sister's husband died two years before Danny's abduction. Life is so unfair at times. Poor Margaret … she hung in there for a few years before she lost her mind. At least she lives. I was so worried she'd self-destruct. Actually, I think I lost my mind over the tragic episode myself. Mike, I've been living in and out of Jim Barley Corn's finest bottles since it finally occurred to me that I may never see Master Danny again."

"Now, that's what I like!" exclaimed Mike.

"You like whiskey, too?"

"No, I hate Mr. Jim Beam and Jack *Dumpy* Daniels, but I respect honesty. You have been honest with me. You could have told me a big tale, but you didn't … you even told me about your vice. And, Matt, you seem to know the horrifying agony of losing a child, having explained how Danny was like a son to you. This is why I am going to hire you. I need a person that can access files and run background investigations on certain people. I need someone to infiltrate from within."

"Lordy, son! You sound like we are after conspirators!" laughed Matt.

"Laugh it up, Matt, but when I brief you in on all I know to be fact, I think your laughter will turn into suspicion, and your suspicion into possible accusations," stated Mike very sternly and boldly. "By the way, how long has it been since Danny was abducted, and where did it happen?"

Matt stirred in his cushioned swivel chair, looked up at the ceiling and rubbed his brow. "About a little over eight years ago. He was a Boy Scout, you know. He loved the Scouts. Patagonia State Park swallowed him whole. I combed that area well, but found very little. 'Managed to track him just west of the Santa Cruz-Cochise County line. The tracks stopped there."

"Tracks ... what tracks?"

"Well, I am good at putting together a criminal scene. It didn't take me long to see the muddled dirt from a scuffle, and broken limbs of bushes. The prints led to an outcropping alongside a hill. Something bothered me about that outcropping of rocks, so I followed the boulders further down the hill and discovered a small tunnel. All I had was a pen light to help guide my way through that dark passageway, yet it sufficed and I came out the other side to a wash. The bed of the wash exposed large tire tracks, like a heavy truck of some sort. I followed those to tracks past Highway 82 and further east to Trench Camp—then Mowry Wash down to the flats of the Santa Cruz River. At Parker Canyon, the tracks disappeared, along with the hope of finding Danny. Matt's eyes turned misty. He stopped talking as Mike sensed a form of blame building up inside Matt. The investigator became business-oriented now, as he quoted a price for his services.

"You want seven hundred a week plus expenses ... hmmm. I'll give you four-hundred-and-fifty a week, and meet half your expenses ... and I'll tell you what days I need you, and what days I don't. I'll also lend you my grandfather's Lincoln, because I know that old jalopy you have out front is a gas hog and may see a junkyard any day now. And, Matt ... you will *not* drink on duty. Am I clear?" Matt took a couple of minutes to tally the offer in his head, as his mind was still a bit foggy from a recent shot of whiskey.

"Ah-h-h, let's see ... car, money, half expenses. I'll take the case!" boomed Matt. The two men shook hands, as Matt drew up the papers. He was still a little loose as he wrote in the figures. After Matt drew up the contract, Mike read it and signed the legal document. He turned and proceeded to leave.

While he was on the way out, Matt asked, "Mike, by the way, have you received any ransom notes for Bobby's safe return?"

Mike hesitated. He envisioned the two thugs that had been at Mr. Brown's store the day Bobby had vanished. "No, Matt, I haven't even received a phone call pertaining to such."

"Well, If you do, we must respond immediately ... *spit-spot!*" exclaimed Matt.

"Thanks for the discount, Matt. Well, I've got t' go!" Mike rushed out of Matt's office, ran to his Jeep, started the vehicle and raced away. He had a pretty little lady to meet tonight, and he was darned if he was going to miss out on two beautiful eyes, lavish auburn hair, lovely rosy cheeks and a great smile, to boot.

Inside Matt's little two-bit shack, the Inspector read over his contract. "Three-hundred-dollars a week!" screamed Matt. Matt grabbed his bottle of Jim Beam. "You, you scoundrel, Jim. See what you made me do! Why I'll … I'll … I need more of this luscious crap!" Matt tipped the bottle and began slurping.

Mike traveled west five miles over the speed limit on Highway 92. As he drove, his mind drifted back to the conversation he'd had with the Sheriff. Why was he acting so harsh? "If the Sheriff's a suspect, I would expect him to act very innocent and kind—feigning, as though he really cares—but he was quite the opposite. I'm confused! Now the good Sheriff doesn't fit the part of a suspect." Mike sat back in his seat uneasily. There were so many 'what ifs' and possibilities.

What really happened to Matt's nephew, Danny, anyway? This question now entered Mike's mind. Somebody kidnapped Danny eight years ago, and Audra's brother disappeared four years ago. "The number four seems to be popular all of a sudden. What is it with four years? Bobby is abducted four years after Audra's brother. Four years prior to Audra's brother's abduction, Danny is gone! I should have asked what Audra's brother's name was when I had the chance." Mike was deep in thought, trying aloud to sort things out— too deep, in fact, for suddenly there were strobe lights behind him, appearing like a brilliantly lit red and blue flashing Christmas tree.

"Great! Mike looked at the speedometer, "Oh Lord! Doing fifteen over the limit. Dang! I was so caught up in thought…. Ah well, I'll take the darned safety course and forget about the points," said Mike to himself, as he pulled off the road and came to a stop. The SUV displayed the word "Sheriff" as the vehicle pulled up close to Mike. The Tahoe slowed down, but then sped on by. Mike's heart felt like it would burst at any moment. "Well, I'll be jiggered! Whoever that was apparently had better things to do then write out a blooming ticket!" Mike laughed inside himself. "Better watch it … I'm starting to talk like bloody Inspector Piper."

Mike turned north on Palominas Rd. and began the last leg of his journey home. As he turned, he noticed the same Sheriff Patrol van sitting idly in a store parking lot across from the intersection. "They're following me now. Maybe they think I know something … or maybe I'm just paranoid. That store is also a tavern, and I'm sure trouble could be brewing inside that the deputies need to tend to." As Mike started down Palominas, the Tahoe's headlights mysteriously lit up as the vehicle slowly pulled out of the parking lot.

Mike, strangely, gave it no further thought, as he had too much work to do before his dinner date with Audra. Mike turned right off Hereford Road, onto Southern Lane, and traveled three more miles to his manufactured house—

could it even be called a home anymore, desolate as it now was without Bobby—a sad house now, that sat on a four-acre lot. As he stepped out of his Jeep, he sighed when he saw the well kept landscaping. Bobby loved chopping down the weeds with his *Weed Eater.* Moreover, he pruned the prickly cypress trees and Colorado piñon pines well as some mountain mahogany that grew in their yard.

Mike noticed the mountain mahogany starting to bud. "Won't be long until those pretty flowers pop their heads out!" Mike smiled. "Just wish my brother was here to take care of this place; he so enjoyed doing that." Mike hung his head as he walked into the house. He quickly constructed a bologna sandwich out of four pieces of bread and three slices of bologna. Then he bounded into his office, turned on his computer and began to surf the 'Net. He drew the symbol he'd seen on the topographic map on a small piece of paper, and figured now was as good of a time as any to snoop out the symbol.

Mike muttered to himself as he tried several different search engines. "Well, I've looked through Greek and Roman symbols, Mayan symbols, and Aztec symbols. I'll bet this is a very easy one, as it just looks like a broken tip of a square pencil with a slanted point ... kind of like a ramp, in a way. Maybe it is just a glitch ... a blotch of spilled ink. Audra's probably right." Mike mumbled on as he typed in the words, *'ancient Egyptian symbols.'* A list of symbols popped up on the screen and one of them did resemble his targeted symbol.

"Hmmm, let's see, it is called a *Maat,* which means *truth, justice, morality* and *balance.* Deities are often depicted standing on this symbol, as if standing on a foundation—shows one of their greatest deities, *Osiris,* standing on this one. Let's see, type in *Osiris.* This picture on the Internet illustrates *Osiris,* the important deity of religion and sacrifice. Points to human sacrifice, also. Sacrifice? Hmmm ... I wonder if they chose this to symbolize the horrible unwanted, forced sacrifices parents have made due to their child's abduction? Surely, the wicked kidnappers don't *sacrifice* all those children!"

Mike's discovery left him feeling very glum as well as stumped ... only more confused than before. Mike reprocessed the information in his mind repeatedly. "I think I'm becoming paranoid. I think Matt might be right when he mentioned the possibility of a conspiracy. There might be more people involved than one in any given abduction, but that is far from a conspiracy."

Mike snatched the phone from his desk and called the library at Cochise College. "Hello, this is Cochise Community College Library. How may I direct your call?" a pleasant-sounding lady spoke. Mike thought it was great to get a real person for a change instead of a recording.

"Hi, may I please speak with Audra, the girl who works at the Information Desk?"

"Sure, I'll patch you over to her. Hold the line for a moment." Mike held the phone anxiously in his hand.

"Hello, this is Audra."

"Audra, this is Mike. You know … the guy you helped with the maps. The one you're gonna see tonight. Man! Am I glad I caught you before you left!"

"Hey, settle down, Big Guy. What's up?"

"I was wondering if you could do me a little favor!"

"What's that, Mike?"

"Could you possibly look through those topographic maps again, specifically the one that shows the Patagonia Lake in the Patagonia Mountains. Look for that same strange symbol we saw today, please," Mike said practically begging.

"Yeah, sure, I'll do that, but you have to pay for my dinner in full … no Dutch treat!" laughed Audra.

"Lady, you drive a hard bargain, but I think I can handle that!"

"Okay, see you at seven. I've got a customer—gotta go, Slow Joe!" She hung up.

Mike paced the floor a little, "Seven. Hmmm, I like that. She sounds more interested than earlier, because she told me around seven-thirtyish. She wasn't sure about me … now she is," Mike gloated.

Mike showed up at the restaurant around quarter to seven. He wanted to appear very punctual and considerate. As he walked into the Country House Restaurant's lobby, his eyes fell upon Audra.

"Well! I thought I'd show you, but apparently you stole my thoughts, girl!"

"Oh, don't beat yourself up over it, Mike. I didn't have anything better to do, anyway, so I got here a few minutes earlier than you." Audra talked on as she held a round map case in her hand.

"What do you have there, Audra?"

"Well, the school has a very good copy machine, so I took it upon myself to copy those maps and bring them here," she explained.

"Wow! Groovy! You sure are thinking, girl!" replied Mike, with excitement.

"I also have another interesting story to tell you, but let's seat ourselves first."

Mike and Audra followed their host to the table, and sat down. The host asked if they wanted anything to drink—they both chose iced tea. Then Audra withdrew the maps from the case and rolled them out in front of Mike. She spoke as she unraveled the maps,

"Mike, after you left I thought a lot about Todd's abduction."

Mike interrupted Audra, "Your brother's name was Todd. I am very sorry," said Mike softly.

"Yeah, and we miss him so-o-o much … we never give up hope. Anyway, I remembered that Todd's group camped at Talkali Lake, but it was always a ritual for some of the boys to hike the north side of Natanes Plateau near Black River, so the map's borders we were looking at did not show that region. I took it upon myself to retrieve the correct map and right here"—Audra pointed at a circled symbol on the map—"is the same symbol we saw on the map, at the spot where Bobby vanished." Audra puffed up glowingly … excited at her sleuthing results.

Mike studied the map carefully. Sure enough, the same symbol lay next to a contour line. It was not obvious but, if one looked very closely, they could see it was the Maat symbol. "Audra, did you happen to bring the map of Patagonia Lake?" Mike became very focused and caught up in the new discovery.

"Of course I did. What do you think I am, a whacky blonde!" protested Audra.

"Oh, just words, Audra; I meant nothing by them!" laughed Mike, oblivious to the impact just a few of his words could have. Audra laughed also as she handed the map over to Mike. Mike almost tore the map in excitement and anticipation. He opened the map and studied it closely. "I don't see it, rats!"

"My boy, my boy! You are really blind. It's right slam-dunk in front of you!"

"I must be blind, cause I do not see it at all!" Mike felt foolish. Audra laughed even louder than before. "Mike, look at the boat launch symbol." Mike looked straight at the symbol. "Wow! How tricky! Of course … they used that symbol but they modified it just a bit to look like a Maat. They are very smart, and you, Dear, are extremely brilliant," laughed Mike. Listen, Audra, I want to go back to where Bobby vanished. I like using the term *'vanish.'* It sounds better, more positive, than *'abducted.'* Anyway, will you go with me? You are very intelligent, and I could use an extra pair of eyes," stated Mike enthusiastically.

"And what else?" Audra smiled, teasingly.

"And I like you, gal. *Ah lahks* you ver-r-ry much," said Mike colloquially, yet warmly.

"Well, in that case, you've talked me into it. When and where do I meet you for this daring adventure?" asked Audra. Mike looked into Audra's beautiful brown eyes. His heart almost skipped a beat as he said, "I'll give you my phone number and my address. We'll leave from my place. Actually, if not for my moral upbringing, I'd invite you to stay at my place tonight, so you would not have to travel so far from town."

Audra looked at the address and laughed. "I didn't know we were practically neighbors. It's a small world, Mike. I live right off Natoma Trail. I'm only a few miles from your house."

"Splendid … right-on! So, it's all settled!"

"Sure, but you'd better be careful!" warned Audra. Mike looked rather confused.

"Careful, about what?"

"I put boys to shame when it comes to hiking!" exclaimed Audra. The two would-be explorers finished their dinner rather quickly. They were both excited about the trip. Mike walked Audra to her vehicle, a two-door, compact, red Nissan Pick-Up.

"Nice truck you have," commented Mike.

"It's very reliable, and that's all I care about right now," said Audra as she looked at Mike's Jeep.

"Great looking Jeep you have!" exclaimed Audra.

"Thank you, it's my little pride and joy. 2003 Jeep Wrangler Rubicon, 2-door, five-on-the-floor, two-tone, over-sized off-road tires, dual disk premium sound, with premium wheels and leather seats ... not to mention, dual air bags, a custom bumper and a moon roof for those romantic nights that I have yet to encounter. And, best of all, it's a four-wheel drive with a winch, so we can pull ourselves out of jams!" Mike laughed loudly.

"Now I can sleep better tonight!" exclaimed Audra. "Oh, by the way, you're coming with me to your first support session next Monday at eight in the evening. I told some of the group members about you, and they are really looking forward to meeting you, Mike."

Mike looked up at the stars—then he looked into Audra's pretty, sparkling eyes. He stepped in closer to her as he spoke, "As long as you're there, I think I could probably sit through a session." Mikes voice was soft and pleasant. A cool breeze caressed both Mike and Audra's cheeks as Mike leaned over and gently kissed Audra's forehead. Audra felt a tingly sensation course through her entire body. She felt lost in time for a moment as she allowed her full, rosy lips to embrace Mike's soft lips. They held each other tightly with their cheeks pressed softly and passionately together. Mike and Audra both felt the need for affection. For once, since Bobby's abduction, Mike found a happy moment. Audra shared a similar feeling as she held on to Mike. Mike stepped back and smiled. "I'll see you tomorrow, pretty woman!"

"I'll be there. You'd just better watch your step though, Buster. My father's a *Green Beret,* you know."

"Well, now ... you've got me shaking in my combat boots!" laughed Mike. They both laughed as they stepped into their vehicles.

Chapter Six

Mike and Audra stepped out of the Jeep, donned a few water canteens and a light backpack. Mike pulled a pry bar out of the back of his Jeep. Audra began to ask Mike what it was for, but she stopped herself. She felt it was none of her business—at least for now. They began the journey to the spot where Bobby had vanished. They spoke a little but, for the most part, their minds focused on what lay ahead.

Audra told Mike all about the mountain mahogany and odorous pines and junipers. She pointed out the cypress trees and explained how they belonged to the rose family. The grama grass and buckwheat grew thick in some areas. This jogged Audra's memory, and she mentioned how she'd once heard that wherever buckwheat grew very thick, there was sure to be silver nearby. She talked about the birds they saw, pointing out Cassin's kingbirds, western kingbirds, tree swallows and several species of canyon wrens and titmouse.

Mike was very interested in—not to mention, rather impressed with—her vast knowledge of nature. Mike did not know so much about plants and birds, but he shared his knowledge of geology with Audra. He explained how tectonic plates, shifting and colliding together, caused the earth to break in huge chunks and jet up out of the ground and fold over themselves, forming the mountains. The volcanic activity during that time left a large variety of igneous rocks and different minerals.

They had walked quite awhile, and talked on and on about nature, when suddenly Mike stopped. "Here it is, Audra. Here is where Bobby vanished." Audra stared down a rather steep ravine, "What was he doing down there, Mike?"

"Well, he was relieving himself, and that's why he didn't want me around. "Dang it all! If only he wasn't so danged modest ... like I'd never seen the male anatomy before!"

"Mike, don't go there! *Don't* blame yourself. My, how we all rode in that train for a long time before we discovered that we were not responsible for Todd's kidnapping. That practice almost tore our family apart," explained Audra. Mike walked down to the greasewood where he had found a piece of Bobby's torn flannel shirt, and the incriminating boot prints.

"Now that's very strange!" Mike shouted.

"What are you shouting about, Mike?"

"I've only been away from this area for a few days and the prints are totally gone. It didn't rain while I was in the hospital, did it?" inquired Mike.

"No, it sure didn't."

"Well, the limbs are still bent over and some broken, but why are the footprints gone?" Mike asked himself and Audra as he crouched down on his hands and knees.

"What are you doing now, Mike?" Mike grunted as he crawled around on the ground, "Aha! The footprints appear as though swept by a tree branch or something like it. Maybe someone took a broom to them. "Look, Audra; look at the sweep marks!" Mike excitedly proclaimed.

Audra looked very closely at the ground. Sure enough, she could see the furrows made by a broom or the leaves from a branch. "Someone came back here, Mike. Someone doesn't want you, or anyone else, to find clues to this rather unique situation … unique and terrible," she added.

"Why? Why would the perpetrator come back to the scene unless there was more to Bobby's kidnapping than meets the eye? I can't fathom your ordinary wicked child molester going back to the crime scene when he gets away *scot-free!* He'd have to be a very stupid man!" Mike exclaimed. He continued on. "I wonder how our expert investigators missed this?"

"Maybe they're not as brilliant as they say they are. Hey, Mike, the swept trail continues towards those big funny-shaped rocks!" yelled Audra, as she began running towards them. Once closer, Mike and Audra had to fight their way through brambles and prickly brush. As they reached the boulders, they both took in a deep breath of fresh air in relief.

"Hey, you weren't just a'kiddin' when you said you were a great hiker. Man! You're making me look bad, girl," laughed Mike, admiringly.

"Yeah, but I'm not toting a big pry bar, either. Mike, why did you bring that thing, anyway?" Audra finally had to ask, her curiosity having gotten the best of her. Suddenly, she stopped talking, as her eyes fell upon something rather peculiar. She walked over and picked up a broken leafy branch. "Mike, look at this. Are you thinking what I'm thinking?" Mike stared at the branch. He turned and looked at the boulders—then he looked closely at the ground below him. The sweep marks from the branch ended at the big rocks before them.

"You know the map reveals that there are supposed to be tunnels all through this area and beyond. We're just north of Highway 83, close to Cave Canyon and the cave itself," grunted Mike as he swung the pry bar into the rocks. Some of the rocks gave way and fell to the ground. "Rather loose, aren't they?"

"Yeah, I'd say so … almost like they were purposely placed there," agreed Audra. Mike stuck the sharp end of the pry bar between a crevice in the boulders and gave a mighty heave. Something within let go and fell, making a hollow sound. A big rock wedged between the crevices loosened a little, also.

"Mike, that hollow sound…."

"I know. We've found a tunnel." Mike pried and pried with all his might, until the rock in front of the crevice gave way and fell back into a dark chasm, leaving a gaping opening to a tunnel.

"Mike!"

"Audra, I wouldn't blame you if you stayed behind, but I've got to go."

"Mister, you ain't getting rid of me that easily!" shouted Audra, as she kissed Mike on the cheek. She was ecstatic. Her heart leapt with joy, for she knew there was a tremendously good chance that finding this also could lead them to discover Todd's whereabouts. They both retrieved their flashlights from the backpacks they had donned. "Mike, I am so eager to get started! Come on, let's go!"

This time it was Mike who was ahead in the game. "Audra, I'm scanning the entrance with the light. I don't want to discover booby traps that would end our trip faster than we started!" explained Mike.

"Oh, yeah! Good idea … glad I thought of it!" laughed Audra, embarrassed a bit that her overt enthusiasm had dimmed her caution for a moment. Mike found nothing but dust, and loose gravel. He climbed into the tunnel and motioned Audra to follow him.

As they made their way carefully through the tunnel, they kept very silent. They knew the abductor might still possibly be around, especially after seeing the swept ground above. The tunnel seemed to go on endlessly, and Mike became a bit worried. He whispered very softly, "Audra, we could get lost in here for weeks and die."

"Well, Hot Shot"—Audra once again taking the lead—"I've been marking the trail with some crayons I brought, just in case we stumbled into a mine or cave. Plus, I have two tubes of lipstick if we run out of crayons!" she gloated triumphantly.

Mike shined his light on the crayon marks, "Fluorescent, no less! Now I *know* I've met my match. Woman, I love you!" Mike whispered, adoringly.

"Well, do you mean that?" queried Audra—herself, not too disinterested.

"Wouldn't you like to know," asked Mike, teasingly. They walked on for what seemed to be another mile. Mike looked at his compass from time to time. They were walking south towards the Coronado Cave. As they walked, they looked very carefully for clues, pieces of cloth, footprints—or anything that might suggest Bobby may still be in the tunnel. But they found nothing. The tunnel became wider and greater in height as they walked. They found hiking very easy now, so they were making very good time.

Suddenly Audra bumped into a large crate of some sort. She shined her flashlight on the crate. *Greater Southwestern Produce.* "I never heard of that one before," Audra said with surprise.

"Hmmm, neither have I. 'Must be an unknown wholesaler. Wonder why someone would store these crates down here? It makes no sense," mumbled Mike.

Audra continued to inspect the crate. She came across other crates also— and then discovered a label. "Looks like a voucher, or inventory list," said Audra.

Mike walked over and looked at the label. "Some of it's in Spanish, but the English reads, *'Fresh produce, healthy, ready for shipment, thirty pollen grains, ten F. gametophytes, please handle with extreme care.'* I can't make out the rest very well … something like *'oli'* or *'Bo'* … I don't know."

"Well, I think we should move on, my husky friend, before it gets too late," warned Audra.

"You have a good point there. You know, this tunnel is pretty big. I'll bet you could get small trucks and other vehicles in here." Mike coughed a little as he spoke, due to the dust in the air.

"Maybe they don't have to drive a truck in here. Look! I found old iron tracks."

Mike excitedly rushed over to where Audra stood, managing to trip over one of the iron tracks, and falling to the ground. His flashlight went flying, bounced off a hard rock, and went out. "Well, you sure know how to find iron tracks in a very safe and convenient way, don't you," laughed Audra. "Are you okay, Mike?" she added, with concern.

"Hey, Sweetheart … it hurts, you know," moaned Mike.

"I'm sorry." Helping Mike to his feet, she again asked, "'You okay, Buddy?"

"Yeah, but my shin feels a bit sore," said Mike as he rubbed his leg vigorously. Mike and Audra recovered Mike's flashlight, a heavy duty *Mag.* "Well, the lamp probably broke, but there's a spare in the bottom of *MagLites,* so I may get lucky." He unscrewed the bottom cover, as Audra shined her light on him. Sure enough, the flashlight contained a spare lamp. Mike set it in place, and reassembled the light.

"Shoot! 'Nothing but nothing; the spare lamp must have broken, too!" complained Mike.

"Give it to me!" Mike handed the light to Audra. She quickly disassembled the light, turning a couple batteries around. She reassembled the light, and shined it in Mike's face. "Always helps to keep polarity correct," Audra grinned.

"You know … I do love you, woman," chuckled Mike. They quickly began walking between the tracks. They had no idea where the tracks would lead them, but they figured they had to lead to an exit somewhere. After almost another quarter mile of hiking through what seemed to be an endless tunnel, they noticed daylight up ahead. They walked faster now. Finally, they came out of the tunnel just above a wash.

"Audra, I know where we are. We're in Cave Canyon. I know the landmarks here. We are a bit south of the road, and a little to the east of, where we parked," explained Mike.

"You know, Mike, this area is ripe for crooks and who knows what else. I never knew this place existed … and right under our noses the entire time! Who would ever believe it? Why it's no wonder the crook got away. Talk about a great hiding place! You would have to know the terrain very well to even think about looking for a person in these tunnels," Audra was fascinated. Mike was, also. Many questions began to race through his bright mind. The two brave hikers walked down into the canyon trail below them.

"Hmmm, plenty of room for trucks and other vehicles. There are tracks, but who knows what sort of vehicle—or vehicles—made them … or who drove those vehicles. Actually, many people drive in and out of here, but they sure don't know anything about an underground tunnel system, that's for sure!" Mike spoke loudly now.

"Yeah, it's very mysterious. This place, and everything about it, spooks me!" shuddered Audra.

In response, Mike put his strong arms around his new friend. Audra melted. She did not know why she felt so submissive to Mike's charm … maybe female instinct. Suddenly their lips met and they found themselves in a world of heart-pounding passion. Pleasure throbbed through the two of them, as they hugged and kissed each other avidly. Passion was uppermost in Audra's mind now; she wanted more of Mike, and Mike felt the same about Audra. They continued, gently clinging to one another … until, that is, the heel of Audra's hiking boot unearthed a metal object, that flipped into the air as she stepped on it. As it stabbed into her ankle, she yelped, "Ouch! Man!"

"Hey! I'm sorry, Audra. I guess I don't know how bad a kisser I am!"

"No, silly, not you. Something stabbed my ankle," Audra explained as she reached down and picked up the metal plate. Mike and Audra studied the plate. Mike looked it over very carefully. Why did the markings and words on the plate look familiar? The blue color of the words even looked like something he had seen before. Suddenly a loud blast from a rifle echoed through the otherwise quiet canyon. The bullet kicked up dust only five feet from where Audra stood. Other shots began ringing out, as bullets suddenly zipped all around them.

"Damn it!" screamed Mike. "God *help us!* We've got to get out of here before we get killed!"

"Shoot! No kidding, Let's head back to the tunnels," hollered Audra.

"No, the bullets are coming from that area!"

Audra looked up to see smoke rising from above the tunnels. "Mike, they're so close. I cannot understand why they keep missing us!" yelled Audra, in a frenzy.

"Babe, I don't know, but I see heavy brush in front of us. We've got to make a run for it!" Mike and Audra raced swiftly to the heavy sage and grass before them. Audra kept right up with Mike as they ran and ran through chunky briars and thick, thorny weeds. They had no time to stop and check for wounds. Adrenaline shot through every fiber of their bodies like never before. Mike and Audra had never been so close to death … never been hunted by a human … never knew what it was like to be the prey … until today.

After running for what seemed to be almost two miles, the couple joined hands and caught their breath. "We've gotta keep walking," gasped Audra, "Got to get to the Jeep!"

"If … if there is a Jeep to … to get to," gasped Mike, as his lungs fought for more air. Audra looked at her wounds for the first time since the race for her life. "Wow! I look like a piece of hamburger!" laughed Audra a bit. She was trying to find some humor in the horror. This was part of her personality portfolio she had developed as a coping mechanism. She found humor to be her best weapon against negative situations.

"I'm glad you are taking this better than me, Audra. Maybe you can comfort me, even though most believe that's the man's job!" Mike cried out, still gasping for breath. They continued on their way. Audra found many ways to make Mike laugh. She told him that he looked like her great, great grandmother when he ran, and she boasted about how she outran Mike to the bushes. Soon Mike was laughing and shooting back sarcasm. Audra knew he'd be fine, and Mike knew Audra was … and would be … okay. They made a great pair. Mike and Audra both perceived this was the beginning of a lasting and loving relationship.

"There it is, Babe. There's our Jeep. Let's go home. I've had enough for one day," said Mike as he put his arm around Audra's shapely waist. Audra put her aching arm around Mike's back, as they marched to the Jeep.

They did not talk much on their way back to town. Audra fell asleep on Mike's brawny shoulder. Mike's mind was in overdrive. He asked himself more questions than he could answer. As he drove, his mind recalled the time when he rode his Honda *Enduro* down a lonely lane. "The lane ... that's where I saw the same words that sign had on it. I know where I have to go now. Tomorrow—unless something else comes up—I'm going to pay the area a little visit," said Mike to himself.

Mike pulled into his driveway and shouted, "We're home, Dear!"

Audra barely lifted her brow, "Oh, and I was having such a sweet dream." She rolled over to her back and lifted her head from Mike's shoulder. It was then that she felt the pain of her wounds. "Oh! Man! I am burning from all the cuts and scrapes. I feel like a pin cushion."

"I think I can empathize with you young lady!" laughed Mike. "Hey, why don't you stay a while and let me nuke you a meal?"

"Better yet, show me your kitchen," replied Audra. Mike hopped from the Jeep and helped Audra out of the vehicle. They both ached all over from their traumatic adventure. They rather limped to the front door. Mike unlocked the door and they walked inside.

Right away, Audra noticed the house needed a woman's touch. The place was not unkempt or messy ... not even dirty, but the interior was drab.

"You need to hire a better interior decorator," giggled Audra.

"Yeah, I'll admit it could use a makeover, but we get along fine. I mean...."

Mike shrugged his shoulders as he walked into the bathroom. Audra felt very feeble. What could she do? She knew the helpless feeling of losing a loved one. Mike returned with a first-aid kit. Audra laughed as he opened the kit. He invited Audra to lie on the couch. Then he began to administer antiseptics and dressings.

After he had finished with Audra, he began mending himself, as Audra wandered into the kitchen to see what she might find there. She found some vegetables, rice and hamburger, helped herself to the cookware and, in no time, the aroma of a fantastic home-cooked meal filled the air. It did not take long for Mike to find his way into the kitchen. "Wow! Smells great! What is it?"

"Dead meat I found in the fridge, along with a spot of rice, water chestnuts, bamboo shoots and, of course, bean sprouts, baby corn and chow mein noodles—heavy on the dead meat, 'cause we burned at least fifty-thousand calories today. Oh, and your salad is on the table. I could only dig up blue cheese dressing." Mike laughed at Audra's description of their meal, *'dead meat.'* He'd never thought of it that way before.

"Well ain't you the little chef!" Mike bragged on his newfound friend.

"Well, when you grow up an Army brat, you learn to improvise, adapt and overcome!" Audra chanted with gusto.

Mike laughed, "I think you're the funniest and grooviest gal I ever knew. Why didn't I meet you long ago?"

"Probably, 'cause I lived in Tucson until a year-and-a-half ago. That might have something to do with your question."

"Glad your Pa decided to move here, Love." Mike hugged Audra as he spoke. Audra responded by giggling, and giving Mike a small kiss on the cheek. She smiled contentedly as she stirred the meal.

Mike left the house and unpacked the Jeep. "Well, buddy, you lost the flash-lights, and left the pry bar out there, and the backpacks, as well. But I guess the discovery was well worth the loss," Mike said loudly to himself as he neatly placed the surviving items in his shed. When Mike returned inside the house, Audra had the meal waiting for him on the table.

They said a small prayer, and thanked God for a safe return—then they dug into the food. They spoke very little until their bellies felt more comfortable. Mike began the conversation. "There is one thing I know for sure now."

"What's that, Kiddo?"

"More than one person has to be behind all this, and I believe we have stumbled onto something bigger than I first thought."

"Why do you say that, Mike?"

"Well, let me start from the beginning … just hear me out, and then you decide if I'm paranoid or on track. You see, the day Bobby vanished, we were on our way to a peak that few know as Tucker's Peak. Now, when we got there...." Mike went on and on, explaining everything in detail to Audra; he told her exactly how Bobby had vanished. He mentioned the dogs, the deputies and, of course, the suspicious Sheriff Joe Tress. He told her how Tress made the men pull the dogs off the hot trail leading to the boulders. Then he ended by adding the remainder of the day's events.

"Wow! Mike! I have to admit that you may be onto something and, further-more, how did they know you and Bobby would be at that spot … at that time … on that particular day? That's more than irony. Mike, we know that Bobby is not in that tunnel—at least there were no signs to so indicate—but what really blows my mind are those crates. You read the words *'F. gametophytes,'* and *'pollen grains',"* said Audra, as she looked into Mike's deep blue eyes. Every time she looked into his warm eyes, she felt so romantic inside. She carefully shook off the feeling.

"So, I read those words. What about them?"

"Do you know what they mean?" Audra asked excitedly.

"Have something to do with produce—probably refer to a plant, or something."

"Good assumption. You are correct, but there's more. Mike, *F. gameto-phytes* are the female reproductive sites of flowering plants known as *pistils*, and the *pollen grains* fertilize the *female* portion of the plant, so...."

Mike stopped Audra mid-sentence, and said aloud, "The *pollen grains* refer to the male reproduction process, or pollination!" Mike sat spellbound.

"Oh, my God! Mike, are you thinking what I'm thinking?"

"Audra, you never cease to amaze me. 'Of course. The *pistils* refer to human girls and the *pollen grains* must be a reference to human boys. Thirty boys and ten girls are to be shipped ... but where?"

"Hey, we don't know that for sure, Mike!"

"Yes, we do. Oh, my Lord! Please, help us! Please God! Those dirty bastards have them penned up somewhere, waiting to be transferred to only God knows where! "Audra, the label also said something like, *'oli,'* or *'Bo.'* What do you think that means?" Mike began nervously fumbling his fingers through his hair. He rubbed and rubbed his head until Audra thought every follicle would release its hold, as every strand of his hair fell out onto the floor and blew away.

"Mike, settle down! We don't know anything ... for sure, that is. Even if what you say is true, we still must have time, because I saw a date, and I know a little Spanish—especially what *Cinco de Mayo* is!" roared Audra.

"Isn't that a Mexican holiday ... Mexico's Independence Day, or something like that?"

"No, it isn't the day they won their independence from Spain. However, it sure confirmed their independence. You see, back in the mid-1800s, Mexico was still very unstable, so the French decided to seize an opportunity for economic growth by trying to take over Mexico. But the Mexicans beat the French army in the *'Battle of Pueblo.'* This victory sealed their independence, and brought much pride to all the people. Today it is celebrated all over Mexico, and all over the United States, especially in the southwest," concluded Audra.

"What don't you know, my brave damsel?"

"Well, I don't know much about nursing, Nurse Michael," giggled Audra.

"Well, at least I know something you don't. Hey! Wait! That's it!" hollered Mike.

"What's *'It'*?"

"Audra, don't you see? Those evil villains are going to transport the children on that holiday, of course. Think about it. When everybody is gathering in town to have a fiesta, those rats—basically unnoticed—are gonna make their move!"

"That makes a lot of sense, brother, because most of our security forces will be focused on their towns, and nobody will be *Cinco de Mayo*-ing in the Huachucas! These people are brilliant!" shouted Audra.

"I know, and that's what really worries me. Somehow, you can bet, someone is making a bundle from this ... a fortune ... off the heartbreak and grief of people that love those children. Those devils should be shot. They don't even deserve a trial. 'Just take 'em out back, shoot them and burn their mangy carcasses!" exploded Mike.

"Maybe with some luck, and help from above, we'll see that day soon, Mike."

"We only have a few more weeks to find out, Audra, and the clock isn't slowing down any since I last looked at it," sighed Mike. Suddenly Audra remembered Mike telling her about the Maat sign.

"Mike, will you please explain that Maat sign in more detail to me," Audra asked. Audra loved mysteries, but she never dreamed she'd actually become involved in one—especially one that could be very deadly. They had been shot at, and chased by bullets through very dangerous terrain. Yet, she vowed within herself that she would stick this out to the very end, even if it took her away from her class work. Something inside her said that Todd was alive, and now there was more than just hope ... there was Mike, and his strong faith.

"Osiris, one of the Egyptians' most popular gods of religion and sacrifice, often stood very tall on those Maats, according to what I read."

"Sacrifice? Like, in humans!" Audra gasped.

"Yeah, I guess so," Mike answered, wary thoughts of what might happen to some of the children, after all, coming to mind. He then continued, explaining how this Maat symbol was an ancient Egyptian emblem representing morality, truth and so forth ... how other Egyptian deities' statues many times stood on those Maats, as well as Osiris.

"Sacrifice...." Audra mused, quietly. She could not get this one thought related to the Maat out of her mind.

"Yeah, the Egyptians did sacrifice humans ... sometimes. Even the Bible speaks about such things. Did you know that, Audra?" Mike turned, jumped up, and swiftly left the room.

"Man! This gorgeous guy is very spontaneous ... like me," laughed Audra.

Mike returned, holding a Bible with rubber latex gloves. "The Book ... the verse ... I wrote it on the cover. I'm glad we had this conversation, as I'd forgotten all about this Bible that mysteriously showed up on my nightstand at the hospital. Thank God, I found it still tucked away in the plastic bag a nurse gave me at the hospital."

"Mike, you're making as much sense as a queer dollar bill. And what's with the latex gloves?" Audra looked puzzled.

"Well, whoever left this on my night stand probably left a decent set of fingerprints with it, and I don't want to take the chance of accidentally contaminating them with my own."

"Here it is, just let me read this to you. Exodus chapter 13, verses 2 and 13:
'Sanctify unto me the firstborn, whatsoever openeth the womb of the children of Israel. Both of man and of beast: it is mine'."

Mike then skipped over to verse 13.
"'And every firstling of a donkey you will redeem with a lamb; and if you will not redeem it, then thou shalt break his neck: and all the first born among men, you shall redeem.'
Why would someone leave this on my stand and, for that matter, who?"

"'Sounds like a sick ... very sick ... joke," Audra thoughtfully commented.

"Actually, Audra, I truly believe somebody I know very well is trying to warn me about something that has to do with Bobby. The passage states that *'both men and beast are mine.'* Now let's make believe whoever this person is has put himself in place of God in this passage. What I get out of it is very clear: *'Stay away; the kid is ours now. He has been redeemed to us and dedicated to us and we own him now, and if you don't stay away, or if you try to redeem him back to yourself, we'll break your freakin' neck!'"* exclaimed Mike coarsely.

"Wow! And I thought I was brilliant!"

"You are. We both are ... and that's why we're gonna find Bobby ... and we may even find Todd, too."

"No! We *will* find Todd!" Audra exploded, with much emotion.

"Now that's the spirit, m' Lady. I love you, Doll!" Mike exuded.

"I love you mostest, Mikey," swooned Audra.

Mike reached over and held Audra gently in his arms. Audra collapsed like a helpless lamb in his bosom. They embraced and kissed each other ... passionately, yet tenderly. Things may have gotten a bit more out of hand than either really would have wanted if not for the interruption of the phone.

"Oh, let it go Mike," said Audra softly.

"Babe, I don't want to lose this moment, either, but it could be an update concerning Bobby."

"You're right. I'm sorry. I mustn't be selfish, tempting as that is at times," replied Audra as Mike lifted the phone up to his ear.

"Hello."

"Hi, is this Mike Taylor?"

"Yes it is. What can I do for you?"

"Well, this is Pat Heyburn, Audra Heyburn's father. She left me your number. I just wondered if my daughter is with you."

"Yes, she is, Mr. Heyburn. We were just finishing dinner and a very pleasant conversation. Your daughter is a great cook. She is also very clever ... and intelligent. You must be very proud."

"Of course I am. But I was a little worried; it's getting a bit late. I know she and you are adults, but she is still my *Little Angel* and always will be. May I speak with her?"

"Of course," said Mike as he handed the phone to Audra.

"Pa." The room filled with silence for a moment. "Yes, Pa, I will." A minute went by. "No, I'm fine." Audra waited for her father to end his response. "Yes, Pa, I will. Yes ... no problem. He's a wonderful man, with a great sense of humor and he's very bright ... yes, and very responsible. He lives three miles from us in the big manufactured house off Cedar Lane. Yes, that's the one. He owns it. Yes. Okay, bye." Audra hung up the phone.

"That's Pa for you. Loves me so much that he just had to poke his nose into our business," laughed Audra.

"That's cool. I wish I had a pa to poke his nose in on my affairs," replied Mike.

"Yeah, I know you do. I'm sorry Mike," sighed Audra.

"Hey, I've got some snooping to do just down the road from here. 'You remember that metal sign that stabbed your ankle today?"

"How could I forget!"

"Well, on the way back—while you were playing *'Sleeping Beauty'*—I was thinking, and finally figured out why it looked so familiar. I saw the same wording and colors on a sign one day—just off an old lane, east of the intersection of Palominas Road and Hereford Road—when I was riding my *Enduro*. I'm going to check it out mañana. You're welcome to come."

"Ha! I'd better be more than just *'welcome.'* I'll be here tomorrow, just name the time."

"Twelve noon. I'm going to church tomorrow, then we'll head over there."

"Well, if we are partners, than I'd best accompany you to church, too ... right?"

"Hey! You're wonderful, Audra!" Mike felt even more excited now. Tomorrow he would stroll into his church with his head held high, as the one he could not help but deem the prettiest girl in town walked beside him.

Mike walked Audra to her Nissan, and she waved goodbye as she drove off. He then shuffled back slowly to his large, desolate house, and found himself pacing the floor after closing the door. He was restless, though he was also becoming extremely tired. His mind felt foggy, yet he fought to keep his eyes open awhile longer. Finally, he gave in to his tiredness, washed himself and dressed for bed.

Before retiring, Mike took one last look out the front window towards the end of the lane, as he locked the front door. He noticed a vehicle parked at the end of the lane. He wondered who it could be. Maybe just a couple of lost people ... or two lovers wrestling around in the car. Mike turned and walked into the bathroom. After brushing his teeth, he went to his room to retire for the night. However, before bedding down, he decided to walk back to the window and check the lane again. The mysterious vehicle was still there. Mike found a flashlight and shined the bright beam on the windshield of the car. The car's headlights came on, and the car slowly rolled down the road.

"Go ahead, you child exploiters! Stalk me, too. I don't care. You won't frighten me away from finding Bobby!" growled Mike, as he gritted his teeth callously.

The Sunday service was uplifting. The pastor preached on faith, through prayer and hope in God. Mike liked the part about holding on, because many times it's the last thirty minutes—when you're just about to give up—that the prayer is answered. The pastor gave true-life examples of this during his sermon.

The people of his church all fell in love with Audra. She seemed to glow with joy and compassion around everyone. Her bubbly personality made her an instant *'Miss Popularity.'* After all the good-byes were said, Audra and Mike walked to the Jeep. Mike opened the door for Audra. She'd started to step inside when a young man walked over to them.

"Hey, Mike!" Mike turned to see Dennis Perris, the Assistant-Youth Pastor.

"Hey, Denny, what's up brother!" shouted Mike, happy to see his friend.

"Not much Bro. Hey, I'm very sorry that I haven't gotten over to see you lately. Actually, I feel very badly about not seeing you right after I heard what happened. I am so sorry, Mike."

"So am I, Dennis. When did you hear about Bobby?"

"Well, I was out of town during that time. I just got back in town yesterday, but I heard about the horrifying tragedy over the news while I was in Tucson. You've probably been told this already, but it's worth repeating. I'm praying for your brother. I'm really praying for Bobby. God is able, Mike. He is able."

"Yeah, I know. Faith keeps me going, Bro."

"'Be all right if I come by sometime soon?"

"What are you doing Monday morning, Dennis?"

"You know what? I've got that day off, due to a district meeting, so I'll see you Monday morning," said Dennis joyfully as he tapped on the roof of Mike's Jeep.

"Well, be there or be square, my friend," chuckled Mike.

"Can't wait to see you. You take care. You, too, ah-h-h...."

"Oh, I'm so rude. This is my favorite—and only—gal, Miss Audra," laughed Mike

Audra extended her hand through the window. Dennis took her hand in his and said, "Wow! They don't make 'em any better than you, Miss Audra." Audra was flattered, but for some reason she did not feel comfortable around Dennis. She searched within herself for a reason as to why she felt this way, but the answer eluded her.

"Thank you, Dennis. You have a nice day, now. We need to get going, but you have a great day," said Audra, perfunctorily.

Dennis waved goodbye as Mike drove off. "Hmmm, you intrigue me, Audra. If I was not observant, I wouldn't ask you this, but since I am ... were you a little on edge around Dennis, or was it my childish imagination?"

"I don't know why, Mike, but for some reason he gave me the creeps."

"Women's intuition, probably," laughed Mike.

"Probably." Audra paused, as though pondering how much more to say. She finally spoke again. "Look, I know he's been your trusted friend for years, but do you really know him that well?"

"Well, we've known Dennis since he arrived here in Sierra Vista over eight years ago, and he's always come across as a straight shooter with us," assured Mike.

"'Wouldn't be the first time I've misjudged a person, though I have only misjudged someone one time in my life ... however, I was just ten at the time."

"Mind me asking who it was?"

"Oh, no, not at all. It was our youth pastor at my Church in Palm Springs, California. I thought the world of him ... bragged on him all of the time. Then one day the authorities arrested him for child molestation. It broke my heart, but I never gave up on God ... just some people," sighed Audra.

Mike didn't know what to say. Finally, he managed to mumble a few words. "Just goes to show you that you never know who the bad apples are sometimes."

Mike helped Audra out of the Jeep. They walked into Mike's house. Audra and Mike changed their Sunday clothes and threw on old shirts and blue jeans. They walked outside and looked at the bright sunny sky. Miller Peak loomed majestic-like above them to the southwest.

"Well, my pretty Little Lady, shall we make tracks on a couple mountain bikes?"

"Love to, but only with you, dear. I wouldn't be caught dead tracking with anyone else."

"Oh, my, now that sounds awful sexy, Babe. You may make tracks on me anytime, especially lip tracks," laughed Mike.

"Cool down, Sport! We have a ways to ride, and you might just get over-heated before we get out the driveway, if you don't." snickered Audra.

"'Be one of the best ways I could think of to overheat. Matter of fact, I think I'd love to overheat right now. Ah, but I have a *mission* today, so we must be *off,*" Mike said, with exaggerated gallantry. Mike knew that if it were not for Audra stepping into his life during this time of great need, he would probably be a wreck right now. She possessed an uncanny way of making him feel secure … and capable. While Mike's mind was absorbed with such thoughts, Audra mounted her mountain bike and took off.

"Hey, lady, wait for me!" bellowed Mike as he jumped on his bike and ped-dled quickly to catch up to his lady speedster. Mike finally caught up to Audra, as he turned left on Hereford Road. "Woman, you trying to kill me or what?" panted Mike.

"Look at those foothill palo verdes, honey mesquite and desert ironwood trees. Did you know that they belong to the pea family?" Audra was excited.

"No, I sure didn't," replied Mike.

"Yeah, they sure do. The palo verdes put out a small yellow blossom, but their fruit is nothing really to crow about. Now, the honey mesquite … Mm-mmm! Their pods produce a rather sweet pea out of which the Native Americans used to make a fantastic type of sweet bread. They would grind up those peas into flour, add some animal fat or oil and water, fry them and, presto! There you go—tasty fry bread!" Audra smacked her lips, recalling its appetizing flavor.

"'Sounds delicious!"

"Mike, it is pretty good. In fact, many Native Americans still make that fry bread, and I had some not too long ago at the fall festival in town. Haven't you ever tried it before?"

"Well, not really. The closet thing I ever got to fry bread is a tortilla."

"Oh! You poor, deprived child," Audra playfully feigned sympathy. "Well, I'll have to treat you to it some day," she added with a smile.

"'You promise?" questioned Mike.

"Hey, as long as you treat this girl right, I'll treat you right!" laughed Audra as they both peddled closer to their destination.

"Hey, thanks for the botany lesson. You really impress me. You sure know your plants."

"Well, I had better … because, my Dear, it's my major."

"Wow! That's cool, I never thought to ask," said Mike, rather sheepishly.

"Goes t' show how interested you are in a gal like me," scolded Audra.

Mike looked at her with a sideways smile. "Hmmm, and do you know what my minor is?" asked Mike.

"Well, ah, no … and that's not fair!"

"Goes t' show y' how interested you are, too. It's chemistry, and if it wasn't for …" Mike slowly shook his head, "if it wasn't for this terrible episode in my life right now, I would be graduating after this semester."

After duly commiserating, Audra looked to her right, at a tall mountain peak just south of them. She cast her eyes towards heaven and sighed. She felt as helpless as Mike, as events of her and Todd enjoying themselves at parks, camping, and horseback riding, or at home watching movies flooded her mind. There had often been other such joyful experiences, including exploring, or engaging in water fights. Audra chuckled inside herself.

The mountain pass Audra's mind suddenly flew to in this reverie had been quite an adventure a few years back. She found herself suddenly reliving the time when her frisky, fun-loving brother had somehow over-stretched his reach out the window of his father's Jeep SUV, as they drove slowly over a very high, rugged mountain pass, leading to Crown King, Arizona. This particularly narrow pass had steep drop-offs on either side of the vehicle.

Todd, Audra and their father had always enjoyed shooting at inanimate targets with a BB gun, so whenever they went camping or exploring, they would bring the air rifle with them. This time was no different. Only, this time Todd had managed to find a position that involved dangling a bit further than normal out of the side window, shooting at some trees and rocks alongside the steep canyon wall. All at once, Audra saw him disappear out the window of the *Town & Country*. His strong calves, with lightning speed, gripped the side of the back door. The bottom half of his legs gripping the door were the only proof that he had not fallen over the steep cliff.

Todd's frantic screams had escaped his father, who was too busy paying attention to driving carefully down the narrow road—not to mention being engrossed in the *oldies* station that was one of his favorites—to hear him. With both music and the wind in his ears, Patrick had been quite oblivious, at that moment, to the activity in the back seat. Meanwhile, Audra had quickly rushed to Todd's rescue. She grabbed his legs just below the knees, grunting and groaning until she'd managed to haul his body back into the Jeep. Her heart was pounding from fright, as she looked into Todd's eyes. They were as big as saucers, and his face was as white as a bleached-out sheet, but he was alive.

Finally, hearing all the commotion, as his eyes caught sight in the rear view mirror of the last moments of Todd's body struggling back through the window, their Pa had hollered out in utter surprise: "What in Saigon's name is going on back there!"

He found a safe place to stop the vehicle, and then turned around to take a good look at Todd. "Leaned over too far out the window with the BB gun, didn't you?" bellowed Patrick, though he was smiling by now, rather enjoying the look on Todd's face … knowing he was now safe from a fate he'd just narrowly escaped.

"Uh-huh … yes, sir! I kinda did!" explained Todd, panting and puffing, a dazed look still on his fear-stricken face.

"I ought to take the butt of that rifle and wallop you up-side the head with it. But I don't think it'd do much good; besides, I'll bet you'll never pull that crazy stunt again!" understanding fear to sometimes be a tremendous deterrent.

"Sir … yes, *sir!*" Todd replied, in the militaristic fashion he'd long admired hearing now and then from his *Green Beret* father. The traumatic look on Todd's face had assured Patrick there'd be no more such nonsense. With that, the trio had broken out into laughter … laughing until they nearly cried … thankful Todd was alive and in one piece, while vowing to be a bit more cautious in the future.

Audra laughed aloud, remembering, as she peddled on, carefully watching the road ahead. Then a gloom settled over her once more, as her mind shifted back in time to that most horrible day … the day when the phone rang off the wall and the authorities showed up at the door. It was awful. The police and FBI never could find Todd. The terrible abduction had sent her mother into a deep state of clinical depression that plagued her to this very day. Rhonda Heyburn, Audra's mother, would wake up night after night, screaming from the nightmares, and the lasting trauma left behind by Todd's abduction. Many times Rhonda ran into Audra's room and held her tightly as she sobbed in her agony, "I'll never, ever let anything … *ever* … happen to you!"

Audra's eyes filled with tears. "Todd is gone and mama's in the hospital. She's living life in a catatonic state. 'What a life. Those bastards!" Audra emphasized the word '*bastards*.' She looked to see a tear streaming down one of Mike's eyes, also. "Maybe due to the wind," she thought, but yet Audra knew better within. They both had much in common, and they both shared a pain, a scar, that would never go away.

Audra steered the cycle with her left hand as she wiped the tears from her eyes with the other. Mike stopped his bike as Audra pulled up beside him. He was very discerning. He knew his own dilemma was opening old wounds that cut Audra clean to her inner heart.

Mike dismounted his bike, set the kickstand and looked into Audra's watery eyes. "Lord, I'm so sorry, Audra. My tragedy is taking a toll on you, also. Maybe I shouldn't have gotten you involved."

"Gotten *me* involved? What! Gotten me *involved!* I wanted this, dang it! Don't you see? Are you that blind? Darn you, Mike! You have no idea what I'm feeling, or what I have felt … the inquiries … the hope that turned to dust, and the unanswered prayers. Oh, Mister, you have yet to learn! My mother's in a catatonic state in Tucson, my father is now a nearly broken man! Oh God, What did I do! What did we do … what does anybody—any parent, child, relative or sibling—do to deserve this?" screamed Audra.

Mike looked into Audra's overflowing watery eyes, and streaming tears, as tears began trickling down his own face, as well. "Nothing, Audra. And I can't answer your question … but I won't give up. I'll die before I give up!" He brushed his fingers softly through Audra's wavy, auburn head of beautiful hair. She fell into his bosom, as they held each other tightly and wept in each other's arms, for what seemed an eternity. Cars and trucks zipped by them, but they could not have cared less; the grief they shared blocked out the world. They felt all alone. Deep inside, their souls ached for honest, pure love, feeling it must exist somewhere in what now seemed a cruel, vicious society—a society that had robbed each of them of a beloved brother.

This love for which they longed was not a yearning for sex—which can be bought, often cheaply, leaving one feeling used and empty—but the purity, joy, richness, and genuine adoration that few ever find, yet all crave. They longed for an untainted and unconditional energetic connection and, as they both stood clutching each other, they felt the vibrant warmth and love of each other's very essence. Their souls reached out and embraced. For a moment, they were one—two lonely hearts, passionately melding together, into one magnificent masterpiece of spiritual unity. This moment was like the beautiful words that come together in a song … capable of melting the heart of the most ferocious beast … or stopping the sun from setting in the twilight of the wide western skies.

Mike pulled gently away and tenderly spoke, "I love you, Audra. I honestly love you."

Audra looked into Mike's soft, blue eyes, tears still streaming down her face. "I love you mostest," she replied, mustering a little laugh.

Mike hugged her again. "No, not this time. I love *you* mostester!"

They both laughed as they helped wipe the tears from each other's eyes.

Mike and Audra returned to their bikes and began riding again. They both felt a renewed strength surge through them. Now Audra fully believed in Mike, reveling in the respect she knew he had for her. Because of this, she could always trust and depend on him. Mike felt the same way about Audra, as he glanced at her again and smiled. He gazed up at the thickening clouds building in the sky, as Audra resumed her lesson in botany. She began to point out other plants and trees. "That bush to your right is cat's claw; it produces long, yellow oat-like blossoms. Hey! There's range rhatany! They're very pretty when they bloom; their blossoms look like brilliant, beautiful little red stars. You know, as a matter of fact, the plants and trees will begin to bloom in April, and they'll continue through June. "Wow! It will be so pretty!" exulted Audra.

"Yeah, and that means, time to break out the antihistamines, if you have allergies," laughed Mike.

"Well, is that all you have to say?"

"No, and I am not totally ignorant. See there?" Mike pointed to some bushy shrubs.

"Yeah, and ...?"

"That's a greasewood. It grows about five feet in height, bearing thorny branchlets, and generates little green flowers. Just to the side of it is some desert rue and buckwheat, along with some asters, and gray rabbitbushes. And ... look! A big sagebrush and a sage willow, to boot!" bragged Mike.

"And everyone of those plants you mentioned—except for the greasewood—all belong to the aster family ... even the aster you mentioned which, by the way, was very general," smirked Audra.

"Well, I give up. You win, Sweetheart. I do know that those sticky bushes can sure give you the itch if their dry leaves and little prickles get down your shirt or in your pants."

"Well, now we both completely agree on something." Audra looked at Mike and grinned.

"Hey! Here's the lane that leads to a big compound I wanted to see today, and right over here is where I saw a sign that resembled the words we saw on that plate that your ankle so rudely discovered Saturday." They walked the bikes over to the sign. Blue words were impressed upon a white metallic background that read, *'County Dept. Dist. Office.'* Audra and Mike studied the sign for a few minutes, trying to make sense out of it.

"I don't get it. *'Department'* of *what* ... and what office?" muttered Audra. Mike had no idea, either, which was why he had wanted to ride back to the compound. Another sign read, *'Keep Out—No Trespassing.'* Mike explained to Audra that he had never seen a *'No Trespassing'* sign the last time he rode his motorbike down this lane. They both wondered why the County had failed to erect a gate at the entrance of the lane, if they really wanted to secure the area.

"There's no gate, but the words on the sign bear a striking resemblance to the words we saw on the plate. Maybe it's nothing … then again, maybe it is. Guess we'll never know unless we do some investigating," said Audra.

"That a girl. Let's get rocking, before it gets too late." Mike and Audra bicycled down the lane towards the compound. Audra looked all around. The lane was somewhat narrow, yet easy to pedal on, due to good upkeep and evenly packed gravel. She saw large cottonwood trees and tall oaks, as well as a variety of berry bushes, but she did not comment to Mike about them; she was more interested in seeing the compound Mike was busy sharing with her. After five more minutes of riding, the compound came into view.

Audra was amazed at the size of the building. "I must admit, it does look like a rather large compound. Man! I expect to see David Koresh walk out of that place at any moment!" she exclaimed.

"Oh, what a pleasant thought, Audra. I should hope not," Mike said dubiously. Hey! Look at those huge iron garage doors! You could fit a large truck through those doors, easily," he observed. The building sat on an eighteen-acre lot. An old red-colored International tractor, with a trailer hitched to the back of it, sat in the front lawn. There appeared to be no one around. The green, grassy yard was in very good condition. Whoever the people were, they took good care of the place. Two large sheds—on-site constructed—stood behind the building, and an eighteen-hundred-square-foot site-constructed brick house was situated just south of the complex.

The building actually resembled a military compound, yet it lacked the fence and gate that you would expect to see around a military installation. Mike noticed some devices of some sort bolted down on top of the building. He looked closely at the box-like devices.

"Hey, Audra, those things on top of the roof look like cameras."

Audra looked at the devices. "You know what? I think they are. They might be watching us on a monitor at this very moment, Mike!" exclaimed Audra.

"Well, 'guess all we can do, then, is smile," Mike deadpanned. As he rode away from the complex, and pedaled over towards the brick house, Audra followed behind. They rode around to the south side of the brick house and parked the bikes.

"What's your plan, Mike?" Mike looked about the building. He was a bit perturbed, presently having no answer.

"Ain't got one at the moment, but I'd *love* to get inside that place. I can't figure for the life of me what it's all about … and why nobody seems to know about it. I've never heard anyone talk of this place since I lived here, and that's twenty-one years."

"That's a long time to be in one place," said Audra.

"Hey, do you think they have microphones in place out here, also?" asked Mike.

"Well, I don't know about that, but those cameras may be wide-angled to see just about every inch of the grounds, and...." Audra stopped talking when she heard a truck approaching the complex. The truck's engine grew louder and louder.

"Looks like we've got company, and that's no small pick-up." Mike instinctively lowered his voice as the two large, commercial straight trucks drove up to the building and into view. Mike and Audra observed them as they turned into the driveway leading to the large garage doors. They were straight trucks—probably twenty-four foot boxes—with reefers located in front of the trailers, above and to the back of the cabs. Blue letters on the side of the white trucks read *'CDO,'* and below the letters Mike and Audra read what appeared to be a slogan or something like it that stated, *'Help us help the hungry.'* Audra quickly looked at Mike and said, "Well, now, are you thinking what I'm thinking?"

"The *CDO* is *County Distribution Office* for the needy and hungry. The reefers on the trucks are used to maintain perishables, such as the produce. The plate you found is linked to these trucks, as well as the produce boxes we discovered in the tunnels," surmised Mike.

"You are too clever ... and we may just be barking up the wrong tree. It's no wonder there aren't any fences or gates; this place is a charitable organization set up by Cochise County, no doubt!" murmured Audra.

Mike's heart sank. Here he thought that he had finally discovered a link ... a clue that would help him blow the lid off a possible connection between the tunnels, the large produce boxes ... and his brother. Now it seemed all too clear that he was leading a wild goose chase. "What about being shot at by whomever?" queried Mike, as the wind picked up and blew his blond hair to the side.

"Aw, 'just some guys that think they found ore or something like gold ... they wanted to scare us away. And, you must admit, it worked."

"But, we know Bobby was forced into that tunnel. The dogs knew that. So did the danged Sheriff! Damn, this is too much!" Mike's voice grew louder.

"I don't know what to tell you now, Mike. Maybe we need to start all over from the very beginning. We do know someone forced Bobby into the tunnel, and we saw crates apparently used to ship produce in and out the tunnel. You know, there are people that live near those tunnels ... not very well-to-do folks, either. I've heard that the foothills of the Huachuca Mountains at one time teemed with illegal immigrants trying to reach the United States. The Border Patrol usually feeds aliens before they transport them back to Mexico, so maybe this is a distribution station that supplies food and produce for the needy, as well as aliens. Now that would explain a lot," deduced Audra.

"Oh, Lord! Well, let's get out of here, then. I just can't believe all this," Mike groaned. When the garage doors opened, the trucks drove inside. After the trucks entered, the huge iron doors closed. "Odd, they'd close the doors to hide produce. It's also odd they would be so quiet about this place and what it does. Usually the City or County would boast of such humane efforts. Hmmm…." Mike had a hunch, and he was willing to stake a claim on it.

As they left the premises, Audra said, "Mike, lots of things are odd. Maybe this place is connected, and the charity approach is just a front to conceal their true dastardly deeds," implied Audra.

Mike did not speak for awhile. He just kept pedaling, his mind burdened with *'what-ifs'* and *'maybes'* again. Just when he thought he might be making some real progress, a monkey wrench is tossed into the works. As they proceeded down the road, they heard a car approaching. Mike commented, "Audra, don't you think it's strange that there is so much activity here on a Sunday afternoon?"

"I never really thought of that, but you do have a point—especially being the County," Audra mused.

Mike rode off the lane, and hid his bike in the tall grass and sage. He did not want to be seen by the driver, or anyone else in the car. Audra followed suit. They lay in the grass until the car passed by them, and then continued on. When the car had driven out of site, they retrieved their bikes and pedaled quickly towards the main road. When they'd reached the end of the lane, Mike stopped and hid his bike again in the thick vegetation. Audra again followed his example, but this time she asked, "Mike, what in the world are you up to?"

"Audra, I'm going to wait awhile and see if another truck comes by—then I'm gonna try and hitch a ride."

"You mean you're going to climb onto one of those trucks! Are you out of your gourd?" shrieked Audra.

"No, Hon; I'm completely lucid. Listen, Bobby would do the same for me. I've just got to find out if we are really barking up a very wrong tree … or digging in the wrong hole." Mike was desperate, and Audra knew it. She tried to talk Mike out of such a silly idea, but with no success. Time passed, and still no truck arrived. Audra was actually hoping a truck wouldn't come, but her wishes were thwarted when suddenly they heard the roar of an engine.

"Well, Mister, your wish is approaching us. I hope you know what you're doing."

"Audra, if you were in my shoes, would you hesitate to do what I am about to do?"

"Touché, my Dear. I would have blown the doors off that place back there," intoned Audra, matter of factly.

"Thank you. I just hope the driver stops for a brief moment when he turns into the lane." Mike crouched down in the tall weeds, waiting. Audra held her breath, as the thought of Mike being run over by a straight truck made her shudder. The large truck pulled into the lane and stopped. The driver had turned a bit too wide, and could not complete the turn.

Like a bolt of lightning, Mike shot out from the brush and rolled under the truck. He grabbed a steel member supporting the leaf springs and axle, and hoisted his body off the ground. He wedged himself between the undercarriage and the chassis, as the truck backed up and began lurching slightly forward. The truck started down the lane to the complex. As the truck slowly rolled down the lane, Mike found it very difficult to hold himself in place. He wished he had a strap with hooks or something, but such a yearning was futile and he knew it. His muscles ached greatly. He remembered watching a movie called *Cape Fear*, starring Robert DeNiro and Nick Nolte. "What a crazy movie! No way could Robert DeNiro have ridden under Nick Nolte's SUV clear to Cape Fear!" Mike laughed, albeit a bit loud for his circumstances. Of course, such thoughts kept his mind off the agony.

Audra watched as the truck disappeared from sight. She understood why Mike had to perform such a dangerous act, but that didn't mean that she was not horrified over what could happen. One slip and Mike could easily fall under the wheels, or possibly become wedged and trapped in the structure and crushed to death. If something happened to Mike, she did not know if she would be able to maintain her sanity. She fought for years trying to keep her health after her brother vanished, and then her mother fell apart. Her morosely withdrawn father was almost a stranger by now. "Please, God, please don't let anything happen to Mike," pleaded Audra.

The huge iron garage door opened and soon Mike found himself inside the building. The truck came to a stop, as the driver turned off the engine. He stepped down from the driver's seat. Another door leading from the building into the garage opened, and a man greeted the driver.

"Well, you finally made it I see. 'Thought you got lost ... or worse," said the man. Mike strained his ears. Did he know the man's voice?

The driver answered, "Would have been here sooner, but I drew a flat back on the Benson I-10 interchange. Luckily, there was a wrecker at *Gas City Truck*

Stop, so he raised the rig and we pulled out the spare, and … Bingo! I was on my way again in no time. Here, I'll show y' the flat. I placed it back under the truck in its cage. You've got t' see it. Come on!" coaxed the driver.

Mike gripped the frame even tighter, as he wedged his body closer to the floor of the truck. His mind raced frantically for some explanation to tell the men why he was under the truck.

> *"Hi, I'm Mike, your friendly straight truck inspector. I inspect trucks for you, so you don't have to. 'Got a problem with axles or springs?*
>
> *"Or, how about those nasty, unbalanced drive shafts? Well, worry no more, 'cause that's what I'm under here for!*
>
> *"Yes sir, That's me … your over-the-road and under-the-chassis mechanic. I'll be with you every mile of the way, so call me—Mr. Mike—the straight truck mechanic today … hey, hey, hey!"*

Mike ran this past his wary mind, and had to laugh just a bit, in spite of his most serious predicament.

"Jack, we don't have time to be looking under trucks for spares. Get the gate open and let's get crackin'! We gotta get the merchandise off this truck and inside … *pronto!*" exclaimed the, as yet, unidentified man.

"Yes, sir, you're right." The driver unlocked the gate and lifted the door. The door rolled open as two other helpers came into the garage and began to unload the crates.

"Be careful with those crates whatever you do. That merchandise is worth plenty!" warned the man.

"You know it, Boss! We'll be extra careful," said one of the helpers, as he took hold of the crate. They lifted the crate and set it on a floor dolly—then they rolled it down the truck ramp and through the metal double doors that led into the complex.

"Only two more crates? Man, are we behind! By this time of the year, we should be seeing at least twenty more heads. I could cuss right now. If we don't make our quota by May, well … I don't have to elaborate on what will happen, but it won't be pretty," growled the man.

"Of course it won't. But, that's not going to happen, now is it, Jack!" This was a different person talking now. Mike wanted so badly to see their faces, but he knew that he would expose himself if he tried to look at them. The man that spoke now had a distinguished voice, sort of refined and yet very clear, like a politician or some public speaker.

Jack looked at his superior and said, "No, no way, Tom; we will make that quota, even if we have to glean the fields ourselves, believe me."

"Now, that is precisely the attitude we like to see and, may I add, there is a bigger bonus for all of us this year. Apparently, our clients on and below the equator are desperate for new stock, so our wonderful investors are quite eager to invest a little more this time around. Their business is going through the roof," Tom smiled and let out a low cynical laugh.

"You know, I love big numbers. When I tell the stockholders the news, I know they'll roll up their sleeves and herd in the bulls and heifers," laughed Jack.

"I'll see you inside, Jack. We have some documents to review—then we have a rather unusual matter to discuss. We have a very small gnat in the ointment."

"Somebody sticking their nose where it doesn't belong?"

"'Just a tad. However, I strongly believe we will not have to resort to death or dismemberment. We'll just contact our consumers, and they'll probably prompt El Niño," remarked Tom.

"So much for the *'Little Gnat'!*" bellowed Jack. One of the men unloading the truck shouted, "Last crate was taken inside." The men entered the building and turned the light off in the garage. Mike slowly lowered his aching body to the floor of the garage. He found the conversation between the men very interesting. Now he knew for sure that these people were not running a charity ward here. This was something definitely less than kosher. They talked in riddles, which made the puzzle a bit more complicated. Mike took a strong mental note of the conversation. He crawled out from under the truck, took out a penlight that he always carried with him, and began to search the back end of the truck. He walked cautiously up the ramp and into the box of the straight truck. Having no fear of intruders, the men left the ramp down and the back door of the truck open. Mike rubbed his sore arms and shoulders as he inspected the trailer. He saw nothing suspicious … just a couple of empty crates. He tried to lift the lids to the crates, but the heavy-duty locks on them held firm. Mike noticed small holes on the sides and tops of the crates.

"I'm not gonna break those locks, that's for sure. And if I try to break into the crates without breaking the locks, I'm sure to make too much noise," Mike whispered to himself, as he snooped around quietly. A faint smell caught Mike's attention. "Smells like the rancid aroma of old ammonia waste. Of course … urine," his nose deftly told him. He looked all around him. Mike scanned his flashlight all over the floor of the trailer, and around each side of the crates, but he saw no indication of animal waste products. Bright blue letters on the sides of the crates read, *'Huachuca Produce.'* "Hmmm, *Huachuca Produce* … I think I've heard of them. Evidently, they are very careful as to how they dispose of the waste material. I wonder if the urine is human or animal?"

Mike found no substantial clues in the trailer other than the odor; no incriminating tickets on the crates, labels or invoices … nothing.

He stepped out of the trailer and made his way carefully to the cab. He
looked at his glowing watch. "I hope they're still in deep discussion about the
bonuses, documents and the gnat they were talking about. I wonder if the
gnat's name is Mike Taylor?" Mike felt a shiver race up his spine. "Grab hold of
yourself, Mike, or you'll develop paranoia. You can't afford to wig out now." Mike
encouraged himself, as he lifted himself up on the running board. He climbed
the access steps on the back of the cab, and hoisted himself to a level where
he could examine the reefers.

He found the nameplate riveted on the left side of the reefer and read it.
"LRA, FLA, name of motor, compressor at such and such, and *ht. P.* Hm-m-m
… wait a minute! I'll bet the faint abbreviation, *ht. P* stands for some type of
heat pump. When I helped some friends work on A/C units, some were combi-
nation A/C-heat pump units. I'll bet this has a reverse valve. Nope. Well, maybe
it does have *some* type of heating element. I'll bet they pump air and heat into
the back of this trailer and—if that's the case—then why would they need this
reefer? They obviously aren't hauling produce, and cattle or other furry critters
wouldn't need heat … or, would they?

There was definitely no sign of animal waste, fur … or even a smell. If I
allow my imagination to run rampant, I'd have to say they are hauling humans
in this truck," Mike whispered loudly, certain of his discovery. He crawled down
from the back of the cab, and slowly opened the driver's door. He winced and
grimaced as though a siren might blast through the silence of the air when the
door opened. However, nothing happened. No horns, whistles or bells
sounded. He could breathe now. Mike crept inside and shined his flashlight all
around the interior of the cab. "Shoot! There has to be something here … anything! They probably took all the forms and notes inside." Mike turned to go. At
least he knew more about the place, and had confirmed his suspicions about
what they were most likely hauling, though he had no conclusive evidence.
This fact bothered him; he wanted some tangible evidence to bring to the
police.

He thought of Raymond Duke, his close friend that worked as a law
enforcement officer for Sierra Vista, as he exited the cab. Suddenly his light fell
upon a clipboard, or binder of some sort, stuck below the passenger's seat. He
reached down and pried it loose; it was a rather nice leather pocket folder. The
folder contained a couple of maps, and some forms. Mike spied vouchers,
labels and invoices, as well as tickets. He shuffled through the forms, hoping to
read something that could shed light on this compound and what they were up

to. Mike read very peculiar passages on the invoices. Then he spotted something familiar:

> *Ship quantity = four crates*   *carrots*
> *Ship quantity = two crates*   *cantaloupes*

He then spotted an asterisk at the bottom of the form. The lines next to it read:

> *Transfer carrots to bee pollen crates, and cantaloupes*
> *to FG crates, upon reaching destination.*

"Now, that's what I'm looking for! Bee pollen sounds familiar, as in pollen grains," muttered Mike to himself. He thumbed through the folder some more, spying a couple of maps within an outer pocket. Mike pulled one of the maps from the folder. He started to unfold it, when he heard some loud voices and shuffling coming from within the complex. He stopped, and quickly stuffed the map and the shipping ticket down the front of his shirt, returned the pocket folder back under the passenger seat and climbed down from the cab. He quietly closed the cab door, and rolled back under the truck, resuming his precarious position beneath the truck just in time.

The double doors flew open noisily, as Jack bounded towards the truck. He was chuckling to himself and whistling a tune. "Must like the bonus he's about to receive," thought Mike. Jack pushed the ramp into place, closed the truck door, fastened the lock and walked up to the cab. As he climbed into the cab, Mike heard him say out loud to himself: "Well, my little veggies, 'looks like I got some gleaning t' do." The iron garage door opened, as Jack started the truck. Mike gasped, as diesel exhaust fumes flooded the area under the truck where he held firmly to the frame. The truck pulled forward, and bounced out the lane. Mike's body felt stronger, more able, than earlier. His findings seemed to revitalize every cell in his body. Mike whispered, "I knew it! I just knew there was more to this place than tractors and trailers. 'Can't wait to show Audra my treasure."

The truck slowly rolled down the lane. Mike noticed that the wind had grown stronger, and the air much cooler. He did not have to stick his head out from under the truck to know that they were in for some icy weather.

Audra walked through the brush to the San Pedro River, which was more like a creek than a river in size. She looked into the shallow waters of the river—then she studied some blueberry and elderberry bushes. She always did love plants, even as a child. By the time she was ten years of age, she knew most of the scientific names for just about every wild flower in the United States. She fascinated people with her knowledge of flowers, trees and shrubs. She had a nursery at home, and it did quite well for some time. She had even sold some cactii and other flowering plants … but her mother's illness eventually got in the way of her work. She began to find herself more involved with her mother—and household chores—as the days passed. Therefore, she finally had to resign herself to the fact that her nursery would have to wait until another day.

Audra peered up at the gray sky. "Funny, how the weather changes so quickly in this part of the state. It feels like it could snow. I hope Mike manages to leave that compound. What if those trucks stay overnight? What if they do? Oh, Lord, we'd really be stuck in a bucket of pig-slop if that happens. I might even have to call the authorities and explain what happened to get him out of there!" groaned Audra loudly.

Her eyes suddenly fell upon a child's baseball cap. Apparently, the river had washed it downstream. The cap was snagged on a branch sticking out of the water. Audra stretched her body out until she almost reached the cap. She gave that up, instead finding a long, thin branch, with which she easily reached out and captured the cap. "*Colorado Rockies* … well, I'm not too fond of the team, but I kind of like the blue bill against the dark cap and the *CR* insignia. 'Guess some kid around here must be a Rockies' fan." Audra shook off the cap, and then squeezed the excess water from it. She held the cap in her hand as she walked back to the lane.

She looked at her watch. "Man! Almost five-thirty! It's gonna be dark in a couple of hours," said Audra aloud to herself. She was becoming more worried as the minutes passed by. Audra looked to her left where she had left the bikes, realizing that she had walked further up the lane than she first thought. Her foot stumbled on a moderate-sized log, as she fell forward. She landed on a prickly bush. "Ah! I could just cuss, but what good would it do," complained Audra as she looked at her right shin. Her blue jeans were torn and—upon closer inspection—she noticed blood oozing from the tear in her trousers. "Dang! That's going to hurt later; 'probably will leave a nasty bruise, too!"

Her ears detected the roar of a truck engine. She looked to see one of the straight trucks roaring towards her. She lay flat on the grass. Her low position enabled her to see a form hugging the frame of the truck. It had to be Mike. She breathed easier now, for he made it back out of the complex garage.

Audra remained flat on the ground, as the straight truck rolled on by her and further down the lane towards Hereford Road. She had begun to rise, when she heard yet another truck approaching. "Oh, my God! The driver of that truck will probably notice Mike when he drops to the ground. I have to do something. She only had a split second to think of a plan. The log she stumbled over came to mind. Like a shot, she raced to the log and dragged it over to the lane. She placed the log across the lane, and then ran into the high brush and hid.

When the driver reached the site where the log lay, he stopped. He knew he could run over it, but he thought of Tom and his car. Mumbling a bit of mild profanity, the driver climbed down from the truck and moved the log off to the side of the lane. That is when it hit him. What was a big log doing lying on the lane to begin with? He jumped back into his cab and keyed his cell phone. "Hey, Jack! Did you pass up a log laying in the middle of the lane?"

Jack answered, "No, the lane was as clear as a bell ... no litter or obstacles."

"Well, I just stopped to remove a rather chunky log off the lane," said the driver suspiciously.

Jack stopped his truck. Mike let himself fall to the ground. He rolled out from under the trailer, and dashed off into the thicket. Mike did not know that Jack had just climbed down from the cab. Jack got a blurry glimpse of the back of Mike's head. Instantly, Jack withdrew a pistol from a shoulder strap he wore, raised it in the air and fired over Mike's head as he shouted, "Freeze!"

Mike was too quick, though. He darted to his left, rolled repeatedly on the ground and then crawled as fast as his hands and knees could take him to the San Pedro River. Mike jumped down into the river, and ran to the other side. He then clawed his way up the steep bank and rolled over the top of the River's levy. Jack fought his way through the tall thick shrubs, but he was not nearly as quick and agile as Mike. Like that, Mike had vanished, as Jack looked around in all directions.

The other driver pulled up behind Jack's truck. "Stupid kids!"

"Hey, remember when we got egged near this end of the lane about two years ago? We laughed at that. I'm sure these were just some goofy high school kids that you probably scared the crap out of with your pistol!"

"Yeah, I'm sure you're right, but y' can't be too cautious, Cain," grunted Jack, as he placed his gun back in the holster. Jack's eye caught a crinkled up piece of paper woven in the thick grass. He started over to it—then he shrugged it off as a piece of litter. He turned and walked with Cain back to the trucks.

"Cain, we got a ways to go, and much gleaning to do, so let's get rolling."

"Right behind ya, Boss. Think we should report this?" Jack looked at Cain and rolled his eyes. "Cain, last thing we need to worry Tom about is how we can't even handle some silly high school pranksters. Now, let's get out of here!" ordered Jack. The two men climbed back into their respective trucks and drove off.

Audra reached the bikes, but she became extremely concerned about Mike when she could not find him. She had heard the gunfire, and knew what it could mean. Audra quickly decided that if Mike did not show up within an allotted amount of time, she would have to report the incident to the police. However, she also remembered what Mike had told her about Sheriff Tress. What if he is called to the scene? Audra decided, therefore, that if she must call someone, she would call the *DPS* and hope for the best. Maybe they would not call the Sheriff. "Right! Fat chance that will happen!" exclaimed Audra, a bit loudly.

When the last truck roared towards Audra, she hunkered down as it passed beyond her, and stopped shortly at the end of the lane, before turning onto the main road. She then watched as a long white sedan, possibly a Cadillac, followed the truck out the lane and down Hereford Road, also. While hunkered down, two strong hands gripped Audra's shoulders. "Ah-h-h!" Audra screamed, as she kicked vigorously. She hit Mike sharply in the shin with her right heel, then she bent over, grabbed his ankle, and gave a strong heave. Mike fell to the ground on his back ...'*Wham!*' He felt some of the wind leave him, as he spoke, gasping, "Au ... Au ... Audra, please! It ... it's *me ...* Mike!" Audra's body relaxed immediately, upon hearing Mike's deep, calm voice.

"Oh, Lord, help us! What are you trying to do! 'Give this poor girl heart failure!"

"Actually, I think it would take much more to give a she-cat like you heart failure. Wow! I haven't hit the ground that hard since my days of wrestling in high school," admitted Mike, still coughing a little from the harsh landing.

Audra looked soberly at Mike, as cold drops of rain began to fall. The sun hid its face behind the dark clouds, as it sank in the western sky.

"Mike, let's get out of here. If you have anything to tell me, it can wait. This place is really getting on my nerves. I do want to see the light of tomorrow. 'You know what I mean?"

"Ten-four, Sergeant! I'm all for that!" They found the bikes, lifted them from the ground, walked them to the lane and rode away swiftly. They spoke very little, as they bounded towards Mike's house. The only thought on their minds was shelter. The rain mixed with ice and snow made the traveling very unpleasant as they pedaled on. The wind was another burden as it blew down from the Huachuca Mountains into their faces.

"We'll catch our death of cold out here if we don't get to shelter soon," hollered Mike over the howling wind.

"No kiddin', Tough Guy! Don't y' just love this wonderful Huachuca weather?" Audra yelled.

"Right now I'm just glad to be alive to enjoy it," screamed Mike, though shivering, as ice and snow cut into his face.

"After what happened, I'll bet you are," Audra yelled loudly over the continuing wind. They rode on, fighting the bitter elements until they finally saw the road that led to Mike's house. They turned down the road, raced into Mike's driveway, and parked their bikes under the porch awning.

Racing to the door, Mike opened it quickly, and both of them tumbled inside. "Whoo-hoo! Now that's what I call *cold* ... cold with a capital *'C,'* Ba-*by!"* shouted Mike. Audra removed her sweater, and tried to dry her wet face and hair with it.

"Hey, Aud, if you want to really get comfortable ... and warm up a bit faster, just use the shower in the master bath. I'll use the one in the back. And, please, help yourself to my mother's clothes; they've got to be much drier than yours! I don't know much about women's clothes, but she looked about your size in height and build," explained Mike.

"She must have been *beautiful!"* Audra laughed, in a self-complimenting teasing sort of way, taking advantage of Mike's comment about their similarity.

"Like I said ... she was your size and build so, of *course*, she was beautiful."

Audra turned a small pirouette, feeling very feminine. She stopped and looked back, questioningly. "Mike, where are her clothes?"

"Oh, I'm sorry. If you walk into the large master closet, you'll see some dresses and women's slacks hanging up, and there is a small dresser in the closet, also, that contains her underwear, and—hey, don't look at me like that! They are all very clean!" laughed Mike. Audra laughed, too, then walked down the hallway to the master bedroom.

"I'll meet you in the family den when you're finished!" hollered Mike. Audra heard Mike but did not reply, so he took that as a possible clue that she had not heard him.

Once in the bedroom, Audra quickly found a clean towel and washcloth. She quickly showered, stepped out of the bathroom with a large towel around her, and walked into the closet. She looked carefully at the slacks and dresses. They were all outdated, but she knew this was no time to be choosy. She found a very pretty, blue dress that was a bit low cut. "Well, I guess this will do," said Audra.

Mike showered and dressed himself very quickly. He also threw on a light blue sweater, then proceeded to relax on the den couch, thinking, as he waited for Audra. The heater was blowing warm air throughout the house, but some of the chill in the air still lingered. Mike laid the crumpled map and shipping form in front of him on a coffee table. He had almost lost the form, as it had fallen out of his shirt when he ran from Jack. He felt grateful that he had been able to retrace his steps, and recover it.

Suddenly, there she stood ... like a model posing for a picture ... her complexion clear and bright, her eyes dazzling like the dress she wore, and her hair beautifully brushed, and shimmering like diamonds. Evidently, she had heard Mike say to meet him in the den. The moderately low-cut dress revealed just a hint of her beautiful and shapely bosom. Mike stumbled for words, but could not find even one.

"Well, how does it look?" Audra demurely inquired of Mike.

His mouth nearly dropped to the floor. "Astonishing … breathtaking … absolutely spellbinding … and extremely sexy! You are a symphony in motion, my Dear. I have never seen a finer sculptured figure on a woman in my life!"

"'Sure you're not over-exaggerating, or being a bit biased?" retorted Audra, gleefully.

"No, Ma'am … I mean, 'No, *Lady!* You make me wish you were a *'ma'am'* … that we were married, Audra!" exclaimed Mike. A thought crossed Audra's mind about Mike's remark, but she dared not speak it aloud; instead, she said, "Thank you, Mike. I'm very glad you like it." Then she added—truthfully, as the clothes had been very stylish in their day, though now outdated—"Your mother surely did have great taste!"

"You know … my mother would have loved you, Audra. I wish the two of you could have met." Then quickly changing the subject, "Hey! I threw some TV dinners in the microwave. They'll be done any minute now." Just as Mike said those words, the microwave buzzed. "Well, what do y' know, speaking of meals and … presto!" They walked into the kitchen. Mike escorted Audra over to the table, pulled out a chair, and helped seat her. He served the meal as elegantly as a TV dinner may be served—on a whim, he'd whipped out his mother's best china—and then sat down opposite the *'Lady in Blue.'* Audra looked into Mike's pleasant eyes and asked a most serious question, for dinner conversation fare. "Mike, how did your parents pass away?"

Mike looked a bit surprised and Audra noticed this. "Mike, I am very sorry if I offended you. I really had no business asking."

"No, I'm glad you asked. It always did help me to talk about it," assured Mike. He told her the entire incident. He explained how they were only to be gone for an evening, but the plane was unforgiving … would not allow for a defect. So, when the stabilizer bar on the back rudder broke off, the plane went into a tailspin … total loss of control with no chance of recovery.

"Later, Audra, the cause was discovered to be due to a factory glitch. The makers of the plane made restitution, but that never brings people back."

Audra sunk her head in her hands. "Seems like there is just too much sorrow in life. I guess we just have to go on with our lives though … go on loving, caring, and trying until we die and go to heaven."

"You said it, girl." Then, very obviously wishing to change the topic of conversation, Mike asked, "How do you like your meal, by the way?"

"It's a TV dinner delight!" laughed Audra.

They finished their meals in silence, washed their dishes, and sat down together in the den. Audra began the conversation about the day's excitement, and Mike was very glad that she did, for he figured a strong review of the events could lead to more clues … clues that they could not afford to forget. Mike pulled open a drawer to the coffee table and retrieved a notebook and pen. "So, you're a copious note-taker?" asked Audra.

Mike nodded. "Very good idea," Audra commended him. "You know, I got a good look at one of those men … the guy coming out the lane in the second truck. He has a round, puffy face with an unkempt beard, that goes from ear to ear. He also squeals a little when he talks, 'cause he was fussing and cussing when he had to move a log."

"A log?" Mike sounded startled.

"Yes, I dragged a log out onto the lane to hopefully stop him, ' cause he was coming up in back of the truck from which you were dangling like a monkey. Had I not done something to slow him down a bit, he would have seen you for sure, as you were disembarking from your luxury cruise!" laughed Audra.

"You've got it! It was a regular Caribbean delight under that truck!"

"I also made out the car. It's a white Cadillac sedan. I tried to read the plate number, but I couldn't. I did manage to see the first letter … and you're not going to like it at all, Mike … not one bit."

"Well, go on … please?" pleaded Mike.

"The first letter was a *'G'.*"

"Oh, gre-e-eat! Now the State or Federal Government is involved in this, also. 'Just wonderful! What are we getting ourselves into, anyway? Audra, I'm afraid this is becoming a rather messy situation. We have big boys and fat cats playing their hand in all this and, if we don't play our cards just right, we might get a visit from the men in black … and it will not be to share tea and toast with them. These people are very dangerous. I even got shot at again today!"

"I know. I heard the shot!"

"I figured you'd say that …'figured you were somewhere close enough to hear. Anyway, let me tell you everything I discovered, and then you tell me if you still believe we're a couple of slouching, flea-bitten, coon dogs barking up the wrong tree." Mike relayed his entire experience. He told Audra everything about the smell in the trailer, the reefer, the conversation between a man named Tom and one of the drivers, named Jack. He explained in as much detail as possible what their voices sounded like—even attempting to mimic them—but nothing rang a bell in Audra's mind. Mike left the den for a moment, and then he returned with a form and a map. Mike set the form on the table in front of Audra. Audra read the ticket aloud:

"*'Ship: quantity, four crates of carrots,'* and *'quantity, two crates of can-taloupes. Transfer carrots to bee pollen boxes. Transfer cantaloupes to FG crates upon arrival at....'* Then she began reading silently, not quite understanding the symbolism … *31° 21'▲::110° 16'◄*. Again, she read out loud: *"Two boxes of flo-ral gifts to be sent to …"* and then began silently again: *12° 0'▼::77° 2'◄'*....

"It also looks like it says, *'two boxes of bee pollen to....'* Each time Audra came to the global location symbolism, she would read silently: *16° 30'▼:: 68° 9'◄*, "and *'two boxes bee pollen to....'* *12° 0'▼ :: 77° 2'◄.'* "I do not really know what all this means, Mike. I'm baffled."

Mike studied the arrows, double colons, and numbers carefully. Then he turned to Audra. "You know, I'm just as bamboozled as the next person."

"Well they are shipping these crates to some destination, and these funky arrows and numbers must mean something … a point of origin, or coordinates … or something," Audra theorized.

Mike rubbed his square, narrow chin. He removed his hand from his chin, and next rubbed his brow with his thumb and index finger. "Of course!" he said, lights suddenly going on. "You're a genius, Audra! The word *'coordinate'* will help solve *this* riddle! If we put our minds *together,* I really think we can solve this mystery. Now, I took Geology in college. Wait here a moment, Audra; I'll be right back."

Again, Mike had left Audra sitting in the den while he sped off to locate something. He returned shortly, holding his geology textbook in his right hand. "When I took this course, one thing I was exposed to was maps and their accompanying symbols. Look here," he continued, as he turned to the back index, and then began thumbing his way to a specific section of the textbook concerning global coordinates. "Look at these coordinates, Audra."

Audra's eyes scanned the page that Mike was holding close to her face. She saw the coordinates 51 6' N 114 1'W. "Well, these are the exact coordi-nates for Calgary, Canada in Alberta; and, 39 75'N 104 87'W is Denver, Colorado, according to this book," noted Audra, as she stole a quick look into Mike's eyes. "You know, Mike, the arrows must be symbolic for north, south, east, and west … like on a topographic map."

Mike nodded his head, "Precisely, Audra. So, now we have found latitudinal and longitudinal and coordinates, used on the globe of the world."

"But, how does this all work out on a globe? It's been ages since I've taken such a rudimentary course like this. I haven't been exposed to this since grade-school."

Mike muttered something, as he rushed back into his room, and then raced back to Audra, excited, and holding a globe in his hands. Audra sat a little per-plexed at Mike's spontaneous behavior.

"Nice looking globe, Mike ... but you're beginning to make me feel dizzy, watching you come and go like a silly yo-yo!" commented Audra.

"Yep, that's me, all right ... a silly yo-yo. Hey, I'm sorry about the wait. Anyway, can you see the faint lines running east and west—as well as north and south—on the globe?"

"'Sure can.'"

"Now, in this Geology class we learned how the latitude lines begin at the Equator, which is equal to zero. Each line is fifteen degrees from each other, so they extend fifteen degrees north—and south—of the Equator, and then thirty degrees, forty-five degrees, and so on, up to ninety degrees, either north or south."

Audra shook her head. "Uh-huh," acknowledging that she understood.

"Okay, for the vertical globe markings—called longitude lines—there is another demarcation line of origin called the...." and here, Mike opened his geology book, shuffling through its pages for a forgotten bit of information. "Ah, yes! Here it is ... the *'prime meridian,'* which is an imaginary line running north and south through Greenwich, England. Anything that is 180° to the west of this *prime meridian* is classified as the *Western* Hemisphere, while anything 180° to the east would be considered...."

Audra interrupted Mike, shouting, "The *Eastern* Hemisphere!"

"Absolutely, Doll Face. This works the same way for the areas north and south of the equator, each longitudinal line being separated by fifteen degrees."

"Well, maybe after another lesson about it from such a *great* teacher, I'll be able to remember this time!" Audra encouragingly complimented Mike, with a smile.

"Now that you've really got the hang of it, let's find out where these shipments are going, Woman!" Mike directed, as he picked up the form with the mysterious shipping directions on it, encoded in global-location symbolism.

"OK, *Professor Mike* ... let's get to it!" demanded Audra, as she looked again at the now not-so-confusing figures on the ticket again. "You know, you amaze me!"

"Okay, the first one here says 31°, 21 ... *apostrophe*—whatever *that* means—and the arrow points north."

"That *'21 apostrophe'* means, my Dear, 21 minutes—or 21 nautical miles—in most cases," explained Mike as he held the globe in his hand.

Audra continued, "We also have 110° and 16 minutes—or nautical miles—with the arrow pointing west, this time. Where does that put us?"

"I'm looking it up on the globe now. Let's see ... thirty-one degrees north of the equator. Move up another mark further for the extra degree, and then a little more for 21 nautical miles. West of the prime meridian, at 110 degrees and sixteen minutes, puts us at about … Whoa! Lord help us, I don't believe it!"

"What! What do we have?" screeched Audra, wanting to be let in on Mike's apparently mind-boggling discovery.

"Look, watch my finger as I draw it out on the globe!" exclaimed Mike. Audra watched carefully—spellbound as Mike again traced the degrees of the latitude and longitude lines that had gotten him so excited. At a little more than 31° north of the equator, and a little more than 110° west of the prime meridian, Mike's finger rested just below Tucson, near the border between Mexico and Arizona. Mike set the globe down and rushed into his room. He returned with the topographic map that Audra had copied for him at the Cochise College Library.

"Audra, this map will give us a very accurate location now, because it has the latitude and longitude written on it, too … like a graph!" Mike studied the lines. "Look!" shouted Mike. Audra looked at the point on the map where Mike was holding his finger. She saw the latitude and longitude degrees written on the map. There was no way she could deny that Mike's theory was proving to be correct.

"Oh, my gosh! That's right about where we were shot at, and right near the cave … and tunnels," gulped Audra. Suddenly she felt weak, bogged down with this mass of suddenly revealed information, yet very excited at what all this could mean. They really were beginning to put the pieces together. Her heart began filling with joyful anticipation for the first time in so long … yet, there was fear, as well. This would be no picnic … not at all, if what they had already been through was any indication. In spite of this, there was an almost unexplainable confidence that they might actually find Bobby—and possibly even Todd—though he had been gone years longer than Bobby had. In spite of this confidence, there was also an underlying fear of the real possibility of ending up dead before they could find them, considering the type of characters that were most likely involved in this apparently highly organized despicable criminal endeavor.

Yes, this was not the ordinary, sole-perpetrator abduction; these abductions had been premeditated and planned very carefully by a most likely mob-related band of thugs. Mike and Audra were definitely outnumbered, in that respect. But, why were these children being abducted, anyway? Where were they being taken, other than the caverns Mike and Audra has so recently discovered.

"Hey, Mike, now let's try to locate where the veggies, fruit, bee pollen and flowers are going. I really do believe that the carrot and flower designations are symbolic of the children. The carrots—or males—become bee pollen, which signifies fertilization, and the letters *FG* have to stand for *'female game-tophytes.'* The flowers, containing pistils, which are fertilized by pollen—origi-nally spoken of as cantaloupes—refer to the girls that are being shipped. The terms, *'carrots'* and *'cantaloupes,'* are just phallic symbols."

"'You mean that the carrots represent the male genitalia?"

"Yes, I do."

"And the cantaloupes?" Mike wondered.

"Probably symbolic of the female breasts. I'm just guessing, now, but it seems a logical explanation," Audra replied.

Now that the matter of the symbolism was mainly settled, Mike swiftly began to trace the globe, finding the locations indicated on the form he had found. *"Two boxes of floral gifts at 12° 0'▼:: 77° 2'◄*. Hmmm, this appears to be Lima, Peru. *Two boxes of bee pollen at 16° 30'▼:: 68° 9'◄* ... that puts us somewhere in Bolivia. And, last of all, *two boxes bee pollen at 4° 36'▲:: 74° 05'◄*, which is Bogotá, Colombia."

"You know how I interpret that, Mike?"

"I have no idea," said Mike softly.

"Think about it. The children appear to be first taken to the cavern, tunnel, or wherever. Then, after that, they are shipped to various final destinations. All those places you called out are in South America. I think the *de*coded mes-sage reads as follows: *'After the children have been taken to the cavern, send two girls to Lima, Peru, two boys to Bolivia, and another two boys to Bogotá, Colombia'."*

"Mike, can you remember anything that the men said about the merchan-dise that may add a bit more to this?"

Mike looked up and down. He thought hard. "Investors, consumers and stockholders were all brought into the conversation. The merchandise brings lots of money to the shareholders. The product is a child ... the child is worth a lot of money. They deliver more boys than girls. "I'm sorry, Audra. All I know is that, for some reason, the children are in high demand—more boys at this time than girls—and they are making some people wealthy. I remember the words, *'Huachuca Produce,'* written on the side of a crate.

"Hey, follow me!" Mike raced to his office, and typed *'Huachuca Produce'* into his search engine, which brought up the following results, which Mike began reading aloud: "A large southern produce market, previously known as *'Greater Southwestern Produce'.''* Commenting, as he read further, Mike con-tinued, "It claims to be a legal charitable organization, and boasts of thou-sands of supporters."

"Wow! How cleverly deceitful!" gasped Audra. They had seen that name, purporting to be a charitable organization, on crates they had run into while in the tunnel they had just discovered. They pondered over this, as they walked back into the den.

Noticing lights outside, they watched as a car mysteriously pulled up into the end of Mike's lane. Only after it came to a complete stop, did the lights go out. Audra and Mike looked at one another.

"Did y' see that? Isn't that odd—especially the way they left their lights on for so long?" asked Audra. 'Not exactly a stealth bomber!"

"Yes, it is rather odd, and I've had it with this guy. He's been doing this every night lately. Audra, do me a favor … act as though you are talking to me. I'm gonna find out who our little spying friend is."

"Mike, I don't think you should go out there!" exclaimed Audra.

"You know, you're probably right. Why don't *you* go?" laughed Mike.

"Well, I'd probably stand just as good of a chance. I knocked you on your butt today, if you remember rightly," Audra teasingly rubbed it in.

"That's what I'm talking about," chuckled Mike as he left the room, making his way to the back door. Mike opened the door and stepped out into the dark night. He noticed, as he sped into the darkness towards the car, how the steady snow and ice had stopped falling, and the wind had—thankfully—died down. He knew the landscaping very well and, for some reason, he had always been able to see better than most in the dark.

As he neared the car, Mike saw that the vehicle was a red Ford *Escort.* "Hmmm … rather small vehicle for such a man," Mike mumbled to himself, observing the rather rotund driver. The man had his window rolled down about halfway, to allow fresh air in, and was leaning over, pulling a donut out of a bag that sat on the passenger's seat. "Yeah, just what the gentleman needs … more *fat* food to feed his face." Then, as he bent over on one buttock cheek to retrieve his messy morsel, a rumble started up within his large bowel. A huge gastric explosion came forth from a mighty crevice between two huge mounds of human flab, sounding as if someone had blown the gasket out of their tuba! Mike nearly blew his cover with laughter, but stifled it just in time. The stench that followed was enough to knock a fly off a manure wagon … even strong enough to reach Mike's nostrils a few feet outside of the vehicle.

This gentleman—an extremely loose description of this particular specimen of humanity—was apparently habituated to such a lifestyle … seeming pleased, while not one whit surprised, at such an occurrence. He was so pleased, in fact, that Mike could not help but think, "How revolting!" at hearing his subsequent disgusting vocal outburst: "Ah, I am a maestro of all maestros!

'Tis the elegant sound of the beau-u-utiful music of relief," the man blurted out, laughing bizarrely.

As he finished carelessly stuffing the donut into his mouth, the man grabbed some binoculars, and focused them on Audra through the den window. "Hmmm, what a lovely dish she looks to be. Well, she's talking to the kid, so I guess I can just lean back and watch the action. Maybe things will get hot and steamy. It gets a bit boring sitting out here, cramped in this tiny car ... I sure could *use* a little entertainment!" the grotesque 'gentleman' raucously laughed again.

Mike noted that his face was interestingly narrow, for a man who was so ... well ... *rounded out*. The man leaned back in his seat, hoping to see some action. He set his binoculars down, fumbled for his camera, and then zoomed in on Audra. Of course, Audra was acting the part very well. She certainly looked like she was talking to Mike. "Baby, you got my engine overheating just watching those plump melons rock, bounce, and roll ... what an animated doll you are!" he laughingly leered.

Having seen and heard enough of this loathsome spy—whoever he was—disrespectfully ogling Audra, Mike's protective instincts kicked in. Suddenly the portly man's door flew open and, before he knew what had happened, he was face down on the wet, cold, icy ground with his arm locked in back of him. Mike held him firmly to the ground with his knee. "Who the hell are you, and what are you doing parking here every night, Mister!" hollered Mike. Mike felt a sudden urge to just wallop the man. Why not take out all his frustration on this disgusting man who apparently thought it was cute to spy on him?

The man whom Mike was having difficulty not thinking of as nothing more than a pig, after hearing his lecherous language, groaned in great discomfort. "Let me go! Come on! I'm *not* your enemy!" he cried out in pain.

"Oh? Then what are you ... some disgustingly despicable sicko that gets off at peeping at people through their windows? Tell me who you are ... *and* what you're doing here or, so help me, I'll break your filthy, flabby fat arms!" screamed Mike.

"Okay, okay! Please, just let up!" The man was almost in tears, his arm still pinned down by Mike. The pain was overwhelming. By now, the man realized Mike really meant what he'd said, as Mike began applying more pressure. "Ahh-h! Phew! Whoa! That hurts! Your uncle sent me to keep watch over you. I know your name. It's Mike Taylor, 'cause your Uncle, Bruce Taylor, told me about you and Bobby ... I know Bobby is missing. That's why he sent me here. He is very concerned!" gasped the pinned-down fat man. His voice was sounding higher and squeakier, the longer Mike held him down.

"What's your name!" bellowed Mike, as he bent the man's arm even more. The man felt as though his entire limb was about to explode.

"My name is Peter Jones. I'm from Palm Springs, where your Uncle just recently moved to!"

"My uncle lives in Boston! Now I know you're lying. I'm gonna break your arms and legs!" shouted Mike.

"No! NO … wait! I can prove I'm not lying. Take my wallet out of my right back pocket. Inside the wallet is your Uncle's business card; he's an insurance agent now. He told me that he was a reckless man who wishes he'd done things different years ago. He moved to Palm Springs to start a *new* life. He would have come here himself, but he thought it might upset you! Oh, God! Please let me go, Mister! I'm telling you, I ain't no enemy here!" cried Peter.

Mike reached into the man's pocket and took out his wallet, as he continued to hold him down. He flipped through it. Sure enough, he found his Uncle's business card. His picture was on it. He actually looked very pleasant in the photo. "Huh … maybe the *crumb-bum* finally did do something with his miserable life, other than chase women and drink all of the time," said a very surprised Mike aloud.

"Oh, he did! He *di-i-id!*" exclaimed Peter.

"Mister, I'm going to let you up, but if you try *any*thing foolish, I'll be happy to carry out my threat."

Mike slowly released Peter, who took in a deep breath. He stood up and held his chest. "I don't feel too good, Mike. You really hurt me! Listen, Bruce wanted me to make sure you don't do anything crazy. He thought you might have tried to take matters into your own hands after Bobby was abducted."

Mike thought, "Hmmm … guess my absent Uncle knows me better than I thought … maybe because he knows what Dad might do in this situation. Perhaps I'm more like Dad than I've thought about, too." This visit had caused Mike to reminisce a bit.

Peter continued, "I was gonna introduce myself to you later. The only reason I've been staking your place out is because I needed to watch your daily routine. I was trying to find out your behavioral pattern. We pros have to get to know those we look after."

"You know, you talk too much. You don't know when to shut up, do you? What are you … some kind of *rent-a-cop?*"

"Among other things, yes I am."

"Well, you can just march your big rear end back to Palm Springs and tell my Uncle that if he wants to make sure I'm all right, then he'd best see to it himself. I don't need you around. You're lucky I didn't really hurt you!" shouted Mike. Mike was very angry. Why did his Uncle pull this stunt on him now? All it did was cause him worries and stress, and it almost led to a few broken bones, to boot.

"I *am* getting out of here, believe me! I don't need money bad enough to lose a limb over it! I knew this was a bad idea. I told myself that before I left, but no, I thought I'd help my friend out. Well, that's what I get for trying to help."

Mike assisted Peter back to his vehicle. As Peter began climbing in, he turned around and looked at Mike. "Hey, Mike, no hard feelings?" Peter extended his hand. The cumbersome man could not help but notice how much Mike reminded him of his all-time favorite movie star, John Wayne. Mike looked a little like him, and talked like him, too.

Mike shook Peter's hand as he spoke, "Well, no hard feelings on my part!" Then Mike let go with a straight arm into Peter's face. His fist landed sharply on the man's long nose. With that, Peter awkwardly fell back into his car. "That's for peeping at my girl through those fancy binoculars you have!" shouted Mike. Peter stood up holding his nose. The blow stung so bad it drew tears to his eyes. Again, Mike let him have it in the nose. But this time he held his punch back; he did not want to kill Peter.

"Ah-h-h! What the ... oh-h-h, I ... ah ... what was that for?"

"And that was for disrespecting my girl. I heard you in here cooing away, like she was some type of object on display for some dirty old man like you! Now get the Hades out of here before I change my mind and break your flabby arms, legs ... and your chubby little neck!" threatened Mike. Peter, in spite of feeling rough after such results from his sleuthing assignment, had never jumped into his car as fast as he did, trying to avoid any further confrontation. He started the engine and peeled out down the road.

For at least fifteen minutes after Pete had left the scene, Mike stood outside in the blackness, looking down the road, pondering the recent scene. He felt good ... he felt badly. He probably could have been a little more merciful to this 'apparently out-of-shape man, who didn't seem such a threat, after all,' his conscience reprimanded him. But—he rationalized—it irked him to recall all the worry this paunchy specimen of a man had put him through the last few nights. It could have easily been prevented, had Peter just properly introduced himself. Furthermore, he'd had no right to spy on him ... and especially his lady. "The nerve of some people!" roared Mike as he walked back into his house, his argument with himself having come to an end.

As he stepped inside the warm house, he noticed Audra slightly trembling. "Are you cold?"

"No, you big goof! I didn't know if that person had a handgun ... or rifle. Though I did not hear anything, there are silencers, you know! Who knew what had happened out there, when you didn't appear for *so* long after that car drove away!" a worried Audra explained.

Mike reached out his strong arms to comfort her. She nestled in and, as he held her, she could feel the heat radiating from his body. She knew there must have been some sort of a struggle, because she could hear Mike's heart pounding, as well. "You and whoever that was out there got into it, didn't you?"

"Actually, it was more like his big nose got in the way. Yes, I held him down until he told me the reason for being here, then I whacked him in the schnoz a coupl'a times!"

"Why did y' do that?"

"I wouldn't have, but I heard him say some distasteful things about you, and he was peeping at you with his binoculars!" Mike briefed Audra in on a few details as he gritted his teeth. Audra felt honored. "So when did you become this chivalrous knight in shining armor?"

"Babe, I've always had it in me blood … Ar-r-r-r! Yes, me bloody veins flow with chivalry from me foots to the top of me head," Mike playfully attempted an Irish accent as he laughed. Audra laughed, too, but—despite how badly she wanted to stay longer—she knew she must go. Her father had rather come to depend on her company during these emotionally delicate times since both Todd and her mother were no longer around.

Audra looked at Mike with dreamy eyes. "Well Darling … my Darling … I must be on my way, or my Papa will be very worried. Good news is that we have a motive—money and wealth … a very common motive—but we still have no suspects and, other than for profit, we do not know exactly why the children are being sent to South America."

"Well, we do have a couple of suspects … actually three: the Sheriff, Jack, and that ugly truck driver that got out of the truck to move the log you some-how *accidentally* dropped in the lane." Mike smiled at the word *'accidentally.'*

Mike fidgeted for a moment, then he said, "You know, Audra, maybe it's time to add another team member. Dennis is coming over here tomorrow morning; he wants to talk to me about all that has happened. He is a very understanding, bright individual. I'll bet he could offer some ideas."

"Yeah, I'll bet," Audra deadpanned.

"Well, you sound a tad unsure and uneasy right now. 'Care to explain?"

"Mike, he gave me the creeps when meeting him Sunday at church. There's something froggy … uh, fishy … about that guy. I honestly think you need to check him out very closely. I know he's been your trusted friend for years, but do you really know him that well?"

Mike pondered the question carefully. In searching his mind for the answer, He realized that he really did not know Dennis entirely. The man was out of town much of the time. He never really discussed anything but his ministry with the kids, or the Lord. Mike finally had to admit that Dennis was actually, in some ways, a rather unique and mysterious character.

"OK, so let's not say too much to Dennis right now," Audra answered, glad she'd spoken up, encouraging him to rethink his idea. "You might be glad you didn't. You could try to check him out thoroughly. If he checks out to be on the up and up, then we could approach him. How's that sound?"

"Well, I guess I could hold off. And … I know just the person to check out Dennis' background. I hired a private eye to handle that kind of footwork."

"A private eye? You never told me about that!"

"Well, I'm telling you now. It just never entered my mind before."

"Well … *getting to know you.*…" Audra sang.

"Oh, give me a break, Audra. Come on … I can't remember everything!"

"I know you aren't perfect, but I'm working to try and increase the odds," Audra teasingly prodded Mike.

"Oh, so now I'm your pet project, your little blond-haired guinea piggy, huh?"

"No, you're my big, lovable, cuddly—not to mention cute—teddy bear, and I'd love to stay and cuddle, but I've really got to go." Audra picked up her bag of clothes. She grabbed them awkwardly and, as she did, the clothes spilled out onto the floor. Mike noticed a baseball cap among her clothes.

"Where'd the cap come from?"

"Oh, yeah … it's a *Rockies'* baseball cap I found stuck on a limb in the San Pedro River. I stuck it between my hip and belt. I almost forgot all about it. Here, you can have it."

"Thanks Audra. I like the *Rockies* somewhat. I'll hang it on my wall." As he paused, he recalled something. "Oh, yeah! We didn't go over that map yet."

"Don't lose sleep over it. We'll go over it tomorrow. I only have to go to college two days out of the week, and I'm going to let Doris, my co-worker, have a few more of my hours. I really don't need the money … I mainly work there to keep my mind focused on things other than my mother's condition and my father's depression. I have really become very interested in our endeavors. I just have a feeling.…" Audra stopped talking.

"What do you mean?" Mike wanted to know.

"Well, that's really all for now, Mike. I've *got* to go!"

"You know, Audra, sometimes you can be a little spooky yourself," laughed Mike.

"Nothing like courting *'a spooky little girl like me,'* right," Audra giggled as she sang yet another portion of an oldie, as she and Mike slipped out the door.

Mike helped her into the Jeep, and then reluctantly drove her home; the house was so empty now that he was there by himself. "But enough of such thoughts," Mike told himself. "We're keeping things above board here."

When they arrived at Audra's house, she said goodnight and walked into the house. Mike slowly drove back onto Hereford Road and headed west towards Highway 92. He turned left on State Highway 92 and drove towards Sierra Vista. Next stop on his agenda was his church. The kids were meeting tonight, and he wanted to speak with some of Bobby's friends.

Mike pulled into the church parking lot, abandoned his Jeep and walked towards the Youth Department. On his way there, he met young Ted Chapman. They almost ran into each other on the sidewalk. "Hey, Mike, you almost flattened me!" shouted Ted.

"Oh, Ted, I'm sorry. Man, my mind stepped into another world for a moment, I didn't see you there," Mike apologized.

"Well, no harm done. Hey, have you heard anything of Bobby?"

"No, Ted. He's still gone, and the authorities don't have a clue."

"Man, it gives me goose bumps when I think about Bobby," Ted exclaimed. "One day he's here and the next—*gone!* He was so excited about the hiking trip you two were going on. Wow! He told us all about where you and he were going … *Tucker's Peak* … and the rock formation you guys had named *'Taco Stand.'* Now, that's a good name!" Then Ted's voice trailed off, as he lamented, "I just can't believe he's gone.…"

Mike thoughtfully rubbed his chin for a moment. "Hey, Ted, did he tell everyone in the youth class?"

"Yes … everyone that was there, anyway. Some guys didn't show up that Tuesday night before he … well … came up missing. But he did tell the rest of us."

"Did he tell Dennis?" Mike tried to sound as nonchalant as possible.

"Oh yeah, he sure did! He even showed Dennis a map of the area you were going to be hiking. He liked to carry those maps with him, so he could show us all the different places you guys hiked. We all loved his hiking stories." Ted looked forlornly down at the ground. The possibility of never seeing Bobby again became all too real for the 12 year-old.

About this time, Mrs. Chapman walked over to where they stood, and said to her son, "Ted I think you'd best be getting along now." Then she looked inquiringly at Mike, concerned. "Hi, Mike, are you okay?"

"I'm getting by," said Mike weakly.

"Well, we've got to be on our way inside. You know we've all been praying for you," she proclaimed as she shook Mike's hand and walked away. Mike remembered the times when Mrs. Chapman would hug him and say how she loved him. Now that Bobby had vanished, nobody at church said these words to him or showed him any affection. They had all become very uncomfortable around Mike, as though he might lose his mind and do something rash. Mike shook his head at this thought. "Why are humans so afraid to show support and feelings for each other? Why is it, during our most challenging times when we need them most, others just don't know what to do? They pull away from those in need, actually avoiding the person. Man! How sad this is."

Other people walked by him, as well. People who used to stop and share with him … spend time with him … now just said a quick *'Hello,'* and offered their prayers. Mike turned and left the church courtyard. He walked back to his Jeep and climbed up into it. He took one last look at the people walking through the church doors. Starting his engine, he looked upward. "Father, please understand why I cannot enter into Your house of worship tonight. I just can't. I feel so alone in all this. The only person who seems to care is little Audra … please make her, and me, strong enough to continue this search. I know this is probably too much to ask, too, but—so far—the cards I've been dealt have been far shy of a full house. Could y' possibly slip me a couple wild deuces, Lord? I just don't know what to do anymore." Mike slipped the Jeep in first gear and headed back home. His heart was very heavy, and his mind frustrated.

As Mike pulled into his driveway, he thought about what Ted had told him. Now he knew that all the children had heard of their most recent hike into the mountains. He also realized that Dennis knew. Bobby had even showed Dennis the precise area they were going to hike, according to Ted. It was then that Mike came into agreement with Audra. He did want to talk to Dennis, and hoped Dennis would stop by, as they had planned the day before. He prayed for this. He had many questions for Dennis, but he knew he had to be discreet. "If Dennis is somehow caught up in this horrifying ring of child abductors, I must not let on that I know much of anything other than what the police have told me."

After entering the house, Mike picked up the map that was laying on the coffee table. He walked into his bedroom and fell upon his bed. His body ached, and he was very exhausted from all the excitement and activities of the day. After resting a bit, he opened the map. There laid before him—big as life—the entire United States. "Hmmm … I wonder if there's any other reason for this big map, other than directions."

Mike studied the map. He saw circled areas with the word *'field'* therein, and underlined. "What now? Another strange code to decipher … or puzzle to put together?" Mike turned the map over. The other side had a small square-shaped cutout portion of a topographic map taped to it. He laid the map to his side, pulled the top drawer of his desk open, and retrieved a magnifying glass. Holding the magnifying glass over the small map, he scanned it very carefully.

Mike's right eye caught sight of a small arrow pointing at something just off the side of East Montezuma Canyon Road. He knew that road well. How many times had he and Bobby traveled through Coronado National Memorial Park via this road? "Hmmm … Bobby disappeared only two miles north of this arrow," Mike mumbled. "Yet another piece to the puzzle. That's all we have … a few weird pieces that make little sense. Maybe there is no sense to all this … maybe I'm just dreaming, and all of this has a very clear and logical explanation. I'm so-o-o sorry, Bobby!" Tears flowed down Mike's cheeks, as he fell into a deep sleep.

Two shadowy figures sat upright at a large desk, in a dimly lit office inside City Hall in Sierra Vista. It was almost twelve midnight, and most people were asleep by now; however, these two men had a very important subject to discuss. One figure spoke from behind the desk, as he sat in an expensive high-backed leather office chair. "I feel it is time you pay your friend a visit. Research his mind, and try to discover all that he knows. We cannot afford to have some little maggot chewing his way into the fabric of what we have built here. Do you under*stand?"* Though his words were by no means refined, the man was possessed of a distinguishingly refined voice.

The shadowy figure sitting at the front of the desk answered. "Please rest assured, you can trust and count on me, Tom. I know Mike very well, and I'm sure I can manipulate any important information from him that will detect if he knows anything, or not."

"Very well spoken. Now, I do not wish to waste anymore time in this dreary chamber, so shall we call it a night … or should I say *'morning?'* The ghost-like figures left the room, locked the door behind them, and disappeared into the night.

Mike awoke with a start. Someone was pounding on his front door and ringing his doorbell repeatedly. Mike glanced at his watch. "Lord, sakes alive! It's already nine in the morning. I must have been very tired. He looked down and discovered his clothes were still on. "Well, at least I won't have to don any clothes this morning." Mike rolled out of bed and half-dragged himself to the front door. He opened the door to see Dennis standing on the front mat, smiling at him.

"Well, can I come in?"

Mike yawned as he unlocked the glass door. "Sure, Dennis. Wow, I was so tired I would probably have slept all day long if you hadn't showed up."

"Well, what are good friends for, if they can't be a pest?" laughed Dennis.

"I'm too tired to answer that sort of question," said Mike as he opened the door for Dennis. Dennis stepped inside and looked around the room, almost as if he was searching for something. Mike noticed this but he had nothing to hide. Suddenly he remembered the map. His mind shifted gears as he tried to recall where he had left it. Mike remembered that he had, thankfully, left it in his room—out of Dennis' viewing. He had been reading it as he laid on his bed, just before sleep overcame him.

Dennis gave Mike a concerned look and calmly asked, "Mike, hey ... really ... I am very concerned about you. I know this is probably a stupid question, but how are you dealing with what's happened?"

Mike sunk back into a recliner in the living room. He searched himself for an answer. "Dennis, I really don't know how to answer that question. I just feel very empty ... and helpless ... like the wind has been completely knocked out of my sails, and my ship's at the mercy of nature."

"I wish I could say that I knew what you're going through, but I don't."

"Oh, Dennis, you don't want to wish such a thing, believe me!" exclaimed Mike.

"Sorry, I guess I didn't really mean that. What I meant is that I wish there was something I could do to help you."

"You don't need to apologize, Dennis. Hey! What did you do in Tucson while you were away?" Mike took in a deep breath. He knew he had to be careful as he asked questions, just to be safe. He did not want Dennis to detect any paranoia or suspicion in him.

"I attended a youth program that was sponsored by a large church."

"Which one?

"Southern Nondenominational."

"What did you talk about, or what did you all plan?

"We were discussing an opportunity for a district camp meeting to be held near Picacho Peak in Picacho Peak State Park."

Mike perked up a little. He and Bobby used to hike the trails in that area. "You know, Dennis, Bobby and I used to hike those trails now and then."

"Yeah, I know."

"You did?" Mike asked, catching himself, sounding a bit too incredulous.

"Yes, Bobby told me all about those trips you and he made." Mike remained silent for a moment, regrouping from his blunder of a moment before.

Dennis finally broke the silence. "Say, Mike, have you been anywhere since that day? I mean, have you gone back out on any hiking trips? You know, to sort things out, or maybe even try and find any clues about Bobby?"

"Well, I did go back out to the site where Bobby disappeared. I looked around to see if I could find even a trace of something that might help."

"Did anybody go with you?"

Mike hesitated before answering, though trying to not hesitate too long, knowing that too much of a pause would certainly be taken as a *'yes.'* Buying some time, he inquired, "Not that it really matters a whole heck of a lot, but why do you ask, Dennis?"

"Well, I noticed that girl with you the other day. Ah, let's see … Audra, I believe is her name … and I just wondered if she may have gone with you."

Mike did not want to get Audra involved so he told a little white lie, though normally loath to do so. "Actually, she wanted to go with, but I told her that I wanted to be alone."

"Where did you find such a gorgeous girl like her?" asked Dennis.

"We met at the library."

"And.…?"

"'And' what? What do you want to know?" Mike paused and, in an attempt to turn attention on Dennis, away from himself, threw out a compliment before continuing. "Wow! Brother, you really *are* concerned about me!" He then explained about his and Audra's meeting. "We hit it off at the library, and one thing led to another. Next thing you know, we're having dinner together."

"What did you two do at the library?" Dennis inquired. Now Mike was becoming a little suspicious … and a bit irritated. He had planned on asking the questions, but here Dennis was, beating him at his own game!

"We studied together. Why?"

"Ah-h-h, nothing … just curious. I guess she must be a nursing student, like you, if you two were studying together."

"Well, we were talking more than studying, actually. She was helping me locate some material and, when we found it, we just started talking. You see, she works at the Information Desk at the library. I needed a reference book, and she found it for me." Mike began wondering if he had just given out too much information, but he'd not been expecting such an interrogation, and it caught him rather off guard. Something felt very wrong. He had to turn the attention back on Dennis, where he felt it belonged … and quickly!

"You know, Dennis, other than serving as our Youth Minister, I really do not know you all that well—even though we have both lived in this district for years. I have lived here all of my life, and you have been around for … what is it … about twelve years now?"

Dennis affirmed Mike's estimation, as it was correct.

"What do you do alongside teaching youth at our church, Dennis? I'm just a bit curious, myself, now."

"Well, you know that we share common ground. We both lost our parents at a young age, and I moved to Sierra Vista later, because I wanted a slower pace of life, and less stress. I used what was left of my father and mother's estate, along with the sale of some property in California, to finance the move and buy a place here. That basically sums me up. I think you know that I work as sort of a courier for the State … and City. I must admit that working for the State and City has helped me come to know a lot of people in the community," explained Dennis as he smiled.

"They sure do send you to many different places. You're gone so much of the time, I don't think your right hand knows what the left hand is doing. Do they pay for all your trips, per diem, and all expenses?"

Dennis began to feel like he was now the one losing at the question game. "Yeah, they do."

"Where all do they send you to?"

"They send me to other reciprocating states, like New Mexico, Texas, Colorado."

"'Ever been to Central or South America?" Mike was pushing his luck now, and he knew it. His big mouth may have exposed him. A strange, surprised look came over Dennis' face … a look that almost asked, "How did you know that?" Mike was not stupid though, because he had just figured out a great reply for Dennis' response.

"Hey, what do *you* know?" Dennis asked, as if Mike had just uncovered some deep, dark secret that he was not meant to know. Then he tried to make a quick recovery, squawking, "I *mean* … what made you say *that?"*

"Well, you are wearing a jacket that says *Salvador* on it."

Dennis, not good at covering up his surprise, responded, "Oh, wow! *I* thought…." Then he paused, curiously adding, softly, as if to himself, "Ah, no … of course not."

Mike caught this, but said nothing, wondering what he did not yet know that Dennis had thought he'd discovered about him and his current—or past—activities.

"No, this is just the jacket maker's name, Mike. If you'll look closely, you'll see that it says *Selvador*, with an *'e',* not *Salvador,* with an *'a'."*

Mike leaned over and laughed heartily, relieved that he had not blown it. "Hey, man! We're getting too personal, I think, and I can tell that it's bothering the both of us. But I like you, Brother, and I think you have a great job, and you do a lot for the kids. I'm just angry … upset at almost everybody these days." Mike recalled the avoidance he'd felt during his last visit to church, which had both surprised and hurt him, as he continued. "I'm especially upset with the authorities, that have not invented better methods to track our missing children down. Do you realize that 2000 children a day turn up missing according to the *National Center For Missing And Exploited Children (NCMEC)?* Who knows where they're going—or if they're being mutilated, sexually and physically abused, or even ... sold!" Mike spoke loudly as he rambled on. He paused before the word, *'sold.'* It was just so unthinkable, that his little brother, Bobby, might actually be sold. He repeated it again under his breath, "Sold ... like objects, not humans." He shook his head.

"What's that friend?" asked Dennis.

"Just muttering to myself. Say, Dennis, d' you ever get a chance to talk to the Mayor ... or the Sheriff, maybe?"

Dennis looked at Mike harshly, as if asking, "Hey! What's with all this questioning?" Mike took note, while also recalling the shocked look on his face when he'd mentioned *'Salvador'* to Dennis. It just seemed there was something Dennis was hiding ... his eyes had even seemed to dilate, he was so surprised at Mike's question.

After what seemed a much longer pause than it actually was, Dennis spoke again. "Of course. I have run into them now and again, but I don't see the Mayor, or the Sheriff, on a regular basis."

"Ah, but you probably do see a few of the County Board members, don't you?"

"Man! You said you wanted to stop asking questions!" roared Dennis.

Again, quick thinking saved the day for Mike. "Dennis, the reason I'm asking you is because I believe they could help us. Now, you knew that Bobby and I were going hiking that day, and you knew the exact location—you and the children in your class. Somebody took Bobby from me, and I know that—whoever it was—they had to have known the exact location, also. I really do not think any of the children would be involved, yet they, or you, could possibly have spoken to someone unwittingly that may not have been above doing such a wicked deed. You would better know how to interpret directions, and map sites, better than the kids, Dennis!" bellowed Mike.

"What, the hell are you trying to infer!" screamed Dennis.

"Dennis, settle down. I need your help, not your temper ... please. I am not inferring anything at all. I am just asking you if you can remember if you spoke to anyone at all about our trip?" Mike knew he had Dennis riled now; he was definitely on the defensive. Mike just knew Dennis had some sort of inside knowledge. He sensed it. Dennis' surprised looks and body language spoke louder than any words ever could.

"I might have said something to the Pastor ... or someone." Dennis rolled his eyes, then looked down. A strange feeling came over him ... a feeling of remorse ... but it was too late to undo whatever he had done. How could he help Mike now? He looked sadly into Mike's eyes. "Mike, I know what you're driving at, but I can't help you. To answer your question outright, yes I did tell the Pastor, but I really didn't tell him exactly where you would be and, honestly, I do not remember telling anyone else. I sense your pain and agony Mike ... buddy ... but taking out your pain on others is not going to help at all. Now, I'm your friend, so I don't mind—although I almost felt like swapping punches with you for a minute there!

"Look, you told me that your neighbor always knows where you go, in case you don't show up at a specific time. Years ago, you told me that. And we have hiked together *how many* times, Mike ... you, Bobby and I. Maybe your neighbor accidentally mentioned the area you and Bobby were hiking to that day," stated Dennis.

Mike looked down at his untied tennis shoes. He was feeling like a heel now, and a tear was forming in his eye. "Why did Dennis start the conversation with so many danged questions, anyway? Was he prying, or was he just genuinely concerned?" Mike couldn't be sure yet. Confusion and frustration filled his mind. He looked over at Dennis with sad puppy dog-like eyes. "I'm sorry, Dennis. I just don't know what to do."

"Hey, partner, just call me whenever you need to talk to someone. I'll be there for you. I have to move on down the road now, but you have my cell number. Feel free to call me *any*time." Dennis asked if he could say a quick prayer. Mike nodded. Dennis left Mike with a very considerate prayer. Mike watched as Dennis pulled out of the driveway and started down the road.

Mike wiped his eye dry and mustered up his confidence again. Thinking to himself about this odd encounter with an old friend, he began muttering to himself. "Dennis, I don't know what to think about you. You seemed rather strange today ... and suspicious. If you are innocent, I hope you will forgive me." Pushing it from his mind at the moment, Mike lifted his phone and called Matt Piper. He had work for him to do.

Matt Piper sucked down his third shot of Jack Daniels, as he looked at the clock.

"Well, me friendly lad, here's to ye," said Matt as he lifted his drink to a little figurine of St. Peter. "Ah-h-h, that'll do for a mite," laughed Matt. He was startled when his cell phone sounded. "Well, now who could that be?" bellowed Matt. He lifted the phone to hear Mike talking on the other end.

"Mr. Piper," began Mike.

"Yes, sir, but can't you just call me Matt."

"Yeah, Matt. Hey, listen ... this is Mike Taylor. It's time for you to go to work. I need you to do a background check on Sheriff Tress ... and on a fellow by the name of Dennis Perris."

Matt interrupted. "The Sheriff! What? Hey, that should be a jolly good snoop for sure, me lad!" hooted Matt.

"I'm going to fax you all the information I have on Dennis Perris ... everything I know about him ... and I'm going to fax a picture of Dennis, also. Do you have a computer?"

"I'd be most illiterate without one, my dear lad! Of course, I do! D' you think I live in the Stone Age, or something?" retorted Matt.

"Great! I'll scan his picture and send it by email!" Animated in anticipation of the findings, Mike was talking somewhat fast; his voice picked up in pitch, as well.

"Okay, lad. Send all the information you can; send it all by email, if you'd like!" the old Englishman suggested. Matt gave Mike his email address, then Mike continued.

"Matt, I want you to follow Dennis around ... tail him. I have reason to believe that he is a suspect, but I want to make sure. I need to know where he goes, what he does, who he sees, and with whom he talks. I would like a thorough background run on him. I don't have his social security number—and I don't know if I can get it—but I do have his home address, numbers et cetera, et cetera ... and et cetera," Mike ordered.

"My, you blast out '*et ceteras*' like a bloomin' Englishman, for sure! Leave his past to me, m' lad. I know how to conjure up more information on a person than the government. I'll have everything on our man, Dennis ... and the good Sheriff."

"Oh, and you may want to tail the Sheriff also, Matt. I have reason to think he may lead you to points of interest."

"This is becoming a very exciting case, indeed, Mr. Taylor. I love it already! Send the information ASAP. Let's get started!" bawled Matt. With that, Matt ended his conversation with Mike and stood restlessly by his fax machine, waiting for it to beep.

Mike quickly faxed the information. He walked into his bedroom, picked the map up off the floor, and scanned Dennis Perris' picture. Within moments, Mike sent the photo to Matt. Mike sat on his bed thinking about all that had happened. He hoped passionately that he'd chosen the right private eye for the job. Mike thought through the conversation he'd had with Dennis, as well.

"I wonder if I missed asking him the most important questions? Did I miss asking him any question that I should have asked him?" Mike lay back on his bed. Just as his head hit the pillow, his phone on his nightstand rang. Mike lifted the phone. "Audra! Hey, thanks for calling. Yeah, I'll be at the support group tonight. I actually look forward to it. Yes, Dennis came by, and I'll tell you all about it later. Sure, see you tonight. Oh, you'll meet me at seven-thirty for a bite to eat first?"

Audra spoke cheerily, "Yeah, let's get together at *The Classic Coffee Shop*. I like their food and music. 'You know where it is?"

Mike felt insulted. "Of course I do, silly; believe it or not, I do get around town now and then. It's near the mall, next to Pat and Bill's, *What's New … Nothing*, furniture store. Pat and Bill own the coffee shop and the furniture shop. In fact, that's where I bought my nice, green leather sofa … also where I've been checking out this neat hutch and curio cabinet."

"All right, already, Okay!" Audra sounded a bit flustered.

"Hey, I'm sorry, Aud. I'm feeling a little edgy today. I always ramble on when I'm anxious. Please forgive me."

"Okay, I'll forgive you. But don't lose your head again, 'cause I won't screw it back on for you next time," said Audra with somewhat feigned sternness.

"Yep, that's me … always losing my head. Anyway, I can't wait to see you tonight. I'll follow you over to the support group after we get done eating," Mike promised.

"Yeah, you're lucky you have a brilliant leader like me to follow," Audra said with chutzpah.

Mike curled his lip. "Yeah, Bay*bah* … you can say that again."

Audra laughed as she told Mike to have a fun day. Then she hung up the phone, leaving Mike thinking about the support group, while he spoke aloud to himself again, as he was prone to do. "Well, Mike you're about to experience something totally new. I wonder what it'll be like to see all the faces of the poor souls that have lost their children."

Mike had a great deal of work to do. He wanted to hang pictures of Bobby all over the town. His picture was in the Post Office and in the police stations, but Mike knew that most people didn't even bother to look through those pictures. He thought, however, that if they saw Bobby's face nailed up on about every other post, they would always remember what he looked like.

Mike gathered up his staple gun and all the posters of Bobby. He'd had them laminated so the first rain would not ruin them. He climbed into his Jeep and drove to Mr. Brown's store, a store conveniently called *Brown's Supermarket*. As Mike pulled into the store, he looked at the price of gas and moaned. "'Seems like the gas train is having the worse luck coming down off the mountain. The way these prices keep climbing, we'll all owe our souls to OPEC.'"

Mike entered the store. Right away Cal Brown's eyes lit up. "Hey, Mike, how y' doing, big guy!"

"Trying to stay alive," said Mike.

"Well, you certainly look healthy. Did y' bring me some posters?"

"Yep, I have them right here." Mike handed the posters to Cal.

Cal looked at Mike and spoke. "I'll take these posters to the Deer Lodge, and the golf and sport clubs I belong to. You're welcome to hang up all the posters you want to around here. I'll help you in any way I can."

"I know that, Cal. Only you and two other people I know can appreciate how I feel right now." Mike felt sorry for Cal. He had lost his son twelve years ago. His boy, Cliff Brown, had been abducted right from his home. Cal and his wife, Linda, woke up one morning and he was gone. They searched high and low, but they had found no trace of Cliff. Of course, they had other children, and they helped to ease the pain, but parents and siblings never get over the emotional scars of missing a beloved child.

"See y' at the support group tonight," said Cal as Mike started out the door.

"I'll be there. I sort of look forward to it. 'Be a relief to converse with those that truly understand what I'm going through, Cal."

"Son, it is. It really is." Cal sounded very sure of himself. Mike walked out and drove away. He had much to do, and the day was wearing on. He stopped at the *Lone Star Café* in Hereford to make sure a poster was still stapled on one of the posts outside the *Café*. He also walked inside for a moment to see if the poster of Bobby still hung by the register. Sure enough, Bobby's picture stared back at him as large as life. The message below the picture read:

Bobby Taylor, beloved brother, please remember Bobby,
a wonderful child missing since March 10 of this year.

Numbers to the authorities and to Mike's personal phone followed the message. Some people may have been reluctant to offer their personal number, but not Mike. He wanted to be the first to know about Bobby, anyway. Unfortunately, some callers were pranksters who told ambiguous stories over the phone, which Mike knew were just a pack of lies. He took note of some of the caller's numbers, which he collected from the caller ID, and turned them over to the police. Raymond actually called these people and told them to expect a call from the FBI. When word spread about these sadistic pranksters actually being interrogated by the FBI, the prank calls ended. However, Mike did appreciate some of the calls he received from those who had lost a young child. They offered their prayers, and spoke of hope, which encouraged Mike. These particular calls helped Mike realize that he was not alone in his grief. There were many others suffering the same fate.

Mike continued driving to Sierra Vista. On the way there, he checked with various small stores and shops, the *Family Ninety-Nine Cent Store*, and the *General Dollar* store, as well as small strip malls and gas stations. All these places graciously allowed him to post Bobby's poster. Finally, he reached his destination, Sierra Vista. Parking the car in the Sierra Vista Mall parking lot, he slowly crawled out of the Jeep and walked over to a large wooden pole. He'd barely started nailing a poster of Bobby to the pole when he glanced at the modernly built attractive mall, and memories of Bobby flooded his mind. Immediately, he envisioned himself and Bobby walking in the mall together, laughing and wrestling with each other, as they strolled past the brightly lit, sparkling display windows of various specialty shops. They walked into the *Harkins Movie Theatre,* and sat down to watch a show that Bobby had nagged Mike about wanting to see. Watching Bobby had made Mike laugh more than the Disney production they were viewing at the time. His big grin, and the way he shifted and rocked in his seat during the exciting scenes, filled Mike's heart with joy. Bobby had been all he had left of his family, and now …

Mike leaned his head against the wooden pole, lifted his eyes to heaven and wept, "Pa, I don't have you or Ma anymore, Pa. Ma … Pa … if you can hear me, please help me! Tell God you've got to. He'll understand." Mike wiped tears from his eyes. Finally, his heart broke and he slumped to the ground, weeping aloud. Some of the folders and posters he held in his hands scattered over the ground. "Oh, God! I can hardly go on. I don't have a family anymore. They're all gone," sobbed Mike. His chest ached from his cries and moans. Suddenly he felt very strange … so light-headed. With this little shred of warning, Mike passed out.

"Mike! Mike, Buddy! Hey, Mike! Mike, can you hear me?" Raymond placed a cool cloth over Mike's head. Mike stirred, as he opened his eyes to see his best friend looking down at him.

"Raymond, wh … where did you come from?" surprised at his appearance, seemingly out of nowhere.

"Hey, big Buddy! Y' had me scared for a minute. I received a call that some drunk had passed out near the east side of the mall and Highway 92. I expected to find a babbling wino, not you, Mike!" With that short explanation of his presence, Raymond sniffed the air tentatively.

"Ah, brother, it hasn't come to that! I'm very much sober, Raymond. I don't know what happened. I was standing here thinking about Bobby and my family when I began to feel a bit strange. Next thing I know, you find me lying on the ground!" As Raymond had not detected any odor of alcohol, he felt a bit foolish. He knew Mike did not drink. Actually, Mike had kept Raymond from drinking when they were growing up. Raymond was a bit rebellious back in his high school days. Mike loved to have fun, too, but he'd always seemed to know when to quit before it grew into trouble. Raymond, being Mike's best friend, would give in to Mike's wishes, staying dry along with him when the guys would break out the booze.

"Heck, I'm sorry, Partner. Shoot, if it weren't for you my Brother, I'd probably have three or four DUIs to brag about when we were in school. Mike, you have been clinging to a lot of sorrow and pain, though. People will do things like drinking to ease the pain, though it's not normal for them to do so. I hope you're not sore at me for wondering."

"No way, you big lug. Oh, my head!" exclaimed Mike.

"Mike, you haven't been taking good care of yourself. I can tell. Your bulky build is beginning to look more like mine. You don't want to end up one scrawny lad, do you?"

Mike laughed with Raymond. "Now, stop knocking yourself. You're one of the wiriest men I know. I saw you hold your own weight before; I wouldn't want to truck around with you, Raymond. Do you remember those three guys down in Tombstone?"

"Ha! How could I forget? You threw them all over the place!"

"No way! Without your help, they would've kicked the Buddha out of me!"

"Yeah, I guess we did make a great tag team, didn't we!"

"And *how!*" laughed Mike, while trying to rub the circulation back into his head.

"Mike, do you need a doctor? I'll take you to the hospital if you do."

"No, Raymond, I think … no, I *know* you are right. I have not been kind to my body lately. I hardly know what sleep is anymore, and Lord knows that I barely receive enough grub, either. I believe my body is finally telling me to take better care of it," explained Mike.

"Hey, the least I can do is drive you around … and I won't take *'no'* for an answer."

"What about your patrol?"

"Ah, fudge! They ain't gonna get all in an uproar over it. Heck, they expect me to be helpful and help prevent accidents. Well, that's what I'll be doing. I don't want you driving all over, weak and ready to faint at the wheel."

"Okay, boss, I'll take you up on your offer. I have a feeling I really don't have much of a choice in the matter, anyway, do I?"

"You got it, my good friend. It's either my way or the hospital's way," laughed Raymond.

Mike and Raymond gathered all the loose posters that had fallen as Mike passed out. They placed them into the patrol car, climbed in, and drove away to the other side of Sierra Vista, near Fort Huachuca. Mike took this time with Raymond as an opportunity to fill Raymond in on some of his findings. Mike knew that if there was anyone left in the world that he could trust, it was Raymond. They pulled up to some wooden poles, got out of the squad car and stapled a poster to the pole. "Shucks, if we had two staplers we'd really move fast!" blurted Raymond.

"It's working out just great with you holding the poster, Buddy," said Mike as he finished with the last staple.

"Looks good," commented Raymond. The men walked over to several other poles, repeating their actions. Mike turned to Raymond, "Raymond, do you have your recorder in the patrol car on?"

"You know it's required, Mike."

"Okay, then I'll tell you what I want you to know out here. Raymond, you're my best friend. I wish we saw more of each other, but you have your life now and I have mine. Hopefully, that doesn't mean we still aren't close. What I'm about to tell might make you think I'm becoming paranoid and desperate, but I can back up everything I say, with good reasons for thinking like I do." Raymond stood silently, waiting for his friend to begin telling him about things he'd learned since Bobby's disappearance.

Raymond's dark hair accented the dark complexion of his face. He was a Navajo, proud of his heritage. He stood five-seven ... not too tall, but every ounce of his medium-sized frame was muscle. He also took pride in his strength and endurance, and his love of martial arts made him quick and dangerous. Raymond was watching the traffic as it rolled by. Some people were rubber necking, as though they were expecting to see Raymond cuff the larger man facing him and whirl him to the ground. He looked west towards the Fort Huachuca gate, just across the road from where they stood. He turned and looked at Mike. Speaking with a calm, well modulated voice, Raymond said, "Okay, Mike, you have my undivided attention."

Mike started from the beginning. He told him exactly what had happened in the mountains, how Bobby had suddenly disappeared after he let out a howl, and how he had tried to find him. He mentioned the rock formation, and crevice that looked like a human nose. Mike then explained the unusual actions of Sheriff Tress. Mike went on for awhile, explaining how he'd discovered the tunnel ... the shooting ... the metal plate that had led him to the compound. He even told him about the maps and the form that he had taken from the truck.

Raymond stood in awe, feeling overwhelmed. Mike had just nuked him with so much data, in such a short period of time, that Raymond had to ask several questions to make sense out of the entire ordeal. "Wow! Mike, you just laid such a huge amount of info on me that it's going to take me some time to sort through all this. You do realize the risk you have put yourself in, when you entered that compound, don't you? And, Mike ... you even *stole* from them! You're still at risk. I swore to uphold the law, Mike, and now you're telling me that you illegally entered into a place that I have been told is a County charitable distributing center for the poor … and actually confiscated County property!" scolded Raymond.

"Can we just say that I borrowed the map and document?" replied Mike.

"Mike, I don't know. Oh, Lord! Mike, you're digging yourself a hole!"

"Tell you what.…" Mike said, as he unzipped a pocket inside his jacket and pulled out a map and a piece of paper. "Here, Raymond; here's the map and the form. Please look at it, and tell me that I don't know what I'm talking about?"

Raymond took the map, opened it, and looked at the United States. He saw the circled areas with the underlined word, 'field,' inside the circles. He read the ticket that clarified what Mike had told him. Raymond had to admit that there seemed to be some validity to it all … actually more validity to what Mike had told him than he thought he would discover, once examining the paperwork Mike had managed to confiscate.

"Well?" Mike looked to his friend, questioningly, for affirmation.

"Well, I admit this does look a little weird. I don't know why they would title produce like this … or why they would code delivery destinations, if it's only produce. And you say these numbers and letters represent latitude and longitude lines and directions?"

"Yes, they are. If you search for where these longitudinal and latitudinal lines take you, they add up to the Southern foothills of the Huachuca Mountains, and various places in South America," Mike knowingly explained.

"You're amazing, Mike … amazing. But, I can't believe that Sheriff Tress would be involved. I think you are probably right about Bobby's abduction. I believe there may have been more than one person involved, but not Tress. Mike, don't you know that he flew immediately out to the scene? Tress was at the Mayor's office when your little brother was abducted. He could have driven his *Tahoe* to the scene but, according to what I've been told, he instead talked the Mayor into letting him use his private chopper."

"You mean the taxpayer's chopper," rebutted Mike.

"Whatever. Anyway, the Mayor and the Sheriff flew out to the scene immediately. Now why would the Sheriff make such an effort, if he were involved in such a heinous crime? If I was involved in such a crime, I'd try to make sure I arrived a bit tardy, don't you think?"

"Well, possibly … unless you wanted to get there in time to make sure something—or someone—must not be discovered," argued Mike.

"So you're saying that the Sheriff hurried to the scene to foul up the search?"

"Now you are beginning to see the light, Raymond!"

"What I see is a paranoid friend who needs to act more responsibly, and stop this nonsense!" barked Raymond, afraid that Mike might be losing it.

"I don't believe what I'm hearing! Raymond, listen! When we were in elementary school, who stuck up for you? Back then, we lived in a time when prejudice was worse than today. 'Remember how some of the kids wanted to hurt you, but I fought for you? We fought *together*, we became best friends. You even told me—always—that if it hadn't been for me, you would probably have become a bitter person that might have turned against the law instead of for it. Dang it, Raymond! I'm asking you to fight for *me* this time! Stand up for me ... please! I don't know who is the real child molester or abductor. Maybe the Mayor himself committed the crime, for all I know. I don't trust anybody and, if you were in my shoes, you know darn well you wouldn't, either!" shouted Mike.

"Then why are you telling me all this?"

"Because you're my best friend. You're like a brother to me. Oh, God! Raymond, who am I to go to? If I can't trust you, then who can I trust?" Mike's eyes began to water, as he couldn't help but become emotional, pleading with his friend.

Raymond bowed his head. His best friend stood before him, falling apart ... but he was making too much sense to just ignore him. Raymond decided to take the risk ... a chance that could ruin his career ... but Raymond knew Mike was correct about one thing for sure: if not for Mike's influence, Raymond knew he would have turned to a life of crime. Raymond looked at Mike and extended his hand. "Okay, Mike. Maybe I'm getting soft, but I'll do it. I'll stand behind you." Mike clutched Raymond's hand in both of his, and then gave him a grateful hug, as a few more tears rolled down his cheeks.

"Hey! Hey, now don't get all mushy. 'People see us, they'll think we're strange or something. Remember, my reputation is at stake here now, Mike!"

Mike laughed aloud. He felt so much better now. He knew he could trust Raymond. He would help him, and Raymond could keep him posted on details, as only someone working on the inside could do. Raymond ... feeling good about taking a risk for a friend who had made such a difference in his own life ... let out with a roar of laughter, too, as they headed back to the squad car.

They finished with the posters, and then drove back to the mall. As Raymond dropped him off, wishing him well, Mike asked him to not leave just yet. "I have something for you, Raymond. I wanted to bring this to you before now, but I just couldn't find the right time. Now I believe it is the right time." Mike ran to his Jeep, pulled out a book wrapped in plastic, and turned to see Raymond standing right next to him. "You startled me, Raymond!"

"I don't want whatever it is that you're going to give me captured on tape, so I figured we'd best stay away from the squad car for now."

"No kidding! Here, brother," Mike said, as he handed the book to Raymond.

"A Bible?" Raymond looked confused. "I do worship ... and read, but I don't think I need another Bible."

"Raymond, someone left this Bible on my nightstand in the hospital. They left it open to Exodus, chapter 13, and had a couple of verses highlighted ... verses two and thirteen. I want you to read those verses, if you would. Then read the footnotes I wrote at the bottom. But, before you do that, please see if you can find a set of prints on this Bible of the person that left it in my room."

"Not a problem, but you probably smeared the guy's prints away by now."

"I only handled that book once while in the hospital. After that, I used latex gloves to carefully open it. It has been covered carefully since then and has not been handled by anyone else."

"In that case, we might stand a good chance of recovering prints, my fine friend!"

"Right-on, brother! And ... thanks for helping me, Raymond," said Mike gravely, with a very steady voice.

"I just hope we both don't end up in the clink before this is over!" chortled Raymond.

Mike smiled, chuckling to himself, as Raymond walked away with the book under his arm.

Upon Raymond's leaving, Mike became a bit more somber. Mike looked at his watch; time was passing quickly. "Only one more hour till I see Audra, Can't wait to see her pretty face again, and I am looking forward to meeting these folks at the support group." Mike walked away from the Jeep towards the mall. He entered the mall and walked down the wide hallway. He had much to think over, and thought a little stroll through the mall would clear his head ... help him think. Mike was focused sufficiently on his thoughts as he walked through the mall that he nearly cut a woman off coming out of *Spencer's Gift Shop*.

"Hey, watch where you're going, buddy!" she angrily chided.

Mike slid to a quick halt, just in time to miss knocking the woman down. "Whoa! I'm very sorry, pretty lady; I didn't see you," explained Mike.

"Didn't see me? I...." The woman calmed down as they caught each other's eye amidst this close encounter, noting Mike's deep blue eyes. "Well, no harm done, I guess." Then, with a flirtatious grin, and sultry speech, she asked, "Sa-a-ay, what is *your* name?"

Mike laughed within himself, being annoyingly used to such come-ons, but he held his aloof posture. "My name is Mike, and it's a pleasure, Miss."

"A pleasure to almost knock me down, huh!"

"No, a pleasure to meet you," Mike smiled.

"Well, it's a pleasure meeting you, too, Mike. My name is Melissa. I'm new in town … just moved here a month ago." Melissa, a very pleasant-looking young woman with dark eyes and hair, hinted, hoping Mike might show her around town.

Mike looked at Melissa and said, "Well, Miss, I'm sure you'll find this a quiet town. Not much really happens here. We do have some fun festivals, and Tombstone's not too far away; I'm sure you would enjoy that western town very much."

"Well, you could maybe show me around sometime, couldn't you … Mike? Maybe we could even enjoy Tombstone together." Melissa blinked her dark Latino eyes at Mike. Her thick eyelashes, luscious ruby red lips, and lovely robust figure almost beguiled Mike into saying, "Sure, I'd love to." However, Mike shook the temptation off and said, "You seem like a very sweet gal, Melissa, but I'm already spoken for, so I'm afraid I cannot."

"Oh, so what … you aren't married, are you?" Melissa cajoled enticingly.

"No, but I really like the girl I'm dating now." Mike wondered how things like this happened … the old *'feast or famine'* syndrome … bad timing, perhaps? "Murphy's Law," Mike muttered to himself, barely moments after declaring himself *'taken.'*

"Murphy … what does Murphy have to do with it?" inquired Melissa.

"Just a saying, that's all. I'm sorry, Melissa. Hey! I could possibly fix you up. I have a very close friend that isn't married, and he's not dating anyone!" Mike said, with exhilaration in his voice.

Melissa considered turning down the offer, but when she detected all the excitement, and saw his eyes light up, she asked, "Is he cute, like you?"

Mike felt his cheeks flushing from the compliment. "Melissa, believe me, you'll think he's a dream boat. He works for the City as a police officer. His name is Raymond Duke."

Melissa became downright excited now. Her father worked as a law enforcement officer for Phoenix. "Why, no kidding! In that case, yeah, I'd be interested," she giggled.

"Great! I'll try and arrange a time. Maybe it could be a double date, if you wish!"

"That sounds like a winner. Here's my number; it's my sister's, as I'm staying with her until I get settled in. She's a nurse, and I just started the nursing program this semester," explained Melissa. Mike thought that Melissa was very outgoing, yet maybe a tad to trusting for being the daughter of an officer of the law. Mike accepted her number and, as he did so, he asked her for pen and paper. He then proceeded to write down his number, and handed it to Melissa.

"Melissa, I really need to go. I'm to meet my girlfriend soon, so I have to say 'bye, but I'll be in touch about Raymond.

"I'll be waiting, and don't forget!" laughed Melissa.

"You never … I'll never forget almost bumping into you!" laughed Mike. They waved as Mike walked away. "Well, that little distraction took up nearly thirty minutes. Even if I slam into another woman, I'll be danged if I blab as long as we just did there!" mumbled Mike.

He walked on, as his mind refocused on recent past events once again. He was trying to sort through his conversation with Dennis, as well as his talk with Raymond. He began mulling details over in his mind. "Hmmm … Raymond said that the Mayor was at the site, too, since he had flown the Sheriff over there. 'Guess the Sheriff must carry rappelling gear in his vehicle, or the Mayor keeps that type of gear in his chopper. I don't know much about helicopters— nor rappelling gear, for that matter—but I wonder why the Mayor's chopper would have that kind of equipment in it, anyway. I'll have to research that later." Mike's mind was awhirl, trying to imagine every conceivable detail about the entire ordeal, not wanting to miss a thing that might possibly be of any help in solving it.

He walked on through the mall until he reached the far end. He turned and headed back to where he had entered the building. "I still feel a bit edgy about Dennis. He just seemed so strange today," Mike just couldn't help mumbling to himself again. "He's never acted that way before. It was like he was on a fact-finding mission … almost as if someone may have asked him to squeeze infor-mation out of me. I wonder if that is the case, or am I really becoming a paranoid screwball."

Then his mind began going another direction, as the word 'sold' again entered his mind. Sold … *sold!* I know those children are being sold, but to whom—why more boys—at present, anyway—than girls? If sex, prostitution and molestation are the motive, 'seems girls would be the prime targets. Money seems to be the primary motive, but I just cannot visualize officials that live in this County doing that … selling children to porn kings, or to cannibalis-tic child molesters. Child porn is definitely a possibility, but why would such sick, deranged people bother to buy children if they're going to kill them in the end? What kind of profit would that be? No, this is too well organized … too planned. Some of our Department heads may be involved, but could the Sheriff actually be involved, in spite of Raymond's hesitancy to indict him? And, what had the Sheriff been doing at the Mayor's office that day? If the Sheriff was involved, then that means…."

Suddenly, out of nowhere, a column jumped right out at Mike … or, so it seemed to him, having received no sensory forewarning of its presence, being so deep in thought. "Ouch! Dang! That really felt good!"

A little boy, walking nearby with his mother, saw Mike ram his head into the column. "Ha! Ha! That was funny, Mommy! The man ran right into a column. That stupid man ran into that great big column!" laughed the little boy as he pointed at Mike.

Overhearing the not-too-discreet child, Mike waved sheepishly at the boy and his mother as he rubbed his head. "Hey, glad I made someone laugh today. Yep, son, you have to be pretty stupid to run into a column, I agree. But, 'funny thing is, the column looked just like my girlfriend at the time. 'Hard way to discover it wasn't!" Mike laughed, though his head was throbbing.

The boy's mother roared in laughter. She, too, had caught a glimpse of what happened, and she appreciated Mike's sense of humor. "You sure you're okay?" she inquired.

"Well, no. My pride feels like you-know-what! Actually, I wish I could crawl into a hole right now!"

"Want to get away … go hide?" laughed the little guy's mother.

"Yeah, but I don't think there are any same-day airfare specials available!" They both laughed. The little boy did not understand this part of the conversation between his mother and Mike, but he did recognize a funny situation when he heard and saw it, so he continued laughing, too. Mike had to chuckle as he continued on his way, rubbing his skull, and chastising himself for being so careless. Once the exit was within sight, he began walking a little faster. After all, 'twas not only his head but his ego, as well, that was sorely bruised and hurting.

Once outside the mall, Mike hurried to his Jeep, jumped in and roared across the parking lot, pulling out onto Highway 92. From there, he made a left onto Fry Boulevard, and then into the coffee shop's parking lot. Mike instantly spotted Audra's little red Nissan. He parked his vehicle and bolted into the *Classic House Coffee Shop.*

As he rushed to the counter, he heard a very familiar voice. "Well … and I thought cows came home late. Where y'been?"

"Come on, Audra, give me a little break. I'm only five minutes late. I ran into too many things … literally, as a matter of fact," he added, not bothering to explain. His head still throbbed from hitting the column.

"Well, Hon, I bought you a meal, so you wouldn't have to. Here … two burgers, fries and a cup of coffee—the All-American meal."

"Thanks, Doll, I'm starving!" exclaimed Mike. His taste buds were going wild, for he hadn't eaten all day. He sat and dove into the burgers. Audra asked

Mike how the visit with Dennis went. Mike asked Audra if she minded him talking as he ate and—since she told him it would not bother her—he began, trying to coordinate, as best he could, his talking with his chewing. Mike reiterated the entire conversation to Audra, and illustrated the look on Dennis' face when Mike had asked him if he had ever been to Central or South America.

"Mike, you sure stuck your neck out on that one!"

"Not really. Like I said, his eyes almost popped out of his head, but I don't think he suspects a thing, because of a jacket he was wearing."

"What do you mean?"

"I saw the word *'Selvador'* written on the front of his jacket, so I asked him if he'd ever visited Central or South America. You know … El Salvador in Central America."

"No kidding! 'Like I'm that geographically challenged!" Audra was a little taken aback.

"Hey, I'm sorry. I didn't mean anything by that; really, I didn't."

"You'd better be sorry, Champ, or I'll stomp your head into the shape of a stamp … you know, kind of flattened out!" Audra gave Mike a *'macho girl'* look.

"Something tells me you probably could," laughed Mike.

"Don't push me, Mike. Remember … my father's a *Green Beret*. He taught me enough to be quite dangerous, if I have to." Mike nearly choked on a fry. Audra laughed loudly, "I didn't mean to scare the air out of you, Tough Guy! Hey, take it easy, Mike!"

"I'm just so hung…." Mike gulped hard as he tried to catch his breath; then he drank some water. "Phew, that's better," he wheezed.

"What else did you do today, besides talk to Dennis?" Mike told her all about hanging posters, and the time he spent with Raymond, but he did not mention Melissa or his run-in with the column at the mall. He also kept his fainting spell to himself. He thought it less than manly to tell Audra that he had fainted earlier.

"Hey, we've got to split. We're going to be late for the support group if we don't buzz on out of here now!" Audra said loudly, as she looked at her watch.

They rushed out of the restaurant, entered their vehicles and drove away. Mike followed Audra to Huachuca Mountain Elementary School where the meetings were conducted. They walked into an annex building just north of the main building. As soon as they walked in, Cal Brown and his wife, Linda—as well as several others in attendance, mostly parents—warmly greeted them. Mike noticed a number of chairs placed in a large circle. After the preliminary introductions, a lady requested that everyone take a seat. Mike sat between Audra and Cal Brown.

"Good evening, folks. Most of you know me. My name is Katrina Adams. I see some new faces here tonight. We do like newcomers to tell who they are, and a little about themselves; however, it's not a requirement so, if you do not feel up to it, we'll understand." Katrina spoke with a very pleasant, soothing voice, which immediately made the people feel very comfortable ... even peaceful, if such were possible in the dire circumstances in which they commonly found themselves. Her well groomed, attractive looks, along with her relaxing voice, instantly won Mike's trust.

A stately black lady sat next to Katrina. She held a brown leather briefcase on her lap. Mike looked at her with interest, not because of her good looks, but because she looked familiar for some reason. Why did she look familiar? He could not place, at the moment, where he had seen her. Mike, therefore, shook off the thought, allowing his mind to return to the session. Katrina looked over at another woman, asking, "Toni, would you like to introduce yourself and share anything with the group?"

Toni rearranged her position in her chair, cleared her throat and spoke. "Hi, my name is Toni." The group acknowledged Toni as they replied with a collective, "Hi, Toni." She continued, "I live in Naco ... you know, just south of Bisbee near Mexico. I lived with my little boy all alone because my husband passed away a year ago due to cancer. Anyway, I'm here tonight because my little boy just recently died from leukemia. My caseworker from the State Child Services thought I should attend these support groups, because I...." Toni hesitated, then caught her breath. "I can't deal with it alone anymore. I've lost two members of my family now, and I don't know what to do!" she cried. Tears ran down her rosy cheeks. She looked to be around twenty-five or twenty-six years old ... too young to bear such grief.

Mike's heart went out to Toni. Here was someone that lost her entire family, also. Linda Brown handed Toni a tissue, as Katrina asked Mike if he wanted to share anything with the group. Mike only wanted to listen; he really did not wish to participate, but he figured if Toni could talk to the group, so could he. "Hi, my name's Mike Taylor. The group acknowledged him, and then Cal spoke up. "I'm glad you're here, Mike." This encouraged Mike, as he continued to relate his story.

"Some of you may know about a little boy that was abducted by s ..." catching himself before he could say *'some'* ...'by a very cruel human being. Actually, I can't help but think of such deranged people as slimy maggots instead of humans." Mike paused, quickly scanning everyone's face.

Audra broke in. "You're doing fine, Mike. We all get rattled and tongue-tied when we first talk about those we've lost."

Mike looked down at his left shoe, thinking, "Hmmm, the lace is untied. Audra saved me again. I don't think anyone knows I was going to say some cruel people. No, I'm just facing paranoia again," Mike said silently to himself. Then he continued aloud, "Sorry folks. I'm a little emotional right now."

Cal put his hand on Mike's shoulder. "Mike, that's why we are all here. That's why Toni came tonight, too." Every person in this room has lost a child due to sickness, violence or abduction. We meet here because those that have not experienced such a terrible, horrendous loss do not understand our emotions. They actually push us away, because they have no idea how to talk to us. Most believe that, if they do talk to us, they'll say the wrong words and offend us, or cause us more pain. They're unfortunately walking on eggshells around us when we most need them to be there for us. But time finally begins to cure that, though I pray time brings your brother back to you." Cal shook Mike's shoulder affectionately as he released his grip.

"Well, now you all know that the little boy who was abducted was my brother. We were hiking in the Huachuca Mountains when it happened. I can seriously relate to Toni. Bobby is the only family I have left. My father and mother died in a plane crash when I was nine. Last year my grandparents perished in a deadly hotel fire in Florida. Now you know how important Bobby is to me; we only have each other left." Mike's voice began to crack, so he said no more.

Katrina looked over the group of people as she spoke. "Tonight I am pleased to introduce you to an individual that has been involved with the *NCMEC* for years now. She is from our lovely national Capital, Washington, D.C. She is here to discuss the topic of missing and exploited children. I realize some are not here due to a missing child, but we believe that our support group can help those who suffer the loss of children due to illness, accidents *or* violence. We all go through the same grieving stages whenever we face a heart-wrenching loss. With that in mind, I now present Ms. Janet Riley. The group clapped as Ms. Riley set her folder on the floor.

"Thank you, Ladies and Gentlemen. I am very happy to be here tonight. I shall be with you dear people for six or seven weeks. During this time I want to be your friend, as we share our burdens and experiences together." Janet spoke in a deep alto voice, her pitch more strident than was Katrina's. "I lost my two daughters in an instant. Nicky was eight, and Brenda ten, when they were abducted from a shopping center in D.C. They were with my mother at the time. No one has a clue as to what happened. My mother was found dead. She had been beaten to death with a blackjack, and the children stolen. The authorities moved quickly on the case, but—when the dust had settled—my two babies were found dead. They had been sexually molested, and then cut up badly, by some horrible human being.

"Mike, I like your description better. Sometimes I think of these people as maggots, also. On the other hand, if we allow these deranged people to turn us into depressed, bitter individuals by harboring hate the rest of our lives, then they win in the end. We cannot love each other when we bottle up hate and anger within us and, believe me, the hate and bitterness grows like an unnatural weed, until the roots begin to literally choke the life out of us."

Janet continued, speaking next to Cal and Linda Brown about Cliff's disappearance. "Cal and Linda, I understand that your son was abducted right from your home twelve years ago. The stages of grieving include denial, anger, bargaining, depression and finally—that proverbial *light at the end of the tunnel*—acceptance. If you don't mind my asking, how have you survived all these years?"

"That's a tough question, which begins to bring back memories, but I believe it is very important to share this with the group," began Cal. "We were both very much in denial after it happened. I'd find myself calling Cliff at times, or walking in his room to get him up."

Linda stepped into the conversation. "I behaved in the same way. Sometimes yet I find myself waking up, and thinking that Cliff is still with us. We did find a lot of strength through our other children, but we also found ourselves drifting apart from one another. I'm not talking about just Cal and me; our entire family was on the rocks. We may have all split apart, had we not discovered that one thing we needed to learn was to stop blaming other family members, or ourselves. Once we learned this, it is then that we began to mend.

"We also realized that the invisible criminal, who may never be found, had somehow become the main character in our home, and was ruining our lives. Though we did not—and still do not—have any clue regarding who it was that perpetrated this horrible crime, he was allowed to control and manipulate us. As long as we let what he had done color our attitudes, this unknown villain—wherever he is, and whatever he looks like—had not only taken charge of our child who disappeared, but also all of our lives. We finally had to learn how to forcefully kick him out of our lives, by beginning to move forward, in the best way we knew how, and not continuing to live in the past." Linda paused, then sighed, as she added, "Now, this was extremely difficult to do, but through much prayer ... and love ... we did it." One did not have to look hard at all to see the lingering pain on Linda's face.

Cal held his wife close to his side. "We don't have any magic wand to wave about healing, but we hope we can offer some healthy advice. When we lost

Cliff, we sort of died with him. We all became a little reclusive. We stopped going out and doing things together. We lived in fear that another horrible tragedy was right around the corner. We grew very suspicious of everybody. In essence, we simply stopped living. Life no longer was a joy. Instead, it became dark and cruel, full of untrustworthy people. When we were finally able to step outside and breathe again, we started to heal. We stopped making the villain the center of our lives, and we began to trust people again. When we did this, we noticed joy slowly, but surely, creeping back into our lives," Cal explained.

Katrina asked the Brown's another question, "Who was the pillar in the family? I mean, who tried the most to bring the joy back? Usually in a family there is one member that is the first to realize that it is time to move forward."

"Oh! That's an easy one," Linda exclaimed. "Cal definitely was. He did his best, shortly after Cliff's disappearance, to set our feet back on track again. He bought and rented comedy movies for us, as well as family games. He tried to laugh as much as possible, even though we knew he, too, was crying on the inside. He even took all the money he had saved up and bought a little market. He thought it would help us as a family, if we worked together, and he was right. I recommend that we should find solace in our friends or other family members. Do something … with somebody, not alone. Keep your minds active. Sure, you are going to cry and feel very upset at times, but you don't have to let it control your lives, or life, and ruin your love for others." Linda's pained face began to soften just a bit as she began recounting how hope had slowly begun creeping back into their lives. This had not been by leaps and bounds, by any means … just a slow, steady lessening of the former excruciatingly painful ache that had filled the void of losing a child, that had not allowed for any joy for so long. This brought some hope to people in the room.

This form of conversation rotated around the room. Soon everyone found himself or herself talking and sharing their feelings. Mike did not say a word further than the short, expected, introduction he'd contributed at the beginning of the meeting. He mainly listened, as his mind began to wander, quietly asking himself questions. "Cal and Linda lost their son twelve years ago. Matt, the private eye then lost his nephew eight years ago. Audra lost Todd four years ago, and now Bobby vanishes four years after Todd disappeared. Now, either the number four is quite a coincidence, or indicative of a distinct pattern. The abducted children had some things in common, as well. They were all boys, and they were all around the same age at the time of their abduction—twelve to thirteen—and all but one lived in, or near, Sierra Vista. Todd had lived in Tucson at the time. What's the connection here? What is it with the number four?"

After analyzing these related facts for awhile, Mike suddenly felt compelled to speak. He looked over at Janet and spoke. "Ms. Riley, you work for *NCMEC,* so you must have stats on missing children, right?" People in the group were puzzled by Mike's question. Why would he ask such a question when they were discussing the topic of dealing with grief? Even Audra looked a bit baffled. Some people wanted to protest, but they knew this was Mike's first time, so they just patiently listened ... wondering.

"Ah-h-h, yes, I do have stats. I have stats with me in a folder, but I must say that you're asking for a rather unusual thing." Mike could see that Janet was definitely taken off guard by such a request. But, as he had no idea if, or when, he might see Janet again, or if she would be willing or have the time to see him, he needed answers now not tomorrow or next week. The clock against which he raced, in his attempt to find Bobby, never stopped ticking; he must hurry ... must gather as much data as quickly as possible.

"Do you happen to have the stats on the number of abducted children during the past twelve years?"

"Yes, I believe so." Janet opened her case and thumbed through her papers, pulling out a small stack from a folder. "I have them right here."

"How many boys were abducted twelve years ago?" asked Mike. Ms. Riley read off the number. Mike then asked, "Now, what happened after that? I mean, did the numbers increase or decrease after that year?"

"They actually stayed about the same," replied Janet.

"What about in our region?"

"They decreased." Mike did not wish to stop, although he knew he was denying people the right to discuss their feelings. He could not stop now. Somewhere, his brother was out there, and Mike felt him inside. He knew instinctively that Bobby still lived, and every second counted. As if to double check her understanding of the information which he had just requested, Ms. Riley asked, "Mike, when you refer to *'this region,'* what exactly do you mean?"

"The mountain region ... you know, the Mountain Time Zone region."

"Okay, that's what I thought you were referring to. And, yes, it did decrease after that year."

"What happened during the next three years?"

"It remained about the same ... until four years later, in '98. It hit a high in 1998 then, after that, it dropped again." Janet looked very interested in Mike. This was no ordinary man, and she knew it. He seemed very alert ... very sharp. Janet became excited, for now she knew what Mike was driving at. She was bright, as well, and caught on quickly. Not wanting anyone to notice her excitement, she acted a little perturbed.

Mike persisted, continuing. "In 1995, what time zone felt the wrath of a higher number of abducted boys?"

"Well, to answer that question …" Janet thumbed through a couple of more pages, as Mike eagerly waited "… the Pacific Time Zone did. Mike, we're getting off the subject here." Janet gave him a stern look.

Mike knew when to quit. "Hey, I'm very sorry everybody; I just got carried away. Since Bobby's abduction, I tend to think there's a bogeyman behind every bush, and I find myself getting a little paranoid every time the wind blows." Mike lowered his head and shifted his eyes to the ground.

"Hey, don't beat yourself up, Mike. Anybody that has been viciously violated feels that way," said Cal. Some others agreed, and dismissed Mike's strange behavior merely as grief, and nothing more. The rest of the session focused back on grief, and overcoming emotional barriers to speeding the grieving process along.

Finally, Audra shared the latest news about herself, her father and her mother. Halfway through her sharing, she broke down and wept aloud. Katrina rose from her chair and walked over to where Audra was sitting. As she passed Cal, she slipped him a small piece of stationery. Katrina knelt at Audra's side and held her. "Honey, let it out. Let out all the hurt." Katrina cried with Audra until the tears had stopped. Mike noticed that Toni, along with some others, was crying, also. Nor did it escape his attention when Katrina had slipped Cal a note.

Next, he looked over at Janet, who sat studying the scene very closely. Mike thought she looked more than a little suspicious, just looking over the group while they cried. As their eyes met, Janet looked at Mike stolidly … a look that made Mike feel very uneasy. He quickly turned away. Finally, the session ended. The people in the group all joined hands, said the 'Serenity Prayer' in unison, and then began going their separate ways. Mike helped Audra out of her chair. He held her hand, as they slowly walked to the door. Mike happened to overhear Katrina saying to Janet, "Well, I hope American Airlines treated you well on your trip down here. When did you arrive in Phoenix?"

"Ah, we'll talk later. I need to get my things together. I have to be at the Windemere Hotel in fifteen minutes. I've got to go … now!" exclaimed Janet. She threw the folder with the stats into her case, shut it quickly and zipped past Audra and Mike.

With that, Mike started thinking about the short conversation that had just transpired between the two women. "American Airlines to Phoenix some time back…. That's it! Now I know where I saw you, Ms. Riley, if that's really your name!" Mike's mind lit up as he shouted the words in his head. He had a lot to digest, and a whole new string of questions that needed answers. He could hardly wait to get Audra outside so he could share his new findings with her.

When Mike and Audra walked a distance from the annex building, Mike excitedly began to speak, but he was quickly cut off by Audra, who had not understood what he was getting at ... what he was trying to find out that might help them in their search. "What was that all about in there, anyway, Mike! You acted as if you were on a different planet. Those people have feelings ... I have feelings! You acted like it didn't even matter to you ... as if only numbers mattered, not any of the children!"

"Wait! I was only trying...." He'd barely begun to explain, when he was again interrupted. He wanted so badly to let Audra know he needed data to verify—hopefully not debunk—his time-zone theory. But her pain would not let her listen at the moment.

"No! Buddy, *you* wait! How could you leave the main topic for the meeting and start cutting open old wounds, monopolizing everyone's time, to boot? Audra mockingly imitated Mike's performance in the meeting: *'Ms. Riley, how many kids were murdered in this zone, or that time zone?'* Oh, Lord! Where's your mind, Mike! Is there any comfort in being reminded of someone's horrible death?"

Mike's male ego suggested he lash out ... defend himself. He, however, wisely listened to the small voice in his head, urging him to calm down, take a deep breath and forget about his pride. Audra was hurting. So Mike adoringly took Audra in his arms.

"After hearing you out, I fear I must have definitely sounded like a mad man in there. But, Audra, it is not fair to judge me so harshly. Audra, I love you; I really do, and I love my little brother very much. I realize that every moment that passes by leaves us with less of a chance of finding Bobby. I have to act very quickly ... I must, or Bobby will soon be far, far away, and then I may never find him. If we have a chance of recovering Bobby—if we actually pin down the ring of people, those who are behind these planned abductions—I honestly believe that we will also find out what happened to Todd. Then, we will also have a great chance of finding many other children who have fallen into the evil clutches of these people. So, you see, I had to ask when the opportunity presented itself! I have no idea when—or even *if*—I will have the privilege another day, so I had to speak out in that meeting. Maybe you don't understand this, but I'm only asking you to try and recognize my situation here." Mike looked tenderly into Audra's eyes as he gently stroked her cheek with the backs of his fingers.

Audra felt a little guilty. She replied appreciatively to what Mike had just told her, as she kissed him on the cheek. "I suppose I was a bit hasty there; call it 'female emotions,' I guess. When Todd disappeared, I would have done the same thing at the time. 'Time' … that's the problem, Mike. Time goes on. Months pass into years and—with it—all your hopes … all your dreams … that one day you'll receive a call and Todd's on the other end, bragging of how the FBI or police have found him, and he's on his way home. In fact, awhile after Todd disappeared, we received some calls from their Agents that stated that a boy fitting Todd's description was seen here, or seen there. Our spirits would soar high in the sky, only to crash land again and again. Finally, the calls just stopped and, as more years passed, we learned to *accept* the truth.

"Then I met you and … and now I am so confused! But, I told you I would stick it out with you to the end, because I believe in you. I love you, too, Mike. Oh, how I love you!" cried Audra. She wept in his arms for what seemed an eternity. Mike's heart went out to Audra, and he found tears streaming down from his eyes, also. Here was a beautiful young woman that surely did not deserve the horror, the agony, of losing a brother.

Mike's body trembled a little as he thought about Audra's dear mother lying in a catatonic state in Tucson, and her father dealing with depression. "She is a brave, strong girl who has taught me how to be brave. God, I really do love this Little Lady. Thank you for sending her into my life." Mike spoke these grateful words as he held Audra in his arms.

Audra looked into Mike's eyes. She loved his pretty eyes. Every time she looked into them, she felt warm and secure. "Mike, let's go home. I think we've both had enough for one day."

"You're probably right," agreed Mike as they turned and walked to their vehicles.

"Hey, why don't you come over to my place tonight. It's about time you met my father, anyway!" shouted Audra.

"Sure, I have time for that. The night's still young!" an excited Mike exclaimed, as he leapt into his Jeep. They hurried down Fry Boulevard, turned right on Highway 92 and headed towards Hereford. Mike followed Audra into a lane leading to a site-built house made of mortar and redwood-colored brick. It had an attractive gable in the front, with an extended two-car garage on the south end; the yard needed a little touching up here and there, but, overall, it was in decent shape. Mike thought the big wishing well out front gave the house a welcoming feeling.

Audra jumped out of the car and ran to Mike's Jeep; "Come on, big man it's time for you to meet my favorite *Green Beret!*" Audra said with enthusiasm; after all, two of her favorite men were meeting each other. Mike followed Audra into her house. He liked the saltine tile floor that covered the foyer; beyond the foyer, the den, carpeted with light beige Berber set off the antique-white walls.

A light tan, leather sofa and love seat leaned against the long den wall. Two carved oak lamp stands stood at the end of the long sofa that supported two ornamented figurines holding artificial flowers in their angelic hands. In front of the sofa, stood a large, engraved, oak, coffee table with a Lazy Susan in the middle. There were some other smaller chairs including a recliner and a rocker, and colorful pictures hung from all four walls. Mike admitted to Audra that he really liked their interior decorator.

"Then, you really do like me, huh!"

"Wow! This is great! You did all this?"

"Yep, I sure did, my Big Hero, and soon I'm going to change it all around again."

"Why? It's already so lovely."

"I like changes. It just makes me feel more free and happy." Mike understood Audra's answer.

"Where's your father?"

"He must be sleeping. You know, Mike, he's just not the same father I knew a few years ago. He doesn't drink, but the doctors have him on some antidepressants and, despite what they say about them, I know they make him tired. All he does is go to work, come home, eat a meal, looks through his files from work and then plops in bed. He lives a very secluded, lonely life."

"What does he do at work?" Mike wondered.

"Well, he's a Commanding Officer; he's in charge of Fort Huachuca's Intelligence Division. I really do not know all the details because he claims much of what he does is classified."

"Being in the *Special Forces* like he is, I can believe that."

"Hey, Mike! Sit down and park yourself a while. I won't seduce or distract you ... I promise," laughed Audra.

"You know, I might just enjoy being distracted!" laughed Mike.

"Yeah, dream on, heap big pipe dreamer ... that'll be the day, all right."

Mike curled his lip Elvis-like as he spoke, "Well, whenever you're feeling frisky Bay*bah*, you just let Big Mike know now, y' hear?" adding that familiar trademark, "Thank you very *much*!"

Audra laughed aloud. "Hey, Handsome, that was pretty good. Anyway, I have some news for you."

Mike perked up, "Go on, Audra; I'm all ears." Mike pulled on his lobes as he spoke.

"I decided to do a little research on *two* counts. First, I surfed the 'Net for a clue that might lead me to the people buying the children. We'll get to the drug situation later. Anyway, during my search, I came across this article and I'd like you to read it," stated Audra, as she took out the article from her knapsack and

handed it to Mike. Mike read the title out loud: *"The New Slavery."* Hmmm...."
He continued reading aloud. "'Says here that....

> *'Slaves in Pakistan may have made the shoes you are wearing and the carpet you stand on. Slaves in the Caribbean may have put sugar in your kitchen and toys in the hands of your children. In India they may have sewn the shirt on your back and polished the ring on your finger.... In Brazil, slaves made the charcoal that tempered the steel that made the springs in your car and the blade on your lawn mower. Slaves grew the rice that fed the woman that wove the lovely cloth you've put up as curtains. Your investment portfolio and your mutual fund pension own stock in companies using slave labor in the developing world. Slaves keep your costs low and returns on your investments high.'*

"Whoa!" Mike paused, while taking it all in, then continued reading:

> *'Slavery is illegal in Mauritania and everywhere else in the world; however, making slavery illegal doesn't make it disappear.*
>
> *'As long as people are controlled by violence and exploited for economic purposes, they are slaves, regardless of whether or not a country's laws recognize the legal ownership of human beings. The number of slaves in the world today is around 27 million—greater than the population of Canada. It is far more likely today that a product of slavery is sold on the global market. For example, there is a significant use of slave labor on the cocoa plantations of West Africa, and the chocolate made from that cocoa is eaten all over the planet. Maybe 40 percent of the world's chocolate is tainted with slavery. The same is true of steel. They're not sure what the average price of a slave is today, but it can't be more than fifty or sixty dollars.*

"Well, that sort of blows our high-priced-sales theory out of the water. Let's see now...."

> *'Such low prices influence how the slaves are treated. Slave owners used to maintain long relationships with their slaves, but slaveholders no longer have any reason to do so. If you pay just a hundred dollars for someone, that person is disposable, as far as you are concerned. In gold-mining towns in the Amazon, for example, a young girl might cost a little over one hundred and fifty dollars. She is recruited to work in*

mining offices, but when she arrives she is beaten, raped, and exploited for prostitution where she may earn over $10,000 a month. If they don't comply, they are killed. One girl was actually beheaded by a miner she would not have sex with. He planted her head on a pole and stood the pole upward as the other miners looked on in approval. Human beings have become disposable tools for doing business, the same as a box of wooden pencils.

'An alarming number of children in Guatemala have fallen prey to trafficking and commercial sexual exploitation. Argentina is primarily a destination country for men, women and children trafficked for sexual exploitation and labor.

'The Government of Argentina does not fully comply with the minimum standards for the elimination of trafficking; however, it is making significant efforts to do so. Government officials should more forcefully acknowledge Argentina's trafficking problem and adopt national policies to address it.

'Bolivia is a source country for men; women and children trafficked for labor and sexual exploitation of thousands. They force Bolivians to work in sub-standard circumstances or illegally migrate, placing large numbers at risk of being trafficked. Bolivian children are particularly vulnerable. Children are trafficked from rural to urban areas for slave purposes, including sexual exploitation. The Bolivian-Brazilian border is also an area of commercial sexual exploitation. Bolivia is a transit country for illegal migrants from outside the region; some may be trafficking victims.

'The heart of the international cocaine trade is located in the Andean region of South America. Virtually the world's entire cocaine base, the intermediate product used to manufacture cocaine hydrochloride (cocaine HCl), is produced in Peru, Bolivia, or Colombia. Cocaine base production in Peru and Bolivia represents about 90 percent of the world's cocaine base; the remaining 10 percent is produced in Colombia. A specific Operation estimated worldwide cocaine production last year to be more than 700 metric tons. Almost ninety percent of the coca leaves—used in the manufacturing

of this massive amount of cocaine—are harvested by adoles-
cent slaves.'"

Stunned by all this enlightening—though very disheartening—information, all Mike could manage was, "I've got to say, *'Wow!'* And what do you say, Audra?"

"I do have some more notes of interest."

"Dear, I hope you have something, because that just blew my mind, and it apparently blew our theory about the profit the ringleaders make on children, as well." Mike felt weak. Now what in the world was he to think?

"Not necessarily, Mike. Let's just speculate for a moment. Okay, we'll use cocaine leaves as the crop and South American children in Bolivia as the slaves. The children are stolen off the streets, or their own parents—according to the media—give them up to pay off debts to the Mafia there. Now, these children are often frail, malnourished and sickly. I read how almost all of the poor children there are not immunized at all and are, therefore, susceptible to anything that rolls across their noses. So they die off quickly, forcing the wicked drug lords to venture out again and glean the streets for children." The word *'glean'* stuck in Mike's mind. "Okay," Audra continued, "so while the lords' thugs are off rounding up more labor, the fields are not being harvested, and the production goes kaput. Mike, what would you do to solve this problem? I mean, if you had old, worn out machines to pick your cotton, how could you solve this?"

"Yes, of course! Such brilliant drug lords, sadly," Mike opined. "The South American Mafia wants us all to believe that they are using their own frail children … that they are buying them at cheap prices … making them appear deserving of little attention from the rest of the economically driven world. But, in reality, they know.…"

Audra cut in, "Yep, they know that to make a lot of money, they have to spend a little, so they buy robust, strong, healthy immunized children from people that we are trying to expose right now."

"And, our kids come well fed, yet most of them have little or no knowledge of the Spanish language. Therefore, they are unable to communicate with the authorities well enough, if they even get a chance, to explain who they really are," Mike speculated.

Stating yet another fact gathered from her much reading, Audra added: "Our children most likely out-produce the sickly children at a ratio of one to three … or more."

"Yes, if one of our children can produce more cocaine than three of the sickly, malnourished children, then the cost of buying our kids earns greater dividends than the cost of dying kids in Bolivia, Peru or Colombia," Mike continued.

"The method of payment is another thing to consider," Audra went on. "The bastards here may be compensated in the form of gold, paper money, or even drugs that they would sell on the streets. But I think that it comes in the form of jewels or metals, because selling the drugs may be too risky."

"You know, Audra, another thing that bothers me are the maps. In order for those maps to acquire the Maat symbol, someone has to be working on the inside, and the car you saw at that compound started with the letter *'G,'* which means it was a government vehicle. It is safe to say some people working for our government are involved in this, and that makes me nervous."

"I know what you mean, Mike. Our government's hands are anything but lily white. Think of all the black operations and assassins we have assigned all over the world."

"Yeah, I still wonder about JFK," blurted out Mike just as Mr. Heyburn stepped into the room.

"Well, you must be Mike," said Mr. Heyburn.

"Yes, sir," Mike said with a smile, as he stuck his hand out to be polite.

"Please, just call me Pat, okay, Mike? I hear, *'Sir'* all of the time on post," he groaned.

"Yes, *Sir* ... yeah ... I mean ... Okay, Pat," replied Mike, a bit flustered. Pat laughed, and so did Audra.

"Now, what's this I'm hearing about *'black operations, our government'* and *'JFK'?*" Pat looked curiously at his daughter and Mike.

"Oh, nothing, Pa. We were just discussing how our government is not completely innocent ... it has room for improvement ... that's all," explained Audra.

Mr. Heyburn knew there was more to the story. "Listen, I heard you two speaking about children and slavery, and I know I wasn't hearing things. Please tell me more about that, if you would," Pat eagerly implored.

Audra wanted to tell her father, but she wondered, if she did, what good it would do, or what further harm it may cause him emotionally?

Mike stared at Audra, "Audra, don't you think your father has a right to know what's going on? Maybe his input would really be helpful."

"I guess you're right, Mike," Audra responded. Mike and Audra told Mr. Heyburn most of what they knew. They left out the part about Mike's stowing away into the compound. They explained their trip through the tunnels, and how Bobby disappeared at the site of a tunnel. Audra produced a few copies of some topographic maps, which had the strange symbol on it. Pat said nothing. He felt overwhelmed and somewhat apprehensive about their findings; however, he had to admit that their story really did seem viable.

Mike handed Pat the article he'd just finished reading, that Audra had copied off the Web site at college. Pat quickly scanned the article. His eyes lit up a bit. He could not deny that there could be some truth to their speculations. Audra asked Mike about the time-zone theory he had brought up at the support group. Now, a bit removed from that setting, she felt like hearing about his theory. So, Mike began explaining what he had concluded, considering the years between the local children's disappearances, to Pat and Audra. "Well, actually I found it very strange that Cal's son, Cliff, was abducted twelve years ago, and then four years after Cliff's abduction Matt Piper's nephew, Danny Thatcher, vanished, especially...."

"Matt Piper? Who in Sam Hades is Matt Piper?" asked Pat.

"He is a detective that lives in Bisbee. Anyway, eight years ago his nephew, Danny Thatcher, was abducted at Lake Patagonia in Santa Cruz County."

"Hey, I recall that case! We were in Tucson at the time, but I remember a recon division being called up to search that area after the abduction," explained Pat. He then signaled Mike to continue. For the first time in years, Pat was feeling a little excitement.

"Then, jumping ahead another four years after Danny's abduction, Todd turns up missing. Sorry, I really am ... and I can honestly say I know the hell you are going through. Now—four years after Todd vanished—Bobby disappears. The number four seems to be of significance here. Audra, you do have a computer, right?"

"Sure, and we also have a DSL connection."

"Great! That will help speed things up!" Mike and Pat followed Audra into the family office. With a quick click on the *AOL* icon, Audra instantly brought up the 'Net service. Pat stood behind them, very much intrigued by their discoveries.

"Okay, type in the number of reported male abductions in Eastern United States in your search engine for the year '94," commanded Mike. Audra, quick as a whip, typed the sentence on the screen. Several selections instantly popped up on the monitor.

"There! Choose *NCMEC* stats on male abductions 1994," instructed Mike. Audra clicked the subject, and an article along with a table of stats appeared. "Let's see, 64,667 missing or abducted males in the East," said Audra.

"Now, do the same thing for Central US, Mountain and, of course, the Pacific time zone," requested Mike.

"Hey!" exclaimed Pat, seeing at once the connection between the four years between local abductions, and the time zones for which Mike was checking stats.

"Anytime," Audra said, waiting for the Central stats; though the DSL was faster than dial-up, traffic sometimes slowed things down a bit. "Okay, 64,312 missing males. Say, why are we choosing *males* for this experiment?" Audra inquired with a look.

"It's not a *male-female* thing, Audra. Because sixty percent of abducted children in the US are females, we will find the calculations a tad easier using males statistics, since their numbers are smaller ... that's all, m' dear ...'tis all," Mike grinned.

"Better not be a *female* thing!" scoffed Audra, laughing. Mike and Pat both laughed at Audra's feigned offense. Audra brought up the stats for the Mountain region. "So, there you go. Hmmm, 98,082 abducted males in the Mountain region, and 64,979 missing males from the Pacific Coast. That is very interesting! What does it mean?"

Mike began with the total number of missing males nationwide for that year. "Look, 292,000 males were abducted during the year 1994. Now, if we add all the numbers from the Eastern Time Zone, the Central Time Zone and the Pacific Time Zone we arrive at...."

Pat interrupted Mike with, "... 193,958. Deduct this from the total, and we get 98,042, which means nearly 34,000 more males were abducted in the Mountain region that year than in each of the other three time zones! Had there been an even distribution among the four time zones, that would have meant an average of 73,000 per time zone. There having been over 98,000 in our time zone, we were more than 25,000 over the average. Awesome deduction, Mike! There's something to your theory." Pat was finally hopeful.

"Repeat the same process using the stats for 1995, please?" Mike asked, getting excited along with Pat by now. When they had finished with the calculations from each time zone, they discovered that a little over 25,000 more males were abducted from the Pacific Time Zone, with this figure repeating itself again for the Eastern Time Zone, as well as the Central Time Zone, in succeeding years.

"Do you see the pattern here?" Mike could hardly contain himself.

"I sure do!" Pat. "The abductions increase across the time zones from east to west, so this year about twenty-five thousand more males will be abducted from the Mountain Time Zone than from the other time zones, and next year this higher number of missing males will repeat itself in the Pacific Time Zone. Wow! Now we can predict the year—and area—that will be hit the hardest in the US!" roared Pat, "... unless, of course, we can somehow stop them! With this knowledge, there ought to be something that can be done now!" said Pat, sounding a bit dismal at the thought of its possibly continuing, in spite of what they now knew.

"Amazing, isn't it?" boasted Mike.

Pat slapped Mike on the back, "'Have to admit, you are brilliant, Mike!"

"And that makes me dog phlegm, huh!" snorted Audra.

"Not quite, my Darling. We'd never have obtained these findings without your fancy fingers!" laughed Mike. Pat joined in. When Audra saw her father laughing, she smiled also, for it had been a long time since Pat had laughed this hard … and long.

"Mike, how did you discover this?" inquired Pat. He became very serious.

"Well, it all started with the four-year spread between the abductions of Cliff, Danny, Todd and my little brother, Bobby. I kept wondering, "Why four years? So, I spent a bit of time meditating on that thought …'*four years.'* I found myself saying those words repeatedly: *'every four years'* … seemed like there might be some insidious system, running like *'clockwork'* … that these abductions in this area occurred via some plan, rather than occurring here every four years by random coincidence. Thinking one day on the College National Football Championship game, played every four years in Tempe, Arizona—the playing location being rotated every year amongst the various areas of the country—it suddenly occurred to me. *Bingo!* But the main tip— verifying my time-zone theory—was this map."

With this comment, Mike took the map of the U.S. out from his jacket and opened it up. Audra and Pat looked at the circled areas in each time zone. They noticed the word *'field"* was underlined in each of the circles. Yet, no matter in which time zone this circled, underlined word *'field'* appeared, it was under a symbol of a clock stating, *'Mountain Time.'* There were varying symbols within each time zone under the word, *'field.'* In the Eastern Time Zone, there was an asterisk; in the Central Zone, there was an arrow; and—for whatever reason, as yet not quite clear—the Pacific Time Zone was void of even the word *'field.'*

"Wow! I see what you mean! Must be the Mountain Time Zone's 'turn' this year. From this map, it appears they make a different map every year. And, when I upload a topographic map of the central US four years ago, look what we see!" Audra looked at her father and Mike.

Mike gazed into Audra's glowing eyes, "Amazing the arrows take the place of the Maat symbol for that zone and that time—then the underlined words *'field'* with the overhead clock must indicate a specific abduction or abductions."

"No doubt, but the main portal of entry these spineless rogues are transporting the children through into the world of slavery this year runs right through our back yard—the Huachuca Mountains," interrupted Pat.

"Wonder why the Pacific Time Zone is void?" asked Audra.

"Probably because they aren't going to hit that area," deduced Pat.

"No, I don't think that's it. Look, the East, and Central US, were already hit, so the old symbols are left alone. But, the symbols for the next region, the Pacific Zone—which is to be hit next year—have yet to be published ... at least on this map," argued Mike.

"Of course!" Pat corrected himself. "We use this strategy in combat: never publish targets on a map until you are about to strike. Mike, you can ride 'shotgun' for me anytime; the Army could use more men like you ... and women like my daughter." Pat happily affirmed both of them, as he gently caressed his daughter's, cheek.

"Pa, I must admit," Audra smiled, "at least you know brilliance when you see it. By the way, 'wonder why we didn't figure this out sooner?" she then questioned.

"Where did you get that map, Mike?" Pat wondered.

Not wanting just yet to reveal to her father how they had obtained this map, Audra spoke up quickly. "We got it from a delivery truck that we believe is being used to haul the children. Mike sneaked into the cab and took it while the driver stepped away from the truck for a bit."

Her father seemed satisfied with her story, so he did not question them any further. Actually, Pat was enthralled at what he had seen. His voice—for the first time in a long time—showed extreme excitement when he affirmingly belted out that which they'd already discerned, "Yes! I'll bet they do rotate abductions from zone to zone. This way, no one—at least those who have not figured out their time zone strategy—can figure out just where they're going to strike next!"

"Of course! The bastards appear to rotate their abductions to keep the authorities hopping around like baffled kangaroos. They cleverly chose our time zones to sector off the regions. Then they chose a pattern, probably so their clients—drug lords or pimps, or whoever they are—in Central and South America can easily keep track of the outfit's movement. This would make the human trafficking operate as smoothly as a well-oiled machine. They would easily be able to set their dates and watches to a precise moment."

Audra shook her head, hardly daring to believe they had figured out as much as it appeared they had learned in such a short time. "Honey, you really amaze me!"

"And, you inspire and amaze me, Lady. Without you, I know we would never have gotten this far," said Mike lovingly. Pat noticed the affection between his daughter and Mike. He had wondered when Audra might finally allow a young man into her life. He had never dreamed the man would share the same horror they had borne for the last several years.

Pat was pulled from his reverie when Mike began speaking again. "You know, Audra, that lady … ah, what's her name … um, the pretty black lady at the meeting tonight … Ms. Rally?"

Audra laughed, "At least I'm better with names than you. Her name is Ms. Janet Riley. What about her?"

"I'm not sure she can be trusted. I'm not sure she is even from D.C. I saw her on my flight back from a medical convention in California, to which I received an invitation awhile back. She sat behind me on flight 454, from Los Angeles to Phoenix. In fact, I was deep in conversation with a lady sitting next to me. I was talking about Bobby, and I told her about the hiking trip we'd been planning for awhile to Tucker's Peak in the Huachuca Mountains."

"Are you sure it was her?" asked Pat.

"Positive. I may be bad with names, but I have yet to forget a face. When we stood to exit the plane, I got a good look at her. Judging by the way she looked at me tonight, I think she may have recognized me, also."

"Hmmm, it would be very convenient for the scumbag perpetrators to have someone working directly with *NCMEC* in conjunction with the government. This would enable them to keep a closer watch on children as well as provide updates on the movements and operations of our authorities," surmised Audra.

Pat told the kids that he needed to get on to bed as, "morning comes quickly, and I have to be at work earlier than usual." With that, he excused himself and walked to the back of the house.

Mike turned and looked into Audra's eyes, "You have beautiful, dreamy eyes, Audra." He leaned over and kissed her full, tender lips—then offered a few words of departure, as he still had a few chores to do at home. Audra looked a bit disappointed, but she understood. She had hoped he would stay a while longer. She was beginning to feel lonely whenever she was away from Mike, for though they had known each other such a short time, they had experienced so much together already, relative to their similar circumstances. She wondered if that meant she loved him, truly loved him. They kissed again, then Mike left.

Mike plopped down on his plush, leather, olive-colored sofa, his mind filled with so many questions, he thought his head would explode. His anxiety was building due to the time that had elapsed since Bobby's disappearance. He began going over the events of the past few days in his mind once again. "Let's see…." he mused to himself. He had left the hospital Thursday evening, seen Audra and the deputies on Friday, visited Matt, and then he and Audra had explored the tunnels on Saturday. Sunday found him nearly shot but, in spite of that, he had managed to confiscate the map and the shipping ticket. Today had not been a waste of time, actually. Then he realized, though becoming anxious, that he had—in reality—wasted very little time. There was no time to waste! But here it was, almost a week later, and he was no closer to finding his brother than he had been the day he started; at least it seemed that way.

Mike began analyzing their findings a bit more—aloud, as he had always been prone to do, as it seemed to be more a bit more productive than remaining totally silent. "Oh, Lord! If they traffic 25,000 strong, immunized, healthy children far below our borders, they surely can't transfer them all at one time, or from only one location. They must have other centers like the one here. Yeah! That has to be it ... there are other centers, as well, most likely also disguised as charitable organizations. They must first divide the children up, and then pass them through in smaller groups, shipping them from various stations.

"We only calculated the boys, yet I have a feeling that these young men are what is considered the prize stock rather than the young women. I honestly believe they are much more concerned about very high labor output, rather than trafficking kinky sex with young teenage girls. However, I could be wrong. I wouldn't put anything past these godless creatures! I think it's time to pay those tunnels and that cave another visit, but this time I have a better plan."

Mike hoisted himself from the sofa, walked into his study, closed the door, withdrew the topographic maps—as well as the shipping forms—and sat down. With his mind completely focused, he studied the material in front of him.

Chapter Seven

Bobby stirred as the door to his quaint room opened. A very lovely looking lady walked into his room. Bobby smiled up at her. She had been extra loving and kind to him since he arrived here. Bobby wondered, "Where is here?"
Yes, where was he? He knew he was in some sort of large structure, and he
knew other children were here, also, because he was granted the opportunity
to visit with some of them from time to time. Maybe these people were telling
them all the truth … maybe they were supposed to be here. The lady walked
over to Bobby and gave him a tender hug, as she kissed the top of his head.
She really tried not to get too close to any of the children, as she did not want
to bond with them, but Bobby somehow seemed to shine out from the other
boys. He possessed a glowing personality, and a rather sharp, quick wit.
These attributes, along with the fact that he was just so darn funny and cute—
his deep blue eyes and dark hair, his dimples and beautiful face—melted the
woman's heart whenever she saw him.

"How are you, Bobby?" The lady's voice was so soothing and pleasant to
Bobby. He grew to trust her, due to her kindness and gentle ways. He also
liked pretty women, like most young boys. He felt safe in her arms.

"I'm feeling fine, but I miss my brother."

"Do you like your room?"

"It's okay. I like the game and play station … and the neat computer center
… and I enjoy Captain Tinker. He's a goofy-looking guy, but he makes us all
laugh all of the time. He is like a funny clown."

The pretty woman hugged Bobby. "You are so funny yourself, Bobby, and
you are very smart. I really believe when you leave here you will be placed in a
position of leadership, due to your talent and brilliance." The woman did not
say this just to make Bobby feel better. She knew the possibility existed, for
some of the boys that had proven to be very brilliant had found positions
above the rest. Her mind then shifted over to Cliff—another brilliant young

child she had helped mentor, who later became a fine leader as a young man—as she thought about this probability.

"I wish I could visit the other children more often, Ms. Kay," Bobby lamented. His eyes looked a little glossy. Ms. Kay hugged Bobby tighter.

"Soon, Bobby, you will. Soon you will see them as often as you wish."

"'You promise?" asked Bobby, a bit more cheerfully.

"I promise."

"But, when will I see my big brother again?" Bobby's eyes drooped a little.

"Oh, Bobby! It seems we talk about this so often. But, then, I can't blame you. I would ask about my brother or sister all the time, too. You'll see him soon, I promise. He knows you are here. You know, he wasn't supposed to tell you about this experiment. You were chosen, Bobby ... chosen, because you are so intelligent, and you have great potential. All those that come here are pruned to become great people in life ... people that make our society wonderful ... and wealthy. Without boys like you, Bobby, where would our country be?

"Now, come eat your dinner, please, Bobby?" Ms. Kay's voice soothed Bobby. He almost felt ashamed that he had asked the question. Ms. Kay knew the mind of a child very well. Her psychological influence over the children was tremendous.

After Bobby ate his dinner, he became droopy and tired. His head felt heavy as he climbed into bed. Ms. Kay tucked him into his bed, kissed his noble forehead, and left him sleeping in peace. "Sorry, but I can't help but love you, my Little Knight," said Ms. Kay fondly. She left Bobby's room and made her way to another child's room to repeat her actions with him. As she walked down the long corridor of rooms, she met Captain Tinker.

"How did it go with the young chap?" asked the kind-looking middle-aged man.

"They ought to pay me extra for all I do ... at least give me a few extra shares!" complained Ms. Kay.

"I can sure empathize with you. Not only do we have to entertain these spoiled brats, but we also have to carry on our duties outside the ward. I feel like a prisoner."

"No kidding! At least the children don't feel like we do. They believe they've really been sent here to become heroes of some sort." Ms. Kay's voice did not sound at all soothing and calm anymore.

"Well, the drugs help in that area quite a bit. Thanks to our good old pharmaceuticals and our wonderful psychiatrists, we can develop new minds," laughed the Captain.

"Well, I have work to do, and so do you, Captain. I'll see you around another bend in this happy, wonderful place," groaned Ms. Kay, halfheartedly.

"Yep, I'm off to make the children laugh in the north wing now. Have fun!" chuckled the Captain.

Ms. Kay turned and walked to another lad's room, a strange feeling of remorse surged through her body as Bobby entered her mind again. After meeting Bobby, she wished now that he had not been chosen. "He's a brilliant boy, just like his brother," said Ms. Kay to herself as she opened up another young boy's door.

Inside the room a blond-haired lad about thirteen years of age smiled and said, "Oh, Ms. Kay, I'm so glad to see you."

Ms. Kay took in a deep breath as she pleasantly and gently said, "Hi, Timmy, I'm so happy to see you." She kissed the top of his head as she spoke kindly, gentle words that made the boy feel very secure and warm inside— then she left. She had other work to do.

A dark figure, sitting in a high-backed chair, picked up his ringing phone in an office located in Sierra Vista. "Hello."

The person's voice on the other end crackled, "We have a problem. The gnat is becoming more like a little sweat bee. He's beginning to unscrew the lid."

"So, he is, eh? Well, we do not wish to panic at this point. That will only lead to more suspicion. The agent we assigned to his case … how did he fare?"

"As far as I'm concerned, he dropped the ball!"

The dark figure leaned back in his comfortable chair. He rocked a little as he spoke, with a rather distinguished low-pitched voice. "'Sounds like he doesn't know the definition of tact and diplomacy. One would think he would have done a better job at this, being a Political Science major."

"To say the least! I told him to be careful. The gnat's a bit suspicious, and he now must use a lot of verbal lotion to smooth him over. 'Guess he just felt too trusted for anyone to be suspicious. Anyway, let's hope the gnat hasn't figured out too much. I *can* tell you that he knows about the time zones. I just don't know how much he knows, though."

The dark figure breathed in deeply. His mind relaxed. He'd been up against amateur sleuths like this before, and this one was less than even an amateur … below the status of a novice … just a stressed-out young punk with a decent scholastic brain. "Listen, let's let the little sweat bee sweat it out some more. Leave him alone; he's on a wild goose chase and, when he realizes this, it will be way too late for him, anyway. Besides—as I said before—if things become a little difficult, we can always trust El Niño," hissed the dark, ghastly figure.

"'Wouldn't want to be in that kid's shoes if El Niño was after me!" the person on the other end of the line replied, with a shudder.

"However, I do not think we shall have to resort to such extreme measures. Rest easy, and do not worry. I am sure we can handle this little gnat," snickered the dark, sinister form.

Chapter Eight

Dennis had committed to turning left before he saw the car swerve to avoid contact. He slammed on his brakes, and came to an abrupt stop. The other driver laid long and heavy on the horn. She held her left arm out the window, in a right turn fashion, and quickly extended her middle finger while shouting profanity. Dennis laughed loudly … long belly-roll laughs. "No harm done, my Sugar Plum!" Dennis continued laughing, as he resumed his left turn into the plaza. He slowly pulled between two white parallel lines, exited his luxury car, walked across the lot, and disappeared into one of the plaza suites. Dennis did not notice the white Lincoln pulling in two rows behind him. The driver in the Lincoln did not bother to egress his vehicle. He, instead, sat in the car, eating a sandwich and drinking Coke from a plastic bottle, while he thumbed through the pages of a book—'*What Every Detective Should Know*'—written by some English author many long years ago.

Dennis walked over to a wooden office door and knocked three times. He heard a few garbled words. The door opened, revealing a thin man about six feet in height. His dark eyes studied Dennis for a moment, as he looked up at him. Dennis, a rather tall, hefty fellow with a big-barreled chest, towered five inches above the dark-eyed man, who had a balding forehead that seemed to glow from the reflection of a wall sconce in the hallway. "Dennis, please sit in the chair over by the water cooler; I will get to you in a moment or two. I won't be long. I need to talk to Raul just a little longer."

Dennis fidgeted a little, shifted his weight to his left side and said, *"No problemo,* Ed; I'll get myself a cold drink of water and wait; I'm in no hurry." Dennis smiled broadly.

"Good, I didn't think you were. Talk at you soon." *'Talk at you soon'* was Ed's favorite cliché. Ed turned and walked back into his office.

Dennis walked over to the water cooler. His smiled faded quickly, when he discovered the cup dispenser was empty. "Oh well …'guess I won't pour myself a cold one, after all."

Ed returned to the chair behind his desk and sat down. In front of his dark, walnut-stained, wooden desk sat a pudgy Hispanic man. "Well, who was that?" the pudgy man asked.

"Just Dennis—here to hand-deliver this box over to the big guy at the post."

"Oh, the funny gentle giant, Dennis, you mean?"

"Yeah, the big clown of the town," chuckled Ed. "Now back to business, Raul. You are in charge of our inventory. Remember … the goodies must arrive on schedule. Is everything in order?"

Raul looked into Ed's waiting eyes. "Sir, we could not be more on schedule. Our friends down South have some sweet tooth," laughed Raul. Ed's eyes lit up some. "No kidding … and lucky for us that they do. You know, our *'Fearless One'* over at the fort said that they are going to sell our candy to the Peruvians. Imagine that!"

Raul stirred a bit in his leather chair before he spoke. "We sell the stuff wholesale, just so they can make a profit by selling retail. We ought to up the ante a little—don't you think?"

Ed did think; he always thought. Sometimes he believed he thought too much. "Nah, they are not going to make much of anything off this deal. You see, our *'Big G'* at Fort Huachuca told me that they are only selling to the Peruvians to bolster better relations … and they've got to act fast, or else."

"Or else? *'Or else'* what?"

"Or else they'll lose the mob's faith in Peru. You know … can't we all just get along?"

"That line is plain getting to Old Amigo. I grow tired of it, but I do understand what you mean. If the hoods in Bolivia and Peru keep banging their heads together like stubborn rams, someone's liable to get more than just a bad headache."

"Well spoken, and we can't afford headaches let alone all-out war between two different syndicates, from two different nations; 'costs us—in money and time," explained Ed.

"So, this shipment will prevent that?" Raul wondered.

"'Bet your hot tamale it will. This is why I want you at the post when the train pulls out. 'You got that?"

"Have I ever let you down, Ed?"

Ed scratched his chin for a second or two. "Come to think of it, you didn't go to my birthday party last year, Raul."

"And, why didn't I?" asked Raul.

Ed laughed, "Because the last girl that popped out of my birthday cake scared you out of twenty years of your life!"

"Well, I sure didn't expect her to rub the frosting off on *me!* That fat ugly woman we picked out as a bad joke thought I was the birthday boy; but, then, I might have thought the same way if I was as drunk and drugged up as she was. Ugh!" Raul shuddered at the memory ... huge, flabby cellulite arms and legs bulging out from her skimpy little bikini ... and all that stinky flab all over his face and body! They both laughed aloud for a few minutes—then they regained their composure. They talked on a little while longer about other issues for about thirty minutes.

Finally, Raul stood up, shook Ed's hand, and left the office. As he shut the door behind him, he looked over at Dennis, who was amusing himself with his pen: "The shot is up ... it's on its way ... and it's good! The crowd is going wild here at the U.S. Airway Arena in Phoenix, Arizona. Dennis Perris comes through again, to save the day for the Suns, with only one second remaining on the clock!"

Raul roared, "That dispenser makes for a great hoop, and the ballpoint pen sure looks like a real basketball to me."

"Hey, Raul Baby ... good t' see you!" laughed Dennis.

"Love to stay and chat with you, Big Fella, but I have to get back to my post. Maybe I'll see you there soon ... that is, if they give you a *gopher* job out my way." Raul snickered, as he walked out the back of the building—delighted within at having denigrated Dennis, calling him exactly what he was to his face ... a *'gopher.'*

Ed stuck his head out the office door and called Dennis inside. Dennis hurried over. He shut the door behind him, and sat in the chair Raul had previously occupied for a spell. The chair still felt warm from Raul's body.

"Okay, Dennis, I need you to run this box over to the big cheese at Fort Huachuca, and be very careful with it. Mr. Hooah—picayunish as he can be—will not be too happy if it gets a bit tattered or torn. In fact, I'm tired, and wrung out, because of staying up half the night worrying about this box getting to the 'Big G' ... so it had better get there ... intact!" Pausing a moment to sigh, the Mayor then continued. "The contents, as usual, are not to be opened by you or anyone but the 'Big G'—period! 'Got that!"

"Right, we'll see to it that no one but Mr. Hooah opens it," Dennis assured him, while tossing in a bit of attitude, with, "Mr. Hooah this, Mr. Hooah that ... whatever Mr. Hooah wants, Mr. Hooah gets. Well, I must say, 'Phooey on Hooey'!"

"Oh, just get the hell out of here, Dennis!" Ed testily barked.

Dennis abruptly stopped chuckling at what he had perceived as his own poetic cleverness. "Gosh, Boss, you sure are touchy today."

Ed frowned, "Dennis, to be honest with you, I only use you because I know your father and—probably because Mr. Hooah knows your father, too—for some reason Mr. Hooah seems to want you around. I only tolerate you; I don't hate you, but I'm not in love with you, either." Then Ed softened his approach, realizing he was being a bit harsh. "Look, Dennis, I know you haven't let us down before, but you just seem too happy at times ... like you've just found the Lord ... or something."

Dennis smiled. "'Kind of like that, Boss, as I do like my job as a *Youth Pastor.*"

"Well, that's another reason I like you. Many people in our fine City seem to like you ... and that helps me sleep better at night," growled Ed.

Dennis' smile returned. "You do, huh?"

Ed rolled his eyes, feeling Dennis was pushing him now, but was amused enough—in spite of that—to let out a genuine chuckle. "Just go deliver the package, Dennis. Now!" Ed shouted.

Dennis turned, walked out of the office, and left the building. Ed plopped back into his chair, and drew in a few deep breaths. "I'll leave when I know he is gone," thought Ed, as he nervously arose from the chair in which he'd just sat back down, and began pacing as he waited for this 'respectable amount of time' to pass.

Chapter Nine

Mike lifted the phone from his desk and pressed the receiver to his ear as he entered Matt Piper's numbers.

Matt sat quietly in his office. He had drunk only a little tonight, for he found himself in a case that mercifully took his attention away from the bottle. His heart was heavy for Mike, for he understood far too well the pain of such a loss. He lifted a sheet from his desk, and was inspecting it closely for possible clues, when his cell phone rang. "Yeah, I'll get you old chap; just hold your britches on!" Matt picked up his cell phone and flipped open the cover.

"Ah, yes, this is Matt. What can I do for you?"

"You can start by running a background check on another person for me, Matt!" exclaimed Mike.

"Goodnight! I'm still in the middle of researching those others upon your request, and already you're dropping another load on me!" bawled Matt, though good-naturedly.

"Hey, do a good job and I'll throw in a bonus."

"Yes, indeedy! What is it you want me to do?" Matt asked, calmed down a bit by the new offer. As they spoke, Mike noticed Matt seemed more focused and more alert.

"Hmmm, maybe the old English drunk still had a bit of pep in him after all," thought Mike. Then to Matt, "Listen, there's a pretty new face in town, a black woman by the name of Janet Riley. I don't have a picture of her, but she belongs to the *National Center For Missing and Exploited Children,* the *NCMEC ...* at least she says that she does. Anyway, she is staying at the Windemere Hotel. I need you to check out her background. I also want you to do a little sleuthing on a compound, or large building, that is east of Palominas Road off Hereford Road. "If you're traveling east on Hereford, you will see a lane veering off to your right just before you get to the bridge. Look for a white sign with blue letters that says, *'County District Office.'* It's supposed to be a charity center of some sort, but I believe it may hold many answers to our questions concerning lost children from this region. See if you can link it to a large vegetable and fruit produce warehouse called, *'Huachuca Produce.'*

"Jiggers fella! Where in blazes do you come up with such uncanny ideas!" bellowed Matt, with curiosity.

"Matt, I have to find Bobby, regardless of how silly I sound at times. I'd give my life for Bobby!" exclaimed Mike.

Matt knew the feeling well, and sighed as he replied. "Okay, Mike, I understand; besides, it's your money. I'll get on it. I also have some interesting news for you, Chap." Before Mike could respond, Matt continued. He sounded very excited. "Mike, I looked into Dennis' background, and discovered our friend leaves a very interesting legacy."

"Go on Matt," coaxed Mike.

"Dennis was born April 20, 1968 to a Robert and Martha Perris in El Paso, Texas. Robert worked for the Government at the time as a Petroleum Engineer. Oil was making big waves in Texas at that time, so he—Robert, that is—had plenty of work. However, as time went on, Texas started dropping out of the competition. Robert found himself stationed in Panama in 1980, where he assisted one of the *OPEC* nations, Venezuela, in South America."

Mike's ears perked up. This was all news to him. "No wonder Dennis became surprised when I asked him if he'd ever been to Central or South America," thought Mike. "Go on, Matt. This is very interesting!"

"Apparently, Martha Perris contracted some sort of infection during her stay in Panama, and she died in eighty-two. 'Sad; the poor chap and his father must have been devastated. However, Dennis and his father continued to live in Venezuela. Dennis attended school in the Maracaibo Basin region of Venezuela, as this is where the Venezuelans produce most of their oil. His life in Venezuela becomes a little fuzzy after that. I did manage to locate him in Bogotá, Colombia later. He studied Political Science and computers at the University of Bogotá. He is very fluent in Spanish, and well educated, of course."

Mike interrupted Matt, "Man, did you find anything odd about Dennis, anything you think is strange?"

"Yes, I did. Your friend moved back to the United States four years after he graduated from college in Bogotá. His father elected to stay behind in Venezuela."

"You mean that Dennis' father is still alive!" interrupted Mike.

"Yes, lad, he is. He probably still works for the petroleum outfit in Venezuela."

"But, he told me that both his parents died in California when he was younger, and he sold his father's estate before he moved here!" clamored Mike.

"Well, then we have another Dennis, or Dennis has a twin brother with the same address, social security number and same visa and passport he still keeps valid, because he does visit South America from time to time."

"The man's a liar: I wouldn't doubt if he carries an alias, also."

"He most likely does if he is that muddy. Dennis works for both the City and State as a sort of *'gopher.'* I followed him today for a spell. He left his rather large, new house and pulled into an office plaza next to a discount store. He left forty-five minutes later with a box in his hands. It's not unusual for a courier to run an errand for the Mayor, but I wonder why he took so long coming back out of the building. And, when he did finally appear, he had only one box!" Matt's voice rose in pitch as he said, *'box.'* "The Mayor walked out of the suite two minutes later. I know it was the Mayor, as I've lived around here long enough to recognize Sierra Vista's Mayor. However, I would have missed seeing the Mayor if your grandfather's car would not have stalled on me. I was going to continue to follow our chap, Dennis," said Matt with a lingering English accent.

"Wow! You sure found out a lot in one day, Matt. I'm rather impressed!" whooped Mike. I was hoping to get the right man for the job, and I believe I have."

"Thank you, Mike, but this is not over yet, you know."

"Yeah, I know. Believe me, I know. Matt, we need to do some research on Ed Braddock, our honest, hard-working Mayor. We may find some interesting news about him, also."

"M' Lad, do you take me for a novice? I did not acquire my rank at Scotland Yard by being lazy and … dull!" Matt coughed as he paused at the end of his last sentence.

"Hey! I wasn't implying anything like that, Mr. Private Eye. I'm merely suggesting we ought to check him out!" Mike defended himself.

"And, I'm telling you that I have already started to do so. Mr. Braddock has an interesting background, as well. His father is an old retired Colonel, and Army medical doctor, who lives outside Sierra Vista. He lives off Carr Canyon Road. Ed, our dear Mayor, lives down from him just a ways. Unbelievably, Ed's father, Colonel Braddock—or Dr. Braddock, whichever title you prefer—was stationed here at Fort Huachuca in 1955, just a year out of West Point. Ed was born a year after this.

"What I found very interesting is that Dr. Braddock spent thirty years in the Army; he was a lifer. I suppose he felt secure with his rank and position, but that, my Lad, is not the interesting chapter. The chapter that whets my appetite is when Dr. Braddock found himself in Panama in 1978. Ed was twenty-three at the time. He had just graduated from Stanford, where he studied law and minored in Spanish. After he graduated, he actually moved to Panama—probably to be with his loved ones—and secured a job as a corporate lawyer at a major Panamanian law firm, based in Medellin, Colombia."

Mike fervently listened to every word Matt told him. He instantly wondered if Ed and Dennis somehow had bumped into each other in South or Central America. Everything Mike thought he knew about Dennis turned out to be a pack of lies, according to Matt's findings. Mike shook his head in disbelief. Twelve years ago, Dennis had walked into the town of Sierra Vista purchased a home, waved a Bible around, until he soon became a Regional Youth Minister, and secured a job with the City and State. Here, all this time Dennis had pretended to be someone that he was not. What was worse was that the year he moved into town was the first year that a child, Cliff Brown, turned up missing. What manner of men are the Mayor and Dennis … really? These thoughts raced through Mike's head disconcertingly.

"Matt, is there anything else I should know? What about the Sheriff?"

"Great Scott, Chap! I was very lucky to assemble all the information I presented you tonight in short order. You have no idea what all is involved in tracking one's past down. Lucky for me, I have the good Queen's stamp of approval on my English shoulders, or I don't think we would have traveled this far," Matt correctly boasted.

"What do you mean by that?"

"You know, Mike, you Yanks amaze me in your transparency at times. The Queen *knighted* me, young man! My credentials … my ability to access confidential information and whatever authority I possess … is international, and shall remain with me unto death."

"I'm not exactly sure what that truly means, but I think you're telling me that where some private eyes cannot step a foot into, you can."

"Precisely, m' Lad, *pre*-cisely!" boomed Matt. Mike liked to hear that. He also believed that this case was building up some of the esteem Matt had lost after failing to find his own nephew, Danny.

"You know, Mike, Dennis grosses eighteen hundred dollars a month, yet he lives in a expensive home and drives a luxurious car. If he didn't receive the funds from his supposedly dead father's estate, then where do you suppose he did dig it up from—just food for thought. I must bid you farewell. I need a little rest now," said Matt, as he yawned over the phone. Mike instinctively yawned himself. He thanked Matt, and hung up the phone.

Mike sat very perplexed … totally frustrated. Now he knew the true meaning of the word *'betrayal.'* He felt the knife of a good friend stab him painfully in the heart as well as the back. How dare Dennis boldly lie about his life and lead everyone to believe he was such a good, godly man! "He's the *'gopher,'* all right. He's definitely the ringleaders' *gopher!"* Mike gritted his teeth. "Okay, you dirty, wretched bastards! Up to now, I feel like I've been walking through land mines, and on eggshells. It's my turn now! You screwed with my mind, now I'm going to twist yours a little." With this, Mike decided that, if he could strike a bit of panic within them, they just might slip up. "If, and when they do," he thought—half aloud again—"hopefully no one will be there to catch them except the law!" exclaimed a very angry Mike.

With that, he pulled out some scrap paper and began to write. Halfway through his second note, the phone rang. Mike let it ring until the answering machine came on. Audra's voice echoed across the room. Mike lifted the receiver. "Hello, Bay*bah!"* howled Mike.

"Well, good evening, Sport. You sure know how to tie a line up! Don't you have call waiting?" asked Audra, with just a little frustration in her voice.

"What's that?" laughed Mike.

"Oh, now insult me!"

"Oh, you know I was just kidding. Actually I don't, but I'm thinking about getting it … just for *you!"* Mike spoke in such a way that Audra wasn't sure if it was in jest or not.

However serious he may—or may not—have been, Audra spoke graciously, "Then you're excused. Who were you talking to … or is that top secret?" Mike began to repeat all Matt had told him in detail and with accuracy. He wanted Audra to know as much as he. He needed her help and, besides, he correctly believed two minds could remember details much better than one.

"Hey, Audra, you want to go with me tonight to run a few errands?" A moment of silence followed Mike's question.

"What sort of errands?" Audra wanted to know.

"When you get here, I'll tell you all about it," Mike enticed.

"What a gyp!" she chided playfully.

"Come on!" Mike laughed into the phone, childlike.

"OK," she relented. "Hey, 'be there in a few! All I have to do is throw on a coat."

Audra hung the phone up, threw on a jacket, and raced out the door. She arrived at Mike's house in no time, wearing a black vinyl jacket and a smile. "Thought you said you had to go home and do chores. I guess you need some help with them, huh?"

"I do, Audra; I need you to watch my back. We're going to the Mayor's house tonight ... and Dennis' house. I called Matt after we got off the phone. He sounded grumpy, but at least he answered the phone. He gave me the address to the Mayor's house. I know where Dennis lives, of course." Mike flung his jacket over his shoulder, and they walked outside.

Audra had begun walking to Mike's Jeep when he told her he wanted to use her Nissan, if it was all right with her. Audra hesitated, and was about to object, when she decided he must have a good reason for such a request, though she did want to know what that reason was. Mike explained that he would tell her as they drove, since they should really get going.

"Oh, why not! We're always going in your bouncy Jeep, anyway!" laughed Audra.

Mike just let out a puff of air between his lips and said, "Yeah, bouncy all right!" As they drove, Mike explained that when he was in the garage at the compound, the men mentioned a gnat that was in the ointment. He figured he must be that *'gnat.'*

"So, they think of you as a wimpy little gnat, huh? That is interesting. That could work in our favor, because they would be expecting little out of you."

"Just what I want them to think, too. If they believe I'm just an ignorant gnat, I'll have the element of surprise on my side." That thought brought laughter to them both. They drove on until they saw the Carr Canyon Road intersection. Audra turned left onto Carr Canyon and headed towards the Huachuca Mountains. After driving a few miles closer to the canyon, Mike quickly blurted out, "Oh, darn, we just passed the Mayor's house!"

"You know, we're in *big* trouble if we get caught doing this, Mike!"

"Not to worry," he calmly answered, asking her to pull over.

As Audra pulled over, Mike was clutching the door latch, beginning to open the door. Noticing this, she cautioned him, "Mike, stop!" She then flipped a switch, ensuring the dome light would not go on when the door was opened. "There! Now when you open the door, you won't draw any attention to us, due to the stupid dome light."

"Good thinking," Mike complimented. "Now you know why I brought you with me."

"Yeah, I can tell you didn't pull too many pranks when you were young," a knowing Audra aptly surmised.

"No, not too many," he had to admit. "'Enough to get by, though," he felt he had to add, not wanting to sound too pristine, or naive, in comparison to his friend, Audra, with whom he was most impressed. As he said this, he was thinking about the *Green Beret* training passed on to her from her father over the years.

As he stepped out of the car and began walking towards the Mayor's front yard, he noticed the house sat rather far back from the road. There was a strong metal, or iron, gate surrounding the house. This did not spoil his plans, though. He took out the note that read,

"We want the bee pollen as soon as possible. Something we did not expect came up. Rush the order to us as soon as you can!"

taping it to the outside of the Mayor's newspaper box, where he felt sure the Mayor would see it. Mike then turned to walk back to the car, laughing inside himself. He knew what repercussions this might cause, but he also knew he had very little time. He walked back to Audra and slowly climbed in. Audra started down the road a ways before she turned her headlights on.

"Well, that was fast and easy!" she exclaimed, just a bit surprised.

"Not a problem, now we only have one more stop to make, and then we can go home and sip on some hot tea or coffee."

"I'll take hot cocoa instead. I've had a bit of a craving for chocolate lately."

"Well, don't look at me if you're having strange cravings. I didn't do it!" laughed Mike.

"Hey! You're awful … even disgusting. Wait till I tell my Pa what came out of your shameless mouth," Audra howled, as she smacked Mike solidly in the gut with the back of her curled fist. Mike groaned a little. Audra could hit much harder than he ever would have guessed.

"Ugh! Now I wish I'd said nothing; you punch like a mule, girl!"

"Yeah, and I was holding back, Mister!" roared Audra. They continued until they came to Coronado Road. Audra turned left onto Coronado, and then took a right onto Ida Lane. She noticed how pleasant the houses looked in the area, but she said nothing. Mike's gesture told her to go past Dennis' house. Since this strategy had worked so well at the Mayor's house, Audra did as Mike requested. Mike opened the door and stepped out. Only one more note to place, with the hope that the notes might instill a little well deserved panic in the villains.

The air was crisp and cool. The weather service had predicted a clear night and a clear, sunny day following, so Mike need not worried about water-damaged notes. He crept close to the house, wondering half-aloud, as he sometimes concentrated better when speaking to himself. "Should I place it in his newspaper box, too, or should I hang it right on his door?" Walking a ways, as he contemplated his plan of action, Mike then crept to the dark area at the corner of Dennis' house. That was his first mistake. He was so engrossed in thinking about the results the note might produce that he forgot about motion detectors … and Dennis' dog.

Lights suddenly flooded the yard as a dog barked loudly. "Dang! I forgot about *Tough Guy!* I'm sure he'd remember me, and stop barking, if I could get close enough to him to let him know it's me," Mike thought. He knew that the entire operation could be jeopardized if Dennis opened the door now, and discovered him prowling around. Quickly scanning the entire area, something large caught his eye. It was his only chance. If this wicked man found him now, it would mean the end of their search, as he knew this bunch of aberrant humanity with which Dennis appeared to be associated could be ruthless killers, as well as kidnappers. "Well, Mike, expect no mercy ... expect death ... and the end of ever finding Bobby, if you're not careful, dude!" he cautioned himself. "They might even kill Bobby, too, if he finds me snooping around ... just out of spite!"

As this last thought was running through his mind, Dennis appeared at the door. He leaned his head out the doorway and peered all around. He walked out of his house and into the yard. *Tough Guy* was still barking, knowing someone was out there. Suddenly he stopped barking, and started running in the direction from which his sensitive nose had just picked up a familiar scent ... the large refuse container which housed his buddy's scent that he had just discovered. Mike remained hunkered down in the dumpster, lest he be discovered.

"Hey, *Toughy ... Tough Guy!* Get your furry behind back in the house! I don't see anything ... probably just those damned worthless cats again!" *Tough Guy* obeyed, turning and walking back to the doorstep. Dennis looked down the road. He saw some cars and pick-ups lined up beside the curve on each side of the road. Then his eyes focused on something that many would call a godsend ... under a dimly lit street lamp sat an orange tabby. Immediately Dennis reached down, picked up a rock and threw it at the cat. The rock bounced off the sidewalk and almost hit the tabby. "You damned, stupid bag of hairballs; get the hell out of here!" hollered Dennis as he reached for another rock. The tabby swiftly ran into the darkness of the night. Dennis muttered some foul words as he walked back to his house. He and *Toughy* walked inside as Dennis closed the door behind him.

Mike sat quietly in the refuse container, feeling that his nose was finally becoming—at least as much as possible—acclimated to the stench, when suddenly he felt some wet, gooey stuff on his hands; then he realized some of it was beginning to seep through his pants. He shuddered to think what it might be. "I wish I'd just taped the darned note to his newspaper box. What a moron I can be at times!" Then Mike's focus turned to wondering how Audra was doing, waiting for him all of this time; then his nostrils abruptly brought him back to his current precarious situation. "Well, Mike, you've got yourself into a real stinky jam this time," he chided. "Now, we're going to have to wait it out for awhile, until everything settles down. How am I going to get out of here, with-out a replay of what happened earlier ... what if *Tough Guy* starts up again?"

Not quite sure what to do yet, Mike sat in the filth, his mind wandering. He saw himself with Bobby again. They laughed and wrestled around like the brothers they were. He remembered their times at Rocky Point, Mexico. "How beautiful the *Sea Of Cortez* is!" he recalled. Bobby and he loved the warm beach and the warm sea. The water almost felt too warm sometimes down there. Mike had wanted Bobby and him to take *SCUBA* classes together, because he had heard how stunning the ocean was in that part of the globe ... elegant coral ... colorful underwater vegetation, not to mention the adventures they would share together.

Mike's mind once again returned to his present situation. He very slowly and carefully lifted the lid from the container. Peering into the night, nothing stirred before him. No one was waiting with a club or gun. Hoping not to set off the floodlights again, Mike cautiously climbed out of the trash. He had just placed his left foot on the ground when the lights came on again. Mike quickly moved away from the house. He knew he had only a few moments before the back door would open again, unless Dennis was sleeping by now. Mike recalled the times when he, Bobby and Dennis had gone camping together. They'd learned at that time how Dennis had a habit of falling asleep very fast, and also slept rather soundly.

Soon Mike found himself walking quickly down the sidewalk. Pausing to glance back, he saw that the light had gone back out. Hearing nothing, as well, he breathed easier as he walked back to the truck. His heart stopped racing as he tapped on Audra's window. Audra's body jolted upward as she awoke from her catnap.

"Wh ... who ... *hey!*" She was dazed for a moment.

"It's me, Audra ... it's Mike." Mike muffled his voice, not wanting to stir any-one in the neighborhood. Audra finally stirred, sat up, and rolled her window down.

"Where were you? I thought you might have gotten lost or kidnapped ... or worse."

"You'll smell what happened soon enough," quipped Mike with a bit of a groan in his voice, as he walked around the truck to the passenger side, and opened the door Audra had by now unlocked.

"Now that you've said that, I thought I could smell something when I rolled the window down. What on earth is that? Is that you? Man, what kind of cologne do you call that?"

"*Essence de Refuse*, mixed with *Prince Dumpster Dive*, along with *Rank Spice,*" Mike quipped humorously, in spite of the revolting situation in which he had found himself. "I had no choice!" moaned Mike. "Do you have something I can sit on so I won't be leaving this *'Essence'* on your seats?" Audra found an old towel she'd wiped the truck down with last time she washed it laying in the back seat, and handed it to Mike without further comment. He slowly climbed into the truck, feeling grubby, anxious to get back home to clean the dumpster residue from his being.

"Were you able to place the note on his box?"

"Well, you needed to be there. His dog barked, when the motion lights came on, so I climbed into his dumpster he stores by the corner of his garage. 'Lucky for us it was there, or I'd have had no place to quickly hide!"

"Not too lucky for *you,* stinky boy! Let's get you home before you permanently stink up my truck." Audra hated the stench, but she had to laugh in spite of that. Just imagining Mike crouching down in a big, smelly dumpster, wading in who-knows-what kind of poop and slop! "Ugh!" she loudly sighed.

"Go ahead, laugh a few more rounds on me ... ha, ha, ha! See, I'm laughing, too! Darn it, anyway, I didn't get a chance to even plant that note, after all that!"

"There's always tomorrow, partner."

"Not tomorrow, we have a very big adventure ahead of us ... unless you don't want to go."

"Oh really? And just what is it that we have to look forward to?"

"Tomorrow we're going to Coronado Cave. I really believe that cave is going to reveal some clues that will shed a lot of light on this case."

"'Unless I don't want to go!' Boy, you bite your tongue! I don't have classes tomorrow, and—even if I did—I'd still go with you. You ain't gettin' rid of me that easily, Brat!" screeched Audra as she held her nose.

Mike laughed at her gesture and said, "I hoped you'd say that." Mike explained that he thought they ought to spend a few hours at Audra's house before going. Mike wanted to leave around three in the morning, or what Audra referred to as 0300 hours. The idea was to get out to the cave site and hike through the darkness when no one was around. The Park Rangers closed the cave off to the public after six o' clock in the evening, but he really did not want to explore the Coronado Cave, anyway. He told Audra he thought the arrow on the small topographic map he had confiscated from the straight truck might be indicative of another cave not too far off Montezuma Canyon Road that cut through the Coronado National Memorial Park. Audra wondered about this possibility herself. The plan was simple. They'd drive to the mountains early, leave the vehicle concealed as much as possible outside the park, unpack two mountain bikes from the back of the vehicle, and pedal their way to the site four miles away. Mike and Audra both agreed that this would draw much less attention.

Audra pulled into Mike's driveway. Mike hurriedly climbed out, as Audra pushed the mountain bikes over to her truck. Running into the house, he paused a moment, turned around, and shouted, "Hey, Aud! We're taking that Cherokee Rodeo parked in my yard over there. It actually belongs to my neighbor, Mr. Eldon. He was a great friend of my parents, and he's a close friend of mine. I told him I needed something with a bigger payload then my Jeep, and he was happy to let me borrow this." Mike was pointing at the tan and brown vehicle as he spoke. Audra stared at the SUV. The dark night hid its colors. She moaned a little, then proceeded to push the bikes over to the SUV, even loading them by herself.

Mike showered quickly, then he raced around the house to make sure everything he'd set up earlier—the timed lights and music—were all in order. He set his Presario 2000 Professional to modem and auto-dial at eight in the morning. He snatched up a duffel bag, checked it over quickly and raced back out of his house, locking the door behind him.

Audra admired how quick and efficient Mike was. She had already loaded the bikes into the back of the vehicle. Being a strong girl who worked out whenever possible, the job had really not been all that difficult. Mike shot an impressed looked at Audra and said, "Good girl!" a little surprised that the bikes were already loaded.

"You make me sound like your pet Lassie. Ruff, ruff!" barked Audra.

"Ha! You are my good girl," laughed Mike, as they both crawled into the Jeep. Mike fumbled for the keys in his pocket. He groaned, wondering why he'd not pulled them from his pocket while standing outside the Cherokee, as that would have been so much easier. Finally, he pulled them free and stuck them into the ignition. The Cherokee started quickly. Mike slipped the vehicle into drive, and the two adventurers were on their way.

As Mike pulled into Audra's driveway, she asked the question that haunted her earlier, but ignored to ask it until now.

"Okay, Mike, do you think the bastards are watching your house, and that's why you want to leave from my house?" Mike hesitated. He surely did not want to instill fear, but he knew he must be honest. "Yes, I do, Audra. I set timers on several lights and a stereo at home, and programmed my computer to dial the Internet at what you would say to be 0800 hours. I want them to really believe that I'm in my house. I may be paranoid, but I don't want the bastards to see me going back to the mountains, because I believe they might follow us and permanently take us out of the picture. I don't want that at all. Do you?"

"Point well taken, I'm definitely all for your idea," said Audra as the Cherokee entered her lane. Mike pulled softly up to the house and shut the engine and lights off.

Quickly and quietly, they dashed into Audra's house. They did not want to disturb Audra's father. Audra asked Mike what he had brought in the large duffel bag. Mike told her that the bag contained canteens, a rugged camera, flashlights, night vision goggles and a pair of all-purpose binoculars as well. "I even have a bag of trail mix and dried fruit and meat to keep up our energy level. Audra coaxed Mike to sit on the sofa, while she changed into something more appropriate for the journey. Mike relaxed on the couch, his hair still a little damp from the quick shower he had taken while back at his house. He felt very comfortable here.

His mind drifted back to the scenes of that night. He'd really blown it at Dennis' house. "Oh, well, maybe one note will cause them as much anxiety as two?" He could hope.

Chapter Ten

Just as Mike closed his eyelids to get some rest, Audra crept into the room. Holding a bayonet to Mike's throat, she said in a low, sinister tone, "You're history, Mr. Taylor!" Mike felt the cold steel blade, and winced at this somewhat macabre surprise. Opening his eyes, he saw Audra dressed in a dark uniform and wearing a ninja-like mask. Mike did not move. Sensing the razor-sharp blade, he knew that one move to either side could cut his own throat wide open.

"OK, you've proved your point. Get it … point?" gulped Mike, trying to not over-react—in his shock—or make a wrong move.

Audra withdrew the knife, sheathed it in a scabbard at her side, and let out a little chuckle. "Hope I didn't scare you too badly."

"No, I always awaken to a knife at my throat. I get off on kinky things like that, you know. What are you trying to prove, anyway, Audra?"

"Here," Audra placed a dark uniform and mask in Mike's hands, "Now, we will be ready for this mission, but we need one more thing to make sure our safety is complete." Audra pulled a 19C Glock pistol from her holster. "Don't worry I have a Glock and bayonet for you, also. I like the Glock 19C. It harbors three safety mechanisms—trigger, firing pin and drop safety. The gun is lighter than most pistols in its class and it has more punch through power than a standard .45. It aims well with a length of a little over six inches, height about five inches, over an inch in width, weighs about 30 ounces with a full clip, and—best of all—it fires 17 rounds. How does that grab you?" asked Audra, as she placed one in his hand.

You're astonishing, Audra, but where did you learn all that … and where did you get the guns?"

"As I said before, my father's a *Green Beret*. You'll be wearing his night combat uniform."

"Where's the beret?"

"You are ignorant, aren't you? Hon, we're not going to a social club, so we won't need to look formal. Anyway, hurry and put these on. My father wore them, and he is close to your size. Might fit rather nicely on you," giggled Audra. Mike quickly left the room, entered the bathroom, slipped out of his clothes and returned, having donned the uniform, bayonet sheath and the holster with the 19-C Glock strapped in it.

"I never fired a gun like this. I am used to revolvers, not automatic weapons like this Glock, Audra! I've never even seen one of these before until tonight."

"Oh, boy!" Audra rolled her eyes. "Look, Mike, I'll explain how simple it is to operate while we are driving down the road. If you have even a general knowledge of pistols, you'll catch on. I'm afraid we don't have time for target practice lessons. I'm sure you'll be fine," assured Audra.

"I hope to God we don't have to use them, Audra. I can just imagine the shock waves a shooting would cause. I wonder what people will think when they see us dressed like cat burglars."

"You, silly! The point is, we dress like this so they won't see us!" exclaimed Audra.

Mike looked at Audra and spoke, "Well, then shall we be on our way?"

"I thought you wanted to get a couple hours of rest," Audra countered.

"So, I changed my mind. It's already twelve-thirty in the morning or—as you would say—0030 hours. If we fall asleep now, we may never get up later. Besides, I'm wide awake now."

"Isn't that odd? So am I. Well, then, let's do it, Soldier!" ordered Audra. They left the house, entered the Cherokee and drove away towards the canyon. Audra felt a surge of excitement, and she loved how Mike looked in a uniform. "Something about a man in a uniform that just makes me tingle all over," laughed Audra to herself.

They turned right on Hereford Road, continued west for about five miles. Then they took a left onto Highway 92. Audra drove the Cherokee because she wanted Mike to have his hands free, as she verbally instructed him in the use of a Glock.

"Okay, Mike, release the clip," Audra began. Mike fumbled around for the release on the clip. "Mike, look at the *base* of the butt,"

Mike checked, and saw something he thought might be what he was looking for. "You mean this?"

"Yes. Now slide it." Still fumbling unsuccessfully, Audra instructed, "No! The *other* way!" With that, the magazine fell out of the clip. Audra continued, "Now, eject any bullet that could be in the chamber." Mike pulled the recoil, and nothing came out. "Okay, it's empty. Now, when you pull back on the trigger safety, the other safety mechanisms release. Slo-o-owly pull back on the trigger." Mike pulled back on the trigger slowly, as he'd been instructed. Once he'd heard a click, he released the trigger, then pulling the trigger as if to shoot, but nothing happened. "My man, my man! When you hear that click, don't *release* the trigger; just keep pulling back on it." Mike did as he was told, and the firing pin made a sharp noise.

"Right-on! Boy, you just passed your first firing lesson on how to shoot a Glock. Now, remember what you learned. You may need it someday! Let's review: Pull the trigger back until it clicks, then pull it further and it fires. In addition, keep your finger on the trigger at all times when you are shooting, or you will mash the second shot and possibly jam it. 'Got it now?"

Mike fiddled with and tested the gun continually for a couple of minutes. "Yeah, I believe I've got it! 'Just passed Glock course 101."

"Good!" shouted Audra.

"This is nuts, though. This whole attire is somewhat weird, like we're about to storm Iraq, or something. All I wanted to do is find clues!" protested Mike.

"Mike! We're not up against sweetie pies here. These jackasses are thieves and murderers. If they see us, do you think they'll walk up to us, tell us how much they love us, and give us a few big hugs and kisses!" hollered Audra.

"Actually, I was hoping they would … but I know you're right," Mike had to agree. He cringed at the thought of shooting another human being, but then he began to think of these men as less than human; how could a truly decent human abduct young boys and girls and do horribly terrible … yea, heinous … things to them! Even if the children survived, Mike knew they would carry the mental and emotional scars for life. Maybe these men were more animal than human, and needed a bullet in the head.

Audra found herself steering into the canyon. They would soon arrive at the site. When they'd driven a couple of miles into the canyon, Mike asked Audra to pull the Cherokee off the main road. Audra saw what looked to be a very lightly traveled trail to her left, leading off Montezuma Canyon Road. She started to turn into the trail when Mike asked her for the odometer reading. Audra stopped the vehicle, and read the mileage to Mike. She then turned the Cherokee off the road and bounced back into a wooded area. She stopped the vehicle and turned the engine and lights off.

"Well, dear, it's show time. I'll get the bikes, if you want to grab the duffel bag," said Mike. Audra reached down, lifted the duffel bag by the handles, and walked to the back of the Cherokee, where Mike was busy unloading the bikes.

As he did this, Audra reached into a pack she was wearing and took out a couple of full magazines. "Mike, take this extra magazine, and load your other one." Mike slipped the full magazine into an ammo pocket above his waist. He loaded the other magazine with fresh cartridges, and then he slid it into the clip. *'Click'* … the chamber was ready to receive a cartridge. Mike took in a deep breath as he turned and faced Audra. He felt a little embarrassed when he saw that she had finished loading her gun in better time than he did.

"Don't let it bother you, Mike. My father loves me very much, and he wanted to be sure I knew how to protect myself, so he's trained me well in weapons and martial arts. Give yourself time, since it's your first experience with a Glock, Mike."

"Should I call you Audra *'Chuck Norris'* Heyburn?" laughed Mike.

"No, call me Commander!" Audra spoke sternly. Mike stopped laughing, and fell silently behind her, as she started back up the trail. Though he did not say it to Audra, he felt secure in knowing what she had just told him. Maybe Audra would actually be able to save him if they found themselves in a life or death situation … something he certainly did not wish to find out, though it could be a real possibility, considering the character—or lack thereof—of the people with whom they were dealing.

Mike handed Audra a set of night vision goggles, and she put them on over her ninja-like mask. Immediately the trail, trees, bushes, rocks and shrubs lit up a bright fluorescent green. With the goggles, they could see well through the dark canyon as they pedaled on. The trip up the trail was short and a bit rough, but soon they found themselves on the main canyon road. They turned left and headed west towards the location Mike had pointed out earlier on the map. Mike stopped Audra for a moment as he retrieved the topographic map, to check their current location. He then produced a foldaway magnifying glass, and opened it to read the map. After taking a few moments to double-check the map, he shouted out to proceed and they began down the road once again.

The night was clear and very dark. The two bikers looked like dark phantoms passing silently in the night. They wound around several sharp bends, as they pedaled closer to the site. The grade of the canyon road became steeper as they traveled deeper into the dark lonely canyon. Somewhere coyotes began to yap with their typically mournful cries. Mike could not help but think about Bobby, upon hearing this. It brought to mind those times when he had told Bobby the reason that the coyotes cried at the moon. It was because they were mad at it, as its light interfered with their hunting, so they fussed at the moon in protest. Bobby, on the other hand, had countered with his own version of their crying at the moon. He said that coyotes howled at the moon because they missed their beloved *'Slewfoot Sue,'* with eyes of blue, who had accidentally bounced to the moon, where she lives to this very day. She is now looking down at all the coyotes with sad blue eyes, as she calls out to them with her broken heart, yearning to be with her beloved coyotes again. Mike laughed audibly at this memory.

"What are you laughing at? If someone's out here they're sure to hear you, 'cause the night is very calm and quiet. Our voices bounce off the canyon walls and echo very loudly, Mike! So, please, keep a grip on your tongue," scolded Audra in a high whisper, with concern for their safety.

"Well, excuse me, Commander! I shall try and maintain from now on." Mike looked at his odometer and—forgetting Audra's recent caution, in his excitement—called out, "We're here!"

"Shhh! My Lord, please be more quiet, Mike! Please! This place gives me the jitters!" Audra whispered as loudly as she dared. With that repeated warning, they both quietly ditched their bikes a ways off the trail, and behind a thicket. Mike tied a large white cloth on a limb jetting up out of the thicket, hoping they would spot the white flag when they returned. After this, they began their search. They walked close together now, and spoke very quietly, when they did speak.

"Audra, according to the map, we should be almost on top of the area the arrow pointed to on the map."

"Well, even with night vision, I don't think finding this place will be a cakewalk."

"You'd be surprised, Audra."

"I am surprised already. I didn't know if we'd get this far."

"You know, if you wanted to conceal an entrance, what would you do?" Mike asked Audra this question, but he, too, was toiling over it as much as Audra. She thought intensely for a bit. As she did so, she happened to lean up against some brush just below a rock structure, which looked a little like half a gable of a house. Suddenly she felt herself falling backwards, gravity sucking her into a pit.

"Mike!" She called out, trying as hard as she could, in spite of the shock of what had just occurred, to use a discreet voice. Mike turned to see Audra struggling to hold onto a sapling. He rushed over to her, clutched her right wrist, and pulled her up. He gazed down at the hole into which she almost fell. He noticed the hole seemed to go only so far, then disappear.

"You know, the slope leading down there is not all that steep. What do you say about having a look?" inquired Mike. Audra nodded, as they started down the dark slope that the thick brush had hidden from view. When they reached what they at first had thought was the end of the trail, their mouths dropped open. In front of them stood a moderate-sized opening like that of a mineshaft, but they could tell that no man constructed this tunnel. The sides were not consistent with that of a tunnel dug out, drilled and blasted with explosives. There was no conformity to this tunnel or cave. No doubt, this was a cave dug out by fast moving water many years ago, when a shallow sea once covered Southern Arizona. Mike took out his flashlight. "Hmmm … limestone … the remains of shellfish and coral. This has to be it, Commander," said Mike duly quiet.

"Well done, Private Pyle," laughed Audra silently.

"Well, gaw-w-wly shazam! I didn't know I had it in me, Miss Audra!" chuckled Mike, as he mimicked the Private after whom he'd just been nicknamed … the most honorable Gomer Pyle, USMC.

Mike took a roll of true tape from his duffel bag. He tied one end of the tape securely around a strong tree root protruding out of the ground near the entrance to the cave. He pulled a rod out of his bag and passed it through the spool. Mike then gave Audra a long, hard look. "It really is show time now, Miss Audy. I have no idea what we're gonna find … maybe nothing. Or, maybe we are about to find a passageway leading to a discovery that will help blow this case right out of the water—or should I say 'right out of the canyon'!" Audra silently held her index finger to her shut lips, once more reminding him of their need to be quiet.

The tape rolled off the reel as Mike and Audra walked cautiously into the cavern. As they wound around a couple bends in the cavern, they noticed how large the cave seemed to grow. It started out about eight feet high at the entrance, then it narrowed a little, but once they had passed a few bends, it opened up into a huge room. The ceiling appeared to be about twenty feet in height, with a width of almost seventy feet or more. It reminded Mike of Coronado Cave in many ways. They saw stalactites hanging from above, and stalagmites protruding out of the floor of the cave. They looked in awe at some of the unusual columns, and almost lost their breath when they saw a rimstone dam holding pools of fresh water. As they walked even further into the cave, they witnessed the beauty of a drapery that covered the roof of the cavern. It was absolutely gorgeous.

"Look at the beautiful crystal-like flowstones that formed these caverns!" exclaimed Audra. She forgot herself, for a moment, to be quiet as she talked. "This is awesome, Mike! I can't believe this cave has never been discovered!" Suddenly she squirmed a little at her own words, as she realized some others already had, and they wanted to keep this cavern a secret for some reason. As reality set in upon her, she became stoically silent once again. Mike lifted the dark mask from his face as he sat down on a large rock to take in the glory of the cavern. He also wanted to steal a well-deserved rest for a moment. Audra sat down beside him. She, too, wanted to break stride for awhile, as well, quietly taking in all the surrounding beauty for a few moments.

Mike reached into his duffel bag, which actually could transform into a type of backpack. He withdrew a pair of night-vision binoculars and scanned the cave. He became a little upset when he told Audra that the cave ended approximately 70 more feet in front of them. He searched the cavern walls all around them, but he saw no other signs that the cavern continued on anywhere. They walked to the back of the cavern, and stopped at what appeared to be a solid sheet of translucent crystalline wall.

"Well, at least we will be given the recognition for finding this natural wonder!" stated Audra excitedly. Mike said nothing. The entire cave gave the impression of something sinister at work. Why would the arrow point to a dead end cavern, unless they just used the cave to store materials and supplies? Why just store materials and supplies in a cave? Why not store their cargo closer to where they operate; and, if it was a storage point, then the supplies could be subject to possible discoverers of the cavern.

"This makes little sense. In fact, it makes no sense at all!" squealed Mike, before remembering their need to explore in relative quietness.

"Hey, just be grateful we've found something!" said Audra with glee. She was still very happy to be in such a beautiful cavern. She began to jump around and sing a little to herself. She—however naively at the moment—did not feel a bit threatened.

"I really thought we were on to something. I just cannot figure out why they even marked this on their topographic map. Dang it, Audra! Now what?" Mike could not help but be angry. Bobby's life depended on him and, instead of moving forward, he felt as if he was falling backwards again … another dead end … another disappointment. However, Audra somehow lifted Mike's spirits and gave him renewed hope when she danced around the cavern, accidentally stumbling on a sharp rock. She then fell forward, and her flashlight flew into the translucent wall in front of her. Instead of hitting the wall and falling to the ground below, the flashlight flew past the wall and landed behind it. The light bounced off the ground a few times then came to a stop. The beam shone in Audra's face.

"What the hay is up with that? I've never seen anything like that before! How can something as solid as a flashlight go through rock?" inquired Audra, with a dumbfounded look on her face. Mike carefully walked over to the wall. He looked for mirrors or something that might reflect an image, but he was at a loss, too. Slowly and cautiously, Mike reached for the wall. Where the wall should have been, Mike just felt empty space. His hand passed through the mirage and he almost lost his balance and fell, for he was expecting resistance. He carefully studied the crystal wall. After thinking the matter through for a few minutes the answer came.

"Hmmm ... the walls of the cavern consist of limestone, mainly from shell-fish. Limestone is made of calcium carbonate grains, or calcite. The walls in this area are very pure in their crystalline nature. I believe what we have just experienced is double refraction. When we, as humans, look at the wall with any form of light, the light refracts off the calcite and produces a double image effect. There is no wall here. We are seeing a false image. Come on; let's go on through. Our search is not over yet!" A new surge of hope entered Mike as he hugged Audra, and then walked through the perceived wall. He looked at Audra from the other side and laughed. Audra could barely see him, due to the weird double image that the wall displayed. Finally, she walked through the wall, also, and joined Mike.

"You know, you really do amaze me, Mike. You're always thinking. I would have never thought of this, nor could I have explained this phenomenon as well as you did. 'May have even turned back, without checking to find that it was not a wall, after all!"

"Well, actually, I wouldn't have either, but I saw a demonstration of this recently in my geology class at college, so it was fresh in my mind," explained Mike. They both remained very quiet for a while. Audra's fear of evil men lurking about in the cavern returned. They rounded a bend and stopped. "Look! A gate," whispered Mike.

"Or, some kind of door," Audra added. "I don't understand." She looked totally bewildered by now; first the *'wall,'* now this door. They tried the door, but it would not budge. Then Audra noticed something unusual. "Mike, this is no normal door. This door has no lever. It doesn't push open, or pull open; it slides open. This is an elevator shaft."

"Amazing! Brilliant deduction, but now what do we do?" asked Mike, as he looked all around him. He walked around, to the side, and down the cavern. Then he spotted a small, wooden, round cover that resembled the bottom of a wooden barrel. Mike ran over to it and gripped the edges. He pulled with all his might. The cover moved ever so slightly. Audra joined him. They both pulled the cover towards them. Suddenly the cover gave way. Small rocks and dust fell from the cavern ceiling above their heads. The dust lightly covered both of them. They brushed the dust from their uniforms. Mike took his canteen and poured a small amount of water on a bandana he was wearing around his neck. He wiped the dust from his night vision goggles and handed the cloth to Audra, so she, too, could clean her goggles.

"I'm reading your mind. You want to go in there, don't you?" Audra did not like the looks of such a dark hole, for all she knew it could be the hole leading to hell.

"Audra, if your brother was counting on you, would you chance going down this hole? I know I might find myself stuck and possibly die in that hole, but it's worth a try. Besides, I think this is probably just another passageway the bad guys used at one time. I think I'll make it, and it may even open up wide enough so I can turn around. You stay here, Audra. I'll go alone. Mike handed Audra the true tape.

"You are very brave, Mike ... and stupid ... but I love you!" Tears streaked down from a scared Audra's eyes, leaving stained furrows on her cheeks from the dust on her pretty face.

Mike looked into her soft, brown eyes. He leaned forward as their lips met. Mike looked up and smiled, "I'll be back. You'll see. It'll be okay." Just like that, Mike disappeared into the dark hole.

Mike found himself sliding downward into the dark chasm below. The cavern floor became very steep and Mike slid faster. His right shoulder collided into the rocky side of the tunnel and his flashlight went out. "Not again," grumbled Mike. He moaned a little in pain as he rubbed his shoulder and, if not for his night-vision goggles, he knew he would lay blind and helpless, groping around frantically in the dense darkness. Momentarily, Mike edged forward. He came to a bend in the tunnel. He noticed the cavern walls and floor were heavily stained—an indication that this tunnel had been traveled quite frequently in the past. The fallen rocks and the loose piles of pebbles and dust on the floor were sure signs that the tunnel probably became a much too dangerous route to pass through, so the people operating here must have dug or widened out another route.

Once Mike had rounded the bend in the cavern, he saw a very faint light below him. "Strange! Where is that light coming from? This is very odd. I'm deep in a dark cavern and I see light!" Mike closed his eyes and shook his head. He slowly lifted his eyelids, only to see the same light shining below him. He crawled slowly around the bend, and looked around him in wonderment. The cavern opened up into a much wider and higher passageway. Now he could stand and walk comfortably down the tunnel. "The entire passageway was probably like this at one time before it partially caved in," Mike whispered to himself. He patted his body vigorously to rid the dirt from the uniform with which Audra had supplied him—then he continued. As he neared what he realized was an opening that led out of the narrow tunnel, the light grew a little more in intensity.

Mike stopped about three feet shy of exiting the tunnel, upon seeing there were some round iron rods barring the entrance. He began to panic a little, for he had fought his way this far, and now a few iron bars might be the factor that would turn him away from his intended mission. He grabbed hold of the end of one of the bars and pulled with all his might … nothing! He tried the top bar and pulled on it, and that's when he noticed that the mouth of the cavern had eroded some around the end of the middle bar. Mike tugged with everything he had.

Suddenly a dark form came from behind him. "Hi! 'Thought this might need a woman's touch," whispered Audra as she grabbed hold of the bar, attempting to help Mike pull it loose. After a bit of a struggle, they sat gasping and panting for fresh air. Catching their breath, they began again, this time working the rod completely loose, and pulling it away from the entrance. Mike climbed through the bars and fell upon the floor of an even larger section of the cave. Audra followed Mike. She landed at his feet and rolled to a squatting position. Mike took her by the hand and helped her to her feet. They looked in the direction of the light, which now glowed much brighter.

"I'm not sure I like this, Mike. What the heck is a light doing shining in the dark chambers of this cave?"

"Very good question. I have a strong feeling that whatever is going on is less than kosher," Mike said with a faint voice. They knew someone was probably posted close to the light, so they talked very quietly as they crept closer and closer to it. Suddenly the passage they stood in lit up as they heard a loud noise of electric contacts kicking in, and the whir of an electric motor. They looked to their right to see the same type of sliding door they had first seen in the chamber above.

Someone was on that elevator; someone would soon walk out of the retractable door—then what?

Mike and Audra quickly hid in a darker area of the passageway, behind an outcropping from the cavern wall. The elevator stopped and the door opened. Two men stepped out of the elevator and onto the floor of the cave.

"They're requesting another midnight run. Apparently, we're behind schedule. We'll probably have a few more also before the train gets a rest," said a fair-haired, weather-beaten looking man. Rough and rugged, he appeared as the kind of man you would expect to see in some two-bit western saloon, or taking part in a Clint Eastwood shootout. The other man appeared younger and more attractive. He sported a well-groomed look and a better physique. "Don't you get tired of working these asinine hours? I can't wait till this silly Mexican holiday is over," complained the younger fellow.

Hey! You watch your mouth, Son, or I'll cut your tongue out and feed it to a stupid Gringo!" shouted the rugged-looking man. His voice even sounded craggy.

"Damn it, Raul! You get too personal. Take it easy. Shoot! You'd think I whizzed in your favorite brand of cereal or something. Don't you ever get tired of being grumpy?" the young man spoke loud and clear. His voice also sounded a bit rough. Both men were anything but soft spoken. They talked about trivial matters for a few minutes and cursed each other from time to time. Mike and Audra had never seen these men anywhere before. They thought it strangely sad that they still had no solid suspects, even when they could see their faces and hear their names.

"If only they would mention a last name," thought Mike. They almost seemed to speak in some sort of code language, too. "What is this *'midnight run'* of which they speak, and why is one of them so excited about the next Mexican holiday?" Then Mike remembered Audra sharing with him about the upcoming *'Cinco de Mayo.'* Were they referring to this holiday?

Mike's skin crawled when he heard the younger man tell Raul, "I still can't wait until March twenty-first is over. We'll be able to breathe a little easier. That'll be the last train out of this hole until *Cinco De Mayo.*"

Raul spoke up, "Ah, yes! March twenty-first ... *veinte-uno* ... birthday of one of Mexico's most beloved presidents, Benito Juarez ... a *fiesta patria!* Hey, Gringo! Let's join the others in the yard. They probably think we got kidnapped, we've been gone so long!" laughed Raul. The two men turned, and began walking towards the yard.

"Well, dang me, dang me, get a rope and hang me!" exclaimed the younger man, as he suddenly stopped, remembering something. "I left my stupid clipboard in the elevator!"

"Just like you, Gringo—always carrying your mind up your behind, never thinking, always forgetting! Go get it, Gringo, so we can finally be on our way!" growled Raul. He sounded irritated ... very annoyed. Mike and Audra watched as the younger man, apparently nicknamed *'Gringo,'* walked over to the stony wall of the cavern, pulled a small swinging door, that actually looked like the wall itself, away from the cavern wall. Gringo inserted his hand into the small door and the elevator door opened. He then quickly closed the camouflaged door that contained the controls, and stepped into the elevator. Over ten seconds went by before Gringo returned with his clipboard in hand. "Okay, my friend, finally we can go," stated Raul with a tinge of an Hispanic accent.

While the men talked, Mike managed to extract his small digital camera from one of the ammo pockets on his vest. He fished it out of the case and leaned forward, ever so cautiously and carefully. If he could just get a good picture of these two, maybe their identities could lead them to the main perpetrators. Mike began to snap the button on the camera when the rock he was holding to balance himself, broke loose from the cornice of the outcropping. He lost his balance and would have fallen right in front of the men if not for Audra. She took hold of Mike's black vest and pulled him back towards her.

This enabled him to catch his balance again. The rock tumbled down onto the cavern base and—worse—the camera fell out of Mike's hand and bounced into a small crevice in the floor, disappearing from sight. Mike quietly let out a long, pitiful groan.

"What the heck was that?" asked Raul a bit nervously as he pulled a gun out from his jacket.

"Ah, come on, Raul! You know that rocks are continuously falling from the roof or the walls of this cave," shouted the younger man.

"Well, Gringo, I'm going to check it out!"

"Go ahead, but you'll have to do the checking without me, 'cause I'm heading to the yard. It was probably just a rat, anyway. They're always running about kicking rocks hither and thither." Raul looked over the area very carefully. He walked a little closer to the outcropping as his comrade walked away.

Raul may have walked over to Mike and Audra, but deep inside he was really just a coward. He put on a good act in front of his outlaw peers, yet when real danger broke out Raul knew how to take care of his miserable, yellow-bellied carcass. He excelled in desertion. This did not bother Raul, for he knew crime too well. He was born into a family deeply involved in crime, and he found out at a young age that other criminals talked a big talk but, when push came to shove, they cared little about him—or anyone else—aside from themselves. As long as they got their share, it would not bother them if he fell over dead. With this thought in mind, Raul turned and walked quickly to catch up with Gringo.

Mike and Audra donned their black ninja-like masks as they raced quietly over to the door. Mike examined the wall for the lid that Gringo had pulled away from the wall. "Here it is—very clever! They disguised the protective guard to the controls with a stony texture that looks just like the cavern wall," whispered Mike.

"No wonder we couldn't find the controls up above," moaned Audra as she looked at Mike in surprise.

"Mike, this is getting to be too much. It's like a bizarre secret agent film or like something out of a *James Bond* movie. I mean, think about it … secret panels, odd trucks, weird men, unexplained compounds, mysterious maps. Need I go on?" Audra said through her mask.

"Well, you can always bail out. I wouldn't blame you," replied Mike as he scratched his right cheek through the dark mask. He found the mask a little irritating against his face.

Audra stood straight upright in front of Mike. She folded her arms in front of her and tapped her left foot on the ground. She looked Mike squarely in the eyes. "Not on your life, Bucko! These intriguing events are the only reason I stick around, and who's gonna take care of your clumsy ass—you? I should think not! You can't even take a picture without falling! No, you're stuck with a superior intelligence like me until this is over," Audra teasingly gloated. "And another thing, Smarty Pants, the reason you're always scratching at your face is because you were intelligent enough to put your mask on in-side-out. You look like you're wearing a huge black jockstrap over your silly head, with two eyes bulging out of the cups!" said Audra coarsely with a somewhat irritated, although amused, voice. Mike, while feeling she might be coming off as quite the feminist—at the moment—nevertheless admired and respected her strong personality.

"Thank you, Dear. Actually I was hoping you'd see things my way," said Mike as he lifted the mask quickly from his head, turned it out the other way, and then placed it back on correctly. Immediately he felt the difference. No longer did the mask feel itchy and abrasive.

"Your way? Oh boy!" Audra blew a long blast of air out of her mouth. "Mike, you're impossible."

"Audra, you're in*credible!*"

Audra smiled. "'Say we stick close to the dimmer lit cavern walls and quickly slither our way out behind Raul and Mr. Gringo. We'll follow them to wherever they're going. I'll bet we could reveal many answers to these riddles if we can find this so-called 'yard'," whispered Audra excitedly, as she turned to race after the two men.

Mike grasped her left arm. "Listen, Audra, that guy named Gringo said that the next shipment leaves on the twenty-first. I think he might be referring to a shipment of children, and Bobby could be one of them. Lord, we are running out of time fast! That gives us only ten days in which to find him. How are we gonna do that? We don't even have a decent lead yet!"

Audra perceived Mike's deep concern. His voice sounded weak, almost helpless … hopeless. "Mike, we'll find a way. Now, I'm not gonna let our two friends get away!" With that, she pulled away from Mike and began chasing after the two men.

"Ah, hold up, Audra. Er, I mean, I'm right behind you!" Mike found racing after his sure-footed sweetheart was quite the challenge. She was very agile and well synchronized. She looked like a scant, shadowy figure against the cavern walls, almost invisible, as though she had trained all her life for operations like this one. Mike hoped his technique was at least half as good as Audra's.

"If anybody gets caught or shot in this caper, it'll probably be me. Audra's too good. Oh, Mike, stop talking negative," Mike grunted to himself, as he tried to keep pace with Audra. Soon they saw the two thugs up ahead of them. Mike gritted his teeth as he thought about the camera he had lost. "What a stupid thing to do! Why was I so nervous and in such a hurry to take a picture? I would have had plenty of time to take many pictures, if I'd not lost my camera! That old cliché is correct ...'*Haste does make waste.*' It sure wasted my camera, anyway." thought Mike dolefully.

"Audra, have you noticed the grade of this path?"

"Yes, we're walking down a slope. Makes walking a little easier, don't you think?"

"Sure does. I don't have a calculator with me, but I would guess for every twenty feet we walk we drop five feet further down into the earth," Mike figured.

"That's probably a good guess. Our two fiends are moving swiftly. They must be a little late for something."

"Maybe they're late for the midnight run," guessed Mike. Audra did not reply. She had noticed that the light up ahead was growing much brighter. "Hmmm, they must have turned, or something," Mike speculated, as the two men who had been walking in front of them suddenly disappeared from sight.

"Mike, I believe we should remain silent as we approach the spot where they vanished." Audra took a small radio out of one of her pockets and handed it to Mike.

"What's this for?" asked Mike as he took the small radio out of Audra's hand.

"Just in case we get separated. Don't lose the channel. This is a special, military-class high-band frequency radio, with a range of twenty-five miles."

"This little mama can reach out twenty-five miles away. Wow!"

"Yes, Dear, and if you lose the channel, just keep *XX* in mind."

"*XX* ... sounds like a rather profane channel!" exclaimed Mike.

Audra laughed a little, "Yeah, the military indulges in smut, don't you know? Actually, *XX* is equivalent to twenty, like your Roman numerals. However, it isn't the same channel twenty as on a normal citizen's band radio. This channel has a different frequency; all the channels on here are different from a CB."

"So the bad guy has a very difficult time trying to intercept the conversation," assumed Mike.

"Bravo, Mike," said Audra as she and Mike turned and proceeded carefully down the cavern trail.

They approached the area where the two men had vanished out of sight. They almost stumbled over a precipice. Steps carved out of the cave's sloping floor led down to a loading dock near the station. Mike and Audra saw an astonishing sight below them. The cave's roof looked to be fifty feet in height. High bay HID lights lit up the area below. A few men appeared to be loading a boxcar. In fact, there was a string of several boxcars all coupled together, waiting to be pulled. Neither had to be an Einstein to figure out that the well maintained track and above rail supported an electric train.

"Mike, this is like a subway system used in Chicago or Philadelphia. These guys are brilliant! This system uses clean electricity, which produces way less noise than a diesel operated train system would, helping them to more stealthily conduct their business.

"Not to mention no fumes or smoke. I wonder how they support this system with energy. Do they have huge generators, or do they actually have a utility line that feeds this place, like the visitor's station we bicycled past on the way in?"

"Oh, God, no!" exclaimed Audra.

"What's the matter, Audra?"

"Look, Mike, they're loading a crate with weapon paraphernalia: *AK-47, AK-74* assault rifle butts, stocks, cartridges, magazines. Lord, they're probably smuggling grenades, rockets, launchers and who knows what, too!"

"And, they're covering the weapon parts with what looks to be candy," whispered Mike. They carefully and quietly viewed the site from the landing, as they lay flat on the ground. From below, the human eye could not see their dark forms.

Audra thought she had already witnessed the worst form of treachery, but the worst was yet to be exposed. Four young men walked forth from what resembled a moderately sized guardhouse or station. They wore strange uniforms, and each held a Russian *AK-47* in his hands.

The *AK-47* assault rifles and uniforms did not upset Audra. The young men inside the uniforms, however, made her gasp.

"My Lord in heaven, look closely at those soldiers, Mike!"

Mike pulled his night-vision binoculars from his vest pocket. "At least these didn't get lost or damaged yet," Mike thought as he lifted the glasses to his eyes. He almost choked on his own saliva. "What! These guys look like young Americans, no older than eighteen or nineteen, I'd say!" Mike's voice rose just a little.

"Young American men in Bolivian uniforms, holding *AK-47s* and guarding the depot and train. Mike, are you thinking what I'm thinking?" inquired Audra, as she turned her head and spoke into Mike's ear.

"There's more to this operation going on here than just abducting children for labor. These boys have been trained for combat. Why would anyone want to abduct young American boys and girls and train them for combat? To have them fight against other South American Nationals? Wouldn't they rather exploit their own children like they do in Central America and abroad?" asked Mike.

"What if that's only a small part of it?" Audra asked.

"Huh?" responded Mike.

"I mean, let's say you wanted to infiltrate a country like Russia, or Iran, or some other country. You want to remain discreet, unknown. You begin by gradually managing a corporate take-over in that country … you know, by buying out huge amounts of stock in that country's marquee corporations, such as the big motor companies and oil industries in the U.S. But there is still a problem, after you've conducted a corporate take-over. Even though you have gained some economic strength in that country, you still need a military stronghold. What better way to weaken a nation then to do so from within its own structure?"

"I'm following you, but not all the way."

"Mike, you have been brilliant, you have brought us this far. You even located and brought us to this underground station. This is literally an underground human railroad, and what I think it's being used for frightens me to death … well, almost."

"Audra, I guess you'll have to be specific. You make it sound like these crazies are not just using our children for labor, but they are using them to fight their wars and ultimately to fight against us, too!" exclaimed Mike, somewhat incredulous.

"Now you're getting the picture. Stay with me, Mike. Pretend we bought out Russia's big companies, and we control a large portion of their economy. We have abducted a large population of their children who, by the way, are still capable of being brainwashed to believe gross lies—especially if influenced by mind-altering drugs and professionals. When the time is just right, we send them back to Russia, or perhaps allow them to be rescued. Now you have a very volatile army programmed to do your bidding within the mainstream of Russia's social structure."

Mike interrupted. "Now, all I have to do is wait until the perfect moment and send the signal that alerts our imbedded army to respond. I have both an invading army, along with the army within the country that I wish to weaken, and bring to its knees—amazing!"

"In a more barbaric third world country, this may not work, but in a country like the U.S., I could see this happening," Audra continued. "We would, of course, open our arms to our own beloved children, thankfully accepting them back. Being natural-born American citizens, they would easily blend back into society's fabric without too much notice. Besides, since we are supposed to be the symbol of humanity, the world would look upon us in disgust if we didn't joyfully accept our own children, in spite of some possibly dubious misgivings." Audra ended her speech as the train pulled forward.

The young soldiers dispersed and hopped into separate boxcars. They stood at the entrance of the boxcars holding their weapons, alert and ready for possible battle. The train pulled out of sight down the dimly lit tunnel. Now all Audra and Mike could see were the shiny tracks leading into the drearily lit rocky corridor. Mike looked at his compass. "The train is heading south ... Mexico. At least we figured that out correctly. They probably unload weapons and children in a depot similar to this one south of the border."

"Mike, we have work to do! We need to confiscate any proof of this place— and what's going on in here—that we can."

Mike looked blankly at Audra, "What do you suggest?"

"That guard house, station—or whatever it's supposed to be—might be a good place to start. I'll create a diversion while you enter it and snatch anything that looks suspicious ... a briefcase, files ... anything."

"Wait, let me be the one to create the diversion, okay? I think that should be my job," explained Mike.

"Why, because I'm a girl?"

"No, because I...." Mike stopped.

"Mike, I love you, too ... but let's face the *facts* here. I'm quicker and more agile on my feet than you, and I can climb better."

"But ...?"

"Case closed," Audra matter-of-factly decreed. "I'll do my part, you do yours!"

Mike put his left arm around Audra, pulling her close. They lifted their dark masks and softly planted a parting kiss on each other's lips.

"Unless we bump into each other before this is all over, meet me at the elevator door," said Audra.

"Promise me you'll show up?" Mike felt weak as he spoke these words.

"Hey, I'll be there ... you had better be there, too! Keep your radio handy, and stay low. Whatever you do, do not let those bastards see you."

"Aye, aye, Commander," whispered Mike, a bit loudly. With that, they split up. Audra began to descend the slope of the cavern from one side of the carved out steps, while Mike chose the other side.

Mike carefully made his way to the bottom of the slope. He used columns, large limestone formations and stalagmites as objects to hide behind as he descended the slope and neared the station below. Finally, Mike made his way to the bottom of the slope. He laid flat on the cold, damp cavern floor behind some stalagmites. While in that uncomfortable position, from time to time, he could see two figures passing by the lit-up window of the station. He also noticed Raul and Gringo standing on top of a loading dock. Apparently, they did much of the grunt work, for they were hauling crates with a floor jack into a storage room carved out of the wall of the cave. From where Mike lay, the high bay lights lit up the entire area quite well. Mike assumed the crates Raul and Gringo were storing must be empty because the men did not have to exert themselves very much when they manipulated the crates. Then they began to move another crate that still had the cover nailed down on it.

"Candy, my butt!" laughed Gringo.

"Ha! It's what's underneath the candy that makes me horny," jested Raul.

"Yeah, I'm dreaming of a white snowy Christmas ... crack, crack, crack and more pure snow, that's the song we sing, you know!"

"You *loco en la cabeza,* Gringo!" laughed Raul.

"You're right, but all this dope makes me crazy, 'cause I get crazy when I get paid."

"And, boy, do we get paid!" chuckled Raul.

"Yeah, I'm happy to haul around these crates!" hollered Gringo in glee. The two happy men disappeared into a storage room with a crate.

"Oh, Lord! More shameful practices uncovered in this already complex situation—not to mention more puzzlement hence tossed into the mix. Is it an organized kidnapping ring, a drug cartel, or illegal weapons trafficking outfit? God, help us! It's all three ... and who knows what else!" Mike mumbled to himself.

Mike's radio crackled as strange noises came forth from the receiver. Mike quickly turned the volume down and looked around his immediate area. Nobody near the building or storage room had responded to the noise of the radio. Relieved, Mike's nerves eased as he tried again to listen. When he still could hear nothing but static and a muffled sound, the numerals *'XX'* popped into his mind. Looking at the face of the radio, he noticed the numerals *'XXI'* were displayed rather than the necessary channel *'XX'* Audra had said they would be using to communicate. Mike switched to channel 'XX' and Audra's voice came in clearly over the radio.

"Mike ... Mike ... Come in, Mike!" Not getting any response for awhile, Audra hoped to God Mike had not been discovered.

"Mike, if you can hear me, please ... answer your radio!" Mike keyed his radio. "Right here, Audra. Sorry, I must have accidentally hit the tune button, or channel switch, or something ... but it's alright, now," whispered Mike into the small radio.

"Great. Okay, I'm in place and ready to create a diversion. Get ready! When you hear a loud noise, the men should come running out of their cozy clandestine quarters to investigate. They'll no doubt head my way. This will draw them away from you and the station. When you see an opening, go for it."

"Understood, Audra … I mean, *'Commander'.*" Mike snickered to himself, then relaxed a bit, listening for Audra's Glock pistol. He assumed, anyway, when she told him to listen for a loud noise, that she was referring to her Glock.

Meanwhile, Audra withdrew a putty-like substance from a plastic bag she carried in one of her ammo pockets. Placing some electronic caps into the putty, which had leads connected to a couple of small batteries and a tiny timing device, she sent up a quick *'SOS.'* "God, we haven't had much luck in our endeavors lately. Please, help us once … just this one time, at least," pleaded Audra. She then placed the *C-4* inside a small crevice within the cavern wall, also jamming a few rocks into the crevice. Audra then looked at her watch and ran towards the station, crouching down between two long concrete platforms, which ran parallel to both sides of the train track. The concrete platforms stood three and a half, to four feet, in height. This provided a deep, long channel in which Audra could hide. Audra looked at her watch again, then keyed her radio.

"Mike, get ready! In fifteen seconds you'll hear the loud noise!" whispered Audra.

"Ten-four, Aud," responded Mike. He hugged the ground even tighter, just to make sure the men would not see him when they came out of the building.

The two men inside watching the station were completely oblivious to what was currently happening just outside their presumably safe abode. The taller of the two, a rather homely, thin-faced man with bulging dark eyes and thin lips, looked at his comrade who was talking about women and money.

"I tell y' my tall buddy, when all this is over I'm heading south of the border. I miss them hot little *chicas* down south! 'Far as I'm concerned, they're hotter than the spoiled brats here in the States, and … who-o-oa! They sure do know how to make my motor roar!" hooted Shorty, a rather ruggedly handsome looking man that loved the ladies. He was stocky, strong and of average intelligence.

"Okay, hot pants, take it easy before you blow a fuse," laughed the tall man.

"You know. I wish we'd see a little more excitement around here. Man! It's just too boring down in this hole!" squawked Shorty again.

"Not me, *'Short Stuff.'* I ain't bored; I like it quiet! I remember too many times when bombs and whistles were going off. I like making money, but I also like spending it. You can't do that if you're dead. This is a fine, smoothly run operation, and I hope it stays that way," said the tall man.

Mike's clothes were soaking up more and more moisture from the cavern floor, and he was feeling rather wretched. "'Wonder when on earth she's gonna fire her g.…" *'Boom!'* Mike did not get the chance to utter another word before a huge ball of fire and flame lit up the tunnel about fifty yards south of the platform. Rocks, dust and pebbles blew out from the cavern wall and smashed into the adjacent wall. This caused a significant collapse of that other wall, also. The air filled with dust, debris and smoke as the two walls converged, and crumpled upon the train track. A large portion of the cave's roof also fell in the blast.

The men inside the station leapt to their feet, ran out the door and down the steel steps leading to the concrete loading dock. The shock wave from the *C-4* sent a small tremor throughout the cavern. Some of the high bay lights swayed dangerously above. One fell, sending blue sparks flying in all directions and taking out an entire lighting circuit, causing an entire row of bay-lights to go out. When the men's feet touched the concrete, they began choking on the dust and smoke that hung in the air. Their eyes burned and watered from the hot dust. They cussed and cursed at the situation as they tried to fight their way through the cloud of debris.

Mike looked on with saucer-like eyes. "When she said loud noise, she wasn't just a' kiddin'!" Mike's goggles helped protect his eyes from the stinging debris, and the dark ninja-like mask he wore actually contained a compartment that held a filter around the nose and mouth area.

Mike saw Raul and Gringo run in the opposite direction of the blast. However, the men guarding the station pulled back and released the charging handles on their *AK-47's*, as they continued toward the blast area.

Mike waited until the men had disappeared into the cloudy mass that hovered in the air, then quickly sprang to his feet and started running towards the station. The damp limestone beneath Mike's feet, however, instantly impeded his forward progress. He fell on the drapery of slippery limestone and slid into a stalagmite. Holding his shoulder and rubbing his knees at the same time, he painfully forced himself to his feet. He continued his mission, but this time with greater caution.

"No, I have no idea what caused this blast, but I don't think it was just an accident!" boomed the voice of the tall gunman. He stood holding an *AK-47*. His thick, dark, bushy eyebrows rose as he spoke with a deep voice.

The stocky gunman, shorter of the two, stood beside his comrade musing, "Might be some freelance competitor. We've had a few skirmishes with them before. Y' never know in this business."

"No way, unless someone turned traitor and decided to open up their own shop. Even then, very few people who are directly involved know of this place. "No, Shorty, no one would be stupid enough to leave the *CDO* and try anything like this, 'cause if someone did leave the club, they'd turn up either in small pieces or a pile of ashes. And, you just had to get bored and wish for some action, didn't ya!" coughed the tall man.

Mike carefully walked up the iron steps leading to the station door. He reached the landing, turned facing the door, opened it, and walked inside. Mike keyed his radio and whispered into the transmitter, "Okay, girl, I'm inside and looking out."

"Good job, Soldier," replied Audra. She had no idea the gunmen were close enough to hear her radio crackle in the gloomy tunnel.

"Did you hear that!" exclaimed the tall gunman.

"Yeah, it's coming from somewhere below the deck we're standing on!"

Earlier Audra had donned another pair of goggles superior to the goggles Mike had given her. She had not told Mike, because she did not want to hurt his feelings, nor did she need him to question her about their origin. The important issue now was that she could see much more clearly with her goggles. She heard the men talking. Her ears became especially alert when she heard the shorter man identify her position.

Audra lifted her Glock 19C from her holster. She raised her eyes just above the top of the concrete platform. She saw some barrels and crates lying on pallets about thirty feet away. From this position, she could see the men approaching her. They walked cautiously, pointing their rifles from side to side. Audra knew that the longer she waited, the less chance she had to survive. Surely the two men were bound to discover her if she did not act hastily. Like a black dart, she leapt off the track and onto the concrete platform. Bullets exploded from the fiery muzzle of her Glock as she ran, dodged and somersaulted behind the barrels and crates. A volley of deadly shots fired from the gunmen's assault rifles answered her bullets.

The taller gunman felt something burn his kneecap as he tumbled to the ground. He reached down to rub his kneecap, but it was gone. Audra had shot it completely off! All the man felt was oozing blood and rigid bone. He screamed, "Ahhh, I've been hit! The bastard shot my kneecap completely off! Damn!" He opened his mouth to shout again, when Shorty saw a bullet rip through his friend's front shoulder and exit out the back of his scapula. Shorty immediately threw himself on the ground, and fired round after round at the crates and barrels.

Mike dashed around the station house frantically. He entered panic mode, for he was finding nothing, and soon the men might return. Mike ran through the station hallways, opening door after door and entering room after room … nothing but disappointing dead ends. Then he noticed one of the doors was locked. He remembered Audra telling him that the Glock had terrific punch-through power. "Well, it works in the movies," Mike mumbled, as he raised the

Glock and pointed it at the lock on the door. He squeezed the trigger, but nothing happened. He tried again ... nothing. "Sheesh! Let's see ... pull back ... pull back on the trigger ... oh yeah, pull back, and do *not* release when it clicks, but keep pulling back." The Glock reset itself as it made a clicking noise. "I've got it! Don't let go of the trigger ... now fire!"

The Glock released one round after another. The speed at which the Glock ejected and reloaded almost made Mike jump out of his boots. He looked down to see the lock, doorknob, and jam ripped to shreds. He kicked the door and it flew open. He raced into the room and found a desk and filing cabinet. A metal briefcase lay behind the file. Mike instantly grabbed the briefcase and tried to open it. "Great! It's locked, too," cried Mike. With no time to waste, Mike rose from the back of the cabinet, and tried to open the file doors. The drawers were locked. Mike threw the heavy metal file on its side. He shot at the drawers, but this only left holes in the cabinet. Suddenly, bullets riddled the windows of the station. Mike immediately fell to the ground. He reached out, clutched the briefcase handle in his hand, crawled out the door, and into the hallway.

Meanwhile, Audra released the magazine from its clip, and replaced it with a fresh one she had been carrying with her in her ammo vest. She knew Shorty was out there ... somewhere ... waiting. She also knew that someone was firing at something ... or somebody ... most likely at Mike. "He'll never make it. He's not trained for this," Audra said silently to herself. "So, Audra, it's do or die time." She reached into her vest, and pulled out a long magazine and gun parts. As fast as she could, she assembled the gun barrel, stock, butt and all—then she inserted the magazine. She picked up a steel rod she had found on the ground, tore a piece of her shirt off, and tied it to the rod.

Audra then raised the piece of the red shirt above the barrels. Shorty saw the cloth and, in his haste to kill the intruder that had severely injured his tall comrade, released a spray of bullets. One of them hit the iron rod, and it flew out of Audra's hand. Now Audra knew where Shorty was, for she saw the flash from his *AK-47* just to her right, next to a crate. With lightning speed, she somersaulted from behind a crate, fell to the ground, and swept Shorty's legs with a volley of bullets. Shorty dropped his *AK-47* as his legs gave way like broken twigs. He lay squealing and cursing. Audra raced towards the station.

Mike's radio crackled. "Mike, keep the hell down. *Don't* get up until I tell you, and *don't* respond until I say it's okay. Key up twice if you can hear me," panted Audra. Audra's radio received two signals as she dodged behind a forklift. She scanned her surroundings, then noticed the murky cloud of dust that once hung in the air had significantly settled. The only remnants left to prove a bomb had gone off in the cavern was one pile of rocky rubble, and a slight fog of particles that still remained suspended, due to their light weight.

She saw three figures circling the station. Each carried assault rifles, yet none of them was in a hurry to enter the building. For all they knew, a small army may be waiting for them to walk through the door. So, the men gathered outside the station in a huddle, speaking quietly amongst themselves. Audra could not make out their words, but she need not have an IQ of two hundred to figure out what they were about to do.

"God, they're either going to riddle the station with a few tons of bullets, or—worse yet—bomb the place!" Her second guess proved to be accurate. The men started to pull grenades from their ammo belts around their waists, when they were startled by a loud shriek. "Got a surprise for you, gentlemen!" yelled Audra with a deep voice, as she ran into the open. She glanced in front of her for a split second as she jumped sideways into the air. Her finger pulled the trigger on the assembled *Uzi,* as bullets roared out of its barrel and chopped at the men's legs. One man managed to squeeze off a few rounds as she quickly fell to avoid them. Audra landed on the ground and rolled back up, ready to fire. The men lay in bloody agony, their legs broken and full of hot lead. One man started to raise his automatic weapon, but quickly lowered it as Audra held her Uzi on him and with a masculine-like voice said, "Try it, and you're dead!" Audra walked over to the would-be killers. One of them reached out for her. She kicked him severely in the head. His whole body jerked as his face fell with a thud on the concrete surface.

The others lay very still. Who was this brutal man before them? They knew this was no ordinary soldier. No doubt, this person endured strict training and was definitely a well-groomed professional. As they looked upon the man in front of them, they were extremely fearful. A ninja-like figure, with an aura of death surrounding him, stood before them. Audra used her well-trained masculine voice. "I was not sent to destroy you. I bring a message from my superiors down south and abroad. We tire from your lack of progress and poor product. You tell your people either you produce at a rate of approval and deliver quality product, or more like me will come and make your lives even more miserable. We already lose too much money and time due to inferior merchandise."

One of the men lifted his head to speak. Audra pointed the muzzle of the Uzi at his face. "But you said you weren't going to kill us," shuddered the injured man.

"You are correct," said Audra, as she kicked the man unmercifully on the right side of his skull. The man fell over almost lifeless. Audra quickly disarmed them all, stripping them of every weapon ... grenades as well as rifles. She then looked upon the only coherent man, who lay in front of her, shaking. She stuck the end of her gun barrel in his face. He shook even more. She repeated this with his skull, his neck, and his spine and lastly she jammed the gun barrel squarely into his rib cage. The man let out a groan.

"Please ... please, don't kill me!" the man pleaded.

"You give me your name, and I won't. I need full name to take back with me for my superiors. If you lie, and don't give me your name, or some credible name of someone running this outfit, more will come and you will die!"

The man's voice began to crack, and he started to cry. "Okay, Ah ... uhm ... please ... my name is Cal Brown," cried the homely man.

Audra drew back. Why would he give the name of Cal Brown? She knew this man! She attended the support groups with Cal. What the hell was going on? Audra paused a moment to gather her wits, and then continued her interrogation. "You ... Cal Brown?"

The homely man answered, "You asked for a name, and I gave you one."

"What do you do?" Audra thrust the barrel of her Uzi deeper into the hapless man's ribs.

"Tell me, what do you do?" she shouted.

The man opened his mouth to speak, but his head felt strange ... dizzy ... almost numb. In a frenzied panic, he reached for his gun.

"Ah, you idiot!" shouted Audra, with a deep voice, as she hit the man harshly in the back of his head with the butt of her weapon. The homely man instantly passed out.

Audra then walked to the top of the steps leading into the station and keyed her radio. "Okay, Hot Lips," she spoke into the radio, in a deep, moderate voice, unlike her own—taking no chances, in case the cavern walls should contain hidden recorders—"you can come out of the station now. Before you do, make sure, if you see any radios, including base radios, that you bring them out ... or destroy them." Mike knew exactly where the radios were; he had seen them while he was searching for files and papers. He raced to the front desk, lifted the base radio over his head, and smashed it soundly on the ground. Suddenly he noticed a book that had been stowed away under the base radio. It looked like a logbook of some kind. He put it inside his vest pocket, and zipped it close. He next lifted a scanner and smashed it. Then he grabbed the charging tray containing several radios and walked out the door.

"Boo!" exclaimed Audra, her sometimes black humor leaving her barely unable to overlook such an opportunity. Mike almost jumped out of his skin. Audra laughed naturally for the first time since the deadly excitement had begun.

"Man! 'You trying to give me an M.I., or what, Audra?"

"O Lord, help us! You almost mottled and turned blue. I'm sorry, Babe, I just couldn't resist."

Mike looked down upon the deck of the concrete platform. He took the radios out of the recharging tray, disassembled the battery packs from them, threw the radios far into the left side of the dark cavern—then he threw the radios into the darkness of another chasm of the cavern. "There, that ought to keep the crooks from talking for a while." He turned, raced into the station house, retrieved the metal briefcase, and walked back to Audra.

As he exited the station, his eyes caught sight of all the bullet holes that riddled the interior of the room. He cringed, when he saw pieces of ceiling and walls hanging only by tape and joint compound, windows blown completely out, and guts blown out of the upholstered furniture. He shuddered when he thought about how close to death he really had been.

Mike walked out on the landing, holding the metal briefcase. "Okay, Commander, may we go now?" asked Mike, as he looked down and to his right. He spied three dark figures lying face down on the loading dock below them, appearing lifeless.

"Did you kill them? I heard all that heavy fire out here. What happened?"

"Let's just say I got the drop on them. I don't think they're dead; however, I did kick and hit them hard enough on their thick skulls to leave all of them with a lasting impression," Audra bragged, though grimly.

Mike heard some faint, painful moans and groans coming from the darkness at the south end of the deck. Audra put her gloved hand over Mike's mouth. "Mustn't worry about them; they tried to kill me, but they'll be all right. All of these cowards will probably live, although they may never walk right again. Their physical disabilities will serve as a strong reminder that, in the end, heinous deeds only lead to death and pain for the perpetrators. Now, Soldier, we have one more small task to perform … a task that will assure the delay of the next train ride out of this station. Follow me," confidently ordered Audra.

Mike followed Audra down the steps and across the loading dock. She began searching for the train yard's electrical service. She asked Mike to help her.

"Where is it?" Audra said in frustration. Now she was confused. She had no idea how to find the service room. Having felt outshone by Audra's superb lifesaving performance, it was now Mike's time to shine. He was now very thankful for the times during which he'd made a few extra bucks while helping friends out. In the past, he'd had opportunity to both run conduit, and pull wire, so he began studying the electrical conduit leading from one high bay-light to another until he found the main junction box. Then he followed the home run to where it dropped into a lighting panel.

From the panel, he traced a two and a half-inch rigid pipe that disappeared into the cavern wall above a metal door. Three four-inch rigid pipes and a few two-and-a-half-inch rigid pipes penetrated the wall.

Mike called Audra over to him. "I strongly believe what you're looking for is behind this door, but it's pretty heavy steel and locked tight. If I had a thin-shank, flat-end screwdriver, I could easily open the door."

"How about a metal social security card?" Audra asked, as she handed the card over to Mike.

"I've seen a card like this before, but I don't remember where," commented Mike as he stuck the card between the latch and door jam. The door opened with ease. Audra and Mike entered the room. Once inside, he found a light switch and flipped the toggle. Light flooded the room. Audra became ecstatic when she saw the two large 2000-amp cabinets, and a couple of 125-kva transformers, sitting in the vault-like room. To her left was an IDF telephone board.

"Soldier, this is it! We're gonna take it all down at once." Mike just stood to her side wondering what she was up to.

"Mike, follow me," said Audra, her voice a bit stern. Mike followed Audra into the electrical room. She made her way over to the large cabinets and trans-formers, opened her vest, and unstrapped a box from her waist. She put the box down on the ground, opened it and began to remove its contents.

"What are you doing?"

"No time to explain. Please take these three pieces of putty and carefully place one on the transformer, one on the electric cabinet, and the last one on the telephone board. Be quick, but handle the plastic with extreme caution," explained Audra. Mike wanted answers, but he knew better ... this was an *'act now-talk later'* occasion. He placed the putty on the equipment, as Audra had instructed. She followed behind him, inserting sharp steel pin-like probes into the plastic globs. Then she beckoned Mike to help her string wire from one probe to another.

Audra skinned the 18-gauge wire, and fastened the bare portion of the wire to each detonator with an alligator clip. The clips held the wire firmly to each probe.

"Okay, now to tie each end of the wire to their designated posts"—speaking as she began doing so—"set the timer, and ... and get the hell out of here! Come on, Soldier ... run!" shouted Audra. They ran across the room and burst through the electrical room door. Mike stopped suddenly. He turned, took hold of the doorknob, and closed the door, assuring that the door was locked behind them.

"Hey! We only have twenty-nine more minutes," screamed Audra. Mike ran toward Audra. He jumped onto the tracks below the train loading dock, then he placed his hands on the top edge of the adjacent Deck and hurtled himself off the tracks and onto the top of the platform. Audra helped him to his feet. They rushed up the carved-out cavern steps to the top of the landing. A by-now-familiar voice echoed throughout the cavern as they stood up on the landing.

"Okay, you filthy ninja bastards, or whoever you are. 'End of the line for you!" snarled Raul loudly, as he trained an *AK-47* on Mike and Audra. Gringo stood in back of Raul. The unsure look on both men's faces told Audra that these men were frightened. They may be good at storage and inventory, but not experienced in heated combat. She did not know this for certain, though, and they did not have the time to explore the subject. What followed seemed like one fast motion. Audra kicked Mike's feet from under him while—at the same time—she drew her own weapon and fell to the ground, squeezing off a volley of bullets.

The entire scene looked like a blur to Raul and Gringo, and the obscure, disabled lighting did not help their vision, either. When they saw the figures in front of them drop rapidly, they began to squeeze the triggers of their assault rifles. Before they could fire one round, a stream of bullets bounced off the limestone formations in front of them and the cavern walls beside them. One bullet grazed Raul's right hand, which held the stock of the *AK-47.* He screamed out in agony, and dropped the rifle. Gringo felt a tingling sensation on the side of his left foot. He looked down to see blood seeping from his boot. He hit my foot!" screamed Gringo.

"Well, he hit my hand, dang it! God, It hurts! Just a flesh wound though. Oooh!" groaned Raul.

"Hey, they're gone!" hollered Gringo.

"They're probably heading up the tunnel that leads to the elevator!" hollered Raul. The two men dashed after the dark-clothed intruders; however, Gringo reminded Raul that they would have to exit out of the cave through the main entrance, so he suggested they should double back, as they might be able to beat them there. Raul looked at Gringo. "Finally, the silly Gringo makes good sense for once." The two men doubled back, but Gringo could not run very quickly, due to his injured left foot; he himself hobbling as well as he could behind his big-bellied friend.

Mike and Audra panted as they ran, both being winded from all the excitement. Their bodies wanted to stop and rest, but their minds knew better.

"Audra, why don't we just hide and let them come after us. We can handle these guys!" exclaimed Mike.

"We don't have time for a shoot out. In twenty-two more minutes the *C-4* is going to turn that electrical room into rubble."

"*C-4?* Isn't that a heavy explosive?" inquired Mike.

"My, you are precocious, aren't you?" Audra smiled, in spite of their dire situation.

"Another talent you learned from your dad?" Mike countered.

"Yes, and if we aren't out of this cave when the *C-4* explodes, I can't promise anything." They ran on for another two minutes before reaching the elevator. Mike swiftly opened the elevator door, and hit the green button. One door opened exposing a larger elevator than they imagined they would see. They jumped inside. Mike closed the door and pressed the button marked '*GL*'—ground level—and the elevator began to ascend.

"Wow, this looks more like a freight elevator than a passenger elevator," commented Mike.

Audra nervously glanced at her watch. If the *C-4* went off now, the elevator would stall, brake or sink back to the bottom floor. They would have to climb out of the emergency hatch, at the top of the elevator car, and shimmy up the cables. "Would we be able to open the elevator doors at the top if that happened?" thought Audra. The elevator stopped and the door opened. Audra let out a sigh of relief. She stepped out of the elevator and scanned the wall. "There it is," said Audra aloud.

"There's what?" asked Mike.

"The hidden cover!" She pulled open the cover, lifted her *Uzi,* and shot out the controls.

"That'll slow them down!" laughed Audra.

"No joke!" exclaimed Mike.

"OK, Mike; let's go. The explosion could possibly bring down the cavern in some areas!"

"That powerful?"

"I don't know. Probably not, but I wouldn't want to be in here to find out!" screeched Audra. They found the true tape, and wasted no time following it towards the entrance.

Raul helped his comrade hobble out of the auxiliary entrance to the cave. "I should just leave you, Gringo, and go on by myself. Aw-w-w, but what are friends for?" he reconsidered, as he continued helping his comrade in crime.

But Gringo lamely protested. "Oh, go on then. I don't want to be the excuse for letting those two pros get away!" hollered Gringo. The word '*professional'* rattled around in Raul's brain. Gringo was right. They were up against two men that possessed a superior talent and intelligence in weaponry. They had made the guards look like rookies, and now he and Gringo had any thought they could outgun, or outwit, these ninja men? 'Hardly.

"OK, Gringo; let's get to the Jeep. They may be pros, but I still have my pride, and we'll have the upper hand if we can beat them to the entrance before they get out of the cavern."

Mike and Audra meanwhile dashed rapidly as possible through the cavern, stumbling a few times in their haste. Once they even fell, but they immediately picked themselves up and proceeded on without bothering to look at their wounds. Their scrapes and scratches began to burn, as they hurried on. Audra glanced at her watch. "Five more minutes and *'boom'!*" she bellowed loudly.

"We're gonna make it! I see the entrance. We're safe!" panted Mike heavily. Mike and Audra climbed out of the cavern. They noticed a cutout path leading up the steep grade.

"Too bad we didn't notice this before. The climb down into the cave would have been easier," said Audra using her male-like voice again.

"Commander, you fell into the pit and I had to save you, remember?" kidded Mike.

"Yeah, Soldier … but at least I *found* the cavern. If it weren't for *yours truly*, you'd still be wandering around like a whipped pup, whining away!" hollered Audra, still using her masculine voice. Her voice stunned Mike, as he helped her out of the pit.

"Well done, Commander," said Mike.

"Soldier, you performed excellently yourself!" boasted Audra, still using her deep voice. As Mike turned to laugh, a light was suddenly shined brightly into his eyes.

"Well, Soldier and Commander, your performance was quite impressive, but not that impressive!" roared Raul from behind the spotlight. Gringo laughed, "Yeah, now we got you! So much for the ninjas." Suddenly a voice bellowed from behind the Jeep, which Raul and Gringo were standing on.

"Freeze! Right now! Let me see those hands reach for the sky, ever so slowly! I said slowly, or I'll blow your freakin' heads off!" snapped the loud officer.

Raul and Gringo slowly dropped their assault rifles, held up their hands, and pleaded for the officer not to shoot them.

"Now, fat man, slowly turn that spot light off. Careful, don't move too fast. My finger's trembling and this gun has a hair trigger!" Raul slowly lowered his right hand to douse the light.

Two officers from the Border Patrol had trained their bright flashlights and guns on Gringo and Raul just in time. The patrol officers had been making a routine pass, when they noticed the Jeep and bright lights. Such activities so close to the U.S./Mexican border usually spelled trouble ... and they were right ... dead right. Just as Raul doused the light as ordered, the *C-4* went off. A huge ball of brilliant blue light, mixed with orange-red flames, blew the door to the vault across the cavern. Tons of rock came crashing down into the electrical room, causing a massive wave of hot air, rock, sediment and dust to burst outward and through the cave's passageways. The cavern became a wind tunnel of deadly hot steam and debris. The ground shook, as gas and dust blew out of the entrance just below Audra and Mike. Quickly they jumped to the side of the entrance, and rolled to safety behind some brush. There was nothing left but molten steel and ash in the electrical room. Even the rigid conduit blew off the cave walls and the bay lights came crashing down.

"What the hell!" shouted the loud officer. The interruption gave Raul his opportunity to make a play at the officers. He quickly spun, dropped to his knees and fired his automatic pistol at the Patrol officers. One of his bullets hit the loud officer, square in the head. The other officer shot at Gringo. Gringo pulled the trigger of his pistol, as he fell back off the Jeep, injured, and landed on the rocky ground below with a bone-crushing thud. Gringo's bullet had not missed its mark; the quiet Patrol officer, defending his stricken partner, fell to the ground. He had been the loud officer's partner for three years now. They had seen a lot of action and excitement together; but tonight would be the last time they would ride together—or by themselves—again. Raul, unhurt, bounded over to the quiet officer, who lay in pain, trying to reach his portable radio.

"Too late for that now!" snarled Raul hatefully. He pointed his weapon at the injured patrol officer. The Beretta echoed through the canyon.

Mike and Audra raced to find their mountain bikes. They considered shooting Raul themselves; however, they had no idea who the other men were and what they intended to do. For all Mike and Audra knew, they might be another rival force. They knew if caught, it could possibly mean their death ... and the chance to save Bobby.

Raul ran to the side of his friend. Bubbles of blood oozed from Gringo's nose and mouth. Raul studied his partner for a moment. He saw a hole in the chest of his lifeless form. "Sorry, Gringo! Damn! I'll avenge you, my brother," said Raul abhorrently. He arose from Gringo's side, and darted over to the Border Patrol's green and white Chevy Suburban. The vehicle's engine was still running. Raul jumped in and yanked the transmission into reverse. He hit two small trees trying to back out. This only slowed him down, but did not stop him. He pulled forward, free of the trees, and continued until he found himself on the canyon road.

Mike and Audra had to stop twice to gather their bearings before they finally spotted Mike's makeshift flag. They raced to the bikes, uncovered them and pedaled to the road. Mike looked up at the eastern sky. He saw dim white light working its way over the mountain peaks. He glanced at his watch and read 4:30 am. Soon the red fingers of dawn would begin their long stretch across the mountains and canyons.

"Mike, we need to get out of here … fast! We can't afford to be seen by the law, or those evil bastards!" shouted Audra.

"I know, Audra … I know. Just keep pedaling. Remember, the road runs almost all the way downhill from here!" Suddenly a large Suburban, its engine roaring, bounced over the curve of the canyon road just behind Mike and Audra.

"Oh, Lord, I don't believe this. Will it never end!" screamed Audra.

"You fools! I'll run over your ruddy, rank rumps again and again till you're both nothing but a grease spot!" growled Raul as he slammed his fist on the dashboard.

"Dang! I bet it's those guys from the cavern. They must have gotten the upper hand on those other men back there!" hollered Mike.

"Mike, he sees us! What will we do?" Audra's heart beat heavily. When it came to firing weapons and hand-to-hand combat, she felt comfortable. However, this was different. She had no control over this situation. Raul held his Beretta out the window and fired at Mike and Audra.

"He's shooting at us!" shouted Mike, as bullets zipped past his left ear making a popping noise.

"Mike, I can't get to my Glock or Uzi!"

"Audra, there's a sharp bend below us. We'll make the bend at a high speed, but they won't without slowing down. After we turn the bend, we'll ride a little further, ditch the bikes and face them down, unless you have a better idea!"

"Sounds like a plan!" shouted Audra as she pedaled even faster. They panted and puffed. They both felt like their chests were about to explode. Bullets bounced off the pavement below them, and Mike felt the burning sting of a bullet as it grazed his arm.

"You, pigs! You swine! This one's for Gringo!" screamed Raul. Raul saw the dark figures disappear. "Oh no! The bend! I forgot all about it!" He pulled his left hand quickly into the Suburban. The back of his left hand hit the metal atop the window frame, causing the Beretta to fall out of his hand. Raul cursed out loudly as his automatic pistol hit the pavement below and bounced off to the side of the road. "Son of a …!" Raul hit his brakes hard, as he skidded forward. He tried everything he knew to make the bend, but his high rate of speed denied him such a convenience. The Suburban slid off the road and hit a yellow oak. The right side of the vehicle crumpled in, but this only served to delay the mad man.

Raul slammed the transmission into reverse, hit the accelerator, and backed away from the tree, tearing off the right front fender. He slammed the vehicle into drive, and roared back onto the road. His eyes were staring ahead, full of hatred. He gritted his teeth, as his knuckles turned white from gripping the steering wheel so tightly. "I'm going to kill you!" screamed Raul as loudly as he could. Suddenly, two dark figures jumped out in front of him. He saw the flames fly out from the muzzles, as bullets sprayed the windshield, front tires, radiator and hood of the Suburban. The hood flew up and buckled over the windshield. Unable to see clearly to follow the road, the Suburban swerved off the canyon road and flipped end over end down the steep side of a gorge.

"Yes! Yes! We did it!" roared Audra, exulting yet relieved at the same time. Mike lifted Audra off her feet and hugged her.

"You're a one-woman army, Lady!" shouted Mike.

"You're not too bad yourself, Angel Face!" laughed Audra. They rode their mountain bikes over to the crash sight. All they could see was smoke and steam rising upward from the crumpled Suburban.

"Mike, where's the briefcase?"

"I had to ditch it back at the bush where we hid the bikes."

"Well, you know what that means?"

"Yes, but we're very close to the Cherokee. Let's put our bikes in it, take off these combat clothes and nonchalantly—as though we know nothing at all—drive back and get the briefcase."

"We're gonna have to, Mike." In minutes, they found themselves alongside the Cherokee. Audra helped Mike quickly load the mountain bikes, and then they shed the dark uniforms, goggles and shirts.

Audra stripped down to a tight jogging suit. Mike wore a white T-shirt and a pair of shorts. He slowly drove onto the canyon road and headed back towards the cavern.

Once they reached the cavern, Mike jumped out of the vehicle, found the metal briefcase and forced it into his duffel bag, which he also had left behind, and raced back to the Jeep. Mike placed the bag and briefcase on the back floor of the Jeep, turned the Cherokee around, and headed for home.

The sun slowly ascended over the eastern horizon. Its long fiery red tentacles crept over the mountains and land, engulfing everything it touched in a brilliance of reddish-orange. Mike looked at the bright rays. He could not help but notice how they reminded him of the bright flaming ball that blew out from the tunnel where Audra had planted the explosives. Mike and Audra talked very little as they drove. For all intents and purposes, they looked merely like two rugged campers coming out of the mountains, rather than a duo of fierce-fighting soldiers, who had just been through quite a night.

When Mike reached Highway 92, he turned right and headed east. He squinted his eyes, as he looked into the bright sun, which had now trans-formed into a huge yellow ball. As Mike turned left on Palominas Road, he finally noticed a red crease on Audra's upper right shoulder, as she was lean-ing on him, nearly asleep.

"Audra, what happened to your shoulder?" Audra stirred a little, rubbed her eyes and looked at Mike. Mike couldn't help but glance at Audra's chest as she turned towards him. He could not help but notice how well Audra filled out her jogging suit. "There's a lot of woman in that suit!" exclaimed Mike to himself. However, his imagination calmed down as Audra spoke. "'Guess one of those pot shots back there managed to graze me. Tell y' the truth, I didn't even notice it until we left the canyon, but why complain?"

"Soon as we get you home, I'll fix y' up, Girl," replied Mike.

"Mike, we were fortunate we didn't get killed. Good thing those guys were just greenhorns, or this whole thing may have had a different ending."

"Speaking of greenhorns, I know you're anything but that. Audra, where did you learn how to shoot like you did back at the cave … and what about the bombs? I know you didn't read how to do that from your grandmother's cook-book!"

"I told you, Mike … my father's a *Green Beret*. He learned from the best. He taught me a lot, 'cause I showed great interest in his profession," said Audra calmly.

"Like father, like daughter," laughed Mike. Mike thought Audra seemed very different from other women, but now he knew she was in a class of her own. He drove on, satisfied. He loved this woman. Audra's answer was good enough for him.

When Mike drove into Audra's lane, Audra told him to pull around to the back of the house. Without questioning her, Mike drove the Cherokee behind the house as she directed him. They stopped just in front of a large patio door. Audra explained to Mike that she did not want her neighbors to see them car-rying anything that resembled combat uniforms, or suspicious-looking dark clothing, into the house. Mike totally agreed, suggesting that the same strat-egy had occurred to him, too, as they drove back from the cavern.

After emptying the Cherokee, and taking their gear inside, Mike and Audra collapsed on the sofa. Audra's father had already left the house to go to work. Audra told Mike he might lie on the sofa, if he wished. His body aching from head to toe, he readily accepted this invitation, as he pulled himself over the end of the sofa and stretched his legs out. Audra left Mike there in the living room, slowly walked to the back of the house, entered her room and plopped onto the bed. They were both physically and mentally drained ... exhausted from the deadly adventure they had experienced.

Chapter Eleven

Mike awoke with a start, sweat dripping off his forehead and arms; even his T-shirt felt damp. He had been dreaming about Bobby ... a nightmare. He saw grotesque, blurry faces carrying his brother into a crate, as Bobby screamed out in agony. They threw the crate, Bobby and all, into a musty old boxcar. They kept piling more and more crates, filled with innocent children, into the car. There seemed to be no end to the crates. They could not have cared less how roughly they handled the crates, as they tossed them recklessly about the boxcar. The children screamed as the evil men laughed louder and louder, and the crates piled up higher and higher. When the children screamed in bloody agony, and the crates gave way and began crushing the tender, living contents inside, Mike woke up.

He glanced over to look at Bobby's picture next to his bed on the nightstand, but it wasn't there. Something was wrong. He sat up and rubbed his eyes. As his eyes focused, he finally realized he was not in his own bed. He looked around the room. "Oh, Lord! That's right. I fell asleep on Audra's sofa. I'm in Audra's house." Mike told himself. Then the events of the early morning began playing back in his mind ... the guns roaring, the men, the cavern ... and the explosions. It all came vividly back to him. He rubbed his face vigorously with his hands. "Oh God, what a night!" Thoughts and questions raced through his mind. What had they done? What would be the consequences? How would the kingpins in such a lowlife operation as the one that they had discovered react to his and Audra's sabotage of their station last night? One thing he knew for sure ... no train would leave that depot for some time. They may have caused over a month of repairs. However, would the outfit choose an alternate route by which to transfer the children, drugs and weapons? Or, would some shipments be delayed? What of the children ... would they risk Moving them? As often was the case, Mike was once again thinking audibly.

"I hope they do, Mike." Mike turned to see Audra standing behind him.

"Audra, you're always startling me! How long have you been eavesdropping on my conversation with myself?"

"Long enough to give you a little input. First, if they move Bobby, we'll know about it. We know they use the large, white straight trucks with the slogan, *'Help us help the hungry,'* or something like that, to haul the children. They'd probably move them at night, so all we'd have to do is watch the roads carefully for these trucks, and follow them to wherever their destination—or destinations—may be. They'd risk a lot by moving the children … money, time … and the chance of getting caught," explained Audra.

"You have a very good point there, and I truly believe the children are somewhere very close to us … very close." Mike was thinking about the complex as he spoke.

"Now, on to another very important topic, Mike. While you were getting your well-deserved beauty sleep, I was listening to the news. Apparently, our little caper last night stirred up a hornet's nest. The local authorities and the press are all over the canyon. Of course, I figured they would be. They closed the park for investigation, so the press must be finding it difficult to get accurate information concerning the actual events that took place. All they know is that two Border Patrol men were shot to death last night. They have no idea who did it, or why. They know nothing about explosions. In addition, incredibly, they did not find Gringo or Raul. Moreover, the officers' bodies were nowhere near the cavern. One was found inside the Suburban, and the other was found twenty feet away from the patrol vehicle." Audra gazed at Mike steadily, as she sat next to him.

"Raul! He lived through the gunfire … *and* the fall!" Mike exclaimed. "He must have crawled out of the wreckage after we left the scene, and managed to notify his superiors. I'll bet they scrambled like bees after someone's britches, when they heard the news. They set the entire fiasco up to look like a simple case of two men having been shot while doing their duty. Now everyone will believe that some aliens or thugs plugged the officers while they were driving, and they simply drove off the road. One officer's remains were still in the vehicle and—to spice it up even more—they dramatically make it look like one was thrown from the Suburban. They are very good. Wow! Now they can keep the park closed for investigative purposes when, in reality, they are repairing the station!" Mike just shook his head at such manipulated deception.

"Actually, this may be a good thing," Audra said thoughtfully.

"You call two innocent officers getting shot a good thing!" Mike couldn't quite understand what she was getting at, at all.

"Of course not! My heart goes out to the force and the families of those poor officers. Mike, if foul play beyond just some bad men with guns was sus-

pected, the inquiries and the investigation that would follow would tie this matter up for many long days, and our evil men might even put the whole operation on ice until who knows when. Then your chances of finding Bobby would
weaken, also. Don't you see these people are desperate? They'll go to any
Lengths to keep on schedule. Last night's cover up is proof of this. These people reacted with impressive speed, and must have gone through a lot of pain
to carefully and swiftly set the stage as they did. But I can guarantee you that
they're very nervous now, in spite of having managed to pull that off to look like
what it did. They're ripe, and ready to make mistakes." Audra sounded very
confident.

"Man, you sound like you have experience in these matters," said Mike.

"I read a lot," replied Audra calmly, with a serene smile on her face.

Mike leaned back into the sofa. "I wonder if anyone saw us leaving the
canyon."

Audra answered Mike's question. "Actually, a couple witnessed a Jeep leaving the area, but it did not fit the description of the Cherokee. It sounded like a
CJ-7, with an open bed. You might want to keep the Cherokee out of sight for
another day or two, just to be safe, though."

"I'm not worried about it. It's my neighbor's down the road from me, and he
rarely even drives it. He stores it in a shed in back of his house, so it won't be
sitting in my driveway, anyhow."

"Oh yeah, I forgot about that. Hey, let's open that briefcase now. I'd like to
see what clues we can unfold this time!" exclaimed Audra. Audra rushed to the
pantry. Mike heard some clinging and clanging, as Audra shuffled through a
tool chest in the pantry. She returned with a small hand mallet and a chisel. "I
think this ought to break the lock off," suggested Audra.

Mike took the mallet and chisel from Audra. He set the case on the floor—
then he placed the edge of the chisel upon one of the locks. He came down
hard and accurately on the lock. The lock softened a little but held. After three
blows, the lock surrendered to the forced strikes. Mike then did this to the other
lock. He achieved the same results. Once they'd lifted the top from the briefcase, they were staring at a folded two-pocket leather notebook. Inside were
file folders, which contained forms and documents. The bottom of the case
contained a couple of maps, a calculator, and a small stainless steel .308
automatic handgun.

"Guns, guns, and more guns!" Audra commented.

"Yeah, these guys really love the wonderful world of weapons," said Mike
sarcastically. He flipped through the papers and forms. Therein they found similar numbers and nomenclature, such as that which they had seen on the
materials Mike had earlier confiscated from the straight truck.

Mike pulled out several other folders. They noticed a different type of information on these forms. They were also very interested in some of the lettering on these other forms; they appeared to be either Chinese or Korean. Audra looked the lettering up on the Internet, discovering that it was Chinese they had run across.

While Audra sat stunned a bit, taking it all in, Mike spoke. "Now we have the Chinese involved. South America was bad enough, but this is getting bigger all of the time. You know, Audra, we started out with an abduction, which then led us to a crime spree of abductions for possible labor purposes. Then we found out that the children are possibly being trained for combat. Then their involvement with weapons and drugs became apparent. Now, we have the Chinese involved, as well. Why? This is just too abstruse!" Mike felt overwhelmed.

Audra picked up where Mike left off. "Well, we've already covered the possibilities regarding the children. The weapons would help in the combat endeavors. I'm sure the children are being used for both labor and combat. The drugs are a prime source of revenue, no doubt." Audra stopped, allowing Mike to add whatever thoughts he might have on the lengthening laundry list of possibilities.

"Didn't we decide that these people probably wouldn't want to mess with risky drug lords and smuggling? Maybe they are not directly involved in the drugs. Maybe the rats are just letting the drug lords utilize the railroad to smuggle the goods into the U.S., and then the drugs are immediately dispersed. The rats would not be readily traced to the drugs that way, and they get a fat commission off the street sales!" boomed Mike. He felt like a case cracker now.

"That is a very good assumption, Mike, but it doesn't explain how the weapons are being smuggled, and where the arms are coming from," Audra pointed out. She went on to say, "There is an interesting shipment that is about to take place somewhere, according to this document." Audra held the document up in her hand. "Some place is about to receive a large quantity of *'FG's.'* You know …'*F. gametophytes.'* Then, after they arrive at the first destination, they are shipped off as '*flower blossoms'* to yet another destination."

"What other destination?" groaned Mike.

"I don't know. Those latitude and longitude numbers are on the paper, in spite of our not being able to read Chinese, Mike! We'll have to check into it. I'll get a globe." Audra marched out of the living room and, this time it was she who returned with a large globe. "I hope this will suffice," she said as she handed it to Mike. Mike studied the globe and told her it would work just fine. Audra read off the degrees and numbers. The first set took them to Panama. The other sets took them east to Beijing, China, along with Chengtu, Nanking, Shanghai and other locations in China.

"Wait, we're saying that many American girls are being shipped to China?" Mike scratched his head.

"It makes sense, Mike. Think about China. What are they presently doing right now?"

Mike searched his mind carefully. His IQ on current affairs was not exactly up-to-date, but it was not that rusty, either. "Well, I know right now that they are trying to take over Unocal, the parent company of Union Oil Company of California. They hold a major portion of our national debt. China is now a member of the World Trade Organization—which definitely gives them more world economic power and the right to more freedom in trade. Some of our major motor companies like Chevy and Ford and U.S. transnational companies, such as certain large discount stores, are heavily invested in China because of their cheap labor—and they practically own the Panama Canal, since we evacuated that area in 1999. They are hoarding tons of gold and other precious metals. China does not want to strengthen the U.S. Dollar by any means. Actually, they are trying to weaken it by staying with the Euro, and inviting other countries to do the same—which would push our dollar further down in value—while making China even stronger than we are. I guess it's fair to say they have us over a number of barrels," concluded Mike.

"That's very well put, my Big Hero, and I believe it ties into our case; maybe not directly, yet indirectly. The main point I'm trying to make focuses on our American girls. Mike, this document reads that over a thousand *'flower blossoms'* are to be sent to the cities in China we found on the globe, and do you know what major crisis China is facing right now?"

Mike groped his chin and rubbed it. He studied Audra. She was out of her jogging outfit, wearing a dark blue pair of slacks with a violet blouse, which made her look colorful and stunning. "Sure is a beautiful woman," mumbled a yet rather tired Mike.

"What'd you say?" asked Audra.

"Ah-h-h, I said ... I'm not sure, woman."

Audra gave Mike a steady looked and frowned. "Do you realize that all the selective abortions of recent years in China has led to a massive wife shortage over there? The Chinese men are buying women from North Korea. This is no public secret and, because of this, North Korea may either become militarily aggressive or collapse from within. This is not implausible. The issue is clear. The Koreans are unable to whet the appetites of over fifty million single men in China. Korean women work hard for these men and, it's safe to say, some American women would, also. I happen to know of a place off the coast of Hawaii that has sold American women to China before. The FBI put an end to that ring, but this makes that ordeal look like a walk in the park."

Mike listened attentively. Audra was making too much sense to take what she said lightly. He thought for a moment then spoke. "We have the Bolivians, the Colombians, the Peruvians and whoever else in South America, and now—*Look out*—here comes China! Audra, what I think we really need to do is to remain focused on our own backyard. The horrible truth is that there are some people—possibly even in high places—in cahoots with these mystery men in South America and China and wherever else they may be. We may not be able to track down the kingpins in other countries right now, but I do believe that we can at least uncover some slime within this country. We already have a list of very hot suspects. We have good reason to believe the Mayor, Dennis Perris, and Sheriff Joe Tress are all involved."

Audra interrupted Mike. "Throw Cal Brown into that list, also."

Mike looked at Audra with eyes glaring in shock. The thought of Cal being involved in such crimes almost staggered him. He'd known Cal too long for a surprise like this. He swallowed hard. "What did you say?"

"Back in the cavern, I asked one of the men for a name. I thought he'd give me his. Instead, he said, *'Cal Brown.'* Go figure."

"It doesn't figure! Maybe he heard Cal's name mentioned in town and used it?"

"I would love to believe that, Mike, but I told him that if he lied, my superiors would know this, and kill him. Mike, after what I did to those men, I truly believe the man. He was so scared, I thought for sure he'd leave a deposit in his dungarees! 'Probably did."

Mike dropped back onto the sofa, covered his face with his hands, and sat silently for a moment. He could not believe … could not absorb such information … that Cal, a man so gentle, kind and understanding could possibly be involved in all this. After all, they had abducted Cal's son! Did Cal allow his son's abduction out of greed … or to cover up his involvement in the affair … or both? He finally spoke. "I … I just can hardly believe Cal could be involved in all this."

"Mike, I don't want to believe it either! But I can't deny what I heard, and under such circumstances that would make it hard for anyone to dare lie."

"And, so, the plot thickens," Mike, overcome with disappointment, commented.

"And how thick it is." Audra walked into the kitchen to retrieve a hot cup of coffee, asking Mike if he wanted a cup, also. He refused her offer, reminding her that he needed to drive the Cherokee back to his neighbor's house as soon as possible, and then he had some chores to do. Audra asked Mike if she could keep the folder containing the *'blossom'* shipments to China.

"Audra, my gosh! Of course you can. As a matter of fact, I want you to keep the metal briefcase, also; it will be much safer with you. We'll take it to the authorities after things cool down a little."

"No, Mike, I don't want the briefcase."

"Audra, when I spoke with Dennis, it felt more like a Russian KGB interrogation than a pleasant conversation. I know they are onto me. If they even imagine I've been around that cavern, they'll waste no time coming after me. They find this briefcase in my possession, and they'll probably kill me."

"Mike, you are paranoid; just put it in a safe place, OK?"

Mike surrendered to Audra's wishes. As he turned to walk out he said, "I'll stick it under the floor in my room. I have a little hideaway there. Then I'll take it to the authorities as soon as I get a chance." Mike walked out the patio door, threw Audra a kiss, and drove off.

Audra stood at the door, a distant look on her face. "Yeah, Mike, I have chores to do, too." She walked into the living room, picked up her phone, and began dialing.

When Mike arrived at his house, he half expected the place to be in shambles. He thought the evil men surely knew about him, and would want to extract anything from his house that might prove him and Audra guilty. However, when the door swung open, the only thing that seemed different than when he had left the house was the coffee smell. What had a pleasant, fresh aroma when he poured it many hours ago now exuded a stale odor. Mike walked over to the coffee table where the stale mug sat in front of his leather sofa. He looked at it and smiled, mumbling, "Maybe I am paranoid. Well, Lord, if you were in my shoes, I'll bet you'd be paranoid, too."

Mike pressed the main button on his answering machine. The display indicated two calls. Mike wondered why there were only two calls on the machine—then he remembered that he had only been away for one night and morning, though so much had happened in the interim that it felt as though he had been away for a week. Dennis Perris' voice boomed over the speaker. "Hi, Mike. 'Hope you're feeling all right. Are you there? Hey! Pick up. Well, I hope you're not sore at me, Mike. I apologize for being so aggressive the other day." There was a long pause, then he continued. "Well, 'guess you're not there. Take care ... and God bless." The message ended with a beep.

Then Cal's voice—Cal Brown, of all people—came over the machine. "Mike, I'm so glad you could make the support group. Next one's on Wednesday. 'Hope to see you. If you need to talk to anyone, you've got my number." Mike dropped to the sofa, tired and confused. He still found it hard to believe that Cal could be involved in all this.

Mike looked out the big picture window facing the Huachuca Mountains. Miller and Huachuca Peaks stood ominously in the center. "Huachuca Mountains ... who would believe that at the foothills of this range lay death and such a horrifying secret? So many suspicious people all conspiring in the mountains." He had to almost laugh, as a fitting moniker for all this came to mind, which he spoke with more bravado than his recent mumbled musings: "It's like one big, bloody *Huachuca Conspiracy!*"

Mike walked slowly to his bedroom. He saw Bobby's picture face down, just as he had left it before calling Matt. Mike snatched the picture up with his right hand. As tears rolled down his cheeks, he tenderly stroked Bobby's face with his fingers. "Bobby, I'm so sorry. I wish ... I ... Oh, God! I can't bear this pain. Why not me!" screamed Mike, as he looked up at the ceiling, as though expecting a reply. Nevertheless, there was no reply forthcoming ... no voice of assurance echoed corner and shout, "Hey, Mike!" There was no banging ... nor any bumping noises ... coming from Bobby's room; no laughter or '*vroom-vroom!*' noises could be heard from Bobby's mouth.

After this bit of reminiscing, Mike called Matt on his cell phone for an update. Matt had little to report; in fact, he sounded rather sharp over the phone. Apparently, Matt was taking the case very seriously, which was good news, in spite of his tone. His drinking binge was over ... at least temporarily. Mike asked Matt to check Cal Brown's background very thoroughly. He also told him to follow him from time to time, as well. Matt protested that an army would be needed to follow all the people he was required to keep track of. Mike, therefore, consented to giving him another $200.00 a week, so Matt could hire a cheap rent-a-cop to help him out.

As Mike hung up the phone, he thanked God that he had plenty of money to fund his endeavors in trying to find Bobby. "God, I've been a little angry with you lately. Could it be you allowed our parents and grandparents to be taken from us so that I'd have the resources with which to find my brother?" Mike laid his head on his pillow. The thought seemed so ugly and cruel ... such a horrible exchange of lives, if this came anywhere near the truth of why things had happened as they did. Mike, therefore, rid his mind of such a thought. He drifted into a state of despair as his eyelids closed. Within just a few minutes, he had fallen asleep.

Audra's father walked through the front door to see Audra looking over some papers she had scattered across the living room floor. "What in blazes are you doing, Little Girl?"

"I've been doing some homework, Dad."

"On the carpet?"

"Yep, and I must say that it makes for a great table."

"Well, I'll try not to step on your project, Audra."

Audra's voice became very sober, as she said, "Daddy, we need to talk."

"'Sounds like a serious father/daughter thing coming up," said Patrick.

"Yeah, we need to talk woman to man. That's much stronger than a man-to-man conversation." Audra laughed at her own words.

Pat sat beside Audra on the sofa. He laid his overcoat on one arm of the couch, hugged his little girl and smiled at her. "She's big and brave, but she'll always be my little girl," he thought.

"Daddy, did you hear anything about two officers getting shot to death in the Huachuca Mountains early this morning?"

"Yeah, as a matter of fact I did. 'Some desperate *'illegals'*—probably. Our post also picked up a tremor from that area. Strange, lot of action in the mountains last night."

Audra stirred uneasily where she sat. She flexed her shapely legs until her knees touched her chest. Audra hugged her knees as she spoke, "Pa, I need your help."

"Need my help? You must have some heavy duty homework there," laughed Pat.

"Actually, I wish it were that simple. Pa, I think … no, I *know* what happened to Todd. I believe he still may be alive."

Pat stood up and walked into the kitchen. He opened a cupboard, took out a glass, and then he opened the fridge, retrieving a cold bottle of Coors *Cutter's*. He poured the non-alcoholic beer into the glass and walked back to where Audra was sitting, having thought about what she said this entire time. Sitting down on the sofa again, Pat raised his glass to his mouth and took a big swallow. "Ah-h-h, yes! Now that hit the spot!" Then becoming serious once again, and returning to the original subject, Patrick said, "Okay, Audra, let's go over this quickly, so I can put you and me both at ease."

"Wait, before you get all worked up, Dad, just listen … please," Audra pleaded.

Pat fidgeted a bit on the sofa, debating how much to say … how much of which he should dare to remind Audra. In the end, he could not hold back. "Audra, don't you remember what happened to you when Todd disappeared … the lampoons, the disciplinary action, the inquiries, the cheap shots—not to mention how it affected your mother? Do you want to start that all over again?"

"My, God, what difference does it make now? I don't belong to them anymore! And I did it for mother … you know that! The doctors had said that she stood a very good chance of recovering from her condition if she knew one way or the other. It didn't matter if Todd was dead or alive, as much as it mattered knowing whether he was alive or not. The nightmares and bitter anguish of *not* knowing where Todd was, or if he was still alive, was that which drove her insane ... and it's driving you and me both insane, too, it seems!

"Daddy, they took me off Todd's case by *force*. I wasn't even supposed to be assigned his case in the first place, because he was ... no, *is* ... my brother. The Department's regulations will not assign agents to a case involving a family member, as they might allow their emotions to hinder progress, or might act irrationally. Well, I took my chances. I said *'Bull!'* to all their stupid regulations, and I got very close to a discovery that led us to Tucson. And I would have gone further, but the darned Department caught up with me, not only taking me off the case, but branding me an insubordinate, finally hospitalizing me due to an absurdly false mental diagnosis. Todd's trail was leading further south, and now I know where. I know *where*, Dad!"

Patrick hugged his daughter as tears fell from her pretty brown eyes. "There-there, Little Girl. You know I love you more than life ... but, Honey, we have to stop living in the past. We need to look to the future. That's why we moved here ... to create a new life, and to start afresh."

Audra's tears turned to anger. In any case, how could her father just throw in the towel without allowing her to explain? She bit her bottom lip. They were living in a make-believe world, and she, for one, had had enough.

"No! We moved out here to hide ... and become recluses. We live in fear ... fear that Mother will never be the same again ... fear of being discovered that we live in fear ... fear of the past. We keep running from it! What shall we do ... keep running? Keep living in fear, never knowing if there was at least a possible chance to find out what happened to Todd? Do we even fear looking for Todd in case, when he is found, he will be found dead rather than alive? What if Todd *is* alive ... and we don't keep trying to find him! If he's found alive, will we then constantly live in fear that the monster that stole him from us will take him away again?

"God knows we're tired of living like this, Pa! You can't keep going on like you do. You are so unhappy and discouraged, not knowing anything for sure. When you're not working, you're all alone ... or sleeping an awful lot ... which can definitely be a good escape mechanism from all the pain you've carried these past few years. I think, too, that Mother deserves to know the truth, good or bad."

Patrick sat stunned ... quiet. He knew every word Audra had uttered was true.

"Wh ... what do you want me to do?" he asked, trembling a bit, feeling so uncertain about coming up with anything viable on his own.

Audra calmed down as she looked deeply into her father's blue eyes that were pleading for answers. For the first time, she realized why she loved Mike's eyes so much ... they looked very much like her father's eyes.

"Daddy, just hear me out, and if I don't make any sense to you—or I sound crazy—then tell me you won't try. But if I do make sense, and what I tell you does seem viable enough to stir in you the belief ... the least bit of hope ... that Todd could still be alive, then you've got to promise you'll help me!"

Patrick sat silently, seriously contemplating Audra's plea while, at the same time, wanting to protect her from a repeat of what had occurred shortly after Todd was taken from them. He had left the post this afternoon, hoping for a peaceful night at home ... and now this. "Okay, Little Girl, I'll listen."

Audra began telling her father everything she and Mike had discovered so far ... about the tunnel ... the metal plate, and where that had led her and Mike. She even revealed their disappointment in some unlikely people—people they previously had thought they knew well ... even admired—suspected of being involved in these heinous activities. She told Pat everything. She repeated some things Mike and she had already told him earlier, but in much greater detail. Then she admitted to him that they knew about ... yea, had even caused ... the slight tremor his Department has detected in the cavern.

Straightaway, she held the shipping forms in front of her father's face and explained what the coded words stood for, how the girls were called 'F. Gametophytes,' or flowers ... blossoms ... roses, and the boys were being referred to as 'bee pollen,' or even vegetables. While showing him the latitude and longitude lines, indicating where on the globe the particular degrees would take them, Patrick's eyes nearly bulged in disbelief—mixed with excitement—when he saw her finger move to certain regions of South America, Panama and even China. As they continued studying the documents together, they realized there were even more messages to be decoded that had previously eluded Mike and Audra:

'Candy canes' referred to AK-47s, 'PEZ dispensers' was code for magazines and cartridges, and 'Graham Crackers' took the place of grenades. Then there were the 'Pop Tart' rockets and rocket launchers. Finally, 'Corn Pops' meant M-16s, and 'Sugar Daddies' equaled AK-74s.

Pat spoke now. "All these dastardly items have been given names that could make one's mouth water. They're all food items of some sort, except for the flowers. And 'Pixie Dust' is probably a drug, like crack, for all we know," he continued. Pat was sharp and someone who caught on quickly. Audra knew by now that her father believed her, but she wanted to help solidify his belief, so she proceeded to produce a magazine from an AK-47 that she had confiscated from one of the gunman's rifles during the conflict in the cavern. Pat looked carefully at the magazine. "All Russian, and apparently made not too long ago, judging by the texture. I know why you need my help now. I remember the other night when Mike shared the time zone theory with us, as well as the encoded use of latitude and longitude lines … I really began to feel a twinge of hope. Now it feels more like a *jolt!* This operation has grown into a monster, and you and Mike are not able to take some steps that I can. Tell me … do you suspect military involvement?"

"Yes, I do, Daddy. I believe that someone with a bit of clout at Fort Huachuca is somehow responsible for the weapons trafficking into Mexico, and further south. The horrible tragedy here is the betrayal of Country, due to greed."

"Audra, I believe that the Chinese, along with some nations in South America, already have some of their men established in high places of our government. It is safe to consider that this is a well-planned operation to weaken the U.S…. economically, socially, militarily, and morally. One day, if this keeps going on, we'll be ripe for a *coup d'etat* and all the men and women behind these heinous crimes have, no doubt, been promised money and high positions of status for pulling it off. Too bad they don't know the enemy like I know the enemy. Their *'reward'* will come in the form of a cheap piece of hot lead between their betraying, buggy little eyes."

Audra and her father talked on well into the night. They took a quick meal break, then returned and began to lay down more plans. Finally, her father told Audra he needed to think about bed. He had grown a bit overwhelmed by the conversation. Yet, as Pat entered his room after showering and brushing his teeth, he felt the steady growth of excitement, and adrenaline pumping through his veins. He even found himself smiling, as a familiar old military tune—about a group of which he was once a part, and still identified with somewhat—began running through his head. He began to sing, victoriously, the old *"Green Beret"* anthem.

Patrick felt great. He now had a revived mission … for his wife … for Todd … for Audra … and for his country. He'd not felt this good since the first Gulf War. He shook his head, almost not daring to believe it. Todd was most likely still around, after all … somewhere. This most assuredly would also mean that he now had a chance of getting his wife back. Prematurely or not, Pat's hopes could not help but begin to soar. This rather reserved gentleman even let out a laugh, as he smiled to himself, recalling how—when life had been more normal than the last few years had been—his wife had such a sense of humor, that he sometimes had referred to her as *'one rip-roaring hoot.'* Feeling rather excited at the moment, Pat lifted his phone from his nightstand and dialed Mike's number.

Mike sat in his office studying all the documents and forms Audra and he had stolen from the cavern. He pondered the word *'stolen'* for just a moment. "Ah, soon the authorities will have all these folders, and I don't think they'll consider it a theft. They would have done the same thing. Why should I feel the least bit guilty about taking something that could save the lives of hundreds— maybe thousands—of innocent Americans?" This thought faded, as Mike's phone rang.

"Hello, this is Mike."

A familiar voice stimulated Mike's eardrum. "Hi! Good evening, Mike. This is Colonel Heyburn." Pat used his title, hoping to capture Mike's complete respect. "Mike, I would really appreciate your company tomorrow around 1430 hours, or I mean 2:30 in the afternoon. In fact, I insist."

Mike stirred a bit uncomfortably. He had really wanted to spend the day snooping for more clues. He had questions that needed answering. He had found a few strange names among the files in the metal briefcase, and he wanted to check them out. He'd thought about asking Raymond to help with this matter. Maybe, along with helping him research the names, Raymond could also check the briefcase and papers therein for fingerprints. Just as he thought of a good excuse to bail out of the Colonel's invitation, he thought about Audra. "Sure, Colonel Heyburn! It would be an honor to talk with you."

"Actually, I've heard you are a fair golfer." Pat's smile traversed the phone lines.

"Well, I'm about average. I have come close to par a few times, though, and once I actually got lucky and came in under. But, I'm a far cry from being a hot competitor."

"'Sounds good to me. I'm no prize turkey myself, Mike. I just want to get to know you better, Son. See you around two-thirty, then?

"It's a date, Colonel."

"And, Mike, please just call me Pat." Mike heard a click before he could respond. He stood there a bit bewildered.

"Hmmm ... introduces himself as *'Colonel,'* and then leaves as *'Pat.'* If he was trying to get my attention, he did a good job." Mike hung up the phone and returned to his work. He took a pen in hand and began writing names, and recently seen strange words, in a spiral notebook.

Five dark figures gathered around a long, wooden table in the back room of a building where special members of the Lodge met. Near the middle of the table on one side could be seen the shadow of a man sitting in a padded swivel chair, with his back turned away from the others, as he stared at a dark wall. Opposite this one staring at the wall sat four others in the semi-darkness.

They had all arrived at the Deer Lodge early in the morning, while most people still lay dreaming in bed. The men said very little at first, speaking quietly among themselves. The shadowy figure that sat alone apparently held a higher position than did the other four, and he had yet to begin the meeting. After another few moments of quiet chatter, the leader—or speaker—turned his chair about and faced his audience. "Shall we begin, gentlemen?" The others acknowledged his presidence over the group.

"Last night, two intruders infiltrated our establishment. We have yet to identify who these intruders are, or what their purpose was for being there. Our security cameras took a beating, but the durable recording boxes did manage to stay intact. We do have a man's voice on tape. We thoroughly questioned the guards. They insisted that the two men, wearing ninja-like outfits, were highly trained professionals, who either work for one of our clients, or want us to believe they do.

"One of them—the man we have on tape—explained that we are not exactly living up to their expectations. Now, I called the good General in Bolivia and explained this problem to him. He seems to be at quite a loss ... or so he says. He told me he would immediately look into the matter ... especially when he discovered how destructive the two men had been. You see, gentlemen, he—as we all are—is in this for profit, and every minute we waste due to this infernal blast in the cavern costs us dearly.

"The General's Chinese allies are very concerned. You can imagine the pitiful looks on their young men's faces when they hear that their American wives will not arrive in China on schedule. This entire incident has cost us in time, money and lives. We lost one of our inventory specialists and, unfortunately, one of the guards opened his obtuse mouth and let a name slip out of it. We had to dispose of such garbage. Anyone that cares to freely give out information about this operation—or the people involved—may join him in the refuse."

"What of the other guard? How is park management responding to the incident?" asked one of the mysterious figures. His voice sounded a bit muffled and syrupy.

The one presiding answered, "The park rangers are of no concern. They still believe our operation is of federal importance, so they are more help than a hindrance. As for the guards, I had them airlifted to a Mexican hospital directed by one of our links in South America. Pretty little Mexican nurses are mending their wounds this very minute ... as we speak, so I am sure they will enjoy their stay. However, two of them will never walk normally again, but we do take care of our own. Don't you agree?" Having seen the resulting consequences of others disagreeing with their superior, all there readily nodded their heads, indicating a uniform consensus.

Another spoke up. "All was not a loss; the last shipment of candy made it across the border, and we did manage to salvage a considerable amount of dust. Also, as no children were being shipped that night, we did not lose any of them." His voice had a familiar ring to it, though Matt could not quite place it.

"True," began yet another, "but now we are faced with a costly layover. Who knows how much we've lost because of these two menaces! Huachuca produce took quite a hit over this; good thing we are a non-profit! Because of that, our beloved—albeit deceived—supporters are stepping up to the plate with lots of money to help us out." The leader now stood up, his face almost visible in the low lighting.

"C'mon you, tin soldier, move your visage into the light like a good sport," thought Matt to himself. He had a good spectator's view, just outside the room where they were meeting, as this room—a small library—had no door. He thought, "They certainly must feel extremely safe here, to meet together without peripheral personnel surrounding the premises." Though the entrance to the dimly lit room wound through a small corridor, Matt still thought the men were unwise to choose a room with no door. Actually, Matt had to admit that he never would have dreamed anyone would be inside the Deer Lodge at this hour in the morning. He knew he would not be here himself, had he not tailed Cal Brown to this place. Mike had asked him to stick close to Cal for awhile, and it had paid off.

After listening to the men talk a short while, Matt knew that if these men discovered him, his body would turn up in a refuse dump, or worse. Wearing a small tape recorder inside his dark overcoat, the sometimes absentminded Matt was fretfully wondering if he had brought his recorder that made no noise when the tape ended, or had he inadvertently picked up the one that clicked when it ran out of tape. He quivered at the thought of being discovered—of his fate possibly being sealed—due to some errant 'click.'

Sneaking inside the Lodge had proven to be easier than Matt had thought it would be. Cal arrived first and unlocked the door to the Lodge. When Cal entered the building, Matt crept over to the side of the entrance and stood in the darkness, which was a good thing, as Cal had returned after only a moment. Cal then walked out into the dark parking lot, and peered down the road, as though expecting company. It was then that Matt had picked up a small limb and tossed it into some brush to Cal's left. As Cal was investigating the cause of the noise, Matt simply opened the door a smidgen and slipped his thin body through it, unnoticed. Once inside, he had found a dark corner in the Lodge, and hidden there until all the men had arrived and taken their places. It was not until he heard them talking that he dared begin moving around, carefully searching all around for a sentry, as he followed the voices to the back room. Now, here he was … after stealthily succeeding to be where he could hear every word … in the precarious position of his life possibly depending on some dratted *'click!'* Matt just could not get that possibility out of his mind.

The leader continued. "We must maintain. We cannot afford to grow nervous now. I explained to the General and Mr. Hooah that it will only take two or three weeks to clear out the mess those two malefactors caused at the station. In the meantime, we will beef up security, and keep training the children. The General is sending some men our way to help clear the cavern. This will speed up the process." The leader stalled for a moment. "Speaking of children, what is the latest update?"

A ghostly-appearing figure at the end of the table spoke up. "They are doing very well; as a matter of fact, a couple of the boys—especially one named Bobby—show an extreme amount of leadership potential." The voice was feminine and very soothing … even sexy. Matt thought that she must be a very attractive lady to have a voice like that … until he remembered some female disc jockeys that had sounded very pretty until he met them in person. "What a disgusting thought!" Matt said to himself, momentarily distracted from his possible *'click'* dilemma. The honey-laden female voice continued. "Bobby is helping me with the others. He is very brilliant … a born leader … and he's truly beginning to believe his brother allowed him to be chosen. His knowledge in self-defense impresses me, as well. He told me that he and his brother trained at the same karate academy."

"Well, well … they did, huh?" said one of the other gloomy figures.

The woman, sensing suspicion in the man's voice, felt she must inquire of him: "And you are referring to?"

"Just going through some combinations in my mind. I am hoping to link someone to the scene of the explosion last night. The guards said that the perpetrators were well trained in combat."

The leader interrupted the conversation. "Listen, the devastation that took place last night was not due to a little *'gnat.'* His girlfriend, as far as I'm concerned, is probably more a potential threat than he; the *'gnat'* is just a nursing student all busted up inside because he lost his little brother. He's going to continue acting paranoid and strange. His girlfriend, on the other hand, has a very interesting background. She once held a spot as a special undercover agent for the government. Our intelligence in D.C. was only able to attain so much information. To probe any further would require express written authority from higher sources, whose cages we really do not want to rattle at this time. We do know that she probably was professionally trained in weapons, and some form of combat, but not too long after graduating from her class, the feds escorted her to a mental hospital where they rewarded her with walking papers. She came close to receiving a dishonorable discharge. I think her father's reputation as a Colonel in the Army, who has an impeccable record, helped prevent such a tragedy."

"Maybe it's the Colonel of whom we should beware!" exclaimed yet another heretofore-silent phantom-like figure.

"Let's not let our minds run amok. The Colonel's alibis are far too strong. How could the Colonel be in two places at one time? He arrived at the Fort at 4:30 in the morning ... the same time the assassins almost killed—if I may use the word—poor Raul here. I personally know the Colonel. I can assure you he knows nothing ... zilch."

"I was there," began Raul, "and I saw what these two men did. It was *not* some wayward nursing student and a crazed ex-agent that pulled it off. These guys moved too quickly ... acted too smooth and clever. No, these guys were pros."

"So, what do we do next?" asked the man with the familiar voice.

"We go on with our normal lives, for heaven's sake! Sure, we will keep our eyes peeled for ninja men, but they are probably in another country by now. The train will run after the twenty-eighth and, with the General's help, we'll soon be right back on schedule again. The next shipment of candy arrives from Clarkdale in two days. I shall store it in the old dump until the cavern is fit for delivery. People, there is *nothing* to fear. Now, let us be on our way.

"Oh, yes ... one more thing." The evil leader stuck his face further into the light as he spoke, and his voice became somewhat sinister, as though the devil himself were speaking. "The kind General in Bolivia has decided to honor us with an appearance of our friend who never failed us yet. He's sending El Niño our way." Murmurs filled the room as the woman and men began to rise. The leader spoke again. "This meeting is over...."

'Click.' The leader looked at the other members, as a trembling Matt silently crept away from the entrance as fast as he could. "Blast it, anyway! I did grab the bloody wrong recorder!" Matt scolded himself, as he made his way back towards the dark corner of the building where he had hidden earlier. He looked back to see lights bobbing and bouncing all around the building. He did not have to be brilliant to figure out that the many rays of lights that shot out through the darkness in every direction were flashlights. Crouching as lowly as he could in the dark corner, he wondered why they did not turn the lights on. The answer slapped him so hard in the face, he felt a little embarrassed.

"You are a bloody, bloomin' idiot, Matthew Piper. Old man, you're getting a tad too rusty. Of course the blokes don't want to flood the building with light!

Why, they'd catch every policeman's eye from here to Tombstone if they did that, and then they'd have to explain why they were holding their little tea party so early, in the dark wee early hours of the morning," said the private eye to himself.

They searched frantically all over the building, while Matt—as crumpled into the corner as he could possibly get to avoid detection—sat there sweating it out. It was not only Matt who was trembling, but the entire group was trembling from the noise they had heard. It's like that when one has less than a clear conscience, you know? Who was spying on them ... how did he—or she—get into the Lodge? Many questions raced through their minds as their hearts beat rapidly and their breathing became more labored. The leader noticed their panic. He sighed, and shook his head. He knew that—unless they kept calm and cool—one of them was bound to crack and slip up ... say a name ... or even reveal their own identity within the group.

"Calm down everybody. There has to be a very logical explanation for this," said the leader.

"And, I think I just found it. Icky-y-y! A big, fat rat!" shrieked the woman. They all shined their lights where the woman was holding hers. There in front of them stood a moderately sized rat. The rat looked into the band of light rays for a moment, as a deer transfixed by headlights, and then he quickly turned and disappeared behind a dark wall.

"Ah, Kay, thank you! Listen, people, if we persist walking around like a bundle of nerves, we will soon become time bombs ready to explode. We are probably up against a competitor, foreign or domestic. I am sure they would love nothing better than to thwart our smooth operation so they can step in and seal a deal with our clients. That will happen if we fold. But if we unite, we will win out in the end. Just go home and get some sleep now. We all deserve it."

The group members all mumbled at one another. They knew their leader was right. They turned and carefully left the premises—all but Matt, for they had unknowingly locked him inside. Matt sat in the corner still, expecting at any moment to be discovered, having no idea that he was now all alone in the dark, dreary confines of the Deer Lodge. He dared not step out from his corner, lest he be discovered. So, he elected to sit tight and try to breathe easily, thankful he'd not been discovered up to this point ... never before having felt so indebted to one measly old rat as he was this morning.

"Easy does it now, Matt. Lon-n-ng silent breaths ... like this," Matt silently coached himself. Suddenly it happened. "Ahhh-*choo!* Oh, man! I'm dead!" Matt squinted his eyes tightly, ready for the bullet to enter his gullet, or the painful knife to slice through his bloody British throat. However, silence followed Matt's sneeze. After a minute or two, he forced his left eyelid open just a hair, looking somewhat like the Chinese inspector Charley Chan, studying a legal form with an eyeglass. Seeing nothing, Matt studied his environment a bit more. "Well, I'm still alive. They must be gone." However, Matt remained seated awhile longer; he did not want to rush out just yet. What if one of those diabolical men or woman had come back for something they'd forgotten? Or, what if they had heard him sneeze, and were waiting for him to reveal himself before letting him know he indeed had been heard? Matt could be sure of nothing, due to that dratted machine he'd brought, with its nerve-wracking *'click!'* Poor Matt was still quaking in his inspector boots, though it had been quiet in the Lodge for quite a spell. "I am just a bit old for these late night parties! Ah, well. I am alive." Matt elected to wait it out a little longer before daring to try the door.

Chapter Twelve

A young man no more than thirty years of age lay in his warm, heated waterbed. He looked up at the ceiling, trying to clear his mind, so he could sleep. However, sleep would not come … it seemed hopeless. He had yearned for a mission for weeks, yet no calls … no notes in the mail—nothing. "Maybe I do my job too well. I leave no *'comebacks,'* while only eliminating those that pose a true threat. Maybe I should not be so thorough. I could leave a little debris behind. This would allow an open door for more work to do." He spoke with a Latino accent. His high cheekbones, chiseled-out jaw and face, along with his thick, dark well groomed hair, composed a look which could be considered nothing less than dashing. In certain places—his bronze complexion only adding to his manly beauty—he had even been mistaken for a celebrity; he certainly had similar leisure time, as someone of such status might.

He lived in exurbia, just outside La Paz, Bolivia … a location chosen knowing the Bolivian officials cared little about the poor, for the most part. Here he would not be harassed. Officials never frequented this part of town, suspecting no one to be involved in any major criminal activity. Their visits to this part of town were mainly the rare response to a small fight, or petty theft. He was here, in part, because his mother and father lived here, also. He remembered the days as a young boy when his father would preach from their *casita* to people in the pueblo. His father certainly knew how to make *El Señor—Dios—* come to life, carefully using his gift of gab. Eventually, they were able to build a chapel, in which the people of the pueblo could gather to worship. The young man laughed within himself, recalling when he had told his father that some day he would make it big, and then he would help his poor mother and father. His father, a very loving man, held his son close to him and said, "God always provides, my son. If you become rich and famous one day and can help your Papa and Mama, then I guess we won't complain."

As a boy, the young man studied much harder than others did. Though his father needed him very much in the fields to help him with the cotton, rice, sugar and fruit, he made sure the boy kept up with his studies. He felt defeated at times, for his father had to compete with some well-to-do farmers and traders. Not owning the large transport trucks some of the others owned, his father would make deals with the men, allowing them a commission from the crop sales, if they would take his staples to the market for him. Papa could not afford to pay to transfer the crops by train. Their life of hardship changed somewhat when Manuel, the young man, grew older. Papa's prodding him to keep up with his studies had paid off; having earned terrific grades, he found himself in a university in Bogotá, Colombia.

While there, he met some very interesting people. As time went on, he became familiar with the Colombian-Bolivian Mafia. His superb intelligence landed him a position in the syndicate, where he soon learned about weapons and explosives, becoming an expert in sabotage. Yet his heart yearned for adventure. He loved action. He also had an uncanny way of reading people ... and locating them. The Mafia's despots, who were at one time leaders in the Colombian Cali and Medellin drug cartels, noticed this and, after assigning him a few missions of espionage and assassinations, they realized just how excellent he was. Manuel was very versatile. He could change a condition to suit his needs very well, and he easily adjusted to his adversaries' techniques to counter his enemy's plans. Nobody was as good as Manuel was. Due to his unpredictable nature, his colleagues dubbed him *'El Niño.'* Manuel's adversaries began to tremble at this name. Sometimes his superiors' antagonists would give in to an agreement at the mere mention of *'El Niño.'* Because Manuel had become such a force with which to reckon, he found himself in a position to name his own price.

However, Manuel knew better than to boast too loudly. The prices for his service were steep, yet reasonable, according to syndicate standards. He found himself growing quite wealthy. Never one to be stingy, Manuel gave much to his family. Even though he told his mother and father he was a successful young executive for a large legal firm, his father sensed Manuel was not telling them everything. This son of a preacher laughed, and hugged his father, when Pedro Martinez, Manuel's father, would question him about the money.

Manuel stirred a little, causing his half-motion waterbed to send soft waves over his spine and neck. "Ah-h-h!" he emoted, in no hurry to get out of bed. He began thinking again about the day his father had said to him, "Promise me, my Son, no matter where you are, or whatever you do, you will always put God first in your life." Manuel saw the hurt look in his father's eyes when he could not answer him. He saw the tears … he knew he had broken his Papa's heart that day.

The phone rang and Manuel quickly answered it. "Yes," said Manuel.

He recognized the General on the other end of the line. "El Niño, you must pack your things for travel. I have a flight already booked to take you to Bogotá. There we will discuss your next mission. After we talk, you tell us what you shall need for this op." He heard a click. The phone went dead as his fax Machine turned on and spit out a few documents.

Manuel became very excited. He jumped to his feet and pulled the flight confirmation from the machine. "Ah, yes, finally I am needed again. Oh! This letter speaks of the United States. Wonderful! I love the beautiful ladies in America," Manuel spoke aloud, in his charming Latinic accent the ladies just adored.

Matt tried to find a comfortable position in the dark corner; however, it eluded him. He finally gave up and decided it was time for him to take his chances, before his crouching position became permanent; after all, he was no *'young punk,'* anymore. He rose quietly to his feet and walked into one of the offices in the Deer Lodge. He pulled a small penlight from his shirt pocket and searched the room. His eyes fell upon a plush leather chair. He had barely started walking towards the chair when he stumbled, sending a metallic-like noise bouncing off the walls. "Shhh, be quiet or you'll wake the dead, Matt!" he chided himself. He sat on the chair, catching his breath. While he rested, he noticed his body and hands shook more than usual. He tried to tell himself it was just nerves, yet Matt had faced tighter predicaments than this and never shaken so much. He gave in, finally admitting the fact that his body was undergoing a long detoxification period, and that he would just have to endure. "Should I? No. Yes, I should. But what if I'm heard talking? OK … I'll call," he finally decided, thus ending this argument with himself. With that, Matt dialed Mike's number.

Mike lay sleeping in his bed when the phone rang. He jumped with a start. Sweat running down his face. He wiped the sweat away and answered the phone. "Ah … Mike here. Hello?" he answered, questioningly, this being a rather unearthly time for a phone call. Mike heard a faint noise coming from the phone. "Hello," he said again. Hearing more muffled sounds, he continued, "I can't hear you too well." Then Mike noticed he was talking into the receiver end of the phone. Quickly he turned the phone around and began speaking into the correct end. "Hello?"

"By Jove, m' Lad! There you are … finally. I just wanted to let you know that I'm stuck in the Deer Lodge. Can you get me out?"

"No, the only person I know that can is Cal Brown. I'll call him." Then Mike caught himself, his brain beginning to focus in on the conversation.

"Wait, I can't do that! I think he's a suspect."

"Mike … Lad, clear your mind. I must have awakened you."

Mike looked around the room. He rubbed his eyes and face. He tried to wake up, but his mind felt fuzzy … a little numb. Mike resorted to an old trick he'd learned long ago that he knew would help him wake up. He lowered his head between his knees. The blood flow returned to his brain, and he began to speak more coherently. "Okay, Matt, tell me what happened."

"Well, I followed Cal to the Lodge and managed to sneak inside, and tape a very attractive conversation between some very interesting people. I wanted to come over now so I can share the tape with you, but I'm rather stuck here. If I try to exit the building, I'm sure to set off the alarm, and then I'll have to make a dash for it. If I do that, I might be spotted. I'm not exactly the sprinter-type these days, Mike."

"Listen, Partner. It looks like you're stuck there for the night. I wish there was something I could do for you, but I'm afraid I can't. I think if I were you, I'd wait in hiding until the caretaker or janitor opens up the building in the morning. Then, while the janitor is busy in another room, I'd sneak out, and walk away nonchalantly, as though I knew nothing. How far away is your car from the Lodge?"

"Ah, it's just down the road a short ways, parked on the side of the curve."

"Good. At least there's no worry that it will be towed away, but is it in sight of the Lodge?"

"Not really, you'd have to walk out to the main street to see the vehicle."

"Well, let's hope someone arrives at the Lodge early in the morning. When you are able to get out of that place, let me know. I'd like to meet you somewhere in the city. The Sierra Vista Library may be just the place to meet, Matt."

"Sounds like a plan. But, I really do detest the idea of spending the night in this wretched place!" Matt groaned.

"Hang in there, Matt. It will be over sooner than you think," Mike said, as he laid the phone on the cradle, and fell back on his bed.

Mike could not help but laugh a little, in spite of Matt's precarious, yet silly, predicament. He also felt for sure now that he had made the right decision in hiring this man who, it appeared, would go to great lengths to get information for him, even to he extent of putting himself in jeopardy.

Mike looked at the brilliant stars through his bedroom window. He thought of Bobby again, as he lifted the bed covers over his body and closed his eyes. "The nights are still rather cold in the middle of March," Mike told himself, as he rolled over on his pillow.

The sun's rays crept slowly through Mike's window as it rose, settling upon Mike's eyes. He awoke, squinting his eyes, and furrowing his brow, in response to the sun's bright rays, and then stared at his clock. "Seven-thirty. Hmmm, no call yet from Matt. Well, Matt, I sure do hope you're out of that deer cage and safe by now," Mike verbalized, to no one in particular. He quickly shed his clothes and walked into the shower. When he turned the cold-water faucet on, water immediately sprayed out the showerhead and over his head and back. "Darn lever is jamming again," muttered Mike. "Sure wakes a body up, though." He made quick work of the shower, changed into clean clothes, groomed his hair, and was just beginning to brush his teeth when the phone rang. Toothbrush still in hand, Mike sped over to the phone and answered it.

"Mike," began Audra, "I hope you have a great time with my father today." Mike rolled his eyes, extremely grateful for the reminder, as he'd forgotten all about his golf date with Pat.

"Oh, yeah, I think we'll hit it off just fine but, you know, I was hoping that you'd come along, Audra."

"I would, Mike, but I have to run into Tucson today and see my mother. I won't be back in time to hit a golf ball, but I will make the support group. I hope you do, too."

Mike did not allow Audra to detect discouragement in his voice. He really wanted Audra to golf with them, but he realized trying to force Audra into it would make him come across as being selfish. "Yeah, I'll try to make it there, Audra. I hope you have a good visit with your mother. You know, Kiddo, I want to believe that your mother can hear what you're telling her. She may even understand some of what you tell her, also."

Audra lowered her head, wondering how Mike could say this, though she realized he'd not met her mother to see the extreme state of catatonia in which she existed.

"Well, aren't you full of the faith," Audra responded, in a rather snippy tone.

"Yes, Audra, and it's pretty powerful. It's gotten me this far in life. It's brought me through our parents' plane crash, grandparents' loss to a deadly fire, and I believe it will also see me through this crisis. I'll walk away with Bobby in my arms yet," said Mike emphatically.

Audra was taken back a bit. She did not expect Mike to react this aggressively. However, she knew she had been a bit sarcastic, helping precipitate such a response. She ruefully apologized to Mike for her cattiness. She then wished him luck in the golf match, assuring him that she really wished she could be there with him. With a cheery, "Good-bye, My Man! Hit one for me!" she hung up.

Mike walked back to the sink, finished his dental hygiene routine, and walked into the living room. Pulling a pair of hiking boots from a shoe rack, he slipped them onto his large feet and walked out the door. "Well, next stop's to see Raymond at the police station," said Mike to himself, as he walked out the door, locked it, and jumped into his Jeep.

As he traveled down the road, it felt good to be in his Jeep again. He took pleasure in his sporty vehicle. He had spent a considerable amount of time customizing it himself. He and Raymond had worked on the lift kit together and, whatever they could not do, their friend, Mark—an ace mechanic, and owner of *Marks Auto Repair Shop*—found a little time here and there to help with. Mike liked Mark. He was old-fashioned honest, and so was his wife, Maggie, who owned the *Antique Mall* next to her husband's repair shop. He thought about them as he drove to Sierra Vista.

Then his mind wandered to something he'd rather not have thought about. Having always considered him a straight shooter, Mike couldn't help but grit his teeth in anger when Cal Brown came to mind. Clutching the steering wheel tightly, Mike yelled, "I can't believe you'd do this to me, Cal! Lead me to believe you are such a wonderful guy, when all along you've been living a lie ... a vicious lie! If you are truly associated with these lowlife maggots, then you probably even sold your own son down the river! If you were here right now, I might just have to pluck out your little beady, squirrelly eyes!" His anger grew, as he imagined Cal laughing about his little brother, Bobby's, abduction ... laughing and counting his pile of blood money. Mike could only imagine how much money these vile, Despicable men had obtained over the years, through the theft of innocent children, and the smuggling of drugs and weapons. His anger began subsiding, as he further envisioned himself self-righteously attempting to even the score, by punching the living daylights out of Cal. Now, this vision even brought a smile to Mike's face, in spite of the present circumstances.

His mind was so preoccupied that he did not realize a Sheriff's Patrol vehicle was sitting off just, to the side of the road, near a sign. He sped by the patrol vehicle at a rate of sixty-seven miles per hour. The strobes lit up, as the patrol car pulled onto the road, and started after the speeder it had spotted. Upon seeing the strobes, Mike pulled over, and began withdrawing his wallet from his pocket, before the Sheriff—or one of his deputies—could even come near his vehicle.

Mike strained his eyes, trying to look through the heavily tinted glass. Straining even harder, after a bit, he could still see nothing through the darkened windows. "Wow! Those windows are wonderfully tinted! How could a crook shoot an officer if he couldn't see him? Well, I'll soon find out if it's the

Sheriff himself, or just one of his deputies. Sure looks like the Sheriff's Tahoe, though," an exasperated Mike muttered, thinking about a ticket's effect on his points, thus his insurance premiums, over the next few years. The Tahoe sat behind Mike for over ten minutes with no one exiting it. Mike became a little unnerved, wondering what was up. Why didn't the Sheriff just get out of his vehicle, give him his speeding ticket, and get it over with, so he could be on his way? "Come on, Tress! Give me the darned ticket so I can haul my buns out of here. What do you think I'm gonna do, argue with you?"

Suddenly Mike saw the Sheriff's window open slightly, as a white envelope fell from the window to the ground. As the envelope hit the ground, the Sheriff turned back onto the road, hurried down Highway 92 and was out of sight in no time. When the Sheriff's patrol passed by Mike's idle vehicle, Mike saw a tall, thin man sitting in the driver's seat. "What the thunder was that all about," Mike wondered aloud. A slight case of anxiety overtook him after the Sheriff left. Cautiously, Mike vacated his Jeep and slowly made his way over to the envelope. The wind tossed Mike's hair about, kicking up dust into his eyes as he walked to where the envelope lay. The envelope shook a little in the strong wind, as though it would take flight, but not enough that it blew away. Picking up the envelope, Mike walked back to his Jeep, closed the door, and tore into the message whose delivery method had been most unusual. Inside was an unsigned note that read,

"Stop meddling. There are EYES watching over you.
Leave this case to professionals—or else!"

"Yeah, if I left it up to you turkeys, Bobby would be heading to Bolivia or Brazil in thirteen more days!" Mike quaked at the thought. The number thirteen did little to calm his fears, try as he might to not be superstitious. Then Mike remembered the trading post in the town of Palominas. The Sheriff had behaved in a similar manner that time, also. Mike's suspicions rose higher than ever before. "I'll see if Raymond will scan this for fingerprints, but I have a feeling the Sheriff is not stupid enough to write a letter and place it in an envelope without using gloves."

Mike pulled back onto the road, and continued his trip into town. He thought about the new names and codes in the folders he had studied last night. Who was Mr. Hooah? Mike knew that this man was a very important cog in the wheel, if not the main cog, for the papers stated that before operations and shipments transpired, *'Mr. Hooah must be notified.'* Apparently, Mr. Hooah was the big cheese, the chief coordinator … the man with all the smarts and ingenuity to keep the corrupt ring running smoothly. Audra and he had figured out the flower and vegetable symbolism on the shipping orders, but what on earth did the 'candy canes' and 'Pop Tarts' stand for? What about the other candies mentioned? More puzzles and more codes. Mike thought hard. "Hmmm, due to their shape, the candy canes *could* be guns. Could the Pop Tarts possibly be bombs?" Mike's mind was fast filling up with questions that needed answers. Then he thought about his challenge for the evening. He really had planned on going to the support group when he'd told Audra that morning that he would be there. So he would, but not with the motive of receiving recovery support for his grief. His plan called for a ride on a 650L Honda XR Enduro, to possibly travel in places his Jeep would not be able to go.

Mike turned right off Fry Boulevard onto Coronado. He traveled another two miles to the Sierra Vista Police Station and parked his Jeep. Mike glanced at City Hall just to the left of the Station. He felt a little paranoid as he stepped out of his Jeep, imagining His Honor, the Mayor, running out of City Hall scream-ing: "There he is, Sheriff. Shoot the bastard!" as he remembered the *'... or else!'* warning contained in the roadside-delivered note. "I wonder how quiet things were down at City Hall the day after our *'Operation Dumpster Dive'*," laughed Mike to himself.

Mike next entered through the glass door of the station, and walked over to the receptionist. Looking at Mandy from behind the bulletproof glass window that surrounded the reception area, he smiled politely. "Hi, Mandy, how're you doing today?"

Mandy looked up and, seeing Mike, smiled from ear to ear. She always did have a crush on Mike since childhood, but she found it so difficult to express her feelings towards Mike. Her pretty, dark eyes, wavy dark hair, and shapely face glowed as she said, "Mike! I thought you'd be in here every day, trying to find out more about Bobby."

"Mandy, I call you all the time! I think that ought to tell you something."

"Yeah, I suppose you're right, Mike. I guess I'd do the same thing."

"Besides, Mandy, I know that if your officers, or the Sheriff, stumble onto anything, they'll let me know about it."

"True. Well, what have you been up to?" Mike swiftly ran the question through his mind. He must be careful about such questions. The wrong answers might lead to suspicion, and suspicion to questions he did not care to answer.

"To be very honest with you, I've been nailing up posters of Bobby. And I also have returned to the sight from which he was abducted ... twice."

"And ...?"

"And I found a tunnel, but no Bobby ... although, I think he may have been forced into the tunnel after he was abducted."

"Yeah, the Sheriff wonders the same thing."

"What?" a curious Mike shot back quickly.

"Oh, nothing, really." Mike looked steadily into Mandy's pretty eyes as she blushed. Mike's eyes always had melted her into soft butter. "Okay, Mike, the Sheriff came by here, and I heard him talking to the Police Chief. I don't think they even paid me much mind. Anyway, I heard Sheriff Tress tell Chief Geracci that he had discovered an opening near the sight where Bobby vanished. He said that he saw boot prints from a couple of hikers that must have found the tunnel before him. Anyway, according to the Sheriff, he climbed into the tunnel and followed it for a ways, but said that after walking about thirty feet into the tunnel, it came to an abrupt end, so he gave up the search."

"Did the Chief happen to ask why he and his deputies had not found that tunnel the very day my brother was abducted?"

"Well," Mandy put her finger to her lip as she thought over the question, "Come to think of it, he did; the Sheriff said something about the dogs and the Mayor. I don't really know because they moved further away from me as they spoke." Mike looked at her and smiled. One thing he remembered about Mandy was that she was a very talented talker, a trait that had earned her the nickname *'Mega-Mouth'* in high school. Mandy had just opened her mouth to speak again, when Raymond walked out of the back of the station and began speaking.

"Hey! There you are, Mike. You were supposed to be here fifteen minutes ago."

"But I *was, Officer!*" Mike answered his friend, with mock trepidation in his voice. Then he explained, smiling, "'Jest got caught up in pleasant conversation with old Mandy here, Buddy."

Raymond looked at Mike and winked, "Oh-h-h, I understand now."

Mandy put her hands on her hips and turned to Raymond. "Do I detect a little derision in that voice of yours, Bucko? And you, Mike … what do you mean, *'old'!*"

"Me?" Mike asked. "Uh, just that you're an *'old'* friend, Mandy; that's all."

"And you, Raymond?" Mandy turned back to Mike's friend now, awaiting an explanation of her previous question.

"Hey, Mandy, you know that I know better than to rattle a hurricane's cage!"

Mandy frowned, "What! What exactly is that supposed to mean?"

Raymond laughed, "Actually, I don't know, Mandy. I just speak what comes to mind sometimes."

"Well, 'don't know as I like what *'just came to your mind'* this time, Raymond," she replied.

"Well, Mandy, when you figure out what it means, you let *me* know," said Raymond, as he stepped away from Mandy, signaling Mike to follow him through the heavy, locked bulletproof doors leading into the back of the Station.

As Mike and Raymond slowly walked away towards the doors, Mandy looked down at the floor and began repeating Raymond's words. "I know better than to rattle a hurricane's cage ... a hurricane's cage? So now 'Mega-Mouth' is a hurricane. Hmmm ... actually, I kind of like that. 'Makes me sound *tough* ... and *m-e-ean! Gr-r-r!* Though I'm not tough and mean, 'might come in handy sometime if suspected of being so," she gloated with satisfaction.

The two men went through the back doors, leaving Mandy still talking to herself.

Raymond led Mike into his office. "I know you're anxious to know the results of the prints." Mike stared at Raymond. He was too anxious to speak. "Well, Mike, I have some good news and some bad news."

"I'll take some good news right now, please," pleaded Mike.

"I managed to pull a good set of prints from that Bible. One belonging to you and one put there by...." Hesitating as though he purposely wanted to build Mike's anxiety level and raise his blood pressure, Raymond finally continued, "... by Dennis Perris. But I do also want you to know I did not pull his prints from a felony chart. I only found his prints easily because of the fact that he was a military brat that carried a Visa and Passport. Dennis cannot be traced to anything unethical, other than a ticket for running a red light. Mike appeared calmer than Raymond expected he would.

"I am so fortunate to have you as a friend," began Mike, as he took a piece of paper out of his wallet. "Hey, Raymond, don't you think it's time you dated?"

"What?"

"No, really. I knew the prints probably belonged to Dennis. Now all I've got to do is find out *why* he put that Bible on my nightstand."

"Maybe he was just trying to comfort you, Mike."

"Raymond ... her name is Melissa, and she is very interested in meeting you. She is also very pretty. I don't think you should throw this opportunity away, Buddy."

Raymond stared at the number and name, then he spoke, "Mike, we're talking about Melis ... dang it! I mean we're talking about Dennis! OK, let's get back to the main topic here," a flustered Raymond said, attempting to recover.

Mike laughed, " I knew when I mentioned a hot woman, you'd fall apart, you shy devil, you."

"Ugh! You're incorrigible, Mike!"

"And, don't I know it. Anyway, I interpret the highlighted scriptures to mean:
'We've got Bobby. He's been redeemed to us, and if you try
and do anything about it, we'll break your neck!'
Raymond read the scriptures again, and had to admit that—if they placed themselves in God's position—it did sound like that, but then Raymond saw it

another way, also. "Perhaps, Mike, Dennis is trying to imply that, since every-thing belongs to God, God will take care of Bobby and watch over him."

"Why'd he use a Bible to tell me that? Why not just.... Whoa, Nelly!" Suddenly Mike remembered something very important. "Wait a minute! Dennis slipped up, Raymond."

Raymond pulled back and stared at Mike, "What do you mean?"

"Listen, Dennis told me that he was out of town when Bobby was abducted. He said he was in Tucson ... that he saw it on the news there. Now, how could he be in two places at the same time? How could he be in Tucson and at the hospital?"

"Maybe he drove all the way to see you at the hospital but, when he got there, he saw you were completely out of it, so he left the verses he was going to share with you on your nightstand."

"If Dennis hadn't made a point of saying that he was not in town at the time, I could believe your assumption. But, like I said, he made it clear he was sup-posedly not even in town on that day."

Raymond's face wrinkled, "Uh-huh. Dennis is either very confused, or he is lying. But why?" questioned Raymond.

"Or, he's been set up." Mike added.

"This is becoming far too complicated, Mike. I can hardly keep up with it anymore!" grunted Raymond. Raymond sat down in his swivel chair and whirled around a couple of times, as Mike reached into his pocket and pulled out a note ... a note that only added to the already present confusion. "Hey, my friend, read this."

Raymond read the note that Sheriff Tress had thrown out the window of his Tahoe, after getting Mike's attention. "Looks like someone wants you to know they mean business about Bobby's case. Where did it come from?"

"It was a present from the good Sheriff."

"What!" Raymond's head fell back in his chair as he listened to Mike explain what all had transpired alongside Highway 92. Raymond just shook his head in disbelief. Mike asked Raymond to dust the note and its envelope for finger-prints. Raymond had to laugh. "He'd have to be one of the dumbest sheriffs this side of the Mississippi to write a note without latex gloves on. But, I'll do it for you, Mike."

Mike's cell phone sounded. He answered the cell phone to hear Matt carry-ing on about how nobody arrived at the Deer Lodge until late in the morning. "Some old cracker came in with some rat traps and began laying them out hither and thither. I finally managed to escape when he walked into the back of the Lodge. Phew! What a grand old night on the town it was, m' Lad."

Mike laughed at the old man's sorry predicament, glad he'd come out of it in one piece, and told Matt that he had a couple hours he could spare at the library.

Matt responded, "Actually, my kind fellow, I'm already at the library. I'll be waiting for you."

"Okay, Matt, I'll see you in two shakes." Mike studied Raymond's face for a second before telling him that he needed to meet up with a friend at the library.

"Your sexy new friend?" asked Raymond.

"Buddy, don't I wish. No, he's an old gent from Britain. We have a few things to discuss."

"Well, I never … bloody leavin' me for a Brit, eh?" Raymond responded, trying his best to mimic an English accent.

"Keep working on that accent, Raymond, and I'm sure Hollywood will soon find a spot in the funny papers for you." They both laughed.

As Mike opened the office door to leave, he turned to ask Raymond a question. "Raymond, you told me that the Sheriff flew out to the site where Bobby vanished in the Mayor's chopper. How did the Sheriff get down from the chopper? Does the Mayor have rappelling gear in his helicopter?"

Raymond laughed, "No, of course not! The Mayor's pilot almost landed the chopper on the ground, so Tress could step off the chopper safely."

"Ah-h-h! I see. Don't I feel like the idiot now." Mike began walking out again, when he thought of yet another question. "Raymond, why was Tress at the Mayor's office?"

Again Raymond laughed. "Mike, stop killing yourself over the Sheriff. He was called to the Mayor's office on a routine breaking and entering. If you knew Tress, you'd find out the Mayor and him are not as close as you think they are."

"Well, it never hurts to ask." With that, Mike walked out of the station.

Mike journeyed down Coronado road a little further until he reached the Library. He pulled into the parking lot and stepped out of His Jeep. As he walked across the circular cul-de-sac in front of the library, he looked up at the trapezoid-like arch above the big glass doors. He always admired the architecture of the building. Most libraries Mike had seen looked like big cubes, as well as many city halls and police stations, but Sierra Vista took pride in their newer buildings. City Hall and the Sierra Vista Police Station were both rounded, with classy overlapping gables. Mike pulled one of the glass doors open and stepped inside. He waved at Gladys and Terry at the Information Booth, and walked around the Library looking at all the tables and cubicles. He'd never thought to ask Matt where he would be perched. As he stood there a bit puzzled, a strong hand gripped his shoulder. Mike jumped a little, as he spun around to see Matt, standing there grinning at him.

"My, we are a trifle jumpy today, aren't we?" Matt suggested, in his loudly whispered British accent.

"I swear, if you ever do that again, you'll be wearing my fist in your mouth, Mr. Pied Piper."

"No need to get rude, young man. How was I to know you are such a squeamish bawl baby? I meant no harm."

"Ah, just forget it, Matt. Now, let's get down to business," said Mike roughly, being a bit embarrassed by the uneasy interchange. He still felt the urge to plaster Matt one ... but why? Mike told himself to calm down. He took in some deep breaths as he asked Matt where he'd like to sit. Matt told him he'd rather stand, as his heroic deeds of the night before had left Matt with legs as stiff as boards. He was not sure at all if he could bend them sufficiently to remain seated ... or at least get up if he did dare sit.

"'You have the tape?"

"Of course!" Matt handed Mike the tape.

"Hmmm ... a 3-mm cassette. You do know how to make my life miserable, don't you?" Mike ungraciously complained. I hope I can find a tape player for this," he continued.

Matt, perturbed over Mike's seeming ungratefulness, gave Mike a hard stare. "Mike! I could have been dumped into a pile of refuse, like these people claim they do to some but—thank God—I made it! I manage to get your information, and all you can do is grumble about a silly recorder? Here! Borrow mine!" Matt fumed.

Mike sheepishly shrugged his shoulders. "I'm Sorry, Matt. I'm just getting so nervous as the days go by. I really think I know where Bobby is, yet I can't get to him. Worse, if I do try to rescue him and I'm wrong, then the wretches will know I am onto them. Then they'll move Bobby to some other location, and...."

"Mike, one minute at a time, I say. The only news I have for you besides this tape is that I did find out a little about our man, Cal. His childhood background is typical; nothing really exciting to report. He remained an average Joe. For some reason, Cal never seemed to get a break in life. He tried so hard to get ahead when he was very young, but some people are just born subject to an unlucky star ... or, possibly, none at all. Yes, I dare say that Cal must have been born under the *'black hole'* sign. Then one day in desperation, our Mr. Brown joined the Army, and wound up in El Paso, where he met someone we know about already. Can you guess?"

Mike wriggled a bit as he thought. "Ah, I know! It was Dennis' father, Robert!"

"My, how good you are, Mr. Taylor! Anyway, apparently the two became very good friends. 'Remember my telling you that Robert was transferred to Panama, when the United States still policed that region? Cal stayed behind in El Paso, and years later we see him barely making ends meet. Well, one day he gathers his things and moves his family west, to Sierra Vista. In Sierra Vista he is met with the same fate ... until one of his children disappears."

"Cliff!"

"Yes, Cliff leaves the picture and overnight our Cal somehow gathers up enough brass to purchase a store. I checked into his financial portfolio at that time and discovered that not only was our dear Mr. Brown flat broke without an asset to his name, but he was also drowning in a sea of debt. Now, call it coincidence or whatever you want, but I find his overnight success story a little too good to be true. Giving Cal the benefit of the doubt, however, I also checked to see if he came into some form of inheritance. 'Wish I could say a rich uncle died and left him all that plunder, but such is not the case."

"I am not surprised to hear that. Matt, Listen, I am very grateful to you for all you've done so far. Stay on it Matt ... please. Here's a little extra for all the trouble you had last night." Mike slipped a hundred-dollar bill into Matt's hand. He said goodbye to Matt and left the library.

Matt looked at the crisp Benjamin Franklin. "My stars Ben, old chap! You and I are out to celebrate our great escape from the Lodge! Oh, you don't say! Why, yes, a little twist of lime does sound rather nice. But let's not upset the apple cart ... not just yet." Concluding his imaginary *tête-à-tête* with old Ben, Matt pocketed the bill and proceeded out the library, not too far behind Mike. Matt had more sleuthing to do, and a bottle of whiskey would only serve to slow him down. He needed to keep his wits about him, so he abandoned the thought of a whiskey sour.

Mike drove east on Tacoma Road to Highway 90. He followed Highway 90 left, and headed for home. He liked going back home this way when the opportunity arose. The drive, though not as scenic, was much more peaceful. This way he missed the traffic rush and lights of the city.

Mike began talking to himself, as he normally did when he was attempting to maintain his focus on a given topic. "It seems like this Robert Perris is becoming more and more a central link in all this. Whenever Matt has traced someone's history, 'seems it's discovered that Robert Perris is a factor. It's like he planned it this way. How exactly did this happen? Did he hire into the South American Mafia, or did he just stumble into it? Or is it much more complicated than that? One thing we know for certain is that these ruthless individuals, so far, all seem to have a common denominator—Robert Perris—and Dennis is his son. Hmmm ... like father like son, a chip off the old man's block, is he?"

Mike rolled that last thought around in his mind. He did realize that Dennis somehow played a role in the crimes, but his role seemed much lighter than the others' roles ... at least at this point, according to all Mike knew at the moment.

He began replaying that evening at Dennis' house in his mind. "I saw another side of Dennis that night. He had never hidden the fact that he didn't care much for cats, but 'guess I never realized the extent of the personal vendetta he had towards them. Anyway, he just seems ... different. He acts like someone has placed him under a lot of stress, and he doesn't know how to deal with it. Maybe Dennis had other reasons for lying than what meets the eye. Perhaps it has to do with his being trapped ... involved, due to his father ... so he can't find a way out, knowing a little too much? Plus, the ring being his only source of *real* income, he can't quite bring himself to cut the cord?"

Then another thought regarding Dennis' recent actions entered Mike's mind. "Maybe Dennis left the book on the nightstand as a warning rather than a threat, and all the questions posed to me the other were part of yet another attempt to warn me? I don't know what to think anymore, but we certainly have plenty of steaming hot suspects, and the time to act boldly is close at hand. We have so much documented proof from Matt, and also that metal briefcase was a super find. I don't think we'll have a hard time convincing the FBI." Mike smiled to himself, even daring to chuckle. For the first time since that heartwrenching day Bobby disappeared, and his search began, he knew he and his partners had the upper hand.

Mike was feeling hopeful as he turned right onto Moson Road. He found himself whistling loudly as he drove down Moson, a stretch of road that cut through the desert flatlands between the Mule and Huachuca Mountains. He glanced at his watch. "One in the afternoon ... plenty of time to get spruced up for a golf match. I just hope I can impress Pat. I can't afford to muff up my chances with the Colonel's daughter. Maybe if I focus very hard on the game, I can give him a challenge he'll admire." Mike drove on, his mind quieted for the moment. He knew Bobby was still alive, and he also knew—deep within his soul—that he was not far away. With all the evidence he now had in his possession, he felt confident of a positive outcome. He actually felt optimistic and less panicky. He even breathed easier.

Dennis leaned against the dark sedan he'd driven to a small airstrip outside of Hereford. A private owner maintained and operated the airstrip, only allowing certain individuals and associates—such as the mayor and friends— to use the airstrip. The airport was a bit smaller than Sierra Vista International, but it was very efficient. Dennis watched as a 1978 Cessna 421C *Golden*

Eagle II approached the landing strip. He admired the twin props and the sleek style of the nose and fuselage. As a child, he had always enjoyed watching planes take off and land. The white plane with a charcoal-colored trim around the outer rudder and like belly circled the landing strip twice before it made its final approach.

Manuel looked out the small porthole-like windows of the plane. The scenery reminded him a little of the flat bush lands he would sometimes land in when flying with some bush pilots in Central and South America, with similar tall brush and thick range grass waving in the wind. "Much less primitive ... not as exciting," he muttered.

When the plane landed, and two men had lowered the stairs to the ground, Manuel helped an older lady step down from the stairs. Once on the ground, he handed her luggage back to her, and smiled, his dimples thus becoming apparent.

The lady immediately saw how handsome Manuel looked. Blushing, she said, "Thank you, young man."

Manuel took her hand in his, gently rolled it over and exposing the backside of her hand. He then lowered his head in a bowing gesture, and tenderly kissed her hand. "My fair lady, 'tis a custom where I come from."

"Helping me with my luggage, or the kiss?" playfully asked the attractive elderly lady.

"Both, my dear," Manuel suavely replied.

The lady's face turned a shade redder. "You are very charming. If I was younger, I'd kidnap you and take you home with me."

"Oh, but it would be my pleasure! You look stunning, my lady." He spoke with a very pronounced Latino accent that made the woman's blood run warm. She blushed even more.

"Unfortunately I'm happily married with my first grandchild on the way," she gushed, as a young girl, rather taken in by the unexpected flattery.

"Your first? Congratulations! This means you have much experience. Do they not have a saying in your country ... ah, let's see ... oh, yes! "Older women make better lovers."

"Older women make *beautiful* lovers!" exclaimed the woman, feeling suddenly abashed upon realizing what she had just said. However, in spite of this, she began to feel very young. This charming handsome man knew all the right lines. "Uh, thank you ... ah...." She suddenly paused, realizing she did not even know the name of this man with whom she'd been tremendously enjoying this banter.

"The name is Señor Martinez, but you may call me Manny."

"My name is Joan. Thank you for inspiring me, Manny. I must be on my way, though. I have so much to catch up on! I wish I'd sat closer to you in the plane. You really know how to lift a girl off her feet, Manny," she smiled brightly.

"It is our custom," Manny repeated with a smile, as the two departed ways.

Dennis stood beside Manuel by now, having observed a little of the conversation between Manny and the attractive older woman.

"Hi, I'm Dennis. I am here to transport you into the city. May I help you with your luggage?" Dennis reached for Manuel's suitcase.

"You may carry that one, but this—this carry-on—remains close to me when I travel. It is very special to me."

As they walked to the sedan, Dennis asked, "How was your trip El ..."

"Stop, right there!" ordered Manuel. "Do not say another word." His voice, so charming only a few moments ago, suddenly turned sour and very harsh. "You are *not* to call me that. Do you understand!"

Some of the color left Dennis' face. For a moment, he thought Manuel was going to literally rip his head off. "Ah-h-h, yes sir, Manuel."

"Very good. You are a fast learner. You shall address me as 'Manuel' ...'Señor Martinez' ... or 'Mr. Manuel Martinez.' If you are ever caught using the name that almost slipped from your tongue, I shall personally see to it you never say that name again! Are we very clear?"

Dennis' pride swelled a little. He wanted to strike out and tell the Latino what he really thought about his silly behavior, yet he bit his tongue and held his peace. "Yes, Mr. Martinez, we are very clear."

"Thank you. I believe we shall be good friends, after all. You know, Dennis, the last man who defied my wishes, lost his tongue ... somehow."

Dennis shuddered within at even hearing of such a hideous consequence for a mere slip of the tongue. "Who is this man, anyway?" he pondered within himself. "He acts so calm and cool one moment, then strikes out in anger the very next." Manuel's comments having squelched the conversation, Dennis said very little as they continued walking towards his vehicle. He held the back door open for Manuel, as he climbed into the sedan. Then Dennis opened the trunk, carefully placing Manuel's suitcase inside. Opening the driver's door, he also climbed in, trying to relax, in spite of the trepidation Manuel's speech caused.

"I'll have you at the Windemere Hotel in no time, Manuel. I'm sure you'll find the Windemere's environment to your liking. It is one of the finest hotels in town." Manuel stared out the window a few moments after being addressed, looking over his entire surroundings ... the mountains, the stylish manufactured houses, and the fields blanketed with thick straw-colored range grass, just waiting to turn green. Preoccupied with taking mental pictures of all this,

Manuel was, therefore, deep in thought when Dennis began what would become nervous ramblings.

"You don't talk much, do you?" Receiving no answer, as Manuel was lost in deep thought, Dennis began to believe he could get more words out of a saguaro.

"Huh, what?" Manuel finally realized Dennis had spoken to him.

"I said you haven't spoken much since we left the landing strip."

"Ah-h-h … Dennis, right?"

"Yep, that's my name. Don't wear it out," laughed Dennis trying his best to lighten up the tense atmosphere.

"Sorry, I am so tired from my long flight, and that puddle jumper back there was far from relaxing. I am not staying at the Windemere Hotel. I reserved a room at the Palatine Motel." Dennis stirred in his seat. He felt very uncomfortable around this enigmatic man he knew little about. Now, he realized the short trip to the hotel, which he looked forward to, would become a longer trip to an alternate motel. Dennis groaned a little inside himself. He wondered why an important figure like Manuel would choose cheaper quarters at the Palatine Motel. Finally, Dennis' curiosity got the best of him.

"Why Palatine Motel, Mr. Martinez? I think you'd enjoy the hotel."

"I am not here for enjoyment, Dennis, although I do mix pleasure with business from time to time … depending on how pretty the ladies are. I am here strictly on business, and I have my reasons for how I conduct myself, and why I choose what I choose. Now, just drive on, please. I am very tired."

Dennis, feeling the strong rebuff in these last words, hence wanting to make his displeasure known, was about to turn to Manuel and say, "Well, excuse me all over the place, my Excellency. I did not know you were so particular!" Then he pressed his tongue against his front teeth, recalling Manuel's earlier words. The thought of going through life without a tongue made Dennis very uncomfortable, so he shrugged his shoulders and said nothing.

Both men remained very quiet during the rest of the trip, other than for the necessary instructions from Manuel. Dennis learned he would not be driving Manuel all the way to the Palatine Motel, after all, as Manuel liked to be in control of his own transportation whenever possible, once he arrived at his destination. Therefore, Manuel asked that he be driven to Long Leaf's Automotive Center off Fry Boulevard. When they arrived, a man quickly sprinted out of the dealership, and met Manuel, as though he had been watching for them through the large display window. As he helped Mr. Martinez from the vehicle, Dennis began exiting the sedan, as well. However, Manuel motioned him to stay put, so Dennis opened the trunk via the dashboard control. The sandy blonde-haired man that walked out of the center handed Manuel a set of keys, helped him retrieve his luggage from Dennis' sedan, and into a sporty-looking GT Mustang. In no time, Manuel was on his way.

"Man, he didn't even have to sign one paper for that vehicle," an amazed Dennis mumbled to himself, as he climbed out to close the trunk that neither of the other two gentlemen had remembered to shut. "Thanks so much, by the way, guys." Then turning his attention back to Manuel, he mumbled some more. "Someone sure takes care of that guy properly." Happy to have been relieved of his charge, Dennis could even laugh now. "Ah! I feel so-o-o good. 'Just knew I'd feel so much better, once that pesky man was out of my sight!" He could feel his respiration and heart rate slowing down to a comfortably normal rhythm.

Manuel pulled into the Palatine Motel, walked calmly into the registration area, and handed the clerk a hundred dollar bill, as he told the clerk he wanted to choose his own room. He then informed the clerk of his further wishes. "I want to be left alone. Unless, or until, I call for service, you keep your maids *away* from my room, okay. 'Got that?" he asked, as he handed the clerk yet another hundred-dollar bill.

The clerk looked puzzled, but why should he argue with someone that tips so well? "You've got yourself a deal, Sir! Is there anything else I can do for you?" he asked, wanting to be compliant with such a good tipper.

"Yes, there is. I shall be staying in room 217. I will pay you for rooms 218 and 216, as well. I need those rooms in which to conduct business. I also expect a direct phone line in and out. And, please see to it that a daily newspaper is delivered at my doorstep, early each and every morning."

"We carry the Sierra Vista Daily Herald," the clerk matter-of-factly informed Manuel.

"That will do just fine. Thank you." The clerk told Manuel that it was a pleasure, as he left the office. Manuel then drove his car near to the far corner of the motel. He liked the height and location, as he could easily survey his surroundings below, and yet not be seen easily. "Excellent, all is in place and ready," he congratulated himself. "Now, my first stop will be the cavern."

Mike stood over the golf ball concentrating on his form and technique. Both he and Pat played the first nine holes quite well. Pat *'birdied'* the first three holes and Mike parred. The next five holes placed them almost neck and neck. Finally, hole nine opened up for Mike. He *'eagled'* this hole and Pat parred. The score was Pat two under par and Mike one under par. Pat took pride in his technique in golfing. He had won some tournaments in his time, so he thought Mike would be an easy challenge. However, Mike knew the Naco golf course very well, and Pat had only played one time in his life at Naco. Actually, Pat had seen no use in golfing since Todd vanished. Now, barely beating Mike with no room to spare, he realized that he was much rustier that he'd thought.

Mike glanced at his watch, as the game continued. "Four o'clock," he nervously thought. "I really wanted to golf with Pat, but I also wanted to research those papers a bit more. I've got to find out what those other codes mean." Mike grumbled softly as he hit the golf ball with his number three driver. The ball sailed into the air—an admirably straight shot down the fairway—stopping just before the right turn leading to hole eleven. "There it is. What a beauty!" Mike exulted.

"Impressive, Mike. But I'm getting a little limbered up now, so watch this! *This* ball is going to land right in front of yours," boasted the Colonel. Pat lined up, and took form. *'Whack!'* The ball sailed through the air majestically, with a bit of a backward spin. It touched down just in front of Mike's ball, bit the ground and—just as he had predicted—rolled a little further ahead.

"Dang! I never saw a ball do *that* before!" Mike could hardly believe his eyes.

"All in the wrists, my son … all in the wrists." Mike liked it when Pat called him *'son.'* He wasn't sure if it was just a nostalgic wish or reality when thinking that Pat's voice sounded somewhat like his father's deep, pleasant voice. Whatever it was, he had to smile at Pat, as the tall Colonel patted him on the back. Except for the last two remaining holes, the other holes had proven to be very much like the first eleven—they parred and birdied. Finally, Mike's concentration lapsed a bit at holes seventeen and eighteen; first, he hit one over par at the seventeenth hole and then even sliced the ball going into the very last hole. Letting his mind wander from the game had cost him four extra shots. Pat experienced a little difficulty, also, but he managed to par seventeen and hit just two over on the eighteen hole. The final score … Pat one over par and Mike five over par.

"Hey, hey! Not my best game, but not my worse game, either," shouted Pat. Mike sighed. "I really thought I had y' there for a while, Pat. The last two holes ate my lunch."

"Mike, you play like a regular. You used no handicap and you finished only five strokes over. That's great! Look at me … I've played golf all my life and I still hit one over."

Mike laughed loudly as Pat said, "Son, you've just got to learn who the master is, and take your beatings like a good soldier." Mike laughed even more now, learning from whom Audra had picked up that pet name she'd called him.

"Well, guess it's time to bug out of here, Pat. We've got a ways to go to get back home."

"Now, where're your manners, young man? The Colonel wants to stop in at the *'nineteenth hole.'* Are you going to deny him this privilege?"

"Of course not; let's head in." The two men plunged their putters into their golf bags, stepped into the cart and proceeded to drive in the direction of the clubhouse. Soon they were lost in laughter and conversation. Mike forgot all about the time as they drank some colas and *O'Doul's*. During their conversation, Pat explained that he and Audra had spoken in detail about everything that Mike and his daughter had been up to.

Mike felt awkward. "Now what?" he thought.

Pat seemed to read his mind. "Mike, please don't be worried. After talking to my most trusted and favorite young lady in the world, I believe Audra and you. I know something is going on around here, and I want to help. Frankly, I always did believe there was more to Todd's disappearance than what the authorities knew. I wanted to snoop myself, but so many things happened after Todd disappeared, that I found myself almost entirely incapacitated. I'm willing to do everything in my power to help you find your brother, and if that means stepping on toes or insubordination, then so be it," growled the Colonel, as he lifted his mug of *O'Doul's* and toasted Mike.

Darkness crept silently over the land east of the Huachuca Mountains. The flats below the Huachucas always grew dark earlier than normal due to the high mountain range. As the last shadows cast from the sun disappeared, a dark phantom-appearing figure walked quietly to the back of Mike's house. This dark form withdrew a small drill from a pouch they carried, and drilled a hole in the middle of the deadbolt securing Mike's back door. Releasing the bit, and sliding a long, slender *easy-out* in place of the bit, they then selected the reverse button on the drill. The teeth of the *easy-out* bit into the hole that had been drilled into the deadbolt, and easily turned it. The bolt slid free. The phantom then stuck a thin steel wedge between the door and the jamb of the regular lock, and with one quick jerk, the door swung open, allowing entrance into the presently unoccupied house.

Once inside, the intruder raced through the house as though it were daytime, and began rummaging through the living room sofa, throwing the cushions and pillows all over. The drawers in the kitchen fell to the floor. Next, the dark form left every cabinet door open, apparently leaving no stone unturned in searching for their quarry. Dashing into Bobby's bedroom, the trespasser then tore through the bed and its covers. This same action was carried out in Mike's office and bedroom. Not yet finding what they had come for, the mysterious intruder savagely pushed Mike's bed to the side, and began walking across the area of the floor the bed had covered.

Suddenly, the thief stopped and pressed down on the floor. Something under the thief's foot felt a little spongy. Quickly, the floor was examined carefully with a penlight; it seemed a bit raised in one area. Grabbing the carpet and pulling hard, they were yet a bit surprised when a portion of the floor gave way, and they nearly fell backwards. Shining the penlight into the compartment, the intended treasure was apparently spotted. Proceeding to withdraw a metal briefcase from below the floorboards, the mysterious intruder fled out the back door, disappearing into the night.

Pat drove into Mike's driveway, and dropped him off. "Beat y' again next time, son!" laughed the Colonel.

"Beggin' the Colonel's pardon, but I think the only thing that saved your butt today was just sweet little ole *Lady Luck.*"

"Luck, my smelly foot; all skill, Mike ... 'twas all skill." Pat was laughing, as he backed down the driveway, and headed for home. Mike never had seen Pat so happy since he met him. Thinking about the game as he walked into his house, his thoughts abruptly changed course, as he turned on the light and stood shocked to see his place in such a wreck. Pillows, cushions, books, and other items lay strewn about. He raced into the kitchen to discover nearly all the drawers had been pulled from their respective slots, as well, and were lying about on the kitchen floor. "Oh, no, the briefcase!" screamed Mike, instinctively realizing what it was that some uninvited intruder had been seeking. He dashed into the hallway leading to his bedroom, stumbling over an object as he flipped the light switch. Mike fell to the ground, but quickly recovered from the fall, only to see before him a sickening sight ... one that caused his emotions to fall as quickly as he had fallen over whatever object had tripped him up in his haste, as he ran in the dark. His bed had been pushed off to the side, and the cover to the under-floor compartment forced open, exposing nothing but an empty space where the briefcase had once lain.

"Oh, God, please let me open my eyes to see this is only a mirage!" Mike closed his eyes and opened them again, but this did nothing to change the reality before him. "Oh God, I'm sick. We had the upper hand ... we had strong evidence. Now we're back to square one, Lord! All we have now is our word and a few maps and shipping forms. And, worse yet, I put all those forms back inside the case for safekeeping. I wish I'd put them in a safety deposit box at the bank. Why am I so stupid!" Mike's eyes watered as he whined; his heart sunk ... it began pounding rapidly, as he entered into a bona fide state of panic. Mike lowered his head between his legs for a few moments to regain his equilibrium. He then walked into Bobby's room and turned the light on. "They even tore up Bobby's room! Whoever it was somehow seemed to know that that briefcase was here."

Mike walked to the back of the long house and entered the mud room, where the washer and dryer stood. He instantly realized how the crook had entered the house, as he looked past the back door that had been left ajar, and into the darkness beyond his yard. Mike took in a hearty deep breath. "Since you guys know me now and want to play like *this,* I'll play your game, but I'm going to be making up the rules from here on out, not you." Mike turned away from the door, and walked to his closet. He retrieved his duffel bag. Then he unloaded his bag onto his cluttered bed. He reached up, grabbed his black ski mask from the top shelf of his closet, and walked back to the bed. Before him lay his night goggles, leather gloves, a *.38 Rutgers* revolver and shoulder holster, along with mace, and a sap.

He then turned to the corner of his room and, seeing his cane standing against the wall, spoke excitedly, having nearly forgotten about it while collecting his gear for the next phase of his mission. "Oh, yes! I must bring that, too!" He loved canes. This had been his weapon of choice when he trained at the Karate institute. Sitting down for a moment, he took some time to think through his plan carefully. "I'm no Chuck Norris or VanDamme, but I'm no wimp either. I've won my fair share when sparring. Where do I start, though?" Mike was rather in a quandary.

Manuel moved methodically through the noisy cavern. He laughed a little when he thought of the guards at the entrance to the cavern. How easy it was for him, a foreigner to enter the cavern. All he had to do was say his name, and that Mr. Hooah had sent him, and they quickly let him pass. "This Mr. Hooah definitely carries a lot of weight here, although I am quite certain the guards were informed about my coming, as well," Manuel thought.

The noise from all the men repairing and clearing out the cavern echoed loudly throughout the dark chambers, as Manuel took the elevator down to the station below. Two large diesel generators sitting outside, with long cable feeds stretching into the cavern, fed power to the working men inside. Manuel stepped out of the elevator and looked all about him. The Americans that met him there briefed him in detail about what had happened in the cavern. He committed the details to memory. He believed the human mind was the greatest tool, choosing not to rely on forms and papers.

As he inspected the cavern, Manuel purposely began to think like the two intruders might have, trying to get inside their minds. Apparently, nobody else had any idea yet who the saboteurs were, or why they had been there, except to sabotage the operation … but was that all? Why had the men chosen not to kill anyone? Why had they spared the cave, when they could have completely blown the place out of the mountain? And why was there a logbook and metal briefcase missing? "They apparently just wanted some form of proof of what goes on here, maybe," Manuel spoke aloud, as he pondered such a conclusion.

Manuel walked over to the outcropping behind which Audra and Mike had hidden not so long ago. He squatted down behind the rock, realizing as he did so that this location would provide a great place to hide from people coming out of the elevator. He also noticed that the outcropping carried signs of having been disturbed just a short time ago. He shined his bright flashlight on the huge rock formation. "Yes, they were behind this piece of stone. There is a fresh break in the rock, and … why, here's the piece that broke off!" Manuel said, as he picked up the small rock that showed signs of recent breakage. Finding that the rock he'd just picked up fit into the fresh break he'd found like a puzzle piece, Manuel shined his light on the ground below him to see what else he might find.

Carefully searching through the pebbles and dust, he noticed the ground had indeed been disturbed. Surely, the men had hidden behind this outcropping in the cave. Then he noticed his light being reflected back to him off some object. Stooping down again, he found there was a crevice in the floor. "Ah-h-h … so now I know you are not saboteurs! No, my silly ninja men, you are spies or a couple desperate well trained people looking for clues. So, you wanted to take pictures, eh?" Manuel retrieved a telescopic steel rod from his jacket. He pulled the rod into a longer stick and fished it through the crevice. When he thought he had a good grip on the handle of the camera, he pushed the top button on the rod, which triggered the strong vice at the end of the rod to close. The jaws of the vice closed around the handle, and Manuel carefully began to pull the camera out of the crevice. His face lit up and his eyes widened as the camera was start-ing over the lip of the crevice. "I've got you!" he exulted. Suddenly, Manuel moaned, "Ay, caramba!" as the camera slipped out of the jaws and plummeted back down into the crevice, falling further than it had been before; it was now out of sight, unrecoverable. *"Caramba, caramba,* and more *caramba!"* shouted Manuel. He stood up retracted the steel rod, stuck it back into his jacket, and walked on.

Manuel stood upon the loading dock of the station, studying what remained of the devastation. He saw some South Americans hard at work alongside Mexican laborers as well as some white men. He walked into the station. He saw where exploding rocks had fallen through the station roof smashing tables and office furniture inside the building. Outside Latinos worked eagerly to repair the damaged conduit and electrical equipment. They were told that a big bonus awaited them if they finished the work in three weeks. Manuel knew this and he chuckled to himself, "My American partners probably don't expect the men to get this done on time, but they know not how fast and accurate we Latinos work. They will pay the bonus, that is for sure."

The laborers had respected his request to leave the station alone until he arrived, so it remained as the explosion had left it. Manuel investigated each and every room of the station meticulously. Then he came to the room where Mike had found the metal briefcase. Glancing at his watch, he realized two hours had already passed since arriving at the cave. He had expected it to take awhile. He continued his very methodical search through the rubble. Turning over yet another chunk of mud and sheetrock, Manuel spied a small penlight. He bent over and fished the light out of the debris, examining the light carefully. "Interesting ... a small MagLite. Well, one of the ninjas was very unwise to drop his little trophy here." Manuel grinned, his face taking on a sinister look; he had a good idea who the guilty party might be, and this might help confirm this. Carefully he pocketed the penlight, and walked out of the station.

Next, he strolled across the loading platform where all the shooting transpired ... an area he had also ordered remain untouched until his arrival. Here he saw the magazines and *AK-47s* and *AK-74s* strewn across the dock. Whoever did this apparently knew something about Russian ingenuity, because the assault rifles had been disarmed very quickly. He walked further into the passageway leading towards the area of the initial explosion. The laborers had cleared a large portion of the mass of rubble to provide passage in and out of Mexico. Manuel easily jumped off the platform and onto the tracks below. He carefully studied the dark corner of the channel through which the tracks ran. "If I wanted to remain hidden, this would be a good place to hide. It's no wonder they spotted the spy running from this spot."

His eyes then caught sight of something that—in the dark—resembled a snake. Upon closer investigation, Manuel saw the strange object was a durable elastic strap. "This strap held a face mask of some sort on the face of one of the spies, I would guess." He used the term spies now because he positively believed the ninja men were not sent to the cavern by an angry or jealous competitor. He believed these men operated under their own initiative. His mind envisioned agents from the FBI or the ATF, agents that received enough training to pull this off ... *special* agents. Manuel lifted the strap up to his face, pretending to put the strap on himself. He smelled the strap: he even tasted it. "Ah, my senses are tingling! Now it is time to talk to the guards."

Shorty sat quietly near a fan in a small connex near the entrance of the cave. The connex housed a table, a few chairs, a water dispenser and a small fridge and microwave. He sat listening to some tunes when Manuel walked in. Not knowing Manuel from the other Latinos, Shorty blurted out, "Who the hell are you, Amigo!" as he spit a gob of tobacco out of his mouth. Manuel sat down calmly beside the short white man, saying nothing. He smiled very casually.

"Well, what do you want? And I ain't gonna ask you again; who the...."

Manuel held up his hand, "Please, please Señor Shorty, stop with this macho act. If you must know, my name is El Niño."

Shorty swallowed his chewing tobacco and began choking. "I ..." he choked again. "I apolo...." Shorty could not but cough and choke some more, as some tobacco juice—in his shock at learning how he'd addressed El Niño—had inadvertently made its way down his windpipe. Finally able to speak, Shorty respectfully addressed Manuel. "Sir, I apologize. I thought you were just one of the Mexicans or one of the other laborers."

Manuel did not like the way he had just referred to his brother Latinos as *'just Mexicans or laborers.'* "Apology accepted this time, but let it *not* happen again."

"I promise I won't. I really am truly sorry."

"Yes, I'm sure you are, my friend. Now, I have a few questions for you."

"That's me, always willing to help."

"Yes, I am sure you are. I am glad you recovered well from your little shoot out with the bad guys, or was it bad *guy*?"

"Well, it was only one guy we saw at the time."

"How tall was this ninja-like man that shot at you?"

"I'd say about five-nine or five-ten, maybe a little taller. I don't know for sure; it was dark, and the guy was rolling around so much."

"Did he speak at all?"

"Not to Too-Tall and me. That's my partner's name. He stands about six-eight, so we call him *'Too-Tall,'* but his real name is Greg. Some of the others, who are not here, said that he had a deep voice; I guess he talked to them. He told them that he was sent by his superiors, et cetera. He mentioned something about inferior products and being behind schedule ... stuff that makes you think that one of our clients are pretty disgusted."

"How did this man carry himself? Did he have broad shoulders and muscular looking arms?"

"Well, he wasn't too broad in the shoulders, he did not sport huge arms, but his legs were well defined."

"Thin at the calves?"

"Yes."

"What about the waist?"

"Kind of slim in the waist. I don't know because...."

"Because it was dark, " moaned Manuel.

"Yes, it was."

"Did his hips sway when he walked?"

"Maybe, come to think of it ... a little. Look, Mr. Niño, I was rolling around in pain. I mean, I don't want to sound disrespectful or anything. I want to help, but all I saw were blurs more than anything else, and the other guys are too banged up to be here. They could help you more than I. They mumbled something about the person talking a little like a Chinaman. Now that could explain the size and shape of the man right there." Shorty rubbed his aching calves.

"So, he swept your calves, did he?" Manuel sympathized.

"Yeah, he sure did. Oh God, it hurts at times!"

"Well, my little friend, I must leave you now. I will tell you this. You are very fortunate to be alive ... all of you. Don't you think it is strange that these men did not kill even one of you?"

"They said they only wanted to warn us, not kill us."

"*Both* men said this?"

"No, the shorter one did."

"So, you did see the other?"

"Barely. He was taller ... about six-four, maybe, unless he was wearing thick-soled boots. His shoulders were quite broad, and he looked very husky."

"Mr. Shorty, you have been most helpful. One more question before I go."

Shorty moaned loudly. All the questioning was making his head ache, and his calves burn. "What?" asked Shorty.

"Don't you find it rather peculiar that these people would wish to blow up the place if they thought you were behind schedule?"

"Of course. I thought about that. That's the reason I believe they are not one of our clients. I'm convinced they are an angry competitor trying to muscle in on the action."

"Of course, you do. That does sound more likely, I have to admit. You are very observant, my friend," said Manuel as he turned to walk out of the connex and exit the cave. Shorty reached around the back of his calf and with the supine area of his hand, he rubbed his calf again. Manuel stopped. "One more thing."

"Yeah," groaned Shorty.

"Never, ever ... never call me El Niño to my face again, and never, ever again refer to my Latino brothers as *'just another Mexican'* or a mere *'laborer'* again. You talk too much, my friend, and I do not like people that talk too much. 'Last person that called me El Niño after I told him not to, lost his tongue.

Manuel stepped out of the doorway, walked out of the cave, and over to his car.

Shorty pressed his tongue against his front teeth. "Yeah, I think I like it better in my mouth. I'll make sure I call him...." Shorty stopped and gulped. "He didn't give me his real name; now what'll I call him when I see him next time?"

"Okay young men, gather around the mat over here," ordered a tall, burly-looking man. He sported a balding head with a little gray hair on each side, yet he was pleasant to look upon. This unique look had earned him the nickname *'Mr. Clean.'* The children liked and respected the man. He was strong and assertive, yet kind and intelligent, also. The young men gathered around the gym mat, as directed. "Gentlemen, as you know, you have been uniquely chosen from other children for an extremely important mission in life. At this academy, we instill rigid self-discipline, and wisdom, as well as the ability to follow orders and complete tasks that are set before you. We also believe that the human mind is our ultimate weapon. Using the mind along with sufficient combat training will insure your safety. "Today, we will all learn more self-defense techniques that may one day save your life.

"Bobby and Donny, front and center." Bobby walked out to the middle of the mat. Donny followed him. Mr. Clean produced a rubber rifle shaped like an *M-16* with a rubber bayonet molded to the muzzle. He handed the mock rifle to Donny, who was standing patiently in front of Mr. Clean. "As you know there may be times when you face hand to hand combat where your enemy will lunge at you with a bayonet clipped to the end of the rifle. I shall demonstrate a technique to disarm our enemy and hold him at bay with his own weapon, possibly even kill him, if need be.

Donny, thrust the bayonet into my stomach." Donny reluctantly thrust the rifle at Mr. Clean. Mr. Clean quickly snatched it out of his arms with one hand, and spun it around at Donny, who now stood there with a foolish look on his face, feeling rather embarrassed. "Donny, I want you to make believe that I really am the enemy. I want you to thrust that rifle at me as though your life depends on it, okay?"

"Yes, sir," shouted Donny. The thirteen-year-old boy gritted his teeth. Now, he was ready and meant business. The other boys stood tense as the drama began to unfold before them. Bobby watched closely. He and Mike had often practiced self-defense techniques like this. "Eee-*YA!*" Donny shouted, as he thrust the rifle with all his might. Like a streak of lightning, Mr. Clean had stepped to the side, and swept his feet, quickly twisting the rifle away from himself and out of Donny's hands, as Donny fell backwards onto the mat.

When Donny looked up, he found himself staring at the business end of the rubber rifle.

"Wow!' Donny said, amazed. The whole group of kids roared as they clapped their hands.

Mr. Clean helped Donny to his feet. "Thank you, Donny, for the demonstration."

"Sir, will I be able to do that soon?" asked Donny.

"Sir, you will be able to do that and more by the time you are ready to begin your mission. In fact, I want to prove to all of you young men that you will leave this academy as a solid soldier. Bobby is now going to demonstrate to all of you that the size and strength of another individual can be used against him," shouted Mr. Clean. Mr. Clean looked at Bobby as he held the rifle in his hands. His pupils dilated just a little bit, as Bobby timed Mr. Clean's fervent thrust perfectly, and he soon found himself face down on the ground, with Bobby holding the rifle to the back of his assailant's neck.

"Sir, you are my prisoner!" shouted Bobby. The other boys looked on in admiration, clapping their hands and shouting.

From his compromised position on the floor, Mr. Clean turned and smiled up at his young protégé. "As always, well done, Cadet," laughed Mr. Clean.

Mr. Clean had recently found himself breaking a significant rule; he was becoming attached to Bobby. This was a very serious violation, but he found it difficult not to, as Bobby was different from many of the boys. He bubbled with life; he effervesced with optimism and spiritual health, making him truly a delight to be around. His strong personality had earned the respect of all the other children. He was a leader, and Mr. Clean and all the others at the compound realized this. They spoke about this within their group meetings, and had decided to do their best to keep him around, somehow. If they could only brainwash him into believing in their cause, maybe their superiors would give in to their wish, just this one time.

Ms. Kay walked into the gym where Mr. Clean was holding his training session with the children. The gymnasium had been built one sublevel underground. The compound contained three sublevels. Each level equipped to train the young boys for combat before they arrived at their destinations in South America or elsewhere. The first level contained the gym, the second, classrooms and the third, a shooting range and obstacle course. Ironically, all this was secretly paid for by the taxpayer's money. As she entered, Mr. Clean was explaining how Bobby was proof that they, too, would learn such moves and techniques themselves.

"So, you see how Cadet Bobby used my own strength and weight against me? He stepped quickly to the side, secured the rifle in his hands and tossed me forward, in the same direction as my initial thrust. This threw me off balance, allowing Bobby to twist the rifle from my grasp and step behind me. Of course, he did sweep my right leg, as well. All of you cadets will learn these and more techniques in time."

"Ah-h-h … hmmm." Ms. Kay quietly interrupted the session. Mr. Clean turned to see Ms. Kay holding a video in her hand. "Bobby, you are needed. Walk with Ms. Kay."

"Yes, sir!" replied Bobby.

As Bobby walked out with Ms. Kay, Mr. Clean returned to his speech, "As I was saying …"

His voice faded from Bobby's ears, as Ms. Kay led him out of the gymnasium and into the corridor leading to the top floor. "Bobby! Guess what arrived!" exclaimed Ms. Kay.

Bobby's eyes grew as big as saucers. "The video! Mike sent the video!" hollered Bobby in glee.

"Yes! So why don't we watch it together?" Bobby looked like a child receiving a present on Christmas Day as he and Ms. Kay walked into a conference room. Ms. Kay closed the door, turned on the television set, and inserted the video in the VCR. For a minute, nothing but fuzz appeared, then there was Mike's face. He looked very healthy. His faced glowed as he spoke.

"Hi, Soldier. I told you I'd send you a recording of myself when the time was right. I want you to know how proud I am of you. As I explained in the first two letters that I sent you, this was necessary. Bobby, I hope you are not angry with me. I wanted to tell you that you were chosen for special missions, but there was so little time and I was instructed to remain silent until now. I do not do the choosing. Our government does this. Your high achievements as a young child, and your unique background, molded you into a perfect candidate for this special U.S. project. I know this must have been tough on you at first, but your profile indicated that you would adapt to the program very well.

You belong to an elite squad of young men that will soon be needed to guard our country. This is a top secret military operation designed to protect the United States from our enemies that we now know will soon strike from the South up from Central and South America. You may soon infiltrate these countries to thwart the enemy's mission to weaken our nation. Bobby, I am more than proud of you, for all Americans shall one day owe their freedom to you and all the other young men and women that were chosen for this brave and selfless operation to save America. I only have a little time left to talk with you. I want you to know …" Mike took in a deep breath, and his eyes turned glossy. "I want you to know that I love you very much. I … I didn't want you to be a special agent in the Elite forces. I was being selfish, but I finally decided to let you go, for the sake of our country." Mike wiped a tear from his eye.

"Well, Sport, you have always wanted to be a *Green Beret*. Now you're going to be more than a *Green Beret*; you're an *Elite Beret*. When this is all over, we'll see each other again. Actually, I've been told that I shall see you before they assign you to your special task." Mike laughed a little, as a tear ran slowly down his left cheek. He then smiled and said, "See you soon, Soldier. Remember, I love you very much." The tape went blank and fuzzy again.

Bobby looked into Ms. Kay's pretty eyes. "I knew he'd send the video like he said he would in the letter. I miss him *so* much, Ms. Kay! I really want to see him in person. I guess I'll have to wait, though." Bobby hung his head down and sighed.

Ms. Kay held Bobby close to her. "Oh, Bobby, this is so hard on all of us. You do know now that your brother does love you very much, and he will see you again soon. Just think ... after your training, he'll watch you walk tall and proud across a military platform as you stand before the Commander and receive your official document as an *Elite Beret*." Her gentle voice and kind words filled Bobby with new hope. He could not wait to graduate.

Then Bobby said words that almost melted Ms. Kay's heart. "I pray every night that God will soon let me see my brother. Do you think God hears me?"

Ms. Kay was silent for a moment. What could she say? That she didn't believe in God or that He can't hear Bobby's prayers? "Yes, Bobby, I think God hears your prayers."

"You know, Ms. Kay, I really love you. I am so grateful God sent you into my life. It'd be so lonely here without your pretty face and kind voice. I pray for you every night, too."

Ms. Kay almost broke into tears when Bobby told her this. She collected her emotions and held her breath for a moment. She had not expected this from Bobby. "How did I ever let myself become so attached to Bobby?" thought Ms. Kay, yet she knew the answer. Deep within herself, she knew. Bobby was the son she had never had a chance to enjoy. He reminded her of Jerry in so many, many ways ... his cute dimples, dark hair, and his bubbly, so-alive personality. Ms. Kay hugged Bobby and said, "I'm praying with you, too, Bobby. Remember, I'm praying too."

Chapter Thirteen

Mike buckled his back strap that held his cane onto his back. The sheath, which housed the cane, resembled a thin quiver. He had fashioned the sheath himself out of hard leather long ago. He checked the time. "Seven-thirty already. Good. The meeting will soon begin, and I'll be there, all right, but I won't be crying and shaking hands." Mike tucked his ski mask into his jacket, and walked into the darkness. He opened his attached garage door and pushed his XR 650L out of the garage. He mounted the motorcycle and looked into the starry night.

"Well, God, you know what I've got to do. I'm only asking for a little help … just a little." Mike inserted the key in the ignition and turned it to the right. The starter kicked in, the bike lit up, and Mike roared down the driveway and onto the road.

Audra sat next to Toni, the new woman that had lost her dear child to leukemia, and her husband to cancer. Beside her—where she had expected Mike to be sitting—sat Carolyn Watt, a one-time nurse that had lost her only child. A horrible man had abducted her and driven off swiftly in his Stingray. Carolyn had seen the abduction and quickly called it in to the Phoenix Police. Within minutes, the police were roaring after the man, sirens screaming, but they did not know the psychotic man was suicidal. Upon hearing the sirens, the man knew the police would capture him. He, therefore, had driven his vehicle through the gate of the Catalina Parking garage that stood next to St. Joseph's Hospital, raced to the very top of the garage, pushed the gas pedal to the floor, running head-on into the cement barricade that encompassed the top floor of the garage. The Corvette flipped end over end, as it went over the side of the tall garage. No one had survived.

Audra became anxious and worried about Mike. She retrieved her cell phone from her beige leather purse and called him. Mike felt his cell phone vibrating inside his jacket, but he let it vibrate until it had stopped. He was in no position to answer the phone at the moment; besides, he did not feel like answering it, anyway.

Janet Riley stepped into the room with Katrina Adams. They both looked very attractive together, like models waiting their turn at walking down the runway. They walked over to the table together and took their seats in front of the group. Cal looked at Audra and said very gently, "Where is Mike? I thought he was coming."

Audra did not know how to answer his question. She fidgeted around for a little while in her seat then said, "Actually, I don't know. I thought he was coming, too. Maybe he feels out of place right now, or too hurt to talk effectively. I mean, he did act a little weird last time. I think he needs more time, Cal." She sounded a bit cold and careless, unsure of how to address Cal after their strange cavern meeting.

"I agree. I thought he seemed a bit odd myself," stated Carolyn.

"People, this is a support group. I have been to many meetings, and I can assure you that Mike is groping right now. He'll come back here when he's ready," said Janet.

"What do you mean by groping?" asked Toni.

"Toni, have you ever told yourself something more could have been done for your son?" Toni looked at Janet with glassy eyes. "Yes, and I still believe if I had been much richer, he would have been saved, as I could have afforded to buy him the best medical care. But, I'm just a poor Hispanic woman, barely making ends meet," cried Toni.

"Tonight, we are going to be discussing this very topic. Katrina and I discussed this topic earlier. We were going to speak on other cases and how others have adapted to the loss of a child, but we have some new people here, so we have chosen the topic, *'Groping,'* or what some refer to as *'Denial'.*" Janet spoke clearly, when she talked, so all could understand.

"How are we groping?" asked Toni.

"Toni, when we start telling ourselves more could have been done, 'I should have done this or that,' 'If only....' or 'It's my fault....' we are, in essence, groping; we are denying the true cause, and fix our minds on a false assumption. It is these assumptions that hinder us from healing," stated Janet.

"I agree entirely with our guest. I find myself groping from time to time, even though my son's abduction took place many years ago, but I also find ways out of groping. For example, I recently made friends with a young boy who sort of ... well ... reminds me of my missing son," Katrina interjected. "We share a unique bond. What I mean by *'groping'* is this: If we continue groping for a solution to a past event that possibly eluded us, that will hinder our healing and keep us in despair. We find it is easy to remain in this groping, but if we choose to look for things in our lives that make us happy—like people, family and friends—we'll find these things also," Katrina concluded, with her smooth, sweet voice.

As further conversation ensued, Mike sat outside under a tree. He'd concealed his bike behind a large bush, and sat waiting for the meeting to adjourn. He did not at all trust Janet Riley, and tonight he would prove why.

Mike's thoughts went to Bobby, as he sat under the large pine tree. He wondered what he was doing, and if he was lying in a cold, musty, dark room somewhere far away. Maybe he imagined all this, and Bobby's abduction was no different from the next one. Maybe he had lost his mind, and he was dreaming this up as he wasted away in a mental institution in Tucson, like Audra's mother. Maybe even Audra was just a figment of his imagination ... a shapely feminine figment, at that. Mike told himself to stop thinking that way. "This is too important to be thinking about such topics as pretty women," Mike briefly chastised himself. Many thoughts passed through Mike's mind ... strange thoughts that made little sense. His mind drifted back in time to when his parents were still living and brought him much happiness. He remembered his mother smiling at him, and his father throwing the ball to him. "Watch the ball, now. Keep your eyes on the ball, or you'll miss it. Don't be afraid of it, Mike." His father would tell him. Then there were the bike rides, the picnics, and all the trips and laughter he had shared with his parents which now flashed through his mind. Then the reality—the utter sadness—of their deaths entered his mind. Finally, his mind came back to the present. "Maybe I have a right to go nutty ... should be allowed the privilege of losing my mind," said Mike aloud. As he leaned against the tree trunk, a squad car passed by, but they could not see Mike under the tree, as his clothing was too dark.

Audra began to feel very uncomfortable when Cal talked about his son, and how much he missed him. He explained how he dealt with such a great loss, how horrible it had been at first, how he groped for answers, also. Audra burned inside. She wanted to jump up and say, "You might as well have murdered your own son for the pleasure of money. You fool these people, but you don't fool me!" She squirmed in her chair as he went on. Cal's wife, Linda joined in, explaining how strong Cal had been through the terrible crisis.

"Yeah, I'm sure he laughed all the way to the bank over Cliff," thought Audra to herself.

The group broke up earlier than usual. Nobody else besides Cal and Linda had felt like talking about their denials and groping. Janet and Katrina looked at each other as if to say, "Well, that was a bust. Better luck groping around next time." Maybe they should have assigned another title to their topic. The people, a rather quiet bunch this evening, rose and walked out the egress of the annex building. Soon all had disappeared into the darkness.

Janet told Katrina that she again had to hurry to the Windemere Hotel. She left before Audra and Katrina did, quickly darting across the school parking lot and climbing into a Mercedes. She turned on the engine and drove away, not seeing the motorcycle that had moved in behind her. Mike kept his headlights off until they were in traffic. He then followed Janet south on Highway 92, expecting her to turn into the hotel. However, she passed up the hotel and continued down the highway.

"Hotel, huh? Well, let's see where you shall take me, Ms. Janet, or whoever you really are," said Mike. Mike was wearing a dark helmet, which helped conceal his head, also. He remembered the day when he rode into town to purchase a helmet. He really had wanted to buy a light-colored full-faced helmet, but at the time, they only had a black full-faced helmet. He bought it because he had been very eager to ride his new bike. Now he was glad he had bought the dark helmet.

Janet drove south until she came to Carr Canyon Road. She turned right onto Carr Canyon Road and proceeded west. Mike fell back, as he did not wish to invite suspicion. He watched from a short distance as Janet's vehicle disappeared around the first bend. Immediately, Mike throttled the accelerator and zipped around the bend in time to see the Mercedes disappear around another bend. He kept up this cat and mouse game until he saw Janet slow down in front of the Mayor's house. She almost stopped, as she passed the Mayor's driveway, then she sped up and pulled into a lane a few houses down from His Honor's house. She backed out of the lane and headed towards Highway 92. "Great! She turned around," moaned Mike. With his headlights off, he looked around him for some place to ditch his bike. He saw a small trail leading off the road. He slowly rolled onto the trail, hid behind some tall grass, and shut off the engine. He covered his taillight with his hands, to extinguish any chance of Janet's headlights reflecting off the bike's taillight as Janet drove by. Now he wished he had chosen a three-quarters helmet instead of a full-face model, because he would have been able to wear his night vision goggles with his helmet when he rode in such darkness.

Mike started the engine and roared back onto the road. He turned left and drove past the Mayor's house again. "'Wonder what she was doing here, anyway?" Mike noticed that the note he had left the other night no longer hung on the newspaper box. He laughed a little, then turned his Honda around and quickly caught back up so he could keep an eye on Janet's car, while maintaining his distance. Janet pulled off the highway and headed west on Peter Canyon Road. She drove a few miles up into the canyon, and then turned into a dark lane. Mike followed her taillights as far as he dared, then he ditched his bike behind a red elderberry bush, and hung his helmet over the taillight of the motorcycle.

He crept very cautiously up to the house. When he reached the house, he saw the Mercedes parked in the lane in front of the garage. A tall iron fence encompassed the property around the house. Jagged arrowheads shot up towards the sky from the top of the iron pickets. "Cool," Mike muttered sarcastically. "Now all I have to do is spear myself like a whale." In frustration, he let go with what sounded half moan and half laugh, at the absurdity of this venture. He was not about to give up, though … not after he'd come this far.

Mike put his night goggles on, and walked around the outside of the iron picket fence until he found a place where the bottom of the fence had rusted away, from weathering. He cautiously kicked out the remnants of what once was a sturdy fence. He dropped to his belly and squeezed under the fence. When he reached the other side, he quickly rose to his feet, ran over to the side of the adobe structure and crept around to the back. He hugged the exterior wall of the house as he inched closer to the back door of the garage. He frowned as he tried the door. He thought Janet probably would have locked the door after entering but, to his surprise, the door was unlocked. Without questioning the motive behind the unlocked door, Mike entered the garage and skulked over to the door leading into the house. "Maybe she was in such a rush, to go to the bathroom or something, that she forgot to lock the doors." He tried the door; this inner door was also unlocked. Slowly he pussyfooted into the house, as he ever so gently closed the door behind him. Wooden steps led to a landing above. The landing invited him to vulnerability, but he had to try it, anyway.

Mike then began holding quite a conversation with himself. "What if she catches me? What will I tell her?

> 'Hi, remember me, Mike Taylor? Well, have I got a deal for you! You see, I was just passing by and I knew you would be interested in why I couldn't make it to the meeting tonight....'

"No, that wouldn't work. Uh, let's see....

> 'Hi, I needed to talk to you, since I missed the meeting so—by using my ESP—I found your house, and then I....'

"Face it, Mike; you're in for it, if she catches you. But, since I have my mask on, if I'm good enough, she won't see me—even if she does see me. That really did sound like an oxymoron, didn't it? Mike, you'd just better hope she doesn't have a gun!"

His on-edge nerves were definitely cluttering his mind. Mike slowly crept up the stairs, his heart pounding, and peered over the landing … nothing. The house seemed void and lifeless. Mike hurried across what appeared to be the family room; he wanted to locate an office or a room that possibly served as an office. As he passed the kitchen, he heard Janet talking on the phone. "Yes, I passed his house." She paused. "He's still flying the flag." She paused again. "Yes, if there is any change, I'll let you know." She turned to face the door leading to the family room. "No, he did not show up tonight." Janet sat down on one of the kitchen chairs. "Yes, I'll stay in touch. Goodnight." She finally hung up the phone, folded her hands in her lap, and sat quietly.

Having found no office yet, Mike walked to the back of the large house looking for a desk, or anything that might hold documents or papers. He carefully opened a door midway down the hall. He looked inside to see a small filing cabinet, a desk and a computer. "Aha!" He walked over to the desk and looked in the top drawer. "Bingo! That was easy. I knew she was in on it. These forms prove it." He quickly folded up some of the notes, and tucked them into his front pocket. Mike turned and walked out of the room. He scurried quietly down the hallway and carefully made his way past the kitchen. As he was about to walk down the stairs and exit the house, he saw a shadow behind him. In a flash, he dropped and swept Janet's feet from underneath her. Janet fell with a thud, as she had not been expecting this move at all when she saw that someone was in the house. She held a .45 automatic in her hands when she went down, and the gun went off as she hit the floor. Mike jettisoned down the stairs and out the door swiftly, as if a bull were right behind him and gaining. He slid under the fence in record time and bolted for his bike.

As he mounted his bike, he heard a shuffling noise in the dark ... the sound of feet running over gravel. "Lord, she is one tough lady. She's fast, too." Mike hit the start button on his bike. The Honda immediately responded, as Mike gave the throttle a quick torque and spun the XR around, tearing down the lane. Janet fired her gun in the direction of the sound. She heard something like glass breaking as the noise of the motorcycle faded into the darkness.

"The SOB! I'll probably need a regiment of chiropractors for this aching back! Well, I know you're not a killer, or you would have killed me back in the house. Hmmm, I wonder ... yes, I hope you got what you wanted. You are a desperate young man and, boy, are you in for a surprise! Oh, the back! How it does *'tickle'*."

Mike rode almost a mile before he turned his headlights back on. As he turned left onto Highway 92, he thought about what he had seen. Glancing quickly as he'd pulled the documents from the desk drawer, his eyes had caught a familiar symbol on a photographic map that was among the documents. The map represented areas in South America that were now familiar to him and Audra, due to the documents he had earlier managed to confiscate from the Huachuca Produce warehouse. Topics of human trafficking were highlighted on some of the document pages. Yes, Janet was deeply involved ... very deeply.

Mike's heart rate decreased a little as he neared Hereford Road. Excitement filled his mind and body as he turned right on Hereford Road. "Next stop, Audra's house," said Mike in anticipation. Mike turned the engine and headlights off as he pulled into Pat and Audra's lane. He coasted to a stop near the side of their house. Just in case someone had tried to follow him, he thought it best to hide the motorcycle from view. Mike took his goggles off and started to hang them over his right mirror, when he finally saw the bullet hole. As there was very little traffic on the road, he'd not consulted his rear view mirror on this trip, so had not noticed it. "Man! She meant business back there. I could have been killed! 'So much excitement, I didn't even realize she'd shot at me." After examining the gaping hole in his nearly annihilated mirror, a queer, weak feeling overcame Mike. Another few inches to the left, and he would still be back there in the bushes ... only very much dead!

Mike glanced at his watch, as he rapped on the door. "Ten thirty. Hopefully someone is up."

Audra pulled the front door open, as she turned on the outside porch light. She freaked when she saw Mike standing on the landing with a dark ski mask on, "Ahh! Wh....!"

Mike quickly took his mask off. "Oh, Audra, it's me, Mike. 'Sorry about that; I completely forgot about this darned ski mask."

Audra caught her breath. "Thought that was you, Soldier. Why weren't you at the meeting tonight?"

"I had business to tend to."

"Look at you! You look like a cat burglar or something."

"Well, the business I tended to required this get-up."

"More spying ... and without me! Well! Don't I feel jilted."

Mike looked at Audra and smiled. "May I come in? I have so much to share with you. I practically got killed tonight confiscating the notes I have in my pocket."

"Really! You must tell me all about it. We missed you at the meeting, but nobody really talked very much, except for Cal and his wife. The man makes me ill. I hate to be around him since we've discovered what he did. I could puke on him. Come to think of it, I almost did." She rambled on, as Mike unstrapped the weapon from his back, and removed his dark shirt exposing a light blue T-shirt. Then he took off his shoulder holster and gun, and rolled it carefully within his dark knit shirt.

"Guess you really were serious tonight. Where did you go?" Mike took the folded papers out of his pocket and handed them to Audra. She took them in her hands, finding them to be a bit damp from sweat. "Ugh! You sweat hog. They're all damp from your perspiration ... unless, of course, you took a quick dip before you arrived."

"It's just sweat, my dear, and—like I said—I almost got killed tonight. I had a right to sweat."

Just then, Pat walked into the living room, "Hey kids, what's up?" Mike looked a little surprised to see the Colonel standing in his PJs, smiling broadly at both of them.

"Ah ... Pat, you're up a bit late, aren't you?"

"What do you mean?"

"I mean, don't you have to work tomorrow?" Mike wondered.

"Yes, I do, but my presence will not be required until 1200 hours."

Audra broke into the conversation, "Hey, what is all this? The photo on this letter looks sort of like a military map of some kind." Pat snatched the letter from Audra and studied the map. Audra drew away. "Well, please ... be my guest!" she huffed, with exaggerated upset.

"I will," chuckled Pat. Mike almost reached for the paper—then he remembered Pat's assuring words at the club. He relaxed and listened. "These are military aerial photos, possibly storage or personnel bunkers ... maybe even camps or compounds. The broad areas look to be well secured and guarded. These people are either trying to keep something from escaping, keep trespassers out, or both." Pat walked over to an end table beside his recliner. He pulled the drawer open and extracted a large magnifying glass. He walked back into the light where Audra and Mike stood. "Why don't we all have a seat at the kitchen table? I think we'll all feel more comfortable, and possibly discover more light in there."

"Good suggestion," said Audra. They all walked into the kitchen and took a place at the table. Pat recommenced reading the photos. As he scanned the photos, he noticed grid lines and numbers, degrees and directional points. The compounds came into view more clearly under the lens. The buildings and surroundings looked well capable of supporting human life.

"Get the map, Audra, please ... my map." Audra raced into her father's study, thumbed through some paperhangers until she found the map to which her father had made reference. She ran back and laid the large, flat map on the table before Mike and Pat.

"My military strategical map of the world ... ta-*da!* I can pin down a cockroach in the middle of a sandstorm in East Africa with this," laughed Pat. Mike thought his globe was impressive, but this map looked downright complicated. All the lines and numbers seemed complex ... even confusing. Pat handed the magnifying glass to Mike, asking him to read off the numbers and degrees.

"Sixteen degrees, 30 nautical south, sixty-eight degrees, nine nautical west," Mike read.

"Okay, we're in Bolivia. Now, I'll trace the grid on the photo. Fifteen degrees, 45 nautical south, sixty-seven and then 0 degrees west, puts us right here on the map. To be exact, it puts us ten degrees east of La Paz, next to the Rio Mamore in Bolivia. This compound is precisely east of La Paz. Right here." Pat pointed to the map with his pencil. Audra and Mike looked at the area.

"You know, the letters talk a lot about human trafficking and arms smuggling. There are some coded messages, and we even see the Maat symbol that we've seen on other documents. Whoever these people are, they have sure done some homework here." Audra paused for a moment. "Mike, where did you get these?"

Mike gazed around the room, wanting to avoid the question, but he realized his position, so he gave in. "I followed Janet Riley to a rather nice, roomy house off of Peter Canyon Road. I sneaked into the house and confiscated them."

"You mean you *broke* into the house?" scolded Audra.

"No, I walked in. The doors were unlocked," retorted Mike.

Pat stared at Mike, puzzled. "That's odd. Why on earth would she leave her doors unlocked ... unless she was expecting ... yea, enticing ... someone to walk in?"

"Oh my gosh, Mike! She knew you were following her. She purposely left the door open to catch you!" exclaimed Audra.

Pat looked down at his map as he leaned over the table. "She either set you up, hoping to catch one of the men responsible for the explosions in the cavern, or she works for the good guys. Judging from what I see in front of us, I'd say the latter is probably the most likely answer. These are reconnaissance photos taken from a sophisticated spy plane—possibly a Stealth—to avoid radar detection. I can't imagine why the enemy would take secret shots of their own back yard."

"You're telling me that Janet is a *'good guy'?*" Mike asked, incredulously.

"Good *girl,* you mean," snapped Audra.

"Yeah, that too," Mike added, smiling at his rather insignificant *faux pas.*

Pat said, "I can't be sure. I'm only saying that the evidence here weighs in her favor."

Mike felt really stupid—even silly—now. "If that's the case, then I surely have misjudged that woman. If so, I can't now help but feel like I broke the law."

"You did, silly. But, if you hadn't, we wouldn't have the photos. And I think the photos are pictures of the compounds where they keep our children," explained Audra, her voice dynamically filling the air. She continued, excitedly. "We have really come far in this caper! We know almost exactly the locations to which the children and arms are being shipped, we know how they're being shipped, and we even have motives. We also have possible dates of shipment, and we now know what many of their code words mean."

Mike interrupted, quizzically. "But, I don't know what some types of candy refer to."

Audra and Pat both laughed. "They refer to the weapons, Mike. *'Candy canes'* are assault rifles, *'PEZ dispensers'* are magazines, and *'Pop Tarts'*— which are pastries, not candy, by the way—are either grenades or some other type of explosives. You see, Audra and I studied all this the other night." Pat, having a competitive nature, had to chuckle at having one up on Mike.

"I knew *'candy canes'* were *AK-47s*. I knew it!" exclaimed Mike, triumphantly.

"Anyway, before I was so rudely interrupted," Audra reminded the guys, "I was going to add that we know all this, and more, yet we really only have one solid suspect, along with the faces and only first names of a few strange men."

Mike's eyes lit up. "Wait a minute! Maybe we do have a little something else by which to track down the heathens. I have a tape recording of a meeting that took place at the Deer Lodge between a few of our wicked friends."

"What! How did you pull that one off?" Audra was impressed.

"Actually, a friend of mine did it. He followed Cal Brown to the Lodge, then he sneaked inside and managed to tape the meeting, somehow. Anyway, I have the small recorder and tape on me as we speak. I'm going to keep it on me, too, as my house was broken into earlier this evening." Mike stopped and looked at Pat, as he finished. "It happened while we were golfing, so I've got to be extra careful."

Audra looked at her father wide-eyed, then she looked at Mike. "Your house … broken into? What did the devils want?"

"They took the metal briefcase, after rearranging all my furniture and silverware. They must have been very experienced to find it. I thought I had hidden it in a perfect spot, but I guess if you have been in the trade a long time, you learn every hiding place in the burglar's book of ethics. And to think, I was going to take that case into the authorities. No offense, Pat, but our golf match delayed that opportunity, possibly for good," groaned Mike. Pat and Audra remained silent, imperceptibly redirecting the conversation back to the recorder.

"Mike, let's have a listen to that tape," said Pat. Mike ran over to his jacket next to the front door and fished out the tape. He raced back and placed it on the kitchen table, clicked the *'on'* button, and turned up the volume. They all sat there, completely absorbed in the mysterious conversation, with their ears focused on every word. At times, they had to strain to hear every word being said.

Audra wanted to shout out Cal's name when he said, "All was not lost. The last shipment of candy made it across the border, and we did manage to salvage a considerable amount of dust, and no children were being shipped that night, so we did not lose any of them." She remained calm for the sake of her Dad and Mike, who were both listening intently to every word the tape contained.

"The voice of the man doing most of the talking sounds very familiar," Mike thought to himself. Mike and Audra both thought the woman's voice sounded familiar, but they could not quite place her. A rather startled Mike—hearing for the first time of Audra's past occupation via this tape—studied Audra's countenance as they heard the main speaker say, "His girlfriend has a very interesting background. She once held a position as a special undercover agent for the government. Our intelligence sources in D.C. were only able to attain just so much information." Audra gave Mike a stunned look; after all, this is not the manner in which she'd planned for Mike to learn of her former occupation.

Trying to lighten this serious revelation a bit, Mike mimicked Audra's recent serenading she'd done, upon learning some information about Mike. He began singing, *"Getting to Know You...."*

However, it was a most serious Audra who interrupted him, stating, "Mike I suppose you have a right to know I once was a special agent for the FBI. I was discharged because I wouldn't keep my nose out of Todd's case. We are not allowed to become involved in a case in which we have a personal stake. Well, I made it my business to become involved."

"So they fired you," Mike interjected.

"I prefer to call it an *'honorable discharge'* but, yes, they let me go. This is part of my past I didn't want you to know. I was going to tell you, anyway, but not just yet."

"Well, now I know why you are so combative in nature, Sweetheart—probably why you know so much about weapons, too, I presume."

"Yeah, working at one time for the FBI does allow one plenty of opportunities to learn many things."

Mike put his arm around Audra and kissed her cheek. "I'm sorry, Audra."

"You mean you're not angry at me for keeping you in the dark?"

Mike laughed, "Not at all! I love you too much to be angry with you. I just wish the Feds had reconsidered. You would have found Todd and discovered this evil operation long ago, if they had."

Audra felt honored by Mike's kind words. About the time Mike finished his reassuring remarks to Audra, the recorder clicked off.

Once the tape had finished, Pat's voice boomed boisterously. "Wowee! Now, this is getting very interesting." Pat looked squarely into the eyes of his daughter and Mike. "I know who the main speaker in that meeting is, and you ain't gonna believe it. I can hardly believe my ears! At first, I only had my suspicions, but when he mentioned he knew me personally, my suspicion turned into reality. Get ready, kids; World War *III* is about to begin!"

Chapter Fourteen

Audra and Mike lifted themselves off their chairs at Pat's words. "Pa, you have our complete and undivided attention! *Who* are you talking about?"

Pat shifted a little in his chair. He looked up at the ceiling as though he really did not want to divulge the information. He finally looked into Audra's eyes. "Audra, does the name General Howard T. Blake ring a bell?"

Audra fell back into her chair. She swung her head from side to side in disbelief. "Oh, Daddy! Not the good General! No! Tell me it isn't so! Ple-e-ease, Daddy!" Audra felt fluid beginning to build up in her eyes. "If it wasn't for General Blake, you know what would have happened. He helped us out considerably during one of the worst crises in our lives. I just can't imagine he'd be involved. Of all the people, I … I just don't … I can't understand." Tears that had been slowly welling up began pouring from her eyes. Mike sat helplessly by. He did not know how to react to the scene before him. He did not know General Blake, or what he had done in the past for Audra and her family. To Mike, the General was now a prime suspect, however, and a very good connection to the weapons trafficking, no doubt.

Pat hated disappointing his daughter like this, but felt he had to explain to her the reality behind all the misery their *'good General'* could have put a stop to but, instead, had allowed. "Audra, honey, listen, we cannot look upon him like we used to. Sure, I realize how much he did for us, but that was *before* we knew about this. We have to put what he did for you and me behind us now. 'Food for thought, girl … I want you to think this over very carefully, and then tell me how much *the 'good General'* actually *helped* us. Now that you know he is apparently involved in this criminal activity—possibly even a leader of this ring, as well—how does this make you feel about the General and Todd's abduction? The General knew all along about Todd. He even could have *prevented* his abduction! You know that all your research into this heinous case led you to realize that Todd's abduction was *planned out!*" Pat put much emphasis on the last couple of words, as he was becoming livid, realizing once again all that had happened, which the General had helped cause, that he just as well could have prevented.

Audra stared at her father, still in shock, finding it hard to believe what she was hearing ... that someone who had appeared so caring, a winsome gentleman—at least outwardly—could be so entangled in something that had destroyed countless lives.

Pat took a deep breath, trying to remain as calm as possible, then continued. "With this in mind, dear girl, think about where we would be today—not only you, me and Todd, but your mother, as well—how we'd be living if nothing had happened to Todd. Think about the hell the *'good General'* allowed us all to go through!" Her father was shouting by the time this last statement spewed forth from his lips. He was angrier than she had seen him in a long time.

Audra began searching her mind for memories. She thought about the hospital, the trials and hearings, how her dignity was stripped from her unfairly as her accusers gloated. They never experienced the abduction of someone they loved very much. How dare they judge her so harshly! The only thing that had saved Audra from prison, and from living a life of dishonor, came in the form of a seemingly very understanding man by the name of General Blake. He had appeared to stick his neck—and reputation—on the line for Audra, when her career had been jeopardized for the sake of her missing brother. Now the truth stood bare, right in front of her. The General's former image dashed, the truth showed him for what he really was ... a towering tyrant, and shocking symbol of total debauchery.

She wiped the tears from her drooping eyes and said, "Well, now we have two prime suspects, anyway. I wonder how he gets his greedy little mitts on Russian assault rifles, grenades, rocket launchers, mortars and who knows what else?"

Pat scratched his head and rubbed his jaw while Mike just fidgeted in his seat, looking perplexed. The scenario that was playing out before him left his head in a whirl. His mind went blank from overload.

"Okay, let's see...." Pat's excitement began to grow, as he purposefully withdrew his attention from the sidetrack on which the General—by virtue of appearing on the disconcerting tape—had led them, back to their current discussion. "Now, Clarkdale was mentioned in that Lodge meeting. I'll be back in a flash," he spoke, as he ran off to retrieve something. Pat was becoming very animated, as he always had before any important military mission, and he knew that this mission could be the most rewarding of all time. He raced into the study, took down a book from the middle shelf, mumbling as he fumbled through the pages. "No, not that one; see *'Zinc production due to scarcity,*

scarcity during WWI and WWII'," he self-advised, as he lifted yet another book, throwing the first one down on the floor. "I'll clean up later," he muttered, hurrying to find his intended information. "Yes! *'Mills scarcity during WWII.'* 'Got it!" he exulted, racing back to show something to his daughter and Mike.

Audra and Mike, by now, were just staring at each other. They had little to talk about at this time, still digesting their individual reactions to the revelation of Audra's previously hidden—to Mike, that is—vocation. Besides, they were both busy, marveling, as they watched Pat; he'd not been this lively in ages. Pat removed his map from the table, opened the book he'd just scrounged up, and slammed it down onto the wooden surface. He leafed through its pages, stopping somewhere midway in the book. "These books are kind of like U.S. Military historical bibles. I used these a lot when I studied at West Point. Here is what I want you to see. Actually, I'll read off some excerpts concerning scarcity:

> *'Economic Spotter: Resources During World War II Key Economic Concepts: In World War II pennies were made of steel and zinc instead of copper and women were working at jobs that men had always been hired to do. Why? The answer is simple. During war times, scarcity forces many things to change! The United States government started a rationing program during World War II. Families could buy only so much gas, sugar, meat, and other goods. By rationing food in this way, the government could make sure that adequate supplies of food would be available for the war effort.'*

Pat continued to explain: "Mills such as those in Junction, Colorado; Preston, California; even Clarkdale, Arizona, opened for business, giving precedence to steel and zinc production, rather than copper. Zinc alloy products helped to reduce the burden for copper products, that were needed at that time for the war effort."

"And?" Audra asked.

Mike's previously blank mind was suddenly aroused, hearing Pat speaking about some of the changes war brings to a country, and he took no time to see if Pat had been planning a response, but blurted out. *"And* ... there is the plant in Clarkdale yet today. I saw it from the Clarkdale train, as I rode through the Verde Valley. The Verde River supported the manufacturing of steel and zinc at that time."

"Very good, Mike," Pat commended him. But, let's say that we've been told the mill has been closed when, in actuality, it is still operating secretly under the careful eye and scrutiny of our *'good General.'* It was no secret that these mills not only produced steel coins, but also produced weapons to aid in our war effort."

"Hold on, Pa! You're saying that the mill is still open and they're pumping out *AK-47s,-74s*, and who knows what out the door ... even now! How could they implement such a thing? How could they alter the plant to produce Russian weapons? Where would they find the molds, and so forth?" Audra was puzzled.

"Well, on 25 December 1991, while we celebrated Christmas, the Russian flag was lowered from the Kremlin and, by the end of the month, the Soviet Union had passed into history. The Baltic States gained their independence, now that the Russian KGB and the Politburo were practically liquidated. Divisiveness among the military grew, leaving the Baltic States ripe for plundering. Boris Yeltsin was too busy justifying his leaning towards liberalization and democratization to properly watch over the affairs of these newly free states, which were not accustomed to governing themselves, and could not quite do so adequately. It is safe to say that, at this time, our evil crusaders, along with black market operation officials, plundered this area, confiscating arms, as well as the hardware and equipment necessary to manufacture the assault rifles, mortars and grenades. The molding equipment, presses and plates were most likely shipped here via cargo freights, then smuggled into the States from Panama, possibly through stations, like the one we have here. In our case, it doesn't really matter how they smuggled it in. What matters is that they did get it into the States, and set up shop," explained Pat, calmly and clearly.

"Fascinating.... So, now all they have to do is fill the molds, fine-tune the end products, and transport the goods about three hundred miles away or so to the foothills of the Huachucas, pour a few sweets over the crates, and ship 'em across the border as *'candy!'*" roared Mike.

"This is getting so deep, it's filling my wading boots," commented Audra.

Her father put his muscular arm around his daughter and hugged her tightly. "Before this is over, Sweetie, it's bound to get deeper in here."

Audra looked affectionately up at her father, "Now, why was I expecting you to say that?" she chuckled.

Mike remembered a question he had wanted to ask Pat earlier. He looked directly at Pat inquiringly. "Pat, What does General Blake's middle initial stand for?"

"Thomas," replied Pat.

Mike raised his right eyebrow. "Well, now I know who Tom is. General Blake's deviant associates sometimes address the General as *'Tom,'* also. I heard one of his cronies call him *'Tom'* when I was hiding under a truck inside the compound."

Audra interrupted Mike. "Yeah, I'll never forget that day!"

Mike became excited. The puzzle was finally piecing itself together. He jumped out of his chair, excitedly suggesting their next move. "Let's make a play! I mean, let's take all this to the authorities. We have the tape, and we can easily lead them to the cavern. We have a big player now ... General Blake. I'll bet he'll squeal his head off to save his butt!" exclaimed Mike, jumping up quickly from the table.

"Not good. Not good at all," said Audra quietly, as she reluctantly burst Mike's bubble. "Mike, think about what you are saying. The recorder is not admissible evidence. The judge would throw out the recorder as an attempt to defame the parties speaking on it. For all intents and purposes, the skit on the recorder could be just that ... a skit ... a silly play. We can't provide pictures, or films. By the time search warrants are issued, the cavern would look like an abandoned mine, or worse. They might blow it up, and the children would no doubt be taken to Never-Never Land ... a place that only God Himself would then know about.

"Of course, we would have some questionable maps, letters and symbols to throw in front of the court ... adding to their entertainment. Hell, we may even present a case so fascinatingly incredible that Hollywood might buy theatrical rights to the case!" jeered Audra.

Mike sat back down and pondered her words. He wanted to curse, but he literally bit his tongue.... "Audra, honestly ... did you have to be so danged blunt?"

"Yeah, I did. I'm sorry, Mike. It's just that I don't want to see you make a mistake similar to the one I made not too long ago."

"You mean Todd—right?"

"Yes, I became entirely too gung-ho, letting my emotions override my better judgment," Audra ruefully warned him, sadly thereby reminding herself, as well.

"My daughter's right. We can't go to the police now, or the FBI, or any other agency. Mike, we will make a play—a discreet play—one that will flush these loony birds out of their comfortable nests and into our waiting sights. And, it will all start tomorrow when I talk to Sergeant Sterling Crowe, an old miner and cowboy. "I think he knows more about Fort Huachuca and the landscape around it than the mountains themselves. "Remember that the key goal is to decapitate the monster. We have to get the ringleaders, or they'll just run off, hibernate for a little while, and then start up again later, once things have cooled down."

Pat placed his strong hand on Mike's right shoulder. "Mike, you look like you've had a rough night, and it's getting late. Why don't you just sack out here for the night? We'll all be able to think much more clearly after a good night's sleep."

Worn out from all the activity of the last several days, as well as the thoughts that had been overtaking his mind since hearing of Audra's past career, Mike smiled gladly at the thought of not having to drive home, though it was not all that far. He looked thankfully into Pat's eyes, "Sure, why not? I've secured my house, soundly. I really don't want to be alone tonight, anyway." Mike suddenly remembered a question he had wanted to bring up earlier. "Hey, you know, the people in the recording mentioned a Mr. Hooah, several times. What kind of name is that?"

Pat slapped Mike on the back. "Good question, Mike. 'Sounds to me more like something we use in the army when we're at a loss for words ... or to signal attention or acknowledgment; other than that, I haven't got a clue."

Everyone being pretty much talked out, after an emotion-packed evening, they all left the table, and started getting ready for bed.

Mike laid down on the carpeted floor in the living room. "Well, Bobby, you now have a very intelligent colonel, Colonel Pat, at your disposal. We're gonna find you, Little Brother." Mike closed his weary eyes and fell asleep.

Early Thursday morning, as the first rays of dawn's dim pallid light began to creep across the sky, somewhere in the distance, a coyote howled ... a nighthawk screeched loudly overhead ... as a dark blue GT Mustang II pulled into the long lane leading to the compound off Hereford Road. Two drivers stood outside their straight trucks, discussing basketball, when they espied the Mustang pulling into the lane. They carefully watched the car as it approached them.

"'Think that's the guy," hollered Jack.

The other driver squinted his right eye, as though looking through a telescope, and responded, "Aye! We were told some dude would be here just before dawn," he growled. This was the homely driver that Audra had seen exit his truck to move the log that she had placed in the lane.

Jack looked up, then he looked at Cain, "Hey, Cain, did y' ever meet this guy before?"

"Nope! 'Never set eyes on him before; been told he's a Chicano, though, if that helps any," Cain carelessly spoke.

"I wouldn't get racist if I were you. Chicano or no Chicano, he was sent here to help us so, in light of that, I think we should welcome him as a guest." Jack always was the more proper one of this duo.

Cain continued his rant. "Don't know why we need him here. Heck, we could probably handle any problems around here ourselves."

Jack gave the rotund man a queer look when Cain said that. Jack liked Cain, for the most part, but he did not care for his bigoted ways … calling other races names and such. He never forgot the day when Cain almost got them both killed in Montgomery, when his big mouth spilled out a politically incorrect name for some black men that were gassing up their trucks at a Flying J's Truck Stop, off Interstate 65, just south of Montgomery. Before they knew it, they had been looking down the muzzle of a gun and, if the Highway Patrol had not pulled into the truck stop just then, who knows what species of flowers they would be pushing up right now.

They kept a weathered eye on the car, as it crept slower.

"Come on, dude! We ain't got all day and night!" moaned Cain loudly.

"Come off it, Cain," Jack tried to mollify Cain's irritation, lest it be apparent as their guest arrived.

Cain looked at his friend and resumed his complaining. "What? Is *'dude'* a bad name now, too? Maybe I ought to call him, *'Your Majesty,'* huh!"

Jack shook his head. "No hope for the clueless, stubborn fat man," he mumbled.

"What'd you say?" Cain seemed moody for some reason, and Jack knew this was not the time or place to be rude. The vehicle came to a stop in front of Jack's truck. A slim-looking figure exited the vehicle, and walked slowly towards Cain and Jack. The man carried a cane in his right hand that looked more like a sign of royalty, than a walking aid. "Huh, maybe we *should* call him *'Your Majesty.'* he looks the part. His cane even looks like a king's scepter," said Jack.

The approaching figure held his posture like a very proud count. His dark, unbuttoned cloak blew open as he approached the men. His attire, walk, and the way he held himself as the wind swirled added an aura of mystery to Manuel's persona. He resembled a phantom in the night, a soft-walking apparition, rather than a flesh-and-blood man. "This guy already gives me the creeps," said Jack softly, out the side of his mouth.

"Gentlemen, is it not a beautiful morning for a nice little chat?"

Cain stepped back a little. He did not like this man. He did not like his looks, even if he was very handsome, and the morose man definitely did not like Manuel's blissful attitude. "If you say so," he mumbled in obligatory fashion.

"God does show his glory in the early morning hours, don't you think?" Manuel gave Cain a piercing look that would cut a man's heart out if looks had such a capability. Cain felt anger, tinged with fear, welling up within, as he watched this enigmatic man closely.

"Sorry for our rudeness, Mister. My name is Jack and this is Cain." Jack pointed at Cain, as he extended his hand.

Manuel shook Jack's hand, keeping one eye on Cain. Somehow, Manuel sensed Cain's fear and anger, and now he was toying with the stout man. Cain's anxiety inched up a notch, unable to avoid Manuel's intense stare.

"I assure you, gentlemen, our interview will be quite painless. I just need a few pieces of information, and I shall be on my way," Manuel assured them.

"What kind of information?" asked Jack. Manuel tucked his cane under his shoulder. "The kind that goes back almost a week ago, when one of you witnessed a man running through the thick brush. I'm sure you haven't forgotten already, for one of you did fire his gun at him."

"I didn't fire it at him," Jack was quick to explain. "I did fire it above his head, utilizing the fear factor, as it seemed it was just some silly high school punk pulling another prank. We get them around here now and then. They mean no harm, but we do not like them getting too close to the center, so we get a little rough from time to time," explained Jack, as he looked into Manuel's eyes.

"Hey, Bubba! We don't have all day. We've got t' get going, so why don't you take what Jack said, and go. Nothing happened here that day, so we're out of here!" Manuel making no move to leave, Cain ordered, "Move your car!"

"Who are you?" a now-curious Manuel inquired.

"I guess you can't hear, either, can you? You heard Jack tell you my name. I ain't gonna repeat it, and I don't take orders from a...." Cain was abruptly stopped. He barely saw a flash, as he heard a *'thwack-thwack'* noise. His left kidney felt like a poker had stabbed him, and his *solar plexus* burned like fire. He began choking, as he held his rotund stomach. Slipping to the ground, Cain continued wheezing and gasping for air. Jack stood in awe and horror at the uncanny speed Manuel possessed. He had never seen a man use a cane as Manuel did, at such a tempo, and with superb accuracy.

All social niceties aside by now, Manuel matter-of-factly asked, "Shall we proceed, gentlemen?" as he explained, "You see, I do not have all day, either."

"Well, I don't see why not. Please excuse me, but what is your name, sir?" asked Jack.

"Names are rarely important but, because I like you both, I shall tell you. My name is El Niño."

"So you're El Niño; I've heard a lot about you," said Jack. Cain still lay on the ground. His had regained his breath, but his back and sternum were sending series of harsh, painful signals throughout his body, and he felt the urge to urinate.

"Ah ... I hope from what you've heard, that I meet your expectations."

"I am honored, Sir. You surpass my expectations, and you have my fullest attention. Besides, I'm just a truck driver; I'm not a fighter."

"Come, do not put yourself down, and never say you are *'just* this or that.' Say what you are with pride. Anyway, I am not here to breathe philosophy into your lungs, or to fill your hearts with gladness. I need to know what this man looked like."

"Well, it happened over a week ago, and it was getting dark."

Manuel rolled his eyes. "Why does every interrogation have to start this way?" he wondered. "Come on ... take your time ... think."

Jack replayed the entire evening over again in his mind, then he spoke. "The man was young, tall, husky and, I believe, he was blonde. At least he looked blonde, unless he had a light-colored cap on. But, I'm pretty sure he didn't."

"Ah-h-h, where did he run to?"

"He ran into the San Pedro River, right over yonder," Jack said, as he pointed in the direction of the river.

Cain moaned as he painfully got up on his feet. He then excused himself, and walked into the thick brush. He relieved himself in agony. It felt like he was urinating fire. "Oh, man ... ugh!" hollered the large-bellied man.

"Don't fear, my friend; the pain will go away ..." then pausing before continuing, Manuel added, "... in a week or two."

"Thanks for the wonderful news," groaned Cain.

"And then what?" asked Manuel, as he walked beside Jack's truck.

"What do you mean?"

"I mean, what else did you notice? 'Anything? Did you see anything else, anything at all ... another person, a piece of cloth, or something he may have dropped?" Manuel caressed the side of the truck with his right hand.

"I did see a piece of paper ... actually, a letter," replied Jack.

Manuel bent over and looked under Jack's straight truck. He scanned the undercarriage very carefully with his eyes, as Cain returned to join the two men. Manuel opened the top pocket of his cloak and fished out a penlight. The bright beam from the flashlight lit up the right leaf spring, axle and frame members. "Did you happen to look at the letter?" Manuel rose and walked slowly to the other side of Jack's truck, as he awaited Jack's answer. He whistled a Spanish tune, as he made his way around the back of the truck, stopping just in front of the left rear tire.

"No, I didn't look at it."

"Why not? Did you not think it odd that he'd leave a letter behind?"

"When you put it that way, yes. But we were already late, and it just looked like a crumpled up piece of trash." Jack moaned a little as he spoke, feeling awkward and foolish for his perceived oversight. Manuel was making him out to appear very dense.

Manuel continued, "Hmmm...." as he scanned the left frame of the truck near the left axle. "So you were driving this truck ahead of Cain here, and stopped to make the turn at the end of the lane?"

"No, I backed up, and then made the turn."

"Oh, you backed out, but you were ahead of Cain?"

"No. I mean ... of course I was ... yes." Jack was becoming just a bit confused now; Manuel's piercing inquiries could have that effect on people at times.

Cain cut into the conversation with a very submissive tone in his voice. "Yeah, I was in back of Jack. I also remember having to stop because someone, or something, put a big log over the road. I would have run it over, but I wanted to be helpful."

"Did you see who did it?"

"No, I didn't," Cain ruefully admitted.

"Do you think the trespasser did it?" asked Manuel, as he stood up straight and faced Cain.

Cain knew better. "Sir, I don't see how he could have. Jack saw the kid running up ahead of him. He'd have to be in two places at once to put the log there, too. I figured there were two, maybe three, pranksters ... one up ahead of me and one or two in the weeds. They're probably still laughing at us," chuckled Cain, softly, as he'd become somewhat subdued, following the episode with Manuel's cane.

"Hmmm. So, Jack, what is missing from your truck? What did you lose?"

Jack looked very dumbfounded. How did this man know anything was missing? Jack said, "I lost a map, a shipping ticket, and an inventory sheet."

"What was on the map?"

"The United States. Places I go to ... places I'm going to go to."

"Nothing else?"

"There was a small picture of a topographic map on the back of the larger map of the United States," replied Jack, a bit reluctant to even answer, by now. He was getting a little frustrated at himself.

"Easy, Jack; you are doing very well. Better than I could, even. You know what my next question is going to be, I'll bet."

"Yes: *'What was on the small map?'* The answer is, the topographic area of a delivery site."

"Ah-h-h, you mean Coronado Park?"

"Yes," replied Jack. Manuel shifted his weight to his right side. "'You know your right rear undercarriage of your truck is much cleaner than the left. Does that make any sense?"

"No, it doesn't. I don't understand."

"It's nothing … unless you pick up hitchhikers that way." Manuel stated this very calmly. Jack looked at the ground below him. He tried to make some sense out of Manuel's words, but could not, as his mind worked differently than Manuel's. He lacked the experience and interrogation skills—not to mention the analyzation skills—which Manuel seemed to have been naturally born with.

Manuel turned to walk back to his Mustang. "Gentlemen, it has been a pleasure. I truly enjoyed our conversation. Before I go, though, I have another question for you both."

Jack and Cain turned toward Manuel. Cain winced as he once again felt a hot flash of pain shooting through his kidney, and continuing to traverse down his ureter. "This is going to be a long *'couple of weeks.'* Thanks so much, Manuel," he moaned within himself.

"Gentlemen, do you not think it very odd that it was soon after you lost the map to the site of the cave when the two intruders exploited it?"

"Just a weird coincidence, probably," said Jack. Cain folded his arms and leaned against Jack's truck for support, rubbing his kidney gently from time to time. It seemed Manuel was not finished asking questions, after all. "Jack, isn't it odd that your map disappeared right after you saw the kid … the *'prankster,'* as you call him?"

"Yeah, but if you're insinuating that he could have done it, then he must have broken into my truck and stolen it!"

"Oh? Even when your truck was inside the compound?"

"Ah-h-h, no. I usually leave the truck unlocked when I deliver inside that building, but he would had to have broken into the garage to steal anything, then," surmised Jack, as he scratched the side of his neck. His anxiety was growing with every passing minute.

"You really do need to have the left rear undercarriage of your truck looked at. It does not match the other side, which is much greasier … more dirty." With that, Manuel turned and began walking away towards the Mustang again.

"Whatever you say, Mr. El Niño," sighed Jack.

Manuel quickly turned back, staring intently at Cain and Jack. "One more little detail," said Manuel sternly.

"What, Mr. El Niño?" asked Cain and Jack, simultaneously.

"Never, ever … never, do you hear me … never call me *'El Niño'* to my face again. The last person that called me that name, after fair warning, lost his tongue. When he found it, it was—as you say here in the United States—too *'gross'* to be sewed back on. Manuel left them with that final thought in mind. He sat down in his Mustang, started the engine and peeled out, leaving Jack and Cain coughing in a cloud of thick dust.

After the dust settled, Cain glanced over at Jack as he wriggled his tongue around a bit, then touching it against his front teeth. "I think I like my tongue where it is!"

Jack stuck his tongue out, then swiped his lips with the end of it. "I have to agree with you, Cain. 'Think I'll keep mine also." He paused, then suddenly, "Hey!"

"Hey, what?" asked Cain.

"Shoot! We didn't get his real name. Now what do we call him if we do see him again? Certainly not El Niño!" Jack exclaimed, savoring the thought once again of his tongue remaining in his mouth.

Meanwhile, Manuel sped back to his motel. He wanted to rest a bit for his next—more pleasant than the last—job. "Ah, yes, it is time for you and me to become acquainted, my pretty little dove. Americans ... they are so dull. I do not understand how they always overlook details that lead to the obvious. We shall soon meet, Miss Audra. You are an astonishing woman," laughed Manuel, as he held up the elastic strap she had inadvertently left behind in the cavern. He gently stroked, and then deeply sniffed ... *"Ah-h-h"* ... the pleasantly perfumed strap, as he drove west on Hereford Road.

Mike thought about all the errands he had to accomplish, as he torqued the throttle of his motorbike. The sun hovered just above the ground, spraying its brilliant color-laden golden rays across the desert landscape. Mike loved watching sunrises and sunsets. He imagined God—in the morning—carefully taking up, first, his flaming red paintbrush. Then, with His utmost divine precision, gently stroking the canvas of the earth's surface below, adding a few touches of some of the most magnificent shades He's created: magenta, violet, purple, reddish-orange. Finally—in a unique and awesome crescendo—His earth below happily awakens to the bright, blissful fireball of dazzling whites and intense yellows. He likened sunsets to sunrises in reverse, with God pulling back one stroke of His magnificent brush, as the colors recede from their former brilliance and intensity to a bright crimson, against a beautiful turquoise sky. Finally, the heavenly brush withdraws from the face of the earth as darkness rests upon the land, and only the faint glitter of God's beautiful gems, resting on a blanket of black velvet above, are left to provide but a faint glow of hope below.

While holding these tranquil pictures in mind, Mike came up a classy blue Mustang that caught his eye as he passed it. He shortly thereafter turned left onto the road that led to his house. He had much to do. There was a door to repair and calls to be made. He possibly had a few visits to make, also, but his energy level had been revived, after a peaceful sleep at Audra and Pat's home. Now that Pat was involved—an expert in combat and military tactics, a man that had connections in and out of the United States—Mike felt a renewed hope within. Colonel Patrick Heyburn was a war hero in the Gulf, and a chief Special Forces advisor in Afghanistan after 9/11. Now Mike had a team and, though he would not have minded taking a leader's role, he had no qualms—thought it a rather wise decision, in fact—about giving this role over to the much more experienced Colonel Heyburn, who had recently seemed to come back to life.

Audra stirred from her bed. What was that infernal noise? "Oh, yeah ... the alarm. 'Time to prompt myself and get going; got classes today.'" She yawned, stretched her arms and forced herself out of bed. She was not a morning person. She heard her father talking on the phone as she walked to her bathroom. "Wonder who he's talking to?" she thought, as she reached down and turned on her faucet, adjusted the temperature, and splashed clean, cool water on her face. "Ah-h-h, yes! Nothing like a cool splash to awaken the mind." She reached for a towel and closed the bathroom door.

Pat heard Audra's shower turn on as he spoke to Sterling Crowe, a one-time Sergeant Major in the Army, who somehow had managed to stay at Fort Huachuca during nearly his entire career. Pat and Sterling had hit it off well from the start. They shared much in common.

Pat learned that Sterling had been stationed over in the Gulf, and assisted in mountain/desert military tactics for some of the ground forces that were deployed to Afghanistan. After the Gulf War, Sterling found himself back in the States. He'd expected to receive a transfer from the Fort to another post but, when his orders came through, he discovered the commander at Fort Huachuca liked him too much to set him free. Sterling retired four years after Pat arrived on post; however, he and Pat stayed in touch. They visited in each other's homes from time to time. Sterling, a true friend, did all he could to encourage Pat through all the tragedies that had befallen him and his family, but he could only do so much. He had witnessed the Colonel slipping into despair, feeling helpless to assist his friend out of his emotional darkness, as their visits and phone calls decreased.

Sterling was, therefore, rather surprised when he heard Pat's voice explode with great enthusiasm over the phone. Sterling had to actually slow the Colonel down, as Pat rambled on with questions concerning the Post, and possible old bunkers or storage depots, sheds or small warehouses in and around the Post ... or even off the Post. "Pat, please slow down. Your words are traveling at the speed of light. I can't keep up!"

"I'm sorry, Sterling. 'Tell you what ... are you busy right now?"

"Ha! Just what I need is some more excitement in my life, you know?"

"Yeah, I do know, and that's why I'm calling … to add a little excitement to your boring life."

Sterling could hear the smile in Pat's voice. "Good! Where are we going?"

"You're going exploring with me. I'll explain when I get to your place. We'll take my Jeep. Put on something durable, 'cause we may have to tramp through some heavy brush and thorny bushes."

"Sounds exciting. What are we going to explore?"

"Well, that depends on you."

"Huh! What do you mean?"

"Like I said, I'll explain when I get to your house." Pat hung up his phone, turned and walked out of his room and into the living room. He wore his camouflage fatigues and a cap. Pat received a call from General Command earlier in the morning, informing him that the major he was to brief at 1200 hours could not make the briefing, since there was a glitch in his TDY form that needed to be corrected. Pat rejoiced at the news. This meant his presence on post would not be required at all today. The entire day was his. He lifted a green duffel bag from the tiled floor, shouted *'goodbye'* to Audra through the bathroom door, locked the door on his way out, excitedly bounded into his Jeep, and rolled out the driveway. A blue Mustang passed by him, drove a bit further down the street, and parked alongside the road.

Pat pulled into Sterling's lane. He lived off Ramsey Canyon Road about three miles west of Highway 92. He lived alone in a light red brick house, typical of houses built in the late fifty's … rather square, but very cozy. His wife, Jackie, had passed away two years earlier, leaving Sterling with a broken heart, but not a broken spirit. People loved Sterling's healthy vigor, and bubbly personality. He appreciated both adults and children. Since his retirement, he had become involved in coaching and scouting. 'His' kids called him *Sergeant Pain*, a pet name originating from his coaching style … he demanded discipline from his players. However, they loved him dearly, because they knew he cared about them.

Sometimes yet he wished he could have had children … and, hence, grandchildren … but, unfortunately, the mumps Sterling had contracted as a young man had left him sterile. This played on Sterling's pride, but Jackie had loved Sterling with all her heart, building him up and supporting him in all his endeavors, no matter how trivial. Oh, how he missed her! When his country had called him to go into Afghanistan, he remembered jokingly trying to stuff his lovely Jackie into a big luggage bag.

"Now, what would you do with little old me over in Afghanistan, Big Boy?" laughed Jackie, heartily.

"I'd dig us a little fox hole and, for once, be able to stay warm at night."

"Maybe even hot," giggled Jackie.

"And sweaty, even," laughed Sterling.

"O-o-oh! I feel that feeling coming on, you big Stud Muffin, you!"

"Well, what can we do about it, Honey Bunny?"

"Come closer and I'll show you, Studly," Jackie had crooned in her most enticing voice. Their lips met, as they tumbled over the pile of clothes on the bed. Soon clothes were flying everywhere, as they both gave into passion.

Someone was knocking loudly on the door. Sterling awoke from his reverie, holding a couch pillow tightly in his arms. He sighed, as he often did, when he discovered it had been just another dream. "For one fleeting moment, I thought I had you in my arms again, my Queen ... my Love." As Sterling was moving slowly, having been abruptly awakened from a deep sleep, the pounding began again.

"Okay, Pat, hold your cantankerous pants on, will you? I'm coming!" shouted Sterling. He yawned, stretched, shuffled to his front door, and opened it.

"Morning, Sterling! 'Ready to lead the expedition?"

"Now, that's what I'd like to know. D' you mind telling me what you mean by suggesting I lead this adventure?"

"Sure, but you must promise your complete confidentiality ... that you will not tell a soul."

"Oh, boy ... one of *those* adventures! 'Reminds me of our days in the Gulf."

"I wish it were that easy."

"Pat, what on earth do you mean?" Sterling paused. Noting Pat's seriousness, he added, "Okay, you have my word. I give you my oath of silence."

"Remember when Todd was abducted?"

"How could I forget?"

"Well, I met the lad whose little brother was abducted earlier this month. He's dating my daughter right now. Anyway, this is my story in a nutshell." Pat quickly related everything he knew, without going into detail. He even showed Sterling some of the inventory sheets, and played the tape that Mike had let him borrow. Pat had dubbed the conversation onto two separate discs, which were well hidden back at his house, so he was not worried about carrying the tape with him.

"Wow! That, Colonel, is too heavy ... but not for me. You can count me in, Pat. Now I know why you are so interested in trying to find the possible location of some serious hidden contraband. Well, let's get going. I do have a few good places in mind. They are on Post, but not right in view." Sterling grabbed his jacket, and threw it over his shoulder, as the men bounded out the door.

Audra slipped into a light windbreaker, grabbed her chemistry book and school supplies, then tucked them into her tote bag. She locked the front door behind her, and walked over to her Nissan. She opened the door, threw her tote bag on the passenger seat, and started out her lane. She turned Right on Hereford Road and headed into town. She had left an hour early, so she could stop at the *Lone Star Café* and grab a quick breakfast. She loved their omelets and coffee. Her mouth watered as she neared the restaurant. She pulled into the restaurant, and parked her truck. She did not see the blue Mustang, slowly passing by, that disappeared down the road.

After her tasty breakfast, Audra said goodbye to Sherrie, her friend and waitress, dropped a generous tip on the table, paid for her meal and left. She thought about the day ahead of her. She thought about many things. Her father's vitality seemed to have returned, for one thing. While this made her very happy, she also knew a positive outcome would bring about an even greater healing … not just for Pat, but for her mother, too. Is it likely that Todd is still alive … that he is down there somewhere working in the jungles, or holding an *AK-47?* She shuddered at both possibilities. Many thoughts filled her mind, as she drove down the highway past a gas station, a car dealer and a shopping plaza. Turning right onto Colombo Avenue, she was only about a mile from the college now, and was soon pulling into the campus parking lot.

Once there, she retrieved her tote bag, turned and looked at the white administration building/testing center, and then she walked to class. A blue car slowly drove past her Nissan and pulled into a parking space, five vehicles down from Audra's spot. After Audra had vanished out of sight, Manuel stepped out from his Mustang with a briefcase, and walked over to her truck. As he turned to walk between her truck and the vehicle parked next to her, his briefcase fell open. A book fell out, and several loose papers scattered across the parking lot in the wind. He quickly dropped his briefcase, attempting to retrieve the far-flung papers. Some pretty, young female students that stood nearby offered to help him.

"Ay, caramba! I am too clumsy. I should have checked the latch on the case more carefully. 'Too much in a hurry!" laughed Manuel. The teens handed him a few papers, and ran to gather some more. With their focus entirely on the papers that had taken flight, Manuel quickly took a valve stem remover from his shirt pocket and—in what seemed merely a second—he loosened Audra's valve stem on her right rear tire, until it slowly began to leak. With speed and ease, he slipped the valve stem remover back into his pocket, as he continued to retrieve his papers. His smooth, agile movements were too quick for the human eye to perceive. Finally, the students had helped Manuel recover every loose paper.

"My lovely ladies, I am so honored by your generosity. You are so kind to help an oaf like myself," laughed Manuel loudly. His bright eyes and charismatic persona, along with his very handsomely chiseled face, immediately won the girls over. They were both charmed and infatuated. One of them, a pretty brunette, giggled and said, "We are happy to help you. Are you a student here, or an instructor?"

"Oh, I'm sorry, young ladies. My name is Manuel. I am just a humble instructor, here on business. I am looking for the Dean, Dr. Faring; we have an appointment. Seems as though the good dean wants to discuss how the Spanish Literature, Philosophy and Language course may be revised. Apparently, he believes the existing one is not up to par ... not dynamic enough, so to speak."

"Well, we'll take you to him. We're going right by his office." Manuel gave them all a cheerful look and said, "Oh, no, that is quite alright. I like challenges. I think I can manage." The girls insisted. They would not take *'no'* for an answer. "Okay, let's march on, then. Lead the way, girls," Manuel spoke, with bravado. They all walked towards the Dean's Office together. The girls felt like they were walking on air, as Manuel's charm and great looks had easily mesmerized them. When they reached the Dean's Office, Manuel bid them farewell, and thanked them kindly for their help. The brunette handed Manuel a note. Manuel took it as he walked into the building quartering the Dean's Office.

"Ay caramba, I hope this does not take too long. If only I could just hand this man a book and leave." Manuel stared at the note. "She does not know me, yet she gives me her name and number. 'Call me. I think you are very hot!' Girls in the United States ... so simple, so naïve. "Tis no wonder they make for such unchallenging prey." Manuel chuckled as he wadded up the note, tossing it into the nearest refuse.

Manuel had called Dr. Faring earlier from his motel. His call was no surprise to the Dean, as Manuel had met him once before, while on a visit. Actually, he had made it a point to meet the Dean. Manuel knew that, at any moment, he might be needed in Sierra Vista, and Manuel always believed one should have a good reason for conducting business in a town, other than seeking retribution for someone's misconduct or terrible deeds. He made it a point to nurture similar contacts in every city, country, state or province where he conducted business. This gave him a solid legal reason for being in these different regions, in case the locals ever became suspicious of him.

When Manuel called, he had found the Dean was excited for such an opportunity. He quickly told Manuel to pick the time and day. Manuel's contacts in Sierra Vista had provided him with a list of class schedules and times for all students whose last names started with 'H.' Therefore Manuel had known Audra's schedule before calling the Dean, and planned accordingly. His organizational skills—of which this was just one small example—amazed all that knew him. Before nine in the morning, he had already interrogated Jack and Cain, made sure Audra left for classes, and set up an appointment with the Dean from his cell phone, as he drove to the college. "I amaze myself at times," said Manuel in self-congratulatory fashion, as he opened the door to the Dean's Office, smiling at the attractive receptionist. After introducing himself, it took only a moment for Manuel to manipulate the receptionist with his charm. Yes, American women … very simple in 'la cabeza.' "They need some Latino in them," Manuel mused.

Pat looked at Sterling as they tuned left onto Buffalo Soldier Trail. "Sterling, do you have any idea yet as to what 'old dump' the General may have been referring?"

"Actually, Pat, I've been thinking about that since we left my place, and I finally do believe I have an answer." Pat's eyes lit up with anticipation, as he coaxed Sterling to go on.

"You know, Pat, a long time ago when Chief Cochise—the Apache leader—declared war on the white people, he began raiding settlers and folks around San Pedro Valley. So, the Army set up a camp near the Huachuca Mountains to defend the settlers, and travelers, from the deadly Indian raids."

"Wasn't that back in the mid eighteen-hundreds?"

"As a matter of fact, yes, it was. Cochise campaigned against the Army from about 1862 through 1877. The Post was only meant to be a temporary site, but we soon learned how important the strategic site really is. Although the Army later closed over fifty forts and camps in the southwest region, they retained Fort Huachuca. In 1886, it became the advanced headquarters for military operations against Geronimo. Later, it served to keep down outlaw and renegade Indian activities. Today it serves in testing of electronics equipment and as an intelligence school."

"Well, I know that," Pat said, suggesting it might be better for Sterling to tell him something he did not know.

"I know y' do, Pat. The point I'm trying to make is that when the Army closed all the other forts around the Huachuca foothills, they didn't take everything with them. I remember an old shack that sits near a trail that veers to the right, off from Hines Road. You know the road that cuts through the Huachuca Canyon?"

"Yeah, I know the road. It's primitive, but not difficult to drive on."

"Anyway, Colonel, I think that shack is a good place to start. I really can't recall seeing another shack built as sturdily as this one. It is very well fortified with solid brick and mortar. It appears to be currently maintained ... at least the last I saw of it."

"When was that?" asked the Colonel, as the guard at the main gate saluted the Colonel and waved him in. Pat saluted back quickly and drove on. They both forgot about the question as they rode on by the guardhouse. They drove one way on Squire Avenue towards the main Post, past an elementary school to their right, and a closed Army health care center to their left. Driving down the road past a rubberized blue running track, they linked up with Winrow Avenue. They soon found themselves passing the Provost Marshals' station and the MP station. This was the Fort's old section. Old sandy peach-colored military army barracks lined the preserved streets. They saw and heard no signs of people in this area, and the surroundings were so quiet that one might get the impression they stumbled into a military ghost camp.

Pat and Sterling traveled on until Christy Avenue veered off into Hines Road. Soon the pavement gave way to gravel, where two bright yellow, swinging, pole gates, used to barricade the canyon road, stood secured in their open positions. A white sign with large, red lettering read: *'Warning: Do Not Enter At Night.'* They proceeded through the gate, and further into the canyon. They passed up other signs indicating the name *'Huachuca Reservoir,'* signs warning of horseback riders, signs telling of nearby campsites—such as Camp Navajo, Camp Pima, Camps Yavapai, Coconino, Greenlee—and so on. They noticed a couple of swing sets standing within the campgrounds for the children. They continued driving past all the campsites, deeper into the canyon. Soon they found themselves among many tall oaks, sizeable poplars, some aromatic pines and spruces, along with many healthy-looking hawthorns, brittle brush, mountain mahogany and various berry bushes. Pat noticed the robust growth of trees. "It amazes me how large these trees are. Get a load of the massive size of those oak trunks ... and look at all the tall cottonwoods!"

"I'm not surprised. You see how steep the hills become, as we enter further into the canyon?" Pat looked at the high peaks composing the steep foothills. Some peaks were smooth, rolling pinnacles, covered in golden grama and range grass. Above the tree line, and further towards the top of the mountains, small cedars, pines and rounded shrubs, known as Mexican manzanitas, grew. Most were seen spread out in thin groves. As Pat studied the scattered foliage growing near the high peaks, the answer came to him in one word: 'runoff.' "Ah, the water runs rapidly off the slopes and into the canyon below, so the trees here are well watered, but only the ones that are able to survive the rapid runoff grow higher above."

"Very good," Sterling commended his friend.

"I noticed that there are some dead oaks in this canyon. I wonder why?"

"Too much water at times … possibly sickness or lightning strikes. But the Army does do a good job of clearing out waste and dead trees. This is why we don't see a tremendous amount of overgrowth. Hey! There's the road to our right!" exclaimed Sterling. Pat stopped quickly. The force of the sudden quick stop lifted both men from their seats.

"Easy, Colonel, please; my bones ain't what they used to be."

"Well, Sergeant *Creampuff,* I certainly do apologize," Pat said, employing their occasional sarcastic, teasing way of communicating. Sterling laughed a little, as Pat drove onto the gravel road and started up a hill. The road showed signs of recent travel, and it seemed to be partially maintained, but the way was less comfortable than that for which they had hoped. It wound through gorges and smaller canyons between the foothills. Then it started downward and turned back up again. Finally, Sterling told the Colonel to stop. Sterling jumped out of the Jeep and began to scout around for the old abandoned bunker. Colonel Heyburn seized his green canvas duffel bag and began following Sterling. They stomped through heavy brush and stooped under tree limbs. After a short, brisk walk, Sterling pointed at a structure. Erected In front of them, built into the side of a hill stood a solid block wall with heavy slurry and mortar poured over it … the ammo bunker. They walked up to the wall. They both saw a heavy-duty armored lock, securing a thick, heavy metal latch. "You'd need a bomb to blow that lock off," said Sterling. Pat shifted his weight to his left, as he withdrew a camouflaged object out of his duffel bag. "What's that?"

"Oh, just a little present I obtained over my years in service. Actually, it's state of the art … a laser probe. Watch this." Pat opened the box-like container, exposing a small monitor and a keyboard that resembled a notepad. He unwound the wire from the thin probe and placed it inside the key slot of the lock. Then he pressed a few keys on the board. The monitor displayed many numbers and letters as the laser flashed slightly within the slot. Finally, the words, *'scanning complete, insert plate'* flashed on the screen. Pat pulled a metallic-like plate from a slot below the screen and placed it onto a hard rubber pad just to the side of the monitor. The words, *'READY TO INITIATE'*—all in caps—flashed across the screen. Pat removed the probe jack and closed the metal lid.

After a few moments, the lid opened, and Pat pulled out a key with a narrow handle. Sterling looked on in amazement. He asked if he could look at the key. Pat handed the key over to Sterling, who held it in his hand, marveling. He shook his head and said, "This is unbelievable! 'Like out of a James Bond movie. The key seems to be very solid and strong, too."

"Special metal alloy," Pat explained, as he took the key back from Sterling, placed it in the key slot, and turned it. The lock readily released. "See, child's play, the computer scanned the inside of the lock and determined the shape of the key hole down to the last micrometer on each tumbler, then it cut alloy with a special laser, sort of on the order of a micro plasma cutter, and ... *voila!*"

They entered the bunker carefully, half expecting an encounter, but as they walked across the cement floor, they realized the bunker was very quiet, void of any personnel.

"Do you think we're in the wrong bunker?" asked Sterling.

"Your question may be a bit premature. Let's continue our search in here," Pat suggested.

They walked throughout the bunker, shining their lights all across the room. "Think we've been had, Colonel!" Sterling impatiently blurted out.

Pat walked to the far corner of the bunker. "Y' think so? Shine your light over here, Sir!"

Sterling joined him in shining his light at whatever it was Pat had found. "Well, Colonel, when did the Russians invade Fort Huachuca?" asked Sterling as he stared at a brand new Russian *AK-47* magazine. Sterling was bending over to pick up the magazine, when Pat extended his arm out and held him back with the palm of his left hand.

"Let's leave it be. As a matter of fact, I think we should leave this place just as we found it ... totally undisturbed."

"Sounds like spy versus spy," laughed Sterling.

"Yeah, kind of like that, you might say. This magazine, for all we know, may have been left here on purpose. They come in, see it moved or gone and ... Bingo! They know someone's found the place, figured how to gain entrance without blowing anything up, and has been tampering inside."

"Bingo! You're right, again, Pat."

"Yeah, Bingo!" repeated Pat, as they both rose to evacuate the bunker.

"Well, that went smooth as silk," boasted Sterling.

"You're not just a'kiddin'! You know, Sterling, I get the willies when an operation is completely void of any resistance."

However, did it really go that smoothly? Nearby, under a thick manzanita bush, lay a camouflaged form of a man, his face covered with paint that matched his surroundings. He trained his Elite IR pro hunting scope on

Sterling and Pat, as he adjusted the intensity illuminated reticle ever so slightly, until the two men came into perfect focus. He tightened his right index finer against the trigger guard of his assault rifle and smiled. Quietly he said, "Bang, bang! You're both dead!"

Mike called Matt, his hired private eye, for an update. Matt answered his cell phone while sitting in a sub shop eating a bologna, pastrami and cheese sandwich. He answered the phone with a little food in his mouth. "Ah, yes, Mike!" The detective knew it was Mike when his name and number appeared on his phone display.

"Matt, please tell me you have some news." The private eye laid down his sandwich, drank some soda and began.

"Well, my fine fellow, I checked up on our Sheriff; the fellow appears to have a solid background. 'Came from a solid family that lived in Bisbee all their lives. His father was a law officer, as was his father before him. The only time there was a discrepancy came about when he beat a man a little too brutally for hurting a young child, but the people of Bisbee and Cochise County stood firmly behind him during that time. I would have, too. The man had broken both the young girl's arms, and probably would have killed her if our hero, Sheriff Tress, hadn't arrived on scene."

"How old was she?"

"Five," explained Matt.

Mike cringed. "That man did deserve a thrashing. Sounds like our Sheriff is more a hero than a crook. I don't know what to think about him now. What about Janet Riley?"

"Mike, now, she is a mystery, for sure. Without proper identification, or at least a bloody good picture of her, I cannot pin down her background to anything. My assistant followed her to what he described as a compound of some sort, outside Hereford, near the San Pedro Bridge. The place you wanted me to investigate … I can't link it to Huachuca Produce. So far, it checks out as a charity warehouse for food and clothing. Oh, yes! Huachuca Produce is a large non-profit agricultural plant, headquartered outside of Brownsville, Texas. Anyway, my assistant said that it looked like she was just surveying the area. Maybe she took pictures also, because my assistant saw her holding something like a camera in her hands. He watched her from a distance, with a rather pricey telescope I let him borrow."

Mike fidgeted a bit, and then asked Matt if he'd managed to dig up anything on this El Niño guy. Matt's response was not complete, but did add a little spice to the conversation. "My lad, I researched every available archive and form I could get my mitts on, but all I can come up with is bits and pieces of a man that is known by the alias, *El Niño,* in South America. Apparently, he's some recluse the police in Bolivia believe is called upon by the Syndicate in Colombia and Bolivia. Nothing is for certain, however. Dennis is not up to much, nor is the Mayor, so far as we can tell. They see each other on short occasions. Perhaps you may want to talk to Dennis when the time is right. He may be more help than a hindrance. Just act as if he's still your friend. You could deceitfully pry some imperative information out of that hole in his face," laughed Matt. Mike listened to every word Matt said very carefully.

Then he said, "Perhaps you're right. I just may talk to Mr. Perris." Having no more questions, Mike said so long to Matt, and hung up his phone.

Manuel sat patiently in his Mustang, reading over forms and material that the Dean had given him. Manuel had found the conversation more stimulating than he expected. The Dean knew a great deal about Spanish philosophy, as well as culture. The more they talked, the more amused Manuel became. They parted on very good terms, with plans of meeting again sometime. When Manuel left the Dean's office, he could not help but notice that the secretary was seeking her own good terms, as well. While Manuel had been meeting with the Dean, she had spruced up her hair, and refreshed her make-up. What's more—only reinforcing Manuel's perception of women in the States—she bent over, revealing much more cleavage than Manuel had noticed when he first walked in. She winked, swooning, "I hope we see you very soon."

"I shall be counting the minutes," Manuel said, toying with this woman he could detect was attempting to entice him.

"Really?" replied the secretary with glee.

Manuel leaned over, took her hand in his, gently caressed and kissed it. "'Tis a custom where I come from."

Kicking her shoes off, almost instinctively, as her body quivered with delight, she whispered, with a smile, "I get off at four-thirty."

Manuel stood up. "What kind words, and such a tempting invitation. Ah, but I am very sorry. I think it would not be wise for me to mix business with enchantment tonight."

"Perhaps another night?" pleaded the secretary.

"Perhaps, my Little Dove," Manuel further toyed with her.

The secretary, at hearing these words that gave her at least a small amount of hope, felt faint and a little flushed. Her eyes fluttered as she watched the handsome well built Latino walk out of the office. As he stepped out the door, the secretary excitedly said, "Oh-h-h, what a cute rear!"

Manuel laughed at the foolish behavior of the secretary, as he settled back into the plush seat of his car. "Manuel, you know what consorting with women can lead to. How many men do you know who threw their lives away because they could not keep their male appendage in their pantalones? 'You remember Ricardo? My, such talent and potential he had. Ah-h-h, but he could not leave the ladies alone. Everywhere that fool went, he left a legacy of broken hearts. One day, however, one of those little doves pointed him out to the police. He lost his cover that day. Aye, in court, ten other women pointed him out, some calling him this name, and others that name … all names given to the sort of men that committed the wicked crimes of which he was accused. What a fool! He simply had no power over his little ferret," laughed Manuel.

His eyes suddenly caught sight of Audra, bounding quickly towards her Nissan. He gazed at her in awe. Her very feminine form and picturesque face filled his heart with great delight. "Oh, my! God himself must have created the word *'beautiful'* to describe this angel." Having even thought the word *'God'* brought back to Manuel the words from his father, "My son, Manny, promise me that no matter where you go, or what you do in life, you will always put God first." Manuel shook the convicting words from his head, as he watched Audra get into her pick-up. She started the truck and had driven just a little ways when she stopped. Manuel backed out of his parking space, and drove up behind her truck. His little caper had worked. The flaccid tire contained no air at all.

Audra jumped out, and ran around to the back of her truck, "Shoot! Dang it, anyway." She quickly turned to walk back to the cab of her truck to make a call, running right into Manuel, who had by now gotten out of his car to see if he could help. As she walked, she threw her hands up in the air in frustration.

"Oh … ah-oh!" Manuel shrieked in surprise. "You got me good there, young lady!"

Audra stepped back. She felt just horrible. "Oh, my gosh! I am so sorry. I did not know anyone was so close!"

Manuel—his hand holding his nose—said, "Oh, it is nothing; just a little tingle. I thought maybe I might help, but I guess I only managed to stick my nose in the wrong place."

Audra moved closer to Manuel. "Let me see your nose, please."

"Of course," Manuel obliged, dropping his hand from his face.

Audra gasped. It was not because of the small trickle of blood coming from Manuel's nose, but because she had never seen such beauty in a man's face before … and what eyes he had! "Is this a movie star in front of me?" thought Audra. Manuel's mild Latino accent served only to accentuate his charm and exceptional looks. "Please, let me help you," Audra gushed, excitedly. She rushed to her cab and removed a clean cloth from her glove compartment. She then found a bottle of spring water. She soaked the cloth with water and handed it over to Manuel.

"Please, take this; it should help." Manuel took the cloth from Audra, and applied it to his nose.

After a minute or two of Audra's 'first aid,' Manuel laughed, "Suppose I can double for Pinocchio?"

"Huh? With your looks, you could double for Cary Grant … or Clark Gable," a flustered Audra blurted out, much against her better judgment, not wanting to lay her thoughts bare. Thinking to herself, "Oh well, at least I was honest," she did not let herself dwell on her slip in judgment. As for Manuel, he was too busy considering his nose, to assign to her the same foolhardiness as he did to many women from the States, who often tended to go *'gaga'* over the appearance with which he had been blessed from birth.

"I don't think my standing here, holding this silly rag to my nose, will accomplish the task at hand," laughed Manuel, as he opened Audra's front door and moved her seat forward. He found the scissors-jack and lug wrench, and then removed the jack handle from under the hood.

As Audra watched, her heart beat rapidly. "Not only is he a very handsome man, but a gallant one, also." Manuel soon had the spare down from the tire rack. He chocked the front wheel with large rocks, and proceeded to jack up the right rear end of the vehicle. In no time, he had pulled the flat tire from the drum, and replaced it with the spare. He lowered the truck, reassembled the tire rack and put all the equipment away.

Audra walked over to him, asking, "Well, what do I owe you?"

Manuel smiled brightly. His smooth, boyish-looking face lit up. "Dinner tonight, of course!"

A school security cart pulled up by Audra and Manuel. A diminutive, gray-haired elderly man inquired, "'Everything all right?"

Audra assured him, "Yes, sir; we were just discussing where we are going to have dinner tonight, following this gentleman's kindness in tending to my flat tire."

The guard looked irritated, having no patience for anyone's blocking the parking lot, for whatever reason. "Well, do it off the lot. You're holding up the show here!"

"We'll be delighted," replied Manuel as he helped Audra into her truck.

"Follow me! Oh, I didn't even get your name," said Audra.

"Manuel Martinez." Manuel extended his hand.

Audra took his hand, replying, "My name is Audra Heyburn. Thank you very much. If you follow, I'll lead the way to where we can get better acquainted."

"That sounds like a wonderful idea!" exclaimed Manuel. Manuel jumped back into his Mustang, as Audra led the way out of the parking lot.

Chapter Fifteen

Pedro Martinez stood before a large crucifix in his small church in La Paz, Bolivia. He prayed earnestly for the children of their city. Many were being taken by force from the street, and he knew where they were going. He was pouring his heart out to God about the matter, when suddenly a young boy no more than eleven or twelve burst through the church doors. The young Bolivian staggered down the aisle and fell at Pedro's feet. Immediately Pedro took the child in his arms. He carried him in front of the altar, and gently laid him on a front pew. His wife walked in carrying a pitcher of water Pedro had asked for earlier. "Hurry, Rosa! Bring the water over here!" Rosa quickly walked down the middle aisle to her husband.

"Oh Lord, it's young Cruz Herrera. Is he okay?"

"I don't know, Rosa. I was praying when he...." Pedro paused as he lifted his arm up. Blood from Cruz was running down his forearm to his elbow.

"Oh, Jesus help!" shouted Rosa, as Pedro quickly took his shirt off and ripped it into large pieces. He took the pitcher from his wife, poured water over a section of his torn shirt, and removed a burlap jacket from Cruz. Cruz's shoulder was saturated in blood. Pedro tore the boy's shirt open at the left shoulder, exposing a horrible sight—a bullet had hit the boy. The gaping hole and mangled flesh—that mushroomed out in the front of his shoulder—revealed with certainty that the bullet had entered from his back.

Pedro placed the wet cloth over the boy's wound. "He has lost a lot of blood, Rosa!"

"But, will he make it?" Rosa cried.

Pedro looked at Cruz, as the boy tried to speak. "I ... I left it."

Pedro talked very calmly to the young lad. "Cruz, try not to talk. We are here; we shall help you." Rosa looked on in horror. This was the tenth time within three months that a child had come to them, hurt badly by the wicked men at the cocoa farms. They knew the evil General's men exploited their young children. These horrible, animalistic men cared only for money, and to quench their filthy sick desires. Children were only dollar signs to them, as they worshipped power and wealth; nothing else mattered in their demented facsimile of a *'life.'* The men had no real love of life—for the frail children, or anyone else.

Other than using these young children for slave labor, the General's men would also steal many young girls, and used them as sex slaves. A few of these poor little girls would sometimes break free from their captors, and find their way to the church. Up until now, the Martinez family had managed to save most of them, and see them safely to the authorities. Though the Government of Bolivia would frequently help the children, it did little to eliminate the cause. This angered Pedro and many other people, who were too poor and defense-less to head a strong revolt.

What also made the poor people of Bolivia very angry was all the false propaganda the world was being told about them. The Bolivian media fed the Americans, and many other nations, horrible lies about parents selling their children to the syndicate for money, or to pay back debts owed. The media made them sound as if they loved money and drugs over their very own children. All the lies and false propaganda, along with the murdering of innocent children, wore down the patience of Pedro.

Pedro looked down at young Cruz, as he writhed in pain. Placing his hand over Cruz's forehead, he yelled to Rosa: "He's on fire! Oh, I don't know … oh, God! Please help us … *now!"* cried Pedro.

"We must take him into the house and clean his wounds well. I'll get bandages and antiseptics," shouted Rosa, stressed from the dire situation.

Holding Cruz in his arms, Pedro walked behind his wife, as she led the way out of the small church and into their house. Pedro's youngest son, José, stood by the doorway to the kitchen. "José," began Pedro, "run … get Señor Herrera! Tell him his son came to us, and he is badly hurt!" José looked at young Cruz in horror, as he replied, "Yes, Papa; I go right now." Then he ran as fast as he could, out the door and down the road.

Pedro laid young Cruz on his bed as Rosa rushed in with cold compresses and cleaning agents to cleanse Cruz's wounds. "Papa … I got away, Papa," a weak Cruz tried to speak.

Pedro comforted Cruz. "Son, try not to talk. We are here by your side. We won't leave you."

"Is Antonio okay … is he?" Pedro did not know what to tell the young boy. Pedro knew Cruz was probably talking about Antonio Rodriquez, Cruz's best friend. They both had turned up missing two weeks ago. Señor Herrera, Cruz's father, had spent an hour each day in the chapel since that time, praying for his son's safe return, and now this. But at least he was alive. Pedro's heart carried a heavy weight for his people. While he preached joy and peace to these poor farmers, his words sounded so hollow at times. All the joy and peace of which he spoke seemed only for those that chose a path of wickedness. Sometimes Pedro had a difficult time believing that anything other than death could provide this elusive joy and peace.

Cruz opened his eyes for a moment, as Rosa applied more bandages. "If only we could have reached him sooner," said Pedro. Señor Herrera followed José swiftly into the Martinez's residence. He arrived to hear Rosa speaking to Pedro.

"Sh-h-h, my husband; we will see him through this. God will see him through."

Cruz opened his eyes, as he now spoke sweetly, and so calmly. "See them, Papa? They are so beautiful! See how they reach out ... *angeles ... ellos vengan por mi ...* yes, they come for me, Papa ... the angels."

Señor Herrera rushed over to his son's side and held his hand. "My son, my precious *mijo!* You've got to make it! I will sell everything I own, and get you to a hospital. They will help. You will be fine!"

"Papa, my friends ... they are st ... sti ... still there. The men are *very* bad ... *muyo malo.*" Señor Herrera fought back his tears. He tried to sound courageous, and encouraging, but—as the minutes passed—he found this to be a most difficult task. He was losing his son, and he knew it. "Papa, they come for me. I see them ... *los angeles!*"

"Oh, God, please! Not my little Cruz, also!" his father cried. Cruz's grip on his father's hand weakened. Tears flooded Señor Herrera's eyes as he said, "Go with them, my child ... my only child. Go be with your sister and brothers. Yes, you may go with the *angeles.* I shall see you very soon, my precious son."

Cruz became very cold and sweaty. The color left his face, as his breathing became heavy—then it slowed down, until it had almost stopped. Finally, his pupils became fixed, as his body went limp, and his breathing stopped altogether. "Yes, my child, you are with the angels now. No more pain ... no more sorrow ... will you ever carry on your little shoulders again, *mijo.*"

Señor Herrera looked down at his son, as tears ran down his cheeks and onto his son's lifeless body. He wept for his son for more than an hour, as he held his bloody body in his aching arms. His moans and cries of agony penetrated the walls of Pedro and Rosa's house. People outside even heard his cries of bitter grief. He caressed his son's forehead as he wept. This was his fourth child he had lost to the syndicate. The evil kidnappers had now killed his precious Cruz, as well ... the only child that he'd had left on this earth.

"Oh, Lord, how long must we bear these terrible, painful burdens, as the people of the world turn their heads the other way? We are but poor, humble people, but we dearly love our children. I beg of you, God! Please, help us; bring us a miracle! Show the world how we love our children ... how we need help. Send us someone!" His words bounced off the walls, and drifted into silence. Was there no answer to their pain? Were they truly abandoned by the world ... even God, possibly?

Señor Herrera finally rose from his long vigil with his son. He looked at Pedro. Pedro felt it, too ... the despair ... the deep anger. Suddenly, something inside both these men snapped. Pedro had daily witnessed the agony of his flock's sufferings and pains, and now Señor Herrera had lost all of his children. What did it matter to Señor Herrera if he lived or died? Pedro shared a little of Señor Herrera's philosophy. He would rather die, also, than continue watching the evil that took place all around him and those he loved.

They walked out of the house together, saying very little. Rosa ran after Pedro, pleading, "No! Pedro, no! I know what you're going to do. I know where you're going; you cannot just throw your life away, as if it were *nada ... nothing!* You have family ... you have me!"

"It is because of you and my family that I must go. I will not stand by and do nothing anymore. I must go. You know I must!"

"Please, Pedro! Let the police handle this, not you!" cried Rosa. She threw herself before him, and cried out for him to change his mind. She urgently begged him; they both knew the viciousness that would often occur when the syndicate was crossed. Pedro lifted Rosa to her feet and hugged her very tightly. She began to breathe easier, thinking, "Maybe Pedro will stay."

Pedro kissed his wife gently. "All that I am, and all that I have ever wanted to be, has been stripped away by these barbaric men who lie, steal, cheat, and take the lives of our children. Today it was young Cruz; tomorrow it may be our Joseph." He spoke of José, as South Americans, sometimes—favoring Americanized versions of their names—would refer to their children, themselves, or each other, using such names. "Forgive me, my precious wife, but I must go. I will be back. I promise!" Rosa sat down beside the dirt road, crying. She watched as the distance between her and the men swallowed them up.

Pedro and Andrés Herrera began loading as many bottles and jars as they could find into the bed of Andy's two-ton truck. The truck had wooden rails encompassing the bed. The rails came in sections, and were made to fit into slots or grooves, so they could be lifted up and away from the truck. Andy and Pedro's activities attracted the neighbors' attention. Soon others walked over to where they were loading the truck. Once they discovered the cause of their labor, something had snapped within them, also. Andy and Pedro were like the spark that had ignited a wildfire. The village men, and even some women, joined their endeavors as they, too, loaded their trucks or pick-ups with gas and bottles.

They also mustered up as many firearms as they could. Most of their rifles were very primitive compared to a Russian *AK-47*, but this was not about to stop them. They cheered and roared, as they quickly loaded their vehicles and started towards the evil General's camp like a mad convoy of determined warriors. Pedro and Andy led the furious mob down the road towards the cocoa trees. Rosa watched, as the vehicles roared past her, with the people screaming and yelling for vengeance. Pedro looked at Andy, "'Vengeance is mine; I will repay, saith the Lord.' But we are the Lord's children, so—as family—part of that vengeance is ours, too!"

Andy shouted out, "Amen!"

Two guards struggled with two young twelve-year-old girls. They wanted their disgusting evil way with them, but the young girls were very frightened and wanted nothing to do with such ugliness. The grotesquely wicked men had abducted the young girls only two days before. At first, the hideous creatures made themselves out to seem like nice guys that just wanted to give them both better lives, but the day following their abduction—after the girls had had a chance to eat and bathe—the men began to make sexual advances toward them. They did not know how to respond to this. They thought the men must be just playing at first, but as the men's behavior became more cruel, the girls realized they must surrender to their disgustingly debauched sexual wishes, or possibly suffer even death.

One of the guards released his belt and began taking down his trousers, when he heard the noise of many engines heading towards them. The guards were both high on cocaine and unaware of their surroundings. They had only one thought on their mind ... the young females. Thus preoccupied, they had carelessly left their weapons outside, leaning against the guard shack. The hideous man that had taken down his trousers was just about to expose himself to the girls, when he noticed the noise growing louder. In a drugged stupor, he fumbled around with himself until he managed to secure his pants around his waist. He hurriedly zipped up his pants without realizing that a part of his T-shirt was hanging out of his fly.

The other man fought to get up, but was also in such a drug-induced stupor that he had lost his equilibrium, and fell back down laughing and cussing at the girls. The man sporting a white flag out his fly walked outside, investigating the noise, only to see a convoy of vehicles rushing his way. He shook his head and slapped his face, panicking, as he raced inside to retrieve his assault rifle. He looked at his partner, who lay there giggling, as he reached out trying to grab whichever one of the young girls he could get his hands on. He was mindlessly using all manner of profanity, as he fumbled about. Almost every synonym related to the female genitalia came forth from this foul, despicable man, as he groped for the little ladies. Scared out of their wits, they could be seen huddling together in a corner of the room, as far away from this poor excuse of a man as they could possibly get. The man who was baring an unintentional fly flag shouted at his comrade, "Get up! Get up, you moron!" Where are our rifles?"

The foul man turned and laughed even louder. As yet more debauchery flowed from his lips, the foul-mouthed mammal bellowed, "I am up!"

The man with his T-shirt hanging out of his fly remembered where they had left their rifles. He turned and ran out the door to get them, but he was too late. He found himself looking down the hollow barrel of a .305 bolt-action Winchester. The man holding the rifle squeezed the trigger. The rifle recoiled in the man's hands, as the bullet ripped through the man's skull, exiting from the occipital lobe, and blowing a portion of his brains onto the wall behind him.

The other guard, attempting to gather a few of his immoral wits about him, as he reached for a pistol from his shoulder holster, found it was not there. He was horrified when he discovered it was missing. During all the confusion— garnering courage from hearing outside what they felt might be their res- cuers—one of the young girls had dared move from the corner in which they were huddled, and had managed to pull the gun from the holster of the drug- disoriented man. The man turned and looked at the child holding the gun on him. "Give me that you, little...." *'Pow!'* As the gun went off, the young girl screamed. The vile man fell to the ground with a very odd-looking expression on his face. He kicked a bit—then went limp.

"Alisa ... Linda! Oh what a happy day! Praise God, we found you!" shouted Pedro, as the girls ran into his arms. They rushed the girls out of the shack, confiscated the *AK-47s*, and continued on their way.

What happened after that became history. The syndicate's thugs had never witnessed such a hostile, angry mob ... men and women fighting for one thing ... their children. This was an honest war ... a war with no political agenda, or hidden meanings. This war was not fought for territory or money. This was a war based purely on love. This war brought into question the adage, *'No war is a good war.'*

The trucks next barreled into the camp, as the men heaved their Molotov cocktails at other guards that came running out of small shacks, huts and build- ings all around the camp. The air became filled with the sounds of gunfire, when the villagers, as one, released fire on these disgustingly evil syndicate hirelings. Gunned down while running to gather their arms, their number was many, and they began dropping like rancid maggots off a poisoned carcass. Others of these hideous men stood frozen in fear, looking transfixed into the eyes and faces of their assailants. Weren't these the cowards from the village ... the people who shuddered when they had entered their town and stolen their children? Look at them now. They are certainly not the same people ... their countenance had taken on a definitely different aura. Previously, when the evil men had entered their town, they saw fear on the faces of the people; today they saw only anger and hatred. They saw people with snarls on their faces, eyes squinting with deadly intent. The General's soldiers—completely taken off guard—fell quickly before this multitude of villagers. Some managed to get a few rounds off, wounding a villager here and there—one villager even losing his life in the blazing battle—but, in the end, the victory clearly favored the justifiably angry parents.

Following this upset, the village men had broken into an ammo dump and confiscated every weapon, round, and mortar to be found in the bunker. They were careful to leave no weapon or cartridge behind in the camp. The only thing that was left behind was a motley group of fifty-two dead men that had worked for the General. Next, they found their children ... what a happy day it had become! Almost one-hundred-and-fifty children were saved that day. They laughed and smiled, as the villagers packed them into big station wagons, or the beds of the large trucks they had driven there. Some of the villagers had driven empty trucks just for this purpose.

They had found the children malnourished, tired, and very weak from being overworked and underfed. But, nonetheless, they were safe now in the arms of those who truly loved them—at least for awhile, and hopefully forever. As most of the villagers were making their way home with their priceless treasures, some had stayed behind and were busily dowsing the trunks of many cocoa trees, and the foliage surrounding them, with gasoline. Once this task had been accomplished, they then hurriedly lit the trees, leaving behind nothing but smoking trees and dead men. They even burned the camp to the ground.

Unbeknownst to the villagers, two of the General's men had survived the holocaust, and would be able to report the identity of the purported malefactors. While knowing they had to report this terrible defeat to the General, they were in no hurry, for the General was not known for his benevolence. He struck fear in the hearts of many. His lust for power and greed led only to one blood bath after another. The two men knew—though their lives had been spared in this meleé—they would now be at stake, due to the General's wrath at his men's ineptness, shown through failure to defend their camp, as well as their quarry. What were they to do? They certainly would lose their lives, if they left the camp to dwell in the village. They had no place to go. Finally, after some deliberation, they called the General and explained what happened.

The General maintained his temper as one of his soldiers explained in detail how the villagers had sacked and burned the camp to the ground. The General told them to stay put; he would send in some reinforcements, explaining that he understood it was not their fault the villagers had defeated them in a hellish battle. He suggested they were needed to keep an eye on the situation, ordering them to return to the demolished camp, and make sure no further damage took place. He also asked the men if they knew who had led the people into battle. One of the men remembered having seen Pedro among the group. His face was easy to remember because, for a long time, Pedro had been one of only a handful of villagers who had enough guts to stand up to the men when they went into the village. The General's men never really took him that seriously, because he was a preacher. They just laughed him off, and went on their way.

"General, it was that preacher man that led these lunatics!" exclaimed one of the men.

"I want to make sure I heard you correctly. You are telling me that Pedro led this mob!" the General asked incredulously. Are you *positive?*" he nearly shrieked.

"Yes, sir, very positive. Without a doubt, it was that Pedro fellow."

"Thank you, soldier. You may return to your post now," said the General.

"Yes, Sir." The ruffian hung up.

General Montiego slammed his phone down so hard the plastic cradle broke, and the phone crumbled. Then he let out a loud shriek. "I want those villagers to learn that if they do this to me, they will pay dearly. This will surely put us way behind!"

His comrade and Intelligence Advisor looked at the General and said, "Sir, we can make up the losses in cocaine sales, or raise our cocoa prices a tad. We are charging a little less than Africa, so if we raise the beans a couple more cents a pound, we'll catch up in the long haul. It's nothing to be distraught over."

"I do *not* want to wait for the long haul. I do not have the patience. I want Pedro and all the others to know we will not tolerate such behavior. I am putting you in charge of this operation. See to it that Pedro is fairly warned, but do *not* kill him. The fool believes that his God can help him! Let him know it's not his *God* that protects him; it's only because of who he is related to that we do not kill him … *no* other reason! Remember … you may kill anyone but Pedro or any of his family members. Am I clear! Do try to buy him off, if you can. Offer him something he can't refuse."

"General, we believe that—even under intimidation—we may not be able to buy off Pedro, the *'Padre'* ... nor able to stop his crusades against our business. After all, he is a preacher. Allowing himself to be bought off would not quite align with his ... uh ... with his principles."

The General stood up. He towered over many, sporting huge shoulders. Twisting his lean mustache, a nervous habit he had acquired that appeared when he became angry, the General now rested his huge hand on his Advisor's shoulder. "My comrade, we are very close, you and I. We are like brothers. You do know who Pedro is, don't you?"

"Yes, General, of course! How many years have I know Manuel? Do you think I could know him all these years, and not know that Pedro is Manuel's—El Niño's—father! Yes, I know we must consider that carefully when dealing with Pedro.

"Yes, indeed! For you certainly would not want to be known as the man who killed El Niño's father. Would you want to irritate a man that has an extremely volatile reputation ... a man who, it's been said, is to have squared off against six men at once and killed them all with his bare hands?"

The General's comrade swallowed hard. Now he knew why the General wanted him to take care of such a delicate matter. They would not at all like to place themselves in a position where they might end up a victim of Manuel's wrath. Perhaps the General even hated Manuel—purveyor of fear that he could be. But then the General seemed to hate nearly everyone, anyway ... especially children. As his mind considered these thoughts, they were confirmed by the General's own words.

"I wish we didn't need the poor village children at all. They are only good for labor—and not much, at that—and for entertaining my men. Those children from the village are almost worthless! In fact, all those children from the poor cities of Bolivia and Colombia come to us so frail and malnourished, to begin with. We're constantly throwing their shriveled up little bodies into the furnace. 'Seems it's costing us more to be rid of their sickly bodies than they'll ever make for us in the fields!" We need some strong, healthy children. We could sure use some fresh meat from the United States about now. That would surely double our profits—even triple them.

"General you must remember that we are a little unstable now. We sold too many arms to the Peruvians, hence, we are a bit weak. I think we should allow time for adjustment and reorganization," cautioned his Advisor.

The General—as he was prone to do—scoffed. "We are never too weak to kill all the pitiful, poor little cockroaches like the villagers!"

Chapter Sixteen

Mike, Pat & Sterling sat at the Colonel's table discussing their day. The Colonel explained how he and the Sergeant had found the arsenal. They firmly believed this cavity built into the side of the hill was still being used now and then to store weapons. Mike—being his usual cautious self—inquired, "Do you think anybody saw the two of you out there sleuthing around?"

The Colonel answered quickly, "Are you kidding? We were in and out of there like two ghosts."

"And how!" Sterling chimed in. "I must admit, we've still got what it takes, eh, Pat! We located the storage bunker in no time, easily unlocked the entrance, reconned the interior, and even managed to get in a game of golf before we left the Fort," he boasted.

"I even took photos of the place with my digital camera … very clear pictures; gotta love the night lenses in these cameras," Pat said, as he handed Mike the camera.

Mike looked at the photos. "Very sharp … nothing but empty space. I do like the picture of the magazine, though. Where was that?"

"Where *is* it," Sterling corrected, adding, "We left it there, figuring it best to not leave any sign of our having been there."

"By the way—begging the Colonel's and Sergeant's pardon for interrupting—where is the Colonel's daughter?"

"She said she had a few errands to run in town. Said she'd be back by eight or nine this evening," explained the Colonel.

"Hmmm, must be some heavy shopping going on."

"Women and sales … get along like fries and pies," laughed Sterling.

Pat steered the others back from the detour on which Mike had led them, suggesting, "I think we need to talk business now. We have much to discuss. Sterling and I have put our heads together, and we agree that the kingpins on both sides have to be drawn out into the open for this operation to be a success. However, how do we bring this two-headed monster to the surface? We have to wake it up … shake it up … and entice the two heads into a serious disagreement."

"There might be three heads," began Mike. "The Chinese are involved also, remember."

"Pat looked at Mike, "Son, I do realize that, but right now we have more knowledge and understanding of our foes in South America and the United States. We know who some of the important players are here, yet we are somewhat in the dark when it comes to South America, let alone China. Let's focus on two for the time being."

"Certainly," agreed Mike, not wanting by any means to question, or argue with, Pat's superior military experience, which he lacked.

Pat leaned back in his chair thoughtfully. "We could bomb the beast. That would wake him up."

Sterling shifted a little to his side. "If you're referring to the bunker, we could blow up the arsenal, pissing off the General, and make it look like South American nationals did it."

"Yes, that might spread rumors and distrust," Pat replied, indicating that Sterling had indeed understood his original comment about *'the beast.'*

Mike carefully entered the conversation once again. "Yeah, but wouldn't that just lead to vehement denials … or, to their responding in such total ignorance, that their innocence might actually be apparent? This so-called General in South America would certainly become wary, when accused of such treachery, having not been the one who committed it. However, I wouldn't be so sure that his repeated denials, or lack of knowledge, would be enough to bring them all out into the open, looking to settle the accusations once and for all. Plus, it might not be so convincing on another count, as well. After all, what would the syndicate gain by blowing up their own supply of assault weapons?"

"Good points you've made, Mike," said Sterling, commending his thoughtful analysis. The three men sat in silence for a bit, deep in thought.

Mike was the first one to break the silence. "Maybe we could try an indirect approach. 'Say we contact an outside source to try and quickly establish an account with both our friends here in the States, and in South America. Then we ask to meet up with the leaders, and high-ranking officers, of both parties to develop trust *and* a contract. The date is set and—as they gather—we storm the meeting, hence, saving the day!"

"Good idea," thought Pat, "*except* that it would take three months and lots of money to orchestrate such a plan, two more months for our present-day heathens to check out our group, and another month to set up such a conference. When they finally did come together to discuss the stipulations and conditions of any possible contract, the true kingpins would send their cronies in their stead to haggle over terms. They're, unfortunately, a bit too wise to allow themselves to all be found together in one place, anticipating just the sort of incident of which you speak, Mike." He then added, "We really don't have six months to implement such a plan, anyway, before we need to act."

"Well, it was just a thought," said Mike. The conversation turned into a ping-pong game of words and ideas being volleyed between the three of them ... or golf, if you will, at times. They considered many ideas, but often—when they really thought they had hit a hole in one—the ball would land in the sand trap.

Sterling leaned his chair back and cupped his hands behind his head, feeling rather uninvolved, as it was mainly Mike and Pat who were still volleying ideas. Rising and telling the two other men that he needed to stretch, Sterling then walked into the living room, where the television was on, faintly lighting up the family room. Though the sound was turned down when Sterling walked into the family room, the pictures blazing across the screen immediately caught his attention. A caption below the fire and smoke flashing all over the screen stated, 'Aftermath of assault on a Bolivian camp outside La Paz, South America.'

He quickly turned the volume up, as the spokesperson for the National and International News Channel explained how Bolivian civilians had stormed what appeared to be a military-like camp, just outside a village ninety miles east of the capitol city, La Paz.

"Hey, guys! Get in here ... quick! I think you need to see what's on television!" Curious, Mike and Pat stormed into the room post haste. They looked at the screen displaying fire, smoke and occasional explosions. The camera left the site of the massacre, focusing in on a reporter posted in a village not far from the carnage that had taken place at the camp. Pat quickly dispensed a tape into his VCR, and pressed 'record.'

"We're here now, standing beside one of this village's most respected individuals. His name is Pedro Martinez. He explained to us earlier that this was a desperate mission to rescue their beloved children from the clutches of the Bolivian syndicate. I was told that he, along with many others of the villagers, recently risked their lives to save their precious children from the clutches of what they refer to as vile, sadistic men. These men to whom they refer have been hired for the sole purpose of abducting young children to be used as slaves on the cocoa farms that proliferate outside their village, near the Rio Mamore."

After this introduction to the scenario being presented, the reporter then held the microphone in front of Pedro, who looked as though he had been in a recent battle. His handsome face was covered with dirt and soot, blood trickled down his neck, and his clothes were torn and ragged. The world was in for an unexpected education ... a shocking, but necessary, revelation ... when the compassionate, yet outspoken, pastor, Pedro Martinez, finally was given a chance to speak.

"We are a humble and hard-working people, who live very modestly. We do not have ... we do not need ... the luxuries those that live in European countries or the United States have. We love our children dearly, and it pains us that the media often has not correctly portrayed this, but just the opposite. Living here, we face a very sinister, evil syndicate, and our government refuses to recognize this problem, though these wicked men have stolen many of our beloved children, who are used as slaves on their cocoa plantations, to harvest cocaine and cocoa beans. People like you come here, and hear many things. It has been reported that we have *sold* our children, because we were indebted to these vile men ... that we loved money more than our children! We face a greater challenge than the world knows, being constantly terrorized, and in fear of losing yet more of our children. Yes, when people like you come here, and they hear many things, it isn't always the truth that wins out in the end. I don't know ... there may be a few people who have sold their children but, if there are, I don't know who they are. I know almost all of the people in this village, and cannot think of one who would ever do that. Look right over there to your right. 'You see the children?"

The cameras immediately turned and focused on the recently rescued children, who looked dirty, thin and weathered by the elements. In spite of how they had fared during their captivity, their faces were happily aglow now, smiling brightly, because they were finally home. After thoughtfully scanning the faces of the children, the reporter spoke. "Yes, they do appear happy, though definitely appear as though they've been through a battle!

"Yes, Sir. The children definitely have been through a battle. When they were taken from their homes and families, every day in the cocoa jungles became a battle for them. Though the government has not helped us, and has often blamed us for our children being held captive, and working the cocoa fields, we have managed to save them from this life of slavery. Risking our own lives to rescue them has proven to the world that the media reports that suggest otherwise are so wrong. Sir, I pray you will tell the world the truth ... that we do love our children ... enough to die for them. Look at their happy faces. Please, do not allow the lies about our children being unloved ... and sold ... to be told any longer. Such lies might help some sell their books, newspapers, and rumor-laden magazines, but they do not help us at all."

"Yes, we have to agree heartily with Señor Martinez about these villagers loving their children," the reporter replied, in answer to Pedro's impassioned plea. "It is apparent, as well, that the children indeed know they are loved. It shows in their faces, in spite of all that they have been through."

As if on cue for the camera—though that was not at all the case—the children came running over to where the reporter had been interviewing Pedro, thus confirming the essence of their conversation. They gathered around Pedro, hugging him as the grandfatherly figure he was—and had been for so long—to many children of the village, shouting with gleeful laughter.

The reporter turned to his cameraman. "Truly, we have witnessed today a glorious heartwarming reunion between parents and their children. There is also speculation that these people may not have to fear as much for their lives, as they have in the past. A huge arsenal containing many assault weapons, cartridges, rockets and grenades was completely blown up today by these desperate villagers, as they launched their attack on the men that had abducted their children. According to some sources, the slaveholders sustained many casualties, as they were completely taken by surprise. Almost all of the children that had previously been abducted from this village just outside La Paz have been rescued. This has been AJ Sloan, reporting for *International News Today*, live, from Bolivia."

Another reporter, speaking from *International News* headquarters, appeared on the screen, discussing the pros and cons of the situation. Pat scratched his chin … his mind searching for an answer. Suddenly he snapped his fingers. "Hey, guys! I know what we can do! Can we get our hands on any *AK-47* contraband?"

"Come on, Colonel; you and I both know that *you* know where to find loads of that stuff!" exclaimed Sterling.

"Darned right, I do!" Pat answered, acknowledging he'd asked, in his excitement, a nonsensical question to which he already knew the answer.

"What's going on, Pat?" asked Mike, just a mite confused by now.

"Don't you see, Mike? They blew that arsenal outside La Paz to smithereens. It was one huge arsenal … might have been a big enough loss to coax our sinister South American general to request more weapons from the U.S; we know where they're manufactured here. If, as we suspect, the villagers did take all of the weapons the *'good General'* may be crying out for these weapons really soon."

"And …?" asked Sterling.

"And, Sergeant Major, we shall make sure that the *'good General'* receives his due," Pat explained, delighted with himself and his exquisite plan.

The Sergeant laughed, "Ha! Of course! Now I follow you. 'Nothing worse than having your weapons malfunction right in the middle of a riot suppression."

"In this case, more like a total rebellion," laughed Pat.

"Okay, already, what the heck are you two talking about?" interrupted Mike, feeling rather left out, confused and perplexed, to say the least.

"We're talking espionage and covert action, against treason. We'll call it *'Operation Dumpster Dive'* in honor of you, Mike, my Son!" laughed Pat.

"Sounds kind of stinky to me, like we're gonna raid a big city refuse dump," cackled Mike, remembering his disgustingly smelly encounter with Dennis' dumpster.

"Ha! What a hoot! I can see us now, bouncing around in the city dump, dodging hungry rodents and used baby diapers," roared Sterling.

Pat joined in. "Yes, let's hope that if anyone hears the moniker assigned to our escapade that that's what they will believe, also ... that it's nothing more than *'a hoot'* ... one immensely odorous local operation."

Changing the subject back to the serious matter at hand, Pat asked, "What do you think is the easiest—and fastest—mechanism to replace on an *AK-47*?"

Sterling, having much firearms experience, quickly gave his opinion. "Well, the gas piston wouldn't be the way to go, and the danged rifles have large parts, making them fire under practically any conditions. Heck, y' can throw them in mud, sand, water ... almost anything ... and they'll still shoot. If I wanted to sabotage the *AK-47* rifle, I think it would be the magazine ... yes, the magazine. We'll replace the magazine springs with faulty springs that wear down quickly after firing, causing the bullets to jam, and leaving the General's men helpless. The kingpins will get very upset when the weapons malfunction, leading to yet another embarrassing defeat."

"Great idea, but what we need to do is just replace the magazines, entirely. We need to get in and out of that dump as fast as possible, without leaving a trace. I have just the men in mind for this operation. We'll confiscate a load of *AK-47* magazines, and rig the springs off post. Then we'll take them to the ammo dump and exchange them with the good ones. Heck, we'll even make sure they look the same in color," Pat, the detail-oriented man said.

Mike began to understand what Pat and Sterling were talking about. "I see what you're saying now. Wow! Won't the General's *'brave,'* child-beating men be surprised? Ha! They'd be better off with peashooters," roared Mike.

Audra leaned back in her booth in the cozy restaurant, and laughed as Manuel explained how his day had started out that morning, with papers flying everywhere.

"That is so funny, and I thought I was a klutz ... president of said club, in fact."

"I assure you, dear, I probably make you look like the athlete." Manuel's accent tingled Audra's ears. Manuel slipped his arm around Audra's shoulders. He noticed a little resistance—then Audra shied away.

"Sorry, Audra, I am too forward."

"No, Manuel; it's me."

"No, it's me."

"No, it isn't. It is me, Manuel."

"Okay, I give in. It's you. So you are spoken for?"

"Yes and no. I mean I really like Mike. I think I love him."

"Oh, you just *think* you love him?"

"I mean, I do love him. He loves … I love … well, we're close! Besides, I don't kiss on first dates!"

"Audra, did I try to kiss you?"

"No, but the shoulder 'thingy' … and that."

"The shoulder *'thingy'?"* Manuel wondered.

Audra suddenly became quiet … her demeanor grew serious. "Manuel, do you believe in God?"

Manuel blinked, in surprise. Whence came this unbidden reminder of home? He began to think he had the wrong cat up the tree. How could this ditzy girl be linked to the sabotage in the cavern? With such a question, she sounded like she did not at all know what she wanted. All Manuel wanted was a piece of information, so he could put his file together and go home. But now the pieces to the puzzle were not fitting together so well. He had read the reports given to him on possible local suspects, and he knew Audra's background. He had thoroughly checked it out; now he was beginning to understand why the FBI had decided to give her a mental dismissal from the agency.

"Of course I believe in God! My father is a preacher. I'd better believe in God," sighed Manuel.

"Did your father ever preach that God always comes first?" Audra inquired.

Now Manuel knew where the conversation was heading … towards an attempted conversion. He envisioned Audra imagining him holding his arms in the air, crying like a baby, as she laid hands upon his unredeemed head.

"So-o-o, 'you want to convert me now or later?" Manuel wryly quipped.

Audra laughed, "Who said anything about a conversion. I was only asking a question. You haven't answered it."

"I put God first … when I *can*. Sometimes things get in the way. Hey, can we please talk about another subject. What about your pretty parks here? You have been to Coronado National Park haven't you?"

Audra's brow wrinkled. "We were discussing God and, now he wants to know about Coronado National Park," she groaned to herself. Then to Manuel she replied, "Yeah, and it's very beautiful. Hey, didn't you say you were from Texas University?"

"Yes, but my family lives south of the border."

"How far south?"

"Oh, far enough … Mexico City." Manuel was not telling a complete lie. Some of his relatives did live in Mexico City.

"Have you ever been to South America?" Now Manuel felt like the fool. How did he let this woman direct him into a corner? He nervously began biting his bottom lip. Thought he rarely did become anxious, when he did, it was the bottom lip he would choose to chew on. This did not miss Audra's immediate notice. After all, she had interrogated many people during her career in the FBI as a Special Agent, learning many such things for which to watch while questioning someone. Yes, her training—included sixteen grueling weeks in the academy, and in Quantico, Virginia—along with her tour through Hogan's Alley, had left her with sufficient skills. Her physical, academic, weapons and judgment skills had earned her a spot at the top of her class when she graduated. She continued to excel in her achievements. Later, she was transferred to Frederick, Maryland, where she received intense intelligence training.

Then her brother was abducted, and her world came to a screeching halt on its axis. Her career plummeted, as she refused to comply with the Agency, whose staunch regulations would not permit her, as family, to be allowed near his case. However, she would not—just could not seem to make herself—stay out of Todd's case.

Audra cogitated on what she saw for a bit. She did not know this handsome man very well. She did not even know his last name. But this much she did know, and thought to herself: "Manuel is nervous. It appears he might be hiding something. He wants to tell me, but he is being very careful right now."

"Actually, I have been to Panama to study culture, just before the United States gave up the Canal. Why do you ask?"

Now it was Audra's turn for a comeback. "Well, it's just the way you talk … I mean your accent. It is much more distinguished from that of others that live here, or close to Mexico. I just wondered if you spent any time there."

"Sounds as if you have been there yourself, young lady, " Manuel replied, noting her linguistic prowess.

"No, but I know people that live in Bolivia, and they have a similar accent."

Manuel released his bottom lip from the clutches of his teeth. How did he get himself into such a predicament? Was he not supposed to ask all the questions that would pry into Audra's background, not his? Instead, Audra seemed to be the one in charge. He began to realize that Audra had manipulated him from the beginning; this gal knew what she was doing. He had just been taken in … he had fallen for one of the oldest tricks in the book: *'Allow others to think you are a complete airhead, then hit them up when they're most vulnerable!'* He marveled at the woman sitting in front of him. She had answered his main question without realizing it—confirming her aptness for interrogation, thus giving credence to her background—but she also had managed to pull more information out of him than he had planned on sharing. She certainly was not the silly redhead he had—at first—thought she was.

"Oh, how inconsiderate of me," Manuel gushed, trying to change the subject from his place of residence. "My name is Manuel Fer*nan*do," he went on.

Audra made a mental note of the name, though she felt he was not being honest. He said it almost too mechanically, as though he had rehearsed the line. However, she did not let on about her observations.

"Well, Manuel Fernando, I have truly enjoyed myself, but I really must be getting along now. I have homework to struggle with."

"What subject?" Manuel queried, wishing to sound interested.

"Chemistry and Plant Biology."

"Oh, I love Chemistry! Perhaps I can help you, as I will be around for a while. Dean Faring and I still have much to talk about."

"That's right, you did say you and the Dean were trying to revise the Spanish program at the college. Right now, I'm studying reaction rates and equilibrium. Do you know about that?"

"Sure, but it matters if it is an exothermic or endothermic reaction. The real trick is to figure out how long it takes for the reaction to occur, keeping in mind that—after the reaction—the elements reverse reaction, to an equilibrium status."

"You sound as confusing as my professor, Manuel. Hey, 'you want to walk me out to my truck? I've gotta get going." They rose from the booth as Manuel dropped a ten-dollar bill on the table. As he pulled, the bill out of his wallet, Audra noticed a piece of paper inside his wallet that looked foreign to her. She said nothing, but she kept the picture on the paper in mind. Manuel paid for the meals, and the two walked out together.

The night was dark. Only the lights from the buildings nearby them lit their way, as Manuel walked Audra to her Nissan. Audra unlocked her door, as Manuel opened it for her. She sat down on the tan vinyl seat, and then she rose again, and was standing outside her truck. "Manuel, please remember, always put God first in your life. You will see someday that it will make all the difference."

Manuel fidgeted uncomfortably. "Audra, may we at least remain friends, since Mike has already made his claim … maybe even close friends?" His words sounded more like a despondent person's plea, than a casual question.

Audra sensed this. She, therefore, reached out and pulled Manuel's cheek close to her. "Of course, Manuel," she said as she kissed his left cheek.

"Maybe we can see some sights together, huh?" Manuel wore a tentative boyish smile as he spoke. Audra smiled back at him, reassuringly.

"Sure, I'd like that, but you'd have to put up with some of my friends ... like Mike, or whomever."

Manuel hugged her closely. "'Sounds like an invitation. I would like to get to know Mike. Here is my card; it has a phone number on it, by which you can reach me."

Audra took the card, climbed back into her Nissan, pulled out of the driveway, and headed south on Highway 92.

Manuel looked the other way. The words of his father had come back to haunt him again. This time they took the form of a very beautiful lady ... named Audra. *'Keep God first in your life,'* she had admonished ... yea, reminded ... him. "How ironic," thought Manuel, considering his reason for trying to contact her in the first place. The words kept running through his mind as he walked to his Mustang. Manuel opened the door to the Mustang and sat down. "Keep God first in your life," he chanted, singsong style. He shook his head as he started the engine and pulled out of the parking lot. Manuel knew nothing of the riot that had taken place in the camp beyond the village of La Palo, where his family lived—on the outskirts of La Paz, Bolivia.

Audra's Nissan coasted to a stop, to the left of her father's Jeep. She glanced at her watch. "Eight o'clock; I'm not too late." She really did want to be in on the action inside. Knowing her father and Sterling were going to try to find the possible storage site where the crooks were storing the illegal weapons, she wanted to be around when they made their plans, but for some reason she had felt compelled to visit with the new face in town. Voicing her thoughts aloud, as she walked up the stairs to the front door, "Though I hate to admit it, perhaps I'm just close enough to being shallow that his great looks won me over."

Mike met her at the door, opening it as she began climbing the steps. Thus, hearing the last few words she had spoken to herself, he did not mention this.

"Hey, Sugar! Where've you been?" Mike glowed, as he looked into Audra's eyes. "Just think, Mike ... this is your gal ... at least, I think so," he silently mused.

She felt a bit uncomfortable ... even guilty ... as if she had committed adultery.

"Oh, just having a bite to eat with a friend," she replied, hoping he didn't have too many questions. Mike let his curiosity show now, by asking, "Male or female?"

"Male. I just met him today. He's a professor in Spanish Literature and Philosophy. He's here to help the Dean at the College revise the Spanish program."

"Hmmm ... and you just happened to be in the right place ... at the right time?"

"Actually, yes; he helped me change a flat tire," she calmly explained.

"Oh, and then you made a day of it, in return, huh?" Now Mike felt like teasing, realizing how ambivalent he actually felt regarding his secured status with Audra.

"So to speak, yeah; but it was only an innocent visit, Mike ... nothing else."

"Well, anyway, we've been laying out some plans inside, and I can't wait to fill you in. 'Gotta, tell you, Audra, I'm glad your father, his friend, and you had a groovy day, because I sure didn't. All I did was work half the day on my house, but I did find out more about Janet, the Sheriff, our Mayor and Dennis. I'm starting to think that Dennis may not be as involved in all this as we think. I'm gonna talk to him and get to the bottom of all this. Janet did take a picture of the compound, but she didn't go inside ... and I found out a smidgen about El Niño."

Audra interrupted Mike. "Tell me about this 'El Niño.' Did you get any sort of a description?" Audra's ears now stood up in anticipation, recalling for just a moment her gut feeling about her new friend's possibly bogus name, in spite of how charming he might have seemed.

"The only thing I know is that El Niño is known as a possible strong arm for the South American syndicate. He lives like a recluse, until called upon to perform a job for them. I don't know any more than that."

"Your friend, Matt, is pretty good at his job isn't he ... like some sort of private eye, huh?" Audra asked.

"'Sort of. But he hadn't been working in a while. That's one of the main reasons I hired the man."

"'Glad he's a man, or I'd get a little suspicious," laughed Audra, reassuring him, after noting his slight insecurity about the Professor, Manuel, with whom she'd just spent some time over dinner.

Sterling and Pat were sharing old war stories when Mike walked back into the kitchen with Audra. "Well, my little Pussy Cat, where in the dickens have you been!" laughed the Colonel.

Audra smelled a faint scent of beer on his breath. She saw five empty bottles of Coors Lite on the table. "Looks like you're having yourselves a wonderful time."

"Sure are," Sterling answered. "Your Pa and I had a very productive day, and we're laying down plans. Here's to *'Operation Dumpster Dive',"* hooted the sergeant.

Audra knew it only took about one-and-a-half bottles of beer to make her father feel a little loose. "Okay, Pa, how many?"

Her father held a bottle in his right hand, between his ring finger and pinky, as he held up his index and middle finger. "Two, Darling, not counting this one … I mean, counting this one."

"Well, you'd better not overdo it. I'm not gonna call in for you if y' can't get up in the morning." Audra looked a little sternly at her Pa, but then had to laugh. They hugged each other tightly. She was very happy to see him finally letting go, and enjoying himself for once.

Then Audra's thoughts began going over other recent events. She thought it rather strange how a terrible tragedy, like Bobby's abduction, has brought Mike first into the library, and then into her own lonely life. That something so heinous as an abduction could lead to love, and a chance for happiness again seemed so ironic … nearly unbelievable. "God, please work all this out … please," she prayed silently, as her father kissed her cheek tenderly.

Mike then led Audra into the family room, where he rewound the tape they had recorded from the news earlier that evening, as he explained a bit of what she was about to see. The tape arrived back at its beginning, Mike pressed, *'play,'* and Audra became engrossed in this news video they had made. As her attention focused on the events in La Palo, Bolivia, and she listened to the interview between the news reporter and a preacher named Pedro—whose looks oddly reminded her of Manuel—Audra wondered.

Once the video had ended, Mike began explaining the plan cooked up between her father, Sterling, and himself … though it was actually Sterling who had conceived the idea of switching out the *AK-47* magazines. They talked late into the night, and then Mike—though reluctantly—returned to his empty, foreboding house.

Mike walked through his house carefully, half expecting a phantom to pop out at him at any time. After the break-in, Mike was left feeling a bit timid in his own house. He hated walking on eggshells in his own place. "After all," he thought, as he timorously walked into his bedroom and looked at Bobby's picture, "a man's home is supposed to be his haven … his castle … not a fearful prison!" Yes, that is what it felt like often in the nearly two weeks since Bobby's abduction … solitary confinement. Being alone in this big old house that was now void of anyone but Mike was sometimes depressing. However, Mike did not give in totally to the devastation that he might have for—though his brother's absence had gone past the normal time of expectancy for a safe return—somehow he knew Bobby was alive. He just knew it.

Mike's phone rang. Mike picked up the phone, "Hello."

"Hey, Buddy, this is Raymond. I have some more news for you."

"'Can't wait to hear," Mike responded.

Raymond fidgeted with a piece of pepperoni pizza on the other end. "Hey, first I want to thank you for giving me Melissa's number."

"You're very welcome."

"She's a real sweetheart. We hit it off right from the start."

"Oh really!" Now Mike wanted to hear more.

"Yeah, as a matter of fact, she's coming over tonight."

"Well, aren't you the stud!" Mike teased his friend.

"Hey, it's nothing like that, Kiddo. We're just going to watch a movie and call it a night … that's all," Raymond assured Mike.

"Ah, don't get all worked up. I was only joking! Anyway, what's the news, *Compadre?*"

"'Turns out I pulled a very good print off that envelope. Well, actually I pulled several. Most of them were yours, but then I found a thumb print of someone else, and guess who that thumbprint belongs to?"

"Our wonderful Sheriff!" Mike's voice escalated, knowing he'd pinpointed it.

"You rat, you just stole my line," Raymond jokingly whined.

"Hey, I could read your mind through the wires, man!" laughed Mike.

"You know, what puzzles me is the print itself. It's almost like he purposely placed his thumbprint on the envelope. That's how clear the print was."

"Where was the print on the envelope?"

"At one of the end corners," Raymond explained.

"No other prints … nothing?"

"There was a smudge mark on the other side."

"Was it on the opposite side of the envelope?"

"Come to think of it, yeah, it was," Raymond said, thoughtfully.

Mike lay back on his bed. The whole thing had a smell to it he did not like. Why would the Sheriff purposely leave his print on the envelope? Did the Sheriff think Mike was so stupid that he would shudder, and throw the note away? Anybody with a few brains would want the envelope checked into, if there was a threat involved. Mike said very little, as Raymond rambled on about the arrests he had made lately, and how he and Melissa were going to go here and there together.

Eventually, Raymond got back to the subject of most interest, at the moment, to Mike. Asking Mike if he was going to file charges … a grievance …

against the Sheriff, he added, "You know, you have the right—and proof—to make his life miserable for a while," explained Raymond.

Mike considered this. In the end, though, he decided that pressing charges now meant life in front of a lawyer, focused on litigation, rather than on his brother, Bobby. Who knows what ramifications it could lead to. "Raymond, don't you see. Even *if* the Sheriff did plant his mark on the envelope, it would be for the reason of wanting me to file a charge, distracting me from my first priority ... that of finding Bobby ... and possibly learning too much—in their estimation—about their sickening child-abducting operations."

"That would be a first," balked Raymond, having to disagree with his friend.

"Think about it. I file a charge and everybody in the County learns about it. I'm on the news portrayed as a paranoid young man, alleging to be harassed by the Sheriff. There's proof ... or so we think ... a threatening note slipped into an envelope that has the Sheriff's prints on it. It wouldn't even hold up, unless there were prints on the note, as well. Did you find any prints on the note itself?"

"Only yours and mine."

"Okay. 'You know what? I don't even think the Sheriff wrote the letter. I don't know how someone got his prints on the envelope but, if you wanted someone to find your prints, why not leave them on the note, also?"

"You answered that earlier. Because he could say that someone had planted the prints on the envelope. But the note is a different story all together."

"Well, Raymond, my buddy, this would be such a merry-go-round I'd be riding, so I'm not going to deviate one iota from my prime objective of finding my brother."

"I don't blame you, Mike. Hey, if you need anymore help, just let me know."

"You've got it, Partner. Take care," Mike concluded.

"You, too." Raymond hung up the phone, and the line went dead. Mike rolled over on his back and looked at the ceiling. Every time he turned around, another piece of the puzzle turned up short or missing, or it just did not fit at all. "Is all this going to work out somehow?"

Chapter Seventeen

Two dark, shadowy figures, dressed like La Palo villagers, muttered some words in Spanish to each other as they opened the door to the small church that Pedro had built himself to serve the people of La Palo. His church had become a haven, as well as a place to worship. For many years, Pedro had preached from the pulpit of this church, and the people loved him. He worked hard and served the people well. Whenever a person in the village had an honest need, Pedro would reach out to help. Today, as the men approached Pedro, who was kneeling at the altar praying to God, he heard them and looked up.

Rosa sang a hymn as she worked: *"En la cruz, en la cruz, do primero vi´ la luz...."* Rosa was normally a happy woman, in spite of their life of hardship. As she sang, she prayed, too: "Thank You, Jesus, for the cross ... for showing me your light." From where she worked—in a shack behind the small chapel—she could not see the front of the church, so did not see the men approaching her husband inside the chapel. They slowly made their way down the middle aisle and knelt beside Pedro.

"Señor Martinez, how are you this evening?" asked one of the men calmly.

Pedro held his hand up, in a *'please, give me a minute'* gesture, as he prayed.

The men knew better than to interrupt a prayer, but they were anxious to state their business and leave. The massacre that had taken place just hours earlier made them a bit nervous about being in the chapel; maybe an angry mob would rush in any moment and kill them both. However, the General had sent them to do a job, and they knew better than to disobey orders. The General was looking for some quick results ... a quick conclusion to the upheaval that had transpired earlier. He calculated a quick end to this sort of rebellion, if he could win over Pedro. He believed every man had a price, no matter who they might be. The price may take on the form of money, jewels or gold, for some. For others, family status, protection, or material acquisitions was their price.

Pedro completed his prayer. He then turned and looked at the two men, portraying villagers, who were kneeling beside him. "What can I do for you, my brothers?"

"Actually, it is what we hope we can do for you, Reverend." The man who spoke wore khaki burlap-like pants and shirt, with a plain-looking poncho around him. His face was fair to look upon. He appeared well groomed and clean. The other, who remained silent as they talked, was gaudy and untidy. He even smelled of body odor, but Pedro was used to this, so paid no mind. Many men frequently came to him desperate and broken. To Pedro, nothing but a person's soul mattered, and he could not turn away a man in search of the truth, or a person in need. When the pleasant-looking man insinuated he wanted to help Pedro, Pedro knew this man had not come to his church seeking help, nor food for his soul. Pedro looked intently into the man's dark eyes and said, "Now, I know why you have come. I knew you would come, but I did not expect you so soon. Could you not even wait a few days?"

"Reverend, try to put yourself in our place. We only...."

Pedro held up his hand to stop the man, and said, "I would never want to be in your place. You see only the physical world, having no respect for things belonging to the spiritual world, because you cannot comprehend it. As you will not try to understand, you go in life hating and hurting others, until you yourself die and are forgotten by this physical world. Worse, as you have not fed your spirit, your spirit dies in the end, as well ... a very sad, lonely end."

"Oh, that was so beautiful, my Reverend, so divine," the malevolent man said sarcastically. "Listen, you fool! We want peace. We were sent here to parley, not kill or maim anyone. We offer you gifts ... gold, money, whatever you may ask for, as long as it is within our means to give it." Pedro knew such an offer always had a catch ... a reciprocal price, usually too high to pay. "What is it you want me to do?" he inquired, skeptical at their attaining any real resolution to this encounter.

"It is quite simple. We know, Padre, that you were the one who led the raid upon the camp. We also know that you are—uh, let's say—very influential in this village. We only wish for you to agree to keeping the peace in the future, in return for our proffered benevolence."

"I will *only* keep the peace if you stay out of our village, and leave our children alone!" Pedro's voice began to rise in anger at their attempt at bribing him.

"Whoa, Preacher! Are you sure there's not something we can for you in exchange for your agreeing to not bother our camp any further? Let's be reasonable, friend."

"I am no friend of a child molester ... a slave holder! Any man that can laugh while a young, innocent girl is being raped is *no* friend of mine!" Pedro yelled, enraged at their disgustingly insensitive bravado.

"Why, Reverend, I am very disappointed in you! How can you accuse us of this, when you do not even know us?"

"I know your kind, and that is *enough!*" Pedro, restraining himself, so wanted to strike out at this less-than-compassionate creature standing before him. How dare these men come into God's house, trying to make wicked deals with him! "You're asking me to just look the other way, while you steal our precious children!"

"Reverend, you keep the peace, and we will not have to harm you, or your family. We will pay you handsome sums of money, and I will stretch my neck out on the chopping block for you. I promise, we will not take children without offering a wage. We will pay wages to the children. This means they will no longer be slaves. I will see to it personally that the young girls are not mistreated. I will also let the children visit their families."

Pedro had heard enough of his gross lies. As the man continued to drone on, Pedro shouted, "Away from me, you scum ... you horrible creatures of hell! I have heard enough of your lies. Do you take me for a complete idiot ... a fool? I will not bow to you, or to your leaders. There will only be peace when you leave us be!"

"Then you make a bitter mistake, my foolish friend. You could have had a big farm, with trucks and tractors. Your dreams were so close to you, but you let it all go, out of selfishness. One last time I ask you ... I even ask kindly. Please, Pedro ... take our offer, please ... I beg you!"

Knowing that it could cost him dearly, Pedro was being anything but 'selfish,' as the cruel man had suggested. "Your offers are full of blood, and dead children's bones. I cannot. I will not." Pedro was courageous ... determined.

"So be it!" The well groomed man motioned to the uglier, unkempt man. The man began beating Pedro. Pedro struck back, managing to land a few solid blows from both of his doubled-up fists on the face of the violent man. Blood spurted forth. The gaudy man lost his temper, pulling a rigid pipe from his side. As he swung with fury and vengeance, the one who had done the talking shouted, "No!" though he was too far from the out-of-control man to grab the pipe from him. The pipe, therefore, landed fiercely on the crown of Pedro's head. There was a cracking sound, like a dry limb breaking in two.

Hearing the commotion, Rosa rushed in through the back door of the church. She heard the pleasant-looking man say, "You fool, Pepe! You could have killed him!"

"No, Scorpio, he is alive," Pepe countered.

Pedro groaned a little, and moved slightly.

"Come, let's get out of this place," said Scorpio. The two men hurried out of the church, disappearing into the darkness of the night.

Rosa rushed over to her husband. Pedro tried to speak to her, but everything seemed like a dream. Something was dreadfully wrong. He faded in and out, in and out, and could not seem to form the words he tried so desperately to speak to Rosa. He did not know he had suffered a cracked skull and, as his brain hemorrhaged, he looked softly into his wife's beautiful Spanish eyes and said, "I love you, Rosa. I tell you, I'll be back. I tell you, young Cruz is right … I see the angels …'*los angeles,*' Rosa, I go home now." His head fell to the side, as Rosa held him in her bosom. He looked into Rosa's eyes, and whispered some last words—then his spirit lifted. She screamed out in extreme sorrow, and bitter grief, as she rocked her husband gently in her nearly numb arms.

José, her youngest son, ran through the church doors and joined his mother. He looked down at his father, who lay limp in his mother's arms. "Mama, is Papa all right?" Rosa looked up at her son, her face completely wet from tears. She shook her head, and wailed all the louder. José felt sick all over … his knees grew weak. When he saw the blood running down his Papa's face, he knelt beside his mother and wept, uncontrollably.

Manuel recorded his daily events in his electronic notepad. Soon he would have all the proof and information he needed for his superiors to construct a plan. They might even order him to carry through with the assassination. This bothered Manuel … a lot. He tried to clear his thoughts of any attending emotions, but she was very different from most other women. Audra reminded him of his mother … so kind, so sweet … so … so spiritual. Her words also haunted him: *"Remember to keep God first in your life,"* she had kindly admonished him, bringing to mind once again his father's words. How could he kill someone like Audra, who possessed such qualities? It would be like killing his own mother, or father. Manuel deposited these thoughts in the back of his mind, shut off his light, rolled over on his side and closed his eyes, attempting to sleep.

Two hours later, he woke with a start, his phone echoing loudly throughout his room. Manuel mumbled to himself, "I told these fools here not to call me in the early hours of the morning." He grumbled some more, as he lifted the phone and placed it to his ear. His mother tried to speak to Manuel but, alas, she had to give the phone to her daughter, who had arrived from La Paz.

"Manny, are you lying down?" Manuel was no fool; he knew something terrible had happened. He saw a vision of his father, as Annette began to speak again. "Manny, Papa … Papa.…" Her voice trailed off, as tears flowed. Manny heard the grief and agony in her voice. Annette regained some of her composure, took in a deep breath, and finished. "Oh, Manny! Papa is no longer with us." She then began to cry heavily.

"What! No! How!" Annette, though she did not wish to speak about the horrible incident, felt her brother, Manuel, had a right to know what had happened.

"Oh, Manny! Papa has been attacked by some of the villagers. He was praying in the chapel, Mama said. Then she heard some commotion, and ran into the chapel, just as they were leaving. She said she thinks two men did it; she's not sure, and she is very upset. She cannot even think straight right now. She is in terrible pain, as we all are. She is calling for you. She needs you, Manny!"

Manuel wanted to ask questions. He wanted Annette to coax Mama back onto the phone so he could ask her about the men, but he knew that—in her condition—such a request would be futile, and only deepen her present agony. The sorrow in his sister's words added to his own grief. His body grew weak. The numbness started from his spine, and fanned outward, until he could barely move his head and arms. "Tell mama I will be on the next flight to La Paz."

"Oh, Manny," Annette said, sniffling, "I can't wait to see you. Mama will be encouraged when I tell her you are coming." Manny told Annette he loved her, asked her to tell Mama he loved her very much, too, then hung up the phone.

"How dare these men touch my father! Do they not know who my father is? Do they not know the consequences that will now follow? It is hard for me to believe some 'villagers' did this. The villagers loved my father; he met needs … he loved them. The people would be committing suicide, by killing my father." Manuel spoke these words out loudly, as though he was talking to someone and, as he leaned back down in his bed and looked up, he realized just who that person was.

Manuel could not sleep. He stayed awake throughout the remainder of the night, trying to put his father's death in perspective. After searching the Internet, and discovering what had happened at the camp outside La Palo the day before, he found the puzzle pieces fitting together rather rapidly, and quite accurately. As he read about the massacre, his mind shifted to the General and his thugs. Then he read about the interview between the press and his father.

Manuel's father's name appeared before his eyes ... right there on the Internet! "Pedro Martinez, a preacher, and said to be one of the leaders in the courageous attempt to rescue the villagers' children from the greedy clutches of inhumane slaveholders, had this to say to the world." Manuel read the words his father said. "Truly, I am proud of you, Papa. How can I make up my failures to you now? What can I do? How can I come close to being the man you were, Papa ... the man you still are? For, one as brave as you will never really die."

Manuel lay back down in his bed, trying to gather his wits about him before calling the International Airport in Tucson. When he did, he discovered the next flight out to Bolivia would not depart for another day yet. He called home, and told his sister to meet him at La Paz International, around two in the afternoon the next day. Manuel then began pacing the floor, both impatient over having to wait so long for his flight out, and deep in thought over his father's senseless demise.

As he paced, Manuel's mind drifted back in time, to the days when he had first met the General. Since the first time he had sat before the General, he remembered his words clearly. "Manuel, I am so delighted to have you as an employee, working for our noble cause. I extend my appreciation to you. I have been told you are extremely intelligent. My primary Advisor has nothing but positive reports concerning your expertise."

"Thank you, Sir," Manuel had replied.

"No thanks necessary at this time. You can thank me later, by proving you are capable."

"Of course, General."

"Fine—then I have a few missions for you." He had then handed three photos to Manuel, which he had studied carefully. Then the General handed Manuel a binder.

"The binder you are holding in you hands is actually a compilation of reports on all the habits and activities of these ringleaders in Colombia. It is their historical biographies, containing the names of all their family, friends and relatives. It also contains everything they have done in life, what foods they enjoy ... even their toiletry habits—all the information you will require to become very familiar with these men. Apparently, these men do not wish to play ball with us; they are being a bit defiant. They thumb their noses at us. We have tried to reach a diplomatic agreement with these men but, so far, all our agents have failed. We turn to you as our last hope for a peaceful arrangement."

"I shall return with a contract that, I am sure, will suit your needs," said Manuel, with a tone of confidence.

The General had immediately liked Manuel's positive attitude. Most of his men used tentative words, such as, "I shall do my best," or "I will see what I can do," but Manuel sounded like he already had a plan in mind. The General smiled. "I like your attitude. I am looking forward to your success." Then the General had said something Manuel would never forget. "Remember this, Manuel, and never forget it." He looked straight into Manuel's eager eyes. "Remember, no matter what anybody tells you, every man—yes, even every woman—has a price. The key is to find that price, and then implement it properly."

As Manuel's mind pondered the General's words of long ago, he lifted himself off the motel bed, and walked slowly across the blue padded carpeting. He knew deep in his heart that the villagers had had nothing whatsoever to do with his father's death. His mind's eye could, at this very moment, see the General sitting at his desk, as he nonchalantly ordered his thugs to pay the good preacher a visit. His mind then filled with destructive thoughts of what he would do to these horrible men ... men who would dare violate him and his family. Angry, tired, and discouraged, Manuel rubbed his face as he sauntered towards the bathroom, contemplating the shower that might help him wake up.

His mind suddenly was jerked back to the present with the loud ringing of the desk phone, which almost jumped off its cradle as it rang. He stood motionless, debating answering it, or climbing into the shower towards which he'd been headed. The last thing he wanted to do was talk to one of his superiors ... or one of the kingpins here in Sierra Vista. Reluctantly, he lifted the phone. He spoke with a soft voice, "Yes?"

"Manuel, this is Audra. How are you doing today?" A sleepy Manuel looked at the clock on his nightstand near his bed. It read eight in the morning. He did not realize so much time had already passed since Annette had called him from Bolivia.

"Audra, I am so happy to hear your voice!" Manuel spoke from his heart. He had nothing to hide this time.

"Manuel, some of my friends and I are going to Carr Canyon for a little R&R. We were hoping you'd come along. You said you wanted to see some sights, and meet some people; well, here's your chance. Manuel thought about this for a moment. He did have a day of 'nothing' on the schedule, since he had completed his report. He also wanted to escape his grief. He needed to let go; this would do him some good.

"I would be delighted to," he replied.

"Great! We could meet you at your place, or you could come over to my house, and we'll leave from my place," Audra said excitedly.

"How about the latter?" he suggested.

Audra gave Manuel the directions to her house, as he played along. Of course, he already knew the route, but he was careful not to let on. After giving Manuel the directions, she told him to be at her place around ten, then she hung up. Manuel turned and walked into the bathroom. "Now, why did I do that?" Manuel asked himself, questioning his own motive.

Colonel Patrick Heyburn stood in front of a team of six Army Rangers. He looked at the Rangers with a stone-like face, showing no expression. The Colonel roared at the soldiers, "Men, you have been chosen for a very unique assignment. Your country is counting on you! You must commit the details of this mission to memory. Sergeant Major Crowe is handing the details to you in pamphlet form. You will study this pamphlet today, and commit it to memory. You will commit every line, every page number, period, semicolon, colon and site location to memory. You will destroy the pamphlets after you have done so. Men, we cannot fail in this mission!"

One of the Rangers noticed the heading, *'Operation Dumpster Dive,'* and could not squelch—though he tried his best—a smirk that had crept up into his face. The Colonel saw this, and addressed him accordingly. "Specialist Downey! So you think this is funny?"

Quickly wiping the smirk off his face, and standing at extreme attention, Specialist Downey replied with militaristic fervor: "Sir! No, sir!"

The Colonel then became extremely serious. "Men, I asked for professionals for this job. I wanted seasoned *Berets,* but the Army and CSA saw fit—upon the advice of the Commander of USASOC—to place *un*seasoned Rangers from the 75th Regiment at my disposal. Now, I am here to tell you that this is no small pie-in-the-sky mission. You must not fail! This extremely top-secret operation cannot afford to fail. I am not at liberty to tell you if this is just a drill, or a viable mission. Because the success of this mission is so crucial, I am going with you. Not only will I join you in this mission to rate your performance, but I will personally involve myself, as will Sergeant Crowe here."

The Colonel then removed a magazine from a large, tough green canvas bag. He looked at one of the Rangers and said, "Here, catch." The Ranger instinctively caught the magazine in his hand.

"What is that, Ranger?" The Ranger turned it over in his hand, and hollered, "A magazine to an automatic Russian *AK-47,* Sir!"

"Very good." The Colonel held another magazine in his hand. "Men, all these bags you see before you are filled with magazines. In your pamphlets, there is a colored photograph of a Russian magazine. You are to break down these magazines within these bags, and replace the inner spring with the spring that has been taped alongside the magazine."

The Colonel looked at the Ranger to whom he had tossed the magazine, and hollered, "Specialist, do you see the spring taped to the magazine?"

"Sir! Yes, Sir!"

"Well, don't just stand there like you're right in the middle of watching a *'Three Stooges Go to War'* slapstick comedy; break it down and replace the spring! Now!"

"Bu...." the Ranger began, not realizing they were to begin immediately.

The Colonel shouted indignantly. "Now, Ranger! Not tomorrow ... *now!*"

The Ranger immediately grabbed his 20-in-one tool, and went to work. He was very nervous ... sweat dripped from his brow ... but in less than three minutes, he had managed to disassemble and reassemble the magazine, with the new spring inside.

"Hmm, you did well, soldier. Men, you have just witnessed one of your buddies tearing apart and replacing the spring-loading mechanism in the magazine. He did it with a primitive tool, also. Now you all will perform this task but, fortunately, with precision equipment, that should speed up the process some.

"The Sergeant and I are counting on you, also. I want to reiterate the importance of this operation. To fail means loss of lives. When this mission is over, you will discover its importance. 'Remember, you must commit your instructions to memory, burn the pamphlets, and finish with the magazines. The magazines *must* look exactly like the magazines displayed in the photo inside your pamphlet. You will now be transferred to the west bunkers to complete your initial assignment in this operation."

As the Colonel began to walk away from the Rangers, he stopped, turned around, and asked: "Men, what is our motto?"

"Rangers lead the way!" They all shouted, loudly and proudly.

"Who are the best soldiers on the face of this planet?" the Colonel continued.

"Seventy-fifth Regiment, United States Rangers, Sir!" screamed the men.

"Will we fail our country, our women, men and especially our children tonight?"

"Sir! No, Sir! Darkness is our friend. We will not fail!" shouted the soldiers once again.

"Men, you are dismissed. I shall link up with you ETA twenty hundred hours. I expect all of you to be ready, and well motivated."

Sir! Yes, Sir!" they screamed one more time. They knew this mission was an extremely important one. The Colonel had just made this very clear to them. To be under the command of a Colonel was a privilege ... a great honor.

The men turned, and quickly hustled towards their bunkers in the hills. One Ranger jumped into the transport truck and followed the other Rangers.

Pat turned to Sterling, "I'm not going to ask how you managed to find all those magazines and the faulty springs."

"Colonel, it was a snap. When you've lived around as long as I have, you meet many strange characters."

Pat patted his main man on the back. "You amaze me. I just hope we get a break."

Sterling looked down at the sandy ground below. "I hope we do, too."

From the pinnacle of a hill just south of Pat and Sterling, the same well camouflaged figure that spied on them at the old ammo bunker the other day, trained his scope on both soldiers below. He looked down the scope of his rifle as his index finger tightened again around the trigger guard, "Bang! Bang! You're both dead!"

Chapter Eighteen

Audra and Manuel talked vivaciously, as Mike quietly kept his eyes on the road, driving carefully up the winding road that led up to the Huachuca peaks looming above them. Raymond and Melissa followed behind them. Melissa sat very close to Raymond. Now and then, she kissed him on the cheek, as Raymond kept a careful eye on the road. Mike noticed this affection a couple of times, when looking in his rearview mirror. He had to laugh just a bit. "Well, those two are sure making some sparks fly between them," he thought. Occasionally they stopped their four-wheelers when they came upon some as yet unmelted snow, stopping just long enough to enjoy a few delightful snowball fights on their way up the mountain.

Manuel found himself laughing, in spite of his sorrow, as he and the others plastered each other with snow. The happy faces of the group reminded Manuel of the joyful times he and his family had shared together when he was a young lad. Those were the times before they had built the highways near his village … the times when they were poor, but very close … the times before the raids, and the fear of being adducted by evil men, had come into their lives.

At nearly eighty-five hundred feet above the town below, the scenery was breathtaking. Manuel commented that he had never seen such heights, and beauty, as he gazed upon today. The spread-out buildings and vehicles on the highway below looked like little matchboxes, and small, moving ants. The county maintained this mountain road very well, unlike many roads Manuel had traveled in South America. He recalled a trip in the Andes Mountains that had ended up being more than exciting. As the car had slipped off the rutty old road, falling over the side of a very steep cliff, only a tree had prevented his plunging further to his death. He had climbed out of the car, and up the steep side of the cliff. No sooner had he reached the top, than he heard the limbs below snapping loudly. The car rolled the rest of the way over the cliff, and vanished below. Manuel could not see, but only hear, the loud twisting of metal—and clamoring of rocks—far below him.

The group was still laughing, as they climbed into their vehicles and headed back down the mountain. They stopped at some picnic grounds below. Raymond soon had a fire blazing in one of the pits, as Melissa and Mike carried the food and condiments to a table. Manuel helped Audra with the paper plates and plastic ware.

"Audra, this has been an exceptional morning ... an exceptional day. I shall always remember this day." Manuel spoke softly ... thoughtfully, thinking of his Papa.

"Hey, it's not over yet," she commented. "We still have plenty to eat."

"Yes, and I am starving. I can't wait to sink my teeth in one of those hotdogs or hamburgers!" The aroma of the cooking red meat and hotdogs filled the air.

As they dug into their hot, tasty mesquite-smoked meals, covered with spicy sweet condiments, Melissa called out between chomps on her hotdog, "Hey, Manuel, you must go with me and Raymond to Bisbee tomorrow. We're taking a train ride through a huge copper mine, called the, *'Queen Mine Tour,'* that is filled with the wonders of some of nature's most beautiful minerals."

Manuel put his hamburger down onto his plastic plate. Here he was, enjoying a wonderful meal with these happy folks, when he should instead be grieving over the loss of his father. He looked around at each one, then spoke. "I ... I wish so much that I could, but I will not be here tomorrow."

Audra gave Manuel a strange look. "I thought you were going to stay longer."

"I was, Audra, but I received a call in the wee hours of the morning. My sister called to tell me that someone has killed my father back home. I would be on my way now, but my plane was delayed." Manuel's voice had became very sad ... sober.

Mike said, "I sure know how you must feel. I lost both my parents in one night, and I lost my brother right before my eyes, practically."

Manuel cast a long look at Mike. Here was a young man who knew the definition of loss, yet he did not seem bothered to share this with Manuel. Did it make him stronger to do so, he wondered.

"Mike, may I please walk with you for a moment?"

Mike quickly said, "Of course." Mike and Manuel walked away from the group and disappeared into the confines of the heavy wooded brush.

Audra stared at the others. "Wow! That sure fell on me like a bomb!"

"No, jive! Poor guy, he must be dying inside. I hope Mike is able to lift his spirits," said Raymond.

Melissa suddenly did not feel so happy or hungry. She had grown to like Manuel, even in the short time they had spent with him.

Manuel stopped next to a ponderosa pine. He turned and began talking. "Mike, I can't help but feel for you, also. How do you go on? I mean ... I don't know if I could show the courage you have shown. You lost your family, and now your brother. How old was your brother?"

"He was only twelve, going on thirteen, when he was abducted a few weeks ago. We were happy together. After losing our parents a few years ago, we just lost our grandparents, too—less than a year ago—in a huge fire, but Bobby and I had each other and God. We made the best of what we had ... each other. We were very close. The faith that I have in God, and the knowledge that one day, no matter what—even if I never see him again on this earth—I will see him, and all my loved ones, again in eternity. Well, I guess it is this that keeps me going on with my life. Manuel, I don't know if what I'm about to say will help you. I don't know if it will even make sense."

"What is that, Mike?" Manuel's curiosity was piqued now.

Mike looked very serious at Manuel. His eyes turned a little misty as he said, "My father told me something not too long before he died, and it has made a lot of difference in my life. He said, 'Mike, promise me, Son, that—no matter where you go in life, or what you do—you will always put God first in your life.' Well, sometimes I feel like doing just the opposite. But, I made him that promise, and I truly believe that, because of it, I still have my mind, and some form of hope."

"Such a strong promise ... such familiar words, too," Manuel muttered softly.

"What do you mean, Manuel?" His words had left Mike the curious one now.

"It is ironic. My father shared similar words with me. Looking back, I should have taken him up on his words. Unlike you, I did not, and now I feel I have deserted him ... even though he is dead."

"It is never too late, Manuel ... never," he said, reassuringly.

"Mike, you do not know me. It is too late." Mike put his large, strong hand on Manuel's right shoulder. Manuel hardly ever let another man touch him, other than his father, but today he found Mike's affection comforting. "My friend," Mike looked squarely into Manuel's eyes, "I tell you from within my heart and soul, It is never, ever ... never too late."

Manuel noticed the tear in Mike's eye. He sensed his sincerity. He found himself shaking inside. He felt like a strong presence outside him was trying to reach him. His heart leapt, and he felt warm all over. He wanted to cry. He jerked away from Mike, and walked off into the woods. With a voice not quite his own he said, "Please leave me alone, Mike. You don't know me. You have no idea what kind of life I've lived ... or still live!" Mike tried to say something, but Manuel walked further away, wanting to be left alone. Mike turned, and walked back to the others.

Mike sat down on the table bench, pondering the scene that just taken place in the woods. He hoped Manuel would soon join them. The others asked Mike what had happened. Mike said very little. A few scant words of explanation came from his mouth, "He feels convicted," and he left it at that.

Melissa just stared away. Raymond and Audra looked at each other, continuing to laugh and eat. After they finished, they cleaned the area and began putting the supplies back into their vehicles. Manuel was back from his walk by now, and joined them, digging right in. He quickly helped them carry as much as possible. Actually, he did most of the work; he insisted, apologizing for his earlier behavior. The others told him not to worry at all, as they understood his circumstances, and were very eager to support him.

When they pulled onto Highway 92, the vehicles went their separate ways. Mike, Audra and Manuel drove off in the direction of Audra's house, as Raymond and Melissa headed back into town. Manuel helped Mike and Audra carry their gear into Audra's house. He bid them farewell, and was about to leave, when Mike said, "Manuel, we shall be praying for you and your dear family during this time of sorrow and grief. We hope one day to see you again."

Manuel's heart was touched. Here were complete strangers, willing to pray for him and his family. He thought about Mike. He had no hatred for others. He loved people. He did not deserve to have his little brother stolen from him. Manuel shuddered at the thought of what he might do, to anyone who would steal his little brother. Then he thought about his father. He wondered what he would do to his father's murderers when he found them, and he knew he would. It was just a matter of time. "Perhaps when I know more about my father's tragedy, and I have settled his estate, I will return one day. Until then, my friends, I, too, shall keep you in my prayers. But please do forgive me, as I am not much of a praying man."

Audra laughed a little, "That doesn't matter, Manuel. I'm sure God is happy to hear even a few words now and then."

Manuel chuckled a bit, also, as he disappeared into his Mustang and roared out of the driveway. Mike turned, and held Audra in his arms. "I'm very glad you and Manuel bumped into each other, after all. Now let's see about getting your spare fixed. I'll get it down from the rack, and put it into my Jeep; then we'll go to town, and let a discount tire shop repair it while we shop."

Audra smiled. "'Sounds like a plan; I'd like to get in a little shopping."

Mike was not much of a shopping fanatic, until he had met Audra. For some reason, it seemed an all right activity now. "Great, then," he said. Mike pulled the tire from the rack. He looked at it, expecting to find a small nail, or something, and then he pressed down on the tire firmly. He heard a small hissing sound. "There you are. Hey! It's coming from the stem. The stem must have gotten cut, or something." Upon careful examination, Mike noticed the valve itself was leaking. He walked over to his Jeep, and retrieved a valve stem remover from his toolbox. Mike bent down and tightened the valve. "Man, that was one loose valve stem. 'Wonder how it worked its way out like that?" Mike pulled out a small, portable compressor and plugged it into the power outlet in Audra's Nissan. The compressor kicked on, and soon Audra's tire was aired up to specs. Audra ran out of the house, expecting to go shopping. She saw Mike jacking up the back of her Nissan with his own hydraulic jack. "Have your tire on in a jiff," he said.

"Same tire?" she wondered, curiously.

"Of course. The valve stem was just loose; 'wonder it didn't blow out of the valve!"

Audra's mind shifted back to the events of that day her tire was down. "It wasn't low when I left yesterday; it was low when I came out of class."

"Well, somehow between your house and the school it apparently worked itself loose. You know, that is very odd," mused Mike.

Audra began to reevaluate the 'coincidental' meeting she had had with Manuel that afternoon. But, she would tell Mike about that later, as her mind was on shopping at the moment. "Come on, hurry your buns up; we've got some shopping to do!"

"Shopping? I already fixed your tire myself. All I have to do is tighten these lug nuts, and it's done," explained Mike.

Audra thought about the tire again. "A loose valve stem, hmmm.... I wonder how that happened. Maybe my meeting with Manuel was not so coincidental, after all," said Audra silently. Her mind again played back that day at the college.

Eight dark figures moved like nocturnal cat-like creatures through the trees in Huachuca Canyon. They moved with ease, and uncanny swiftness, as they neared the arsenal that Pat and Sterling had found a couple of days before. Since Pat and Sterling had discovered the ammo dump built back into the hill, they had kept surveillance on it. They witnessed several Jeeps and transports roll up the twisting road, unloading pallets with crates on them. They did not know for sure if the crates contained weapons, but they were willing to venture a gamble on it.

Tonight, the Rangers carried large packs on their backs, filled with the faulty magazines they had rigged earlier. They wore combat helmets with masks, complete with night vision and infrared optical lenses. They could see very clearly, as they swept through the darkness of the night. Soon they surrounded the arsenal. The Colonel carefully and quietly whispered to the Specialist heading up the group of Rangers. "Sergeant Kelley, inform your troops to move in fifteen minutes. Tell them to study the perimeter, and take a few thermal shots of the interior. Also, I have detected some movement outside; apparently, a guard has been posted. My infrared scope is picking up a human form inside, as well. Remember … this operation must not fail! If it does, I will personally ship you and your men off to Fort Benning, Georgia, with the worse recommendation you could ever imagine."

"In other words," Sterling quipped, "you'll wish you had signed up for the Girl Scouts, if you and your men fail."

The Colonel chuckled at how Sterling had finished his thought. "I couldn't have said it better myself."

"The Colonel and Sergeant Major need not worry, Sir. My men never fail." Sergeant Kelley was then off in a flash.

"Can you believe we're posted in front of a stupid dump, beside a *stupid* hill, when we could be enjoying the women in town!" exclaimed one of the privates—with a somewhat limited vocabulary—who had been assigned guard duty over the ammo bunker.

His partner walked out of the bunker, and sat down next to his disappointed friend. "Well, Private, not all of us have that luxury. Just be thankful you have a job in the States, and you're not in Iraq right now, guarding an ammo dump there."

"At least it'd be a little more exciting," the first one began to speak again, when a slight *'phhht!'* sound came from the tree line. Both guards slumped over, and fell to the ground. Like a quiet storm, the Rangers moved in. Pat noticed one of the men pulling a couple of half-filled flasks of whiskey from his bag. He poured a little whiskey over the men's heads and into their mouths. Then he stuck a thin needle, attached to a syringe, into each of their waists.

"What are you doing?" asked the Colonel. "Sir, when these men wake up, not only will they smell like they were drinking until they passed out, but they'll actually have alcohol in their bloodstream and terrible hangovers, to boot. They'll actually believe they've been drinking."

"Huh. Amazing! I like that. You guys are pretty good."

"Sir, we're the best, Sir!" the Ranger responsible for this part of the escapade responded.

"Hey, now! Don't get cocky, Specialist; the night ain't over yet," Colonel Heyburn cautioned.

"Yes, Sir," replied the Ranger.

Soon the Rangers were inside. They swiftly found the crates of magazines, opened the locks with ease, and began replacing the good magazines with the faulty magazines. Pat walked amongst the Rangers, taking mental notes of their progress. He noticed there was only a sketched outline where the magazine, which he'd cautioned Sterling against picking up a couple of days, ago had once lain. "It was indeed a plant, just as suspected," he mumbled to himself.

Sterling helped load and unload the crates. He had not had so much excitement in a long time; it made him feel young and useful again. Thirty minutes later, the Rangers were packing, and shipping out. They had closed, and locked, all the crates they had opened. They then evacuated the bunker, locking the doors behind them. They left the bunker looking spotless and clean, as if nothing at all had happened. They had replaced every magazine in the entire arsenal. As the Rangers were taking a route back to the post, other than that on which they had come, the Colonel asked if the trails they had left on the ground were being swept. The Ranger looked at him and replied, "Of course, Sir. We never leave a stone disturbed." Pat laughed at this twist on the old cliché, and said, "I know ... you guys are the best."

"The best! Yes, Sir, that we are," the young, confident Ranger replied.

When Pat and the others reached the post, Pat pointed out some of their minor mistakes he'd noted as he wandered among them back in the bunker. Then he told them they would know if their operation was a complete success or not in a few weeks. "Men, you might as well know that this operation may not have been a drill. As I stated before, this is to remain *'classified'* until further notice. Now get some well deserved rest." With this commendation, the Colonel walked away.

Manuel sat quietly in the seat of the passenger plane. A man sitting next to him tried to strike up a conversation, but Manuel was in no mood for that; his mind was with his family. How ironic it seemed. Instead of flying back to hug his father, and kiss his mother, he was flying back to mourn his father's death ... to bury him. He thought, too, about the people he had left behind in Sierra Vista. They were very different from his superiors he served there. He thought of Mike and Audra as real friends. But, how could he befriend those he must fight, or even kill? By now—if all the events had not played out as they had—he would have left Mr. Hooah with all his facts about Audra, Mike and those helping them, and been on his way home. However, a voice within him would not allow him to do this. He had, instead, leased a safety deposit box at the City Bank in Sierra Vista, and put his notes in that box. He held onto one key, and hid the other back in Sierra Vista. There was a good reason for doing this. He must scrutinize all possibilities before he turned Mike and Audra over to Mr. Hooah. "First things first," said Manuel to himself.

Manuel looked at the familiar ground before him, as he fiddled with a little penlight clipped to his front shirt pocket. The lakes, rivers and trees all sang out to him in one accord. Soon he would be home. He leaned back in his seat and sighed, as he clicked his penlight on and off. As his eyes focused on the small light, his face suddenly lost all expression, as he momentarily remembered the little MagLite he had found in the cave. He had given it to some hooligans that worked for Mr. Hooah. By now, they must have traced the serial numbers back to Mike. "No!" his thoughts screamed. "They will ruin everything if they harass Mike now!" He broke the airline's rules, using his cell phone to call the thugs, who were—at this very moment—implementing his orders.

"So, Bruce, you still can't remember where you bought this flashlight, or who you gave it to? You're telling me you never owned it? You never saw it before in your life? *Liar!"* the hefty man screeched, as he hit Bruce across his face again. Then he sunk his fist into Bruce's gut. "Listen, credit cards don't lie, people do!" Bruce found his plight a bit hard to comprehend. One minute he was enjoying a nice Chinese dinner he had ordered from a neighborhood Chinese cuisine and, the next minute, his doorbell rang. Now, here he sat on his own sofa, as three well dressed morons beat him severely. They shouted curses at him, and blamed him for an explosion that had happened in some remote place he knew nothing about. "I don't know, Bruce, I really don't know. I come here trying to be a very understanding guy, and how do you treat me? You *lie* to me!"

Bruce's mouth began swelling up, as he spit pieces of his teeth and flesh from his bloody mouth. He tried to speak, "I ... er ... I thell ya, I dunno; I jez ... I may have loz one, but I dunno wha' you mean. Blow up ... blow whuddup?" he asked, confused.

"Bruce, I don't even want to talk to you anymore!" the man barked disdainfully, as he cocked his pistol. "This has been one boring conversation, from the very beginning!" Before he could pull back the trigger of the already-cocked gun, his phone rang. " Yeah, whadda ya want!" he yelled, upset at being interrupted.

"Listen, I don't know who you are, but I will find you and cut out your ugly tongue if you ever shout in my ear again! Now, you are to ignore any lead the Mag flashlight led you to. The flashlight is *no* longer a problem; it was purchased with a stolen credit card. If you have harassed *any*one about the light, you have been fools. You don't need to beat up innocent people. Please tell me you were able to figure this out."

"Who is this, anyway?" the man holding the cocked gun asked, ignorantly.

Manuel became very upset. "You idiot! I have your name and number. This is El Niño and, when I see you, I shall kill you myself. I hear someone moaning in the background!" The phone went dead. The hefty man, filled with fear, raced over to his partners and told them they had to leave immediately. They left Bruce lying in pain, badly bloodied, and bolted out the door. Bruce winced in agony, as he crawled to the phone. Pulling it down from the counter, he dialed the police. As he waited for help, he remembered—he had purchased the light as a gift for Mike.

The 747 jet landed on schedule at the La Paz International Airport. The large plane taxied off the runway and pulled up to the extended corridor. Annette greeted her handsome brother with a kiss. "I am so glad you are here, Hermano. We've all missed you terribly! I wish you could have been here when all this happened. Mama thinks that if you had been here, all this wouldn't have happened at all."

Manuel looked a bit puzzled. He wondered what his sister was talking about. "Annette, forgive me, but I have been very busy in the United States. What do you mean, 'all of *what*'?" Annette looked surprised. "Manuel, haven't you kept up with the news?"

"Not other than what I read on the Internet. I have been working too much, I suppose."

"Papa was on television … there was a raid. I tell you what … let's get your luggage into my car. Then I'll tell you all I know—you need to know." Annette and Manuel found the luggage claim, and retrieved his one lone suitcase; he always traveled light. They walked out of the airport and to the parking lot. Manuel paid the guard and they were on their way. When Annette pulled onto the main freeway, she began to tell Manuel the whole story, beginning with young Cruz stumbling into Papa's chapel, after being shot. She told how he had fought for his life, as Mama and Papa helped him as much as possible, but died shortly after his father arrived. She told how the people had become very angry … and much violence had followed. She explained that there had not only been a raid, but many had been massacred. Bombs were used, fields were burned, and an arsenal was sacked and set ablaze.

Manuel sat back in his seat, his heart feeling very heavy. Now he understood what his mother meant when she said that if Manuel would have been around, none of it would have happened. She may have been right. Manuel's innate diplomacy was very good at redirecting the villagers' anger, yet deep inside he knew that he would not be able to stop their fury forever. However, he had never dreamed that his own father would die as a victim of their wrath. Manuel had always managed to keep his family safe from the clutches of the General; he and the General had a pact ... a deal. He had many questions now, and he knew the person he solely trusted and believed in, his precious mother, would provide the truth.

He knew the time was not right for such questions. He would wait until he had buried his precious father—then he would begin his research. He would find the men, and kill them with his bare hands. Only a painful death would do for such creatures that would dare touch any member of his family.

Chapter Nineteen

Mike sat anxiously on his olive-green sofa in his living room. Normally, he thought of himself as a patient person, but when the Colonel told him that they must all await the criminals' next move, Mike argued in his mind that there had to be something left to do. Matt recently told him that his assistant had managed to take a decent photo of Janet Riley, with a zoom lens, stating that he would get right to work on her picture and Manuel's. Mike had to laugh, when he thought about how he had managed to take Manuel's photo. While they were up on the mountain, he'd calmly walked over to his Jeep, pulled his digital camera from beneath the front seat, turned and snapped a shot of Manuel smiling face, as he was throwing a snowball at Melissa. Then he set the camera back down under the seat, and lifted a water jug to quench his thirst … the main reason he had walked over to the Jeep.

Mike could not help but fidget in his seat. "There must be something else I can do!" His mind seemed to be spinning in circles, like a roulette wheel, and would not be quieted. Finally, the ball fell on Dennis Perris. "I know! It's Sunday; I'll invite Dennis over for another chat." Mike walked over to his phone, and called the church. Cynthia Stevens, the church receptionist, answered the phone.

"Hello, Shiloh Valley Church. How may I direct your call?"

"Cynthia, this is Mike. Do you know if Dennis is still at the church? He usually sticks around for a while, cleaning and setting up things for next Sunday."

"We missed you at service today," she said with concern.

"Yes, I wanted to be there, but I had many things to do. I did make it to Sunday school, though." Mike really did not feel like discussing trivial matters, but he wanted to be polite.

Cynthia started to go on about a few other subjects when Mike broke in. "I'm sorry, Cynthia, but I really do need to speak with Dennis."

"Oh, yeah, that's right! I'll see if he's still here." She hurriedly dropped the phone, and walked off. Mike could hear much shuffling, and many voices, echoing in the background.

After what seemed to be seven or eight minutes, Mike heard the phone scruff across the counter, as it was being picked up. "O-o-oh, my ears," he moaned, as Dennis' voice boomed through the receiver.

"Mike! Hi, Partner! This is a very pleasant surprise. 'Saw you go into the Sunday School session, but I missed seeing your face in the morning worship service."

"I'm sorry I missed you, too," Mike replied politely. "I just had to get away, Dennis. I had a lot to think over in my mind; that's why I'm calling you now. I really need to speak to a friend today. I know I've rather avoided you recently, but I just didn't feel like talking much to anybody lately. Could you come over today when you get finished at church?"

There was a slight pause. "Well, I was invited to lunch with the pastor."

Mike sighed. He was just about ready to say, "Oh, well, better luck next time," when Dennis spoke again.

"Hey, tell y' what … when I get done eating, I'll come over to your place. How's that sound?"

"'Sounds like a winner, Dennis. What time do you think that will be?"

"Oh, no later than about two this afternoon."

"Great, I'll be here." Mike hung up the phone and began to think about how to approach Dennis with all his questions.

Manuel stood silently over his father's casket. The poor villagers had chipped in and purchased a very nice casket for their preacher. This touched Manuel's heart deeply. As he stood there, Manuel was again beginning to feel things in his heart he knew little about. He could not understand why he felt them; he could not begin to comprehend the origin of such emotions. Why did he feel this way? Was his heart becoming soft? It had all started when he met Audra and her friends. The words Mike told him seemed to haunt his soul, as well. Before him stood the villagers, weeping loudly for their pastor. Some of the women fell to the ground, crying in agony. Even the men could not hold back their tears. Señor Herrera fell to his knees, holding his face in his hands, as he wept bitterly. Pastor Miguel Garcia stopped now and then to take in deep breaths, as he preached the memorial service for Manny's precious father.

Earlier Manuel had asked the funeral home for the cost of the casket and their services. The owner, who had known Pedro very well, had charged the villagers only what it had cost him to purchase the casket. He donated his services. Manuel looked at the old man with watery eyes, as he handed him a large envelope. "I give you ten thousand Bolivianos. Pay the people back their money, Paco, my friend, and you keep the rest for your services. I want my father to have a service that matches the man he was ... honorable and very noble."

Paco tried to give Manuel back his money. "I need no money like this to give Señor Martinez a very honorable interment. A man such as your father already earned such a burial."

"Then consider it a donation to the people and yourself." Manuel turned and left Paco's establishment.

Manuel's mind focused on the service once again. His mother was burying her noble, pretty head in Manuel's bosom, wailing despondently. Manuel tried to hold back his emotions but, as the service continued, he found himself losing his composure. He, too, began to weep a little. Finally—after all the eulogies, testimonies and the memorial service ended—the village people lined up and gathered around Pedro's final resting site, which was beneath a wide-spreading, beautiful almendra tree. When the people looked up at this giant tree, they would always remember Pedro and what this giant of a man had stood for.

Manuel approached his father's grave. He knelt down and looked down into the cavity in the ground at his father's casket. Below him lay the hard-working man who had always believed in Manuel ... the man who had shared his dreams ... the man who had held onto hope, when others in the poor country of Bolivia had none. Here lay the man who knew not despair ... the man that gave so much and asked for so little ... the man that, somehow—through all his toils and back breaking labor—made sure Manuel had received a very sound education.

Manuel lifted a small piece of earth to toss on his father's grave, sadly participating in a custom symbolically giving up a loved one's body back to the earth whence it came ... and the finality of it all. His mother also picked up a handful of dirt, and painfully dropped it onto her husband's casket. His sister and brother did so, as well. However, Manuel just rolled the soil around in his hands ... hesitating to toss the dirt upon his beloved Papa, as he felt it was not all over ... yet. He looked upon the casket of the man he loved more than life, and then he spoke these words very softly: "I will avenge you, Papa. I will avenge you." He could not throw the sod on his father's casket. To Manuel, it seemed it would be an insult ... like throwing dirt in his father's face. He also felt very unworthy. Custom, or no custom, he could not.

The words of his father began to haunt him, as he looked once more upon his father's earthly tomb. "Please, Manny, promise me that no matter what you do in life, or where you go, you will always put God first." A tear flowed down

Manny's cheek as he said, "Yes, father, I one day will make this promise, but not yet … not yet." He placed the soil in his coat pocket, and rose from the ground. Then he walked over and joined his family, as others gathered around Pedro's gravesite.

Mike's doorbell rang. Mike looked at the clock. "Two-thirty, not bad timing."

Mike opened his door to see Dennis standing on the doorstep. "Hi, Mike, may I come in?"

Mike looked Dennis directly in the eyes—then he looked behind Dennis and said, "Certainly, Dennis, please do." Dennis looked behind him, then faced Mike and walked inside.

"I made some coffee; care for a mug?"

Without responding to Mike's offer, Dennis looked around at the house. It looked much tidier than the last time he had visited. "'Looks like you must have hired a maid, or something. Your house really looks nice, Buddy."

Assuming the lack of refusal of his coffee offer was a 'Yes,' Mike handed Dennis a mug. As he stood up to accept the coffee from Mike, his head towered about three inches above him. He was a tall man, with a slightly round physique. He loved to laugh. At times, when he would tell jokes and stories, Dennis laughed loudly … a belly roll type of laughter. They at first spoke about trivial matters, and laughed about past events they had shared together. Then Mike abruptly changed the subject.

"I guess you've been really busy with your ministry, Dennis."

"Boy! You're not just a'kiddin'! It keeps me hoppin'. I have been to so many districts lately, that I can barely keep track of it all."

"I'll bet. Hey, I know I've been avoiding your calls lately, Dennis. I want to apologize for that, but there are reasons. I haven't felt much like talking to anybody until now."

"Oh, please … I do understand, Mike. If I were in your shoes, I probably wouldn't want to talk to too many people, either."

"Thank you, Dennis. But, there is another reason, also. Dennis, I am a little upset at you."

Dennis immediately stopped drinking his coffee, sat it down on the table in front of him, and gave Mike his full attention. "I'm sorry … what did you say?" Dennis, caught off guard, did not expect this.

"Dennis, when we last spoke, you told me that you were in Tucson, when I was here in the hospital. But, one of the nurses I spoke with told me that they had seen a man, fitting your description 'to a T,' walk into my room, and then walk back out. She said you had a book in your hand. *This* book," Mike emphasized, as he held up the hard-covered Bible that had Dennis' prints on it. Mike knew he was gambling; he knew someone else might have planted the Bible, in an attempt to frame Dennis, and make him appear suspicious. Mike also had made up the story about the nurse.

As Mike spoke, Dennis had picked up his mug and began drinking again. As Mike finished, he set it down on the table again. He leaned back on the couch, in a relaxed fashion, taking in a deep breath of air.

"Okay, Mike, you've got me. I was in Tucson when I learned the paramedics had taken you to the hospital in Sierra Vista, so I drove back to Sierra Vista, found the room you were staying in, and I entered your room, hoping to talk to you. I felt so badly about what had happened."

"What time was that, Dennis?"

"Probably around eight in the evening; it was just before visiting hours ended. When I didn't get to talk to you, since you were out like a light, I just left the Bible there for you. I guess they must have given you some pretty powerful stuff!"

Mike stirred in his chair a little. He had not thought much about this before … exactly how he would approach Dennis … so, he chose his words carefully. "Dennis, why did you highlight the thirteenth chapter in Exodus … the second and thirteenth verse, in particular?"

Dennis sat on the couch, acting a bit nervous. "I was hoping those words would somehow comfort you. I don't know. I could have chosen a zillion other verses, but I was upset, and fumbling for verses. Those verses speak about how children are like gifts from God … dedicated to God. I thought you would see this and, somehow, it would comfort you."

"Hmmm, okay. But why didn't you just tell me in the first place that you had been at the hospital?" Mike pushed, as someone with nothing to hide would have just told him, or so it seemed.

"I know I should have, but I just didn't. Actually, I should have done many things, but I just feel so … funny. I mean, I feel awkward. I'm afraid I'll say the wrong thing, and only hurt instead of help."

Mike shifted in his chair, nervous about his next move … the big nuke he was about to drop on Dennis. "Dennis, I bumped into a friend that knows about your father. I know he's still alive. I also know you've been to South America, and that your mother passed away in Panama. Why, Dennis … why did you tell me your father is dead, and that you've never have been to that part of the globe?" asked Mike, with a bit of pain in his voice.

Dennis fell back into the soft sofa cushions, feel as though he'd just had the wind knocked out of him. His eyes fell upon the carpet. Now what could Dennis say? Mike had caught him in a rather bold lie … several, in fact. What was he to do? Dennis took in more air as he calmed his nerves. "Mike, I had to lie to you, and I wouldn't blame you if you never speak to me again, but the truth is, my father *is* dead. He is dead, as far as I'm concerned. I hate what my father has become. He is not a very nice guy. He is involved, heavily involved, in the syndicate in South America. I think he's even killed people, or had them killed. I never knew this until I accidentally stumbled upon some strange papers on his desk one day. Well, he would have to walk in on me at that time. He knew then that I had discovered his terrible crimes. We got into a huge, screaming argument about it. He even threatened me. I told him that—unless he changed and got out of such a lifestyle—I didn't want to be around him anymore."

"What did he do?" asked Mike.

"He laughed, and then he said he *had* no son. He gave me a huge wad of money, and set up a healthy checking account here in Sierra Vista, under my name and ID numbers. Then he told me to report to Mr. Braddock, our Mayor. According to my father, the Mayor had some work for me to do. Yeah, some work. I run around like a silly chicken, with its skinny neck half chopped off, delivering stupid papers, or whatnots, to everybody—including Tom, Dick and Harry.

"Mike, would you want people to know that kind of background? Would you want people to know that your father is a low-life scumbag? He may be worth millions, for all I know, but he isn't worth a plug nickel to me. I pray for him, and hope for the best, but it would take some huge miracle to change him.

I do still visit South America, and Central America, from time to time, but I keep it under my hat because I'm afraid it could lead to questions that might expose my father, and what he really is. To be frank, I think my father knows the Mayor here, and that is why he sent me to this city." Dennis stopped. He put his hands up to his face, and rubbed his cheeks vigorously.

Mike sensed the father and son love-hate relationship. He just sat in his chair for a few moments, lost for words. As the two just looked around the room, gawking at pictures—and at each other from time to time—Mike saw tears in Dennis' eyes. The tears flowed down his cheeks onto the carpeting below him. Mike gazed upon his much-burdened friend, feeling foolish. For so long, he had misjudged this man. If only Dennis had told him about his father long ago.

Mike rose from his chair, and sat down beside Dennis on the couch. He put his hand on Dennis' shoulder. "Dennis, I am so glad you finally got all that out in the open. I feel so much better about you now. I thought some bad things about you before today. I am no longer upset at you, though I am a little angry with you for not telling me this sooner. But, hey, like you said before, 'What are friends for, if they can't be a pest?' 'Remember that?" They both laughed, as Dennis wiped a tear from his eye.

It was late in the afternoon when the last villager, Señor Herrera, left the Martinez residence, and walked sadly down the streets of La Palo. Manuel looked in on his mother, as she lay on the sofa in the living room. Manuel had paid a contractor to build this room; he had paid for others, too. The house additions were a gesture of his gratitude for what his father and mother had worked so hard for and given to him. His heart ached heavily. He had planned on surprising his father this year at harvest time; he'd planned on purchasing a big farm truck for his Papa, just like the ones his wealthier neighbors owned, so he could take his own harvest to market. Now all of this seemed so meaningless.

Manuel gritted his teeth. "He gave, gave and gave even more, but received very little in return."

His mother overheard these words coming from the mouth of her son. She called Manuel over to her, and began to speak with a very soft, loving voice. "No, Manny, your father received more than he gave."

Manuel looked at his mother in surprise. His shoulders drooped, as he looked down at the wooden floor. A small coat of dust had collected on the floor, taking away some of the beauty of the calisaya wood. "Mama, please tell me … what do you mean?"

His mother kissed his cheek and then spoke softly and lovingly to her precious son. "Your father worked very hard, this is true. He also gave to everyone almost all he had. But, in return, Manny, he received many gifts from the villagers. Listen, Son, most people in the world give out of their abundance; they give many times because they want something in return, but the people here gave out of their poverty … they gave out of love. Manny, do you know such love?"

Manuel squirmed a little. He thought about all the sacrifices Papa had made for him and the family. "Yes, Mama, I do know such love. Papa showed me this love, and so have you. I think I understand."

His mother smiled, "This is so good to know, my Son. It is what your father wished for."

"But, Mama, he was killed by two villagers! I cannot forgive this act of betrayal!" Manuel's voice rose in anger … in agony.

Rosa grabbed her son and hugged him. "You were not there! You do not know what you are saying. The men were no more *villagers* than is the President of Mexico! They were strangers from some place; I know not where. I was there … I heard them speak. They talked liked Colombians. They called each other 'Scorpio' and 'Pepe.' Believe me, Manny, no one in this village killed Pedro. You should have been here the day he and the villagers saved the desperate lives of our children; you would know none of the villagers would do this to your father. The people all fought together to rescue the children. Your father was one of the leaders; he and Señor Herrera both led the way. I am proud of your father. He gave to the people what they needed most—courage and dignity. They regained them both that day, and I feel they will never again lose them. This is everything your father ever wanted … he wanted the people to start believing, and hoping again, that one day God would fight for them. Don't you see? It is true. We have more respect for each other, and our lives, than we ever had for years. Just before your father died he said, "Rosa, today we begin to win back our freedom, our pride."

"Mama, what else did Papa say?" Rosa began to weep profusely, yet she managed a few more words, as tears flowed unchecked from her eyes. "Oh, Manny!" She held her son close to her. "Papa looked up into my eyes and said, 'Please, my sweet, precious wife, tell Manny no matter what he does in life, or wherever he goes, to always put God first.' Those were the last words that came out of his mouth before he died, Manny; Papa was thinking about you when he died, my Son." Manuel held his mother in his strong, muscular arms as she continued to sob. She cried for what seemed to be an hour, as she fell asleep in Manny's bosom. He tenderly laid his mother softly on the sofa where they had been sitting, and gently placed a pillow under her noble head.

Manuel opened the door quietly, and slipped outside. A gentle breeze blew through his thick, dark hair. The sun was setting in the west. He noticed how similar the colors were to that of Sierra Vista, as the sun sank behind the tall mountains. He walked away from the village. He did not know at first where he wanted to go. He just wanted to leave. The names of Scorpio and Pepe echoed through his mind. These men worked for the General, and he knew them well. Something inside him was beginning to change. Try as he might, he could not hold it back. Maybe he did not want to. Maybe he had finally found what he had been searching for all his life. He walked, and walked, and walked all through the evening, until he found himself next to the small river—Rio San Juan—where he and his father had happily fished together when he was quite young. Visions of very happy times with his father danced through his head.

"Oh, Papa! You are the best papa in the whole world!" laughed little Manny.

"Oh, Son, I am sure many sons say that about their papas, all around the world."

"Maybe not, Papa 'cause they don't know you. If they did, they would say the same thing!" laughed Manny, as he splashed his father with the clear water from the river. Pedro and little Manny soon found themselves in a wonderful world of laughter and joy, as they splashed through the cool water.

Pedro picked Manny up, shouting, "Now for the big splash!" Then he safely threw Manny—who could 'swim like the proverbial fish'—into the deeper water, announcing, "Here comes Super Tuna!" They laughed and laughed together about that one.

"Hey, son, I see some red horses! Let's see if we can catch them. The fish love them, you know." Manny rushed to his father's side. He jumped up on the bank and tossed his father the throw net. In no time, his father had caught a host of the red-finned little minnow-like fish. They laughed heartily, as they emptied the small fish into their buckets. "Now, we will catch fish so big, even God will want to dine with us tonight!" laughed Pedro.

"Yeah, God and all our friends," Manny added. "Mama will be more than delighted with our catch!"

"Of course! Mama loves fish, too. I will cook them for her when we return, and let Mama rest. She has been working too hard lately. Come on, my Son. Let's go further down the river. I know a place where the fish are so big, you need harpoons to kill them!" Manny and Pedro laughed so hard they almost spilled all the water from their bait buckets.

Manny became aware of his surroundings once again, following this delightful reverie into the unencumbered past he recalled experiencing with his beloved Papa. He remembered all too well these happy days in the sun with his dear father, who did not smoke, drink or cuss. He was truly a gentleman. Manny sat upon the bank of the San Juan River, burying his face in his hands. No longer could he hold back his anguish and grief. He wept bitterly. He was alone … away from everyone but God. Manuel looked up into the stars and said with a choking tear-filled voice, "Forgive me, Papa. Forgive me, Father." Then he wept louder as tears ran like streams down his cheeks.

"Son, He already forgave you the moment you returned," said a kind, sober voice.

Manny looked up to see a familiar face. "Señor Herrera, what are you doing here?" Manny wiped the tears from his face with the sleeve of his shirt.

Señor Herrera spoke gently. "I, too, remember the days in the sun with your father. Remember how you and my sons would come here often and—many times—we would fish this river together. We all shared much laughter and joy together here. It is no surprise that fate brought us together tonight at this magical place to mourn your father's death."

Manuel choked on his own words a little. "Yes, I remember that. How long have you been here Señor Herrera?"

"'Long time … before the sun began to set today. I have been here thinking and thinking about what to do next. I am trying to think like Pedro. I ask God, 'What would Pedro do?' Now you come to the river. I think God sent you. Manny, will you stay and lead us?"

Manny thought about these words. Yes, he could stay and lead the people, but this would disable him from dealing with his enemies directly. His heart was with the people yet he knew, in his mind, he could serve the people more efficiently if he attacked the enemy head-on. Manuel sniffled as he spoke, "Señor Herrera, I can help our people greatly, but I cannot do so by staying here. I must use the methods and skills God has given me. We are up against a very powerful and evil force. I cannot stay here and wait for the enemy to come to us. I must go out and meet our foe head-on in the battlefield. You have heard of General Montiego?"

Señor Herrera cringed at the mention of the name. "Yes, I believe most know him. He is very evil, though he pretends to be a generous man. Your father told me about this vile man. Manny, your father gave us back our pride and dignity. He was a great man. He gave me hope, and courage to go on. Now his death has given me more strength to see the battle's end. I shall never allow one of our precious children to fall into the wicked general's clutches again. I came here asking your father what to do next."

"Well, I know what to do next. You must lead the people here. You must be their pillar. Papa always trusted you, Andrew," Manuel began, calling him, as they sometimes were prone to do, by an Americanized version of his Spanish name—Andrés. He fought for you. Now his spirit cries out to us the words, *'courage,' 'hope,'* and *'faith'* … more than ever before. Señor Herrera, the General is a very rash man … his anger is fierce, and his retribution swift. His fury is upon this village. You must somehow keep all the villagers united. The people must stand at guard, ready for a vengeful attack at any time."

"We believe we are ready, as we have all the weapons from the arsenal we raided when we liberated our children," explained Señor Herrera.

This knowledge gave Manny hope. "Then you must see to it that the people keep their arms next to them at all times. Do not leave one pistol unloaded, or one grenade out of sight. I will go forward and do battle with our foe the way I know best. Together, we shall conquer this evil tyrant, and his wretched men," said Manny, adamantly.

Great hope and faith flowed through Señor Herrera's entire body. Manuel's vibrant words had touched his very soul. Andrés spoke with a strong, fighting voice, "Yes, yes! Let them come. Let the wicked villains come. We shall triumph! If the General attacks us, he shall fall, and what a mighty fall that will be! Manny, we have one on our side who is much more powerful than the General. Your father knew this. He preached about Him all of the time. We have God on our side. God is our source, and we have more than enough!" shouted Señor Herrera, excitedly.

Chapter Twenty

Bobby and the rest of the young boys, along with a few chosen girls, walked through the chow line, picked up their food, and found their assigned tables. Bobby looked at Timmy, Brad, Donny and Susan. They all had become close friends. Bobby asked Susan and Timmy if they missed their families.

Timmy said something Bobby thought very strange. "Actually, I don't remember them very well."

"Come to think of it, I don't remember my family very well, either. I see their faces sometimes, and I can feel them, but I forget their names at times. I am happy here. I know where I really belong now, and I have many friends here. I like it here." It was Susan speaking this time, confirming Timmy's observations.

"So do I," agreed Timmy.

"Don't you like it here, too, Bobby?" asked Susan. She looked at Bobby with a glow on her very cute little face.

"Well, sure, but I remember my brother, Mike, pretty well … though I sometimes forget some of the things we did in the past."

Bobby looked all around him, and picked up his chocolate milk. He stared at the others, as they gulped down their milk. The adults managing the compound told the children to drink all of their milk, be it white or chocolate, as they wanted the children to grow very strong, and healthy bones. Bobby walked over to the water fountain and poured his milk down the drain. He filled his carton with cool water, and returned to his table. Mr. Clean was watching the children from behind a large, decorated one-way mirror.

"Wonderful, my kids! You're all drinking your beta blockers, and mind-enhancing tonic, like the good children you are," he thought. He didn't see Bobby dumping his out. The children had no idea their memories were being chemically erased.

Early Monday morning, Manuel received a call from a very familiar voice. "You're needed immediately at HQ. Your presence is required no later than three o'clock this afternoon. Be there!"

His cell phone became silent, as he looked around the room in his moderate hacienda outside the village of La Palo. Manuel stumbled out of bed, and began brewing a strong pot of Bolivian coffee. He thought of the more robust Colombian brands, but his mind referred back to the memory of his father. "Papa, I will always buy only your coffee beans, and only what comes from your fields," Manuel spoke, as though his father was standing in the room next to him. "Yes, I truly love your coffee, Papa."

One item he hated was '*coca.*' It brought to mind too many horrible, nightmarish memories. He never could understand how plants could bring about the deaths of so many people, or why people could fall in love with their addicting effects. This included the last legal drug known to mankind, as well ... alcohol—made not from a plant leaf, as was cocaine, but from grain. "Take away alcohol, and all hell would break loose on this planet," laughed Manuel sarcastically, recalling a few details he'd heard about a time now known as '*Prohibition,*' which occurred in the United States decades before when alcohol had been outlawed for a season.

Then, the thought of his father's death entered his mind once more. His words once again haunted Manuel. "Yes, Father in heaven, I *will* ... one day." Manny shook his head. "Surely I am finally losing what little mind I have left. I only hope I can hang onto its remnants. Lord, just let me keep my mind long enough to accomplish a few last feats; that is all I ask."

Manuel lifted his cell phone and, within minutes, Annette's voice came over the line.

"Hello, Manuel."

"Yes, Annette, please come over to my place. We must talk, now. Hurry, please." Manuel ended the conversation.

Annette turned in her bed. She had told Rosa she would stay on a few days to help with Papa's affairs before she left for home in La Paz, because Manuel had to leave soon, and he had entrusted her with their father's estate, knowing she would do the right thing. Of course, he wanted everything to go to the family, especially his mother. He knew that he was the eldest son, and it was his responsibility to see these things through, but times were changing. He felt no shame in allowing Annette to handle the affairs. She had humbly accepted this.

Annette wondered what it was that Manuel could be wanting, so early in the morning, and why he was being so secretive. She jumped out of bed, and hurried through the house. She splashed some water on her face, drank a cold cup of coffee, and then bounded out the door, not even pausing long enough to change into her clothing. She climbed into her car, and raced towards Manuel's house.

Manuel poured the hot, dark liquid into his mug. He lifted the steaming russet-colored fluid to his nose and took in a deep breath. "Ah-h-h, that smells so good ... just like the fresh grounds that Papa used to make in the early morning hours. Manuel sat down at the kitchen table, picked up an old local newspaper, and read about the massacre that had taken place while he was still in the United States on business. He felt a sort of pride and dignity filling his person as he read: "Truly the villagers had waited too long for this noble cause."

He flipped through the pages until he found the piece on his father. The Bolivian paper did not say much about his father. They mentioned that he was thought to be one of the rebel leaders, who had helped free some workers in the cocoa jungle twenty miles outside the La Palo city limits. There was also mention of a labor dispute, and a violent protest over unfair wages. Manuel slammed the paper down on the table. "The corrupt media in Bolivia can never print the truth! The people will believe anything. They make it almost sound like it was all the villagers' fault. The lying, freaking idiots ... nothing but pawns! I'll bet they didn't even air the truth over television; 'probably made it sound like a 'breaking and entering'!" God, help us all!" Manuel groaned.

Annette knocked loudly at the door. Manuel hurried over and opened the door, to see his sister standing in a robe. "Come in, Annette. Goodness, you must have flown here!"

Annette walked in and plopped down on one of Manuel's love seats near the sofa. "Well, you sounded very anxious to see me, so...."

"Actually, I am. Please follow me, Sister. I have to show you something, and I have such little time. I must be in Bogotá by three this afternoon. I have a very important client to tend to." Manuel spoke as he walked to the back of his house. Annette carefully followed behind. He moved a somewhat heavy bookcase over about three feet, and lifted some wooden slats from the floor. Annette watched. She said nothing. Manuel carefully removed a briefcase and a wooden box. He opened the box, exposing many gold coins ... half of them, priceless Spanish gold coins. Then he exposed the contents of the briefcase. Annette's eyes lit up when she saw the gold coins and the money.

"I estimate a million Euros worth of bills in here. We both know that gold is beginning to make a huge wave around the world today, so I collected these gold coins, accordingly. Annette, I am about to embark on a ... well ... a very unpredictable adventure. I show you this because, if anything should happen to me, you will know where it is."

"Manny, how did you come into all this?"

"Oh, careful investments, studying the market, knowing when to buy and sell. This is a collection of what I've accumulated over the years while working. I tried to give much to Papa, but you know Papa ... so proud ... so set in his ways."

Annette ignored Manuel's remark. "Manny, I am no *'estupido.'* You're showing me this because you're going after the men that killed Papa, and you know you may die doing it. What about me, Manny ... what about Mama ... and José? We have already lost a father. Do you think it is fair we lose a brother, also? Why don't you just take this money and get away. All Papa ever wanted for us was our freedom and, for the most part, he saw to it we got that, but the price was very steep. Papa wanted each of us to be like him ... a person with hope, and full of love ... to be able to enjoy life, and—at the end of it—to know where we are going!"

"I honestly think it's too late for me, Annette. Your brother is wicked, but I *will* avenge our father."

"My stubborn Brother! Don't you know, after all these years, as the Son of a preacher, that it is *never* too late!"

"'*Never too late*' ... yes, that *is* nice to know. Then there is still hope."

"Of course there is, Manuel. With all this money, we could all leave this place and make a new life."

Manuel liked that idea. It made him feel very free for the first time in many years. Then he thought of the murders, and the other children, yet alive; he thought about Mike, Audra and young Bobby, Mike's little brother. They deserved freedom, also. Why did he feel this way? What was happening to him? "Annette, you will never understand why I must do what I know in my heart is right."

"No! What is wrong with you, Manny? Who taught you to be like this, anyway? Name the person that made you like you are today, right now, as you are standing in front of me! If you tell me who has influenced you to behave like this—to put your life on the line for a vindictive cause—and I believe in that person, I will do as you ask of me!" Annette screamed.

Manuel lowered his head. He bowed in reverence, as his mouth clearly uttered these words: "My, God, and my Captain, taught me this, and a man here on earth I called 'Papa' ... a brave man known as Pedro Martinez," proclaimed Manuel, as tears filled his eyes.

Annette stepped back. She drew her elegant fingers to her lips. She felt all the anger in her drain out of her body, as she became limp. She walked over to Manuel, and threw her arms around her brother. She knew very well that this could be the last time she would ever see her precious brother alive. Manuel lifted her chin up so he could look into her lovely Latino eyes. She smelled like a flower, yet looked much prettier than a rose as he said, "I love you, my dear, sweet Sister, and I am counting on you to take care of Mama and Joseph," Manny implored, as that is what Manny sometimes called his younger brother, José. "Will you do this for me, Annette?"

Annette's voice filled with melancholy. "My dear Brother, of course I will. Hold me, Manny ... hold me tightly, as if there were no tomorrow ... I am afraid there may not be ... for you, dear Brother," she cried. Manuel held her tightly in his strong arms, as they wept upon each other. Deep within himself, Manuel knew that—once he left her—he would see her no more in this life. Annette somehow knew this, too.

The brass double doors of the elevator opened, and Manuel stepped inside. A gentle-looking elderly attendant, wearing a dark blue uniform with a nametag stitched above the front pocket of his shirt, greeted Manuel. "What floor, Sir?" asked the old man.

"Top floor."

"Oh yes. Right away, Sir." Whenever the attendant saw someone as important-looking as Manuel requesting the top floor, he knew better than to delay. Only the finest diplomats and representatives were invited to the General's suite on the top floor. The man pressed the lever, and soon the elevator began its ascent to the General's large penthouse-type office. Manuel tipped the attendant, turned, and began walking down the all-too-familiar corridor. Two of the General's guards quickly encompassed Manuel.

"Sorry, Sir, but we are ordered to check briefcases, and frisk people for weapons."

"This is ridiculous! I've never been frisked before when I visited the General. Wasn't he expecting me?"

"Yes, Mr. Martinez. He knows to expect you, and so did we. This is only a precautionary measure, I assure you," stated one of the guards. He pulled an automatic pistol out of Manuel's shoulder holster and said, "Follow us. We'll give you your pistol back, under the General's orders."

"Oh, man ...'*Happy days are here again*' ..." sang Manuel, as he followed the guards to the suite. One of the guards held his card up to the reader, and the door made a slight clicking noise. They opened the door to a huge, luxurious room. Expensive paintings and tapestries hung from the walls. In the middle of the room stood a huge, exotic fish aquarium trimmed in gold. The frames around the paintings were all trimmed with gold-plated wood. The floor was tiled white marble, laced with sapphire-like stones. Manuel turned to see the General sitting at his massive desk, made out of cocoa wood and solid calisaya wood … so well polished that it gleamed when light hit it. Behind the General stood a figure looking down at the sights far below. Scorpio stood at his right side.

"Well, well, Mr. Martinez. It is so good to see you. I wondered when we would meet up again. You and I need to see more of each other, but you don't make enough mistakes … unlike Scorpio here." Scorpio looked the other way and rolled his eyes. "Did my guards frisk you?" the General inquired.

Manuel stood silent for a moment, looking at Scorpio, as many pictures of death flashed through his mind. How many ways could he kill Scorpio? He thought about the half-second kill. No, that was too merciful. How about the ten-second kill … the one where the victim sees his heart before he keels over. No, still too merciful. He imagined cutting up Scorpio into little tiny pieces. Yes … one finger and appendage at a time. He laughed inside of himself, as he played this scene over in his mind. "I will do it right in front of the fat General's eyes, then I will lay the pig himself on the butchering block, and saw on his fat body, also," Manuel thought to himself.

The General motioned to his guards. They hurried over to his side. "Give Manuel back his weapon … now!" the General ordered loudly. The guard who had taken Manuel's pistol pulled it out of his pocket and handed it over to Manuel.

"As you wish," said the tall guard.

"They do not know all my friends yet, but in time they shall," the General lamely explained. "I am sorry if they inconvenienced you," the General apologized.

"Apology not required. We go back too far to let such a little thing like that upset me."

"Manuel, I heard about the horrible fate that befell your family. I am very upset, and very sorry," the General said, as he offered his condolences.

"Tell me who did it, Manuel, and I swear I shall kill the swine with my bare hands, slowly until they beg for their lives!" exclaimed Scorpio.

"Oh, I'm sure you would, Enrique," said Manuel, with more than a touch of contempt in his voice.

"What do you mean by that?"

"Just that I am sure you would make them beg for their pitiful lives; that's all I meant."

Scorpio opened his mouth to speak some more, but the General held up his hand. "Okay, that's enough. Manuel, have you any leads?"

Manuel looked away from Scorpio, whose real name was Enrique, then he looked at the General. "I have no idea. All I know is that two ungrateful villagers entered the chapel in La Palo and killed my father. If I find them, I will be the one who kills them with my bare hands! I could not care less for these ungrateful beings. They should die and be out of our way!"

"Then it will not bother you if I tell you that we are seeking retribution for what was done at the camp. You see, Manuel, I cannot tolerate this behavior. Already we are behind in production. Now we have lost many, many assault rifles."

"I told you we should have retained the last shipment of rifles and ammo," said the General's newly appointed Advisor, whose name was as yet unknown to Manny, as he stared out the window. "I also think it is a mistake to fire upon the villagers now. If you want to seek retribution, wait until all this has cooled down a little, then hit them." The Advisor kept his face to the window, so Manny did not get a good look at it, to be able to recognize him in the future.

"Not this time," began the General. "I will not let the pigs live out the week before I strike back. They must be taught a lesson as soon as possible … one they will never forget!" hollered the General. "Now, I have contacted our Chinese sources, but General Genghis told me they cannot provide us with the weapons we need anytime soon. So, I spoke with Mr. Hooah in Huachuca. He is willing to barter with us. He is going to expedite a shipment of arms this very night across the border. If all goes well—and I am positive it will—we will have the weapons within twenty-four hours," roared the General.

"I still believe we should hold off," said the Advisor.

"Advisor, I know you mean well, but this time I will be in charge of the operation myself. You remember how well you fared last time?" the General smiled.

"Yes, Sir; you may be right." The advisor paused, "… I hope."

The General looked at Manuel. "Your family will certainly be spared. Anyone that even sets foot on your family's property will have to answer to me. That goes for my highest ranking man, to the peasant foot soldier. No one, under any circumstances, is to lay one finger on the Martinez family!" ordered the General. Manuel looked strangely at the General. Here was a man that had caused the death of his father, and he was being asked to take him at his word about how his family would be protected. How ironic!

The General, still intently gazing at Manuel, said, "Is there anything you would like to add?"

Manuel wanted no more than to pull his gun out and blow their heads off. He even pondered the idea for a brief moment. He knew he could kill the General and Enrique … possibly even the Advisor, too … before he himself was felled. However, another idea was forming in his mind. His father once had advised him that when you run after cattle you may get one, maybe two, but— if you take your time and work around them—you can build a fence that will hold all of them, and then you can claim them all. Manuel was building that fence, but not for cattle. He was carefully designing a *'fence'* by which he would trap the men on both sides of the Equator.

Manuel said, "I shall return to Sierra Vista, Arizona. I have not yet completely finished my report for Mr. Hooah. I have a little left to do, but I am close, very close. I would like to leave tonight, if possible; I do not wish to tarry any longer. Each moment I am away gives the enemy more opportunities to, once again, sabotage our operations in the United States."

"Go with our blessings, Manuel." The General was very pleased to grant Manuel his wish. Manuel turned to walk out. "Guards, please see Manuel safely out of the building. I shall arrange a limousine to escort you to the airport. Do you have everything you need for your trip?"

"Yes, it is all in my vehicle at this moment."

"Very well, then. Leave your car here. When you get back, I shall see to it you drive from here in a sparkling new Porsche.

"Thank you, General. You are too kind."

"Let's just say that I believe a happy employee makes a great employee. Oh, and remember what I always say, Manuel."

"Yes, every man has a price," said Manuel.

"Very well spoken. We bid you a very safe flight." Manuel turned and walked out the door. The guards escorted him all the way to the lobby, and into the waiting limousine.

The General turned to his men and smiled in relief. "That went better than I had hoped. Now we have Manuel out of the way. When we attack the village, we will kill all the pigs, sack the town, and burn it to the ground!" he shouted, as he made a tight fist and waved it in the air.

Chapter Twenty-one

Colonel Heyburn crouched down, not far from the road that led from the main canyon road back to the old arsenal. He was well camouflaged behind some trees, foliage and berry bushes. After he and Sterling—just days ago—had found the bunker to be currently used, though it appeared from a distance to be abandoned, Sterling had directed Pat to another exit from the post, rather than returning through the main gate, or the east gate. As they drove south through Huachuca Canyon, Pat made the comment that the road seemed to go south forever. He had been anxious to get in a round of golf before they left the Fort that day. When they'd arrived at this alternate exit, they realized—though well concealed—that someone had used it recently; many track marks leading from the exit were proof of this.

Pat, hiding silently in the brush, on the cold canyon floor, began to wonder if he ought to leave, as his presence here was not actually required; he had only decided to survey the area out of avid curiosity. Earlier in the day, he had noticed several light transports rolling south on Christy Avenue, and had thus ordered one of the Rangers to recon their position and report back. When the Ranger told him that they had parked the transports outside the old bunker, Pat knew that General Blake was preparing to transfer the weapons.

"Well done, Ranger," Pat had commended him, upon receiving this useful bit of information. "Tell the other men this is no time to sit around and get fat and lazy. There is a very strong possibility all of you will be required very soon, and I'll need you to be alert, and mentally sharp. Stay off the booze, and keep away from the women. I can't afford any weak-kneed men."

The Ranger had shot a rebellious look at the Colonel for one split second, and then shouted, "Sir, yes, Sir!"

The Colonel, recognizing the look on the Ranger's face, then said, "Son, you fail to understand that I was your age at one time. I served in Intelligence, and in the Special Forces, before you were even a thought in your father's mind. My hormones were running overtime back then, as are yours today; I witnessed some of the finest falling into temptation. It is a tragedy when your buddy doesn't show up the next day when you're called to take up arms, and rush into a forward zone. You really miss him when the bullets are flying around your head. You get very pissed off, too, when you return to hear your prodigal buddy talking about his exotic night with some dizzy hussy, while you were busy dodging bullets and tracers all day long. Are we clear!"

The Ranger, standing at attention, his face—this time—emotionless, replied: "Yes, Sir, we are crystal *clear,* Sir!"

"Thank you, Ranger. That is all," the Colonel said, dismissing the Ranger.

Pat laughed under his breath, recalling this earlier, comparatively mild, confrontation with the young Ranger. The roar of engines disturbed the normal sounds of the night. The lonesome cries of the night birds had stopped. The transports neared Pat's position. He crouched down lower, suddenly worrying, "What if they have infrared scopes?" As though hugging the ground would help, the Colonel laid as flat as possible on the cold, damp earth. He lifted his eyes just enough to see the vehicles stop at the intersection connecting the main canyon road and the road leading to the old ammo dump. There was a short exchange of words between the drivers of the vehicles; the driver leading the way got out of a large Hummer, and walked back to the other drivers. He waved his arm in the air a bit, pointing at something, then he quickly returned to his vehicle, rolled onto the main canyon road, and headed south to the old concealed exit.

Pat watched as, one by one, the vehicles turned onto the main canyon road and disappeared into the darkness of the canyon. He slowly lifted himself from the ground and cautiously stood to his feet. "Ha! This *Green Beret* still has what it takes!" laughed the Colonel. Then, he felt the cold end of a gun barrel being poked into the back of his neck.

"Bang, bang, Colonel! You're dead!"

Mike paced the floor at Audra's house. "Really, Mike, if you keep that up you'll wear a path in the carpet," laughed Audra.

"I can't help it. All we've done is lie dormant for days on end!"

"You're hallucinating, Mike. It's only been two or three, at the most. You make it sound like weeks."

"'Might as well be weeks; I can't stop myself from pacing. I want to do something. I've got to do something!"

Audra smiled as she sympathized, "Mike, you're hopeless. Pa said to lay low … be cool. We have to wait for them to make the next move now and, if that means a month, then I guess we'll just have to suck it up, and wait."

Audra was being impractical, and Mike knew it. "A month, huh?"

Audra smiled as she coaxed Mike over to her. "Maybe ... three? No, Mike, you know I'm just being ornery; I'm sure things will break soon. Heck, the way it's been going, I wouldn't be surprised if it all happened tonight," she realistically stated.

Mike gave up his pacing, and sat down next to Audra. As she ran her soft, graceful fingers through his hair, he calmed down some. She pulled him towards her. They'd just begun to kiss, when a sharp rapping on the door startled them. Audra raced over towards the door, as she yelled, "Who is it?"

Blimey! Don't just stand there asking silly questions, young lady. Let me in! This is Matt Piper. I was told to come tonight!"

Audra wrinkled up her face, questioningly. She did not know any Matt Piper, although the name did sound familiar. She gazed over at Mike.

Mike returned the gaze, with a startled look on his face. "Ah-h-h ... I forgot to tell you about Matt."

"Colonel Patrick Heyburn, you are coming with me!" ordered the masculine voice, from behind Pat's back, where he'd put a gun to the Colonel's neck. Pat immediately realized he had been followed; this was probably one of the General's men. He thought about where this might lead. He knew that if he tried any quick move, the man was sure to blow his head off. He also knew that the General could not afford a military inquisition right now. Most likely, the General would kill him, and destroy his body, so that it would never be found, anyway. Pat shuddered uncontrollably, as they walked, feeling weak and helpless in the presence of his captor.

"Come, Colonel, we must not keep the others waiting."

"Yeah, we must not do that, but I would really appreciate it if you would kindly point that thing in another direction."

"If that will make you feel better," the gunman coldly answered his captive.

"For some reason, I think it would," Pat said, his words laden with emotion.

"Very well then." The man lowered his gun.

The Colonel fell quickly to the ground, sweeping the man's feet out from under him. Then Pat quickly plunged the palm of his hand into the nose of his would-be assailant, while stripping his rifle from him. Pat stood over the shadowy, dark figure that lay below him, holding his nose. "Well, Mister, like I said ... I still have what it takes. Now, you and I are gonna have a little talk."

Before he could get another word out, Pat heard the sound of an air rifle, and felt a sharp object sting his neck. He reached up and quickly pulled the dart out of the back of his neck. Then everything went black.

Suddenly, Janet Riley was standing above the Colonel, and the mysterious man who was still holding his nose. "Okay, Weasel; help me load our friend here into the Jeep. You really weaseled yourself into it this time."

"I didn't expect him to be so quick!" he wailed.

"I guess he really does still have it in him. Let's get out of here before they see us. We can't afford to attract any attention to ourselves."

"Yes, Sir!" said Weasel, as he and Janet lifted the Colonel upon their shoulders, and made their way to the hidden Jeep. They lifted the Colonel up, and dropped him into the back bed of the Jeep—then covering him with a heavy, green tarp—and drove out of the brush that had concealed the Jeep. Soon they were down the road, and out the post gate. They crossed Highway 90, turning onto Fry Boulevard, heading south.

Audra opened the door to see an elderly man sporting a woolen coat, with a plaid cap on his head. His face bore quite distinguished features, along with a handlebar mustache. Sounding very British, he looked the part of Sherlock Holmes through and through.

"I wasn't expecting you, ah-h-h...." Audra stammered.

"The name's Matt Piper, as I recall stating earlier, just after I rapped on the door with this here cane. Mike suggested I come by tonight. I suppose he wanted me to meet you. You must be the charming Miss Audra he keeps bragging on."

Audra felt a bit flushed, though flattered. "Yes, I am Audra."

Matt smiled at her and said, "May I come in?"

Audra opened the door, and stepped aside. "Please do. I've been dying to meet Mike's friend that supplies him with all the leads he's been telling me about. As a matter of fact, I remember your name now. You're the detective who lost his nephew. I'm really very sorry, and I know how you feel."

Matt looked into Audra's lovely eyes. "I know you do, young lady. I know about your brother, Todd."

"Would you care for a drink or a bite to eat?" Audra politely inquired.

"I might be fitting for a whiskey Mac, and a ganteau."

"A what?" asked Audra.

"Oh, dear! I'm sorry. One can't always get his way. A *'whiskey Mac'* is a mixture of ginger, whiskey and a spot of wine, and a *'ganteau'* is a cake. But, as they say, you can't have your cake and eat it, too. Actually, a glass of soda ... any kind ... and a few crisps—or potato chips—sounds very nice."

Audra left Matt with Mike, and sauntered out into the kitchen. She returned with a tray of chips, cola and French dip. She sat the tray down on the table in front of the sofa, sat down next to Mike, and said, "Please, help yourself, Matt."

Matt took a chip in his hand, scooped down into the dip, and started munching away, as Mike began the conversation.

"Audra, I asked Matt over here not only because I wanted you to meet him, but I also wanted you to hear what he has to say about our friend, Manuel."

"What do you mean?" Audra leaned forward, intently listening.

Matt spoke between bites. "Mike emailed me a photo of our friend, Manuel. I had already connected—well, sort of connected—Manuel to the syndicate in South America. The photo basically confirmed this. Upon talking with the Bolivian police, and other Bolivian authorities, I was able to diplomatically squeeze some information out of them. I then emailed a photo of Manuel. I must say, they did not seem very cooperative; however, when I mentioned I personally knew *El Dueño de Policia* in La Paz, they became most accommodating. They told me his name is Manuel Martinez, a one-time brilliant student at Bogotá University. He resides in La Palo, or so they believe, which is a barrio outside of La Paz. At any rate, he does go by a few aliases. He is known as Manny, Emanuel, Martin and El Niño. Strange name ... *El Niño* means 'the little boy'."

"Yeah, kind of like the El Niño weather pattern ... but that's another story," said Audra.

Mike looked at Audra and asked her if the name rang another bell. She put her right index finger to her lips and thought aloud. "Hmmm, let's see. That name does sound familiar." She paused for a moment, then her memory came alive. "Yes! I remember now! When we were listening to the tape of the meeting in the Lodge, I distinctly remember hearing them mention that name."

"Excuse me, dear, but don't you mean *my* tape?" Matt asked, eager to be given credit for his harrowing derring-do that had obtained them that tape. "I was the bloody bloke that almost got my bloomin' head shot off that night!" protested Matt.

"More than that, we know that this man, *El Niño,* is the one we know as Manuel Fernando," Mike spoke, still sad at having learned of the deception.

"Or Manuel Martinez," confirmed Matt.

As this same thought crossed Audra's mind, she felt something stir inside her. While she believed Manuel had lied about his name, he had displayed genuine friendship before he had rather abruptly left the United States. She explained this to the two men, but they were not thoroughly convinced that her intuition was intact.

"Men in his line of work are very charming, as well as very good actors, Love," said Matt.

"Well, so are you, my dear private eye, but that doesn't make you a criminal!" retorted Audra.

"Do I detect a bit of admiration in your voice?" asked Mike.

"I don't know," Audra moaned dejectedly. "Maybe you're both right. Maybe he's just a low-down, dirty crook, aching to be hung. Maybe he lied about everything. But, I just have this feeling inside me that tells me he is not what we think he is … at least, not any more." Audra looked away from the men, as she thought more about what she had said.

Mike sensed Audra's concern for Manuel, yet he dismissed it as merely a girl infatuated. Then he told them about his conversation with Dennis. "You know, I really think Dennis is one confused man."

Matt bit into another chip, as he looked first at Audra, then at Mike. "I believe he is, too. Everything that I have found out about him leads me to believe that he does not know as much as we first thought he did. He may know a little, but I don't think he is a main cog in the machinery."

Mike and Audra thought about this, as they both dug into the chips and dip.

Manuel paced the floor in the motel. He had paid the motel for a three-week stay in advance when he last arrived; therefore, when the cab dropped him off at the motel, he did not bother with the clerk, but walked straight to his room. He spent much time working hard on a plan of action. What could he do to bring the kingpins together?

Audra had been right. Manuel's heart was changed. Maybe it was God … maybe it was the words of his beloved father … maybe it was Audra, Mike and Melissa's honest feelings towards him; or, maybe it was all three combined. Whatever caused his change of heart had left a strong, lasting impression. The conscience he couldn't remember ever having had before, had surfaced in a mighty way.

"I know … I could tell the Generals Montiego and Blake that they have to meet, in order to develop a plan of action against the saboteurs. Maybe they would meet together, if I lied, and told them that there were many saboteurs. No, I should tell them that the enemy wishes to parley, but only with them. *"Ay, caramba!* This is not going to be easy. I think, my pretty Little Dove, Audra, and my good friend, Mike, that it is time we lay all our cards on the table. I must do something else. Annette, please be there," Manuel plead, punching her number into his phone, as he fell across his bed.

Pat's eyelids felt like pieces of lead, as he tried to decipher his blurry surroundings. He thought he should be dead but, as the room began to come into focus, he realized how alive he was.

"Well, little Goldie Locks awakens!" someone Pat did not know said, rather sarcastically. Pat turned his head slowly, to see a man with a bandage on his nose.

"Who are you?" Pat wondered, grateful to be alive.

"They call me *'The Weasel'.*"

"Well, Mr. Weasel, apparently you couldn't weasel your way out of a bloody, swollen, fat nose, could you!"

"I'll give you that much, Colonel, but that's all I'll ever give you again. 'Guess you still do have a little left in you." The man's face lit up a bit when he said this.

Actually, the Colonel detected some respect in Weasel's voice when he spoke. As Pat looked at Weasel, he could not help but think how the name fit him so well. Mr. Weasel had small, squinty eyes, and a sharp, pointy nose. His blonde hair brushed back into a ponytail only added to his martin-like features. As Pat's mind cleared, he discovered his hands were untied.

"Why are my hands free?"

"What! Do you think we're uncivilized here, or something? There is no need to restrain you. I do not think you are dumb enough to try anything, as you are in a building that is well secured, with people who like to shoot now, and ask questions later."

"Weasel—or whatever your real name is—I don't really like you, and I don't like who you work for, either … or what you do. So, let's stop pretending to be friends. I know what you all are up to, and you also know that I know, so why amuse yourselves any further? I'm not capable of telling you anything you don't already know. And, even if I were, I wouldn't tell you."

The door opened, and Janet Riley stepped in. "Oh, I love it when a man shows such courage and bravery."

"Oh, you do, huh? Well then, I must be making you feel hot, Sweet Cheeks," Pat replied, sarcastically.

"Really now, Colonel, if that did it for me, I'd keep Weasel here talking to you for days. Patrick James Heyburn, born of a James and Cathy Heyburn, your father is still alive in Tucson. Your mother unfortunately passed on three years ago. I am sorry to hear that. Your son was abducted eight years ago, and your wife is living a hellish life in an institution. You have a brilliant daughter who, I think, got the shaft while serving as a special agent in the FBI."

"You talk like you know her."

"Audra? Oh yes, she graduated three years behind me."

"What!" Pat was incredulous that his daughter's classmate had turned traitor.

"I don't think I need to spell it out, Colonel." Janet waved her hand, signaling another person to step inside. The door opened, and Cal Brown stepped in.

"I don't believe it! Now I know I'm amongst a brood of vipers. You pitiful excuse of a human, Cal!" screamed the Colonel.

Too long Cal had suffered the pain of carrying a secret that only he knew, but could share with no one. Cal had held his anger in long enough. "Shut up, Colonel, and listen to me!" Cal shouted, with great emotion, as Janet left the room. "You have no idea what the hell I've been through for years, but now you're going to."

The Colonel was taken off guard for a moment before he replied. "What I know now, Cal, is that you sold out to the General and the syndicate in South America, just like your friends here."

"That goes to show you that you don't know me at *all!*" Cal screamed out.

"I'm all ears, and it looks like I'm not going anywhere anytime soon, so I guess I won't mind listening to some forked-tongued disgusting scum, like yourself!"

Cal collected his composure. He knew the Colonel had every right to behave aggressively, having nothing to go on but what he'd seen. He would act the same way towards his neighbor, if he thought he had sold his own son down the river.

"Pat, just hear me out, please, and then—if you still feel the same way about me after I explain myself to you—I'll give you my permission to slap me silly."

The Colonel grunted before he spoke, reluctantly. "Okay, let's have it, Cal."

Cal sat down in a chair in front of Pat, and began his narrative. "Pat, twelve years ago my son, Cliff, was abducted. I lost more than a son that day … I lost my mind, my family, and my health. You see, Sir, there was a reason behind Cliff's abduction, and why it was allowed. Now, I know you may not believe me, and I don't dare give a rat's hairy butt if you don't, but I was blackmailed. I knew a Robert Perris, father of the Youth Pastor here in Sierra Vista, Dennis Perris."

Pat piped up. "He's another suspicious character."

Cal laughed, "Dennis? Ha! He's just a small gopher. His Pa kicked him out of the house, and sent him here as an errand boy. He doesn't know a thing, as far as I can tell." Silence filled the room for a moment. Then Cal took a deep breath, and continued. "Anyway, Robert and I had met while we were both stationed in El Paso, Texas, while in the Army together. I became a desperate man. I barely had enough bread to put on my table to feed my family. Then I received a phone call from an old friend."

Pat jumped in, "Robert!"

Cal sat back in his chair, allowing himself to relax a bit, pleased that Pat was at least giving him his ear for a few minutes. "Very good, Colonel. Yes, it was Robert Perris. He told me that he had people in Sierra Vista that could help me out. He sounded very excited over the phone ... said he'd lined up a job for me, and that soon my financial status would greatly improve. Well, how did things improve? 'Not much ... not much at all. I was given a job running errands for the Mayor—like Robert's son, Dennis, does now—and still drowning in debt."

Pat interrupted again, "So, you decided to trade your son to the syndicate, and sell your soul to the devil!"

Cal shrugged his shoulders. "Worse. The Mayor and a couple of men that looked like Latinos came to my house after Cliff's abduction. They said they had to speak to me in private. We met in a dark shack, just outside Tombstone. They told me if I did not bow to their wishes, they would kill my entire family and me, so I felt *forced ... compelled ...* to give in to their corrupt organization. They set me up financially and made me purchase a store that they use as a land base for laundering money and trafficking drugs. This is what brought these people into the picture."

"You mean Miss Hot Stuff and Weasel," Pat guessed, not knowing Janet's name.

Janet rolled her pretty, dark eyes and said, "Hey, the name's Jane, and this is Special Agent...."

Weasel quickly piped up, shouting, "Weasel! Call me Weasel."

"OK, If you insist," Janet replied. "Colonel, meet Special Agent Weasel."

"Unfortunately, we've already met," Pat commented, glaring at Weasel.

"Hey, you're complaining? I have been following you all over the place ... to the old bunker and all over town ... through shrubs ... and all I got out of it was a puffy nose!" Weasel whined.

"Pat, we know that you are onto something really big here. At first, we thought you might be part of the ring, but then we put two and two together and—with Cal's help—we know you are setting something up," explained Jane.

Cal looked at Pat with pleading eyes, "Pat, please ... my son's life, and thousands of other American children's lives, are at stake here. The FBI has been the best thing that has happened to me since Cliff's abduction. The only hope I have in life—that keeps me going—is receiving pictures the syndicate sends me of Cliff ... I've had to watch him grow up only in pictures. Do you think I don't understand what you're going through? Yet, if your son wouldn't have been abducted, we would not be so close to possibly putting an end to all of this!"

"Wait! Are you saying that you and the FBI could have stopped this ring years ago?" Pat asked, incredulous that they would let it continue, if this were so.

Jane spoke up. "Pat, if we would have blown the whistle years ago, we would have a few drugs in our hands, and maybe one or two people, and the underground operation would have moved elsewhere. We would be right back to square one. We had to be patient, and wait. Our only question is: What do you know, and what were you doing at the bunker?"

"How can I trust you? You almost killed Mike!"

Jane looked pitifully down at the floor. Then she raised her head. "I aimed over his head but, in all the confusion, I forgot how steep the pitch is leading out of the lane."

"You should aim a little higher next time. Don't you agree!" exclaimed Pat.

Jane realized how weak her story sounded to Pat. She gave up.

"Okay, Weasel … Cal … let him go. He's right. Our badges and stories aren't enough. If we were working for the General, I'd shoot you right now. Get out of here!" screamed Jane.

Pat got up and left the room. He soon learned he was inside a house. He walked to the door, half expecting to be shot at any moment. However, having made it out of the house in one piece, Pat then walked down a dark lane, which led to Peter Canyon Road. He panted a little, as he walked the steep incline leading to the main road. "Well, she wasn't lying about how steep the lane is, anyway," grumbled Pat. His wallet and cell phone were still in the same pockets as he had left them. He called his daughter, and told her where he was. She responded by telling him that she would soon be there to pick him up. He continued walking down the road towards Highway 92.

"That's that; we've lost the edge now. All that research, and for what?" grumbled Weasel.

"Well, he'll change his mind. I know he will," said Jane.

"I hope so … I really do hope so. Our children are depending on it," said Cal, with a very sad voice.

"Well, at least the Mayor's flag is still flying."

"That gives us some hope. At least another load of abducted children haven't arrived yet," Cal said remorsefully.

The three hung their heads and sighed. They had hoped the Colonel would comply. Yet, it is hard to trust when you have lost so much in life; they could hardly blame him. This was the thought that entered their minds, as they slowly walked out of the room. Jane laid her gun down on a countertop, and wandered off down the hallway, as Cal and Weasel found the sofa a nice place in which to slouch down. "Guess we just wait," mumbled Cal.

"Guess so," replied Weasel.

Chapter Twenty-two

Around two in the morning, Bolivian time, the General picked up parts to an *AK-47* from out of a crate in the back of a large transport truck, and quickly assembled the assault rifle. He was very pleased that the weapons had arrived so quickly from America. He gloated over his private airstrip, hidden in the cocoa trees, as he inserted a full magazine into the clip. He squeezed off a long volley of shots. The faulty spring in the magazine held, as it had been rigged to hold for a short period of time … just long enough to give them confidence, before it would then malfunction.

"Ah-h-h, yes! That's music to my ears. Let's get these assault rifles into my men's hands. We attack Wednesday, at dawn … like Santa Ana at the Alamo!" shouted the General.

His Advisor shrugged his shoulders, and looked away from the General. "The General is surely a jackass," he thought to himself.

Meanwhile, the General's Commanding Officer shouted orders to the other soldiers standing nearby. Floodlights above them lit up the strip, as the soldiers quickly jumped into the trucks, and started towards a camp not too far from the village.

"Advisor, it will not be long. Soon the entire village will be nothing more but rubble. The villagers will soon learn to never again revolt, or defy me, and we shall have all the children we want to harvest our fields!" shouted the General, confidently.

His Advisor calmly said, "Yes, Sir … yes, all the children … and all the goodies."

The General looked at his friend, and slapped him on the shoulder. "Cheer up. You sound so pessimistic."

On Wednesday morning, just before the sun's first red ray of light stretched forth its finger across the sky, the General's men let out with a loud cheer and a roar, as they descended upon the village of La Palo. They had no idea that they were racing to their death, knowing not that the villagers had confiscated all the grenades and weapons from the ammo dump in the camp during their recent raid. They thought the people had blown them all up.

They also did not know that Manuel had called his sister, and warned her about the possible raid that might take place at anytime. He told her to inform Señor Herrera about the storm of men ready to hit them. Annette wasted little time. Then Señor Herrera and Annette warned all the villagers to be on guard. Wherever the villagers went, they carried their assault rifles and grenades. As they worked, they stacked their weapons nearby, under blankets or camouflaged by sticks or branches.

The bell in the village rang loudly, even before the General's troops touched one foot upon the village soil. The men, women and children of La Palo jumped to their feet, clothed and with *AK-47s* in their hands.

The General's troops stomped into the village, waving their rifles and shouting curses at the people. They opened fire, expecting no return volley, but their eyes opened wide, as the people screamed back at them, as they fired their weapons. Señor Herrera led the villagers, as bullets filled the air. Then, to the horror of the General's troops, their rifles suddenly stopped firing. They shouted at one another in shock … totally confused. "My gun won't fire!" yelled one.

"Mine won't fire, either!" screamed several of the other evil soldiers. One by one, they began falling to the ground. One soldier became very desperate. He slammed the butt of his rifle on a rock. It went off, with the bullet hitting him in the neck. He looked at one of his comrades, with bugged-out surprised eyes, as he gasped for air like a blowfish out of water.

"You fool! You shot yourself!" his fearful comrade shouted.

The soldier clutched his bloody throat, and fell lifeless to the ground.

"A-h-h-h!" the people raucously screamed, as they fell upon the soldiers, with the fury of a hurricane. The General's soldiers cursed, and cussed, at their deplorable situation. They screamed, as they tried to fight the bullets and people off with their bayonets. However, the villagers kept advancing upon the troops, firing round after round. The troops began to drop in bloody droves to the soil beneath them, yet the villagers were relentless. All the fear with which they had lived for so long had turned into anger and hate. They were determined to bring an end it now … today! How dare the General steal their children, and what they had worked for all their lives? Did he not know they were men and women of honor … a people with dignity? They cheered and hollered as they fought.

One of the General's sergeants shouted to his fellow soldiers, "Throw your grenades! Throw your grenades!" Then his head exploded, as a bullet ripped through his skull. The troops tore the grenades from their belts, and threw them at the people of the village. The grenades went off, sending shrapnel and debris flying dangerously into the air. Some of the village men fell to the ground, holding their faces and screaming, while others died on impact. Yet, the villagers were not to be denied their freedom.

Señor Herrera shouted, "Return fire with your grenades! Throw your grenades *together,* at my command. Quick! Stand in line on the ridge above, and pull your pins. Okay, throw your grenades ... now!" Suddenly, the General's soldiers saw the sky raining grenades down upon them. They tried to leap for cover, but they were too late. Shrapnel was flying all around, as the wicked soldiers screamed in bloody agony. Some men were literally blown apart, when the grenades landed on their heads, or bodies. All around the soldiers, impeding their vision, rose a huge cloud of dust and smoke, as the villagers kept pounding the men with grenades and bullets. Women dropped what they were doing and ran to help the men. They loaded the magazines, and carried fresh linens and water to the wounded. The villagers fought the General's troops well over two hours, yet it was one of the shortest battles of its magnitude in Bolivian history.

"Retreat! Retreat!" cried one of the General's men, as a bullet ripped through his chest. In response to this cry, the men began running to their trucks but, when they got there, they found the trucks full of villagers who opened fire on them. Bullets roared once again, as soldier after soldier fell to the ground. Finally, the firing slowed down, and only a few shots could be heard now and then, as some of the General's soldiers had hidden behind—or in—anything they could find. The villagers hunted down and found these men, showing little mercy ... wasting no time in shooting them, lest they be left alive to turn again on the villagers.

In this deadliest of battles, occurring on the twenty-second of March, not one of the General's men survived the brutal fight. Almost five hundred men— some permanent employees of the General, and some hired mercenaries— lay rotting in the warm Bolivian sun. The villagers suffered five casualties, and fifteen were wounded. The people of La Palo mourned the dead as heroes.

Chapter Twenty-three

Manuel pulled slowly into Audra's driveway. He called ahead to ask if he could meet her and Mike at Audra's house. She hesitated at his request before she said, "You know what? I think you should come over." The way she handled herself on the phone clearly indicated to him that she knew something about him. As he inserted his cell phone back in its case, Manuel thought, "Maybe it is for the best. Now, what I say will not come as quite such a shock to them."

Manuel stepped slowly from a rented Firebird; not the car he had really wanted, but at least it was available. He walked up to the doorstep, and knocked on the door. Audra opened the door to see Manuel's bright, handsome smile and deep dimples. His wavy dark hair glistened in the sunlight. "Ah, hello, Audra."

Audra looked into Manuel's pretty, dark eyes. She could not help but notice how they sparkled. "Manuel, please come inside."

"No, I think I should like to stay out here and talk. Is Mike here, too?"

Mike walked over and stood next to Audra. At this point, he did not feel much like being diplomatic, but he knew better than to let on that he knew whom this imposter was that stood before them. "Hello there, Manuel; 'good to see you again. Are you feeling okay? I mean, I am sorry about your father … that you had to leave on such a sad note. I guess you must have some more business to tend to here, or you would have stayed back in Texas."

Manuel detected a little contempt in Mike's voice. "Yes, I do have business here. That is why we must talk."

"Well, we are all ears, my friend," Mike said, condescendingly.

Manuel felt a bit ill at ease. He knew Mike was being belligerent, but why? Did he know who he was? Manuel shrugged off the thought, and got right to the point. His way was the direct way. "Mike, you don't sound like yourself. Are you feeling all right?"

Mike thought over what Manuel had said. "Don't blow it now," he told himself. Then aloud, he said, "Manuel, I'm just a little upset today. Forgive me. It's been over two weeks now since I lost my little brother, and I'm beginning to...." Mike looked away. The thought of losing Bobby forever burned into his heart. His eyes began to tear as he looked off in the distance at the Mule Mountains.

"Uh-h-h, Audra ... Mike ... Bobby is the main reason, among a few other reasons, that I came back." Mike was now confused, his body filled with grief and anger at the same time. He thought about what Pat had told them when he returned from his little meeting with Jane, Cal and the man called Weasel. Mike studied the ground until his eyes fixated for a couple of minutes on a strong-looking stick on the ground, thinking of what he was about to do. He hardly heard a word of what Manuel was trying to say. Then, with lightning-like speed, he snatched the stick in his right hand, spun it around like a fast-moving baton, and struck Manuel below his knees, sending him to the ground.

"You won't make a deal with me like you did with Cal Brown, you piece of *slime!*" screamed Mike.

Manuel looked up at Mike, as he lay there rubbing his shins. Manuel knew Mike did not want to maim him or he would have gone for his knees instead, so just maybe he could reason with Mike. "Mike, stop! I am not here to fight, and I don't know what you're talking about!"

Audra looked on in horror. What could she do? Should she hit Mike or Manuel over the head? She loved them both, but she knew she loved Mike more; and, why was she allowing her emotions to make such a decision, anyway? Wasn't this the notorious *'El Niño'*? Is he not the bad guy? Why *did* she like him ... because he was handsome? She did not know him well. He could have killed many people, for all she knew.

Mike stood almost two inches taller than Manuel, with broader shoulders and bigger arms. "Mike, stop! Let Manuel talk to us!" shouted Audra. Manuel groped for his cane he kept inside his coat. He reached into the scabbard sewn into his coat, and clutched the cane.

Seeing Manuel reaching inside his jacket, he strongly suggested, "Manuel, you can talk to us from where you are. What do you know about my little brother?"

Manuel studied Mike's every move as he spoke. "I know that you have very little chance of getting him back, unless you listen to me!"

That was it! Mike swung the stick at Manuel again, who instantly drew forth his cane, blocking Mike's blow. Then he immediately jumped to his feet, ignoring the throbbing pain in his shins. Mike thrust, twirled and jabbed the stick at Manuel, but Manuel was very good, also. Mike had prevailed over many opponents in sparring competitions; he was thinking that Manuel would be just another.

Manuel twirled his stick so swiftly Mike could barely see it. Mike felt something sting his back; he returned the favor, by swatting Manuel in the back, as well. Manuel spun around and swept Mike's legs. As Mike fell to the ground, he quickly rolled, and slapped Manuel's feet very harshly with his stick. Manuel grimaced in pain. "He is very good ... like me," Manuel thought, as he twirled and struck Mike's arm with his cane, just as Mike was trying to pick himself up off the ground from the former blow. He fell back down onto the ground.

Mike's right eye caught sight of Manuel's cane, slicing the air above his head. Mike blocked the blow, lifted himself up off the ground just a bit, managing to deliver a hard fist to Manuel's inner right thigh, just below his groin. Manuel fell backwards. Then Mike rushed in, slamming blow after blow into Manuel's midsection. Manuel grunted, as he balled both of his fists together, dropping them heavily onto the back of Mike's neck, as his knee kicked Mike in the chest. Mike felt the wind leaving his lungs, as he fell.

With more fight left in him than Manuel thought any man could muster, Mike grabbed hold of Manuel's ankles, tossing him like a rag doll. Manuel landed with a loud thud. An average man—following such a landing—would have laid on his back gasping for air, but Manuel worked out frequently, and often practiced countering such techniques. He knew how to fall. When Mike sent him on his back, he slammed his forearms into the ground to counter the force of the fall, preventing the wind from being knocked out of him. Yet, while he had studied martial arts for years, he was up against a very good opponent here, who not only knew martial arts, but was very good at wrestling, too.

While Manuel was yet on the ground, Mike began to put a stronghold on him. Unexpectedly feeling Manuel's elbow hit him sharply in the ribs, Mike rolled over to flip Manuel on his side, so he could pin him. He saw the muzzle, but it was too late.

"That's quite enough, tough guy! You've proved yourself. Now, get the hell off me, or I swear I will blow your brains out!" shouted Manuel. Both men were bleeding, and gasping for air. Manuel held a Taurus .40 automatic Brazilian pistol on Mike.

Mike settled down, as he looked at the gun in Manuel's hand. "You shoot me and you will never see South America again!" shouted Mike.

"No, but it might make me feel good all over."

Audra had stood silently by long enough. "What the hell is this going to accomplish? What has it accomplished? All this macho bull-dung is solving nothing. What is it you want? Stop it! Mike ... Manuel ... stop! *Stop ... now!*"

"Hey, I came to talk, not fight, guys. Look, Mike, I could blow you away, and could not care less about what happens to me. I have nothing to lose, unlike you. You have your brother to consider. You have Audra, and other kind people all around you, that you take for granted. You whine and whimper over Bobby, and you do not see all those around you that love you. I feel sorry for you ... I pity you. They want to help you, and—damn it—so do I! Now, here, take the gun." Mike looked into Manuel's eyes. He started to reach for the gun, but something stopped him. "Take it!" screamed Manuel. Mike slowly lifted the gun out of Manuel's hand. "Okay, you win. Shoot me!" Manuel yelled. Mike backed away, and aimed the gun at Manuel. "Okay Amigo, aim it at me and pull the trigger." Manuel's voice grew soft, almost gentle. Why did he want to die?

"What! Are you suicidal?" yelled Audra, tears beginning to flow down her cheeks. "Are you both suicidal? Please, stop all this lunacy! I can't stand to see either one of you get hurt. Don't you know I love the both of you? Please, stop!" Audra pleaded.

Mike lowered the gun, and handed it to Audra. She wiped the tears from her eyes, as she released the magazine, and unloaded the chamber. She had to quietly laugh, in spite of herself, when she saw the magazine and chamber housed no bullets. Manuel had again put on a very good act. She said nothing to Mike.

"All right, all right," gasped Mike. "I'll listen. Let's talk."

The noise outside woke Pat up just in time for his ears to pick up some voices talking about a village raid gone awry. He dashed into the family room to see the same reporter he had seen a few days ago talking about the bloody raid on the camp outside La Palo. He raced outside to where his daughter, Mike and another young gentleman stood. "Hey, Mike, Audra, come in here quickly."

"But, we're ... *'cough'* ... busy talking," said Mike.

"Let the talk wait," Pat suggested. Studying Mike and Manuel, he knew—from their bleeding cuts and tattered clothing—that they had been fighting. "You two can kill each other later. You have to see what the media is showing on television. That village called *La Paso* or *La Palo*, whatever it's called, is in the news again. 'Looks like another battle took place there today!" shouted Pat.

Manuel ran over to where Pat stood, excitedly asking, "Please, Sir, may I see, also!"

Pat looked puzzled, but answered, "Sure, and while you're inside, I'll get some bandages and iodine; it appears you boys could sure use it."

Manuel laughed a little as he said, "We were just showing each other a few friendly wrestling techniques."

"Uh-h-h … *'techniques,'* huh? Looks more like it was a very realistic per-formance," said Pat, suspiciously.

They all bolted into the living room to see some clippings of the aftermath around the village. The reporter for the International News Channel … *INC* … was speaking. "The people in this village have now made their awesome pres-ence known twice within the space of one week. As confirmed earlier, over five hundred men perished today in what appeared to be a suicidal raid on this poor village. The men that stormed the village have been again linked to the Bolivian syndicate.

According to the people of *La Palo*, these men marched into the village with Russian *AK-47s*, hoping to take the village by surprise, and kill all the people. They believe this is the act of one of the syndicate's kingpins, seeking retribu-tion for the villagers' actions just days ago. Now, all that is left of the kingpin's army and a number of possible mercenaries, as well, are dead men. Not one man is reported to have survived the wrath of the villagers. Experts at this grisly sight say that the Russian weapons malfunctioned during the raid, ren-dering the syndicate's forces virtually defenseless against the villagers' contin-ued barrage of bullets and grenades. Five villagers, all older men, died here today, and fifteen sustained minor wounds. We asked one of the leading weapons authorities what happened today.

"Apparently, the magazines were flawed. After carefully disassembling a number of these weapons, we discovered that the coils inside the magazines were defective. This is good news for the villagers, bad news for the other men. This is very unlike a Russian *AK-47*. These assault rifles, which are operated by a gas-filled piston, have very strong parts that are slightly larger—and spaced further apart from each other—than you would find in most weapons of its class. This makes them virtually impervious to water, mud, and many other elements that are often the cause for most other assault rifles to jam and malfunction. We have never seen a weapons malfunction of this magnitude before."

"So, in your opinion, what caused such a malfunction?" asked the reporter.

"We have not determined this as of yet, but there is strong evidence that this is a manufacturing problem. The steel, or whatever alloy was chosen for manufacturing the springs, was apparently weak. We will know more later."

"Thank you, Sir," the reporter thanked the expert, turning back to the amaz-ing story at hand. "Call it a glitch, call it a manufacturing error, call it whatever you want, but what these villagers are calling it is *'an act of God!'* The villagers have been celebrating, and thanking God, near the small chapel where Pedro Martinez many times preached the word *'freedom'* from the pulpit. He and the five villagers who died today are being mourned as heroes. This is AJ Sloan, in Bolivia, at the scene of an attempted massacre gone awry.

"Yes! Thank God, my family is alive!" shouted Manuel. All eyes turned on Manuel, expecting an explanation.

"This is why I came back ... why I am here. You did this, Colonel, didn't you? You rigged those magazines. You are brilliant! You see, the evil General in South America killed my father!"

"Wait! Hold on ... you're going too fast," said Audra.

"There is a wicked man that calls himself *'the General'* in Colombia and Bolivia," Manuel began. "He also controls a portion of Venezuela. He is very evil. Have you not heard of the General? I know you have been trying to solve this mystery. I even know you, Audra, and Mike, were the ones who blew up the cavern.

"Mike, you stowed away on a truck, and entered the compound. I know. I figured it out, when I saw the truck underside was cleaner on one side than the other. I am not like those *'estupidos'* who run the operation on this side of the border. I was sent here to find the saboteurs, and buy them off or kill them, but so many things happened so fast. Finally, the General had my father killed, and I know he wants to kill my family, and me, also. I stayed up days and nights trying to figure out a way to manipulate both evil parties into a trap. They are very violent people. They might kill one another if we plan things just right. Now this bloody battle has taken place, and many of the General's hired men are dead."

"Well, you sure did your homework, Manuel!" exclaimed Pat.

"Yeah, I'll say! You amaze me," said Mike somewhat hesitantly.

Manuel sensed his distrust. "Mike, you need to put away your fears for awhile. I know you have been through a lot, but if you don't start trusting people who want to help you now—*right* now—you will lose your little brother. Besides, you have nothing to lose, and a brother to gain. If I am bad, you lose, but why would I bother to walk in here and expose myself? What would I have to gain?"

"I don't know; maybe to kill us? Maybe you want to throw us off the trail?" Mike knew in his heart that he was wrong.

Manuel laughed, "Yeah, that must be it!"

"I believe him, and I want to know what we can do," Pat offered. "Now that our *'Operation Dumpster Dive'* has been a complete success, the next move is to get the bad guys into a mutual meeting. Both kingpins from both sides must be at this meeting, or it will not work. If we can't get them both together, we'll get some, but not all, of the slime. Now, I have some contacts in Panama that may be able to pose as Bolivian nationals, and people I know here, as well, that might be able to help."

Manuel interrupted, "Listen! Many accusations, cuss words and threats are being exchanged between the top dogs already. I know the General. He will be very willing at this stage to visit the man who sent him pea shooters instead of assault rifles."

"I think they could have done better with pea shooters and water pistols myself," laughed Audra. They all chuckled at her statement, as Manuel resumed talking.

"Anyway, you may do what you think is necessary to persuade the villains here to show at the meeting. Leave the grotesquely rotund General to me," Manuel said, contempt showing in his voice for the man who had taken his father from him.

Mike gazed at Manuel with a very serious look on his face. "Manuel, do you know all the people who are in back of this, here in the United States?"

Manuel looked down at the floor, then into Mike's anxious-looking eyes. "Mike, my contacts in the United States are very limited. I do know that General Blake is one, and Ed Braddock is another. As a matter of fact, a note he found on his newspaper bin added much to his anxiety."

Audra snickered, " I wonder who put the note on his box?" Mike and Audra laughed, recalling the subsequent disgusting encounter with Dennis' dumpster.

Manuel continued, "I know about the drivers, and some of the men in the cavern, only because I needed to interrogate them. These are the only people I know of. However, I must admit my own guilt, too. Under the direct orders of my superior, General Montiego, I long ago coerced Cal into joining our organization. I helped set up Cal's store. We blackmailed him and—for some reason—I feel very guilty over everything I have done. I guess … no, I know … that my father's words have finally sunk into my thick, stubborn skull."

Pat coaxed everyone to the kitchen table. Manuel liked the Colonel. He knew a tough bird when he saw one, and he knew he would not want to be on the other side, fighting a man of his experience. He also was feeling very young for some reason, as if God had given him a new chance in life, to make up for all the wrongs he had committed. While his father was yet alive, he talked much about freedom such as this, but Manuel's philosophy on freedom had always seemed to revolve around many acquisitions such as money, land and material items. This feeling was so new to Manuel, and he was learning that he very much liked it. Pat told his daughter to fetch the metal case. This caught Mike's attention, and he sat up straight, wondering what case might appear to which Pat had referred.

Audra left the men, and returned with a metal briefcase. Mike sprang up out of his chair. "What the heck! You ... Audra? You have a lot of explaining to do! That's the briefcase I confiscated from the cavern!"

Pat motioned for Mike to sit back down. Mike quietly returned to his chair, as Pat explained, "Mike, we had no other choice but to make you believe the bad guys had stolen the case. You were millimeters shy of handing over the evidence to the authorities. If you would have done that, the lid to this case would have been blown clear off, and our chances of catching all the slime bags would have been thwarted."

Mike looked at Audra and Pat in bewilderment. "Wait, you mean when we were playing golf, Audra was breaking into my house? You could have told me about this, rather than breaking in."

Audra turned to Mike. "Mike, you were *vehement* about turning this case in to the local authorities. We couldn't risk the chance. You know you wanted to turn that case in more than anything else!"

Mike looked gravely down at the floor. "You're both right. I was thinking of Bobby and myself. I was going to blow the lid off this case. I don't think that I would have listened to you. I wanted it to end ... I wanted my brother back, not thinking about anyone else, I guess."

"And, you're gonna get him back!" Pat said, with emphasis. "We're all going to get our children back ... and we're gonna get the evil crooks, too," stated Pat, sternly.

Mike looked at Pat inquiringly. "Well, what's the plan, Colonel?"

Pat gave Mike a very reassuring look, as he began laying out the plan. "Okay, we're gonna call this one *'Operation Double Decapitation.'* We'll need the FBI's assistance and, Mike, make sure your private eye stays off the whiskey sours. We're going to need his help, too. Get ready! We're going to bring our enemies, foreign and domestic, to their cowardly impotent knees! We'll shut down *'Huachuca Produce'*—and all the dark, discreet trafficking— permanently.

"Here's what we're gonna do," Pat continued. "When I'm done talking, we'll refine the plan, as needed. Are we clear, Soldiers?"

Manuel liked this very much. He became very excited as Pat went on and on, intelligently drawing out a very workable arrangement. Manuel saw a flaw here and there, but he would wait until the Colonel had had his say. Manuel looked at each of the others gathered around this table ... they were his friends. His heart was warm. This feeling came on strong—that new feeling only experienced recently—the feeling of worthiness ... the feeling of joy, and rebirth. Manuel's face was glowing; it was an angelic look. Audra caught sight of this, but said nothing.

Manuel knew he had work to do ... work that included recorders, PCs, and a Chinese female saboteur (professional assassin, and member of the Chinese Intelligence HQ) named Ming Chow—a women who knew General Blake in an intimate sort of way, to put it mildly.

Chapter Twenty-four

General Montiego angrily paced the marble floor in his high-rise suite. "This is an outrage, a treacherous travesty. I shall have their heads for this. I'll personally enjoy torturing the General in America myself!"

"We need more information. We should not resort to an armed strike, without knowing the full details. We must gain knowledge of what ensued in the United States before we take any aggressive action," said the Advisor. The Advisor stood a husky six-five, with solid shoulders, and a thick chest. He had entered the syndicate over twelve years ago, as an Anglo from America. The syndicate had found a position for him as the Chief Petroleum Engineer for a large oil firm in Venezuela. Even before he took the position, he knew the syndicate operated the company. He actually worked directly for the syndicate, arranging covert diplomatic relations with OPEC and the political figureheads throughout South America.

The Advisor would also entertain, from time to time, the despot-like lobbyists loitering within the corridors of power in Washington D.C., while trying to swing the votes of Congressmen in the direction of their special interest group. He was very good at what he did. His clever advice, along with the cunning way in which he knew how to manipulate others, soon swung the support of many of the officials in the syndicate's direction … a major reason why the government is so lax when it comes to laws inhibiting slave-holding and drug smuggling. His efforts soon earned him a position beside the General himself. Many called him *'El Poco General,'* or just *'Poco General,'* which means, *'The Little General.'*

"This is all the information I *need*, Poco!" screamed the General. Having lost his composure, he grabbed an *AK-47* from behind his desk, pointed it at the granite walls that encompassed his suite, and fired off round after round. The bullets shattered the large, exotic aquarium, sending glass flying, and water and fish gushing all over the floor. The men standing in the General's quarters quickly fell to the floor, as the hot metal ricocheted off the walls, and splattered all around them. The noise of the assault rifle echoed loudly throughout the room. Finally, silence replaced the loud roar of the rifle ... that is, until the General shouted, "Get up off the floor ... all of you, you cowards!" Slowly the men rose from the floor. When all were once again standing at attention, the General pointed the assault rifle at one of his guards.

Poco held out his hand in protest. "He did nothing to cause this!"

"Poco, this is all the information, and proof, I need to know we have been betrayed!" The General squeezed the trigger. The guard closed his eyes, as his heart beat heavily. He swiftly made the sign of the cross, expecting to die. Nothing happened. Try as the General might, the rifle would not fire. "See! It jammed! The Americans betrayed our loyalty. They deserve death!" The guard pulled himself together, and sucked in a deep breath. Every major event of his life, along with many indiscretions, had flashed before him during that most critical moment which, he'd thought, would be his last. His knees were weak, and his arms tingled all over. The General merely looked at him and said, nonchalantly, "Thank you for your kind assistance in my demonstration. You may sit down now."

The Advisor stuck to his guns. "Sir, I implore you. Before you waste more lives ... before you act in angry haste and direct an assault on the General in Huachuca ... wait until we know more, and things cool off. It cannot hurt to linger for awhile. We can send our intelligence into the Huachucas, and discover what really happened."

The General began pacing the beautiful marble floor that once had sparkled. Now, debris from the granite walls, and water from the fish tank, lay all over it. Some fish splashed about in shallow puddles, while others were dying, unable to breathe from lack of water. The General gave his Advisor's comments much thought. He knew he already had his most intelligent man in the Huachucas at this very moment. "Maybe Manuel could use a little help at this time," thought the General. He was just about to take Poco up on his advice, when his private phone rang. This line only rang if there was a very urgent message being delivered. The General swiftly snatched the phone in his hand, and held the receiver to his ear. Manuel's voice captured the General's full attention.

"General, Sir, we have a very delicate matter here in the mountains. This matter, I assure you, will require your presence here."

The General listened to every word very carefully. "Go on, Manuel." Poco, having heard Manuel's name mentioned, listened carefully to the General's conversation.

Now came the true time of testing; would Manuel be able to persuade the General he was needed in the Huachucas? "I have reason to believe that the Americans may have staged the bombing in the cavern," Manuel continued.

The General quickly spoke up, "Why would they do this? How would they benefit?"

"General, think of it. I know the Americans are dealing with General Genghis, our Chinese associate and other nations, also. The Chinese own the Panama Canal by de facto, and much of the wealth in South America. Now, I have intelligently interrogated all the men involved, concerning the bombings and all the strange events that have taken place here. I have put together a very convincing report, containing all the proof you need to realize that the Americans are planning a coup. The men that actually bombed the cavern were Chinese. The Americans knew you were going to sell the previous shipment of arms to the Peruvians. They know how greed works; they invented the word.

"General, they knew you were in transition with the Peruvians, and the relationship was yet a little weak at the time. They sent spies into the village to rally the people. You fell into their trap, as they know ... they have heard ... of your volatile nature. You stormed the village, and they knew—anticipated—that you would. They knew you would desperately need arms, so they rigged the assault rifles to malfunction and sent them to you, knowing you would seek quick retribution against the villagers."

"I don't understand. Why?" shouted the General.

Manuel became irritated. He knew the General was an idiot, but he was proving himself to be a complete moron. He held his composure as he spoke. "General Montiego, my friend ... my leader ... please listen closely to me. Lately we have taken our American contacts too lightly. Even our Chinese associates are beginning to believe America is ready for collapse. The Americans are not complete fools, though. They know that if they can prove strong and worthy to the Chinese, and our neighbors, they will be able to stretch their slimy tentacles further south into our country. Today, they technically take orders from you and our colleagues. Tomorrow, you may find yourself bowing to their demands. It has happened all the time throughout history, captains and kings, General."

"What do we do?"

"You contacted the General here, did you not?" Manuel inquired.

"Of course! But, he denies everything. He sounded very upset and confused about the whole thing."

"Of course he does. I called upon him, also. We had a very interesting conversation. I caught him in a few lies. As I said before, he is very willing to discuss this matter personally."

"I agree, but he will not come here, and I do not wish to set foot on American soil." The General scowled slightly as he spoke.

"I understand. This is why I have arranged for both parties to meet on neutral ground. General Blake is very willing to convene with us within the subway … the cavern. Look, we are so weak now, a pack of baboons could take us over, and hire us to pick the lice off their furry butts, yet—if we act now and meet these people on neutral ground—we can beat them at their own game. This may be our only chance to put an end to all of this."

The General stood silent, as Manuel's words sunk into his mind. Manuel made all the sense in the world at that instant. The General trusted Manuel very much, as Manuel had proven himself worthy repeatedly. General Montiego knew the Americans had betrayed him, and that the stage was being set for covert action by the American underground network to overtake his organization. He cursed verbally and said, "Why didn't we see this coming? Manuel, I shall be calm and discreet. I will meet with the General and his pigs. We shall act as though we know nothing. We go in good faith, but we leave with many American heads in our duffel bags!" The General slammed the phone down.

Paco looked the other way. He had lost the edge again. "I must have lost my touch, but where did I lose it?" Paco asked himself, as he sat down in his dusty posh chair—dust caused by General Montiego's rampaging *AK-47* demonstration.

Chapter Twenty-five

Pat rang the doorbell to Jane's house. After a minute or two, the door opened. Jane looked at Pat with her soft brown eyes. "Well, to whom do I owe the honor of your presence?"

The Colonel studied Jane's smooth face and pretty eyes, and said, "To a man named, *'Little Boy'.*"

Jane looked dumbfounded. "Come on in; we hoped you might change your mind. They walked across the foyer, and the living room carpeting, and into her kitchen.

Weasel was sitting at the table, with a languishing look on his face. He came to life when he saw the Colonel. "Colonel Heyburn! Man! We prayed you'd change your mind, and come back!"

The Colonel could not help but notice two faint, yellowish-black rings around Weasel's eyes. "Hey, that's some real cool-looking camouflage."

"Look, I'm not here to argue or be difficult. I know who you are now. Jane, 'you know Mike Taylor?"

Jane's brow rose at the mention of Mike's name. "Yes, we did meet on a couple of occasions."

"Well, he told me about you. He did not trust you. I—at first—did not, either, but one of Mike's friends discovered that you are a Special Agent, and a man known as *El Niño* has convinced us that we should cooperate together to bring this horrible evil empire to its knees."

"I know of El Niño. I knew he was here lurking about. However, we have nothing on him; he is too clever to leave any dirt, in which to sweep him up. He probably is one of the most guilty of the bunch, but his background is cleaner than mine," stated Jane.

"Well, you don't want to sweep him up now, anyway. He is working with us."

Jane and Weasel's eyes lit up. *"What?* No!" Both Jane and Weasel shouted at the same time. Pat calmly told the two agents to take a seat. When they were all seated, Pat explained the entire story to Jane and Weasel. He told them their plan, and how they expected the two-headed monster to meet in the cavern to which Mike and Audra had carefully drawn directions. He explained how Manuel had already contacted both Generals Blake in the States, and Montiego in South America, to arrange this meeting. According to Pat, the stage was set, and the pawns placed strategically in a row; they had left nothing to chance. Pat laid out the times, dates and locations of everything for the agents. Pat then showed them the basic layout of the cavern, and its surroundings.

Pat didn't know what to think of what he saw next. Jane laid a blueprint on the table in front of him of the compound near the Palominas Bridge. The print revealed a few sublevels, as well as ground level, and above. The compound was built like a large hotel, with a cafeteria above ground, and with a gym, strategic center, and some sort of range below. Pat became angry as he looked at this print. "Why, you two bit brainless cops! You've known all along where the children were being held hostage? You could have stormed the compound *long ago*, and put an end to all this!" screamed Pat.

"Patrick Heyburn … Colonel … *Sir!* Listen to me!" screamed Jane, trying to calm Pat down, as he began carrying on. "Yes, we could have run in there like a barrel full of heroes, and walked away with medals, as the public gloated over our proud accomplishment. But, what would we have really accomplished? Sure, we would have captured a few smalltime crooks—the butcher, the baker and the candlestick maker—maybe even the poor matron herself. However, the kingpins would still be alive and well, laughing at our feeble little escapade, while they sipped whiskey sours from their little beach chairs somewhere in the beautiful islands of the South Pacific, or elsewhere. Pat … oh, Pat …! Had we done this, we would only be right back where we'd started, only further behind the eight ball, as the criminals would be just that much more attuned to our operation, and more cautious!"

Pat sat back down. She had made a very clear point. He was very impressed. He hung his head. His words were a bit broken when he spoke, "Yeah, I see your point. You have a way with words Jane, but what a sacrifice, knowing where the children are at this moment, and yet…." he couldn't go on, and became silent.

Jane put her arms around Pat's neck, and hugged him. "When all this is over, Colonel, I truly believe you'll be laughing again."

Pat squeezed Jane's forearm affectionately. "I pray you are right, Jane. I really do."

Jane hugged Pat again. Then she stood upright and said, "And, I am not just an ordinary agent; I pull some weight within our organization, and I can muster up the manpower and muscle. You just keep providing me with the intelligence."

"Will do, Jane, will do," said Pat.

"By the way," Jane wanted to know, "who is Mike's friend that uncovered me?"

Pat looked back at Jane before exiting the house. With a British accent he said, "A bloody, bloomin' Inspector from Scotland Yard, named Matt Piper." They all laughed, as Pat left the room.

On the morning of the twenty-fifth of March, before the sun crept over the eastern horizon, three straight trucks roared down Hereford Road, and stopped before they came to the driveway leading back to the compound. Jack, Cain and the driver following behind them, Scott Bentley, stepped down from their trucks and walked towards a red Firebird.

"Well, here we go again," said Jack.

Cain rubbed his kidney. "Man, my kidney still aches a little from the last time we had a meeting with this guy."

Scott walked up to the other two men. "Is this the *El Niño* guy we're suppose to meet this morning?" Scott was excited to meet the legend himself. He had heard how this man could pluck one's heart out and feed it to them before they fell to the ground. "I've heard a lot about this guy," began Scott. "He's supposed to be bad ... bad to the bone!"

Cain rubbed his kidney a little more, as he warned Scott, "Just don't call him *'El Niño,'* what*ever* you do!"

Jack laughed. "Ah, Cain! Y' should have let the kid find out that like you did—the hard way."

Cain straightened his back, still rubbing it, as he retorted to Jack, "You know, you're right; 'guess I'm getting too soft in my old age."

Scott looked at the two other drivers with a blank expression on his face. He had no idea what they were talking about but—even as inexperienced as he was—he knew, by the way they spoke and behaved, he had better not call this man with whom they were soon to meet up, *'El Niño.'*

Manuel stepped out of the Firebird and approached the men very slowly, as he had done before. A nighthawk screeched above them as a coyote let out a lonesome howl. The wind kicked up a little, fanning Manuel's hair. Once again, his appearance took on a mysterious phantom likeness in the predawn darkness. He waved his cane in the air, as he walked closer to the men. Cain cringed when he saw the cane, and rubbed his kidney more vigorously. Scott looked on in awe.

Manuel now stood in front of the men, smiling, "Well, you are all here now. I am impressed with all of you. I thank you for your kind cooperation. Oh my! I left a very important item in my car; I must retrieve it. I shall return in a snap!" Manuel then turned to walk back to his car. In a flash, he fished his Taurus automatic pistol out of his holster, spun back around towards them, and pointed the gun in the faces of the three men. Their eyes lit up like headlights, as they peered down the muzzle. "Take off your coats and hats, throw them aside, and plant your ugly faces down on the ground ... all of you!" Nearly frozen with fear, they were, hence, complying rather slowly, when Manuel shouted again, "I said get *down* ... unless you want to eat some hot lead for breakfast!" Noting Jack's slow response, Manuel kicked him in the knee. As he reached for his knee, Manuel hit him in the head with the cane he was holding in his left hand. Jack fell to the ground, moaning. Seeing that, Cain and Scott quickly fell flat, hugging the asphalt. They knew they were not going to receive help anytime soon from any passersby.

Out of the morning haze, from some thick weeds and brush, climbed three stealthy figures, running parallel to the lane leading to the compound. They raced over to where Manuel and the three men were, and began holding weapons to the drivers' heads. Forcing them into the heavy brush, they made them all lie down flat, with their heads up against a tree. "I said, put the top of your thick skull up against the trunk of that tree or, I swear, I'll blow a hole in it!" Audra used her masculine voice as she shouted this command. Cain quickly did as Audra had told him. "Now, hug the tree!" Scott began to raise his head in protest. Audra kicked him sharply in the back of his head with her combat boot, and he fell unconscious. Audra quickly wrapped Scott's arms around the poplar tree, and cuffed his wrists tightly with a pair of heavy-duty metal hand-cuffs.

Cain turned to look at Mike. He began to curse when suddenly he felt a burning sensation in his kidney. Manuel had hit him once again with his cane. Cain fell, holding the same kidney as before. He grunted, "No, not again. Come on, have a little mercy," as he began to feel the urge to urinate.

"We'll show you the same mercy you have for the children!" hollered Mike, as he cuffed Cain's arms around a tree trunk. Jack did not bother to argue. He fell to the ground and hugged a tree, as another dark ninja-like figure cuffed his hands, also. Manuel placed some strong duct tape over the men's mouths, gave each man a rap over the head with his cane, and walked back to his car. The three dark figures dressed in black combat uniforms stood in front of Manuel.

"You guys—and especially the lady—are very good!"

"Me, too," said a familiar voice with a British accent. The soldiers wore dark masks over their faces.

Manuel chuckled at this interesting Brit, who had endeared himself to the trio, "Yes, Old Man … you, too."

"Well, I guess the good Queen's royal combat training really does come in handy," laughed Matt.

Manuel looked very serious as he soberly spoke to his comrades. "Look, this is it. This is the day. We have planned this in detail. The FBI is working with us, and your father definitely knows what he is doing. I respect him very much. Mike, 'no hard feelings about the other day I hope. Now … I must go, my friends. The Colonel needs me. You know … he reminds me of my father."

Manuel had turned to leave, when Audra latched on to his arm. "We love you, Manuel. We are more than grateful to you."

Mike looked at Manuel. "There will never, ever be any hard feelings between, us, Manuel. I know your heart now. Please, be careful, and take good care of the Colonel for us."

"Maybe he will take good care of me. But, we shall see. Look, you must go before the sun rises! I must be on my way, too."

Suddenly Audra instinctively pulled Manuel's head down, and kissed his lips. Mike understood this moment. It was not a kiss of passion; it was a kiss of honest love.

Manuel looked into Audra's eyes and gently said, "Maybe in another life … maybe." He jumped into his Firebird and left.

Mike, Matt and Audra took off their black ski masks, and put on the drivers' coats and caps. They climbed into the trucks that were still idling and pulled out. Matt struggled with the gears. They growled loudly, as he fought to slip the truck into first gear. "Come on, you bloody old bucket of ungreased bolts! Come on, Betsy, give me a start!" The truck finally slipped into gear, as he turned down the lane. "That 'a girl, old Betsy. Treat me like a man, and I'll buy you a set of new rubbers, I will!"

Jack glanced helplessly at Cain. He wanted to shout, "This sure gives new meaning to the saying, *'Oh, go hug a tree'*."

The security was a bit light at the compound, being a Saturday, and many of the men were on their way to the cavern. Only two sentries stood by the large metal garage doors leading inside the big building. They saw the trucks and the drivers and—like many times before—they opened the automatic doors to the compound. The trucks turned, and pulled forward, to back into the garage.

Matt was feeling a little insecure behind the wheel of his truck; it had been a long time since he had maneuvered anything this large. He hoped it would be like riding a bike … and it was, to a certain extent. Carefully, he spoke to his truck. "Come on, Betsy, ole girl; make me a proud daddy." The truck slipped easily into reverse, without a groan. "Ah, you make me proud! Yes, I'll give you some very handsome little box trucks, if you treat me right. Now, back up gently into the garage. Make me a proud papa." Matt backed up carefully into the garage, without one miscue, as sweat ran down his forehead and one cheek.

One of the guards approached Mike's cab. He began talking before he looked at Mike. "Okay, Jack, I'll help with the crates."

"No, actually I have a better idea. You shut your mouth, get out, and open the back gate. Then we'll discuss the crates." The guard looked up at Mike. He was reaching for his gun, when suddenly his head felt queer. He fell to the ground with a thump.

Audra smiled. "'Got t' love a stun gun!" Mike fumbled for the key to the back truck gate, as Audra taped the guard's mouth tightly shut. When he found the key, he opened the gate. He and Audra lifted the guard into the box of the truck. Audra almost screamed, before she turned to see Matt smiling at her.

"My, didn't mean to cause you grief," Matt apologized.

"Where's the other guard?" asked Audra.

"In the back of my truck, behaving like a good little boy. He was quite the cooperative bloke, he was. Walked politely into the back of the truck, and allowed me to tape the hole in his face shut very nicely. Of course, my Webley-Fosbery automatic .45 revolver helped motivate him … just a tad."

Audra looked at the detective's revolver. "Very ancient. I'll stick with my *Glock*."

"Harrumph! How rude," said Matt.

They hid in the darkness behind the doors. The double doors to the large garage opened, and four men stepped inside. They were dockhands. "Oh, gentlemen, will you kindly—and quietly—step up into the back of the truck and lay down. No sudden moves … unless you like the taste of lead."

"Huh? You fire that, and everyone in the building will come rushing in here," laughed one of the laborers, who swiftly fell limp to the ground.

Audra laughed, "'Gotta love tazer guns, too!" She ripped the sharp probe out of the man's chest, and ordered the other men to load their co-worker into the truck. They hastily did as they were told. Matt taped their hands behind their backs, their mouths, and then taped their ankles together. Finished, he then shut the door on them. Mike peered inside one of the open crates, and gasped. Inside the crate lay a soft pad, with a bed protector on it; on top of the protector, he saw a syringe and small bottle of Valium. Instantly he knew their protocol. The abductors would shoot the children up with Valium, and load them into the trucks. While the kids slept quietly, the drivers would transport them to the compound. The bed protectors were self-explanatory.

"Okay gang, let's get what we came for," said Matt. They turned, donned their ski masks, and fled into the building right in front of a surveillance camera.

"Shoot, they'll see us!" Audra shot the camera with an odd-looking gun.

"What the hey!" Mike said, startled again at Audra's amazing ingenuity.

"Little gift I kept, compliments of the FBI; it's a high-frequency jam gun. You can't see the invisible rays, but that camera is frozen in the same frame. All they'll see is the same picture until the camera is reset."

"Okay, Jane Bond, I think we need to spread out from here and locate the kids," Mike suggested.

"I agree," said Matt. Audra did not like the idea of separating, but she knew—in order to cover the building quickly—they had no other option.

Manuel pulled up to the cavern entrance. He looked at his watch. "Five-thirty in the morning; what a lovely day for a storm. Ah-h-h, yes! I am in plenty of time for this wretched meeting." He looked into the hills above him. "Colonel, I hope you and those Agents are in position," he said silently to himself, as he entered the cavern. Two sentries looked at him. Immediately they stepped aside, for they knew Manuel from times before. In fact, Manuel had visited them last night. He told them he needed to go over some facts in the station before today's meeting ensued.

Manuel bid them good morning, but the men held their peace. "Come now, soldiers, it is such a beautiful morning … much too beautiful to be so glum."

One of the guards managed a smile, but still did not say anything.

"Americans … too macho to notice beauty, anyway. If not for some of their señoritas, they would know no beauty at all. What a pity." Manuel continued into the cavern. He studied the walls carefully. In his mind, he saw these walls crumbling to the ground. He wondered how Mike, Audra and their friend, Matt, were doing. They had to get in and bind the people in the building. They could not afford to have even one of the kidnappers send a distress signal.

The entire success of the operation rode on the shoulders of these three people. The Colonel had wanted to use the Rangers; however, Manuel's *'slip-in-and-slip-out'* plan had seemed much more efficient. It would be much quieter, allowing less chance of being seen. Also, Audra and Mike already knew the building from the outside, and they had studied the print of the inside. This was a good thing, as the Rangers had had no time to recon the area, which would have left much more of their operation open to chance.

Manuel spotted Shorty, and walked over to him. "Good morning, Shorty. How are you feeling?"

Shorty remembered what Manuel said about his name and people who had allegedly lost their tongues. He pressed his tongue against his front teeth, as he groped for a name. "Ah … ah … ah-h-h," he stammered.

Manuel looked disgusted. "Please, Shorty, we are not at a *dentista's* office. If you cannot find a name for me, just *'Sir'* will do."

"Ah, yes, *El* … er, I mean, yes, sir … Sir!"

"Not too many *'Sirs,'* Shorty, or you'll have me looking behind myself, expecting to see the General. Oh, and speaking about generals, are they beginning to arrive?"

"Yes, Sir! The big guys are coming in from both ends of the cavern."

"Ah-h-h, how sweet; like one happy family."

"Yeah, one happy family," the guard reiterated, thinking otherwise.

"I suppose I should find a seat among them," Manuel thought aloud.

"Yes, Sir; maybe that would be a good idea."

"Yes, you may be right." Manuel slowly turned and walked towards the station. He gripped a small, slim, hard-plastic device in his hand, inside his jacket pocket. All he had to do is lift the cover from the device, and the hills would come alive with Agents, the Colonel most likely leading the way.

Manuel stepped inside the renovated station. It looked very nice, and bigger than it had been before. "What a shame; it may very well all collapse again." Manuel chuckled a little at the thought. He felt another device in his pocket … a small radio transmitter. When he had walked into the cavern last night, he had told the men he wanted to walk the premises to make completely sure the area was void of any unsafe places from which an assassin could hide and shoot. Actually, he had used that time to plant bombs all over the cavern. He had been carrying the bombs in his briefcase, so was in no danger of their being detected, as no man dare lay a hand on Manuel's briefcase, if he valued his life.

Manuel knocked on the conference room door. A guard answered the door and asked for Manuel's name. "Tell the General Manuel is waiting." The sentry left and quickly returned. He opened the entrance, as another guard quickly ran to retake his post outside the door Manuel was about to enter. The guard was furiously trying to zip his fly, apparently having just returned from relieving himself. Manuel chuckled and walked into the room.

"Ah, a sight for my sore eyes," laughed the big-bellied General.

"And you … a sight for mine, also, " laughed Manuel. He looked over the General's shoulder to see Scorpio, and the General's Advisor, along with some of the General's other dignitaries and guards. The room was very large, so many could sit at the table at one time. Even the General was impressed by the size of counter.

"Now, we are all together. One big happy family!" The General came alive, because he felt very secure whenever Manuel was around; after all, Manuel was the best.

The men spoke about family, and of trivial matters. They laughed and joked around a little; even Scorpio joined in the conversation. They did not bring up *La Palo,* or anything negative, for they knew that time would come soon enough.

The door opened, as General Howard T. Blake, Ed Braddock, Cal Brown and a lean, dark-haired, slim-faced, tough-looking man, wearing a long over-coat—along with some of the General's thugs—walked into the conference room. Manuel looked at both sides, and knew the war would soon begin.

"Tom … General … we meet again in person," said Montiego calmly. There was a slight note of distrust in his voice.

"Yes, it has been too long, hasn't it? I'd like you to meet Cal Brown here, and Jim Peters. You already know Ed."

Montiego bowed his head politely. "I'm honored."

Paco looked at Ed and Cal. "Well, Ed … Cal … it has been quite some time. You guys look very handsome today."

Cal stared into Paco's eyes. "How is my son, Robert?"

Robert held up his hand. "Because we are friends, I will allow that name to be used here, but it really means very little to me now." Robert Perris reached into his coat pocket.

Ed reached into his coat, as well, but Blake stopped him. "Really, Ed, that won't be necessary."

Robert pulled out a few photos, and handed them to Cal. Cal's eyes watered, as he looked upon his twenty-one-year-old son. "Cliff, you turned out to be a fine-looking man," said Cal, as he stroked the photos with his fingers. The photo showed Cliff standing next to another young American lad. They were both smiling … each had one arm around the other's neck.

"That's Eric standing next to him," Robert explained. "They live next to each other. They both think they are in the American Elite Forces. Believe me, they are very well fed, and happy. Cliff is married with a one-year-old child. Lucia is the name of Cliff's wife. They are very much in love."

Cal sighed as he looked at the pictures. He knew he should be very angry with Robert and Montiego but, for some reason, he did not feel so angry. Now he was a grandfather, and that thought made him happy. Robert showed him another picture of his granddaughter and daughter-in-law. The baby smiled up at Cal, and Lucia was very pretty to look upon. Cal sniffled a little, then wiped his nose. "You told me I would see him one day," aware of how tentative such promises could be.

Montiego cut into the conversation. "That depends on what takes place here today, gentlemen."

Mike was wishing now that he had with him one of those guns Audra had—the high-frequency jam gun variety—as he stared at a dark bubble housing a camera. How was he going to take it out? Maybe they should not have split up, after all. Then he remembered why Manuel had told him to pocket some paint. Mike grabbed the thin paint can, and raced over to the camera, quickly spraying the bubble. "I hope that doesn't trip the alarm," thought Mike. He knew a little about the data line running to the smoke detectors. He knew if some of the dust, or mist, managed to pass the eye beam inside the detector not too far from said camera, the fire alarm panel would go into trouble mode, but he had to take the risk.

However, the paint did not travel far, so nothing happened. Maybe he was safe from detection, after all. Mike moved swiftly down the long corridor. He opened door after door to the young boys' rooms. The boys were still in bed, sleeping. He awoke them. One of the boys—a very handsome-looking black child—looked at him and asked, "Who are you?"

Mike saw the military-like clothing, folded at the foot of the bed. He remembered that the boys were possibly being trained for combat; he remembered the plan Manuel and had Pat devised, to ensure that the children would obey them, without causing a scene.

"I'm Colonel Taylor, soldier. What is your name?"

"I'm Donald Stevens, but everyone calls me Donny."

"Well, this is a drill, Donny. You are to instruct the other boys to meet in the large garage. Hurry! Suit up, and go!" A child in the bed next to Donny overheard the conversation, and jumped out of bed. They donned their clothes in the wink of an eye. "Look men, this is a covert operation." The boys stood at attention, as though they knew what that word meant.

Chad, the boy next to Donny, asked, "What does that mean again?"

Donny looked at his friend and said, "It means it is a secret assignment. We have to be very quiet, and we have to make sure the others are, too."

"Correct, Donny. You'll make a Colonel yourself one day." Donny gloated, as the two boys slipped into the dimly lit hallway. Mike turned and walked out of the room. He began his search again. He looked into another room, and saw a very familiar face.

Audra disabled the security camera above her, and entered a child's room. She woke the lad up and, with her fake masculine voice, repeated the same words that Mike had said to Donny. Soon the children on her side of the building were all gathering themselves together.

Matt found his mission a success on the floor above, as well. In very little time, many of the children were filing into the garage.

Bobby jumped into Mike's waiting arms. They hugged each other tightly, as they both wept. "I knew you'd come. I knew it!"

"Bobby, we have very little time to get you out of here. We have to leave!" Mike looked up, to see a large group of young boys, and a few girls, staring at him.

One of the girls looked at him and said, with a mild voice, "Are we going home now? I thought we had a mission to go to."

Mike's heart melted. The children were being brainwashed. He took the girl in one arm and Bobby in the other. "This mission is over now. We're going home ... we're *all* going home."

Montiego was becoming irritated. The meeting was going nowhere. Both sides were denying anything they might know about the cavern saboteurs, and the malfunctioning rifles. Tom was speaking. "Look General, you have no shred of evidence to support that we staged a bombing in our own cavern...."

"Stop! Stop right there, Blake," Montiego interrupted. General Blake's face showed that he did not appreciate the disrespectful way in which the South American General had just addressed him. General Montiego continued, "It is our cavern, not just yours, which makes the bombing that much more irritating. We worked very hard to build this cavern, right alongside your men!" Montiego's voice rose.

Manuel shifted the conversation in another direction. "Gentlemen, please ... you have proven only to give me and yourselves nothing but migraine headaches. General Blake, you knew of the shipment to Peru. You also knew we were making changes ... that we were in a transition period. You knew, too, that if there would be a good time to implement a counter plan to muscle in on our organization, this would be the perfect time. Now, you want us to try and prove that this was your motive, and we want proof that you did not rig the rifles, sending many of my General's men to their horrible deaths."

Both generals began to speak, but Manuel held up his hand, stopping them. "Please, I have listened all morning to your petty bickering, and it gets us nowhere. I wish for only ten—maybe fifteen—more minutes of your time." Both generals nodded their approval.

Manuel began his monologue. "For days, while many shameful words were being angrily fired back and forth between my General and you, General Blake, I was busy investigating the cavern ... busy researching everybody, and *'leaving no stone unturned,'* as you say here in America. Now, I discovered something very interesting. You see, the cameras in your cavern here, have a built-in photo and audio recorder. Not all the cameras were destroyed and, for that, I must take my hat off to you, General Blake. As you like very expensive cameras, that conceal the tapes and audio recordings in an extremely durable box-like structure made out of material not unlike those which conceal tapes on a large passenger plane, I was able to put together a portfolio of pictures and some recordings of the saboteurs." Manuel took out some photos from his briefcase, along with a recorder. He placed the recorder, and an envelope containing the photos, on the table before the men.

"Now, let's listen to the voice of one of the assassins." Manuel played the tape.

"I was not sent to destroy you. I bring a message from my superiors, down south, and abroad. We tire from your lack of progress, and poor product. You tell your people to either produce at a rate of approval, and deliver quality product, or more like me will come, and make your lives even more miserable. We already lose too much money—and time—due to inferior merchandise."

"So, some guy with a deep voice spouting off at the mouth," said Blake.

Montiego agreed with Blake, for once. "I agree with Blake. This gets us nowhere again!"

"Wait! This does go somewhere. Thank God for computers, which can break voices down into tiny microscopic fragments. As no one person has exactly the same size of vocal cords, everyone has a unique voice. I have had this voice analyzed by computer, men, and the computer has linked this voice to Ming Chow."

"But, she's a girl!" Blake immediately got quiet, realizing what he'd done. His eyes widened, wondering how he could correct this *faux pas ...* retract his comment.

"General, how did you know Ming is a girl?"

"Well, the 'Ming' in the name sounds ... well, it does sound feminine."

"I have male friends called *'Ming,'* General, but they don't have this voice. This voice belongs to Ming Chow, a special top agent that works for the Chinese. These are her photos. Do you recognize her, General?"

Blake stared at the photos. His throat felt very tight. He could barely swallow. Why had he gone and said the word, *'girl'?* Fate is so strange, so unpredictable ... just as are words. Only one wrong word from a person's mouth could mean life or death. The General was beginning to realize this, in a most uncomfortable way.

"I do not recognize the pictures, no."

"Are you positive?" Manuel insisted.

"Yes, very."

"General, this agent is trained for Chinese special operations, the word *'covert'* more than applies to her. She is in and out of places so quickly, it's a wonder your cameras even caught her. As I said before, 'good thing you like expensive cameras. But then, again, the citizens of these United States paid for them; you didn't. I also know you are excellent at fudging books and accounts."

The General squirmed in his chair. "How could Manuel know anything?" Blake thought to himself.

Manuel continued. "Our organization has her on record. Here is a photo of Ming, from our files." Manuel showed all the men in the room the photo. Montiego nodded.

"Ming's greatest specialty is espionage-slash-sabotage. She has trained her voice, as well as her hands, feet, and mind. Your men described her physique to me very well. Now, let me play this tape differently. You see, this is a very expensive recorder that takes the voice the computer has analyzed and, through many series of steps I do not quite understand myself, arranges the voice particles in such a way that it can uncover the disguised voice." Manuel began playing the tape again. The recorder stopped, started and stopped again. It clicked and hummed a little, then it began to replay the voice over again. The same words came forth from the recorder's speaker, only this time they heard a woman's voice. The voice sounded a little like Audra's, but with a higher soprano-like pitch.

"That, gentlemen, is the true, unadulterated voice of Ming Chow, the saboteur that was in this cavern the night of the bombing, and the night the men almost lost their lives ... but they didn't because it was a stage!" Manuel's voice rose loudly.

"You are a bold-faced liar!" shouted Blake. "You can't prove any of this!"

Manuel had had enough. He was seeing red. "General, I have given you more time than you deserved to come clean! Now, I want you all to take a good look at Miss Ming in this photo. Do you recognize the man she's draped all over in the photo?" As Manuel held up the picture, Blake's face grew instantly pale. He knew the score now. His hand reached quickly for his Beretta.

Bobby, Mike, and the other children raced down the corridor as quietly as they could. Some of the children's minds were a bit hazy from the drugged milk they had been drinking for a good while, but they managed to keep up, anyway.

Audra turned a corner in the hallway, and walked through some double doors, the children following her. She opened the doors to see a large, bald-headed man grinning at her. She raised her Glock, but the man was very quick. His foot came off the ground faster than Audra's eyes could detect his movement. Mr. Clean had knocked the Glock out of Audra's hand, before she knew it. The gun landed on the ground to her right side. As she dove to retrieve the pistol, Mr. Clean caught her in midair, lifted her above his head, and sent her sailing across the hallway. She braced herself, managed to roll over onto her feet, and hit the ground.

The children stood mesmerized by the combative moves they were wit-nessing before them. Mr. Clean approached Audra, who had—by now—gotten back up. He gritted his teeth, and kicked the toe of his boot at Audra's head. She quickly spun to the ground, ducking the karate kick, and slammed her balled-up fist into her assailant's groin. The man grimaced, but this did not stop him. The children began to encourage both Mr. Clean and Audra, as they thought they were watching just another drill. Mr. Clean grabbed Audra's hair, and lifted her face up. He cocked his massive arm back to deliver a fatal blow.

Audra butted her head forward as fast and hard as she could relieving the pressure off her head. She then managed, somehow, to sweep the man's legs with her hands. The man fell to the ground, still holding on to Audra's hair. He began to pull her hair until he actually felt it tearing from her scalp. But Audra's body, full of adrenaline, did not feel the pain. She moved swiftly forward, allow-ing the man to pull her hair. Mr. Clean pulled Audra up to his chest, thinking that she was at the stage of giving up, but his face filled with surprise when Audra thrust her fingers into the man's throat. As he started gagging and chok-ing, Audra clamped her teeth over the man's hand that held her hair. She bit down hard until she felt her teeth come together through the sinew and gristle of the fatty part of the back of the man's hand. Blood spurted, as he let go of Audra's hair.

Several guards now bounded into the hallway. They drew their pistols. Just as they did, the air filled was with one round after another. The guards fell to the ground, moaning and groaning in pain. Mr. Clean jumped to his feet, and ran off down another dimly lit corridor. Matt, who had arrived in time to shoot the guards, shot a few rounds in the direction of the fleeing man, but he missed.

"Like I say, nothing beats a Webley-Fosbery," boasted Matt, as he handed Audra her Glock. Other children stood behind Matt, looking shocked and confused. Below them, they saw a small puddle of blood, and blood was running from Audra's scalp.

"Matt, the man got away. He's sure to call his superiors. We've got to move fast!" Audra screamed.

"So much for in-and-out, without being seen!" Matt lamented.

The children still looked confused. Audra managed to smile through all her pain and agony. "It's a lifelike drill. We decided to put on the most realistic drill you'll ever see before any real combat." The children fell for Audra's deception. If they had known she was actually fighting for her life, they might have panicked or—worse—joined the bad guys.

Bobby and Mike ran ahead of the other children, hoping to make a clean get away to the garage, but they were mistaken. Captain Tinker and Ms. Kay were there, barring the way. They both held Russian *AK-47s*, pointed at Mike and the children. "That's far enough! We are well trained, and well armed. Give up, or get shot!"

The General's gun roared in his hand as Scorpio, Robert Perris—known as *'Paco'*—and some of their men returned fire. Manuel quickly hit the ground, and rolled out the door. The guard outside took aim at Manuel, but he was too late. Manuel caught him between the eyes with a bullet. The guard fell over, on top of Manuel. Manuel threw the guard off to the side, and dove behind a file in the hallway, just as another sentry fired his *M-16* at him. The rounds blew open the file, and scattered paper everywhere.

Ed screamed at the man, as he sported his *.44* automatic. He did not want to fire any rounds. "Stop!" he screamed. "We can still settle this without killing each other. Jim, Cal, Robert … stop!" Not about to listen to the Mayor, Jim pulled an *AK-47* out from his overcoat. He had made a small fortune keeping the Sheriff from investigating any strange goings on in the park. He had always managed to direct the deputies away from a scene that might lead them to suspicion; this was his job. He would also stage false alarms, whenever General Blake wanted the Sheriff and the police far away—away from the area through which they would travel when they were trafficking children, drugs, and weapons. He also had a clever assistant—an emissary—someone from the Sheriff's department. Jim raised his assault rifle, and had begun firing off rounds, when Scorpio shot him in the chest with a cartridge from a 9mm Taurus. Jim went down firing, one of his stray bullets hitting Montiego in the shoulder. The General flinched, but he still kept firing. All Montiego's troops, and Blake's soldiers, heard the shooting.

Manuel now rolled out from behind the filing cabinet, and shot the sentry that had held him captive for a few moments. He then lunged through a window, falling on the loading dock below. He let out a groan, as he grabbed and held his wounded arm, scurrying off to hide behind some large calcite pillars in the musty cave. Soon Blake's hired mercenaries, and Montiego's troops, met in front of the station. They did not even have to ask themselves why they were shooting at one another. "Dirty, filthy, Bolivian scum!" yelled one of Blake's men, as he opened fire on Montiego's men. The return volleys from both sides almost shook the cave. Manuel could hardly believe all the bloodshed, all in the grand old name of mammon, otherwise known as *'money.'* He crouched further down behind the pillar, as the shooting continued, even escalating.

"Ms. Kay, what are you doing?" asked Bobby, surprised to see her holding a gun on him, his brother, and the other children. "Is this part of a drill?" he further inquired.

Mike looked down at his little brother sadly. "No, Bobby, this is not a drill, and she is not Ms. Kay. Her name is Katrina Adams. She supposedly works for the *National Center for Missing and Exploited Children.* Well Ms. Kay, Katrina—or whoever you are—now I see how you can keep up with all the statistics, and what the bureau is up to, when it comes to our beautiful children. You are always one step ahead … but it's now time for your empire to crumble."

"Oh, and you're going to do it?" laughed Ms. Kay, still holding her *AK-47* on them.

"No, not just me, but—as we speak—your superiors are probably being gunned down by Bolivian forces. Yes, you see the *'good General'* Montiego is at this moment showing his gratitude for all the nasty little guns you sent him that have caused many of his men to die!"

"You lie!" she shrieked.

"No, you lie, Katrina. You lie to *all* these children. You make them believe you are a wonderful lady, when you are a beast … a wicked demon!"

"Shut up! Shut your mouth or, I swear, I'll blow it off your crazed face!"

Bobby, still having feelings for Ms. Kay who had been kind to him, walked towards her, unafraid. "Ms. Kay, why are you so angry at my brother? Ms. Kay, when I first came here, I was so scared. You were kind to me, and I fell in love with you." Tears were falling from his eyes. "You were like the mother I did not have. Please tell me you are not a mean woman?" cried Bobby.

"Oh, Bobby, you are the son I should have had. I love you, too. Please, Bobby, remember the video of your brother?"

Bobby, in his mind, saw Mike's face on the video. "Yes, of course I do."

"Well, Bobby, this is kind of like the video. Mike is here to see you off to your mission. We planned this. All you have to do is come to me, and we will leave to go to the train; Mike will soon join you."

Mike began to believe she was mad. "Bobby, if you saw me talking on a video, it was probably like one of those computer images, or something like it. You know … like *'Jar-Jar Bing,'* in *'Star Wars'.*" Mike could not believe he was talking like this, but what else could he do? Katrina was doing a great job of exaggerating!

Bobby stood there, very confused. Should he go with Ms. Kay, or go with Mike? His mind drifted back to the video that day. He did remember something different about Mike—but what was it?

"Please, Bobby, come to Mommy," Ms. Kay implored. "Mommy loves you."

Captain Tinker himself began to wonder about Ms. Kay. Bobby moved closer to her, still confused.

Mike warned, "No! Bobby, no … don't go to her. That wasn't me in the video. Bobby, you're my brother. I love you!"

Ms. Kay remembered her precious son. He was a lovely boy … so dear to her. They shared so many wonderful days together. Then one day she saw her son lying dead, in a dumpster. His body was bloated, and stained with dry blood. She cursed the wicked criminal, or criminals. After that, she sought solitude—then she had run into Ed Braddock. He told her how she could help with young boys. She jumped at the opportunity. In her crazed mind, she really did believe that she was helping the poor children find better homes, in a mission somewhere south of the border.

"Bobby, I have decided to go on your mission with you," Ms. Kay tried again. "You see, Bobby, this is a mission. You and I can live together in love and peace. We'll walk the shores together, and ride bikes, and swim … just think how happy we'll be. Come, my Son; come to your mother. They took you from me years ago, but God has brought us back together again." Ms. Kay held out her hand. Her voice was so gentle and sweet … so heavenly. Bobby ran over to her and hugged her.

Mike could hold back his emotions no longer. He cried, "Please, Ms. Kay! I know you are hurting very much inside, but don't you see that you'll be *just* like the horrible people that killed *your* son, if you take Bobby from me?"

Ms. Kay thought about the words *'horrible people,'* and how being referred to as such … compared to such vile people … really stung. "They were evil, wicked child-killers … like Richard here! He calls himself *'Captain Tinker,'* to make the children laugh, but he really *hates* them." Her voice then rose in pitch, as she madly screamed, "Don't you, Richard!"

Richard began to stutter. "I ... I ... I do ... I don't know. What are you talking about, woman? I don't *hate* them! Yes, I *do* try to not love them. You ... you're crazy, woman!"

Bobby had been thinking, as this scene took place. He realized now what it was about the video that was strange. Mike had always had a little mole, just below the left side of his mouth. In the video, the mole was on the opposite side. Wiser now, Bobby looked at Ms. Kay. "Ms. Kay, come with us. You can be my mother, if you come with us." Bobby was playing along now, and it had begun to work.

"Yes, I could come with you." Feeling placated, she lowered her *AK-47*.

"Woman! Get your mind together," Richard shouted. "You're crazy! You can't go anywhere with anyone. You're staying here, even if I have to shoot all of you!" he continued to shout, very frustrated.

"No, you aren't shooting *anyone!* You're an evil man, and I hate you!" screamed Bobby. He ran at Richard, swinging his fists at him. Bobby was so angry, he gave no thought to the rifle in the man's hands. Richard turned the gun on Bobby.

"No-o-o!" Mike let out a long, loud scream, as the hallway filled with the echo of the deadly rifle. In the confusion—and being in a dimly lit corridor—Mike did not know what had happened. He fell to his knees. "No, no, no-o-o!" Tears filled his eyes. He had promised Bobby he would always watch over him. He thought he could save him but, in the end, it appeared he had failed miserably. Mike held his hands to his face and cried. Suddenly an urge filled every fiber of his being.

He knew he did not have anyone now. No family, and no loving relatives. He had nothing to lose, but his life ... and that did not seem important to him anymore. He grasped his *19C* Glock. He knew death was knocking at his door, and he was determined to rise up, and meet it, shooting and yelling. He was sure that—if he could shoot both of these wicked people before they got him—then the other children would be safe.

Mike jumped to his feet, with his Glock held in front of him. It was then that he saw Bobby standing over Ms. Kay, weeping. Bobby was alive, after all! It was Ms. Kay Mike had seen falling, as the rifle rang out in the dimly lit quarters, not Bobby. "Oh, Ms. Kay, I love you!" Bobby cried. The other children gathered around Bobby and Ms. Kay. A short ways away, Richard also lay in a pool of blood. Ms. Kay had not only turned on the children's nemesis, but had—at the same time—stepped in front of Bobby, giving her life for him. She managed to caress Bobby's cheek with her hand, as she spoke with an angel's voice, "My son, I shall see you again. I shall...." She coughed a little ... the bullet had penetrated her chest; there was little they could do. "I shall always ... love you

... Bobby." Her head then rolled over to her left shoulder. Mike thoughtfully closed her eyes.

Manuel listened to the shouts and screams of Bolivian and American men. The automatic weapons kept firing, and occasionally a hand grenade blew dust and debris all over the cavern. One American ruffian yelled as he threw a grenade. The debris from the grenade ricocheted off the walls of the cave, flew back and struck the American ruffian in the head. He crumpled over, dead. Bolivian deviates, and American deviates, were actually killing themselves off with their own grenades. Six men had blown their own brains out before they ever realized how deadly the grenades were. Bombs were also filling the air with a cloud of dust, causing the men to choke and wheeze, but the men were so enraged, they kept firing, regardless of how bad the conditions became.

Manuel reached into his pocket and pulled the signaling device out. He thought about using it but, deep in his heart, he really wanted the men to kill off each other, rather than blowing up the place with the bombs that had been planted the previous evening. This would rid the world of the evil men, once and for all, yet this was not part of the plan. He had said he would assist the FBI before he left for the meeting, and they were hoping they could capture some men alive, for interrogation purposes. Maybe some of these men would lead them to other sources within both the American and South American syndicate; besides, Cal's life was at stake here, too. With some reluctance, he signaled the FBI. Soon Agents were pouring down from the foothills, and moving in on the cave. They met up with heavy resistance at the entrance. Shorty and some of Blake's men were determined to keep the FBI from entering the cavern. General Blake's men shot many FBI Agents, as they tried to work their way into the cavern.

Pat yelled out, "Fall back, men, fall back! You're taking on too much fire! Let my men and me handle this." The agents gave up their positions, heeding Pat's orders. As soon as the Agents stepped away, the Colonel ordered his men to launch smoke bombs and teargas into the cavern. The rockets left the launchers, and whistled into the cave. Soon much of the cavern became nothing but a huge cloud of gas and smoke. Yet—having learned a grave lesson from the last bombing—the men inside the cavern were prepared for even this, each of them carrying a gas mask with them. They quickly put them on.

Manuel now ran out from his hiding place, under the cover of this cloud, and struck one of the smugglers across the head. The criminal fell to the ground. Manuel stripped him of his gas mask, and put it on, so he could breathe. He looked at his watch. The Colonel seemed to be losing the game.

He was surely making a valiant effort, but soon the cavern would be saturated with angry South American Nationals. The General had ordered these men to enter the cavern from the Mexican side, and take over the cavern, if they had not heard from him by nine in the morning. Manuel saw the time was already eight forty five. The men would soon be pouring in from the south side of the tunnel.

The noise of the previous several minutes had somewhat quieted down. Manuel stumbled through the debris and wreckage, finding bodies of men lying dead all around him. Some were still alive though, but badly wounded. When Manuel reached the station, he found little evidence of life. He could still hear the battle raging outside, but the Colonel did not fire any more smoke bombs or teargas into the cavern. Maybe he knew this might lead to Manuel's death … or maybe he was out of smoke bombs and teargas. Whatever the case, Manuel noticed the smoke and gas escaping through the roof of the cavern. "Clever. The Americans finally figured out they needed an exhaust system to filter air in and out." Soon the cavern became virtually smoke free once again. Manuel entered the station, and walked cautiously towards the conference room.

When Manuel reached the room where the massacre had begun, he found the door had been blown completely off its hinges. He stepped inside, saw Scorpio lying on the table face down, blood dripping from a gaping hole in his head. The others were also dead, or dying. Blake looked up at Manuel, lit a cigarette, and managed to take one puff before rolling over dead. All of Blake's men and Montiego's men lay in thick pools of blood. Then, he spied Cal. Somehow he had managed to escape the deadly crossfire.

Manuel walked over to Cal. "You have only a few minutes to get out of here before you die for sure, Cal."

Cal turned to see Manuel. "Well, we did it, didn't we?"

Manuel looked closer at Cal. Why didn't he get up off the ground, and make a run for it? "Cal, get out of here! There are more coming; they will be here any moment!"

Cal sat up and smiled at Manuel. "You know, I was not a good man. I should have been stronger. I should have told Robert to take a hike. I was weak, Manuel, and it led to my son's abduction. But, hey! I'm happy, 'cause I know my son is alive, and he is happily married … and I'm a proud grandpa, too. I'm a grandpa, Manuel."

Manuel opened Cal's jacket, exposing a bullet hole in his gut. Now he knew why Cal did not try to leave. He had only minutes to live. "You want to retire a hero?" he asked Cal.

"More than anything, right now," Cal told Manuel, very seriously.

Manuel handed Cal a grenade. "Here, Cal. When those child molesters come in here, don't give them any satisfaction."

"Hey! I'll blow them to hell with me!" wheezed Cal.

"No, Cal; you're not going to hell."

Cal laughed, and it hurt. "You are funny. I like you, El Niño."

Manuel laughed. "I usually tell people not to use that name, but just before you pull the pin, tell them, '*El Niño* sends his regards'."

Cal coughed some more. "Will do, my friend, will do."

Manuel left Cal, and walked out of the station. He heard the shouts of men coming his way from the south end of the cavern. It would not be long now. He clutched the transmitter. "Soon all this will only be a memory," Manuel said loudly.

Manuel began walking towards the cavern entrance.

"Nice to see you're still alive, Amigo."

Manuel instantly recognized the man's voice. Before he even turned to look at the man's face, he said, "My dear General, so nice to know you are alive, also." Manuel turned and looked upon the big man, as he spoke to Manuel.

"Well, it's just you and me until my other men arrive, and they'll be here very shortly. You know, Manuel, I've been thinking. How did you put all that information together? How did you get that photo from our files? You know ... the one of Ming? It did not dawn on me—until halfway through all the shooting—that I, alone, had the key to that file, and that you had not asked for it. But then, I know, too, that you are a very intelligent locksmith, as well as one who knows about photo transpositions and audio recordings. You know, I never did really check you out thoroughly when we hired you. However, I did have the office run a very quick check on you.

Anyway, while everyone else was busy killing each other off, I was hiding in a freaking spider hole out here. You are extremely brilliant, and more, Manuel. The surveillance cameras above the files filmed a figure that fits your description very well. You stole that photo, and rigged the recorder!"

Manuel stepped away from the General, not sure what to expect.

"I applaud you," continued the General. "I wanted full control of both the American and South American underground in this operation, and you handed it to me on a silver platter. You also got rid of much dead weight in our organization. All my leading men became mere leaches, but not you. Together, we shall rule the underworld as the new leaders of both sides of the Equator. You shall receive riches beyond your wildest dreams, my dear *El Niño!*"

"What about General Genghis?" Manuel wanted to know, more out of curiosity than anything.

"He is thrilled over the news." General Montiego waived his cell phone. "The greatest invention since crack cocaine; I've already contacted him and his officers. With the foolish Americans out of the way, they will have to deal only with us. We now own the entire enchilada! No more interference ... *we* set the prices. We'll give China discount oil via unscrupulous methods and, with China's help and other OPEC nations, we'll raise the price on the Americans. We handle all the trafficking, and we receive all the profits. We continue with our current plan, only now we will be able to act more quickly, and bring the American Empire crashing to its feeble knees within a few years!" The General laughed at his own ill-perceived shrewdness.

"You are mad," Manuel aptly assessed. The men were almost upon them. Manuel stood silent. His face grew very sober, stone-like. He looked deep into the eyes of the General.

"General, you told me more than once that every man and woman has a price. Well, I really gave a lot of thought to your philosophy about humans and, do you know what?"

The General, still upset by Manuel's words—why would he call him 'mad'—responded more out of curiosity than thought. "What is that, Manuel?"

Manuel spit some dirt out of his mouth, all the while keeping his eye on the General. "You are right, General Montiego. Every man does have a price, and yours comes very cheaply. It costs less than one Boliviano."

"What does that mean? Show me what you're talking about?" asked the General anxiously.

Manuel did show him, as he raised his *.40* automatic. "Your price comes in the form of a cheap piece of metal, called *'lead'.*" Manuel's gun roared. The General's faced turned white with surprise—then he fell to the ground.

Manuel had very little time. He saw the troops rushing towards him. He knew, too, that they would shoot anything that moved, for these were the General's orders. Manuel darted into the darkest corner of the cavern, as some of the men saw his shadowy figure slip behind a large stalagmite. Shots began ringing out all over. Once again, the cavern became a war zone. Manuel rolled in and out of the sharp rocky formations. Bullets ricocheted off the stone walls around him. A piece of stone clipped his side, and he cringed in pain. He knew he had to make it to the entrance for any chance of survival.

He could hear shouts coming from the entrance and he knew the Colonel had broken through. However, the Colonel was too late. Manuel saw only death and destruction awaiting the Colonel, if he and his men were to enter the cavern now, as the General's troops far outnumbered the Americans. He gripped the transmitter; he must make it to the entrance soon, if he was to save his life and the Colonel's life.

Chad Rook, otherwise known as *'Mr. Clean'*—having escaped Matt's poor aim in the dimly lit corridor of the complex—frantically tried to reach Blake, Ed or anybody belonging to the conspiracy but, try as he may, he could not contact anyone. He had no idea the Mayor, Blake, and most of their associates, lay dead or dying in the cavern. Finally, Chad managed to contact an individual they only referred to as *'Khaki,'* due the color of his uniform he wore on a daily basis. Khaki stood next to his vehicle, looking off into the mountains that concealed the cave. He had wanted to go in with the Mayor and Blake, but General Blake and the Mayor had told him to make sure the law stayed away from the cavern. He remembered the words of General Blake. "I don't care if you have to shoot the deputies; just don't let them get near the cave!" Khaki was thinking about the General's words, when his cell phone vibrated in his pocket. "Yeah," replied Khaki.

"Khaki, this is Sergeant Rook; you've got t' get over here, pronto!"

"Over where?" Khaki inquired.

"Here … the compound! Get over here to the compound, and be quick about it! All hell is breaking loose! I've got intruders running amok all over the place! Round up some of your thugs and get over here, before the children and these ninja-like people carry them all off. Hurry! I need back-up, like, yesterday!" screamed Chad, irritated at his density.

Khaki looked at a deputy standing nearby, and said, "I've got an emergency call! I've got t' go!"

The deputy nodded and said, "Hope it's nothing too serious. 'Catch you later."

Khaki jumped into his Chevy Tahoe, and raced towards the compound. Khaki called one of his hired gunmen, and explained the situation. "You all have been standing by as I ordered, right?"

The gunman smiled, as he spoke over his cell phone. "Of course, Amigo; we were hoping for a little action today. We could use the extra money, and the target practice. I, and my three other men, will leave whenever you want us to."

"Very good. Get over to the compound, as soon as you can. We have big trouble brewing!" Khaki shouted over his phone, as he drove north on Coronado Memorial Road.

The man on the other end of the line looked at his men and laughed. "Let's blow this dump; we're needed at the compound! 'Looks like we're gonna have us a little fun today!" The hired gunmen were already geared up, and anxious for action. So, they dashed out of the mobile home they were temporarily living in, and jumped into a Hummer. They laughed and cheered, as they sped towards the compound.

Mike looked into the faces of the children. The children stood frozen with fear, and perplexed. Mike assured the children they would be okay. "Follow me kids; we've got to get out of here, now! Everything will be all right, I promise, but we've go t' get moving … fast!" he pleaded, as he repeated himself.

Mike held out his hand to the children. One of the little girls took hold of his hand, as Bobby released his grip on Ms. Kay. He stood up, wiped a few tears from his eyes and shouted' "Come on, everybody! Ms. Kay gave her life for us. Let's not let her down now. Let's *go!"*

The children found new hope, and strength, from Bobby's words. They all shouted, "Yes, Sir!" They followed Mike, Bobby and the little girl, as they stepped around the lifeless forms of Ms. Kay and Richard.

Meanwhile, Matt and Audra led another group of children into the garage. "Where's Mike?" shouted Audra, frantic that he may have gotten into some sort of trouble.

Matt bestowed a clueless expression, and shrugged his shoulders. "I have no idea. He probably ran into trouble, like we did earlier!" only adding to Audra's worry about the exact same thing.

Audra felt the urge within to go back inside the compound. Then she looked around at all the children for whom she felt responsible, and wasn't sure what to do. Matt and Audra had gotten most of the children this far; however, they were not out of the woods yet. They must get them into the trucks yet, and as far away from the compound as possible. She had a very difficult decision to make … risk going back in to try to save Mike and the other children, or get the children who were already filing into the trucks away from here, to safety. "Matt, 'think you can handle things here for a few minutes?"

"I'll do my bloody best, but if any other blokes show up, I don't know if I'll be able to hold them off for long!"

Audra shouted, "If I'm not back in three minutes, leave without me!"

"Great Scott! Lady, what do you think I am?"

"Three minutes!" screamed Audra, as she dashed back into the building. Mike and the children were stampeding through the last corridor leading to the dock, when they saw Audra rounding a corner coming in their direction. She aimed her pistol at the children … or so it seemed.

"No! Audra, it's us!" screamed Mike. "Drop to the ground!" Mike loudly ordered the children. Audra stumbled over a small box, or container of some sort, which had been left in the corridor. She tried keeping her balance, but her momentum and gravity carried her to the floor. They saw fire blazing from the end of Audra's 19C Glock, as they heard the gun roar. They all quickly ducked to the ground, expecting to be pelted with lead. While on the floor, they heard a loud *'Ping!'* and then the sound of something falling—*'ka-lunk'*—to the stone-tiled floor.

The corridor grew deathly quiet. Audra's bullet had struck Mr. Clean's assault rifle. The weapon flew out of his hands and bounced harmlessly into a vacant corner of the hallway. Mr. Clean reacted with terrific speed, capturing the first child he could reach with his left hand, as he drew his bayonet and held it to the child's throat—Bobby's throat! Mike looked on in horror, as Mr. Clean pressed the sharp, steely knife against his brother's throat. "Is there no end to this madness!" screamed Mike within himself.

"Now! The party's over … and, *you …*" Rook looked at Audra, "you filthy …" he wanted so much to say it—the *'B'* word, the mother of all dogs—but the look on the children's faces prevented him. "You … you hussy … you mother of dogs!"

Audra's knees grew a little weak. "I wish my bullet would have hit you between the eyes, where I aimed!" screamed Audra. Audra looked at young Bobby with eyes that said, "I'm so sorry, Bobby. I stumbled … I fell … so, I missed my mark."

Mike blurted out, "So, what are your plans now, mister … whoever you are?" The kids looked on in disbelief and abashment.

"What are you doing, Sergeant Rook? Why do you have a knife at Bobby's throat?" asked cute little Susie, one of Bobby's close friends with whom he had often eaten lunch within the compound.

Rook did not know what to say at first. He held his cool, thinking before he spoke. What could he say? A baleful smile crept across his face, which a moment ago had looked very sullen. "What did you think this was kids … a carnival … a kiddy ride to the romper room? This is *reality*, and these people here are your enemies. These people are terrorists—evil undercover agents, from the most wicked country in the world! We've got to eliminate them. *This* is your mission!" The children looked more puzzled than before. They stared at Mike, then at Audra.

Mike quickly tried to refute Rook's lies. "No, children, we are here to take you back to your *families!* We are here to save you. There *is* no *'mission'* … there *is* no war. There never was. This man took you away from your families by force. He wants to sell you to wicked people far away from here." Mike pleaded with the children, who were now even more confused than before.

Maybe Sergeant Rook is right," said Donny Stevens. The children—confused from their *'conditioning'* while at the compound—began taking tentative steps towards Rook. Mike and Audra glanced at each other. "What now?" their eyes seemed to plead. Bobby stood frozen, as even he pondered the words

Rook had just said. Bobby—still held by Sergeant Rook—shifted his weight just a bit, thinking some uncomfortable thoughts. Then his nose caught a familiar scent coming from Rook's hand and face. Why hadn't Bobby notice this scent before? Maybe he had just not thought about it, if he had encountered it before at the compound. Maybe he had never been close enough to Rook to notice it before now. Or, it even could be … maybe … that Rook had somehow chosen this day to wear it for the first time since Bobby's abduction. Whatever the reason, he now became fully aware of the aroma that was busily triggering a distinct memory. It was a sweetly odorous spicy smell … the scent of the *'Old Spice'* he remembered Mike wearing at times—until, that is, Audra had gifted him with her favorite men's cologne. Bobby, while no connoisseur of colognes, recognized this scent all too well.

Bobby's full senses were coming back to him. He recalled how angry he had been at Mike, when his captors led him to believe that Mike was involved in—had allowed—his abduction. He was sure now that Mike had nothing to do with his abduction, and he also knew why. The man who had taken him away from Mike this very moment now held Bobby in his evil grip; he knew it … he smelled him … he could not mistake Rook's odor for anything else. Suddenly Bobby let out a piercing cry, *"You,* Sergeant Rook! *You're* the one who took me from Mike! It was *you* who kidnapped me that day in the Huachuca Mountains! You dirty liar!"

Then to the children—emboldened by his discovery—Bobby shouted, "Hey, everybody! My brother is right! We were forced here! Our families did not deliver us to them, or make us come here for *'special training.'* I know, because Sergeant Rook kidnapped me! Didn't you Sergeant Rook … *didn't* you?" screamed Bobby.

Rook stood there, dumbfounded. The children respected and loved Bobby. He stood out as their leader. The children frowned at Rook, as they tended to believe Bobby. They started yelling and screaming at the malevolent man. As they closed in on Rook, he loosened his grip on Bobby, and lifted the pressure off the bayonet. Bobby had hoped for this moment. Before Rook managed to even burble, Bobby slapped Rooks right elbow violently with the palm of his right hand. The hand that now held the bayonet loosely against Bobby's throat sprang forward and away from Bobby. Bobby instantly dropped to the floor. Mike advanced with uncanny speed, and caught Rook under the chin with a right upper cut, sending Rook backward against the wall of the corridor. Rook's head bounced viciously off the cement wall. He fell to his knees, and began to rise. His bayonet fell out of his hand and fell—*'clank'*—to the hard floor. One of the kids picked it up, and threw it as far as possible down the dimly lit corridor. It clinked, clanked, and skidded to a stop many feet away from the action.

Audra trained her Glock on the villain, though she dared not pull the trigger, for the children and Mike were busily ganging up on Rook, like a swarm of mad killer bees on an aggressive intruder. Audra could find no way to take a clear shot. The children jumped on the man who had dared to take them away from their beloved families. They kicked and punched Rook wildly. Rook managed to toss some of the children to the side, and reach his *AK-47* assault rifle. He took aim at Donny Stevens and pulled the trigger—nothing. The bullet from Audra's Glock, that had hit the rifle earlier, had rendered it harmless.

Mike shouted, "You son of a...." as his right fist met Rook's face. Mike felt the skin tear, as flesh and bone gave way to a deep bloody cut. Rook fell backwards, thrusting the rifle at Donny in complete, blind anger, as he fell. Donny swiftly stepped out of the way, clutched the rifle by the stock with both hands, pulled with great force, and quickly twisted the rifle away from his body and out of Rook's hands. Rook fell forward onto the granite-like floor. Without hesitation, the children piled on top of Rook and began severely beating, kicking, scratching and biting him.

Rook screamed in agony. "Get them off me. Get them off!" Mike hesitated—seemed rather like poetic justice to him. "Ah-h-h ... help me!" screamed Rook.

Audra dashed to the scene. "Children, stop! Stop, before ... before you turn completely into one of *them*. Don't stoop to their hideous level!" Audra aimed the Glock at the wretched creature that was now beneath the swarm of angry children. The kids stopped battering Rook, and turned to Audra.

Mike looked down at the pitiful creature. "You don't know how much I want to kill you. I wish you would try to make a move ... do anything to give me an excuse ... so I can take the pleasure, you bastard!" shouted Mike.

Rook panted, breathing heavily, as he lay on the floor. Blood poured from deep cuts, tears and gashes in his face, arms, head and neck. His left eye oozed with blood and clear fluid. Apparently, one of the kids had almost gouged his eye out. "I don ... I don't feel right," he moaned. More blood gushed from his neck, in time with his pulse. Mike looked down at his enemy. He actually felt pity for the fool, whose gash in his neck was gaping, wide and ugly.

Mike turned back to the children. "Let's go, kids. Let's go home ... for sure, this time." Mike sounded weary, but relieved ... thinking it would all soon be over.

Rook took in a deep breath, mustered up all the strength he had in him, and lunged at Suzy, who had dared speak up, as he held Bobby in his grip. This vociferously mad man was not about to give up, in spite of his having sustained near-fatal wounds. "Ah-h-h ... you witch! I'll kill you ... *all* of you!" Instinctively, Audra raised the Glock—*'Bam!'* The shot echoed throughout the chambers. Two words entered Rook's mind before he keeled over and died: "The Bit ...!"

The children sprang to their feet. Behind them lay the body of a man whom they had thought was a good man; they felt little remorse for the man they had thought cared for them, having learned the attention they had received from him was based on nothing more than selfish, mercenary desires. Now his vile intention was to shoot them all ... a desire expertly thwarted by Audra's quick instinctive reflexes.

"Come on! We have to get to the trucks. Now!" screamed Audra, as she helped Mike lead the children out onto the loading dock. They all ran into the huge garage, which actually looked more like a warehouse, where they found themselves looking straight into the eyes of five men, barricading the wide entrance of the large garage. Standing front and center of the armed men was Deputy Jeff Seagle. Seeing him—one who had purported to be his friend—made Mike's blood run cold.

Four of Montiego's men walked cautiously into the conference room where the insane bloody massacre had taken place. They looked around, and saw nothing much but puddles of blood on the floor, and red-stained walls. Bodies of dead men lay on the floor, or draped over the office furniture. They slowly began poking the bodies with their bayonets. When they got to Cal, he opened his eyes. As he let go of his hand grenade, and watched it roll under the men's feet, he said, "Surprise! This is how we welcome our guests in these parts. Welcome to the United States!" The men raised their assault rifles, and were about to fire, when one of the men saw a metal object roll under his feet. He screamed at the others, "Get out!" and lunged for the door himself, but the warning was too late. The grenade exploded, burying hot shrapnel and debris deep into the bodies of all four men.

Manuel heard the explosion as he ran. "Good bye, Cal," said Manuel, as he hurried to the entrance. He saw Colonel Heyburn ahead of him, scurrying his way. "Go back, Colonel! Send your men back!" Manuel held up the transmitter. Pat took a good look at it, and immediately shouted, "Men! Retreat—get out of the cavern—*now!* It's gonna blow!" The men saw the look of horror on Colonel Heyburn's face, as he kept shouting the words, '*Retreat! Get out of the cavern!*' at them. They did an immediate about-face, ran back out of the cavern, and dove behind rocks and brush. Colonel Heyburn soon joined them. As Manuel dove out of the cavern, he pressed the button on the transmitter while his body was still airborne. The electronic detonators on the bombs lit up. The huge explosion rocked the entire cave, and shook the ground beneath the feet of the Colonel and his men.

Montiego's troops were hopelessly trapped. Large limestone boulders, and huge stalactites and calcite columns fell upon the men, instantly killing them and pinning them to the ground. Huge balls of reddish-orange and blue flames engulfed all the men inside the cavern. The dazed and confused men scarcely knew what had hit them. Some died painlessly, in a molten pile of rock and rubble. Others screamed in horror and agony, as hot flames melted the flesh off their faces and arms. Smoke and flame belched out of the mouth of the cave. The entrance shook and crumbled, and a huge column fell upon the train that sat in front of the station, crushing it to the ground.

Just moments before the blast, a sizeable gap led into the cave. Now, a hole just big enough for a man to crawl through remained. Manuel sat up, and looked around him. He saw the bodies of Agents and American soldiers sprawled out over the ground ... men and women who had given their lives for the greatest cause he could think of. They had given their lives for the back-bone of America ... her precious children. As Manuel sat there, thinking of getting up and surveying his surroundings, he found himself struggling to get up. Something was dreadfully wrong! Colonel Heyburn walked over to Manuel, and looked down at his brave friend and ally. Pat saw red fluid flowing from Manuel's side. When the bombs went off, they had sent many objects flying through the air. Pieces of rock, metal, and rebar became deadly bullets and missiles. A piece of hot, deadly, half-inch rebar had rocketed through the air and speared Manny in the back, as he lunged out of the cavern. The narrow rod had entered his lower back and exited out his front left lower quadrant.

Manuel looked up at Pat. "I am ... I ... I ... I don't feel so good, Colonel. Do you think ... think it's ... it's too ... too late for me?" His speech became labored.

"Too late? Medic! Get me a medic ... *now!*" hollered the Colonel. One of the Colonel's men crept over to the Colonel's side and said, "I'm sorry, Sir. We underestimated the resistance. We only had one medic with us, and I'm afraid he took a lethal hit from a bullet during the battle."

"Damn!" Pat turned to Manuel. "Hang in there, Manuel ... just hang in there. The Colonel took off his shirt, and ripped it to pieces with his strong hands. He applied the torn cloths to Manuel's wound. "You'll make it, Manuel. I'll hold these compresses on you all the way to the hospital, if I have to!"

Manuel nodded, to thank the Colonel, as he was becoming a bit weak. He looked into Pat's eyes and—in spite of how weak he was—felt he had to say what he was thinking. "You know, you remind me of my father, Colonel. He was a strong man ... a preacher ... who obeyed God. He also was a ... a very fair man. He fought hard for people ... like you do, Pat."

Manuel began to drift away. "Manny, don't try to talk too much. Save your strength. I'll have you safe in the waiting arms of a pretty nurse in no time," Pat promised, praying with everything in him that he could keep that promise.

Manuel groaned, "Listen, Pat, the night we planned ... all this ...'you remember I gave you ... my sister's number?" he inquired, as he fought for every breath.

"Yes, of course, I do."

"You must remember ... to call her. Tell her you need ... those maps and papers ... in the box under my floor ... back *home* ... in La Palo. She knows where it is." Manuel had to pause, as he'd been talking quite a bit. "It has all the locations and ... and names of the camps ... camps the children have been taken to ... over all these years. You ..." Manuel hesitated again, as he tried to gather more strength, "You may be able to ... to save many of them, Colonel." Manuel took in a few more deep breaths, and then he began talking a bit oddly.

"My father once told me a story ... a story from the Bible ... about a man who ... who killed very good people. I think his name was Paul. He did many bad things, 'cause ...'cause he thought he was doing ... the right thing." Manuel coughed. "I've done many ... many bad things, too. I feel like Paul. 'You think I ...?"

Pat was no theologian, but he did believe in forgiveness. "Manuel, as far as I know, God loves anybody that calls on Him."

Manuel's body jerked some, as he coughed again, and choked. "Father ... mi Dios ... forgive me," Pat heard him whisper. These were Manuel's last words, as he slipped away from the land of the living and into eternity.

"Damn!" Pat exclaimed, deeply disappointed. Men, see to it that this man's body is well taken care of. He was one of the bravest, most intelligent ... and noblest men I have ever known." The Colonel, not wanting his men to see the tears welling up in his eyes, walked slowly away from this tragic scene.

Mike could not believe his eyes. He felt sick ... disgusted. "What a day full of surprises this has been already!" he thought, "... and it's barely halfway through." Before him stood someone he'd thought of as a friend ... clearly aligned with the enemy. He inquired of Deputy Seagle, "So, you sold your soul to the devil, huh, Jeff?"

"Devil? I don't believe in fairytales. Look, Mike, I tried my best to warn you to stay out of it, but you just wouldn't let it go."

"I thought you were on my side, Jeff," Mike spoke with disdain.

"I was, Mike. I didn't want it this way. I thought if I patronized you, I could lead you off the trail. I knew you wanted to find your little brother so badly, that you'd try anything to get him back. I hoped you would fall for the note, but no; you were too brilliant for that."

Mike studied every inch of his situation and, from his angle, he saw no way out.

"Okay, hot shots! I'm through talking. Drop your weapons, and kick them over to us, now. I mean it! Do it *now* ... unless you want to watch some of these children drop, instead!" shrieked Jeff, loudly. He relished the position of power he held over his hapless, unlucky victims. One of the hired gunmen trained his *AK-47* on the children.

Mike looked hatefully at Jeff. "You're a slimy, wormy little maggot. I'll bet you would shoot a child, and laugh about it later. I thought you had a family, Jeff."

Jeff scoffed. "Hardly! I just told you that to win your trust. These brats are no skin off my chin."

Regardless of what Jeff said, Mike, Audra and Matt knew the children were worth money to these wicked men. If they gave into their wishes, the children would indeed be spared. They also sensed Jeff's cold, cruel nature. They were beaten. They had given it their best but—in the end—their best was not good enough. Mike slowly dropped his weapon to the ground.

"What was your role in all this? Since I know you're going to kill me, anyway, why not tell me?"

Jeff liked boasting about himself, so he felt honored by Mike's request. "Four words can sum up my role: 'Keep the law away.' You know what a deputy makes?"

"No," said Mike.

"Not enough. I make more money in one month, in this racket, than I do in an entire year with the Department," laughed Jeff.

"Yeah, a real dirty cop. What about the Sheriff?" asked Mike, as he, Audra and Matt kicked their weapons over to the gunmen. The children stood silent, once again dazed, scared and confused. Some were crying a little ... they wanted to feel safe ... they wanted it all to end. They wanted to go home.

"The Sheriff, huh?" Jeff smirked. "You really thought he was in on it, didn't you? Naw, the old man's too straight. But, he did come in handy. You see, the Mayor persuaded the Sheriff to pull the dogs away from the rocks that were concealing the tunnel. He told the Sheriff that he didn't want the media and the public to believe we have incompetent dogs."

Mike lowered his head for a moment, and stared at the cement floor. All along, he had really thought the Sheriff played a corrupt part in the conspiracy. Mike had misjudged Tress, and felt sorry for this misjudgment. But then ... then he remembered the torn cloth from Bobby's shirt. Mike looked up at Jeff.

"Okay, if—as you say—the Sheriff is not in on this, why then did he switch the cloth from Bobby's shirt with another piece of cloth?"

"Well, Mike … I'd say he merely forgot which shirt pocket he had put it in. You must have seen our forgetful Sheriff pull the wrong rag out of his shirt pocket just before the paramedics shot you full of dope. He finally realized he had pulled the wrong piece of cloth out of his shirt pocket, and got the right one out. But you didn't know about that, because you were too busy visiting 'Never-Never Land'," laughed Jeff.

"You must think you're very clever," said Mike.

"Hey, not that I'm bragging but—as you are fully aware by now—I'm not the one who's about to eat a few rounds from an AK-47 for breakfast," Jeff roared in triumph.

Two of Jeff's hired gunmen were in the process of reaching for the weapons the trio had kicked over to them, when the sound of fully automatic rifles filled the air. In less than three seconds, all five deviates had collapsed on the ground, their bodies riddled full of holes by M-16 U.S. assault rifles. Six dark figures rappelled straight down from the rafters above them. They moved like sleek, dark panthers stalking their prey, as they probed the bodies of the men. After making sure the area was secure, one of the men dressed in a dark uniform said, "United States Rangers, Specialist Thomas Kelley at your service."

"My father sent you!" Audra exulted, with much relief and appreciation.

"Yes, Ma'am! The Colonel told us you might need a little assistance, after all. We arrived and took our positions shortly after you entered the compound. We also notified the local authorities." It was then that they noticed the sirens screaming in the distance, as they neared the compound.

"Bloody sounds like the cavalry is on the way, also," hooted Matt. Squad cars flooded the scene, and surrounded the complex. Raymond bolted out from his vehicle. He scanned the area carefully, as he approached the Rangers and the people inside the compound.

The Chief of Police himself strolled over to where the children and their rescuers were gathered. He looked at the children. Many thoughts raced through his mind, most of them about how he wished he would have known about the compound years ago. He finally spoke. "It is very difficult to believe something like this has been happening for so long, right in our own backyard! Raymond, you are to be commended."

Raymond looked at Mike and Audra. "No, Chief. Mike, his friends, and our Rangers are the heroes."

Mike piped up, "No, the real heroes are all these wonderful children you see here before you!"

The children roared, as did the police and the Rangers. Specialist Kelley shouted, "Children, lead the way!" At these words, everyone present shouted, and cheered even louder.

Chapter Twenty-six

The time: 2100 hours, the location: top secret U.S. military base, Camp Cocoa, in southern Costa Rica, north of Panama. Colonel Heyburn walked before a small group of military officers, made up mostly of Captains and Lieutenants. A Sergeant First Class called out loudly, "Group, *ah*-ten-*shun!*" Immediately, the soldiers stood at attention, and saluted. Colonel Heyburn looked at the men, all tough and ready ... men specially groomed and trained by Elite U.S. Military Intelligence and Special Forces. Among these Elite Officers stood the six Rangers that had assisted the Colonel during *'Operation Dumpster Dive.'* The Colonel liked what he saw. "At ease, men. Take your seats," he then roared.

"Men, you have been briefed already. There is not much more I can say. You already know your company will be split into separate platoons, and trans-ported to designated areas within the periphery of several South American nations, which include Venezuela, Brazil, Bolivia, Colombia and Peru. I have been informed that you and all your men know your directives by rote. You have memorized the maps, and locations—I hope you have—for this is a very serious assignment, and a very brave man sacrificed his life, delivering this information to us." A vision of Manuel Martinez flashed through the Colonel's mind.

Colonel Heyburn continued, "Do not underestimate the enemy. You are, for all practical purposes, entering a hostile forward area. If you allow yourself to be caught, you may be shot. This is a highly classified military covert operation to rescue what rightfully belongs to us ... our children. I want you to put your-self in the shoes of the men and women that have lost their children to the evil enemy you are about to encounter today. They have no conscience, and they hate you. They stole our children from us, and one of their top agendas is to weaken us ... even if it means using our own children against us.

"Now, you and your men will parachute below radar from A400 military transport planes. The public has been told that these planes were to sit on the shelf until 2010, but a fleet is at our disposal now, compliments of the UN. These planes, as you know, are equipped to carry over one hundred fully geared and armed soldiers. Your task is to subdue the enemy, and render them completely defenseless. Only certain, highly trusted, government officials within these nations know of our mission. This is one of the reasons for the shallow drop. The other reason is that intelligence suggests that the syndicate maintains a radar system of some sort, however primitive it may be. Once the enemy is disabled, we will notify the government officials and their nations—then we can fly at normal altitudes.

You will not need worry about a long-term assignment; this is an in-and-out mission. Once we obtain our primary objective, we are to alert the Navy. The USS Reagan, Eisenhower and Roosevelt are sitting in international waters, not far off the coast of Peru. They are sailing a bit light, gentlemen, because we need all the deck space and quarters' space that we can get. As you know, God willing, we may find ourselves airlifting thousands—even tens of thousands—of abducted United States citizens to safety aboard these carriers. If we have to fill the skies with every chopper we have to retrieve our kids, then so be it. I hope that many will be transported to this base, where C-5 cargo planes will be waiting to take our kids home from here.

"Once the Navy is alerted, they will fly in the *CH-47D/MH-47E Chinook* heavy-lift helicopters. From here, the MI-26 cargo choppers will suffice.

"This is a nighttime operation. Keep your heads clear and remain alert. These filthy child molesters may not be well trained, but they are not to be underestimated. According to Intelligence HQ, they are not one bit aware of what is about to befall them, so we do have the advantage of total surprise.

"Men, look at these Rangers behind you." The officers turned and gazed upon the six men. "I want you to remember, *'Operation Just Cause.'* Before the red dawn, members of the 75th Ranger Regiment were deployed in Panama, where they surrounded and captured Manuel Noriega. They were in and out. They sustained no casualties. Some of you refer to these men as yearlings ... men that want to be important cogs in the machinery of the Special Forces, to which you, Officers, already belong. If the Rangers can do it, I believe you, Elite Officers—and your men—can, too.

"This mission is very special. *'Operation R-O-C,'* or *'Operation ROC(k),'* if you will—Rescue Our Children—must not fail. It will not fail. I will be joining you in this mission, for this involves some of the most—if not *the* most—consequential military operations in our history." The Colonel looked into the eyes of the Officers, with utmost gravity. "Gentlemen, do you have what it takes? Are you ready, and motivated, to kick the butts of these cowards that have abducted our American children? Are you ready to beat the snot out of these poor excuses for men, who get off on pushing around little children, and molesting our little ladies?" The men stood up and shouted their anger in unison. They could hardly wait to get their hands on the hideous creatures who had stolen their kids!

"I'll see you on the landing strip. Godspeed, men ... let's show these 'low-lives' no mercy. Our little men and women are counting on us. I, for one, am not about to let them down!" bellowed the Colonel. "Move on out!" shouted the Colonel. The men charged out of the room and raced to their assigned platoons.

At 2145 hours, the A400 military transport planes rolled into position. One plane after another took to the dark skies above, heading south to their destinations. Soon these fearless soldiers from the skies would drop upon their unaware and unsuspecting foes. The soldiers were pumped and more than motivated for this mission.

The *Elite* soldiers did not say much as they neared the drop sites, but in their minds, they saw the enemy before them. They heard the cries of their beloved little young men and ladies calling out for help. One of the soldiers chanted aloud,

"You can mess with the best, and put us to the test, but
when you mess with our children, get ready for your death."

Soon all the soldiers were chanting these words, as they tightly clutched their M-16s until their knuckles turned white.

Annette tossed in her bed; it was the wee hours of the morning. Days ago, Colonel Heyburn had spoken with her about Manuel and the battle that had taken place. Annette was more than willing to help Colonel Heyburn. She had found the paperwork identifying the campsites just where Manuel had said they would be, scanned the information into Manuel's PC from his house outside La Palo, and then emailed the information to Colonel Heyburn. She was eternally grateful to learn from Pat Heyburn that her brother had died honorably, with a prayer on his lips.

In the early morning hours, after the prop planes carrying the American soldiers had lifted off the ground, hoping to rescue America's greatest treasure, Annette Martinez lay in bed, staring up at her bedroom ceiling in the little village of La Palo. Her mind was once again troubled, and full of remorse, as she focused on Manuel. She heard the sound of turboprops from a low-flying plane approaching. She jumped out of bed and ran outside. She stood near the chapel her father had built, as an A400 flew overhead. "Get them! Get them all

... for Manuel ... for the children!" she shouted. Tears filled her eyes, as she watched the plane disappear into the night.

"We have a visual on a potential drop site fifty nautical miles bridge side," shouted the pilot of the A400.

A tall captain ordered his men to prepare for the drop. The men all stood up, as they held onto the side of the plane. "We're jumping from one-hundred-and-twenty feet. 'Piece of cake. Get ready for hook-up, men. It's *'Geronimo'* time!

One of the soldiers turned to his buddy and said, "Next stop, men's lingerie!"

"Shut up, and move on!" shouted his friend.

"Hey, you know my butt always itches before a shallow drop like this."

"'You know what you are?"

"What?"

"You're the main character in the last chapter of the book entitled, *What's the use*?"

"Now you've hurt me ... you've really hurt me," said the soldier who had started the repartee, as he hooked onto the static line, checked the chinstrap on his helmet, and began his jump. He rolled into a fetal position, waiting for the heavy yank from the line. The line extended a short ways, then yanked the soldier's entire back piece of his T10 parachute packtray. The 50-pound break cord, woven in and out of loops on the main packtray exploded—*'Kawoosh!'* The top piece pulled off, exposing the entire canopy and lines at once! The top piece stayed with the static line, trailing out the jump door. The full force of the wind inflated the canopy, and extended the stretch-out lines, almost instantly. The soldier landed on the ground a bit harshly, but was soon up and running.

In less than fifteen minutes, the entire small platoon had located each other and fallen behind the tall captain. The captain looked at his men, "Okay, José! We park ourselves until we hear from the Colonel. We are all moving in simultaneously, so these suckers won't be able to relay any message to another camp."

"Where are we, Captain?" asked one of the soldiers.

"Somewhere in Bolivia," replied the captain, as he searched the area with his strong night-vision binoculars. "I see signs of the road ahead leading to the camp. 'Knock, knock, maggots; we're about to huff and puff, and blow you to hell!'" exclaimed the Captain. The men fell at ease, and waited.

As the men waited for the Colonel's signal, many other drops were taking place in remote areas of Peru, Venezuela, Colombia and even Brazil. Almost forty more minutes had passed before the Colonel's signal came through to the Captain in Bolivia. His cell phone vibrated. The Captain laughed as he answered the phone. "No, Sir, I wasn't laughing at you. I didn't expect a phone call. I thought you'd use one of our expensive radios. I'm just laughing at the situation." The Captain paused. "Yes, we are ready." He paused again, as Colonel Heyburn offered more instructions. "Yes, we will commence *'Operation ROC'* in ten minutes. Understood."

The Colonel spoke clearly into the phone. "All other platoons have been notified. They are all ready to engage the enemy."

"Apparently, we were the last platoon to drop," the Captain commented.

"Okay, Captain Greer, pump up your men. In ten minutes I want that camp liberated!"

"Aye, aye, Colonel. We aim to please, Sir!" The Captain hung up and then relayed the message to his men. They arose, and disappeared into the darkness.

At approximately 0130 hours, all platoons simultaneously—and swiftly—raided the camps, striking with the lightning speed of deadly cobras. Before the enemy soldiers could raise a rifle barrel to fire, they soon found themselves surrounded by American Elite Special Forces soldiers. Other men spread out and were busy locating many American children, whom the wicked men had been using as slaves, or special servants. Some discovered a few young American men toting *AK-47s*. They had been briefed about this possibility, and told what to say.

One *Green Beret* looked at the young American soldiers, who believed they were on a special assignment for their country. "Sir, this mission is over!" he shouted. The young abducted Americans looked at the soldier before them. Here stood another American ... a true *Elite* soldier. In their minds, they thought they were on a true mission. When they heard the soldier's words, they lowered their assault rifles, and saluted their fellow American soldiers. "Men, we need you back home now. Come on, let's go home. Our families are waiting."

Colonel Heyburn raced over to a building that looked like a confinement center of some kind. Kelley, one of the Rangers, watched his back as he planted a small explosive on the lock of the door. As the small bomb exploded, the doors flew open. Two guards that worked for the syndicate fired round after round at the smoking entrance, then they ran outside to see where the dead men lay, but they found no bodies. "Up here, *slime* balls!" hollered the Colonel. They turned swiftly to fire at Pat and Kelley. The Colonel and the Ranger beat them at the trigger, riddling them with bullets. The kidnappers fell to the ground. Colonel Heyburn fished out a flash grenade as Kelley joined him at his side.

Then the Colonel saw the figure of a young man holding an *AK-47* in his hands. The young man looked at the two American soldiers and said, "Surrender now, or I'll shoot!" Pat saw Kelley's hand move slowly to his side as he whispered, "I can take him in a heart beat. The way he holds his rifle indicates he hasn't been trained any better than these other idiots."

"Stay your hand, Kelley. I know this man."

Kelley became confused. How could the Colonel know someone he had never seen before? "You what?" whispered Kelley.

He's my son! I knew he would be here; that's why I chose this camp." Pat looked into Todd's eyes.

"Todd, your mission's over, son. I'm here to take you home."

Todd turned a bit scarlet, then he spoke. "Your voice sounds familiar, especially when you called me *'son.'* Are you Americans?"

"Yes, we are. You were sent here on a mission, weren't you?"

"Yes."

"They told you that you were chosen especially for this mission?"

"Yes." Todd saw something familiar about the man that stood before him. His mind played back his past. The man's face looked very familiar, and it filled an empty place in his mind. "Father?" Todd said, with an incredulous pitch to his voice.

Pat had not heard this precious name from Todd in many long years. His eyes began to water as he said, "Yes, Todd, I am your father ... Colonel Patrick Heyburn. And, you are my son, Todd Heyburn. There are two lovely women waiting for you back home."

Todd lowered his assault rifle, sounding relieved. "Then this mission is really finally over."

Pat looked lovingly at his son. "Yes, it is all over ... completely and forevermore. Let's go home, son." Todd ran into the arms of his father. Though he may have been brainwashed, he still knew deep inside him that his family loved him very much. They embraced each other, as tears rolled down their cheeks. Kelley thought about his own little son at home. He, too, found himself wiping a tear from his face.

Todd pulled back and looked into his father's eyes. "Pa, is the mission over for all of us?"

"Yes, son, it sure is."

Todd looked at the dead men. "I thought these men were on our side."

Pat knew just what to say. "They were in a way, but they turned against us. They attacked us back home. They tried to kill your sister and me, but we won. Now it's time to win here."

"You've got to follow me. Let's get the rest of the children." Todd ran ahead of them, as Pat and Kelley followed. He led them to a well built square building. "This is an underground bunker. Many children are down there, but so are the Brazilians. I can get inside, but I hope you guys are really good, 'cause I don't think they'll surrender without a battle," Todd warned.

Pat looked at his son proudly. "Lead the way, Son!"

Kelley spoke up, "Now, that's a new one, *'Lead the way, Son.'* Rangers always lead the way!"

"No, not this time, Ranger," laughed Pat. Todd opened the door and stepped into the bunker. An angry enemy soldier greeted him. The evil man started to lift his assault rifle, when a sharp object unexpectedly sank into his throat. He dropped his weapon, and clutched his throat.

Kelley raced over to the man and twisted the bayonet buried in the man's neck. "As I said, Rangers lead the way!"

"Okay, Ranger, lead the way," quipped the Colonel.

Kelley laughed, saluted the Colonel and said, "With pleasure, sir." They hurried down into the bunker. Kelley was just about to turn into a passageway, when he heard someone talking.

"Come on, little soldier girl. Give daddy a little sugar and spice." One of the wicked abductors was trying to coax a young American girl to acquiesce to his lasciviousness. The girl bit the man's hand as hard as she could. Blood spurted from his wrist, as he pulled his pistol from his side holster. "Why, you little...." then he fell to the ground, clutching his throat; Kelley's bayonet had again found its target.

"You're very good with that," said Todd.

"All of us Rangers know how to throw around a bayonet. Actually, it's a hobby of mine," Kelley responded.

The rescued girl just looked at Pat. She was crying and very scared. Pat looked at the young lady with caring eyes. He thought of Audra, as he looked gently into her eyes and said, "Honey, we're the United States Army, and we're taking you home to be with your mom and dad."

She looked up and smiled broadly. "'You really mean it? I'm going home!" She waved her hands in the air, as Pat reached down and hugged her.

Three men came around the corner of the corridor towards the four Americans. Pat quickly pulled the pin from his flash grenade, swept the girl into his arms, and shouted, "Hit the ground and close your eyes!" *'Kabla-a-am!'* the grenade went off, filling the corridor with super intense light. The evil soldiers fell to the ground, groping and crawling around like helpless blind men.

Pat, Kelley, Todd and the twelve-year-old girl ran past the guards and stormed into the rooms inside the bunker. When they entered the rooms, they encountered many American children. "It's truly unbelievable. It's wonderful and horrible at the same time!" exclaimed Pat.

"I know what you mean," replied Kelley. Soon Pat and Kelley, with the help of Todd and some of the older children, rounded up the remaining kids in the bunker. The children quickly rushed after the Colonel, Kelley and Todd, as they led the way out of the bunker. Todd and Pat stormed out, together shooting at half-drunken guards, and dodging bullets. Kelley tossed several hand grenades into a group of angry sentries, which blew up into small pieces of hot metal that felled most of the guards. Todd and his father fired their assault rifles at the remaining guards. The atmosphere grew quieter. Only a few shots could be heard now, coming from the jungle where the cocoa trees grew. Soon many American and Brazilian children rushed out of the thick brush and trees. Their cheers became loud roars, as American soldiers escorted them into the camp. The Brazilian children were eager to go home, and the American children clung to the men, their saviors.

It was a day to be remembered throughout time. The American Special Forced had simultaneously stormed more than thirty syndicate-operated camps, and liberated the young captives. Only ten American soldiers sustained wounds. Not one child or American soldier perished in *'Operation ROC.'* The skies were clouded with large Chinook heavy-lift helicopters, which were modified to transport one-hundred-and-twenty children each, after they were stripped of their heavy weapons, vehicles and equipment. Many *MI-26s, MI-8s,* and other heavy cargo choppers were also sent in to aid in the airlift. Together, each camp had averaged between twenty-five hundred and four thousand American children. Most were slave camps. However, some were special camps set up to brainwash and train young American boys and girls who had demonstrated military potential. These were the children General Montiego and his foreign associates had planned to use in their diabolical plot to infiltrate the United States.

The massive airlifts continued throughout the morning and into the evening. Never had there been such a rescue operation of this magnitude. Many children were flown onboard the carriers, as some of the cargo helicopters had flown in from these large ships; however, the majority of the cargo choppers that flew into South America had come from regions north of the Panama Canal. Children were then airlifted to cooperative airstrips in South America, and boarded C-130 turboprop cargo planes, and huge C-5 jet cargo carriers. When viewed from below, it looked like an all-out air strike from the United States.

In many exurbias throughout South America, the day had started like any other day. Women brought their men and young little children water and what little food they could muster to the fields. Outside cities such as Bogotá, Colombia; Puerto Ayacucho, Venezuela; Cochabamba, Bolivia; Lima, Peru and as far south as Paraguay, poor, hard-working villagers—men and women, like Pedro's family in La Palo—worked what little land they had with cut up and calloused hands. Not too many people wore smiles in these villages ... nor did one child over ten years of age walk the village streets. The evil General—and greedy, wicked syndicate leaders like him—had stolen their greatest treasures, abducted and put them to work in the jungles harvesting cocoa beans, leaves and coffee ... leaving the people with nothing but broken hearts.

Since this had happened, the men, women, and younger children, who were still at home, worked side by side. Sometimes they lifted their weather-beaten faces and looked out over the village ... as if they were hoping to see their children returning ... while tears fell from their eyes. They remembered the beautiful days when the laughter of children filled the pueblo; but not today ... maybe never again. They missed their sons and daughters bitterly. What could they do? Their government feared the syndicate; they dare not cause waves, lest the syndicate rise up against the government, and end the lives of the puppets that walked the corridors of official buildings, and pretended to be for the people.

"Jorgito, let me have the hoe now; we need to get back to work. The cotton will not weed itself," said a poor farmer to his son, as they returned to work from a short siesta. Little Jorgito obeyed, bending over and lifting the hoe from the ground. His father looked upon his son with saddened eyes. He feared the day might come when the evil men would take Jorgito from him. The people were so poor and defenseless; what could they do? His thoughts were brought back to the present, when the sound of a large cargo helicopter was heard, its blades noisily slicing the air above. The huge chopper landed in a clear patch of land near them.

Once on the ground, American soldiers stepped out of the chopper, and began helping the village children from the chopper down to the ground. The people dropped their hoes and sickles and ran to the children. They saw familiar faces all around them. Oh, what a blessed day, what a glorious jubilant day it was! The little *muchachos* and *muchachas* raced into the waiting arms of their grateful parents. The people lifted up their faces to heaven as they gave thanks, with tears of great joy running down their cheeks. The children cried out, "We're home, Mama! We're home, Papa! The brave soldiers from the United States found us, and brought us home."

The American soldiers stood tall and proud near the villagers. The people gathered around the brave soldiers. Tears filled their eyes as they shouted, *"USA, USA, USA!"* The soldiers smiled, and humbly bowed before the people. Most of the soldiers joined in the celebration. They danced with the children, and hugged them tightly. Then they took to the skies again to deliver more children to their rightful families. Scenes such as this were taking place all over the entire continent of South America. People danced and laughed throughout the land. The United States, and all the nations of South America, recognized this day as the *National Independence Day for Children*.

When the children from the United States once again set their feet on home soil, they were not only greeted by a huge host of members from the media, but thousands upon thousands of US citizens also cheered them on. People from all over the nation roared and cheered for their young little heroes, as they stepped off the carriers and the planes.

The National Guard escorted the children to hospitals throughout Orange County, California, and in other states, for check-ups. While some did arrive ill, and a few others were a bit malnourished, the majority arrived back home healthy, and extremely eager to see their families. The joy experienced by the waiting family members was unimaginable. This wonderful, pure, incomparable joy swept the entire nation, and even spilled over into many other countries near and far. The globe seemed like a warm ball of hope and love for days.

When the company of soldiers arrived in the United States days later, they, too, stood in awe at the masses around them. Streamers and confetti floated down from overhead. Only the return trip from World War II could have matched this celebration. Fireworks lit the skies, as cannons roared. The exuberant celebration that had taken place when the children fist arrived back home had begun all over again. Colonel Patrick Heyburn—and his son, Todd—stood on stage amidst a very large, extremely happy crowd. After the Colonel had recognized the crowd, and given a short, very upbeat, briefing of their major success in South America, Todd and Pat hugged each other in front of over 265 million cheering Americans. Tears flowed from the eyes of millions that day, for they felt the dawn of a new, hopeful day. Their government had brought back to them the greatest gift a country could ever wish for ... they had brought America back many of her missing—and sorely missed—children.

On a warm, sunny Sunday in Tucson, Arizona, Todd, Audra, Mike, Bobby, and—of course—Colonel Pat Heyburn walked into the room of Mrs. Rhonda Heyburn. Mike whispered to Audra that he was feeling a little awkward about visiting her mother during such a tender reunion. Audra responded that, as far as they were concerned, he was family. After all, Todd might not even be home now if it had not for Mike, and his unflagging energy invested into their shared situation, even when it might mean risk to him—thinking back now to his undercarriage hitchhiking on a straight truck early in their investigation, for starters. Audra knew she could never be more right.

Rhonda Heyburn sat staring blankly at the floor below her. She said nothing, as they approached her. Audra hugged her mother. Pat stroked her hair, as both he and Audra spoke tenderly, "Mama, there is someone that loves you very, very much, who wants to see you." Tears rolled down from Audra and Pat's eyes. The doctors' hopes had come to pass. It was almost too good to be true. Even Pat could hardly believe his ears when he heard Rhonda try to speak ... the first time in so long.

Though she spoke some, Rhonda was still in somewhat of a dream state. Her mind was playing back the times when she and her son had walked on beaches, and laughed over silly movies, and apple pies. Birthday parties and Christmases of long ago filled her head, as well. She was, without any doubt, in another world. Yet she saw Todd's face just as clear as day, and was puzzled. "There he is ... right in front of me ... but he barely speaks to me," she was mumbling, though her family could not quite distinguish what it was she was trying to say.

Then she paused. Many thoughts silently raced through Rhonda's head, as she lay there. "He just looks at me ... with those pretty eyes of his. He looks older now. I always wondered what he would look like ... when he grew up to be a young man. Thank you, God, for allowing me this special privilege." Then, sensing a bit more of the reality of the situation, Rhonda's thoughts became more intense. "Oh, my! He's talking to me ... he's touching my hand ... he feels so ... so real! He is telling me he is home now ... to stay. Wait! He really ... he really *is* talking to me! His voice is very clear." Rhonda was not totally sure but what she may be seeing or hearing things that were not so, but it seemed—more than ever before, as she had lain there so long, imagining—that Todd was standing right there in front of her.

Meanwhile, Todd kept calling out repeatedly, "Mama, I love you. I'm back! Papa found me and brought me back. I was away, but I'm here to stay now, Mama."

Rhonda began mumbling again ... softly, as she had not spoken in so long. "He's warm ... and sweet. He is very handsome and tall ... like Pat. He is my ... my son!" Then the realization broke through ... and tears began to flow down her face as she finally realized that—after all these years—she was no longer dreaming, but that her son was really there ... in person. Now, she was no longer softly muttering, but spoke loudly, with excitement: "My son, you have come home! Oh! My son, my beautiful boy ... my *boy!*"

Todd's eyes swelled, as he and his Mama hugged each other tightly. Audra and Pat finally broke down and wept, having kept their emotions in check while investigating, and carrying out the children's rescue. Now they were home with the family all together ... home, where they could once again relax ...'*let it all out,*' so to speak, and those pent-up emotions readily surfaced at a time like this. Rhonda turned, and looked upon her husband and daughter. "My husband ... my precious daughter. See, God has brought Todd back home to us!" They fell into each other's arms, weeping and laughing at the same time. Audra, Todd and Pat witnessed the world stand still that day.

Mike and Bobby wept, also, and hugged each other. Mike whispered, "Come on, Bobby. Let's leave them all alone to their special miracle." Bobby nodded. The two brothers left quietly, as the Heyburns proceeded to hug and kiss on each other, sometimes talking all at once ... just, in general, enjoying the renewed company of each other. All of the family was finally together once again.

The next few days that passed saw remarkable changes in Rhonda. She became like a young girl again. She laughed heartily, as Todd helped her exercise her legs and arms, which had atrophied while in her catatonic state. However, she was coming along better than the doctors had anticipated, for love works wonders ... love brings laughter and joy ... true love wants for nothing. Indeed, true love it was that had emboldened those who had risked their lives to bring all the children home ... that which had saved Rhonda from possibly an entire lifetime of this make-believe state in which she had existed for what seemed—though it had not been—'*forever.*' Todd reached over and kissed his mother, as they continued exercising. She was enjoying it immensely ... and she was going to be fine.

Meanwhile, Audra and Mike kept dating. Bobby admired Audra

tremendously, and especially loved hearing the stories of Mike's and her cavern-prowling escapades. You could say he fell in love with her. At first, she was like a big sister but, when he found out she was six years older than Mike, he looked upon her more like the mother he'd been missing now for several years.

"So, I heard you might sign back on with the Agency. 'Guess you really impressed Jane Riley. In fact, you must have blown her away, Audra! I didn't know she was a top, *top* Agent. Yep, 'sounds like the FBI really does wants you back."

"Yeah, they gave me their utmost apologies, and practically begged me to come back." Audra could not help but boast a bit, remembering her dismissal.

"Well, I guess that means I may not be seeing very much of you?"

"That depends," Audra replied, uncertain as to exactly what her future held.

"Your *'That depends'* sounded nearly like a question," Mike noted.

"Actually, it was. You see, the Sheriff needs a seasoned deputy, now that our *'dear friend,'* Jeff Seagle, is no longer available, so—if certain people around here really want me to stick around that badly—I just might think about hiring on with our good Sheriff Tress."

Mike's eyes glowed, as he squeezed Audra closer to him. "You know what still kind of bothers me about the entire crazy mystery we were up against?"

"What?" Audra wondered aloud.

Mike kissed Audra and said, "There is still one mystery which remains."

"Ah-h-h, and what is that?" Audra returned Mike's kiss, as she asked.

"The head honcho that led the ring here in America got away," Mike said, as he once again returned the favor that had been returned by Audra.

Audra said, "Maybe he never really existed. Maybe his name was just a code word," she suggested, as she planted another kiss, this time on Mike's cheek.

"'Seemed, actually, more like they were talking about a real person." Mike returned Audra's affection, as he spoke, this becoming a playful game by now.

"I guess perhaps we'll never know," Audra replied, as she kissed Mike again.

"Yep, the *'big cheese'* got away. He's probably in the Bermudas, sipping piña coladas by now … laughing, and working out his next big, diabolical plot."

"Mike?" Audra stared into her man's eyes.

"What?" asked Mike.

"Close your eyes, keep your comments to yourself, and kiss me … really *kiss* me."

"Now, that's one demand I know I could live with," Mike chuckled heartily, as he swept Audra partially off her feet, and passionately embraced her.

Weeks passed. Mike received word that a huge celebration was going to take place at Veterans' Memorial Park in Sierra Vista … a celebration in honor of all those who had participated in rescuing the children. Mike, curious, asked the committee why they were holding it at the park in his town. They told Mike that if it weren't for him and the good people of Cochise County, this wonderful day would never have been possible. Besides, Mike was to be the guest of honor, for—the truth revealed—it had been his deep love for and devotion to his brother that really led to the capture of the evil men, and had led to the success of *'Operation ROC.'*

As the celebration time neared, Mike became a bit nervous ... and reluctant, for he believed the true heroes were the kids themselves. This gave him an idea, but he did not share it with anyone.

On a crisp, windy morning, the mill clerks informed the Superintendent of the steel plant in Clarkdale, Arizona that he had a large group of visitors waiting to see him.

"What visitors!" Suddenly he found himself surrounded by Agents from the FBI and ATF. A short, stocky man walked over to the Superintendent. "Hi there, Ben. 'Guess this is the end of the line. I wouldn't make a fuss if I were you. You see, we have some heavy guns aimed at this place. Right now, we would love the opportunity to blow this mill right off the face of the earth."

"I really don't know why I'm in trouble. I work for the government," Ben commented, naively.

"No, Ben, you only thought you did. This fact has already been taken into consideration."

A tall, attractive, tough-looking black woman walked into Ben's office. "Come. Let's all leave this death hole. This is nothing but a mill full of death and carnage.

Weasel lifted his hand, and pointed at Ben with his index finger. He lifted his thumb, signing indicative of holding a gun. "Bang, bang, your operation's dead," he intoned, sans any emotion.

Janet Riley escorted Ben out of the mill, as other Agents flooded every section of the plant. The days of manufacturing Russian weapons—or weapons of any kind—in Clarkdale, Arizona were finally over.

Just by chance ... or perhaps not ... one afternoon, as Audra, Mike and Bobby walked into a convenience store near the Intersection of Hereford Road and Highway 92, they stumbled upon Bobby's Youth Pastor, Dennis Perris. He was on his way out of the store. Bobby saw him and quickly shouted, "Hey, Big Dennis, what's up!"

Dennis seemed in a bit of a hurry but, nevertheless, he stopped and started speaking to his little admirer. "Hey, Bobby, it's great to see you! What a super surprise! I'm so glad you're back home, Little Buddy!" Mike and Audra walked over to the two carefree guys, and joined in on the conversation. They laughed and talked together for more than a few minutes.

Mike then looked at Dennis and said, "Hey, Den, why don't you come over to my place tonight? We're going to have a regular party. Well, actually it's just gonna be Audra's family and us two bachelors." Mike hugged his brother as he said, *'bachelors.'* Bobby liked this ... it gave him a grown-up feeling, being included with the men. They were all expecting Dennis to jump at the invitation, for Dennis had seemed like a new man lately ... seeming relieved to know that the authorities had finally caught the bad guys. When the children had been rescued, a large burden seemed to fall from Dennis' shoulders ... as if his soul has been freed.

Dennis laughed, and appeared as if he wanted to say 'yes,' but with reluctance in his voice, he declined, saying that he could not make it. "Actually, people, I need to go home and better organize myself for a journey on which I'm about to embark."

"Journey!" exclaimed Bobby. "Where're you going, Dennis?" not sure if his friend was going on a trip, or leaving permanently, from the sound of things.

"Well, Buddy, you see, I got a call from the East Coast. There's a company in the East requesting a good spokesperson. They liked my resume I sent to them, said they want to hire me—sight unseen, and I like the sound of the money they're offering to pay me, too."

"'Sounds good to me," Mike interjected, thinking that after all that had happened—including the Mayor for whom Dennis worked being one of the indicted parties—a change might be good for him.

"Yes, it does sound good, Mike. Anyway, they expect me to be there in a couple of weeks, so my hands have been, like, really tied up lately with the house ... packing and so forth. So, I'm afraid I just won't be able to make it tonight, Bobby ... Mike ... Audra," politely addressing each of them, as he turned down the invitation. To be honest, after all that's happened, I want to get out of here for awhile. Think about it, Mike. How would you feel, if you'd been working for a bunch of terrible people, like I was, and you didn't even know it? Then one day, you wake up to the truth. On top of that, you discover that your father—also a crook—is dead."

"Yeah, I see your point, Dennis. But, this is so sudden."

"The job offer was very sudden."

"What about your house? Is it in the process of being sold?"

"I'm leaving it in the trusty hands of a realtor."

"Well, shucks, this sure is a surprise!" Mike offered.

"Hey, I'll see you all again some day ... probably. I still want to remain active in youth ministries, so I'll be getting around from region to region ... and coast to coast."

Mike, Bobby and Audra looked a bit overwhelmed. Bobby looked up at his friend, Dennis, who—for years—had been his Youth Pastor, and Sunday

School teacher. "I'm really gonna miss you, Dennis. I'm at a loss for words!" Bobby pined, sadly.

"I'm at a loss for words, too, Bobby," laughed Dennis nervously, "and I'm the one who's leaving!"

Bobby held his hand to his forehead and saluted Dennis, *"Understood and Acknowledged,"* said Bobby, in militaristic fashion.

Dennis returned the salute. "Yes, Captain! *Understood and Acknowledged,"* he barked, in an exaggerated manner. They both laughed loudly as Dennis rubbed the palm of his hand over Bobby's dark hair.

"Well, I sure am glad I got that out today," Dennis' voice seemed to crack a bit. He rubbed his face, and bid his three friends *'Adios'* for the day. Dennis walked out the glass door, and climbed into his vehicle. The engine started. He honked his horn a few times, as he pulled out of the store's driveway.

The trio walked out of the store behind Dennis and watched his car turn right onto Hereford Road. "Strange. Why is Dennis going back to his house using Hereford Road," said Mike out loud.

"Maybe he's taking the scenic route back?" suggested Audra.

Audra and Mike had decided Dennis might just be a likeable guy, after all. They felt much better about Dennis now, in fact. Dennis had made a lot of sense by choosing to leave. Mike could understand why he needed to spread his wings. Mike turned to the others and laughed, "Well, there goes one big, funny guy."

Suddenly something clicked in Mike's mind. He turned and looked at Bobby. "You and your being *'at a loss for words,'* and then your, *'Understood and Acknowledged'* ... where did you say you got them from?" Mike was not sure if Bobby had heard them while interred within the kidnappers' compound, or if Mike had just overlooked his use of such phrases prior to this time.

"Hey, I told you way before I was even kidnapped, who I got that from. Don't you remember Mike? Dennis says it all the time," explained Bobby, unaware of its meaning, or connection, to all that had just transpired.

Mike smiled wryly, his words unconvincing, as he said, "Yeah, good ole Dennis." Then a thought entered Mike's head. Hmmm ...'*Loss of words ... Acknowledged.'* Pat told me that when a person is at a loss for words in the Army, he says, *'Hooah,'* sounding out the acronym for *'Heard, Understood, and Acknowledged'* ...'*HUA.'* 'Hooah'—spelled out phonetically, and conveniently converted into a surname—also can simply mean *'acknowledged.'*

"Oh, help us God!" Mike screamed out, in sudden awareness.

"Mike! *'Help us, God,'* what!" Audra needed to know.

Mike began repeating the thought process he had just gone through regarding Dennis, and his syndicate name. Bobby had no idea what his brother was talking about, but Audra knew.

"Come on Audra ... Bobby! We have to stop Dennis!" hollered Mike, as he coaxed Bobby over to the Jeep.

"What the heck is going on!" Bobby wanted to know, as he dashed after his brother and Audra.

Mike did not say anything. He just grabbed his cell phone and the Jeep keys from his pocket, as he bolted towards the Jeep, with Bobby and Audra running beside him. "Bobby, you stay here! Audra and I will chase down Dennis!"

"Why? What's this all about?"

"Just stay here. I'll be back soon!" Mike yelled, as he jumped into the Jeep.

"Hey, Bro, last time you left me alone, I disappeared!" shouted Bobby, fear beginning to grip him.

"On second thought, hurry! Get into the Jeep!" Bobby jumped into the Jeep, alongside Audra. Mike raced around and practically dove into the driver's seat. He started the Jeep and sped off. Mike's mind was so engrossed on catching up to Dennis, that he almost sideswiped a car when he turned out of the parking lot. The car honked unmercifully at him, as it veered off to the side of the road, successfully avoiding him.

"Hey! You don't have to kill us in the process!" shouted Audra.

"Sorry, guys. I'll do better; I promise. Audra, here, take the cell phone, and call Raymond. Maybe he's on duty. If he is, tell him what we're doing, and what road we're on." Mike gave Audra the numbers to Raymond's cell phone, then went on. "It all makes sense now. Dennis was gone on long trips many times."

Audra cut in, "Yeah, when he was gone, he was coordinating all the activities in the other time zones."

"Exactly. I don't know why I couldn't put this together sooner," said Mike, irritated with what he perceived to be his own density. He was very angry with himself for not solving this one before now.

"You couldn't figure it out, 'cause I wasn't around, Bro!" laughed Bobby, trying to figure into the equation.

"The kid's definitely got a point, Mike," said Audra. Bobby laughed, but he still didn't quite understand what was going on, though it had been he who opened Mike's eyes while speaking the phraseology taught him by—or caught from—Dennis.

Audra kept trying Raymond's number until she finally heard Raymond's voice. "Raymond, 'you on patrol now?"

"Heck yeah, but I'd rather be at a movie with Melissa."

Mike left the road for a moment. "Hey, Mike, you are trying to kill us!" screamed Audra again.

Mike looked at Bobby and Audra. "We'll be okay. 'Just a little nervous."

"'More like a *lot* nervous!" Audra protested.

"Hey, Raymond, we're after a very serious criminal here. Listen, we're heading east on Hereford Road, just off Highway 92. Can you get your guys to cover all the exits off this road?"

"Audra, who you chasing?"

"The leader of the kidnappers who was never discovered ... until now, that is!"

"I'll be danged! You have my fullest attention. 'Sounds like Mike is driving."

"Yeah, he's trying to kill us before we can catch up to the crook," Audra chuckled, nervously.

Bobby was now realizing whom they were talking about. "Dennis is a *crook?"* thought Bobby, though he spoke nothing, needing time to digest such a thought.

Raymond told Audra, as he signaled his back-ups, "Tell Mike, I owe you and him one, anyway. Thanks to you two, I got a big promo. I'll probably get another one, if you turn out to be right about this guy. So, thanks! 'Be right there."

Mike saw Dennis turn left on Moson Road. "Audra tell Raymond the suspect just took a left on Moson. Tell him we're gaining on him ... quickly!"

Audra lifted the phone to her mouth to speak again, only to hear Raymond say, "Tell Mike I caught every word he said. He has a *big* mouth," laughed Raymond.

"Raymond, I wish I could laugh with you, but this guy is probably well armed, and very dangerous!"

Overwhelmed to learn this of someone he'd so long admired, Bobby could no longer hold his silence. "Dennis, armed and dangerous!" Bobby shouted, aghast.

Raymond heard Bobby shout Dennis' name. "So, you're after the big, funny guy, huh?" jeered Raymond. "Let me tell you what...."

"Raymond!" Audra interrupted. "He may not be so *'funny'* when you have to try and subdue him. We know he is our man."

Raymond felt small for laughing at them. "Audra, look ... I'm sorry. But why don't you all just let me and the other officers handle this? We may even be able to wait until after things cool down some."

Audra interrupted Raymond. "Look, Ray! We cannot afford to do that! If we don't take him now, we'll probably never get another chance, and the brains of this operation will have gotten away for sure this time!"

"Understood! We'll cover all exits off Moson Road."

Audra looked at Bobby and Mike. She stared at Dennis' vehicle in front of them. "Thank you, Raymond. Please, try to hurry!"

Dennis saw a car closing in on him very quickly. He looked for flashing strobes. No lights or sirens came on. He knew then that it was not a patrol car. But who could it be? Then he thought of Mike. Maybe Mike had heard something back at the store that shook him up after they parted company. Dennis mulled over in his mind all he could recall of what he had said during the course of their conversation. "No, he couldn't have figured that out ... or, could he ... did he?"

Dennis sped up, but could not outrun whoever it was who was tailing him, as they soon pulled up alongside him. Dennis saw that it was Mike, frantically signaling him to pull over. Many thoughts raced through Dennis' mind as he drove. He was not an idiot. He knew Mike was not the police and, anyway, what evidence did they really have on him? None whatsoever. Even if the police did show up, they would need a search warrant to search his vehicle without good cause. Dennis lifted his foot off the accelerator to slow down, but not before Mike had had a chance to behave rather irrationally, as he reacted to Dennis' failing to stop when he had motioned for him to do so.

Making sure everyone was buckled in, Mike yelled, "Hang on! We're going for a spin!"

"Mike, we'll roll!" screamed Audra.

"That's what heavy duty roll bars are for, Sweetie!"

This did not mollify Audra much, to say the least. "Mike, you're crazy! Bobby's in the Jeep with us!" Mike acted as if he had not heard a word. He quickly overtook Dennis, and then slammed on his brakes.

"Damn you, Mike!" Dennis squealed, as he hit his brakes. It was not in time, however, to avoid smashing into the heavy metal bumper on the back of Mike's Jeep. The Jeep swerved, but Mike managed to keep it on the road, as Dennis lost control and nose-dived into the ditch. Sand, dirt and gravel flew up over the windshield of Dennis' car. He tried driving his vehicle out of the ditch, but to no avail; his spinning wheels only buried him further into the soft sand. In desperation, he kept spinning his wheels, as he tried to rock his car free.

Mike jumped out of his Jeep and started to run over to Dennis, without thinking. Then his sensibilities took over, and he stopped suddenly. "What if he has a gun?" he thought. Mike slowly, carefully began walking over towards Dennis, who was by now getting out of his car.

"What the hell are you doing, Mike? Trying to get us all killed!" Mike did not answer, but studied Dennis very carefully for any signs of a weapon.

Mike glanced inside Dennis' car. The only thing he saw worth noting was a folded map lying on the passenger seat. "Well, Dennis, you got away before I could tell you a few things that I didn't get a chance to say back at the store."

Dennis was becoming irritated now. The longer Mike held him up, the longer it would take him to get to his real point of destination. He had a meeting back East, all right, but not for a respectable job. He was to be in Miami tomorrow to coordinate the trafficking of drugs into the Gulf States.

Mike took the undiplomatic, direct approach. He thought about all the children who had died, due to this man's greed; the thought sent him into a rage. "Mr. Hooah, your days of abducting children, and trafficking drugs and weapons, end today!" screamed Mike, loudly. Bobby heard these words. So, Dennis *was* Mr. Hooah. Bobby had heard that name mentioned while at the compound.

"You blithering idiot. I'm not this Mr. Hooah!"

"Bull! You thought you could get away with it, huh, Mr. Hooah? Well, Bobby figured you out. He knows who you are and, now, so do I. You slipped up, you child-molesting pervert! You know all about the maps and symbols, the drugs and weapons trafficking, and the child abductions. 'Got t' hand it to you, Dennis … you even had me fooled for a long, long time. You diabolically misused the sacred title of *'Youth Minister'* to keep track of as many children as possible, as well as to give you the liberty of migrating from region to region … setting up your illegal trafficking centers … while you hypocritically waved *'God's Good Book'* frantically in the air!"

"You have a wild imagination, hot shot, but that's *all* you've got. You can't prove a thing. Even if I *were* this Mr. Hooah, I am much too valuable to the U.S. government to ever be held behind bars."

Mike glanced at the map on the passenger seat again—then his eyes fell on the trunk of Dennis' car. "The trunk … maybe the trunk holds proof," he thought. Mike was willing to gamble on it. He looked crossly at Dennis. "What do mean, *'If* you were Mr. Hooah'?" Not waiting for an answer, Mike motion to Audra, as he spoke. "Audra, blow the lock off Mr. Hooah's trunk!" he screamed, livid with Dennis by now.

Dennis' face turned red with rage, as Audra aimed her Glock horizontally at the keyhole. "Don't do it Audra. I have friends in very high places that help me coordinate the trafficking. How do you think we're able to code the maps and run the operation so smoothly? We have many affiliates working on the inside. I am just the tip of the iceberg. Many despots within our government arena have high-ranking seats within the Chinese and South American parties. You're all fools who do not know the danger you're in. I won't see one day behind bars. As much as you hate me and despise my presence, I am a very necessary evil in the establishment."

He took a short breath, and continued his rant. "Now, Audra, I like you, but if you touch my luxury car, I'll press very heavy charges ... and I'll see to it that you and your family all disappear ... forever! There won't be a shred of your flesh to find, let alone your meager body!" Dennis was desperately hoping that his bluff would work.

"If you think you can manage all that, then you really are a big chunk of the iceberg, not just the tip, aren't you? Well, *'Mr. Iceberg,'* your big plans just bit the dust ... melted into oblivion ... for we've hurt you badly. All your men—from grunts on up to Generals Blake and Montiego—have been killed, or incarcerated. You're worse off than when you started, and every last one of the American people is aware of the entire evil underground empire. It would take many lifetimes for anyone to even think about starting up another similar evil operation. No, you're through, Dennis, and you know it."

"Go ahead, Audra; he's just bluffing. Blow the trunk open!" screamed Mike. He squared his broad shoulders with Dennis.

"No! Don't do it! If you stop now, I'll just go on my way, and forget about all this. If you two don't back off now, I won't be responsible for the actions of my superiors. I don't run the show, you know. How do you think people like me were placed in our positions? How do you think a General took command of a small post like Fort Huachuca? In case you don't know, I'll tell you. Some of our government officials—from the ATF up to the CIA, including some of our great leaders that walk the corridors of our White House—are in cahoots with many of the world's biggest crime lords. They run the show. They call the shots ... and I can't guarantee the safety of your lives!" shouted Dennis.

"'You know what, Dennis? This is what I think of your *'guarantee'!* You're going down!" screamed Audra, as she pulled back on the trigger several times. *'Blam! Blam! Blam!'* The noise of Audra's Glock filled the night air, as the trunk flew open, exposing topographic maps, a metal briefcase and large chests. Audra pulled out one of the large chests, and shot the lock open. *'Blam! Blam!'* her Glock rang out again. She retrieved several *AK-47s*, and a few grenades. "Mr. Hooah, you definitely have a lot of explaining to do!"

"You Dirty Hussy! I wish I'd sold you to the sex slaves in South America. I'd love to see what those good ole boys would do to a pretty little thing like you," Dennis leered lasciviously. "Then, after they've had their way with you...."

'Smack!' Mike hit Dennis sharply in the face, as he screamed at him, "No one is going to talk to Audra in such a manner without paying the consequences!" Dennis reached for his eyes, and his nose, from which blood was gushing profusely. Dennis backed up, trying to avoid Mike, as he rushed in for

another blow. "You're not a man, you're a maggot … a maggot that I'm gonna *squash!*" roared Mike, angered nearly beyond words at Dennis' disgustingly sick verbal abuse of Audra. Bobby was watching from the Jeep, where Audra had told him to stay down. Meanwhile, she crept out of the Jeep, shielding herself behind Dennis' car, and holding her Glock close to her body.

Mike discovered that Dennis was quicker—and stronger—than he had erroneously assumed he would be. Without much effort, Dennis lifted Mike off his feet and slammed him to the ground, as he derisively yelled, "Yeah, you jerk! I was a wrestler, too, but I threw around much bigger men than you ever did. Come on, you wimp!" screamed Dennis.

As Mike hit the ground, he rolled to his left, managing to sweep Dennis' legs with his right calf as he rolled. Dennis lost his balance and fell to the sandy ground. Mike found a stick from a cottonwood tree, but it was clumsy, and hard to control. He twirled the stick around, hitting Dennis a few times in the head and gut. Dennis let out a groan. "You have a unique saying that gave you away, Mr. Hooah!" jeered Mike, as he thrust the stick harder into Dennis' midsection.

"I'll kill you!" screamed Dennis.

"You'll have to … if you want to live, you murdering maggot! You spell nothing but death for our children. On second thought, you're not even a maggot; you're just a little piece of maggot dung!" Mike slammed the stick over the crown of Dennis' head so hard, that the stick broke in two.

Dennis muttered something—then he picked up a large piece of the broken stick and flung it at Mike. The small, wooden limb struck Mike in the face. He reached for his cheek, and pulled away a bloody hand; the gash in his cheek was deep. Blood flowed down his neck, and ran down onto the front of his shirt.

Dennis now pulled out an automatic pistol from within his windbreaker. He'd just barely squeezed the trigger, when a bullet ripped through the air. Dennis had been too busy dealing with Mike to notice that Audra was holding a gun on him throughout the fight. The bullet shattered Dennis' wrist, but not before the Beretta he held jumped in his hand. Mike felt something burning in his side. In spite of the pain, his justifiable anger drove him on; he lunged at Dennis, and furiously pounded his fists into Dennis' rib cage, with a flurry of hard punches. Dennis went down, as Mike brought his right knee up into his face. Dennis moaned, and fell face first into the dirt, blood trickling out from his mouth and nose.

Audra and Bobby ran over to where Mike was barely able to stand. Bobby looked up at Mike's face—that had not fared so well against the broken limb Dennis had tossed at him—and grimaced a little. Mike felt odd … lightheaded.

"'Think I don't really feel so good," Mike mumbled, leaning hard on Audra's arm. He heard the sirens; they sounded so far away for some reason. He could see the strobe lights, and saw Raymond and other officers running towards them. He heard Audra say something, and he saw Bobby crying. He said something, too, though he wasn't even so sure of what that was; in shock, he was fading fast.

"What did he say?" Bobby wanted to know, worried at seeing Mike collapse, as rounds of bullets filled the air. For Mike, everything went dark, as he passed out. For now, he was feeling much better, temporarily shielded from the reality at hand.

Not far away from where Mike had passed out, Dennis also lay on the ground … dead. He had tried reaching for his pistol to shoot at the officers, but Raymond and his partner had beaten him to the draw.

Chapter Twenty-seven

Several well dressed oriental men, in highly decorated uniforms, sat around a large, beautiful conference table, made of expensive dark almendra, or almond, wood. The walls encompassing the room were laced with gold, dripping with pearls and gems. The floor was of sapphire stone, studded with small emeralds. Priceless tapestries and portraits hung from the luxurious walls.

The silent men looked at their leader, who had his back turned to them. The finest oriental architects and engineers known to man had constructed the room, as well as the entire massive building that housed the highly ornate room. The table had been built to accommodate many diplomats, and associates, from all over the globe.

Finally, General Genghis, the leader of the Chinese operations headquartered in Panama, stood up and faced his elite men. All eyes fixated on him. General Genghis was the most influential leader in all of China. No other man on earth possessed a lust and power for wealth that exceeded the General's. He also took great pride in his name, Genghis. He considered himself more powerful than the ancient warlord, Genghis Khan. In his own self-assessment, no man equaled his superior intelligence and might. No man dared defy the General. His elite officers trembled as he spoke.

"Gentlemen, we were this close to toppling our foe. We were this close!" screamed the General, as he held up his index finger and thumb, with barely a span between them. Again he repeated for emphasis, *"This close!"* The men squirmed uncomfortably in their posh chairs, being well aware of his explosive temper, and his impulsive acts of violence. At any given moment, he might retrieve a pistol from his military vest and shoot one of them!

"The dates were set ... the time for us to move at hand. The young abducted Americans—trained in military protocol—were almost ready for deployment into the pitiful United States. We should be gloating over victories right now, not licking our wounds! How could we have let this happen? We must now concentrate on regrouping! What can be done?" No one dared move. They all held their breath, hoping the General would not call upon them.

"Colonel Chang, are we still on course? Will we be ready to implement our plan?" shouted the General. Colonel Chang fidgeted in his chair. Despair and hopelessness filled every fiber of his being.

"Ah-h-h, we have a little problem ... a little fly in the ointment, so to speak."

"What problem? What fly?" screamed the General, as he looked down at a crystal plaque in front of him that was shaped like the United States.

"The Americans have gained tremendous worldwide attention, due to the children's rescue. The United States has gained a considerable amount of respect and sympathy, as well, for what they did. The great success of 'ROC' has recaptured the South American's trust in the United States. Thousands of children—from Colombia to the southern tip of Argentina—have been returned to the waiting arms of their parents and relatives. The Americans are being esteemed as heroes ... *heroes,* mind you! Venezuela—as have other OPEC nations—has already begun lowering their prices on oil. They are doing what they can to help the United States in further endeavors to stop the slave trade in third-world countries. Europe has grown closer to the United States, also, and our allies—the South American Mafia—have been severely crippled. Many of General Montiego's men died ... those interred in his camps have been liberated. The General himself is dead. Actually, his camps are now being used as human crises centers for children, as well as for helping to house the poor."

"Get to the point, Colonel! Define what all this means!" screamed the erratic General, hatefully.

"Sir, with all due respect, it means we no longer have any hope of following through with any plot against the United States for many long years to come, if ever. Our campaign is over. We have failed, Sir. The dollar bill is on the rise again, and there is nothing we can do about it."

"Ah-h-h!" the General screamed. "Kill them! Kill them all!" The General picked up the crystal plaque, symbolizing the United States, and violently threw it on the sapphire floor. *'Crash!'* The loud noise of crystal, breaking, echoed throughout the room. Shards of shattered crystal flew in all directions. A large, extremely sharp, sliver of crystal ricocheted off the floor, struck the General precisely between the eyes, and embedded into his forehead. The General screamed in pain, as he grasped his forehead. Blood was running down his face, and onto his hands.

Upset not only by their failure, but also at his own ineptness—indicated by his self-inflicted injury—the General was screeching as he began to speak again. "We wanted to cripple America! We wanted to see it crumble to pieces. Now, look at the crystal plaque ... *in a million pieces!*" His voice rose even more, as he iterated this last phrase. "'You see that? That's as close as we are *ever* going to come to shattering America now!" hollered the General. He looked at all those seated about him, as blood continued to drip to the floor from his forehead.

One of his henchmen reached over to place a bright, clean cloth on his forehead. Grabbing it from him, he again screamed. "Give it to me you, idiot! You are all idiots! You will all die! I will kill all of you! Before I kill you, tell me ... who is it that is responsible for our failure. Who dared defy an emperor?" The men shifted their weight in all different directions. Their General was losing his mind right there before them. One of his elite officers stood up and faced the General.

"Since we are all going to die anyway, I shall tell you. You lost to a man referred to as, *'The Gnat.'*

"The Gnat!" the General shrieked.

"Yes, an insignificant, tiny *'gnat'* has beaten you into submission!" shouted the officer. Genghis dropped into his chair. This was all new to him ... the General had never known what it was to lose before ... never! The words, 'beaten into submission,' echoed loudly in Genghis' head.

"Beaten by a man referred to as a helpless gnat ... beaten by ...'*The ... Gnat.'* Yes, *I* have been beaten by ... a *'gnat!'* Mr. *'Gnat'* beat me ... he beat *me.* Ah-h-h ...! Mr. Gnat *beat* me. He beat us all ... a *gnat* ... a tiny little *insect* destroyed me! How can this be!" They all sat just staring at him, realizing he was losing touch with reality. He continued his diatribe:

"The Gnat ... the Gnat ... the Gnat ... the Gnat ...!"

The men saw something strange happening to their most feared leader. His eyes sort of glazed over and dilated, as he kept repeating, *'The Gnat!'* over and over, and over again.

The General's well trained physician ran over to Genghis. He opened his medical bag and retrieved a sphygmomanometer, stethoscope and a visual probe. The doctor examined Genghis very carefully. Genghis kept repeating the same words, as his physician looked around at the officers in the room. "We must get him to the hospital ... immediately! He has gone into a catatonic state."

"The Gnat," became the last words that came from General Genghis that day ... words that were still echoing through the room, as the doctor tended to the General, as they awaited help. *"The Gnat ... the Gnat ... the Gnat...."*

Chapter Twenty-eight

The day, Monday, May twenty-ninth, Memorial Day … a fitting day for a celebration in honor of all those involved in *'Operation ROC.'* Many elite dignitaries attended the celebration at Veteran's Memorial Park in Sierra Vista. Tens of thousands of people from all over the nation covered the entire area. Large bleachers erected to accommodate a mass of people encompassed the park. Almost five hundred top government officials, including the Governor of Arizona and the President of the United States, attended this momentous occasion. The media crawled all over the vicinity. The police barricaded Fry Boulevard and the surrounding streets. People fanned out into these barricaded streets to take part in one the most glorious events in the history of the United States. Blimps hovered above. Jet fighters roared overhead. Paratroopers exhibited their abilities as they gracefully soared towards the earth with square canopies displaying the brilliant colors of the U.S. flag. The Navy, Army, Airforce and Marines all demonstrated their skills before the crowd.

Around late afternoon, the air shows and demonstrations ended. The Admirals from the USS Reagan, Eisenhower and Roosevelt stepped up on a large stage and addressed the nation. They recognized all the men who had risked their lives to save the children. They introduced Colonel Patrick Heyburn. When Pat stood before the people, he explained how courageous the men and children had been. He called a very familiar person to come up on stage, Michael Douglas Taylor. With the help of his little brother Bobby, Audra, and Bruce Taylor, Mike and Bobby's uncle, Mike began making his way to the stage.

Bruce stared into Mike's eyes, asking as they walked to the podium: "Mike, let me be your Uncle … *please?"* Mike felt a lump in his throat.

He hugged his Uncle and said, "You always were … you always were." Bruce brushed a tear away from his eye, and clapped as Mike faced the crowd, having now arrived at the podium. As he gazed out over the massive crowd, a sudden sharp pain gripped his side. "Is it the wound, or the butterflies darting around in my stomach?" Mike wondered within himself.

When he began to speak, his nerves gave way to boldness. "Ladies and Gentlemen...." A huge roar of applause interrupted Mike's speech. "I didn't say anything yet," laughed Mike. The crowd laughed. "This is one of the greatest and happiest moments of our lives, isn't it?" The crowd stood to their feet cheering Mike's name. Mike held up his arms. He winced a little in pain. Many of the people saw the look of pain on his wounded face. His courage to step up before them won the hearts of all the people in America.

"Today, I stand before you to receive a medal and a reward as guest of honor in this greatest of all celebrations in the history of our free and glorious country, the United States of America!"

The crowd roared louder. They stomped their feet, and thousands on ground level jumped up in the air screaming, *"USA! USA!"* If ever there was a time to be a proud American, this was the day.

Colonel Heyburn held up his hands, as Mike began to speak again. Here stood a brave *'true hero.'* "I am very grateful and honored to be here to receive these awards but, as I stand here before you today and look out over all of you, and consider our entire nation, I say these words from the bottom of my heart ... and I mean them. People ... look by your side, right next to you. What do you see?" Mike put his arm around Bobby's neck. "I see the bravest, most courageous, soldiers that we have in America. I see love and beauty as I gaze upon America's greatest asset and the backbone of this great nation ... our brave, wonderful, precious children. They are what we are all about, and may we never forget this. So...."

All the people shouted and screamed once more. The cheers sounded like an entire squadron of fighter jets flying overhead. Throughout the nation, as people watched by television or listened by way of radio, they felt the pride of what it is like to be a true patriot. Their hearts pounded as their eyes watered. Finally the crowd settled.

"People, my American brothers and sisters, the medals and honors I receive here today I donate to the bravest and strongest of them all ... the proud Americans who really won this battle against evil, the children who were abducted from their families. These children stood strong and brave before their wicked captors. They stood together and—in our American way—they united and supported each other through all the horror the abductors threw at them.

"I have talked with many of these children since they came back. Numerous stories were shared with me ... stories of young girls and boys who would not let themselves fall into despair. They nurtured each other and looked after one another, while in captivity. When we, as adults, would have dropped our heads in defeat, and fallen to the ground, our children lifted their heads to God, and to their country, and they prayed and courageously went forward. Look at your little soldier, Mama. Look at your little brave son and daughter, Papa. Look upon them and see that beside you—and probably just a few heads below you—stand the real soldiers we honor today … the bravest soldiers of the mission. Their story is one of total sacrifice, love and commitment to each other.

We can all take a lesson from these true heroes. They were stripped of family, self, and country; yet, now—now that it is all over—instead of taking, they give even more to us. As sure as there is a God in heaven, these children, and all our children, are our bravest little *Berets*. I say let's honor them. Give them all the medals. Give *them* all our love and admiration because one day, you know, our courageous brave little *Berets* are going to lead our nation." Tears filled every eye in the audience. Even the brave company of *Navy Seals, Green Berets, Marines* and *Rangers* who had taken part in *'Operation ROC'* wept. The tears were not of sorrow, but of great joy.

"My little brother always loved honorable ballads, hymns, and songs dedicated to our country and those who serve to preserve our liberty. He and many other children came up with their own ballad in honor of all the brave children who won their freedom from captivity. It also applies to all our precious children. Today, the *Army, Navy, Air Force* and *Marines* special choirs have joined together on this glorious day to sing to you this ballad." Mike spoke proudly, as he introduced them.

The many men and women of each choir rose, as the accompanying symphony orchestra led them into the verses. Their voices boomed in unison as they sang the beautiful ballad:

> *"Taken from their homes to a distant land—*
> *Led by force from a cruel, dark hand.*
> *They were tough … they would not give in—*
> *'Stronger than any woman or man.*
> *"Our children stayed the course, and stood together,*
> *Where others may have laid down and died.*
> *They did not give up … they helped each other—*
> *Fighting, faithfully, by each other's side."*

The choir picked up in volume and pitch as they sang the chorus, loud and proud.

> *"Pin on all our children the highest 'Medal of Honor.'*
> *They're our pride and joy from sea to shining sea.*
> *They're God's precious gifts—they are our future*

In 'Our country 'tis of thee....'
Through them we all are extremely blessed.
For they are America's shining best."

The choir repeated this chorus, and then went into yet another verse, whose lyrics touched the heart of every American in attendance that glorious day.

"Many tears were shed both night and day—
Hoping somehow, they would all be saved.
Sometimes it seemed all would be lost,
And our hearts would break at the tragic cost.
But our prayers never ceased, from shore to shore,
And as we prayed, they fought and won the war."

Again, the choir repeated the chorus. The next verse—which spoke of the children's holding onto hope, as well as their victorious homecoming—sent proud tingles up and down everyone's spine:

"It took all our faith—it took all our love—
There seemed no hope ... even from above.
But then one day, faith, love and prayers did win,
As our precious children all came home again.
Now that they're here, this is what we'll do
To make our county's dreams come true. We'll ...
"Pin on all our children the highest 'Medal of Honor.'
They're our pride and joy from sea to shining sea.
They're God's precious gifts—they are our future
In 'Our country 'tis of thee....'
Through them we all are extremely blessed.
For they are America's shining best."

Feeling more was needed to sufficiently portray the excitement of the occasion, the conductor led the group—who by now were very much into emoting the heartfelt meaning behind the lyrics—through a boisterously sung refrain, as the people gathered there screamed out in glee, tears running down their faces:

"Yes, through them we all are extremely blessed.
For they are America's shining best!"

The crowd roared and clapped yet more, as the combined chorus finished this meaningful ballad, honoring the returning children. Women's, men's, and children's voices filled the air so loudly that it sounded like a torrent of cries and cheers. They hugged each other, as they continued to weep with joy. Hundreds of *Elite Soldiers* walked among all the children that the *American*

Armed Forces had rescued that one fateful day. They were set apart from the rest of the crowd. As these *Elite Soldiers* walked among the brave little *Berets*, they pinned silver wings upon every one of the children's chests … yes, each and every one of them. Truly, these were the bravest!

Audra, Pat, Todd, Rhonda and—of course—Bobby hugged each other tightly, as the cheers roared louder. Matt Piper, Danny Thatcher and Danny's mother, Margaret, stood behind Mike. Danny was alive! He had brought back with him—as had all of the children—new hope and joy to his mother and his Uncle Matt. To Matt and Danny's right were Cliff, Lucia, and Miguel, with his father and mother, Cal and Linda Brown. Miraculously, Cal had somehow survived the bullets and bombs in the cavern. Many had since speculated over the logistics of his survival. Some believed his body had lain too low on the floor inside the station for the shrapnel to hit him … or suggested that perhaps *'Lady Luck'* had watched over him that fateful day. However, Cal Brown had his own theory. He believed it was because God had wanted it this way.

Cliff hugged his father, who sat crippled for life in a wheelchair. Cal looked lovingly into the eyes of his handsome son he'd not seen in so many years, as he proudly held his grandson, Miguel—or Michael—on his lap. The words came from deep within his heart when he was heard to say aloud, "Thank you God! Thank you for allowing me to pay such a small price to see my son—and his own little family, and for giving me the use of my two arms to hold my boy once again." Tears ran down his cheeks, as Cliff gave his father another affectionate hug.

Overhead, skyrockets filled the air with thunder and shook the ground. *F-16* and *F-15* fighter jets roared over the heads of the people once again. In the background, large Howitzers fired off a volley of rounds, in salute to the bravest *Berets* of them all, the many rescued children of the United States of America.…

The Brave Berets

♦   ✧   ♦   ✧   ♦

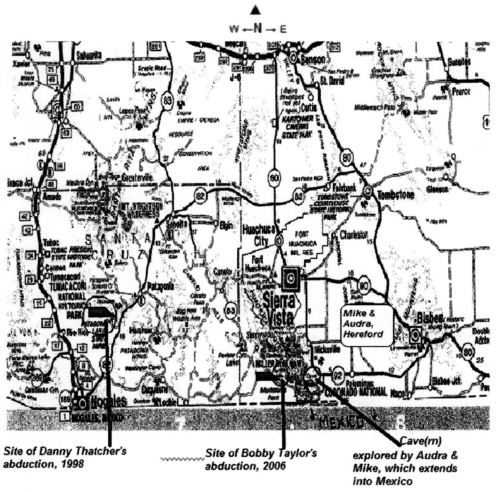

Site of Danny Thatcher's
abduction, 1998

~~~~~~ Site of Bobby Taylor's
abduction, 2006

Cave(rn)
explored by Audra &
Mike, which extends
into Mexico

Note MAAT symbols ◣ on map ... covert symbol used to locate
areas of abductions

The names of Audra and Mike have been [circled]
indicating city of residence

Epilogue

The high-ranking government official sat in his plush political office, staring out the window. He sat very quietly, pondering the events of the last two weeks. He slowly lowered his eyes to gaze upon the bold headlines on the front cover of the Washington Post one last time:

Huachuca Conspiracy Exposed

he read. Casually picking up the paper, he calmly ripped it in half and threw it into the trash container. His lips curled into a sinister smile, as he thought to himself, "So, my friends, you believe you have won, and conquered us. I am not sorry to say that your efforts have only awakened a sleeping dragon. The end is not yet!" He lifted his cell phone from his pocket, and punched in the numbers to make an international call.

Meanwhile, elsewhere in the world, another official was sitting back comfortably, in his expensive overstuffed chair, when the phone rang. Finally, a familiar voice answered the first official's call. *"Hola! Está Pepe."*

The official smiled. *"Señor Pepe, mi Amigo! Está El Endriago. Es tiempo para conversación, mi Amigo. Tu eres lista?"*

There was a brief moment of silence, followed by a sinister laugh. "You may speak to me *'en Ingles.'* Yes, Señor Endriago, we are in perfect position now—we are, as you inquired, *'ready.'* With both generals out of the way, and the Chinese in shambles, we are indeed ready—yes, indeed … *very* ready.

"Good, my friend—very good. Soon we will strike … but not yet. We must have patience. Soon—yes, soon."

Author's Notes

◆ ◇ ◆ ◇ ◆

Although this story you have just read is fictional, it is based on events that actually still occur in our allegedly civilized world. I implore the reader to indulge the author's following notes, which not only give an historical perspective behind this concept of slavery, but current-day examples ... news items. Perhaps such a summary may assist in helping this universal problem make a sufficiently indelible imprint to ensure that these children will never again be forgotten.

◆ ◇ ◆

When we think of the concept of slavery, many of us may automatically picture a cold, ruthless—yea, often heartless—southern aristocrat, beating a poor black individual over his/her bare back with a bullwhip. This was a common thing, prior to the *'War Between the States,'* or what has since come to be known as the *'Civil War'* (1861-1865). The institution of slavery, however, developed in ancient times ... long before there ever was any European migration to what became known as America. Most of us have heard of the horrible four-hundred-year bondage of the Hebrews by the Egyptians. Many of us have seen the movie, *'The Ten Commandments,'* starring the famous actor, Charlton Heston, portraying the Hebrews' savior, Moses, who—with the help of God—led the Hebrews out from that centuries-long, bitter bondage to freedom. We realize that these were basically archaic times, when barbaric tribes and kingdoms flourished upon the face of our planet.

We find it very difficult to forgive these people of their horrible actions; but, after all, the world was in a comparatively uncivilized state, and most were illiterate, in spite of the Egyptian society possessing some knowledge considered rather sophisticated for their times. Modern science and our present day humanitarian philosophy were not even a notion at that time in some people groups. Lacking our contemporary knowledge of mass production via machinery, robotics, elaborate assembly lines, and heavy construction equipment—such as bulldozers, cranes, trains, and our modern forms of transporting people, as well as freight—they had to rely heavily on their own physical labor, and beasts of burden to assist them.

According to most historians, anthropologists, and even theologians, when men first came into existence—whether by creation or evolution—they were basically nomads who traveled about, following their food source like sharks that follow schools of fish in the ocean. Their main concerns were quite basic, and they seemed to be quite happy surviving on the bottom rung of Abraham Maslow's hierarchy of needs ... caring merely for such things as, clothing, food and shelter. We can only surmise that breeding was more a necessity than a sport, or a luxury, during prehistoric times.

Later on, men finally wandered into rich lands that hosted many animals and an enormous amount of staple products. These tribes were the fortunate people who later—because they did not have to exhaust the majority of their energies on activities such as finding food and shelter—began to ask themselves questions we still ask ourselves today. Such questions have led to enormous breakthroughs in science, as well as to the modernization of society. The questions are as follows: Who are we ... what is our purpose, and ... how did we get here?

Thus, with much more time to spare, apart from fulfilling their basic needs, these tribes developed a higher degree of learning. People began to develop an appreciation for math, science, religion, language, philosophy, etc. Men also discovered ways to enhance their strength, using metal weapons. Men learned the art of metallurgy and early forging techniques, such as iron casting. The tribe fortunate enough to find areas where they could think and advance also developed armor and weapons, as well as better construction techniques. Soon stables, blacksmith shops, mills, mining and lumber camps, monasteries, and fishing docks came into existence. The tribe became a kingdom. The kingdom soon sought power. The kingdom also learned that those with lesser knowledge made easy prey.

Primitive tribes, weaker than the now more highly organized kingdoms, would find themselves at the mercy of these more developed cultures. If the tribal people valued their lives, they would either join the kingdom as slaves, or be put to the sword. The kingdom relished the cheap labor slaves offered; however, their labors were not in extreme demand until the kingdom discovered that other empires existed outside their domicile. Now the kingdom found themselves worthy opponents to either overthrow or with whom to barter. Thus, slaves became a much more important commodity as the empires began to trade amongst themselves. The more slaves a kingdom had the more product they could produce—supply and demand—which, of course, brought in more wealth for the kingdom. The kingdom could then invest in greater technology and weapons of destruction. The slaves did all the laborious work of plowing, harvesting and building, so the empire could focus largely on their military, both for the purposes of domestic security and the territorial takeover of another adjacent kingdom, if they felt like expanding their borders.

Merchants, plantation owners, and builders began to realize that the more slaves (cheap laborers) they could afford, the more wealth they could obtain, by regularly utilizing this inexpensive labor. This equates, economically, to today's modern businessmen hiring a cadre of low-wage earners, helping to enhance the company's bottom line, albeit these workers are not slaves ... laborers forced to perform their labors against their own will.

Because it was very time consuming and costly to hunt down their own slaves, or go to distant lands and purchase them, commerce turned to slave merchants—similar to the wicked slave traders that are still, unfortunately, in existence today. These traders would either capture members from primitive tribes, or purchase slaves previously captured by other tribes, at very reasonable rates. They would then transport these captives to some center or commerce, charging the commercial despots there up to three or four times the cost they had paid to acquire the slaves. They often auctioned them off, hoping to amass even a greater amount of wealth.

Sometimes, after a kingdom had become very large and powerful, they would then raid an entire village, sack it, burn it to the ground, and carry back the men, women and children as slaves. The older women, female children and ladies that were considered unattractive were used for labor. The prettier, more robust women became sex slaves, referred to politely as *'concubines'* (secondary wives). This barbaric practice was well accepted, and even boasted of, by almost every kingdom for many years. We oft look back at ancient times, shaking our heads in disgust and disbelief. "How could humans stoop lower than an animal by allowing such devilish, heartless behavior as owning slaves, anyway?" we might wonder.

Well, here is what might be a surprise to some. In our present—purportedly civilized—world, this barbaric institution ... *slavery* ... is very much alive and well. In fact, there are more people enslaved today in the world than the number of those who were brought over from Africa on the middle passage! The population explosion, along with the economic and social vulnerability of large numbers of people in the Third World, gives rise to the glut of available slaves. The result is that the cost of slaves has become cheap—cheaper than at any other time in history! What is terribly appalling, and seriously inhumane, is the child slavery that persists in our supposedly humane modern society.

A very large portion of this outrageous, malevolent form of slavery interestingly—though sadly—centers on the cocoa bean. The chocolate industry is a staggering multi-billion-dollar business patronized by almost every adult and child in the world. In articles that speak about chocolate, and how wonderful it is for everyone—especially the fat cat investors, who manage to avoid mention therein—chocolate ranks way up on the polls with sex and money.

Today the healthcare industry even affirms that chocolate is good for our health—dark chocolate, in particular—even while it is a relatively high-fat product, as it contains a considerable amount of antioxidants that fight against fat-related oxides that are responsible for the beginning of cardiovascular problems. Studies reveal that chocolate contains polyphenols—antioxidant phytochemicals (plant products believed to reduce the risk of cancer)—that fight against heavy fat-related oxides that plug our arteries and veins.

What is even more exciting is that polyphenol flavanoids—which are powerful antioxidants, having more antioxidant activity than vitamin C—from chocolate also contain large oligomers. An oligomer is a mixture of compounds in which two or more smaller molecules combine to form a larger molecule, containing repeats of the structural units of the original molecules. These oligomers can actually prevent LDL (low-density lipoprotein) cholesterol from building up in our arteries, which can—in turn—cause atherosclerosis, or, abnormal fatty deposits and tissue degeneration in the inner lining of arteries. So, out with the bad LDL, and in with the good HDL (high-density lipoproteins). Our beloved chocolate contains plenty of these wonderful good-for-your-arteries compounds. It can actually prevent heart disease!

Further, In 1998 a Mori survey concluded that half the women interviewed preferred chocolate over sex, and that half the men interviewed preferred chocolate to driving a sports car. Yes, from chocolate-covered ants to luscious nougat candy bars, we can all feel very good about chomping into chocolate … or should we? For the ugly truth behind the harvesting of the cocoa bean in West Africa, and in parts of Central and South America, is that the hardworking hands of a child slave harvest a large majority of these cocoa beans.

Of course, the children do not just harvest the beans for our chocolate delights. They also are made to harvest the leaves of the coca tree for the syndicate in these areas for the manufacturing of cocaine, which they then sell to our children in the streets of America. The slavery issue does not stop with chocolate and drugs; there are many children in Brazil, for example, who are making the charcoal that tempers the steel for our metal products, such as leaf springs on our cars, parts for lawn mowers, and so forth. It is safe to say that everyone in the entire civilized world can most likely find some item in their house that was made by a slave ... and most of those slaves are children.

The people who own these children—and women also—are dubbed slave-holders rather than slave *owners*. This may make it sound less horrid, but is it? Experts that deal with the subject of modern day slavery estimate that there are approximately twenty-seven million slaves in the world today—greater than the entire population of Canada. Most of these slaves are children.

Where do they come from? They come from all over the world basically, and—though many people seem to turn their heads, and refuse to believe that such a monstrous institution like this exists—the startling fact is that it does. This situation is not going to improve, either, unless we wake up and do something about it.

In the story you have just read, *"The Huachuca* (pronounced hwã-choo'-kã) *Conspiracy,"* The NCMEC (National Center For Missing and Exploited Children) made a bold statement, in conjunction with a U.S. Department of Justice study. According to that study, nearly 800,000 children were reported to have gone missing within a one-year period. That is the equivalent of more than 2,000 children being reported missing each and everyday. There are those who believe this is just a scare tactic, while trying to persuade people that heavier restrictions are needed for children. One official even suggested that newborns receive microchip implants, and older children receive teeth implants, that can be tracked from many miles away via satellite.

An official in New York stated that this number—2000 children going missing per day—is absurd because, if the rate of missing children were that significant, most of the desks in American schools would be empty. Yet, when we look at the number of schools K-12th grade, and compare them with the number of missing children we arrive at a figure of 7.2 children missing from a school each year (800,000children/110,000schools = 7.2.). This statistic would hardly lead to any empty school buildings, unless these missing children were disproportionately from one area in particular. Children of all sexes, ages, and races come and go in and out of schools everyday—given our notably mobile society—like people in a city park. It is safe to say that any given school would barely detect seven missing children a year. Further, if you add the military, boarding and private schools to this 110,000 figure, the higher total raises the ratio sufficiently that the children per school per year average leaves us with a yet smaller figure, closer to four.

The fact is, 2000 children every day go missing in the United States. Where do they go? Many are believed to be spousal abductions, or relative abductions, or runaways. Even if 80% of the missing children fit this category, this still leaves 160,000 unaccounted for, per year.

The answer is elusive and, after researching the archives and a tremendous amount of data, we see that too many people are taking the wrong approach to our missing children. We should be slamming our fists on the desks of our overpaid, overfed Congressmen and -women, and demanding that more be done, but we are not. Instead, most of us believe—or would like to naively believe—the fallacies fed to us by either ignorant individuals, or a misinformed sector of the media. Excuses for this complacency are (1) the child was unwanted, anyway; (2) an angry parent—fighting for custody—has stolen the child; (3) because the child was unwanted, s/he ran away. This apathetic approach only adds to this tragic crisis; it surely does not lead us to any resolution.

Some of these children are sexually exploited and found dead. This is the most horrendous crime a human could commit. To turn on one's own young is no less than demonic! There has been speculation that traffickers are transporting some of our young girls into China where today—due to the forced birth limitations and, therefore, selective abortion of females during the past few decades—the men in China face a massive shortage of wives. Then there is another unfortunately very viable assumption ... a dark one, at that: that our children are falling into the hands of slaveholders. Authorities have concluded that some of these slaveholders, and sexual exploiters, are even operating within the borders of the United States.

An alarming number of children in Central and South America—Guatemala, El Salvador, Honduras, Nicaragua, Costa Rica, Brazil, Peru, Argentina and Bolivia—have become victims of trafficking and commercial sexual exploitation. In fact, the children that are being trafficked throughout Central and South America are growing in such large numbers, that the governments of these countries are finally attempting to institute programs aimed at trying to effect a decline in the enormous rate of human trafficking. However, this has been extremely difficult, because these governments' law enforcement officers lack a clear acquiescence from political leaders, as well as the resources to aggressively pursue domestic and international traffickers. Therefore, though trying, most of these national governments still have no comprehensive policy to prevent trafficking, although some miniscule measures have been taken, in an attempt to reduce the trafficking of children.

The leaders of these countries are finding themselves up against establishments that pose as job recruiters, recognized by their government as legitimate organizations. Thus, children looking for an honest income are drawn to these establishments, only to be abducted and taken to labor camps—or houses of assignation—where they are sexually exploited. There are over 284 of these deceitful organizations in different Guatemalan cities, let alone the other countries also mentioned above.

When the United States gave the Panama Canal to the Panamanians in December of 1999, a Pandora's box of debauchery was opened. The Chinese became the actual owner of the canal by *de facto.* The *Caza Alianza (CA)* is a non-profit organization with a Latin American network that provides care, rehabilitation, and legal aid services for street children—especially in Mexico and Central America. They have reported that China enjoys reaping rewards from the syndicate, which operates the underground trafficking of children and drugs in this region.

When the United States regulated the activities of the Canal, such heinous acts were uncommon; today, these horribly inhumane acts are commonplace ... traditional. Children are being sent across the Canal into South American countries as slaves to harvest the cocoa bean for chocolate, as well as to harvest the coca leaves from which freebase or crack cocaine is finally made.

Children who are illegally trafficked into Mexico are also being exploited. Reports by the *CA* indicate that some children are even being trafficked into the United States. Greed has bred an extremely cheap network of forced labor. It has also bred the unthinkable sexual molestations of many, many innocent young females in Central and South America. In addition, it is safe to say that many abducted American daughters are in real danger, and many free children are potentially at risk, as you read these very words, highlighting this very real situation.

We cringe at the thought, and do not want to speak of such horror—possibly even shying away from it—yet, there may be many of our abducted sons dying on a cocoa plantation at this moment. And ... filthy men, who are less than human, may this very moment be sexually molesting some of our young daughters who have been abducted—a thought about which it is almost too terrible to talk. However, we must talk about it, because ignoring this will only make matters much worse.

The questions of who the perpetrators are, and why, are being revealed daily; yet, for some reason, we seem to remain in the dark over this poignant issue. Is it because we just do not want to believe it—which we believe is often the case, or is it because we do not care ... not even for our own children? Have we become an apathetic nation of people, who no longer feel it is our responsibility to bring such evil to its knees, or are we willing to fight for what rightfully belongs to us?

While it is true that humans are creatures of habits, vices and addictions, do we unblinkingly allow our flaws in these areas to overpower us, or do we stand up for what is right, and overcome them? Do we take action, or do we passively ignore things going on around us, dismissing them as possibly even a scare-tactic ... a hoax ... contrived ... unreal? Knowing that men and women have lost their lives to bring these heinous acts to the forefront—something one does not even think of doing for a mere hoax—it is now up to us to do something, in their stead, to continue this very real fight.

We wrap this up, by returning to our initial subject harvest—the cocoa bean—and suggest you think soberly the next time you've a yearning for some delicious chocolate entrée. Remember ... you could very well be indulging in some sweet explosion of sheer ecstasy that was harvested by the blistering hands and/or the sunburned back of a dear little slave girl or boy.

◆   ✧   ◆   ✧   ◆

More Facts for Consideration

The following commentary is based on reports made by public experts and officials on the topics of human trafficking, child exploitation, and current-day slavery.

When we think about Florida, we picture the beautiful southeastern sun pleasantly smiling down upon Florida's many beaches as beautiful women, laughing children, and robust men romp and play in the sand, or flounder in the warm Atlantic waters. Who would think that in one of America's most beautiful climates lay a dark secret that is now rising to the surface? According to human rights advocates at the Florida State University, and other state officials, modern-day slavery is alive and well in this sunny state.

Officials discovered people forced to work as farmhands, prostitutes and maids all across the state. All one need do is look for areas in Florida that demand cheap labor to possibly uncover farms that harbor forced workers, otherwise known as slaves. In south Florida, federal prosecutions have indicated hundreds of farmhands who were victims of human trafficking, and a forced prostitution ring identified many young women and girls brought from Mexico. State officials also cited a case of "domestic servitude" in southwest Florida.

Human traffickers bring many illegal immigrants into the United States annually, and either use them for their own deranged reasons, or discreetly sell them to others who require them for farm labor or prostitution rings. The trafficking dilemma does not only apply to Florida; we see trafficking and human exploitation throughout the heartland of the United States, including Midwestern states such as Missouri. The three main destinations for these poor misled, or abducted, people are Florida, New York and Texas. New York officials observe many sexually exploited women and young girls. Texas also is a hot spot for agricultural slave labor and sexual exploitation.

Poor immigrants seem to be the main targets of trafficking; however, more and more United States citizens are also falling prey to traffickers. Our homeless and runaway children—estimated to be between 1.3 million and 2.8 million—find themselves at an increasing risk. Traffickers pose as people that want to help our young girls and boys. After they gain their trust, they export them into various cities around the United States, where illegal rings sexually exploit them and force them to participate in nude parlors, child pornography, and prostitution (survival sex), or use them for cheap labor. We tend to downplay the severity of the licentious crimes because many of these precious exploited children dubbed as *'runaways,'* or *'thrownaways,'* are somewhat frowned upon by society. This is a grievous tragedy. These children did not run from home to join the despicable, filthy porno rings and inhumane activities of the sick and deranged; they usually have left home due to overwhelming abuse and betrayal by those they thought loved them—their fathers, mothers, sisters, brothers, or relatives. Many feared for their lives. Some parents forced them to run away. Others that live under very ugly conditions are lured away by emails from people—traffickers—offering to help them. We can only imagine some of these evil traffickers posing as wonderful officials, who claim they belong to a legitimate organization whose only concern is to help those living a distressed life.

Once the children unwittingly run to these predators, they become easy prey. They are broke, hungry and, therefore, very desperate. They find themselves at the mercy of the wicked traffickers, with little or no means of escaping. They are held bondage by immense fear—fear of life and limb. Their basic needs are met only if they comply with the sinister terms of the ruthless men. With nowhere else to go, and no hope of a better tomorrow, what little willpower they have left after being broken by their home situation is now totally broken, leaving our poor children feeling defenseless and defeated. This hopelessness then leads to their giving in to the evil desires of their hideous abductors—lest they lose even their life.

Complex traffickers take the children across state lines, to avoid detection, into cities teeming with transient males, seasonal workers, military personnel and sex tourists ... deranged individuals that find it fascinating to rape a young little girl or boy. How demonic!

Can you imagine the fear these poor, helpless children live in? They fear their evil lords ... they fear the client and his wicked nature. The fear is so strong, that they develop many emotional disorders; however, the diabolical, heartless controllers give the children drugs, so they may cope with all this debauchery.

This evil sexual exploitation of our children has prompted the U.S. Government to take a stand against legalized prostitution. A growing body of research is showing that prostitution is not only inherently harmful and dehumanizing to women and children, but it also fuels the growth of trafficking in persons ... or modern day slavery. Please bear in mind these evil exploitations do not just affect *'runaway'* children and *'thrownaway'* children ... women, men, boys, girls—people from all walks of life—are at risk.

The U.S. Central Intelligence Agency estimates that 50,000 people are trafficked into or transited through the U.S.A. annually, as sex slaves, domestics, garment and agricultural slaves.

Some are forced into rural areas, such as Georgia and South Carolina, where they find themselves held captive—along with unemployed legal immigrants—inside well-secured compounds, surrounded by fences, barbed wire, and patrolled well at night by dogs and men bearing weapons. As an example, there was one plantation where the owner lured the poor, unemployed, legal immigrants into slavery by promising them temporary work and a fair wage. The owner loaded them into vans and station wagons, took them to his rural plantation, and forced them to harvest his oranges, cotton and sugar cane. Their labors began before daybreak, and their taskmasters pushed them to work late into the night.

These men, women and children never saw the outside world; also, the owner charged them room and board. After harvesting the orchards and fields, the owner of the plantation forbade them to leave. The owner told the forced workers, "You owe me too much money, and must work off the debt." Fortunately, the media and authorities discovered this particular slave camp, and ended the nightmares. They are not always easy to locate, as the traffickers and recipients of abducted children and slaves do not belong to one specific race. They are Caucasian, Hispanic, Asian, and people of various cultures and ethnicity.

Another topic to highly consider is international abductions, or human trafficking. The *'Human Rights Watch,'* a non-profit organization dedicated to protecting the human rights of people around the world, estimates that every year 800,000 to 900,000 men, women, and children are trafficked across international borders into forced labor, or slavery-like conditions. Trafficking includes all acts related to the recruitment, transport, transfer, sale and purchase of human beings. The transaction must be by force, fraud, deceit, or other coercive tactics for the purpose of placing them into conditions of forced labor—or practices similar to slavery—in which labor is extracted through physical, or non-physical, means of coercion. This coercion may include blackmail, fraud, deceit, isolation, threat, or use of physical force, or psychological pressure. Children are exempt from this definition. Those who allow themselves to be smuggled into other countries do not fit this category; however, minors fall under the definition of trafficking, even if the child volunteers. Children are not considered of age to make such a responsible decision.

The UN International Labor Office *(ILO)* reports that Asia has three-quarters of the 27 million people believed to be in forced labor worldwide. This is a very large number of adults and children. When we look at this figure, we might assume that some children from the United States fall into this group. Is it possible that evil traffickers abduct some of our children from the United States, and ship them off to foreign soil? We can only surmise. When we realize the enormous number of children that vanish each year without a trace, we might conclude this is a very likely possibility.

The questions to ponder are—where are they going, and why are they going? If we can answer these two questions, we can come closer to answering the elusive third question: What group in a certain country is abducting them? China faces a tremendous challenge at this time. Due to selective—technically, enforced—abortions, and incentives to spare a son over a daughter, in order to curb the massive population in China, there is a huge disproportionate ratio of men to women. Almost thirty-plus million men are crying out for female companionship in China; this has become an excuse for pillaging North Korean women. It is plausible to believe that some of our own precious young girls and women are actually waking up inside the borders of China after being abducted.

There is another theory, not so passion-related. Countries such as Northern Uganda, the Democratic Republic of Congo, Liberia, Myanmar, Colombia and Sri Lanka, are abducting children—both males and females—to use as soldiers against their neighboring foes. They find children very useful in combat. The children make harder targets for the enemy. They can slip in and out of areas without being detected due to their size. Their aim is very deadly, and they can be brainwashed easier than an adult can. The question to consider here is this: Are any of these warring countries stealing our own young sons and daughters, and exploiting them for combat?

What has been done, so far?

The heinous crimes and horror mentioned above finally prompted our government to pass a couple of Acts, hoping to end, or curtail, this terrible crisis. The *Trafficking Victims' Protection Act of 2000* (P.L.106-386), and the *Trafficking Victims' Protection Reauthorization Act* (P.L.108-193), provide tools to combat trafficking in persons worldwide. The Acts authorize the establishment of the *'Office to Monitor and Combat Trafficking in Persons,'* and the *'President's Interagency Task Force to Monitor and Combat Trafficking in Persons,'* to assist in the coordination of anti-trafficking efforts.

A secondary aspect of the U.S. effort is to strengthen law enforcement's ability to investigate, prosecute, and punish violent crimes committed against children, including child sex tourism and the commercial sexual exploitation of children. The *PROTECT* Act *('Prosecutorial Remedies and Other Tools to End the Exploitation of Children Today' Act, 2003)* was passed by the Congress in April 2003, and signed into law by President Bush. The Act serves as an historic milestone for protecting children, while severely punishing those who victimize young people. Of particular note, the *PROTECT* Act allows law enforcement officers to prosecute American citizens and legal permanent residents who travel abroad and commercially sexually abuse minors, without having to prove prior intent to commit this crime. The law also strengthens the punishment of these child sex tourists. If convicted, child sex tourists now face up to 30 years' imprisonment ... an increase from the previous maximum of 15 years.

The *PROTECT Act* made several other changes to the law, other than jurisdiction now reaching to cover crimes committed on foreign soil, as previously noted. Parallel criminal penalty enhancements are now also in place; these relate to the production of child pornography, as well as arranging and/or facilitating the travel of child sex tourists. Another notable addition is that it extends the statute of limitations for crimes involving abduction, physical abuse, or sexual abuse, to the lifetime of the child. This is something we see as a particularly laudable addition, because—due to the nature of such crimes—children, even adults, often need much time to arrive at a place in their lives where they can even face, much less talk about, such occurrences ... and, often, only with outside help.

♦ ✧ ♦   See *'U.S. State Dept. Trafficking in Persons Report'*t   ♦   June, 2005

What Can the Average Citizen Do?

Let's just speculate for a moment, as this is a major humanitarian crisis ... this is a reflection of our world today. Is this how we want to go down in history ... that we the people of earth loved our children so much that we allowed evil men to steal them from us, without putting up a fight? What does it mean to you when you discover there is an insatiable demand for child pornography and sexual exploitation of children throughout the world? What does this say about us as humans? Into what are we evolving? Why are our precious little children in such huge demand sexually? We do not even have a right to judge another country, when we are just as black- and cold-hearted as they, when we allow this to go on. What does this say about our government ... and the entire world as a whole? We might understand how a few deranged minds exist in the world but—as we study the outrageous numbers involved in the abduction and human trafficking of children—we must postulate that the number of filth-ridden, deranged minds throughout the world is such that it staggers all human understanding.

So, what are we going to do? What can you do? Having presented this question to numerous people, I am sad to say that the average apathetic response was a disparaging commentary on our society today. Approximately ninety percent of the replies can be summed up in these discouraging—possibly even frightening, as we turn our heads away, unwilling to see what is happening—words:

> "Well, you can't do nothing (sic) about it, because we do not
> unite together anymore in this country. Besides, I'm not
> affected by it."

Dr. Melissa Farley is a very brilliant psychologist, and second-wave feminist, studying the effects of global sex trafficking on prostitutes. She believes that these effects are deleterious. She is *Director of Prostitution Research and Education* at the *San Francisco Women's Center*. She is also a leading author on child sexual exploitation. Dr. Melissa Farley has made a bold statement, which this author supports one-hundred percent. I respect Dr. Farley very much; her thoughts, to which I refer, are summarized herein.

Dr. Farley has talked to trafficking survivors, both here—California, New York, and even the American heartland—and abroad. What she discovered was not only the victims having—universally—endured a most heartbreaking experience, but a vast network of transnational criminal elements, perpetuating governmental corruption and, thus, threatening rule of law. These findings support the idea that this is not only a human rights issue, but also a national security concern. In light of these facts, there is much at stake. President Bush and Congress—working closely with faith-based, community and feminist organizations—are aggressively pursuing freedom for all victims of modern-day slavery.

This is a situation that demands more than legislation, however. Dr. Farley has well stated that for all victims of sex trafficking to become free, we as citizens must examine our own cultural attitudes and behaviors, to ensure that we do not contribute to this 'market' for vulnerable women trafficked into prostitution. She sums it all up for us in this statement:

> *"We must look into our hearts and decide we do not want to support this black, evil market in any way, shape or form. We must get rid of our apathy, and be bold. Our children's lives, and our futures, are at stake."*

◆　　　✧　　　◆　　　✧　　　◆

For detailed information concerning human trafficking, child abductions and slavery, please contact the following Web sites. Learn more on how you can help prevent and end these heinous crimes. Do your part ... get involved.

<u>U.S. State Department</u> ♦ Office to Monitor and Combat Trafficking in Persons
http://www.state.gov/g/tip/

<u>Department of Justice</u> ♦ Child Exploitation and Obscenity Section ♦ *CEOS*
http://www.usdoj.gov/criminal/ceos
e-mail: criminal.division@usdoj.gov

<u>National Runaway Switchboard</u> ♦ This is an extremely good resource that will instruct you in ways in which you can become involved.
http://www.nrscrisisline.org/
1 800 Runaway (786 2929)

<u>U.S. Department of Health and Human Resources</u> ♦
http://www.hhs.gov/

<u>Rescue and Restore</u> ♦
http://www.hhs.gov/
1.888.3737.888

<u>Paul and Lisa Program</u> ♦
http://www.paulandlisa.org/
1.800.518.2238

<u>CA/OCS/CI</u> ♦
http://travel.state.gov/family/about/faq/faq
1-888-407-4747
(202) 736-9090

<u>U.S. DEPARTMENT of STATE</u> ♦
http://www.state.gov/

Act now ... get involved with the *NCMEC—National Center for Missing and Exploited Children*—or find an organization like it. Join forces with Mr. Walsh, the host of the hit television series, *'America's Most Wanted,'* and head spokesperson for *NCMEC*.

♦   ✧   ♦   ✧   ♦

How can I help find missing children?

Answer: Take time. Yes, the best way to help *NCMEC* is to take the time to look at the photographs of missing children in the many venues made available to us—including *ADVO* postcards, posters at Wal-Mart stores, in federal buildings, or wherever they may be found. Report any information about those children to *NCMEC's* toll-free Hotline 1-800-THE-LOST (1-800-843-5678).

As an aside—no small thing—just prior to going to press, while shopping at Wal-Mart, we noted their success rate in just over a ten-year period. Nearly six thousand children have been recovered through this particular effort, averaging nearly 600 per each of those years, more than eleven children per week … rescued!

You can also help by keeping *up-to-date* photographs of your own children. After all, <u>one</u> out of <u>six</u> of the children featured in *NCMEC's* photo-distribution program has been recovered as a direct result.

◆   ✦   ◆   ✦   ◆

Also see ◆ http://www.missingkids.com,
for more information as to how you can be of service.

About the Author

In this volume, a man's gift for writing, and commitment to helping guard the hearts of both children and adults come together to intrigue us with a very exciting and spellbinding, yet heartwarming story.

His many short stories about animals and children have touched our hearts throughout the years. Will understands the wonder and love our children bring into our lives, having spent much time with them, while serving as a Sunday school teacher, foster parent, and scout leader. His studies have include pre-med, microbiology, and electronics.

Will is an active member of the *NCMEC, Americas Most Wanted*, and *The Human Rights Watch*. His biography is one of tremendous adversity, and the strong will, determination and human spirit to overcome.

Presently working in the health care field, Will resides with his lovely wife at the foot of the beautiful Huachuca Mountains. We find his driving philosophy summed up within the following thoughts:

> *"We all have the power and hidden strengths within to overcome heartwrenching, tearjerking hardships in our lives. We just need to dig into our souls and pull it out of us. We also need to realize we are human, and this makes us vulnerable.*
>
> *"The main ingredients to overcoming adversity are love, faith and trust: love for others, God and ourselves; faith in believing that love will conquer while trusting that, through God, we already have conquered."*

◆ ✧ ◆ *Ruth A. Markel* ✧ ◆

978-0-595-39835-5
0-595-39835-9

CPSIA information can be obtained at www.ICGtesting.com
Printed in the USA
LVOW10s0311120115

422443LV00002B/507/P